Also by
NANCY JOAQUIM
BUILD ME A CITY
Secrets, Lies and Love In Baron Haussmann's Paris

......an intricately plotted tale that draws readers in
and makes French history come alive......

Joaquim's writing simmers with the glamour and
magic of old Paris.....Publishers Weekly

Nancy Joaquim, a graceful writer, makes the most of an exciting period
in French history, first the Second Empire, then the Prussian Siege of Paris,
and finally, the Commune......

......in the author's poetic treatment, readers get a wonderful
Dickensian denouement...... Kirkus Reviews

SOPHIA
A Woman's Search for Troy

"The Schliemanns are tailor-made for historical fiction because so much
of their life story is almost like fiction itself," says Joaquim. "Before the two
discovered the ruins, most scholars believed that Homer's 'Iliad' was,
to some extent, a historical document."

Many authors — Daniel Boorstin and Will Durant among them —
have written the story of Heinrich Schliemann's finds, but until Joaquim's book,
no one has really delved into the contributions made by Sophia Schliemann.
- Arts and Life, "Tribune" Scottsdale Arizona

SOPHIA SCHLIEMANN
Eien Frau Entdeckt Mykene Published by HERBIG-Munich (In German)

"Nancy Joaquim tells the story of a great love and a woman who steps out
of her husband's shadow into a tension filled archaeological adventure."
- Alfelder Zeitung, Saxony

"Historical novel, true to the actual story, without twisting biographical facts...
smart writing, entertaining, exciting, a cultural-historical reading pleasure."
- Welt Am Sonntag, Berlin

IMPRESSION SUNRISE

This book is for my husband Richard.
With love and thanks for always being there.

Nancy Joaquim

Richard's Dedication To His Wife Nancy

Nancy Joaquim
October 8, 1938 - January 11, 2024

"It only takes a moment,
For your eyes to meet, and then...
Your heart knows
In a moment
You will never be
Alone again.

And that is all, that love is about
And we'll recall when time runs out
That it only took a moment
To be loved
A whole life long"

- Jerry Herman

IMPRESSION SUNRISE

The Romance of Alice and Claude Monet

by
Nancy Joaquim

An Historical Novel

Copyright ©2011-2024 by Nancy Joaquim; Montrose Hall

Library of Congress Number: TXu1-722-463
ISBN: Hardcover   978-1-7377559-3-7
          Softcover   978-1-7377559-4-4
          eBook   978-1-7377559-5-1

All rights reserved. No part of this book may be reproduced or transmitted in any form or by any means, electronic or mechanical, including photocopying, recording, or by any information storage and retrieval system, without permission in writing from the original copyright owner.

This is a work of fiction, based on actual facts. Certain names, characters, places and incidents are the product of the author's imagination or are used fictitiously.

Every effort has been made to trace and contact copyright holders prior to publication. If notified, the publisher undertakes to rectify any errors or omissions at the earliest opportunity.

CREDITS

Front Cover Photo: Impression, Sunrise (soleil levant) (1872)
    Painting by Claude Monet - Antiquarian Images / Alamy Stock Photo
Front Cover Design: Barbara Feighner
Layout and Design: Nile Graphics

First Edition 2024

ACKNOWLEDGEMENTS

I am grateful to all who have come before me with scholarly, well-researched, published work on the subjects of Impressionism, the French Impressionist Painters, and aspects of Claude Monet's iconic life and career. Their numbers are legion, for Impressionism and Claude Monet enjoy a level of popularity unparalleled in the world. I thank them one and all.

The research for this book has been done in museums and at historic sites in France, Italy, and the United States. I thank all those art historians, museum curators, municipal officials, and fellow-researchers who were so very helpful. My special thanks for the outstanding achievements of the following.

Daniel Wildenstein's extraordinary Four-Volume MONET, Catalogue Raisonne; Tashen, Wildenstein Institute, Benedikt Taschen 1996, stands alone in its stunning breadth of content and scholarly research, of which enough may never be said. Mr. Wildenstein's thoroughness in documenting the vast number of Claude Monet's paintings and his attention to related details of Claude Monet's life and work are unequalled.

The late John Rewald, known as a foremost authority on late Nineteenth-Century Art, with more than five-hundred published works to his credit and the gentleman known as the Dean of Impressionism, bore his distinguished title with good reason. I am but one researcher who came to admire the passionate attention he brought to details related to time and place as well as his gift for masterful pose, particularly as it pertains to specific works of painters and their critical reviews during Impressionism's earliest days, events which Mr. Rewald has chronicled with rare clarity and devotion in, among other works, HISTORY OF IMPRESSIONISM, The Museum of Modern Art, New York 1946.

THE NEW PAINTING, Impressionism 1874 – 1886, An Exhibition Organized by The Fine Arts Museums of San Francisco with the National Gallery of Art, Washington, D.C., 17 January to 6 April 1986, Washington; San Francisco 19 April to 6 July 1986, published by The Fine Arts Museums of San

Francisco. In the winter of 1986, exactly one hundred years after the Eighth and last Impressionist Exhibition I had the great pleasure of attending this exceptional event at The National Gallery of Art in Washington, D.C. Paintings included in all Eight Impressionist exhibitions loaned by museums and private collections worldwide, many rarely if ever seen in public, were exhibited in a brilliant array of content designed to transport the Twentieth-Century viewer to those late Nineteenth-Century exhibitions held in Paris on the Boulevard des Capucines, at Rue Laffitte, Rue le Peletier, and Saint-Honore. The human experience of viewing the paintings of Monet, Renoir, Degas, Morisot, Pissarro, Cezanne, Sisley, and Caillebotte as they were exhibited in their lifetimes continues vivid in my memory these many years later. Critical reviews related to each exhibition as they appear in Impression Sunrise have been inspired by the Exhibition Catalogue. I remain grateful to The Fine Arts Museums of San Francisco and The National Gallery of Art, Washington, D.C. for this lasting impression of Impressionism.

I wish to thank the French Heritage Society, formerly The Friends of Old French Houses and its officers. With their cooperation, in 1994 I was introduced to the late Monsieur Jean Marais who, in his final months, kindly and enthusiastically encouraged my interest in this project and aided in my earliest research pertaining to the Chateau Rottembourg, the extent of Ernest Hoschede's collection of Impressionist paintings, his auction of 1878, and his life with Alice and their children at the Chateau Rottembourg. Monsieur Marais brought substance and credibility to the earliest stages of this project, providing me access to photographs and related materials of historic significance from, among other sources, The Bibliotheque Nationale and the municipalities of Montgeron and Yerres. I continue grateful for his assistance.

My visit to the Chateau Rottembourg, an estate which continues to exist today, was made possible through the kind cooperation of the Officers of the Historical Society of Montgeron, France. Their affection for Montgeron and their interest in the Chateau Rottembourg's history along with photographs, maps, and print communications, provided me the intimate lens of historic and geographic accuracy I would not have enjoyed without their generosity. I am deeply indebted to them for leading me through the historic rooms and grounds of the Chateau Rottembourg and the nearby Church of Sainte-Jacques.

It must also be noted that central to my study of Claude Monet, French Impressionist Painting, lives of the protagonists and individuals portrayed in this book, all have contributed to the joy I have experienced. All of which speaks to the great art museums of America and Europe. Their doors and collections have been open to me not because I received special consideration, but because the art exhibited on their walls was on public exhibition and accessible to all interested persons who ventured into gallery rooms with no constraints of time placed on eyes that could never see enough or study enough. Of particular significance to me were The Museum of Fine Arts, Boston; The National Gallery of Art, Washington, D.C.; New York's Metropolitan Museum of Art, The Art Institute of Chicago, The Musee du Louvre, Paris, The Musee Marmatton Monet, Paris, The Musee D'Orsay, Paris, The Hermitage, Moscow, and other smaller American and European museums housing treasures of Impressionism. It was during repeated visits to these institutions that I found myself facing many of the Claude Monet paintings Ernest Hoschede once owned and where I came to respect and admire his taste and unqualified love for Impressionist pictures.

Now a special word on the famous art dealer, Paul Durand-Ruel, without whom no story of Impressionism is complete: How does one adequately acknowledge the life and work of so significant a figure? Is it best to begin by commending his great stores of patience and tenacity and perhaps his courage and foresight in bringing Impressionism to America in 1886, or should one dwell more closely on his human efforts as caring friend, mentor, and frequent loan officer to members of that group of struggling young lions whose work he promoted against all odds and at every turn? In his time Paul Durand-Ruel was a masterful showman and convincing salesman. He was forward thinking, resourceful, and imaginative, and like any good salesman he wanted to make money, which despite a number of serious setbacks, he eventually did. It was, however, his gift for recognizing genuine talent and taking that talent to the right place at the right time that has made Paul Durand-Ruel what we know him to be today: a legend.

No acknowledgment on these pages would be complete without my expression of loving thanks to my husband, Richard, who has been part of IMPRESSION SUNRISE from its inception. Over the years it has taken me to complete the manuscript he has encouraged my every effort with unfailing support and tireless attention, commenting on every aspect of the story as it developed, blending excellent criticism with consistent encouragement and always in keeping with our mutual respect for the world of art and the central protagonists of this story. Our visits together to the Chateau Rottembourg at Montgeron, The House of the Cider Press at Giverny, and the Café Baudy also at Giverny remain treasured memories. This book exists because of him.

Our daughter Vanessa's devotion, high spirits, and sense of humor were most welcome to me as the manuscript grew and developed, at times too slowly for my taste. Her unwavering interest in the project inspired me more than she knows to spend one more hour or one more day sorting through the immense volume of collected research material with which I eventually came to terms and which resulted in forming the soul of this book. I thank her for having the faith in me that I have in her.

Nancy Joaquim

Impression Sunrise
Claude Monet - 1872

"It is I who invented the word or at least because of a picture I exhibited I provided a journalist from Le Figaro with the opportunity to create a sensation. He had some success as you see. "

Claude Monet's answer when asked how impressionism was named. Memoirs of Paul Durand-Ruel
Durand-Ruel, editors
Archives of Impressionism II; Paris and New York, 1939.
p. 339, 340

Pauline Carolus-Duran - Portrait d'Alice Hoschedé. - Magite Historic / Alamy Stock Photo

Alice Hoschedé (1875)
Painting by Carolus Duran

Claude Monet by Pierre-Auguste Renoir- RTRO / Alamy Stock Photo

Claude Monet (1875)
Painting by Pierre-Auguste Renoir

In our life there is a single color
As on an artist's pallette
Which provides the meaning
of life and art
It is the color of love.

Marc Chagall

Claude Monet and his wife, Alice, St. Mark's Square, Venice, October 1908 (b/w photo) - Bridgeman Images

Alice and Claude Monet
Venice-1908

Louis XVI Lyre Clock

Louis XVI, White Marble-Ormolu Clock
Signed "Raingo Frere, Paris", 19th Century.

(authors collection)

Table of Contents

	Circumstances	23
1.	Outrageous Fortune	31
2.	The Street of Pictures	45
3.	The Salon	71
4.	In That Small Café	79
5.	Private Lives	105
6.	Eye of the Beholder	121
7.	A Family Affair	133
8.	Habits Respect, Tradition	145
9.	Turning Points	171
10.	The Dawn Lover	191
11.	The Gare de Lyon	201
12.	The Company We Keep	215
13.	Arrival at Montgeron	239
14.	Birds of Paradise	259
15.	A World Apart	271
16.	The Children's Hour	293
17.	Touches of Yellow Ochre	311
18.	Striations in Color	329
19.	The White Turkeys	341
20.	A Primed Canvas	355
21.	One Brief Shining Moment	389
22.	The Third Exhibition	405
23.	The Unthinkable	441
24.	Vetheuil	489
25.	Poissy	559
26.	Giverny	583
27.	State of the Art	627
28.	A Gifted Man	659
29.	The Rule of Three	679
	Afterword	693
	Bibliography	709

Panhard et Levassor Vintage Car/Voiture Ancienne, England - Chronicle / Alamy Stock Photo

Typical 1900s "Panhard-Levassor" with unknown passengers

CIRCUMSTANCES
(Letter from Jean DeLille)

In those days you didn't need a license to drive a car. In the France of 1900 if you owned a car you could legally drive it. Of course you were not expected to endanger human life, injure animals, or in any way damage the property of others. There was, after all, something to be said for civil behavior, but at the same time there was also something of a wild delight about the whole wonderful business of owning and driving an automobile.

Adding considerably to the novel idea that when one drove a car the world did not end at one's doorstep, was the attractive consideration that until the French Motor Car Act mandated drivers licenses, one was not required to be concerned with the long list of tiresome rules and regulations which came about once the world's love affair with automobiles exceeded all expectations and demand for these engineering marvels reached unimaginable proportions. No, in the France of 1900 if you drove an automobile, you were trusted to do the right thing. No uniformed Gendarme stopped you for speeding, no citations for disturbing the tranquility of the community were issued, and the existence of a stop sign or traffic signal at the intersection of two roads was unknown. Once you were sitting behind the steering wheel and moving, all you had to think about was where you wanted to go, which of itself could be a difficult decision to make, especially if like Claude Monet you happened to live in the remote Normandy village of Giverny where there were intriguing choices to be made between three bumpy gravel roads, one leading to the Church of Sainte-Radegonde, the other two to the equally remote Normandy villages of Vernon and Gisor.

Claude had a car. He thought the automobile was by far the world's greatest invention. In 1901 he ordered a custom-built Panhard-Levassor which took eighteen months to complete and which he was proud to tell me had been tagged at the Paris factory with his name, C. Monet. With a degree of enthusiasm I'd rarely seen in him, he anxiously awaited the vehicle's arrival at Giverny, delighted as a child expecting a new toy as he anticipated members of his large family sharing happily in the carefree joys of touring the countryside by motorcar. Sadly, the euphoria was short-lived. Claude's wife, Alice, did not share in her husband's enthusiasm for the marvels of the automobile. Once the long awaited vehicle finally arrived, she made every attempt to enjoy the novel experience of motoring as she sat beside her husband in the gleaming black Panhard, but it wasn't long before she discovered that Claude was a terrible driver. He was completely reckless and totally seduced by the thrill of motion and speed. She said the smile never left his face as she held on to her hat and he raced along one of the three gravel roads he had decided to challenge that day, heedless of both bumpy road conditions and worst yet, the dangers of stormy weather. As a result of this daredevil behavior and disregarding his wife's clear admonitions, Claude's joy behind the wheel of his beautiful Panhard-Levassor was fleeting at best. Fearing serious injury to one of the children or to her husband and his precious artist hands, Alice took charge of matters and hid the Panhard's starter crank. Skillfully softening the blow, she also hired a full-time chauffeur for less hazardous and imminently more pleasant motoring journeys, such as the weekly jaunt to the market at Vernon which she knew Claude loved and the occasional Saturday luncheon at the local Hotel Baudy where every eye was on them and where many of the aspiring American painters hungry to be in the midst of the acknowledged Master of French Impressionist Painting took rooms, their presence in Giverny an invasion of privacy which did not please Claude at all.

"Why is everyone staring at us?" he would innocently ask on these occasions at the Baudy as Alice smiled indulgently and pretended to study the menu which as the result of several years of Hotel Baudy luncheons she had committed to memory. "They're probably admiring your attractive new yellow vest," she would say nonchalantly, or "they must want to see what you decide to eat. Let's give them a real show today and have the roast lamb with apricot glaze. For dessert we should order the chocolate custard with cream and a tray of those sweet almond cakes you like so much."

Alice knew about such things. She knew about eating a leisurely luncheon in a dining room where every eye was on you. She knew about a successful artist's burning desire for outlets of anonymity, and she knew about the exuberance of aspiring artists hungry for recognition. She knew about chauffeurs and how to go about hiring them. She knew about running fine houses and supervising a staff of servants and gardeners. Most of all, Alice knew about protecting the people she loved and having fun in the process. It was this natural ability of hers, this joy she took in nurturing the lives of the people she loved which to this day remains uppermost in my mind whenever I think of her as I do now. As much as I hate to admit it however, I do harbor one single disappointment in moments such as these when I allow myself the luxury of remembering, and it is one with which I have never come to terms. During all the years she and Claude were together, Alice was content to live in the shadows, to remain in the silent but supportive background. She seemed to prefer that self-imposed state of being, her intelligence and natural spontaneity deliberately hidden from the same circle of admirers and citizens of the world who revered Claude. I should have been more sensitive to the dramatic changes that had occurred in her life, those hundreds of troubling incidents and hopeless conditions which took their toll and eventually affected her view of the world and of herself.

There are people who achieve great things in life. Claude was such a person. He had an insatiable hunger to succeed and the mindset and self-discipline to make that happen. It was different for Alice. She was born into a wealthy family of distinguished French clockmakers and had grown up in the elite world of chateaux in the country and piano lessons every Thursday. Given her background, at first it was difficult for those of us who cared about her to understand her romantic attachment to an unknown thirty-six-year-old upstart Paris painter who, for all his self-certainty, appeared to have absolutely no prospect for success. In our privileged little circle everyone asked the same question: "What does she see in him? He's just another absurd artist with ridiculous aspirations. He's taking advantage of her. Besides, she's married and the mother of five children!"

One of my favorite photographs of Claude and Alice was taken in the autumn of 1908 at Saint Mark's Square in Venice. I like it because the pigeons on Claude's head and the expression on Alice's face convey the playfulness and genuine spontaneity which was so much a part of the joy they constantly found in one another, all its random fragments weathered into quiet, respectful contentment by the time that Venice trip was taken. By then, Alice and Claude had been together for more than thirty years. They had endured one crisis after another. They had faced failure after failure. They had been destitute one minute, rich the next. Life had demanded a great deal of them, but there in Saint Mark's Square, in a picture with pigeons, it is clear to me that regardless of life's circumstances or the passage of years, they had always understood the power of the magic existing between them and how very much they meant to each other. After a while it mattered not at all to their friends that each of them had been married to others when they met and fell in love. After a while it didn't matter to me either.

By 1908 and that trip to Venice, Claude was a solid block of a man with a world-wide reputation and enough money to buy a car, a house, a yacht or anything else he wanted. The struggle was over, yet a few of the old habits remained. He still smoked the strong Caporal Rose cigarettes of his youth, he still drank Calvados after every mid-day meal, and he still awakened at dawn every day. Of course, at Giverny, new habits were established. When he wasn't away on a painting expedition, he painted there every day, but he also found time to watch over his constantly expanding gardens and lily ponds with great delight. Always receptive to innovation and the inevitability of change, in the gardens at Giverny he and Alice experimented with a wide range of the colorful flowering plants which served to inspire many of his paintings. Occasionally turning from his favorite Calvados, he developed a taste for the fine Sancerre Blanc sent to him from prominent vintners of the Loire, and in his later years when his eyesight began to fail he did not falter but painted with greater zeal than ever before. His private life with Alice and the strength they had developed between them to confront and manage all things had made that possible.

Although Claude lived to enjoy worldwide fame and the friendship of a select group of international art collectors and prominent government leaders, it was Alice who saw to the basic details that made daily life the satisfying experience it was for him at Giverny. She took great pleasure in supervising the running of the household and she was very good at the task, especially when it came to planning delicious meals with the cook and arranging the decorative objects she knew were important to Claude. It was Alice who decided to place the Japanese glazed pottery cat given to him by a visiting Japanese admirer on a sofa cushion in the yellow dining room where the walls were lined with the Ukiyo-wood block prints Claude collected with great enthusiasm, and it was Alice who carefully hinged together the familiar comfort of old habits with the trappings of success into the splendid life they enjoyed together at Giverny. Much to his credit and although his eventual fame and the nature of their relationship often kept Alice nameless and hidden away in the background, Claude knew this to be true. After a while, I suppose we all knew it to be true. Under all her gentle shows of femininity, Alice was a strong, resilient woman, and although she and Claude were from two different worlds, the time came when even I, with all my stored up affection for previous lives and glamorous old ways, had to admit they were perfect for one another.

With an eye for all things beautiful and a reluctant grasp of cold reality, after a while I also came to grips with the fact that Alice hardly fit the mold of the French society woman she really was. I still marvel to think that in a manner entirely inconsistent with her upper-class upbringing, she did indeed eventually become what her first husband, Ernest Hoschede, would call "a match for the mountain." On more than one occasion when Ernest and I were in the country hunting together or simply enjoying a long walk, he told me that Alice was exactly the type of society woman Claude and his renegade band of Impressionist painters had sworn to avoid because they had determined such women to be self-centered, controlling, and too insensitive to the demands of the artist's life of constant struggle to be completely trusted. When I remember those words I also recall that back then my good friend Ernest Hoschede was looking at life as he always did, with a nonchalant cynicism that for a long a time I shared. Under it all though, and as life's patterns were irrevocably altered, I really did admire Ernest for never losing sight of what he wanted most in life which was Alice's love.

Odd, isn't it, at this advanced stage of life and on this particular day that I, Jean DeLille, should be thinking about automobiles at Giverny and pigeons in Venice and stirring up old memories that are best kept locked away, but I suppose today I did myself no great favor by returning to that abrupt turn at the top of the Concy Road and those beautifully scrolled iron gates which to this day still lead to the Chateau Rottembourg where all the trouble began. I have no idea what led me there. Since that last heartbreaking day years ago when everything was over, I have deliberately avoided that bend in the road, preferring the somewhat longer approach to my house from the lower Concy Road nearer the station where once each day except Sunday the train still comes from Paris into our picturesque village of Montgeron. Of course, the truth is that my avoidance has been part of a private conspiracy with time. The greater truth may be that I have taught myself to believe a lovely white lie, forced I suspect, by the fragile thread of circumstance to believe that nothing existed for Claude and Alice before Giverny; no splendid old houses at ends of long drives, no loves or old friendships that have died out for lack of interest, absolutely nothing left to restore grand old images and reminders of a glorious past that meant so much and ended too soon. Until today, when I found myself at the gates to lives and loves that no longer exist, I truly believed I had succeeded at last in forever confining my thoughts of Claude and Alice not to the pain and anxiety of the past, but to their idyllic life at the rambling, green-shuttered Giverny farmhouse where amidst their sublime gardens and ponds they found their peace. I have even gone so far as to think of Alice not in the beautiful rustling silk taffeta dresses she wore seated by Ernest in the glow of evening candlelight at their elegant Chateau Rottembourg, but in her big yellow straw hat, cutting flowers for the house at Giverny, Claude smiling as he catches a glimpse of her from a window in his studio.

Now, thankfully, the flood gates can be opened and quite contrary to the power of my former convictions, I can squarely face the flow of events as they occurred and allow myself the wide-eyed clarity to see that Claude and Alice were simply meant to be, their love as easily understood and natural as the running of the tide or the rising of the sun. Frankly, I once thought they had fallen in love here at Montgeron simply because they had found themselves alone together in the romantic August of a difficult year, but now that my final link to such speculation is broken, I can pause and quite honestly see that as is the case with all the successful relationships and marriages I have admired, Claude and Alice found that elusive common ground we all search for. They learned to fill in the missing pieces of one another.

Despite this current run toward reality which I must admit, soothes my heart and eases my moments of reminiscence, time and again over the years I have remained content to tell myself that few settings in the world are more irresistible to susceptible hearts than those of the French countryside in the month of August. I have also regretfully reminded myself that countless heated love affairs begun in the rose-scented summer air at the loveliest of secluded chateaux have quickly cooled as autumn's winds begin to turn the landscape gray and dull. I myself have experienced my share of short-lived liaisons complete with moonlight kisses and passionate embraces under exactly such circumstances and with exactly the same disappointing results.

Have you been to Montgeron? You must come next summer. Yes, come by train in August when Claude came. Be here at that time of year and you will understand. Montgeron is still a lovely country village, small and tidy, about forty kilometers south and east of Paris. The houses nearest the station are modest and set close together. You will see that as soon as you step off the train. You will also notice that the small summer gardens are well-kept and filled with beautiful flowers. It is along the ascending Concy Road that the houses are farther apart, secluded and grand, most, like the Chateau Rottembourg, seductively hidden behind intimidating gates and elusive ribbons of lawn.

It is best to take the train from Paris as we all have for years, out of the Gare de Lyon. It leaves every afternoon but Sunday at one or thereabouts, depending on the mood of the engineer. The gradual, great sweep as you pick up speed and race along into the countryside is almost unnoticeable, but soon, as you gaze out of the window, the landscape of the Brie Valley lies before you and you are riveted by its beauty: the Briard Plateau's dense purple vineyards embracing the hillsides and the vast stands of flourishing woodlands flecked golden in the summer sun. It isn't long before a hot Paris summer and a crowded city train station filled with every contention of the universe can be completely forgotten. It must have been that way for Claude when he came in that August of 1876, quite unprepared for the charm and gracious spirit he would find at the Chateau Rottembourg, unprepared most of all for the thoughtful preparations the Hoschedes had made for him, but Ernest and Alice were splendid hosts. He was invited to their chateau dinners and was introduced to their many friends and family members, most memorably to Ernest's wonderfully flamboyant Cousin Beatrice and her dreadful husband, Marc. Imagine it! All this planned as a result of Ernest's fascination with a renegade band of French painters who were being called Impressionists. He attended their first exhibition in the spring of 1874. I have the catalogue he gave me. That event changed him; changed his view of Paris, changed his view of himself, even changed his view of me. Of course in 1874 I was just a fledgling young portrait painter and he was a secure, distinguished man about town; rich, handsome, married, owner of a successful Paris department store and obsessively drawn to all that was newest and best and most cutting edge.

How I wish I had been more perceptive during that span of years, more attuned to the realities around me and less enthralled by life at the Chateau Rottembourg and Ernest's many grand gestures. And of course, had I paid closer attention to the true scope of his daring as he supported Claude Monet and his controversial colleagues I would have seen his determination and unrelenting optimism as the dangerous mix it really was, but there was no letting up, no letting go, and the beautifully masked, skillfully crafted façade continued unchallenged, slowly but surely weaving its deadly web of hostility and betrayal and inevitably leading to the heartbreaking end of life as we knew it and loved it and expected it always to be.

Jean DeLille, Chateau Rougemont,
Montgeron, June 1927

CHAPTER 1

Outrageous Fortune
1874

That Jean DeLille should find himself the close observer of a past which in its time had dazzled him would not have surprised those who knew him best and were aware of his devotion to Ernest and Alice Hoschede and their Chateau Rottembourg. Of course on that day when he found himself at the imposing gates to Rottembourg, everything about his relationship with the Hoschedes had been over for many years. The winter of life was nipping at his heels and he was an aging country gentleman no longer concerned with keeping pace with what he called "the commotion of the world," taking his greatest pleasure from his country house, his gardens, his books and dogs.

In his day, DeLille had been one of the more successful portrait painters in Paris. Fresh out of the prestigious l'Ecole des Beaux Arts at the age of twenty-five, within a brief two years he had established a reputation as both a gifted artist and witty raconteur, the later talent particularly endearing to his gentlemen clients who often grew impatient with the length and number of required portrait sittings and were grateful for the distraction provided by his risqué disclosures regarding the cabaret music hall venues in which he took great pleasure primarily at the Folies Bergere such as his recollections of the night the very tall, very beautiful bar maid climbed atop the very long mirrored bar and proceeded to lead the group-singing of The Angel and the Child as she slowly removed her apron, her dress with its fifteen small buttons, and every lacy little thing beneath.

Apart from his frequent visits to the Folies Bergere and in sharp contrast to its often rollicking atmosphere, in his studio DeLille followed Van Dyck's serious and elegant example of portraiture, embracing the aggrandized, continental painting tradition of glowing satins and plush velvets on large canvases, subjects arranged in imperious poses and against flattering backdrops, as well as characterizations denoting the highest levels of style and station whether or not these styles and stations conformed to the slightest hint of reality at all. DeLille's appealing work along with his disarming personality had taken him far ahead of his struggling contemporaries, and unlike the endlessly romanticized, garret-bound Montmartre artists painting under desperate circumstances, he worked in a spacious, well-equipped studio in the city. By 1872 he was being recommended by Paris art dealers and praised by critics. By 1874 he was in demand and making enough money to support his mother and sisters in Dijon with enough left over to indulge in more than a few personal luxuries including a well-appointed apartment quite near the Parc Monceau and the frequent company of more than a few expensive ladies of the evening. His routine well-established, DeLille had quickly become that rare Paris artist satisfied with both his work and himself, but as the summer months of the eventful year of 1874 approached, a fascinating new client appeared at his studio door one day, one who would expand his predictable world and introduce him to a very new way of life.

In a surge of farsightedness, a Paris department store magnate and art collector named Ernest Hoschede had decided to have his portrait painted as a Christmas present for his wife, Alice. Having heard of the gifted young painter with a flair for glamorizing his portrait subjects, after a brief meeting he engaged Jean DeLille.

"I have sometimes wondered what would have happened if I had not agreed to paint Ernest Hoschede's portrait," DeLille revealed years later in his published memoirs, his intimate writing style and personal recollections providing an insightful study of a successful, sophisticated man of Paris in the prime of his life. "From the very beginning I liked him," DeLille wrote, recalling his first encounter with Hoschede. "His was a big, magnetic personality, warm and engaging, and I immediately saw him as a highly agreeable portrait subject. This was in large part due to the fact that from the first moment of our meeting he was completely unpretentious. Considering my status as a noted society portrait painter accustomed to the many affectations of the privileged class, this came as a pleasant surprise. He arrived at my studio unexpectedly one day in early June as I was cleaning brushes. There he was, standing at my door without introduction or appointment, a smiling, elegantly groomed gentleman of the city intent on immortalizing his own legacy, or so I thought at first glance.

"Hello! I'm Ernest Hoschede," he called out from the doorway like a seasoned actor who in a split second has stepped onto the stage, prepared to speak his lines and deliver a moving soliloquy on the general disarray with which he could plainly see I was content to surround myself. "I hope I'm not interrupting anything," he said, "but I'd like a portrait painted of myself and word has it that you're among that small circle of the very best in Paris," he added, stepping into my studio and looking around. "It's to be this year's Christmas present for my wife, and it's to be a well-kept secret. Do you think you can manage it?" he asked as I continued to clean brushes at my work table.

"Of course I can manage it. The question is should I?" DeLille remembered answering all too caustically, also recalling that as he had put down his brushes and wiped his hands with a towel he regretted not having disposed of the morning's cup of coffee still on the paint-stained table in the middle of the studio alongside what was left of the crusty roll he had hastily bitten into hours earlier. "From what I can see, Monsieur Hoschede, you do not look terribly frightening and you have come at a good time," DeLille further recalled having said, moving closer to his unexpected visitor. "I have just finished the last of the spring commissions. Please come in and let me have a good look at you. Summer is slow for portrait painters in Paris. Everybody goes away and quite honestly, right now I could use the work. My youngest sister is being married in Dijon at the end of the month and in a weak moment, over one of my mother's delicious Sunday luncheons, I announced that I would be happy to pay for the wedding. Since then, what I thought was to be an intimate family affair has grown into a veritable city-wide festival. At this point, my obligation includes the wedding dress, the traditional croquembouche, the entire formal luncheon, and of course the wines, which must be the very best and most expensive. Please know, Monsieur, that I am grateful to whoever recommended me to you. Shall I send flowers?"

Briefly studying the Hoschede countenance and as yet with absolutely no idea that the attractive man before him was becoming a Paris art collector of considerable note, DeLille found a highly satisfactory portrait subject as he gestured Ernest to a nearby chair. The sum of 5,000 francs for the completed portrait agreed to along with a deposit of 1,000 francs, he continued to examine his new client, commenting on facial features and detailing the expected process.

"Monsieur Hoschede, you seem to have a decent face and I see that all the expected parts are arranged pretty much as nature intended," DeLille began with a smile. "Ah yes! A nose, two eyes, a chin, and hair! That's good. Sadly, Monsieur, with the gentlemen there often is no hair. At those times I despair for a while and then resort to feathered hats and the flourish of military uniforms and helmets. I like to add swords, epaulets, cloaks, plumes, that sort of distracting thing you understand, but yes, I believe I can preserve you for posterity and in time for Christmas. You have quite marvelous hair and you will look very much like yourself without aid of plumes or helmets. Your wife will be pleased with my work. If you like, we can begin our sittings right away; tomorrow, if you're free. A little sketching, a little settling into the composition, only that to begin, and don't worry about confidentiality. I am nothing if not completely discreet."

"On the outside and unlike many of my portrait subjects who said very little during sittings and carried themselves with a steely, touch-me-not quality I found offensive, Ernest Hoschede had a compelling, marvelously outgoing manner about him," DeLille wrote with clear nostalgia, "but what I noticed as with more time I examined his features closely were his marvelous brown eyes. They looked straight at you, almost right through you. So invasive were those eyes, that I was quickly reminded of my most offensive shortcomings such as tendencies toward embarrassing untidiness and disarray, personal qualities for which I suspected even early on, an elegant man like Ernest Hoschede had little patience."

"Promise me you won't tell my friends or competitors that I don't look frightening," he said to me with a dramatically crushed but humorous expression as I took my time studying his handsome face and the luster of his thick, silver-flecked dark hair. "I work very hard to convince people that I am nothing short of terrifying. It's good for business; intimidates the competition; gives all five of my children something to think about too," he laughed with that wonderful throaty laugh of his.

Despite his wish to terrify and intimidate, during that first encounter, DeLille saw something beyond invasiveness in Ernest's eyes, and for a while it troubled him. "It was a quality impossible to ignore," he divulged. "At first I thought I was being overly intrusive as I judged his features, his body mass and height, but it was those eyes. They were never still. They were always searching, inspecting in an almost requisite manner, the way a bird or a hunter instinctively surveys his terrain and immediately judges the range of danger or sagacity. It did not take long for me to realize that in the brief time it had taken him to walk through my door and introduce himself, those eyes had swept over everything in the studio and had not missed a single thing, not the half-empty coffee cup, not the dried crumbs on the table, not the freshly stretched canvases piled up against one wall, the easel by the window, or the colors of the messy old paint spatters on the stone floor. It was marvelous, though, to face this rare individual squarely and study him, suspecting that hours or even days later, every detail of what he had seen would be remembered in a precise delineation of proportion and particulars.

Intense as his eyes were in meeting mine, it would be some time before I would learn that here was a big-hearted lover of life; someone who could be ready for a good time at a moment's notice, even a rough fight if necessary, but from the beginning I felt there was something terribly unsettled about him, something that told me he was not entirely satisfied, not completely happy. I saw it in the gray shadows that occasionally crossed his face and the uncertainty that came and went in those restless eyes as we began to talk. It would be some time of course, before I would come to understand the true depth of what I was seeing in Ernest's eyes on that summer morning when we met in 1874; longer yet before I came to understand the true nature of the deep-seated anxiety with which he and Alice, had begun to live, or that in his disquietude he was not so different from those of us who must confront our demons and deal with them as best we can. Eventually though, I came to know Ernest Hoschede as a man driven by ambition, ego, and an immense need for respect. At first I saw it in the way he sat. It was all in his posture, in the solid set of his shoulders, in the attractive tilt of his handsome, well-proportioned head, in his own confident sense of self when he talked to you or for whatever reason decided to ignore you completely, which from time to time I found he would abruptly do.

He was a substantial, thick-set man with large hands. His quick smile had a way of lighting his face and like so many of us in those precious, defining ears of trial and error, his natural energy and spontaneity had not yet been dimmed by disappointment or tarnished by life's contrivances. No, there was no hesitation, not yet, no faltering in Ernest Hoschede, not then, not on the outside. In those early summer days of 1874 and apart from what I saw in his eyes, Ernest Hoschede had an infectious glow about him and I accepted his portrait commission with clear enthusiasm. An appointment was made, not for the following day as I had suggested, but for the following week which he said would be more convenient. Promptly at ten o'clock on the appointed morning, my portrait subject appeared, and with no small ceremony. He was truly a sight to behold.

Twirling a gold-pommeled cane, he came through my door wearing a magnificently tailored black frock coat and a pale blue satin vest, his attire completed by gray striped trousers, a stiffly starched white collar, and the shock of an expertly knotted bright red silk cravat. It was a well-conceived costume for a man with his easy grace and swagger and I had to admit that he had truly captured the desired worldly, accomplished look I knew we both wished to convey in his portrait.

"I frankly marveled at his natural demeanor," DeLille confessed. "The control, the command, the strength I worked so hard to convey in my portraits were all there in a full human composite of clear decisiveness that made me realize painting Ernest Hoschede's portrait and capturing his complexities was not only to be my most enjoyable assignment, but my greatest challenge, and that was simply because my subject was portraying no adventurer, no military hero or author's fictitious character. He was portraying himself."

"I began by seating him on an armless tall-backed chair. To my surprise, my subject immediately struck his own pose. Amazing me yet again, the pose was absolutely perfect," DeLille recalled. "Without chair arms to support him, which would have given him something to do with his arms and hands, he leaned slightly forward, his shoulders straight, his well-groomed left hand poised on his upper right thigh, the right hand clasping it, his feet positioned a few inches apart, one behind the other, the right foot flat, the left bent at the instep, as if at any moment he could be ready to run. His head tilted ever so slightly, he looked just a bit to the left, his marvelous profile in full view. His gaze was to the window, and it was as if he had found something there to focus on; something so compelling that for a few minutes I was convinced he had forgotten I was there. It was, however, in those few moments as I quickly began to sketch that I grasped the concept for the portrait. It would not be a full-length depiction, but a three-quarter body composition, one taking full advantage of the strong physical subject before me: the sensitive eyes, the full cheeks and perfectly shaped nose, the contours and lineation of neck, chest, and shoulders, and the strong, immaculate hands so authoritatively set."

As DeLille described it, the ensuing conversation on that day was only mildly revealing, but it touched on a variety of subjects, Hoschede's clipped, often disjointed conversational style and his tendency to rapidly run thoughts together at times difficult for DeLille to process. "His sentences were like hot potatoes being tossed about at the fireside," as he put it.

"Paris may be enjoying good times now, but nothing remains static here," he remarked as he settled himself into his pose, his solid gaze to the window. "When I look out there I can almost feel the breath of my competitors brushing hot against my neck. Must be the same with you. Things in Paris are moving so fast right now. Everybody wants to outdo his neighbor, his friend, even members of his family. I'm thinking about adding the new electric lighting in parts of my department store. It's expensive though. One of my competitors has electricity lighting up his windows. It's on until midnight. Have you seen that show on Rue de Rivoli? Nothing more than an effort to tempt the public into buying. Every night the newest merchandise is laid out in bright light for all to see. I understand people actually return the next morning, ready to buy. Where is it all going?"

"And who could that competitor possibly be?" DeLille admitted to having asked, more than mildly interested in exactly who the worrisome competitor of such a man as Ernest Hoschede could dare to be.

"La Samaritaine over there, facing Place de Chateau d'Eau! Their merchandise is cheap and appealing to the new crowd. You know, that bunch that got rich on Baron Haussmann's Paris makeover, the tar merchants and suppliers of construction tools and equipment, the wagon masters and workhorse breeders. They knew a good thing when they saw it. Opportunity yes, and plenty of it to construct all those miles of avenues and boulevards, and what was it? Thirty thousand new buildings? And from what my wife tells me, in addition to its fixation with electricity, La Samaritaine has announced it will be open on Mondays! No commercial establishment in Paris has ever been open for business on Monday! What is happening to this city? And then there's Bon Marche. Now there's another wild attempt at turning Paris into a melting pot of substandard goods and shameless self-promotion. Three store levels of merchandise. People milling about everywhere as if they'd never seen clothing, bottles of fragrance, or housewares before. Next thing you know, stores will be open at night as well as on Mondays. Where is it all going?"

Toward the end of that first sitting, DeLille's talkative subject not only complained about competitors, he also spoke at some length about his great fondness for country life and as he did so, artist and subject discovered the mutual attachment that would bind them together in close friendship for the rest of their lives.

"Thank God I can escape to the country every summer with my wife and children," the man DeLille would soon call Ernest confessed. "Out there at our Chateau Rottembourg I can forget all about this nonsense. Our house is in Montgeron, near Yerres. Perhaps you know Montgeron. Charming small village. The Senart Forest runs along its border with Yerres. Very good hunting in the Senart. Do you hunt? A few of your contemporaries live in the area, Gustave Caillebotte for one, Carolus Duran for another. You must know Duran. Big, flamboyant personality. Glamorous. Always wears a cloak. He's done a nice painting of my wife, Alice. He and his wife, Pauline, often come to dinner. They've been restoring a lovely farmhouse at Montgeron. Perhaps you don't know Gustave Caillebotte. His father is a friend of mine. Martial Caillebotte has been a Justice at the Tribunal of Commerce for some time, but he made his great fortune manufacturing beds for the military. Smart. He's none too happy about his son giving up the practice of law in favor of painting. His mother is the one who encourages him. She gave Gustave one of the first floor rooms in the house for use as a studio. He evidently finds great inspiration at Yerres. He showed me some scenes of the family gardens he's done. I bought two."

That last statement alone should have told me that I was in the presence of a serious art collector, one who cared deeply and bought wisely, but I was completely focused on the project at hand and I paid only passing attention to my new client's casual reference to the purchase of paintings. It was only much later that Ernest's avid interest in the Paris art world would come to mean something to me and it was only when I saw with my own eyes the truly spectacular collection of paintings he was assembling that I understood the depth of what in truth, was becoming an obsession.

"How long does it take to reach your country place?" DeLille asked, caught up in the rapid Hoschede conversational style but wanting to remain engaged, all the while struck by his descriptions of summer days marked by the pastimes of artists such as wealthy Gustave Callebotte who painted outdoor scenes of kitchen gardens abundant with rows of colorful vegetables and baskets of freshly picked strawberries, figs, persimmon, and quinces.

"Montgeron is about forty kilometers from Paris by train. Once I leave the store and get to the Gare de Lyon I can be out there in about an hour, depending of course, on the speed the engineer has decided on for that day. It's usually enough time to do a bit of newspaper reading and enjoy a little nap. Every year, Alice and the children spend the entire summer there, and every week from June to October I travel back and forth between city and country. Must attend to business, you know. Alice loves the house at Montgeron; loves her gardens; grows beautiful roses. Sometimes we spend Christmas in the country. The children pray for snow."

"It sounds wonderful, DeLille, recalled remarking, adding "In Dijon my mother keeps a garden. It's small, but she adds a few new things every year. When I visit her in the summer what I enjoy most is the time I spend every day looking after the garden with her. I've thought that someday I'd like to have a house in the country with a garden of my own, but I'll be needing fewer family weddings before I can think that grandly."

It was during one of the early July sittings that in his decidedly presumptive way Ernest planted the seeds of a very new aspect of life for DeLille. "There's a house for sale at Montgeron," he announced with his confident, broad smile. "It would be right for you, DeLille. It's not too far away from us, on Ruelle des Prez, quite a good house, not a big estate, but spacious enough and airy, and there's a winding stair leading to a charming tower. Nice place for a painter like you to work in. Lots of light up there in that tower. The house itself is constructed of stone and there are gardens. I heard about it coming onto the market just last week. DeLille, you should see it. I could take you out on the train with me at the end of the week. You could stay the week-end with us. Of course whatever timing strikes you as convenient will be fine, but I wouldn't want someone to come along and buy the place before you've had a chance to see it. I think I'll talk to the caretaker and tell him there's an interested party, someone who will do the property justice. I'll ask him to put off anyone who comes to the gate with an inquiry."

"Monsieur, I truly appreciate your suggestion," DeLille interrupted, "but I'm sure a house at Montgeron would be much too expensive for me. I would love a country house someday, but I'm better off to wait. I'm living comfortably here in Paris right now and in addition to expenses for my sister's big wedding, I'm seeing a young lady who interests me very much. If we marry I'll want to buy a house in the city and be close to my studio. All that will be expensive. Also, I believe in maintaining a solid level of financial security, a cushion of ready cash and a few safe investments you understand, something I expect I will continue to do for the rest of my life. Thank you very much for thinking about me. The house you describe sounds wonderful and I'm intrigued by the tower, but perhaps in a few years I will be in a better position to consider the purchase of a country place."

"No, no! You don't understand, Jean! The house I'm telling you about can't be terribly expensive," DeLille's persuasive portrait subject insisted. "It may need a little work and that could affect the price, but from what I can tell it looks like a solid place, good for a painter like you, and even if you marry and set up a Paris household, I'm certain the maintenance would remain affordable, and what a nice wedding present a house in the country would be for your bride. I must say, the whole thing sits quite nicely at the end of the long drive to the large main house. Very impressive in its setting. I'm told it was the estate manager's house at one time. Last week I had a look at it with the caretaker. He lives in the gatehouse. The owners of the estate are Montgeron friends of ours, but they rarely come out from Paris anymore. The caretaker seems to be looking after things. He tells me the manager's house hasn't been lived in for a while. I will say the rooms do appear a bit neglected. A little paint and a few repairs should take care of things. I also think a little rainwater may have leaked into one of the second floor bedrooms. I noticed a few stains on the ceiling, but that sort of thing is easily taken care of, and what's a country house without a leaking roof and a few stains on the ceiling? There's some furniture. It's dusty, but most of it looks to be in reasonably good condition. I saw some tables and a rather nice writing desk. The garden is overgrown right now, but you could have it under control in one or two summers. I know the place must sound a little derelict, but it could be just the sort of project you and your bride would enjoy taking on together: breathing new life into a lovely old house and reviving some gardens. Eventually you could paint there full time, invite your clients. And if the price can be negotiated, which I believe it can, why not consider it? And Jean, we'd be neighbors. We could go into the Senart and hunt together. You must come, and soon. Alice says we could use some fresh young blood in Montgeron. I know she'd like you."

Cautious as he was about incurring financial obligations, curiosity succeeded in getting the best of Jean DeLille. Within the next week he found himself on the train to Montgeron, the proud owner two weeks later of a lovely stone house complete with winding staircase and tower, and on the grounds of an impressively large estate which, although seldom visited by its owners, was magnificently maintained by a team of local gardeners and a devoted caretaker. Unfortunately, the old gardens surrounding DeLille's newly acquired country property did not enjoy quite the same level of attention as did those surrounding the elegant main house. They were overgrown and strangled by weeds but DeLille found himself eager to start in on restoring them.

The long, winding drive leading to what eventually would come to be called Chateau Rougemont was marked by a simple stone post on the Concy Road, not too far from the imposing black iron gates of the Hoschedes' Chateau Rottembourg, and from the day of his arrival at the Montgeron address where he would eventually come to live the year round, Jean DeLille and Ernest Hoschede became the best of friends. For the next three magical summers DeLille was a frequent and favored dinner guest at the Chateau Rottembourg. He joined Ernest and Alice and their family in leisurely summer luncheons and picnics under the glorious copper beech trees of the Chateau Rottembourg estate. He and Ernest hunted together in the Senart, garnering seasonal pheasant, guinea hen, ruffed and hazel grouse, gray partridge, and the ever abundant rabbit and hare. They joked and poked fun at one another's shooting prowess and hunting attire, they laughed a good deal, and through one summer after another they visited at one another's houses almost daily when Ernest was at Rottembourg, progress on what had become a long series of arduous renovations at DeLille's country residence and their increasingly alarming cost the focus of lengthy, but humorous and always good-natured complaints.

When they discovered they shared a minor talent for the piano, the two began a tradition of playing duets after dinner in Rottembourg's rotunda where, from under a sparkling crystal chandelier, a gleaming black Pleyel piano shone out like a beacon from the center of the room. They did rather well with what they could remember of the Beethoven sonatas and Chopin etudes they had learned through childhood, but after a few glasses of brandy or champagne, DeLille took over the piano to play and sing a raucous solo tune or two he had recently heard at the Folies Bergere while Ernest took it upon himself to do a spontaneous little dance.

"I was the far better pianist," DeLille humorously confessed in his memoirs, "infinitely more musical and definitely more accurate, but quite surprisingly, Ernest was a most agile dancer and so taken was he by the success of our spontaneous after-dinner performances, that at their conclusion he would fall into one of the four flowered red chairs nearest the piano and laugh wholeheartedly, clearly delighted with himself and his newly discovered talent for solo dancing."

Alice was embarrassed by both DeLille's dance hall ballads and Ernest's dancing. A capable pianist herself, she also frowned on their attempts at Beethoven and Chopin piano duets which both Ernest and DeLille readily admitted were hardly suitable tributes to their revered composers. Most of all, Alice frowned on their drinking and, as DeLille put it, "I now believe Alice may have been justified in objecting to our drinking, but it is not at all true that Ernest and I were completely irresponsible drunkards, unruly or even mildly destructive. No, we were nothing if not at all times supremely polite gentlemen rather magnificently dressed in our evening attire if I say so myself, and readily engaged in intelligent conversation with guests, but I do admit that after dinner, with the encouragement of friends and the added pleasure of multiple glasses of champagne, we were playful. That must be said. There was just something wonderfully, harmlessly intoxicating about the combination of fine wines, good company, and delicious food being enjoyed in the magic of the French countryside. And how could I not have been intoxicated by that beautiful piano bathed in candlelight in that magnificent house inhabited by those extraordinary people?"

Unlike any other DeLille had ever known or been part of, the environment at the Chateau Rottembourg sparked the senses, and in the hands of Alice and

Ernest Hoschede it did indeed succeed at intoxicating not only its most frequent guest, but every visitor, male or female, avid indulger of spirits or pious creature of abstinence. "Quite simply, there was nothing like it," DeLille wrote, "and if I could be accused of being drunk with friendship, beauty, and love throughout those all too few precious summers at Rottembourg, I gladly admit to frequent and complete inebriation."

As the result of twenty portrait sittings and the several years they enjoyed as country neighbors, Jean DeLille came to know Ernest Hoschede better than anyone other than Ernest's wife, Alice. Even years later, when everything was over and only the debris of anger and blame remained, DeLille would adamantly believe that Ernest was at his best in those early years of the 1870's. In fact, Ernest himself would eventually look back on those years, brief as they were, as the best of his life. He would see them as a time of extraordinary vibrancy and unlimited opportunity not only for himself and his family, but for the City of Paris as well. Prosperous, confident, and supremely optimistic, like so many young men of his privileged circle he was ill-prepared for the consequences of change clearly evolving around him in a city brilliantly modernized and newly transformed.

Portrait of Paul Durand-Ruel (1831-1922) in his gallery, c. 1910. - Heritage Image Partnership Ltd / Alamy Stock Photo

Durand Ruel
1910

CHAPTER 2

The Street of Pictures

By 1874, the dynamic spirit of a forward-thinking powerhouse named Baron Georges Haussmann had settled in and overtaken the heart of an important world capital no longer irrevocably tied to medieval remnants of its historic past. Between 1853 and 1870 and with carte-blanche from Emperor Louis Napoleon III, Baron Haussmann had directed the massive transformation of the City of Paris, an undertaking which had resulted in the elimination of muddy slums, the creation of magnificent parks and gardens, and the remarkable cleansing of the polluted River Seine. The result was nothing short of stunning. When all was said and done, the poet and novelist, Theophile Gautier wrote: "The city is aerated, cleaned, and every day puts on the makeup of the civilized world."

Significantly impacting the application of that flattering makeup, apart from the miles of impressive tree-lined boulevards and long blocks of uniformly roofed Haussmann apartment buildings lining both sides of the Seine, were the Twenty Arrondissements or Administrative Districts which by 1860 Baron Haussmann had created to organize the city as never before, thus replacing a maze of municipal confusion with a series of clear directives across all Paris, essentially making it possible for accurate maps of the city to be created and distributed. For the first time in history, areas on both the Left and Right Banks of the river as well as the islands between, had definition. Further clarifying the city's defining characterizations, a person could immediately be known by the location of his arrondissement, each possessed of a distinction clearly setting one apart from the other.

"Ah, you say you live in the First Arrondissement? You must be very rich!" a resident of the First might hear from his new friends as he sipped his café crème at a table in La Nouvelle Athenes or La Marlette. The First Arrondissement was the Historic District. Here were The Louvre, the Tuileries Palace, Le Jardin du Palais Royal and Place Vendome, nearby a number of elegant, high-rent Haussmann apartment buildings.

As prestigious as The First, the Fourth Arrondissement comprised of ninety-four acres on the tip of the Ile de la Cite, was the island home of the aristocratic Marais. The land, given by Charles the Bald, also known as King Charles II and father of Louis the Stammerer, to the Sainte-Opportune Abbey in 880 for development of crops, here by the Nineteenth-Century were the elegant mansions of Place des Vosges and the renowned Cathedral of Notre Dame. In The Fifth Arrondissement, the Sorbonne maintained educational authority over the Left Bank's thriving academic community as did the University of Paris in the Sixth and the Museum of Natural History housed at the Hotel Guenegaud in the Sixteenth.

Parisians had quickly accustomed themselves to the clarification provided by their twenty new arrondissements and their individual distinctions. They had also quickly adapted to the bright blue porcelain street signs attached to corner buildings, but it was one narrow, unpaved street in the heart of The Ninth's bustling center which by spring of 1874 was attracting the attention of a particular group of Paris residents very much in step with Baron Haussmann's modern Paris, Ernest Hoschede prominent among them. It was this street, within those early years of the 1870's, which was silently and steadily setting the tone and temper of Alice and Claude Monet's remarkable journey to Giverny, and it was this street onto which many of their fellow travelers would tread and make their presence known. It was The Street of Pictures.

The blue porcelain marker attached to the corner building at Boulevard des Italiens identified the old coach road as Rue Laffitte. No different from any other blue porcelain marker attached to any other building on any other busy corner within the Ninth Arrondissement's variety of stylish shops, crowded restaurants, and mirrored cafes, Rue Laffitte's gleaming patch of blue was an accurate directive to the casual passerby, but to Paris artists and their collectors that patch of blue marked the gateway to hope, for in the art galleries tucked between the old mansions lining both sides of the storied passageway into Paris, hundreds of paintings by artists both struggling and successful, past and present, were displayed and for sale. Given the nature of its appealing contents to enthusiastic collectors and the financial opportunities it held for struggling painters, Rue Laffitte was indeed The Street of Pictures, and it was here that the highly unlikely romance of Alice Hoschede and Claude Monet essentially began, for it was also here that in 1868 the Paris art world opened its seductive doors to Alice's husband, the then thirty-year-old Ernest Hoschede.

Beginning with little more than curiosity, Ernest's repeated visits to The Street had, at first, resulted in a growing fascination with the content of its dynamic world and the people connected to it, but even as a young man, Ernest Hoschede was possessed of a burning desire to be connected to all things and all people that mattered in the city of his birth, and in those days the Paris Street of Pictures world mattered. Its gallery addresses were well-known to those who frequented The Street, but whether Ernest or any other urbane citizen of Paris regularly patronized Beugniet at 18, Lebure at Number 12, Detrimont at Number 33, or Durand-Ruel at Number 16, they took pride in The Street's existence, for it did its part in defining the thriving cultural life of Paris. It was different for those whose work defined The Street, those artists who lived and died by its rhythms and flirted with its possibilities. To anxious, struggling painters at work in lonely Left Bank quarters where time could pass too slowly and breed long periods of discontent, The Street of Pictures was no thoroughfare of municipal concern or pride. To them it was a repository of dreams. Well aware of its risks and guises, its moods and temperament, it was within this pulsating world of creativity, constant struggle, and plentiful money that in a remarkably short period of time Ernest's role in the Paris art world developed and fully blossomed.

At the outset, eager to become known as one of The Street's more significant patrons and in possession of a small collection of caricatures and lithographs left to his family by an uncle, he enthusiastically assembled a collection of landscapes and portraits, none terribly important, many not very good, most not at all interesting. By spring of 1873 all that changed when he acquired several important Barbizon landscapes, a large Corot titled *Morning* of particular significance. In rapid succession, the powerfully rendered landscape paintings of other Barbizon artists followed, Courbets and Rousseaus becoming particular favorites. Well on his way to becoming recognized as a highly respected Paris collector and in the process creating a collection of considerable note in a city famous for shaping the tastes of the international art world, Ernest's choices and purchases were soon guided by the distinguished Street of Pictures dealer at Number 16, Paul Durand-Ruel, the paintings Durand-Ruel sold to him financed by handsome profits from the Hoschede Department Store on Rue de Poissonniere, a highly successful commercial enterprise which had been at the center of Ernest's professional life for more than ten dynamic years.

With a tireless drive to succeed and an advance of 400,000 francs from his generous parents, at the age of twenty Ernest had taken over the modest but reliably profitable drapery and upholstery business his father and mother had operated all their adult lives. Openly harboring a dislike for the mundane business of household textiles, in a short time creative Ernest Hoschede had turned to carrying a vastly more selective and expensive range of luxury merchandise which the re-named E. Hoschede's well-heeled clientele insisted was as elegant and tasteful as its charming young owner.

If you wanted the very best in a wedding trousseau or were in need of an exquisite infant layette or christening gown to be handed down through generations, Hoschede's was the place. If you needed a special gift, be it for your wife, your mother, or your Friday afternoon lover, there were silk fringed scarves from Lyon, embroidered shawls and lace mantillas from Barcelona, and gold lockets and bracelets from Saint-Armand-Montrond. For your husband or father or the devastatingly handsome Moroccan gentleman you met last week at l'Orientale and cannot stop thinking about, there were watch fobs, leather gloves, and document cases available by special order. Despite the ready availability of fine epicurean goods throughout Paris, at Hoschede's one could find unique, beautifully boxed provisions imported from several locations across the continent and beyond. There were Swiss and Belgian chocolates, imported coffees and teas. There were delicious jams, jellies, and biscuits from London, all handsomely presented in uniquely hand-painted wooden boxes and tins. There were wicker baskets fitted for extravagant country picnics. There were exquisitely dressed, porcelain-faced Bru dolls. There were fine linens of every description: bed linens, table linens, and tea linens. Wide-brimmed ladies' hats appropriate for promenades in the Bois de Boulogne or afternoons at the Longchamp races dominated a corner of the first floor. Nearby, a colorful assortment of the currently popular feathered ladies' evening headpieces were displayed on mirrored cases, and in a secluded, quiet alcove one could find the required black mourning veil which if more convenient, could be ordered by messenger and delivered by courier to a grieving widow within hours. Hoschede's purchasing agents called on a long list of French milliners, dressmakers, and jewelers to provide only the most beautifully crafted items. Ernest Hoschede would have it no other way. And as his profitable enterprise prospered, so did his personal life.

Not only was there a grand Paris apartment on Boulevard Haussmann, there was the romantic Chateau Rottembourg at Montgeron. There were also the luxuries of butlers, maids, and cooks, and a private train to transport Alice and Ernest and their children and guests to and from their country estate where no personal want or need was overlooked. Established, wealthy, and popular, by the time he was in his mid-thirties, his department store running smoothly, its daily operations in the hands of a capable Managing Director, Ernest found himself with more time and considerably more money to spend on developing his art collection. At Monsieur Paul Durand-Ruel's Street of Pictures art gallery where the paintings Ernest favored were informative topics of conversation, the assiduous dealer's experience and insights provided an increasingly solid foundation for the artistic definitions eagerly sought by his enthusiastic client. Quite in keeping with his penchant for high quality and good taste, Ernest had established a client relationship with an outstanding dealer in art.

Paul Durand-Ruel's expertise was admired and well-respected. Regarded as a Street of Pictures luminary, he was rapidly building an international reputation, but the range of his interests and the sales he depended on were not entirely limited to transactions conducted over expensive Old Master paintings and the sure-to-maintain-their-value Golden Age works of the Dutch and Belgians. He was also handling the work of several unknown painters who had recently formed a cooperative and were struggling to establish themselves within the strict parameters of the Paris art world. Ernest was not particularly drawn to their work, finding their paintings naïve and difficult to understand, but prices were good and if Durand-Ruel was handling them, he assumed there must be at least some talent, and hopefully some future value there. With encouragement from Durand-Ruel, early in 1874 Ernest purchased several paintings by members of the group of seven artists, these paintings adding a very new contemporary dimension to the rather conservative Hoschede collection, at the same time providing fresh conversational topics to flow between dealer and client. So congenial did this dealer-client relationship become, that in April of 1874, Durand-Ruel extended a personal invitation to Ernest to attend the afternoon opening of an exhibition of work by the struggling group of seven unknown painters he was encouraging. They had decided it was time to present themselves to the public and test the Paris art world's chilly waters. Durand-Ruel was assisting the group in organizing its event which was to be held at Number 35 Boulevard des Capucines, in a studio loaned by Felix Nadar, a prominent Paris photographer. Ernest accepted the invitation with pleasure.

Although located in the bustling center of modern Paris and mere steps away from the landmark junction of Boulevard des Italiens and Boulevard des Capucines, the rarely utilized Nadar studio seemed an inappropriate setting for any public exhibition of art in which highly refined Paul Durand-Ruel would have a hand, but ever the gracious guest, Ernest appeared at the appointed hour. He drank the champagne. He chatted with the attendees. He looked and judged and quite contrary to his expectations, what he saw in the poorly lighted setting was not only work of the Durand-Ruel-supported painters, but a mélange of artworks by other artists as well, the exhibition in its entirety numbering far more than the fifty paintings shown by the group of seven who had initiated the event. Although interested in viewing the entire but somewhat confusing presentation, it was the fifty paintings by the core group that captured Ernest's interest and immediately elevated his enthusiasm for what even in the unflattering setting appealed to his love of all that was newest and most cutting-edge. He took particular note of the unknown artists' names which in the catalogue were shown as Pierre-Auguste Renoir, Camille Pissarro, Edgar Degas, Paul Cezanne, Alfred Sisley, Berthe Morisot, and Claude Monet. According to Durand-Ruel, all had worked hard to prepare for the exhibition, some creating new works, others gathering older work deemed appropriate to show, the group of seven fully convinced that with this concerted effort their time had come.

Focused on landscape, portraiture, and scenes of daily life, even in the dim light of Nadar's poorly maintained studio the fifty courageous paintings stood out with their strong colors, bold brushwork, and unpretentious subject matter, their jolting impact so stirring a departure from the perfection of traditionally represented themes of escapism and fantasy that it was here, in the presence of what Ernest considered to be a profusion of highly transformative art, that he experienced the soaring conviction lying in the heart of every sincerely devoted art collector when time and place converge to set the time for choosing. As a result, it was here, and with exciting thoughts of expanding his collection of similarly conceived contemporary paintings much further, that with little hesitation he immediately placed reserves with Durand-Ruel on three paintings: two by the English painter named Alfred Sisley, the third by the one woman in the group, her name, Berthe Morisot.

Much to Ernest's great regret and fulfilling to a great degree Durand-Ruel's personal predictions, the eager group's attempt at attracting public interest and generating sales during its month-long exhibition was a complete failure. Scorched by the Paris press and scorned by the public, the group had, however, succeeded in one thing. They were the talk of the town. At their expense, the art-loving population of Paris accustomed to studio-posed portraiture, religious themes, and depictions of familiar European scenes was quite thoroughly enjoying itself.

"Is that really a crop of blue lettuce?" an exhibition attendee was heard asking of his companion as he stood before Camille Pissarro's *Hoarfrost* and adjusted his spectacles.

"No, of course not," the companion answered with a hearty laugh. "It's a field of cabbages gone bad! Wouldn't you love that horror hanging in your drawing room?"

"What is the woman doing behind the cherry tree?" another attendee was heard to ask of Berthe Morisot's *Cache-cache*.

"Don't you see what is happening?" the gentleman beside him asked with stern authority. "She has dropped her umbrella and wants to cut down the tree and carry it for shade. She is desperately overheated. It must be a very hot day wherever she is."

Although politely commended for their efforts, the comments and barbs ran the gamut of all that could be expected of this oddly intimate style of painting with which the Paris public had absolutely no experience. Serious about their art and respectful of their long cultural history, Parisians were unaccustomed to being confronted by depictions of people caught in simple everyday acts of being themselves and landscapes painted not in the professional studio but out of doors. Mon Dieu!

Driving this public negativity most effectively were the opinions of Paris art critics whose articles were written with clear disdain and widely circulated.

"Not one of these pictures looks finished!" was the opinion of several. "The painters must have been in a great hurry to prepare for this fiasco! Ridiculous!"

"The ballerina is too fat," one critic wrote of Pierre Renoir's young dancer, "and what, or who could she be looking at with those strange eyes? You call this art?"

"The frames are as terrible as the subject matter," wrote another critic, "and the light is dreadful. Fortunately, nothing will come of these radicals. This is not the way we do things in Paris. We have rules. Doesn't everyone know that?"

"First we had the fires on Rue Le Peletier," moaned yet another critic. "Now this. What additional tragedy can befall us?"

"I'll get a stroke from it for sure!" wrote Louis Leroy in Le Charivari of Claude Monet's painting, *Boulevard des Capucines*. "Those spots were obtained by the same method as is used to imitate marble; a bit here, a bit there, slap-dash, any old way. It's unheard of. Appalling!"

Offering at least a modicum of comfort to those left most aghast, the group of seven had wisely and with Durand-Ruel's encouragement, invited better known, more widely accepted artists to join their inaugural effort. Despite his own consistently explosive opposition to being categorized, Edgar Degas agreed that in order to appear credible and attract a larger audience, the better-knowns should be invited to participate in the Boulevard des Capucines event, specifically the group of successful Naturalists who posed human figures and animals in outdoor settings and habitats and whose name-recognition and popularity would surely improve the group's public image. Camille Pissarro disagreed, citing the danger of presenting too wide a variety of styles to the public at one time. Soon convinced, however, that painters such as the well-known Zacharie Astruc, Armand Guillaumin, and Stanislas Henri-Rouart would indeed attract greater interest, Pissarro eventually conceded, soon discovering, along with his colleagues, that the Naturalist presence did absolutely nothing to help the courageous advance of the rebellious, as yet unnamed battalion. All did agree, however, that the Cooperative they had formed had at least solidified their identity as a contentious New Group of Paris Artists worthy of attention, their organizational aims having been seriously set forth and documented well ahead of their disastrous exhibition.

The renegade Cooperative had been formed at the group's Café Guerbois headquarters, its Charter and Articles worked out by Camille Pissarro. So enthusiastic was the group about the formation of its own Cooperative, that it wasn't long before membership was open to any artist who came forward ready to contribute the annual sixty-franc membership dues, the amount payable in installments of five francs monthly for twelve months. Eventually, a roster of thirty members formed the 'Societe anonyme cooperative d'artistes-peinteurs, sculptures, et graveurs,' presenting more than two hundred pieces to a shocked public in the unique spring event of 1874, the nucleus of seven organizing painters showing barely one-fourth the total works in the exhibition, but in their non-traditional themes of quiet landscape, modern life, and contemplative domestic portraiture focusing fully on an adversity "for which we may never be forgiven," as Edgar Degas so aptly put it, a comment borne out by several respected critics.

Attending the opening in the company of Louis Leroy, the revered octogenarian and L'Artiste's long-time art critic, Marc de Montifaud, fingered his well-waxed mustache, adjusted his monocle, and observed that despite what he considered to be the thoroughly French subject matter, this group of painters was being perceived as subversive because "they simply are not preserving the science of painting, the construction of groups, the arrangement of draperies, the beauty of effects, and the artfulness of their means," all of which, Montifaud insisted, were "at the heart of French art." And so it went: the subversive arrangement of draperies, the heartless lack of effects and means and the unforgiveable absence of constructed groups, these disdainful phrases quoted again and again to and by the art-loving Paris public.

Reviled by the influential Paris press, rejected by the public, and discouraged at every turn, the upstart band of revolutionaries took encouragement from one another and from the champion they had found in Paul Durand-Ruel, the only art dealer in all Paris courageous enough to handle their work. At the same time, one courageous patron was emerging, his interest sparked by a particular painting he had seen at the much maligned exhibition.

On May 5th, the very day following the exhibition's close, Ernest Hoschede stepped out of his gleaming black carriage at Number 16 Rue Laffitte, prepared to make a purchase. Breathing deeply of the fragrant Paris spring air and with a twirl of his gold-tipped walking stick he strolled up to the green lacquered doors of The Durand-Ruel Galleries with the smile and swagger of an arrogant Bourbon prince. He was as imposing as the surrounding architecture. Ernest knew this about himself and he enjoyed the affiliation. His narcissism, although unconscionable at times, was not altogether unforgivable, for he was blessed with exactly the particular bearing of which Jean DeLille had taken notice and written of at some length. Of medium height and build, his solidly regal posture in the clear perfection of a May morning was that of a self-assured man-about-town, one on highly favorable terms with the tone and temperament of the city he had lived in for all thirty-six years of his charmed life.

Like the compelling background Rue Laffitte provides him, on this day Ernest Hoschede is fascinating to observe. His thick hair, glossy black and lightly dusted with silver, curls around his ears and brushes ever so slightly against his stiffly starched white collar. His beard is clipped fashionably short, close to his well-contoured chin. Nature has been good to him. His nose is enviably straight and perfectly proportioned to the unusual width of his cheeks. The striking impact made by the agreeable arrangement of these features aside, it is the small crinkled lines that form at the corners of his eyes whenever he smiles that give his attractive face it's winsome playfulness. It is a sexy, devilishly appealing quality that will, for all his adult life, give Ernest Hoschede the persistently jocular look of a mischievous schoolboy.

Paul Baudry - Portrait d'Ernest Hoschedé.- Magite Historic / Alamy Stock Photo

Ernest Hocshede
1876, by Paul-Jacques-Aime Baudry

Ernest is one of the Paris Insiders. He knows the Street of Pictures well. He knows its story and is on good terms with its personnel. Born and raised in Paris, he also understands his city, but this is no ordinary man of Paris content to casually classify locales such as The Street and in doing so foster civic pride. To Ernest Hoschede, The Street is not a destination designed for idle wandering. Neither does it exist for the whims of dilettante painters or the mere acquisitive pleasure of curious outsiders. To Ernest Hoschede, The Street is golden. It has meaning and purpose. It is about the quiet contemplation of color, shape, and space. It is about silence in a cathedral and praying to own every beautiful thing in it. In Monsieur Paul Durand-Ruel's art gallery it is about time at a precious standstill amid a spectacular array of rebellious illusions pressed against carmine-red walls. And so, it is with walking stick in hand and a fresh white rosebud in his lapel that on this May morning Ernest Hoschede saunters into the Galleries Durand-Ruel with a particular painting on his mind. It is *Impression Sunrise*, the 18x24-inch Claude Monet painting which by late spring of 1874 seems to be providing the renegades with a label as of all things, Impressionists. The story is being circulated in the popular Cafe Anglais that standing before *Impression Sunrise* during his one and only visit to the Boulevard des Capucines exhibition, Louis Leroy, the art critic of "I'll get a stroke from it for sure" fame, inquired of the man standing directly beside him what the group was calling itself. Confronted by the title plate under the painting, the man answered, "I would say we are Impressionists. Yes, that's it. Impressionists," said man standing beside Leroy the creator of *Impression Sunrise* himself, Claude Monet.

As was the case with most of its dubious companions, for the entirety of the month-long exhibition, *Impression Sunrise* had generated no interest. No reserves had been placed on it and by closing day it had, along with its rejected accomplices, gone back to Durand-Ruel unsold, but something about Monet's Le Havre harbor scene had reached Ernest. He had to see it again. He also wanted to arrange for payment and delivery of the Sisley and Morisot paintings he had reserved and of course, he would remind Durand-Ruel of the ten percent discount offered to purchasers during the exhibition.

Once inside Durand-Ruel's gallery he found *Impression Sunrise* displayed on an elaborate easel close to the doorway. Clearly, the prominent location of the painting and its title plate were serving not only as tangible evidence of the new group's identifying label as Impressionists, but as a major Street of Pictures dealer's wholehearted support of them.

"Ah, bonjour, Monsieur Hoschede!" came Paul Durand-Ruel's cordial greeting, his welcoming voice ringing out against the accommodating walls of the gallery he and his late father before him had operated for more than twenty years. "I had a feeling you would come by today," he added with a broad smile and a twinkle in his bright blue eyes, "but Monsieur Hoschede, you must excuse the great jumble you see here today. As you know, the exhibition on Boulevard des Capucines closed yesterday and today the paintings have been arriving. I have been given the improbable task of handling most of them with the hope of selling, but right now it's a nightmare. This one has told me he wants his paintings on this wall, that one wants his there. The truth is these paintings could be sitting here for months, regardless of their placement. I really must be out of my mind to be cluttering up my gallery this way, but regardless of the bad reviews there is something about this work I find worthy of encouragement. I watched my father's great success with the Barbizons. Corot and Courbet and a dozen others owe their fame and fortunes to him. I'm hopeful of duplicating that success in some way, but we'll see what happens. In any case, I'm doing my best to make sense of things today. I just hope I can," he added, throwing his hands up as if in surrender. "Do look though, and take your time. Just a few more notes to enter into the ledger and you will have my full attention."

Intent on the accuracy of his ledger, Monsieur Paul Durand-Ruel may have appeared vexed by the day's circumstances, but under the practiced veneer of exasperation there lived an astute art dealer very much at ease in the world of exhibitions and their aftermaths. It was a world in which he had lived at his father's side through childhood and into adulthood and it was one to which now, at the age of forty-three, he brought not only experience and skill, but mastery. Ernest had seen this piqued side of Durand-Ruel before. As a result, his patience as a preferred client was neither being tested nor challenged. In fact, the agreeable smile lighting Ernest's face revealed little of the thundering roar of delight he felt as he surveyed the state of things spread out before him.

"I understand perfectly," he assured Durand-Ruel with a nod, content to be left alone in a leisurely perusal of the landscapes and figure paintings of a cooperative of avant-garde painters whose trust in Paul Durand-Ruel he saw as not only justified, but earned. In conversation with Durand-Ruel he had learned that most of them had been at work for ten or fifteen years and that Durand-Ruel had first met several of them in the city of London.

Taking refuge, as many French citizens did, in the British Capital during the Franco-Prussian War and the dark days of the Paris Siege of 1870-1871, Durand-Ruel had been introduced to Claude Monet and his work through Monet's friend, the artist, Charles-Francois Daubigny, who like Claude and other young men in France, had escaped Paris on the last crowded trains to Calais and Le Havre, crossing the English Chanel by packet boat to avoid both conscription and the deprivations of the Paris Siege. Renoir, Sisley, and Pissarro joined Monet in London, meeting Durand-Ruel through him and like him, establishing a dealer relationship. With a sharp eye for talent and the energy of a circus ringmaster, while in London, Durand-Ruel mounted an exhibition which included several of Claude Monet's paintings along with several by Renoir, Sisley, and Pissarro. The exhibit, although not a money-maker, was not a failure, for in London, Durand-Ruel had found an exciting new group of hungry artists to encourage and promote. They were from Paris, they had no fear of toying with color, shadow, or perspective, and their uniqueness was capable of attracting what every art dealer worthy of the name dreamed of: Attention.

Durand-Ruel liked Claude Monet's work in particular, and upon returning to Paris at the conclusion of the war, he began buying all the canvases Monet brought to him. By the end of 1872 he had purchased twenty-nine Monet paintings for a total advance to the artist of 12,000 Francs, or 2,400 U.S. Dollars, at the time there being Five French Francs to One U.S. Dollar and Five Dollars to the British Pound Sterling. Soon, Monet's friends Renoir, Sisley, Degas, and Pissarro were also taking their paintings to Durand-Ruel and receiving advances ranging from 100 Francs (Twenty U.S. Dollars) to 1000 Francs (200 U.S. Dollars). By the time the Boulevard des Capucines Exhibition had opened on April 15 of 1874, except for Edgar Degas and Berthe Morisot, Durand-Ruel was handling almost all the

New Group's work. Like Edgar Degas, Berthe Morisot chose not to establish a dealer relationship with Durand-Ruel, her preference at the time to sell privately or from the studio of her brother-in-law, the dashing and much-admired painter, Edouard Manet.

Ernest was aware of Durand-Ruel's London history with what the dealer was calling his "young lions," and now that a considerable volume of their work was in his hands following a disappointing Paris exhibit, it would be interesting to see what would sell and what would not. Ernest was fascinated by the process. Some canvases remained in their exhibition frames. Others had been removed from borrowed frames and awaited Durand-Ruel's expertise in providing the frames he felt appropriate. Unmoved by the criticism hurtled by critics at the frames he had selected for the exhibition, Durand-Ruel wisely kept his own counsel and trusted his own taste. He cared deeply about frames and what they could do for a picture, a compulsion he shared with Camille Pissarro who agreed wholeheartedly that the proper frame completed the artist's work as little else apart from a sale, could. With persistent attention, Durand-Ruel also cared about safeguarding the work of the painters he represented, so much so, that many arriving paintings deemed ready for display were being promptly hung by two apron-clad assistants along the gallery's carmine-red walls in the precisely spaced, straight rows upon which the Rue Laffitte dealer insisted. In the wake of the most outrageous and maligned art event any anyone in Paris could remember and in spite of the jumbled state of affairs in his gallery and the deflated spirits of the group of painters he promoted at every turn, Paul Durand-Ruel had never looked happier as he observed the ongoing installations, often and clearly specifying his preferences with regard to sequence and positioning.

"Wonderful to see everything in one place like this today, isn't it?" he said, coming to Ernest's side with obvious pleasure, but Monsieur Hoschede, some of these paintings, even though they have been on exhibition for a month, are not yet dry. That is something I worry about. I kept reminding these artists that it can take a year for a painting to dry completely. Of course they know that, and I really don't know why I bothered myself with such an admonition, but everybody was pressed to the limit and in a big rush to present enough work to show. Some waited too long. Edgar Degas really had us worried. Some of his paintings came in barely an hour before the doors opened. I was afraid to touch them. I was hoping young

Gustave Caillebotte would be ready to exhibit, but he insists he needs more time to feel comfortable showing his work. There's a big talent there. He's bright and already an important part of the group. They love the fact that he is very much in step with their independent philosophy and that he is a collector himself."

"I do wish things had gone better for them," Ernest remarked, his granite-hard gaze riveted on *Impression Sunrise*, which seemed perfectly at home occupying pride of place on Durand-Ruel's most elaborate easel, "but what about this painting?" he asked, gesturing toward the orange-hued canvas, "this Claude Monet picture. Surely the paint is dry on this *Impression Sunrise*. I'd say it must have some respectable age to it by now, wouldn't you agree Monsieur?"

"Ah, yes, I do agree," the seasoned dealer stated. "Claude Monet painted it from a window at his father's house in Le Havre about a year ago, and from the look of things it could be keeping me company for another year, but you know how it is. In the Paris art world, the establishment rules and our art critics have a way of holding the public hostage. Brash, independent attitudes suddenly appearing on the scene don't sit well. Apart from all that though, I somehow remain hopeful, especially for Monet. Is the painting of interest to you?"

"It might be," Ernest nodded, his gaze still fixed on the Monet canvas. "Is that the Le Havre harbormaster standing up in the boat? Strange to stand up in a small boat. Monsieur Monet has an unusual eye."

"Like yours, Monsieur Hoschede," Durand-Ruel responded. "Yes, unusual perhaps, but not strange at all. Clear and unclouded I would say, and yes, quite like yours. Claude Monet is from Le Havre. He knows the harbor and I believe it knows him."

"What is the price?"

"One-thousand francs."

An impish smile lighting his face, the Rue Laffitte dealer began toying with the gold chain of his pocket watch with his thumb, a habit he turned to when evaluating circumstances, the skillful negotiator in him instantly aware of an opportunity for encouraging the sale of Claude Monet's Le Havre harbor scene. Dealer experience had long ago taught him that no one asked the price of a painting unless they were interested in buying it, but in this case the window of opportunity was as unusual as Claude Monet's artistic eye.

Durand-Ruel knew the client standing beside him very well. He knew his tastes and understood his lifestyle. There was no doubt in his mind that Ernest Hoschede lived every day of his luxury-loving life with a burning interest in all that was newest and most cutting-edge, and not only for himself but for his prestigious department store as well. The Hoschede emporium on Rue Poissonniere was as well known for its high quality, fashionable merchandise as for its owner's innovative approaches to marketing and the new innovation of advertising. Distinguished, well-connected people walked into E. Hoschede's every day. They made purchases amid spectacular arrangements of fresh flowers in the three first-floor niches. Ladies came to meet their friends. They ascended the grand staircase and enjoyed luncheon or tea in the elegant third-floor Pavilion, the fine food emporium Ernest had added to E. Hoschede's variety of experiences when a generous attic space requiring the raising of the roof and the addition of clerestory windows was turned into an elegant tea garden lushly planted with a profusion of leafy Dieffenbachia and masses of Dracaena, Lilies, and flowering Anthurium, the thriving array of greenery and blossoms cared for by an attentive, well-paid staff of gardeners. And who could tell? Perhaps a distinguished proprietor's interest in a new style of painting or better yet an exhibition in his store would arouse curiosity enough to generate circles of interest and a few sales. Ernest Hoschede was known to love originality, and if it was circulated that it was he who owned the painting that seemed to be naming the young lions, perhaps the idea of Impressionism would begin to take hold.

"I will tell you this, Monsieur Hoschede," Durand-Ruel began, launching into one of the articulate narratives at which he excelled, his thumb busily tapping at the chain of his pocket watch. "As the show was in progress and for all four weeks of its duration I did my best to sell this painting for Monet. As far as I'm concerned, *Impression Sunrise* is the most notorious painting in Paris right now. Thanks to Monet himself and his completely unprepared comment to Louis Leroy, it has provided a good label for Monet and his group, but no one wants to buy it. Pity! I've told myself it could be too far ahead of its time, too controversial, perhaps too much, but my arrangement with Monet on this was interesting. As you well know, when we Street of Pictures dealers accept paintings from the artists we represent, for the most part we try to provide an immediate advance against the eventual sale price. Monet likes that arrangement. He always needs money; a few hundred francs here, a few hundred francs there. It's the way he survives out at Argenteuil with his wife and son. With this painting it was different. This was the only time he asked me to take a painting without francs passing between us. It could be he was expecting a big response or a lot of money as a result of the exhibition. I don't know. I understand how hopeful he is and I respect his trust in me, but I've told him not to expect too much, especially now. Paris is changing. The whole of Europe seems to be, and in uncertain times people can be slow to adapt to new ideas and new ways of doing things, especially when it comes to spending their money on art. You know of course, that there is talk of recession in Paris. I hear about it every day; from clients and other dealers. I'm very worried about it. I dread the thought of what a failing economy could mean to Paris, and if recession does come, of course it will have a catastrophic effect on the art market in general and on this street in particular. The private sector will run from us as fast as those thoroughbreds at Longchamps on Wednesday afternoons. Of course none of this is news to Claude Monet. He's an intelligent, well-informed man. He knows how things work in this city, but I always feel I must do whatever I can to keep his spirits up. He expects a great deal of himself, sometimes too much. I see unusual talent in him. He works remarkably hard, but he has chosen a difficult life. Worst yet, he and his colleagues could be emerging at a bad time."

Ernest nodded in agreement with the idea that public taste was not easily swayed. He, himself, had tried any number of cutting-edge items at his store, which although favorably received at first had failed to generate sales significant enough to continue supply. Apart from their shared opinions regarding a capricious public's interests, it was Durand-Ruel's view of the growing financial crisis in Paris that was suddenly generating Ernest's immediate concern. If Durand-Ruel was right, the Paris economy of 1874 was faltering and like it or not, facts were facts.

Magnificent as it was under Emperor Louis Napoleon's Second Empire edict and the leadership of his brilliant Municipal Administrator, Baron Haussmann, the ambitious building boom and city-wide seventeen-year-long renovation program of the mid-1800's which had made Paris the most beautiful city in the world, had required massive financing and now, barely four years after the dissolution of the Empire and the abrupt end to Haussmann's renovations, in the elegantly gas-lighted restaurants and cafes along Haussmann's masterfully conceived grand avenues and wide boulevards, worried Parisians could still be heard blaming Haussmann for the country's overwhelming debt and criticizing Emperor Louis

Napoleon's stubborn overreaching vision for the threat of recession. The prospect was difficult to face, but the disagreeable truth was widely known.

As Haussmann's spectacular six and seven-story apartment buildings had risen one after another, and as the widest, most beautifully tree-lined boulevards and avenues in the world had criss-crossed the city at lightning speed, employment had reached a new high, creating a very new class of eager consumer. Responding to this fertile development, a rapid succession of new savings banks had opened to welcome the crush of unqualified, inexperienced customers the conservative merchant banks refused to touch. Easy credit had been extended with a smile and a quick signature and like employment itself, the number of mortgages and loans issued to citizens eager to become part of gorgeous new Paris had reached an all-time high. Since then, borrowing had continued on at an unprecedented level, but now, as the complicated decade of the 1870's had begun to unwind, starting off with the Franco-Prussian War, the devastating austerity of the Paris Siege from which the city had not yet fully recovered, and a subsequent period of anarchy, bloodshed, and political unrest rooted in the rise of The Paris Commune, once prosperous banks were failing, unemployment was on the rise, and Ernest Hoschede was being forced, as were many of his contemporaries, to concede that now and then, inconvenient and unattractive as it was, financial realities must be faced.

"Monsieur Hoschede, the world out there may be changing under our noses, but right now the general public isn't as open to new idea as you are," Durand-Ruel remarked as the two men continued to stand before Claude Monet's *Impression Sunrise*. "No matter what happens around them, most of our citizens prefer to live within the secure confines of time tested tradition and when it comes to art, they feel safest conforming to the unchallenged edicts and opinions of the Paris Salon and its commitment to shepherding public taste, especially when financial jeopardy threatens. Of course, this is not an objectionable condition. Our revered cultural institutions are the envy of the world. Year after year, when more than forty-thousand people attend The Salon, which simply put is the most extravagant annual art exhibition to be found anywhere across the globe, most of them enter the doors of the Palais d'Industrie genuinely relieved to see the same old themes painted and re-painted and re-sculpted and re-drawn, thus reinforcing the belief that the Paris Salon Jury is the best judge of what art really is. Of course, at the bottom of it, I believe the truth is that the general public is more than a little afraid of change. Sometimes I'm afraid of it myself. I wish things were different. Perhaps one day they will be, but right now Paris simply isn't ready to risk stepping away from its satisfying old habits and confronting the new idea of art you see here in my gallery today; this subtle suggestion of light and air, these scenes of ordinary human beings caught doing ordinary things. It just feels to me the timing is off."

A group of chattering men and women came into the gallery. They spoke to one another in Italian, walking slowly across the dark oak floorboards and commenting as they viewed paintings that had formed the Impressionist Exhibition. One of them addressed Durand-Ruel in French and said he had attended the Boulevard des Capucines exhibit. Politely acknowledging the gentleman, Durand-Ruel said he hoped he had enjoyed the exhibition and apologized for the disarray in his gallery, explaining that it was only temporary. At the same time he said he would be happy to answer any questions about the paintings, the artists, and prices. The group proceeded to observe the canvases being hung on the walls, glanced at the long tables lined with unframed canvases, and in minutes hastened toward the door with an abundance of "Merci, Merci, and Gratzi, Gratzi!"

"Well, there it is," Durand-Ruel remarked. "Even foreign visitors aren't interested. Those looked absolutely frightened. Right now, what we have in these paintings is a new idea and nothing more. Very soon there may be no money for new ideas. My late father had a difficult enough time promoting the Barbizons. Fortunately, until his fortunes turned around he sold frames and artist supplies as well as Corots and Courbets. Maybe I should do that. I often ask myself why I am promoting all this, especially now. I'm not making any real money on these pictures, and to make matters worse I walk a fine line here. I am now allowed to reserve paintings before the doors of the annual Salon Exhibition are opened, but it could be that before too long I shall have ruffled enough official feathers to find myself alienated from the very people who provide me with the basis of my livelihood."

Considering the demands of his profession and its many unknowns, it was not difficult to understand Durand-Ruel's tenuous art dealer position, especially when it came to financial outcomes. He put it very well when he said, "And of course, it is always imperative that I carry pictures that will sell. The English landscapes seldom fail me and I confess to a personal fondness for the Flemish and Dutch painters who are bringing in good money today. I do admire the tenacity of those lions, though. They took a big step with their exhibition. It was all their idea and perhaps a dangerous one without the blessing of the powers that be, but they've had enough. They're tired of submitting paintings to Salon Juries and not only being rejected but also being told that their work cannot be exhibited because it doesn't conform to proven artistic principles of the past. Adding insult to injury, they've also been told that since most of them have been at work for years, they should know better. Their impatience right now is easy to understand. Thank God they are secure in the most important thing, and that is their talent. Too bad the institution of The Salon and its juries have installed such a great wall. They may never be able to climb it, but there may be ways to get around it. We'll see. It could take time, though."

"Your observations should make it more interesting than ever to attend The Salon Exhibition this year," Ernest responded with his broad smile. "I'm meeting my wife there later this afternoon."

"Ah yes, then everything you see there will appear in rather sharp contrast to what you see here today. Do let me know though, if you see something you wish to reserve Monsieur Hoschede, and do be sure to look for Carolus Duran's portrait of Phillippe Burty," Durand-Ruel suggested. "It's a beauty; very well finished, and of course it is hanging on one of the more advantageous walls. Monsieur Duran has become a star and a Salon Jury favorite. Naturally, he's selling well and making lots of money. Recession won't hurt him. Other than that, you will find The Salon to be more of the same: some very good, very solid things, some in my opinion not very good or solid at all, but I will leave those determinations to you and to Madame Hoschede, of course. Please do extend to her my very best regards."

"Perhaps it has never come up in our conversations," Ernest responded further, "but Carolus Duran is a country neighbor of ours at Montgeron. He has done a painting of my wife in our garden. In the summer months when we are at the Chateau Rottembourg, he and his wife often come for dinner. My wife is very fond of them."

"Ah, that beautiful country house of yours! I assume you will be spending the summer there again this year?"

"Oh yes. The trunks have come down from the attic and my wife and the children have been busy packing and planning things as they do every year at this time. We all love it there; the freedom of the country, the beauty of the old house, and we have only one more occasion to celebrate before leaving the city. Madame Hoschede's uncle, Julian Raingo, turn sixty in a week's time and we are giving a party to celebrate. Of course, you know how closely knit the Raingo family is. Please do not tell her I said this, but Madame Hoschede is turning the apartment absolutely upside down for the occasion! Today, though, is set aside for The Salon. I'm meeting her there at two o'clock. Julian Raingo, will be joining us."

"Be prepared for the crowds. This year the exhibition is bigger and better attended than ever before," Durand-Ruel cautioned. "I like to believe that could possibly be in some small way due to the upset created by my young lions and the contrasts they represent, but who knows? Every day we do the best we can and regardless of the bad reviews at least their names are out there. We will try again, but it could be a while. I'm afraid that very soon this Street of Pictures could become a rough neighborhood."

Paul Durand-Ruel's realistic views sustained his fragile art dealer position in significant ways, but no one knew better than he that a Paris art dealer's life could be as difficult as the lives of the artists he represented, especially in uncertain economic times, and no one knew better than he that nothing about his gallery, not its carefully painted carmine-red walls, not the nature of its difficult-to-sell contents, not even the woody smell of its hundred year old timbers distinguished it from any other Street of Pictures gallery. Although Paris was unquestionably the art capital of the world, Durand-Ruel's gallery might have been any gallery on The Street of Pictures, the two men standing within the first of its three rooms any two discussing any painting, but on a cloudless spring day tailor-made for optimism, its daring mood was unlike that in any other gallery on The Street. Paul Durand-Ruel had laid his groundwork well and the air was rife with possibilities, but Ernest Hoschede had already made up his mind. He intended to buy the painting that had named a group of renegade painters Impressionists, but not for a thousand francs.

"Five-hundred francs for *Impression Sunrise!*" he called out, opening with those words, the initial stage of the age-old French ritual known to countless generations as bargaining.

Stationed before the painting in question, their voices brittle, their friendship and mutual respect temporarily set aside, Ernest Hoschede and Paul Durand-Ruel were suddenly engaged in heated debate, their back and forth efforts applied to the near tribal ceremony performed by buyer and seller as related to supply and demand, each party equally challenged to displays of charm, dramatic skill, and a complete understanding of the time-tested rules of the game.

At first, befitting gentlemen and conforming to accepted introductory procedures which demanded profusions of "if you please and I beg your pardon," they were terse in the confrontation, polite but serious in the approach, and above all, direct. Now and then they exchanged light-hearted comments and with well-practiced expertise threw their heads back and laughed, feigning shock or insult.

"Ridicule! Impossible! Durand-Ruel chortled as Hoschede once again countered *Impression Sunrise's* one-thousand franc price by half.

"C'est un tragedie, mais la piece avait pendu un peu de sa magie!" Ernest returned, shaking his head from side to side with appropriate drama. ("It is a tragedy, but the piece has lost a little of its magic.")

Between exchanges, the two frequently glared and scowled or suddenly pretended disgust and just as suddenly, as if dueling at dawn on a cherished field of honor, one or the other took a step back to assess the extent of the inflicted wound.

"Monsieur, one-thousand francs is absolutely my best price!" Durand-Ruel finally announced, facing the Hoschede countenance squarely, holding fast, ready to set the rapier at the opponent's throat and prevail in the encounter. "And if I may say so, one-thousand francs is a pittance for a man in your position, Monsieur!"

"That could be true Monsieur Durand, and I suppose this masterpiece, this "scene mysterieuse a l'orange" (this mysterious orange scene) of Monet's is a great bargain at one-thousand francs! It saddens me to say this Monsieur, but I walked past this "homage a Le Havre" at least a dozen times at the Boulevard des Capucines exhibition and I was not the only person to have done so. Did I hear you say you estimated there were two-hundred people who came through the door on opening day? It appears that not one of them was interested enough to reserve, nor was anyone else in attendance during the ensuing month interested enough to reserve. Sad, but before long, the painting will be famous for nothing more than faded splendor. "Un tragedie! C'est domage, c'est un grand domage." ("A tragedy. It is a great tragedy"). Poor Monet. No one cares."

"Take it, Monsieur Hoschede," Durand-Ruel urged, his desire to do his best for Claude Monet paramount. A mere thousand francs and it is yours! We can deliver it tomorrow. You will not regret this purchase and *Impression Sunrise* will make a fine addition to that growing collection you nurture with such care and attention. And who knows? Someday I may offer to buy it back from you. Monet may amount to something. Stranger things have happened."

Silent in the flattering light and unwilling to give an inch, Ernest appeared composed and thoughtful, but as befitting a Paris merchant with an eye for all that was newest and best and a history of getting his way, he was on the brink of decision. His mind racing, his imagination was hard at work as he anticipated the responses of his friends when they saw what was arguably Paris' most notorious painting hanging on one of his Boulevard Haussmann apartment walls, or better yet displayed for the summer at the Chateau Rottembourg where his many visitors would see it and ask a litany of questions. In a matter of minutes, his brasher side had taken over and the heart of the collector beating within him was drumming out that *Impression Sunrise* was an important picture. He had to have it. It was ablaze with color. It demanded attention. It required something of the viewer, and as far as Ernest was concerned it had named the most interesting collaborative of creative artists to emerge in generations, and wouldn't it get Uncle Julian Raingo's blood going when he saw it at his birthday celebration! An admired man of cultured tastes, Julian Raingo was Alice's uncle and the Raingo family patriarch. He was a loyal supporter of The Salon. He was also the Raingo family's financial advisor. Given his status and the esteem in which he was held by his friends and family, his sixtieth birthday celebration was to be no little get-together. His favorite niece, Alice, was planning it as a true milestone event in her beloved uncle's life. Leaving no detail to chance, she had been meeting with florists, wine merchants, butchers, and green grocers, and when all was said and done, in rooms filled with lilies and ferns, there would be lavish toasts and outright pledges of allegiance if the number of invited guests was to be taken as an indication of the influence the elder Raingo wielded. Two tall stacks of engraved invitations had gone out, countless cases of champagne had been ordered, and an elegant buffet menu had been set. Important people were coming and Alice was taking great care in preparing her home for this event, but that was Alice Raingo Hoschede, her talent for carefully detailed planning legendary in her distinguished Raingo family.

"Eight-hundred francs!" Ernest called out to Durand-Ruel, glancing toward the orange-hued *Impression Sunrise* before him and the small black boat at its center as he confidently set the final terms of his bargain. "Please arrange for delivery, Monsieur."

A sensitive man with an unerring eye for pictures and an inherited flair for business, Paul Durand-Ruel observed his client's solid, well-tailored shoulders, the white rosebud in his lapel, and the unflinching directness of his steely gaze. There was no mistaking his intention. He was strong and convincing and Monet was in desperate need of a sale. The dusty building on Boulevard des Capucines had probably been a poor choice of location for the display of his paintings, but it was an initial step and a decisive way forward. Now though, perhaps it must be considered that relationships were important. Wealthy, influential patrons such as Ernest Hoschede were few and far between.

"Tomorrow at two?" Durand-Ruel affirmed, turning to his meticulously kept black leather ledger with two of his favorite words: "Please sign. And Monsieur Hoschede," he added with an agreeable nod, "I shall include the frame as part of our transaction. Unfortunately, I have not yet had time to add the costs of the Morisot and Sisley paintings you placed on reserve into my records so those will be delivered later in the week. Hopefully by then I will have made better sense of the chaos you see here today."

Heading toward the door in long, confident strides, Ernest was pleased with himself. Smiling broadly as he stepped into his carriage, he vowed he would never part with *Impression Sunrise*, never sell it, never trade it, never return or sell it back to Durand-Ruel. It would stand as the hallmark of his collection. It mattered not at all that its creator enjoyed no particular distinction. *Impression Sunrise* was a label. It represented an important step in his determination to form a significantly unique art collection and with continuing guidance from Durand-Ruel it would remain central to an assembly of Impressionist paintings he would add to and enjoy for the rest of his life. Now, with the prospect of adding three more of the rebel group's paintings to his collection, his mood exuberant, Ernest directed his driver to the Palais d'industrie and the entrance to the prestigious Salon Exhibition of 1874 where he and Alice had arranged to meet.

CHAPTER 3

The Salon

Ominous gray clouds threatening rain were gathering over the immense, 850 foot long Grand Palais as Ernest's carriage joined those in the long, slow line of afternoon attendees arriving at the imposing public drive. Hardly a waste of time, the delay provided Ernest as well as every other waiting carriage passenger the opportunity to take in the full spectacle of the incomparable scene. Since its completion in 1855, people had remained astonished by the size and scale of the elegantly columned Palais d'Industrie. In the crowds gathered on the well manicured gravel walkways almost twenty years later, the same air of awe and civic pride remained palpable.

The artworks chosen for the annual Salon showing were selected by a jury's decision and stood as representative of what they and they alone considered to be examples of the highest French artistic ideals. In short, both the jurors and the artworks they selected were the personification of establishment at which the daring rebels were thumbing their collective noses. Not too surprisingly, the powerful Salon juries were delighted to return the gesture. "Subversives!" the upper echelons called them. "Insane!" chimed in the critics. "Wonderful!" Ernest maintained.

In the sea of colorful finery, he spotted Alice and Julian Raingo waiting at the top of an exterior stairway, Julian Raingo's six-foot height standing out in the crowd, his tall silk hat adding readily identifiable inches to his courtly frame.

"Oh, darling, there you are!" Alice called out with her dazzling smile as he approached. "I'm glad you got here before it starts to rain. We arrived just minutes ago ourselves," she added, kissing Ernest's cheek and squeezing his arm. "Uncle Julian has been looking forward to this. Of course, so have I, but it was a long wait in the carriage. There are so many people here today! Do you have the tickets?"

Tickets presented, appropriate familial greetings exchanged, the scope of the Salon Exhibition was the matter at hand, the content of its annual presentation of immense interest to each and every attendee, in particular to privileged Julian Raingo whose personal Paris circle was defined by men in high places, the same men linked to the Institute des Beaux-Arts and The Salon; the similarly privileged men who, like Roman emperors of old, could determine by a show of thumbs up or down, which of the artists seeking approval and acceptance would live and which would die.

Ernest took Alice's elbow and guided her through the maze of people at the doors, proud as he always was, of her head-turning appearance. Pretty and engaging, Alice's beautiful smile conveyed a warmth that drew people to her. She made conversation easily and was particularly skilled at tapping into personal interests. She would ask about one's family, one's children, one's profession or favorite pastime, sincerely interested in the responses of those she engaged. Of medium height and elegant posture, the beautiful clothes Alice wore to great advantage stood as an agreeable accompaniment to the attire of her expertly tailored husband. Her carefully chosen ensemble for the city's most important spring event consisted of a floor-length black silk taffeta skirt and a pale yellow silk faille jacket, its wide cuffs embroidered and heavily beaded in the currently fashionable black passementerie. Under a small black hat and short veil, her dark hair was pulled back in the loose chignon Ernest favored, especially when held as it was, with the pair of tortoise-shell combs he had given her.

Packed floor to ceiling with Salon Jury approved paintings and pieces of sculpture, the interiors of the Palais served as a highly flattering background for well turned out attendees such as the Hoschedes, and this was the intention, the magnitude of the vast, two-story high aisles clearly illuminating former Emperor Louis Napoleon's vainglorious purpose in establishing France's domination in art, not only around the globe, but on a grand scale for citizens of the city over which he had presided with superb Napoleonic excess. And the concept of regal grandeur adrift in overwhelming expanses of space had succeeded brilliantly. Parisians loved the scale of their Palais. The nave alone measured a remarkable 630 feet. The flawless, pale limestone walls set the tone for whatever or whoever was exhibited against them, the palatial serenity of this basic background highlighted by a succession of colorful international flags installed along the entire length of the upper interior pavilion.

Little about the exhibition surprised or pleased Ernest. He and Alice had come to view the Salon-accepted subject matter every year since their marriage eleven years before and little had changed. "It's like coming home after a long holiday, isn't it darling?" Ernest commented to Alice with a wide grin. "Familiar faces, comfortable places. Isn't it wonderful? Look there. Ah, the beloved religious themes awash in the saintly act of supplication. Isn't that Saint Theresa in her ecstasy? I've seen her this way so many times that I'm beginning to think of her as a girl I knew before I met you. I promise, Alice, it really was long before I met you. And look here! The always reliable succession of military portraits! Such a surprise! I have a few myself, but let us examine closely that fine array of uniformed French heroes bedecked in ribbons and medals representing every military campaign in our colorful French history which, I cannot fail to add, we have seen here year after year, again and again! Aren't you tired of it? Let's skip all this next year."

"Ernest, please," Alice admonished in a whisper. "Uncle Julian will hear you. This is a fine array of work. We cannot like all of it. No one can, and you know perfectly well that no other event in Paris generates this much excitement. Look at the crowd here today. And everyone looks so nice!"

Alice was entirely accurate in assessing The Salon as the wildly popular event it was. As eagerly anticipated as any international sporting event or celebrity appearance, it announced to all Europe, if not the entire globe, that Paris was at the center of the art world; that its cultured opinions mattered, that its great gift for identifying genuine artistic talent went unrivaled, and that its citizens had every reason to enjoy and be proud of their cultural leadership.

Quite in keeping with long-established standards, the Salon process for an artist who wished to have his work considered fine enough to be included in this cause-celebre could be nothing short of exhausting. Submitted work was examined by the jury as closely as a physician examines his naked patient for evidence of a rare disease. For weeks, the artists worried and fretted and waited for the results of the examination, and while winners and losers were decided, women from one end of the continent to the other spent hours fussing over what to wear. "This small hat? No, that large one with the big plumes. This dress? No, too somber, too plain. It's Paris! Those feathers? Heavens no! Too gauche! Where is my walking stick? Don't forget your silk handkerchiefs."

Scores of well-to-do internationals: British, Italians, Russians, Spaniards, and Americans descended on Paris for the springtime event, crowding into hotels, restaurants, and cafes, anxious to behold the selections made by the renowned Salon Jury and at the same time absorb all it meant just to see and be seen in glamorous Paris. And as if that were not enough excitement to whet the appetite, this year a tasty fresh ingredient had been added to the heady Paris mix. A group of upstart artists had actually held their own version of a cause-celebre, the dates of their ill-fated debut actually conflicting with those of the Salon for two entire weeks! A deliberate challenge? Impossible!

A renowned French institution and arm of the Ecole des Beaux-Arts, The Salon had reigned supreme for more than a hundred years except for a brief period when ministers of Emperor Louis Napoleon's Second Republic had bowed to public pressure and created the Salon des Refuses which was formed to show artworks The Salon Jury had rejected, a sincerely well-intended venture which was abruptly ended when the artists as well as the public decried the obvious stigma placed on any "refused" artist. Ernest and Alice Hoschede knew the Salon's history. They knew how it had worked for years and how it continued to work. That knowledge was part of being and living in Paris, a city where café-loungers and gossip-spreaders were constantly watching for delectable missteps in the active Paris art world, a condition the Minister of Fine Arts promoted at a hastily called meeting of The Salon Jury of 1874, his tone conveying a rather high degree of displeasure.

"It has come to our attention," he began in one of the more richly paneled Ecole des Beaux-Arts rooms where the Jury had gathered, "that a rebellious group of painters the art critic and playwright, Monsieur Louis Leroy has named Impressionists, are ignoring the time-tested protocol not of mere generations but of centuries, by forming a coalition and presenting a united front, choosing to emerge not from the bosom of the proven Paris art establishment but overnight and under their own insulting independent banner at, of all things, an unauthorized public exhibition held not within the confines of a Salon-des-Beaux-Arts approved location, but at an abandoned photographer's studio on touristy Boulevard des Capucines! This cannot stand."

The Minister was quoted repeatedly, his statements published in newspapers and periodicals, his insistence on maintaining The Salon's solid position in Paris life applauded by a citizenry perfectly comfortable with its exacting edicts and with every intention of supporting its decisions not only mildly, but avidly.

Despite Ernest's cynicism and Alice's admonitions, together with Julian Raingo, the three enjoyed making comments to one another as they viewed the huge number of artworks on display in the vast Palais, Ernest teasing, questioning, Alice politely choosing her favorites, this year's mutually agreed best of the best and just as Durand-Ruel had predicted, the work of their swashbuckling country neighbor and frequent dinner guest, Carolus Duran.

At times, the afternoon became a social affair as well as an art-oriented event. Friends were encountered as they strolled along the aisles and paused to exchange greetings. Julian Raingo's concentration on paintings was frequently interrupted by many of his Paris acquaintances of long standing, those wealthy, well-connected gentlemen who, like himself, examined painting after painting and bronze after bronze, their most vocal responses saved for the Inquisition-themed paintings of long-haired, naked young females kneeling before red-robed prelates who held the balance of fate in their gnarly hands.

"I don't believe I would want one in my home," a nearby woman's strident voice was suddenly heard to state, "but I certainly do wish I had her body!"

"Why, Cousin Beatrice!" Ernest said turning to the red-haired woman standing beside him. "How good to see you, but what a surprise! You're the last person I'd expect to see in this crowd!"

"Well, Ernest my dear," I decided it was high time I saw what all the fuss is about!" Beatrice Pirole announced in her persistently haughty manner as she continued to admire the depicted naked, long-haired Inquisition victim and Alice and Julian Raingo joined in expressing their own surprise at the chance meeting, Beatrice's attire of particular interest, as it usually was.

Ernest's Cousin Beatrice was, by all conventional standards and within her rather straight-laced family, an outspoken woman of unrivaled taste. Having known and been observers of her ostentation for many years, Julian Raingo as well as Ernest, and Alice, were well-acquainted with her ability to shock with astonishing wardrobe combinations of color and style, but it did appear that for this visit to The Salon she had outdone herself, choosing to wear a garish ensemble comprised of a floor-sweeping pink-flowered bright blue cape, its yellow feathered collar worn open over a dangerously low-cut purple dress, the added surprise of a veiled pink velvet hat a suitably shocking statement perched atop her very red hair.

"This Salon event has all Paris absolutely mad! I really don't understand it!" Beatrice announced, twirling her long pearl necklace across the suggestive contours of her ample bosom as she acknowledged Alice and Ernest with a nod and blew a kiss to Julian Raingo with whom she had been acquainted since her days as proprietor of a jewelers shop on Rue Royale. "It has absolutely captivated the interest of the entire city and just this morning at breakfast, my husband suggested I avail myself of the opportunity to improve on what he called "my limited grasp of culture" by joining in the adulation here. I must say, had I known there would be so many paintings and sculptures of nude men, I would have started coming years ago. Julian, why didn't you tell me?"

"My dear Beatrice," Julian Raingo answered with a hearty laugh, "today the Paris art world lies before you in all its beauty and eccentricities. Enjoy it with an eye toward absorbing that world in all its varied artistry, some of it daring and grand, some of it frankly boring."

"Julian, I know you love attempting to polish my image, but you needn't patronize me," Beatrice said in her direct way. "I know I have my eccentricities, but I also know the difference between what is coarse and what is inappropriate. I may not be the refined art connoisseur you are, but this poor young girl I'm looking at in this painting is being tortured not only by her inquisitors, but by her embarrassing nakedness. I can't imagine what she has done to deserve such treatment. Really, this child's lack of clothing before officials of the church in their velvet and ermine is outrageous. Why would any artist want to paint such a thing?"

"My dear, you have successfully captured both the artist's intention and that of the Inquisition itself," Julian Raingo began to lecture in the way he had of assuming artistic superiority. "What we have here is intimidation intended to result in a confession be it true or untrue, but my dear, that is how the Inquisition worked. And the nature of a painting like this really is all about history. These subjectively oriented paintings are not only intended to be taken at face value but at the same time as depictions of history's circumstances, many of them unfortunate. They record events and project emotions connected to those events in ways which if gone unrecorded might be completely lost. We can learn a great deal about history from the visual impact made by paintings like this, and of course as works of art they have their incomparable qualities. Here, let me draw your attention to the artistry of the painting you are examining, the elder Raingo went on, enjoying the opportunity to express his expertise, demonstration of which he said to Beatrice "may add significantly to the truly commendable point of your attendance here at The Salon today," he further offered in an attempt to focus Beatrice's attention on a more classic approach to viewing the large canvas depicting the popular Inquisition theme of naked females kneeling before aged prelates.

"First of all," he continued, "I do quite agree with you that the young lady as a subject is most attractive, but look closely now at the composition: the positioning of the prelates, the brilliant colors of their robes, the well-executed brushwork, the beautiful flesh tones."

"Ah yes, as usual you're right, Julian," Beatrice conceded, taking a deep breath and exhaling slowly. "The flesh tones are truly beautiful, and yes, the brushwork is very well-executed, particularly in the lower torso area I'd say."

"And Beatrice, I would say," Ernest quickly interrupted, "that the most appropriate place for the display of such exquisite Inquisition themes is right here, under the large number of lecherous, presupposing noses surrounding you right now."

Beatrice broke into laughter, nodding her head in agreement with her cousin's assessment, quite unaware of his noble attempt to rescue her from making further suggestive or embarrassing remarks as the group of smiling gentlemen now gathered to view the large canvas in question grew larger and more interested in the ongoing exchange of remarks there was little attempt to disguise.

Julian Raingo's low chortle came as a relief to Alice who knew her uncle well enough to know he did not approve of Ernest's often sarcastic attempts at humor. At the same time, Alice understood Ernest's protective intention. He was very fond of Beatrice. They had been close friends since childhood and as they had grown into adulthood under very different circumstances he often took it upon himself, as he did now, to shield her from what he insisted was merely an unfortunate disregard for the boundaries of polite behavior.

"Well, as I think about it," the elder Raingo continued to Ernest as the foursome walked on, "I suppose there are a few equally appropriate places for depictions of the naked female torso, as for example in The Louvre where Venus de Milo's exquisite nakedness receives daily adulation from hundreds of admirers. Ernest, I'd venture to say you have probably gazed upon that seductive form on many occasions and although as you know, I have issues with your vague ambitions as an art collector, I really don't think of you as a lecher at all."

The smile on Julian Raingo's face conveyed no apology for having reminded Ernest of their opposing opinions on matters of lifestyle and taste, but Ernest was no fool. On a fine afternoon in May, The Salon was no place for challenging a man like dignified Julian Raingo who understood completely the regard in which he was held in Paris. He had stature and reputation, and unwilling to tarnish an otherwise enjoyable experience, Ernest wisely decided against defending himself against the unmistakable insult Julian Raingo had delivered with his incomparable grasp of necessary civility.

They were two very different people, one with his feet securely planted in the past, the other with his in the risky future, but as for Ernest's ambitions and Julian Raingo's assessment of them, no one knew better than Ernest himself that at the moment he was a man finding his own expanded views of the future in sharp contrast with the dark cloud of recession Durand-Ruel had warned of earlier in the day. If the Rue Laffitte dealer was right, dark economic times would affect every aspect of Paris life, especially the operations of an exclusive department store and the wild ambitions of a defiant band of rebels whose paintings the heart of the collector in Ernest Hoschede was beginning to find irresistible, but for the moment there was no need to worry. Tomorrow afternoon Impression Sunrise would be delivered to him and he would rest easy in the knowledge that he owned the identifying flag of the most controversial art movement to descend on Paris in decades. It was enough. For now.

CHAPTER 4

In That Small Café

The rain began just before dawn the next morning, gentle and warm at first, but by noon temperatures had plunged and from the riverbanks of Montparnasse and further north to the quiet quarter of Auteuil and the spine-thin turrets of Saint Genevieve's Abbey, all promise of spring had vanished. So intense were the downpours and accompanying winds, that daily life as Parisians knew it was slowed to a near halt by teeming profusions of carriages, omnibuses, horse carts, and milk wagons maneuvering along soggy avenues and rain-slicked boulevards, doing their best as their drivers cursed and spat, to avoid colliding with one another or striking down those single-minded pedestrians who remained determined to cross slippery avenues and boulevards wherever and whenever they pleased. Oblivious to the inclement weather, at Number 16 Rue Laffitte preparations for delivery of Impression Sunrise were underway.

"The perfect match!" a clearly delighted Durand-Ruel said to his assistant, Alphonse Legrand, as with a broad smile he unrolled two sheets of thick brown paper across the long table in the storage room and supervised the wrapping of the twenty-four by thirty-inch painting he considered to be the most notorious in Paris. "It doesn't happen very often, but when the right buyer meets the right painting there's magic in the air."

"Ah yes," agreed the attentive Legrand, carefully securing the paper with several neat folds and winding lengths of sturdy string twice around to further protect the contents of the bulky package. "Monsieur Hoschede and Impression Sunrise are made for each other, but Monsieur Durand, I wish it would stop raining. I worry about sending a painting out on a wet day. Perhaps we should delay delivery until tomorrow when the weather is better."

"Nonsense, Alphonse," Durand-Ruel assured his uneasy assistant, adding a final knot to the length of string. "We won't be delaying delivery. Monsieur Hoschede will be eager to have Impression Sunrise in his possession, and don't worry. We've double wrapped the painting and secured it well. That should be more than enough protection for the drive to Boulevard Haussmann. It's not so far, and of course we'll go out to the delivery carriage with an umbrella. Besides, the courier is our regular man and there is a big canopy at the entrance to Monsieur Hoschede's building at Number 56. Impression Sunrise will be well protected. Alphonse, the weather may not be cooperating, but as far as I'm concerned this is a fine day. I can't wait to tell Claude Monet he's had a sale!"

"Careful! Careful!" Durand-Ruel admonished the uniformed courier from under his black umbrella as Impression Sunrise was secured in the delivery carriage. You carry precious cargo there. Monsieur Hoschede is one of my best clients and I would like him to remain so for a long time to come!"

It was with a great sense of satisfaction that the enterprising dealer watched the delivery carriage pull away. "This is a good beginning," he thought to himself. "With this painting in his possession, Hoschede will promote the New Group as Impressionists. It's a good label for them and he's a good salesman. He could soon become our strongest ally."

On Rue Laffitte, within view of Durand-Ruel's doorway, a few cyclists braved the wet winds, their hats pulled down low on their foreheads, their long scarves trailing in the wind behind them, their best efforts at avoiding the puddles forming on the unpaved, gravel roadway occasionally resulting in an unwelcome muddy splash. By contrast, on a corner of well-paved Boulevard Haussmann, as if intended to make up in some small way for the sudden wintry spell, bunches of bright yellow jonquils crowded out gaily from the corners of a flower vendor's green and white canopied cart.

Ernest stood uncharacteristically pensive at one of the windows of his second-floor study, his view to the bright yellow shock of jonquils and the glistening wet pavement below. Even under ordinary circumstances rain could put him in a somber mood, but awaiting Durand-Ruel's delivery carriage he was unsettled by more than dismal weather. He was worried, and more than he cared to admit, by the previous day's conversation with Paul Durand-Ruel. He couldn't put it out of his mind. Recession was a term he had only recently been hearing in Paris, and for those involved as he was in a commercial enterprise it was conjuring up a particularly ominous range of unsettling thoughts. Perhaps Durand-Ruel was right and recession was indeed on the horizon. Several times during the past year his own brother-in-law, Auguste Remy, a Paris stockbroker married to Alice's sister Cecile, had discussed the grim prospect with him. Ernest had ignored Remy's warnings as the typical overreaction of a financial mind, but things felt differently now as he evaluated his vulnerabilities with more than mild concern. He ran a successful business. He carried luxury goods. He had a large family and two large households. There were servants and considerable household expenses. If, as Durand-Ruel had said, the private sector was likely to run from Rue Lafitte and its paintings, it was also likely to run from his store and its high-priced goods. Fueling his immediate concern further was the amount of the loan he had been granted the week before by the Union Generale Bank. He had needed prompt funding for the semi-annual volume of merchandise he ordered for the store. He also had plans to increase the store's square footage. The three-story apartment house at the rear of his building was for sale and he intended to buy it. A long-time customer of Union Generale and friend of its president, Christophe Emmanuel, a fifty-thousand franc line of credit with a low interest rate had been quickly approved, more than half the amount about to be sent off to a variety of expert draftsmen, weavers, and artisans across France.

"Hold on to as much cash as you can," Emmanuel had advised as Ernest prepared to leave their meeting, "and my friend, if you have gold, hide it away somewhere, perhaps at that country place of yours. It pains me to say this, Ernest, but make no mistake: financial prospects are looking more dismal every day. Think about re-evaluating your expenses. Cut wherever you can, and if I were you I would immediately close all house accounts at the store and deal in cash-only sales. There's no telling when or how this will end."

Ernest had left the imposing bronze doors of the Union Generale with a number of fresh concerns. The renewed line of credit was one thing and he was relieved to have it, but he had other accounts, substantial accounts with a long list of merchants throughout Paris, and friend or foe, in an economic downturn, creditors would want their money. Pressed to the limit, they could demand it overnight.

Waiting for Durand-Ruel's delivery carriage, Emmanuel's warnings kept repeating themselves in his brain. "Hold on to as much cash as you can, and if you have gold, hide it away somewhere, perhaps out at your country place. Think about re-evaluating your expenses. Cut wherever you can."

Turning away from the rain-spattered window, Ernest unbuttoned his collar, walked to his desk, and took a cigar from the silver rimmed humidor. Striking a match and lighting the tip of the pungent Spanish tobacco, he puffed slowly, trying to force his thoughts away from debt and cash reserves and presidents of banks, recalling instead the far more agreeable transaction with Paul Durand-Ruel which for eight-hundred francs had made him owner of the twenty-four by thirty-inch Le Havre harbor scene painted by an unknown painter from Argenteuil named Claude Monet, the purchase price of 800-francs promptly added to his long-standing account with Durand-Ruel.

He leaned back against the desk and watched the curls of smoke rising to the ceiling, considering the likely reactions of Alice's Uncle Julian to the namesake harbor scene at the upcoming family party. The elder Raingo was a serious collector himself, his tastes classic, his preferences directed toward the Old Masters; to Vermeer and Rembrandt and Frans Hals and the Flemish masters of his Belgian family's native Antwerp and Bruge, and if past experience was to be relied upon, dear Uncle Julian would do what he always did at family gatherings when confronted by the latest example of Ernest's rapidly expanding interest in contemporary art. At first he would look amused as he examined the canvas. A small smile would cross his lips and quickly disappear. He would then step back, fold his arms across his chest, and shake his head while his expression took on a critical frown and he uttered two familiar words: "Unconvincing! Naïve!"

It was common knowledge that Julian Raingo was a staunch traditionalist, but it was also known that he maintained a hearty appetite for news of daily Paris life in all its colorful guises. The new group's notoriety had to be of interest to him, Ernest calculated. With this in mind, he decided that during the celebration he would put forth as many details as possible concerning the group's work, emphasizing their desire to be recognized on their own terms and this time he would not allow Julian Raingo to make his caustic remarks and promptly wander off to discuss other matters with clusters of invited guests, contenting himself with more personally satisfying comments such as those regarding the generosity of his favorite niece's unparalleled attention to detail when entertaining in her home.

Ernest smiled again, recalling Alice's genuine talent for planning Raingo family events and those of the Belgian community in Paris of which the Raingos were a prominent part, but Alice was also of great help to him when it came to entertaining his most discriminating suppliers and purveyors. She planned for every eventuality, and not only on special occasions, but in matters of everyday life. Fresh flowers appeared at the table in the middle of winter. There were impossibly crisp table linens at every meal, and above all there was no shortage of time or thoughtfulness when it came to the five Hoschede children. Ernest was well-aware that his wife's efforts took time and immense levels of energy, but for all her love of order and structure, he also knew that Alice appreciated his own natural spontaneity and talent for surprise. Anticipating her response to Impression Sunrise, however, he wasn't quite sure what to expect. Although tolerant of her husband's recent interest in the newly named Impressionists, Alice was in her Uncle Julian's camp when it came to taste in paintings and she made no secret of the fact that she did not share Ernest's enthusiasm for what both she and Julian Raingo were calling "that strange new art."

"It's something new for Paris to talk about, that's all. It won't last," she had remarked sitting beside Ernest in the black brougham as they left the Boulevard de Capucines exhibition during its second week. "And how dare these upstarts choose dates to conflict with the Salon's! Everybody knows nothing in Paris competes with the Salon. I think it's disrespectful, and of course it just points out that their work isn't good enough for the Salon and never will be. I can't imagine what they're thinking," she had insisted, shaking her head from side to side. "How do they expect to get anywhere? Well, darling, at least Felix Bracquemond's etching of you was well done, but I do think you're much more handsome in your National Guardsman's uniform than he made you out to be."

Ernest chuckled aloud. He knew the popular Paris artist, Felix Bracquemond quite well, and he recalled sitting for the etching. It was intended as a gift for his mother, but before it could be presented Felix had asked for permission to exhibit it along with what he had said was to be a small showing of artworks in which he and a few colleagues were participating at a photographer's studio on Boulevard des Capucines.

Awaiting Impression Sunrise's arrival, Ernest's impatience was relieved by the thought of his pretty wife's memorable profile in the soft afternoon light as she had commented on Bracquemond and the event in general. Her shining dark hair had been brushed away from her face and fastened in a cascade of curls. The close-fitting high collar of the rose silk taffeta jacket she had buttoned over a long, dark blue dress had set off the healthy glow of her flawless complexion to memorable advantage. He remembered that as she had talked and gestured in the flickering light her face had remained predictably animated and a bit flushed. They had been married for eleven years and Ernest still adored the small, determined pout Alice assumed whenever she was displeased or only mildly perplexed.

"Darling, I know how interested you are in these new painters," she said, "but I don't understand what you see in their work," she had said. "Never in my life have I seen such confusion," Ernest remembered she had remarked, slipping her gray kid gloves over her delicate, small hands and gazing out through the oval-shaped, beveled glass carriage windows to the fascinating array of new cafes and shops lining both sides of Boulevard des Italiens. "It was maddening in that terrible old studio. It even smelled bad; dusty and damp!" she had concluded with another frown as the carriage came to a halt at the Café Riche but I know you, my darling. Over these past weeks you've been going back again and again, haven't you? But why? Ernest, you've managed to form a fine collection of worthwhile paintings without adding the work of these unknowns. You don't need any of their nonsense. No one does."

By then, Ernest had indeed attended the Capucines exhibition a number of times, his repeated attendance during its month-long duration and his ever-increasing interest resulting in lengthy conversations with each member of the core group of artists being labelled Impressionists. Along with Durand-Ruel, all seven were deeply appreciative of his enthusiasm for both their work and their effort to succeed without The Salon, so much so, that by the time the exhibition closed, he was being regarded as a serious patron. Unfortunately, at the same time, ongoing published critiques of the calamitous exhibition continued ever more inflammatory, contributing to an overall feeling within the group of failure and the clear suggestion that they would be wise to disband and work on their own. These persistent attacks did not escape Alice's attention. Devoted to reading the weekly newspapers and monthly journals, she could not avoid noticing the stabs of increasingly bitter negativism. All earlier published and widely read blistering criticisms directly following the exhibition's opening paled by comparison to those which as the exhibition progressed to the end of its month-long duration were appearing in print. No one was spared. Claude Monet, Pierre Renoir, Alfred Sisley, Edgar Degas, Berthe Morisot, Paul Cezanne, and Camille Pissarro, all seven painters the art critic, Louis Leroy had named Impressionists in his scathing article entitled Exhibition of the Impressionists, were now being further decimated by an ever more influential list of critics writing for the widely read Le Rappel, Le Siecle, L'Artiste, and The Paris Journal. The obvious intention to put an end to the New Group's very existence could not have been more clearly understood.

"He has a deplorable predilection for market gardens and does not hesitate to paint cabbages or any other domestic vegetable," wrote Jules Castagnary of Pissarro's Le Verger in Le Siecle.

"Obviously this is not the last word in art, not even of this art. It is necessary to go on and to transform the sketch into a finished work," Ernest Chesneau now wrote of Monet's Boulevard des Capucines.

"In addition to Impression Sunrise, Claude Monet has shown four paintings and four pastels," Chesneau put forth in The Paris Journal, commenting on Monet and in particular his Boulevard des Capucines: "At a distance one hails a masterpiece, the crowd swarming on the sidewalks, the boulevard's trees waving in the dust and light, this trembling of great shadow and light sparkling with even darker shadows and brighter lights, but come closer and all vanishes. There remains only an indecipherable chaos of palette scrapings."

"No known judge of art has ever, even in his dreams, imagined the possibility of accepting a single work by this painter who not so long ago was seen carrying his paintings to the Salon on his back like Jesus Christ carrying his cross!" wrote Jean Prouvaire in Le Rappel of Paul Cezanne who, summarily rejected by The Salon, had proceeded to join the Independents and exhibit Etude: Paysage a Auvers, the painting also titled Quartier Four, a Auvers.

Despite the negative critical and public opinion as well as the ambivalence of his beloved Alice and taking advantage of the available ten percent discount Ernest had, nonetheless, reserved Alfred Sisley's paintings of Marly, Numbers 163 and 165 in the catalogue, corresponding notes seen being marked onto catalogue pages by the soft-spoken, eternally observant Englishman, Alfred Sisley himself. Attracted to the landscapes of Pissarro and Madame Berthe Morisot's watercolors and considering their purchase, Ernest had not reserved a single exhibited work of Claude Monet, but once Leroy's Impressionist label had been attached to Impression Sunrise, Number 98 in the printed exhibition catalogue, he had become far more receptive to the canvas whose subject and colors he had initially found profoundly unsettling. He had placed no reserve on the Le Havre scene, but for reasons he himself would never fully understand, he had been increasingly drawn to thoughts of its dramatic impact. Several short weeks after his purchase of the Monet painting, Ernest attended another Durand-Ruel exhibition, this a June showing and sale of Barbizon paintings held in the dealer's gallery rooms where once again, as had occurred on several occasions at Boulevard des Capucines, he encountered Claude Monet.

It was well-known by Street of Pictures Insiders that in his time, Paul Durand-Ruel's father had actively promoted the as yet undiscovered Barbizon painters in much the same enthusiastic way his son was promoting the struggling Impressionists. Now, however, it was also being noted that the younger Durand-Ruel was finding the unsold Barbizon canvases his father had stored away for lack of interest such as those of Corot and Courbet, were now in great demand, astonishingly valuable, and doing a good deal to keep his doors open and a roof over his family's head.

At the well-organized Barbizon Exhibition, Ernest and Claude had found mutual areas of interest, their regard for the New Group's work and Durand-Ruel's support quickly forming a firm foundation for a closer friendship as well as opportunities for expansion of Ernest's collection of Impressionist work to which later that summer and once again through Durand-Ruel, would be added two Monet paintings of the Seine, two of the Saint-Lazare train station, and one of Monet's family garden at Argenteuil. Grateful for Ernest's support of all seven Impressionists and now considering him to be an important patron, from time to time and as a gesture of respect, Claude invited him to join the Impressionist circle in the heart of Montmartre at the Café Guerbois where the rebel battalion had established its rent-free headquarters, formed its cooperative, and hammered out the articles of its charter.

Located as it was, in the busy, workaday area of rundown Avenue de Clichy, the Guerbois at Number 11 could not have been a more improbable destination for the likes of chandelier-loving Ernest Hoschede, but he saw the dirty, smoke-filled Montmartre atmosphere as a setting highly conducive to the revolution they championed.

Described in some detail by the band of loyal combatants as an ideal battlefield, the floor was appropriately covered partly in saw-dust, partly in sand, and creating the appropriately high level of confusion, there was rarely need for a waiter. People simply shouted out their orders for coffee, wine, and cigarettes, and in the unlikely event that food was required, the menu consisted of only two items: boiled potatoes with peas and pea soup with potatoes. Both were surprisingly delicious. Bread, usually warm, was plentiful. Ernest was intrigued by the entire scenario, his fascination further stirred by activity at the two billiards tables which he was told were in constant use from morning to night, the sounds of loudly clicking balls in tandem with frequent explosions of contentious voices, clanking plates, and the haphazard stacking of metal trays compared quite favorably, and much to Ernest's amusement, to shouts of commanders, battleground confusion, and rounds of revolutionary canon fire being set off in the distance.

Like any rebel rendezvous worthy of the name, the Café Guerbois was condemned every year, but just as in more prominent Paris arrondissements where influential relationships meant everything, because the long-time Guerbois proprietor was married to the sister of the local prelate whose mother was the sister-in-law of the former assistant to the kennel master at Fountainbleau who had barely survived a vicious attack by one of the hounds in his care, the Guerbois, along with its next door Montmartre neighbor, the equally ill-kempt Pere Lathuille, had been spared demolition during Baron Haussmann's sweeping mid-century Paris overhaul. Adding to the Guerbois' colorful reputation, confusion continued to exist with regard to its official address.

Known for many years to be located on Avenue Batignolle and at the odd confluence of at least four city arrondissements, the Guerbois' street address had overnight, without notice, and in the much beloved shoulder-shrugging Montmartre tradition of "for unknown reasons," been changed to Avenue de Clichy. Further complicating unruly Montmartre matters, the painters now being called Impressionists had formerly been known as "The Batignolles," their label handily adapted of course, from the street address of their gathering place, but once the Avenue Batignolle became Clichy, named after the Barriere de Clichy, the gate prominently built on the road to the village of Clichy as a tax collection point, they were suddenly left not only nameless, but disoriented. Hardly eager to adapt the damaging identity of a tax collector's gate and become known as Clichys, their new, far more acceptable Impressionist label had arrived just in time.

Ernest took to the Guerbois company immediately, enjoying the spirited camaraderie and edgy Montmartre atmosphere, intrigued at the same time by the unpretentious demeanor and lively conversation of these brash, unknown painters who made no excuses whatsoever for their defensive positions in the Paris art world, their most passionate discussions centered on the inflexible dictates of the Salon, their most interesting exchanges centered on their lives, their families, their gardens, their love affairs, and always their poverty. Clearly, Ernest noticed, they shared a great collective concern. When one or another of them came through the sagging Guerbois door, every member of the assembled group looked up, openly relieved to see that one more week or one more day had passed safely without incident or harm and that their battalion had survived yet one more round of attacks. Assured that a few hasty meals and one or two hours of sleep had sustained energy and allowed the essential process of painting to continue, they relaxed and went on with the important business of being together.

Renoir and Monet, Ernest quickly discovered, had known one another for years. Together with Sisley and a fellow artist, Frederic Bazille who, much to their mutual and lasting regret, had been killed in the early days of the Franco-Prussian War, they had known each other since 1863 and their art student days at Gleyre's studio.

Born at Limoges, Pierre Auguste Renoir's artistic efforts had begun with porcelain painting, but later, as a young emerging painter in Paris, he became enchanted with Fragonard and Boucher and had spent long hours copying their paintings at The Louvre. By 1869, he and Monet were painting scenes of Parisian life at the popular restaurant and bathing spot, La Grenouillere (The Froggery) where, with no intention of doing so, in seven small canvases they had set the independent tone for the outdoor themes of landscape and everyday life which were to become lasting hallmarks of the New Group's collaborative.

Renoir was a slight, thin man with little interest in the daily rituals of personal grooming. Indoors or out he always wore a hat. Highly sensitive to the public adversity being caused by his group, he could become nervous when the Guerbois conversation turned overly subversive, but in lighter moments he displayed a ready sense of humor which most often manifested itself in the irony he found in his surroundings as with great wit he observed the pulchritude of women or the facial expressions of nearby strangers who had no idea how closely he was watching them.

Alfred Sisley was of another type entirely, Ernest had easily determined. An Englishman by birth, he had the fragile expression of a sensitive, vagabond poet. Women loved this quality in him and he was known to return their admiration with "excessive enthusiasm" as Renoir put it. Born in 1839 to a comfortable British family, Sisley too had endured the Gleyre studio experience, and with Monet, Bazille, and Renoir had one day escaped the constraints of traditional methods to paint in the glorious outdoors, never again to return to Gleyre's studio or his stringently structured methods. His family financially ruined by the Prussian war, Sisley found himself completely dependent on sales of his paintings. Meeting Monet and Renoir in London, on his return to Paris he too became a Street of Pictures client of Paul Durand-Ruel.

Paul Cezanne was as intense as his full-beard. Born in 1840 to wealthy parents at Aix-en-Provence, he was well-educated, attending the College Mignet where he met Emile Zola who would remain a lifelong friend. In accordance with his father's wishes, he enrolled in law school but after a short time he pleaded to try for l'Ecole des Beaux-Arts. Distraught by having failed his entrance examinations, he returned to Aix where he worked in his father's bank and at the same time aligned himself with Classical Renaissance tradition, soon turning to the anonymous portraiture that would begin his difficult struggle with self-exploration and the elusive veil of interpretation which critics predicted he would never entirely pierce.

Edgar Degas was the ill-tempered, perpetually moody member of the group. He was also the best draftsman. He had studied at l'Ecole des Beaux-Arts and was gifted with a remarkable visual memory. A devotee of the studio and not the outdoors, he worked on many of his paintings and pastels from memory. Like Claude Monet, he too owed a debt of gratitude to the caricature experiences of his youth. As an adult he loved the Daumier cartoons appearing in each edition of Le Charivari and was an avid collector of them. He had family ties to America and in 1872 had visited relatives in New Orleans, Louisiana where he created one of his most famous paintings, The Cotton Exchange. Victim of his wealthy family's devastating financial reversals and embittered by the ensuing ironies of life, Degas was at his sarcastic best when faced with humanity's many examples which were most obvious to him on his daily walks along Paris boulevards where he could observe activities of the common man, commenting at length and in scathing detail on an endless stream of human shortcomings and physical characteristics with bitter, often embarrassing lampoonery.

Camille Pissarro was the oldest of the group and the constant enthusiast, always wanting to move forward and progress to the next step and beyond to the next. Born in 1830, on the Caribbean Island of St. Thomas in the Danish West Indies, he had been sent to a Paris boarding school at the age of 12, his imagination and abundant talent soon completely taken over by forays into the sweeping beauty of the French countryside. A dedicated lover of nature, he found his greatest pleasure in exploring its endless variations. As a result, he was a prolific painter and turned out canvas after canvas in rapid succession, consistently producing more work than any of his colleagues. Pissarro became a close friend of Cezanne and along with Renoir, Sisley, and Monet, had also met Paul Durand-Ruel in London during the war.

Ernest need not have been told that Madame Berthe Morisot was of a particular class and that she would never dream of being seen at the unladylike, bohemian Guerbois. Apart from its sub-standard reputation, the strict social mores of the times did not gaze kindly upon such provocative places as suitable for respectable women. As a result, Madame Morisot had only a vague idea that her colleagues were meeting somewhere near the Rue Guyot studio of her good friend and soon-to-be brother-in-law, Edouard Manet, one of the new group's most enthusiastic supporters but not at all one of them.

Recently betrothed to Eugene Manet, Edouard's brother, the ever-watchful Right Bank gossip-mill insisted it was Edouard and not Eugene that the beautiful Berthe truly loved and wanted to marry, but alas, Edouard was already married. A resourceful, sophisticated woman, Berthe met with her Impressionist colleagues on her own well-mannered terms, either inviting them individually to her home or meeting with one or two over dinners at the cafes and restaurants she favored and always in the company of Eugene.

Gustave Caillebotte was the youngest member of the group. Highly intelligent, well-educated, trained for the law, and about to become the eighth member of the active core group, he was from a wealthy family. Serious-minded and regarded as the group's catalyst, Caillebotte was a well-spoken, talented young painter and staunch supporter of his colleagues, but he had not exhibited with them on Boulevard des Capucines, his readiness and maturity as an artist yet to be tested.

Claude Monet was rock-solid and direct, his unblinking gaze often piercing and uncompromising. Opinionated but tactful, he was always a gentleman. He had beautiful manners, Ernest observed, and although poor as the proverbial church mouse, he had a taste for good living. Whether or not he could afford them, he was known to like good clothes, good food and wine, and although shyness could quickly overtake him in the presence of strangers, under comfortable circumstances he could carry on a lively, intelligent conversation on topics dealing with everything from politics to Mallarme's latest poems.

Much to his surprise, Ernest soon saw that these meetings at the Guerbois had evolved not at all as the detailed artistic discussions conducted between like-minded artists he had expected, but largely as social occasions and informal opportunities for personal encouragement and reassurance. He heard no lofty oratories focused on artistic technique. There were no forays into the mysteries of color or the vagaries of light. In truth, no one ever discussed anything at all to do with methods or procedures. Of course there were discussions about style, particularly when it came to the styles of successful artists outside the core group such as the currently popular Desboutin, Bracquemond, Astruc, and Beraud. Most significantly, and most often however, when all were safely assembled around the deeply scarred Guerbois table and wine had been poured, it was the edicts of the

Salon, the make-up of its jury, the position of the Superintendent of Fine Arts, Comte de Nieuwerkerke, and what, if anything, it would take to attract Salon attention on their own terms that occupied the newly named Impressionists most passionately. With an undeniable eye to the remote possibility of capitulation and eventual acceptance by the Salon Jury, and despite Edgar Degas' staunch insistence that they never "degrade" themselves by submitting work, visibility had become the group's singular and for the time being, only objective.

"It does not come easily, this acceptance you seek so avidly," the dashing, blonde Edouard Manet advised repeatedly when slipping into a chair beside Monet or Renoir at the embattled Guerbois table, "but you must keep trying with The Salon. Let your name be heard every year in their meetings even if it is not in the most favorable terms, and keep this in mind: There is nothing to compare with the public exposure of one's work at the Salon's Palais d'Industrie Exhibition. It generates interest and sales and isn't that what we all want?"

"Manet's paintings are selling," Degas casually remarked to Ernest on one such occasion, his chin in the palm of his hand as he leaned on his elbow. "Why should he care about our struggle? The Salon serves him well. He lives by it and he will die by it. Look at him sitting there in his beautiful yellow coat. I should paint him in that pose."

"Exhibit with us!" Degas had urged Manet in the Guerbois as discussions surrounding the organization of the first rebel exhibition had begun. "Your prestige would be immensely helpful. Your inclusion would attract a better, bigger audience, and surely you understand that we will never give in to those Salon heretics. We may be struggling for a principle, but we must continue to exhibit on our own and maintain our independence no matter what. Let them come to us."

"No, I believe in what you are doing but I will not exhibit with you and you must face the fact that they will never come to you," Manet insisted, secure in his own successful world. "It is the only way. The Salon is too powerful for you. Enter your work again and again. It is what I do and I am not always accepted. We all learn to live with rejection, but sooner or later the tide will turn. You must be patient and continue to work and submit, submit, submit."

As offensive and insulting as this exchange would forever remain to Degas, other members of the group including Renoir, Sisley, Pissarro, and Monet clearly understood Manet's position and to some degree envied it. Above all, they valued his loyal friendship as well as his frequent financial support when rents came due and the landlady, the green grocer, and fish monger had refused further credit. Along with their loyalty, however, was the constant hope that under the right circumstances Manet would eventually agree to exhibit with them.

"It will never happen. He will never exhibit with us. He will die alone in his Salon world," Degas further remarked idly to Ernest between sips of wine in the shoddy Guerbois, watching the eternally elegant Manet in his eternally fine clothes. "His painting is as magnificent as he himself is; too beautiful, too much for the likes of us."

As yet unknown to Degas at the time of these remarks, Ernest was well-acquainted with Edouard Manet. The distinguished artist made purchases at Hoschede's Department Store. Aware of his patronage and always interested in adding to his art collection, Ernest found it beneficial to make his acquaintance, to the extent that he had invited Manet and his wife, Suzanne, to visit the Chateau Rottembourg. They had come for summer visits, staying for several weeks and enjoying the rural pleasures of the Brie Valley as well as the Hoschedes' gracious hospitality. Alice admired Suzanne Manet's pianistic skills which all listeners, including a somewhat envious Jean DeLille, agreed were considerable. Following Rottembourg's delicious dinners Suzanne often played the Bach Preludes or Mozart piano sonatas at which she excelled, Alice delighted by Ernest and DeLille's somewhat over-zealous applause at their conclusion. During one such summer visit, Edouard painted a portrait of Alice in the garden, during another a study of Ernest with Marthe, oldest of the Hoschede children.

Ernest admired Edouard Manet's sensitivity to the struggle of the Impressionists. They often discussed the group and its challenges. Ernest also admired Manet's appreciation of their courage and talent, and although the popular artist had not exhibited with them, Edouard Manet was a kindred spirit, completely at one with the Impressionist cause and its desire to change the way the public looked at its pictures, even his pictures, but in an odd turn, of late the identities and at times the paintings of both Edouard Manet and the acknowledged Impressionist leader, Claude Monet, were being confused due to the similarities in their names. But for one letter, the spelling of their surnames was identical. In pronunciation they could even sound alike. Time and circumstance would erase the impact of confusion, but to clear the as yet untested air and leave no question,

Monet had begun to sign his canvases with as clear and pronounced a letter "o" as Manet was implementing to similarly emphasize the letter "a" in his own canvas signature.

Quite like Ernest Hoschede, Edouard Manet was known as the consummate Paris 'flanneur,' a recognized man of style who strolled the boulevards and avenues to see and be seen and to remind himself how much he loved his city. Ernest appreciated these qualities of style and pride in the men of Paris. He also appreciated the fact that Edouard Manet's celebrity went far beyond city street life, his place in the art and salon worlds considered just avant-garde enough to pique and just discernable enough to hold public interest. Apart from Manet's artistic talent and in keeping with Ernest's own deep desire to make his own mark in the art world, this may have been the best reason for Ernest to like Edouard Manet, but as if designed for mutual amusement, in the country at Montgeron, both men found they shared a taste for wild game drowning in wine and a great disdain for the exaggerated benefits of drinking water. Ernest's daily responsibilities and pursuits were vastly different from those of Manet, but his interests and passions were not so distant from those of the gracious artist whose social life centered about smart cafes and restaurants such as the Athenes, the Riche, and Tournelles, where proprietors, waiters, and more than a few beautiful prostitutes knew him by name. In terms of Manet's own artistic approach and in keeping with the constraints of his attitudes, he remained alien to the outdoor landscape painting his Impressionist friends pursued with great gusto. So tied to the indoor studio tradition was he, that he had not established a relationship with a Street of Pictures dealer to represent him when it came to promoting sales. He showed his own paintings in his own Rue Guyot studio, his sales emanating almost exclusively from these periodic exhibitions.

In a departure from this norm and through a scenario in which Ernest would acquire several Manet treasures, at Claude Monet's urging Paul Durand-Ruel had visited Manet's studio one afternoon in 1872. Before leaving, he had purchased all thirty paintings in it for thirty-five thousand francs, immediately sending a messenger to offer Ernest Hoschede first choice as soon as they had been delivered to Rue Laffitte. Hurriedly leaving his store, his carriage left waiting at Durand-Ruel's door, in one brief transaction Ernest purchased Young Man in the Costume of a Mayo, Woman with a Parrot, The Street Singer, The Ragpicker, and Embarkation at Boulogne sur Mer.

Soon, Ernest was taking great pleasure in his patron-artist relationships, very much enjoying the companionship of the friends he was making at the Guerbois and offended only occasionally by the behavior of Edgar Degas whose overall rudeness and frequent temperamental outbursts were patiently tolerated or completely ignored, but at the Boulevard des Capucines exhibition where Ernest had introduced Alice to Berthe Morisot, the one female artist whose work was exhibited with that of her male colleagues, Degas' behavior had been found to be intolerable.

A stately, beautiful woman, Morisot was known to have a gift for conversation, a quality which among women of a particular class in the city of Paris was not so much a talent but a well-developed skill along with horseback riding and playing the piano. Convinced that Madame Morisot and Alice would get on well, especially since Suzanne Manet was mutually admired, a frequent visitor to the Chateau Rottembourg, and soon to become Mademoiselle Morisot's sister-in-law, Ernest had counted on the potential of their friendship as a step toward encouraging Alice's greater enthusiasm for his patronage of the Impressionists. As well met and equally adept a conversationalist as Alice was, however, this introduction would not be remembered as one of Ernest's best decisions.

Edgar Degas, resplendent in formal afternoon attire, his black cloak lined in white satin, had escorted Berthe Morisot to the afternoon opening, the tall, head-turning Madame Morisot equally splendid in a fashionably narrow long, black voile dress and one of the severely angular black hats she favored. The two stood side by side at the far end of the first room. Ernest and Alice approached them and Ernest introduced Alice to both Edgar Degas and Berthe Morisot, only to find Degas not only typically unpleasant, but dismissive. A curt phrase or two and he promptly walked away, a gesture that even in the company of gracious Berthe Morisot, was one Alice found insulting and altogether in keeping with what she concluded must surely be the overall rude behavior patterns of the derisive group as a whole. Thinking about the incident in the seclusion of his study, Ernest smiled again. He looked to the clock on the mantel. Half an hour after two. Durand-Ruel's delivery carriage was very late. The driver must be delayed by the weather, he decided, striding across the dark, bare floor and sinking into his favorite chair beside the waiting corner easel, his unrelenting, critical eye taking in every detail of his surroundings which more than any other aspect of his life spoke volumes concerning his personal taste.

The room, although the smallest in the apartment, was its most beautiful. Even in the gray light of a cool stormy day it gleamed like a jewel, its introspective tone set by the dark oak floor which was kept waxed almost black. Reflected against the blazing fireplace, it shone like a fiery opal. The walls were covered in richly textured ruby red baize and against their inviting calm hung many of the paintings Ernest had collected in recent years, the Barbizon School well represented, the older historic portraiture substantial and perceptive, the newer Impressionist landscapes growing in number from month to month.

The frames surrounding each canvas had been chosen with care. Durand-Ruel's obsession with frames having successfully infected Ernest, all were gently gilded and expertly carved, some of cured alder wood, others of lime or pine. The furnishings in the room were few and of high quality, the decorative appointments plentiful, carefully placed, at times whimsical, often in pairs, always important, most with provenance. Under two Corot landscapes a collection of six miniature early eighteenth-century bronze elephants paraded across a hundred-year-old giltwood console table once the property of Napoleon Bonaparte. A pair of bronze andirons once luxuriously housed at Fountainbleau guarded the fireplace, each formed of a rampant lion supporting a shield emblazoned with the symbolic French fleurs-de-lis. A fine pair of intricately carved high-back armchairs, their seats covered in their original slightly worn eighteenth-century Saint Cyr gros and petitpoint needlework, faced each other at the fireside. Ernest's favorite chair, also an armchair, but smaller and upholstered in burgundy leather, stood in the solitary corner where he waited. To one side was the corner easel where he intended to place Impression Sunrise. To the other, a bronze bust of Cardinal Richelieu glared out from the center of a circular marble-topped table strewn with open books and stacks of paper scrawled across in Ernest's bold handwriting. A green woolen scarf was tied around the cardinal's neck, placed there one cold winter afternoon years before and thought far too appropriately amusing to be removed. Nearby, a pair of tall, gilt-bronze candlesticks in the form of fearsome satyrs awaited each day's falling dusk. The room was a haven of peace and quiet. But for the rain pounding against the mullioned windows, the only sound came from the ticking of the clocks. There were two, the name, Raingo, inscribed in florid gold letters across each glistening white porcelain face serving as constant reminders that Alice was a Raingo, descended from the distinguished family of French-Belgian clockmakers.

The Raingo brothers, Belgian by birth and famous for their precise clockworks set into fine art bronzes, had, in one hardworking generation and under both French and British royal patronage, become successful enough to invest in a variety of commercial establishments and blocks of lucrative Paris real estate. Gradually, cramped living quarters above dusty Vielle-du-Temple workrooms had given way to luxurious Paris apartments and fine houses in the countryside. So complete was the family's transformation from working class to landed gentry that on her father's death, Alice had inherited her family's Chateau Rottembourg, the magnificent Brie Valley country estate where every year she and Ernest and their five young children spent the summer months. Distracting his thoughts, Ernest could hear Alice in the downstairs hall.

"Celeste!" she was calling out to the housekeeper in her lyrical voice, "Monsieur Hoschede is expecting a delivery this afternoon. It's another painting. We'll be needing a mat on the floor in the hall before you let the courier in. On a day like this he will have very wet feet and we have just had the floors polished for the party."

Ernest smiled again. There was no one like Alice, he thought, no one with her eye for perfection, no one who cared so much about getting things right, no one with her generous heart, especially when it came to her family and home. The distinguished Raingo family clock business was a particular source of pride, and Alice made no secret of the fact that she treasured the Raingo clocks in her possession. She liked to say that the two in Ernest's study were perfectly suited to the design and use of the intimate room in which her husband spent so much of his private time, the graceful, lyre-shaped timepiece presiding over the room from the center of the marble mantel and the larger figured bronze on the desk fine compliments to a place where introspective hours could be spent alone with one thoughts.

More pensive as he waited, Ernest sat back and blew small, quick, puffs of cigar smoke into the idle air, allowing his mind to wander once again. It was easy to understand Alice's predilection to details of comfort and structure and Raingo family values he considered, once again a close-lipped smile suddenly lighting his face. Yes, as a family unit the maddeningly predictable Raingos had been raised to be steadfast, upstanding citizens, at least socially, and except for Alice and her Uncle Julian they could also be counted on to be boring as hell. He laughed aloud at the thought, but there was no denying that their reputations in the city's large Belgian community of which they were an integral part, were defined by their wealth and impeccable manners and the sort of propriety people expect in old families. Their punctual, evening-attired arrival for Julian Raingo's party was not likely to disappoint. Neither would Alice's preparations which had been in planning stages for weeks. All would be perfection. The buffet supper arranged on silver trays and tall epergnes along the length of the dining room table would create a picture too beautiful to be mercilessly attacked with mere serving spoons. The all-white flowers on the sideboards would be artfully arranged, compliments would fly, and Alice herself, dressed in one of her long, pale gray silk taffeta dresses would appear relaxed and prepared for another of the festive evening occasions on which she thrived. Yes, Ernest reflected, Julian Raingo's sixtieth birthday celebration would be a memorable affair, family and closest friends gathered to raise toasts to a milestone event in the life of a beloved patriarch and Paris luminary. Of course Julian Raingo's close friends, the Lavoies would be there, full of news from London where they were spending so much of their time lately. Notwithstanding the many attractions of the British capital, they never missed one of Alice's parties. Considering themselves to be important collectors, like Julian Raingo they too collected Dutch and Flemish paintings. And then there was Cousin Beatrice who would be attending as well, and thank goodness for her. Hopefully, she would live up to expectations and make her dramatic entrance draped in yards of lace, a spray of brightly colored feathers waving in her tightly curled red hair, her rouged cheeks a bit too pink, her heart-shaped lips a bit too red, her perfume strong and regrettably memorable.

Widowed for a number of years, Beatrice had recently married Julian Raingo's wealthy banker, Marc Pirole, a man who seemed to have been born in Julian Raingo's mold. Like the elder Raingo, Marc was a staunch traditionalist and a financial genius. Unlike sophisticated Raingo, however, Marc was a very boring man. More than any other topic, he enjoyed talking about international monetary values, currency graphs, market rates, and the cost of living in corners of the world few people had ever heard of. Fortunately, fun-loving Beatrice had come along to jar Marc into a livelier more secular life, even a hearty laugh from time to time. He adored her and saw to it she had everything her heart desired. Somehow, though, a fine new house in a prestigious arrondissement, an unlimited personal expense account, and an elevated sense of social prominence had not changed too many of dear Cousin Beatrice's old habits. Much to Ernest's amusement as he recalled their meeting at the Salon Exhibition, she remained an extravagant, outspoken woman who could be relied upon to dress outlandishly, establish herself at the center of any gathering, and promptly spread the most vulgar bits of gossip in absolutely no time at all.

It was rumored that Beatrice and the life-long bachelor, Julian Raingo, had been secretly in love for years. In spite of their very different personalities and polar opposite tastes, no one knew why they had never married when she became widowed, but whatever the reason, they had remained close friends and even after Beatrice's marriage to Pirole, they were known to be frequent dinner and traveling companions, spending weeks together every summer at Biarritz or Trouville and promenading the resort beachfront walkways every afternoon, arm in arm, Beatrice attired in one of her red or black and white striped dresses, an enormous matching hat held down over her red hair in the brisk seaside breezes by a long tulle scarf she tied in a huge bow under her chin. At the upcoming birthday event and with no particular complaint from her husband, Beatrice would not stray too far from the elder Raingo's side, Ernest predicted as he envisioned the proceedings, her company warmly welcomed by the dignified gentleman who adored her unconventional company. If past experience was to be relied upon, Beatrice would flutter her newest lace-edged fan and from behind its protective shield recite her risqué rhymes to him, of which there were many. He would throw back his head, laugh at her rhymes, feign shock at her foul language, and hang on to her every word as she flirted with him, stroked his hand, and made him feel he was the only person in the room if not the entire world. At evening's end they would thank and compliment their hosts on the success of the evening as they said their good byes and stepped out into the night, each reluctantly going their separate ways.

Given Beatrice's unconventionality, on the surface it would seem highly unlikely that she and imminently correct and polite Alice would have developed a lasting friendship, but they did. Beatrice had little talent for making friends, but when Ernest's choice of Alice to be his wife was announced, Beatrice immediately welcomed her cousin's fiancé with open arms. As far as Ernest was concerned, the fact that Alice had learned to overlook his favorite cousin's natural ability to offend was reason enough to tolerate Julian Raingo and his maddening displays of superiority.

"And Celeste, one more thing, please," Alice called out downstairs. "We won't be taking tea in Monsieur Hoschede's study this afternoon. You know how it is when he receives a new painting."

Growing impatient now as he continued to wait, Ernest turned to his desk. On it, in silver frames, was a photograph of four of the five Hoschede children. He examined it closely, as he had hundreds of times in the past, observing every detail captured by Felix Nadar, the Paris photographer Alice had engaged for the sitting. The oldest child, a daughter, was ten-year-old Marthe who looked so much like her mother; yes, pretty and proud like Alice. All three older girls: Marthe and her sisters Blanche and Suzanne, had worn their best velvet dresses and the shiny, silver buckled black shoes they loved. Five-year-old Jacques, the only boy in the family and a year older than Suzanne, sat at the center of the sisterly group. Not quite a year old and asleep in the nursery, Baby Germaine had not been included in the photograph. The four who sat for Nadar had smiled, looking exactly as the children of privilege should look: happy, secure, and part of an untarnished world. Yes, Alice was raising her children the way she herself had been raised, with an abundance of love and considerable attention to the niceties of life. She was a mother who could be overly protective, that much was true, Ernest had admitted to himself many times over, puffing at his cigar once again, but Alice did put all the Raingo women to shame with her intelligence. She was always interesting to talk to and she was, without question, his favorite companion. Of course, it hurt not in the least that she was very pretty to look at and that her personal accomplishments were quite above average. She played the piano, rode horses, read newspapers and novels, attended concerts and openings of the latest plays, and like most women in her circle, she could talk to just about anyone about the latest news in Paris. Adding to her admirable attributes, Alice ran her two households with skill and good humor and she even enjoyed a bit of unladylike risk every now and then, not outright trouble of course, or anything unpleasant that could reflect badly on the family, Heaven forbid, but risk was something Ernest was sure Alice could handle. She certainly had taken a risk in marrying him, at least that was the attitude of both sets of parents who had done all they could to discourage the match.

For her part, Alice's mother, Jeanne Coralie Boulade Raingo, had felt that handsome and charming as he was, Ernest Hoschede was not wealthy enough for her daughter, while Madame Honorine Hoschede felt that pretty and wealthy as she was, Alice Raingo was too opinionated and extravagant for her son.

"She will ruin him! And us!" Honorine had repeatedly complained to her husband once her beloved son's betrothal to Alice was formally announced. "Those clothes of hers must cost a fortune! Did you see the yards of blue silk she wore at your niece's wedding? And a huge matching hat if you please, made to order of course. And the girl has an opinion about everything. She thinks this, and she thinks that, and have you read this book, and have you read that one? She doesn't let up. My handsome Ernest had the pick of Paris. What does he see in that flighty girl? Do you remember that dear little Louisa Nolandes, so shy and darling? Whatever happened to that lovely girl? She was perfect for my Ernest."

The marriage hotly opposed, advice flying in all directions until the last minute, on April 16th, 1863 the wedding took place in spite of parental concerns and without the presence of the groom's parents, Alice bedecked in yards and yards of ivory Brussels lace, the bodice of her dress covered with intricate embroidery, the cuffs of her long sleeves tightly buttoned, her train appliquéd with satin panels edged in seed pearls, news of the extraordinary length of her veil, which fell to the floor from a lace cap delicately stitched with a small coronet of white roses and completely filling the center aisle of The Madeleine, a fresh target for the cynical Madame Hoschede who had received a detailed description of Alice's appearance from the enchanted, wildly in love bridegroom, Honorine unmoved by her son's romantic declarations. It didn't matter. The young couple had been madly, blissfully in love. Eleven years and five children later, they still were. Yes, pretty, strong-willed Angelique-Emile-Alice Raingo Hoschede always found the strength to see things through and she really didn't worry too much. She certainly didn't worry about money. She never had, and why would she? Along with a spectacular fifteen thousand franc trousseau, Alice had brought a dowry of one hundred fifty thousand francs to her marriage and inheriting the Chateau Rottembourg after seven years of marital bliss hadn't changed her, not really, not the way money and ownership of important property changed most people. No, the money and the chateau and the blocks of Paris real estate her Uncle Julian continued to mange for the family with quarterly distributions of income hadn't changed her at all. Alice was his Alice. She was an heiress and of a particular class, but she carried her husband's name and she shared his talent for living life to the fullest. Together they had formed a splendid union of ideas peppered only occasionally by contrasting views of the world, but regardless of their minor, short-lived disagreements, their ongoing love affair had never cooled and apart from Ernest's current interest in Impressionist painting and its chief proponents, they were at one in every aspect of their lives.

Ernest left his desk and placed a fresh log on the fire. He glanced up to the mantel clock once again. Almost three o'clock. A frustrated smirk crossed his face. Where was the courier with his painting? This waiting was a waste of time. He returned to the window with its view across rooftops and spires and in the midst of the pouring rain he began to admire the bright shock of yellow spring jonquils in the canopied vendor's cart across the street. The irony of the scene served to alter his pensive mood. It wouldn't be long now he contemplated with another puff at his cigar, no, not long at all before the weather would turn warm and spring-like again. This rain would pass and in a week, perhaps less, the budded quince and young chestnut trees lining the avenues would burst into flower. Yes, and before too long, bunches of yellow daffodils now so gloriously rare and playful in steely, drab light would seem quite ordinary in warm, bright sunshine. That was it; yes, like life itself at various turns, the weather would eventually right itself and warm into a lasting spring, and as May and early June settled in, Paris would come alive again. It was a city of well-established seasonal habits and this spring would be no different from those he had known all his life. On warm sunny days the flower and wafer vendors would relocate their carts and nest like seasoned old birds at the entrance to the Tuileries Gardens. By then all the public parks and gardens would be freshly planted in their annual riot of color. Borders of red salvia, white marguerites, and silver-leafed eglantine would be everywhere. The fountains would be turned on once again. Sprays of water would leap up into the sky, fan out, and for a few magical days the pace of the city would slow, its inhabitants eager to be outdoors and bask in the novelty of early summer's abundance of sunshine and warm temperatures as they abandoned schedules and paused to admire their cultivated urban carpet. Pairs of lovers would stroll along the tree-lined avenues and boulevards. Arm in arm in a world tailor-made for romance, they would promenade along the pristine walkways of the Bois de Boulogne, resplendent in their newest finery, their daily lives no longer affected by intruding bursts of chilly wintry winds and fickle moods of late spring weather, their receptive spirits hopelessly seduced by the vitality of a city known the world over for its love affair with beauty. Caught up in the allure of the City by the Seine, the most jaded Paris resident would stop to admire the pristine lawns of the Louvre turned suddenly green, brightened and freed from months of winter gloom by adjacent acres of red and pink roses. Lulled by the city's incomparable talent for municipal spectacle, indulgent afternoons would often end with a luxurious pause at the sentinel rows of lime trees in the Luxembourg Gardens where every year scores of tree-swifts flew in from Africa to spend their summers nesting and raising families in the Paris even they found irresistible.

By then, the Hoschede family would be far away from city sensibilities and walks along the Seine, Ernest reminded himself, looking forward to the pleasant prospect of spending yet another summer at the Chateau Rottembourg. How he admired that property and everything about it. In one way or another it was always on his mind, nestled into some small corner where he could dwell on the splendor of the house and its rose brick façade. He especially loved Rottembourg's grounds; its tall cedars, its oaks and willows, the hollows where his children safely played, and its access to the forest where he hunted the small game. The Chateau Rottembourg had become a great source of pride to Ernest, its bucolic setting and candlelit evenings of unhurried pleasure establishing a tradition of lively conversation not always linked by news of Paris galleries, cafes, or theaters, but more often by country news and country habits; by the fine show of white summer roses at the quaint village train station, by the stationmaster's irascible, gossip-loving wife, and by the all-consuming ease and grace of country life.

As he had since Rottembourg had passed to Alice, Ernest would again spend the summer months traveling the forty kilometers back and forth each week by train between Paris and Montgeron. He would attend to business in the city from Monday to Thursday, anxiously returning to Alice and the children in the country by Thursday afternoon. The schedule changed in August when by tradition and across Europe, the entire month was given over to holiday. This was the period of summer to which Ernest looked forward most, Rottembourg's landscape at its beautiful peak, the days of August warm and leisurely, business and its schedules tossed aside and forgotten for more than four idyllic weeks. The sudden sound of the door pull and Celeste's quick footsteps echoing along the length of the downstairs hall startled him, jarring his thoughts away from lyrical summer pursuits and back to the provocative present.

"Bonjour, Monsieur," he heard her say pleasantly to the delivery man. "It is good to see you at last. We expected you hours ago, but oh my! You poor man! You are soaking wet. I am so sorry, but please wipe your feet on the mat. Monsieur Hoschede is waiting upstairs and of course he will understand that the rain must have delayed you. Follow me. Oh my! You are very wet! I do hope you didn't let yourself become chilled. Colds are very difficult to get rid of at this time of year. Before you leave, do come to the kitchen. I'll have some hot tea waiting for you."

"I am so sorry, Monsieur Hoschede," the soaking wet uniformed courier apologized at the top of the stairs where Ernest waited, "but my carriage was caught up in a terrible soggy mess of wagons and carriages on Rue le Peletier. It was all confusion and upset. I have been driving in Paris for years and I have never seen anything like it. People were shouting and angry. More than once my horse reared and shied. When I stopped in the middle of the street and got out to calm him, women shrieked at me and poked their umbrellas in my face. I had all I could do to guard my eyesight. It was terrible. No one was helping anyone else and the heavens kept opening up, but I knew I couldn't let anything happen to your package. I was so glad to know it was safe and dry inside my delivery carriage. I pride myself on the care I take with everything I deliver, and Monsieur Durand-Ruel was clear in warning me to be careful. "Prudemment! Prudemment! " he called out to me as I prepared to leave The Street, but Monsieur Hoschede, I hope you understand why I am so late. In the pouring rain everything was bunched together in the middle of Rue le Peletier for more than two hours and I will say again that I have never seen anything like it; that mass of carriages, horse carts, milk wagons, and people trying to cross from one side of the street to the other in an immense confusion, but here I am at last. My apologies and au revoir, Monsieur Hoschede. I do hope you will be happy with your painting. It has endured a most arduous journey."

"Thank you for your patience," Ernest said to the courier as he handed him a fifty franc note. "I shall be sure to tell Monsieur Durand-Ruel about your careful attention to a painting both he and I very much care about."

CHAPTER 5

Private Lives

Ernest had good reason to appreciate the courier's care with his anxiously awaited painting. The layers of heavy brown paper covering Impression Sunrise were remarkable dry. Not a spot of rainwater had fallen on them. Placing the package on his desk, he quickly slipped away the string and carefully unfolded the sturdy layers of brown paper. Setting the wrapping aside, he placed his latest prize on the waiting easel facing his leather chair.

His eyes riveted on the canvas, he was more fascinated than ever by the prominent role Claude Monet and his Le Havre harbor painting were playing in naming the culture clash that had Paris buzzing. He leaned forward, awaiting the onset of feelings he had come to anticipate. It was always the same with a new painting, the same range of emotions in exactly the same predictable order. First, came the comfort of pure satisfaction in having prevailed in the chase. Next, came pride of ownership. Pure contentment quickly settled in like an enveloping cloud, but vanity soon interrupted, on its forever hubris heels a burst of ridiculous merriment ending in an explosion of delighted, victorious laughter. With the arrival of Impression Sunrise into its triumphant owner's hands, however, a very different range of feelings stirred in Ernest Hoschede.

Non-conformist that he was, Ernest had understood the great potency of the painting's namesake significance in those requisite moments of bargaining with Durand-Ruel and in a short space of time he had felt irrevocably connected to its tangible significance. Now, though, alone with its controversial distinction in the privacy of his own home and as the painting by itself began to undergo the process of his close scrutiny, there was a new, revealing alliance.

Leaning in closer to the easel and ignoring all unspoken rules, he committed the cardinal sin and touched the canvas. He smiled, enjoying the touching, savoring the guilt. Slowly, hesitantly at first, he gently ran his fingers over the brushstrokes of orange sun. He sat back for a brief moment, stared, then leaned forward again and repeated the forbidden process, this time more reverently. Like a lover passionately exploring the wonders of the beloved's shape and form, he tenderly traced the sun's reflections glistening in fiery glory across the pale water. He marveled and admired. He qualified and excluded. He sat back once again and stared at the faceless suggestion of a figure standing alone in the middle of the canvas. "Stupid to stand up in a small boat in the middle of a harbor!" he remembered having joked with Durand-Ruel during their bargaining. How foolish that remark must have sounded to the sophisticated dealer who hadn't laughed at all. Now, in the privacy of a quiet space exclusively his, it didn't seem stupid at all for a man to stand alone in a small boat in the middle of a harbor. No, it wasn't stupid or strange at all, not when a man could stop, stand back in his own world and pause to truly see. Now, the nondescript, featureless dark figure standing alone in a small boat in the middle of the color-drenched Le Havre harbor looked courageous and far from stupid. He bore about him exactly what, in his inimitable voice, Emile Zola was calling for in art at every opportunity: "the human touch, the living corner of creation that makes of art a new manifestation in the face of reality."

Clearly, Impression Sunrise was not at all like other paintings Ernest had acquired and cared about. It was the work of a strong, confident rebel, that much was true, but from the first moments of its arrival into his hands, Impression Sunrise became more, much more than he had expected it to be. It was not the work of an uncomplicated painter. It was the work of a master. It was freedom in a frame, forbearance and permissiveness at a roar, a tantalizing view of jeopardy and faceless hope, a glance across dawn's deep waters into the abject future. In all its complicated simplicity, Impression Sunrise was a portrait of Ernest Hoschede himself. The realization stunned him. Who was this Claude Monet, this freedom fighter, this intruder into his soul?

Ernest reminded himself that his acquaintance with Claude Monet, although increasingly cordial as the recent exhibition month had progressed, had not been motivated by his sincere admiration for the artist's work at all. Throughout its duration he had remained far more attracted to the landscapes of Pissarro and Sisley and to Madame Morisot's intimate domestic scenes, but as Impression Sunrise had been discussed and criticized more and more sharply, his personal curiosity about Claude Monet had grown.

At the Guerbois, he had found Monet slow to reveal anything of himself, instead chatting enthusiastically with his colleagues about their lives and their activities and rather deliberately leaving his own personal life unexplored. Ernest realized that his own inclusion at the renegade Guerbois table was a gesture of great respect and an immense compliment to his courageous support and patronage, but by the time he had purchased Impression Sunrise, Ernest knew Claude Monet only as a cordial but guarded man, an artist whose work consumed him every day from dawn to dusk and one who kept very much to himself. Durand-Ruel had explained that Claude rarely extended a personal invitation and since he was uncomfortable with strangers, that when not painting he chose to spend his time with his family and in the secure company of the close circle of fellow painters who gathered at the Guerbois. Ernest had seen that side of Claude for himself. What Ernest had not seen was that alone with his colleagues, Claude was very different. With them he was jovial and completely at ease, probably at his best. His closest friend was Pierre Renoir and over time he had befriended Edouard Manet, a man whose talent he held in very high regard. Of course he held a great respect for Paul Durand-Ruel whose efforts in promoting him were deeply appreciated, but even with Manet and with his own dealer, Monet appeared to maintain an arm's length relationship. Other than his openness in frankly discussing his constant bouts with poverty and debt, his personal revelations, at least in Ernest's presence, went only so far. His hobbies and private interests apart from painting seemed generally unknown. Ernest never saw him carrying a book or a newspaper, yet he could quote Zola, Hugo, and de Maupassant. Clearly, he admired the intelligent, well-informed of Paris and apart from the familiar company of his colleagues, he appeared to appreciate the occasional company and comments of thinkers, especially when it came to matters of contemporary life, being particularly drawn to new ideas, especially those of popular playwrights, novelists, and poets such Stephane Mallarme.

Impoverished as he was, Ernest had noticed that Claude was extremely fussy about his food, but his friend Renoir may have been one of the few people who could name his favorite dishes, most preferred among them, chestnuts pureed in cream. His singing voice, which was a fine one, Ernest was told by Alfred Sisley, had been heard only by his musical mother and his loving aunt, Sophie Lecadre, during Sunday afternoon family musicales at Saint Adresse, but in fact Sisley had heard Claude singing while painting with him in the forest at Fountainbleau, his fine baritone voice soaring through the melodic lines of folksongs of the Auvergne as he set up his easel and scanned the woodland's light and shade.

Claude had a wife and a son but few people outside the Guerbois circle knew their names. Claude's painting was his life and other than the city of Paris itself, to which he was devoted, painting was all he truly cared about. He did love the rhythm and pace of the city. He drew constant inspiration from it, yet he was not often seen casually strolling the avenues and boulevards, leaving such activity to Degas and Manet who were familiar daily figures along the city's busy tree-lined boulevards. Driven by his work and completely dedicated to it, Claude Monet was, as Ernest was discovering, essentially an aloof individual. The man was unquestionably self-possessed, solid and strong enough to weather any storm alone, but as talented and self-reliant as he was, if recession came to Paris how would he survive? How would any member of his rebel group go on?

Busy with the children and preparations for the coming birthday celebration, it was an hour before dinner that same evening when Alice saw Impression Sunrise. She had dressed for the evening with her usual care, attired in one of the dozen or so long gray evening dresses she usually chose to wear, each designed in a flattering shade of silver, ash, pearl, or smoke. The taffetas crackled when she walked. The satins gleamed in candlelight. The tulles fell to the floor in tier after seductive tier and every evening, the responsibilities of his own busy day set aside, Ernest looked forward to these hours alone with the woman he had fallen in love with at first sight. More than ten years after their marriage he was still drawn to Alice's sensual warmth. Like the admiring lover he was, no detail of her appearance went unnoticed. He admired her shining dark hair brushed back into a thickly wound chignon or curled at the curving nape of her long slender neck, the necklines of her fashionably slim, low-cut evening dresses revealing a good deal of seductive decolletage, her bright smile beaming toward him.

Taking a cue from Durand-Ruel and the prominent display of Monet's painting in his gallery and wanting it to be the first thing Alice saw, Ernest had moved the easel holding Impression Sunrise close to the doorway.

"Oh, another of those," Alice said with a lighthearted laugh as she approached. "I've had a feeling it wouldn't be long before one or two more of the new paintings would be added to these walls."

Standing before Ernest's most recent prize, Alice looked puzzled. "Was this painting at the Boulevard des Capucines exhibition we attended?" she asked. "I don't remember seeing it at all. Of course there was so much going on there, too much, really, but my dear, I'll indulge you once again and do my best to understand your fascination with all this," she said, as Ernest came toward her and she kissed him on the cheek. Drawing her close, he held her tightly in his arms for a long silent moment.

"What is it?" Alice asked, looking up to his handsome face, sensing the uneasiness in him. "Is everything all right?"

She had been perfuming her bathwater with the jasmine oil he had brought to her from the store a few days before. It lingered on her skin and clothes. The intrigue of jasmine suited Alice, its floral allure together with her nearness suddenly succeeding quite totally in distracting Ernest from nagging concerns with lines of credit or presidents of banks or any interest he may have thought he had in sharing his excitement for the latest addition to his art collection. It was just as well. Earlier that day, as much as he had needed additional capital and as enthusiastic as had been about Impression Sunrise, he had begun to regret the sizeable amount of the loan he had signed on to. "It's nothing, darling. It's absolutely nothing," he whispered, "just another silly incident at the store, a customer complaint, nothing important."

In his arms and quickly lost in her familiar melting softness, Alice was the passionate woman he adored. In an instant the familiar fire flamed up between them, igniting the surging wave of desire that in all their years of marriage had never dulled. Her hands slid up along the smooth sleeves of his black velvet jacket to his broad shoulders. Her fingers stroked his cheek and encircled his neck, seeking the tenderness that pressed close to him she always found, knowing that the ardent, unrestrained beyond always awaited them, always vibrant, always theirs alone.

"Tell me what's wrong," Alice gently coaxed. "Ernest, you can't fool me. Something is on your mind and it has nothing to do with this painting," she whispered with another kiss. "It's nothing, really, darling" he whispered back, "just a customer relations detail I must work out. It will be fine. You know me too well, but right now I really would prefer to talk about how much I love you. Now listen carefully."

It was like this between them at day's end, distress and annoyance no matter how worrisome quickly replaced by loving indulgence, the inevitable little hurts and stabs of daily life forgotten as if they had never happened, pangs of disappointment and anxiety lost to soft laughter and tender endearments, the intense ardor flaring up between them heated by ever more ardent kisses and a treasured devotion that over the years had strengthened and grown increasingly playful between them. Making their way upstairs to the bedroom at the end of the second floor hall they were like young lovers. They touched, teased, laughed, and pushed at one another with every step, oblivious to time and place and desperate for the soaring wonder of completeness that came to them in surrendering moments of tender intimacy when the singular, secure oneness they had learned to create in rare, undamaged hours came to delight and possess them.

"Now, about whatever it is that's been on your mind today and we didn't talk about before I landed here in this lovely bed with you," Alice chided later, propping herself up against the bed pillows on one elbow, her hair a loose, tousled frame surrounding her face. "I've decided I'm not leaving this room to see about your dinner without a full confession. You may begin at any time. I'm listening."

In the room's soft candlelight her face glowed. At the age of thirty, Alice still had the radiance of a young girl in love with life, happy with her place in it, and supremely confident in what the future would hold. Her eyes sparkled with vitality. A healthy pink blush crossed her cheeks. "I'm glad you have the painting you wanted, though," she conceded with another kiss. "That should cheer you up, and before this night is over I promise to go back to your study with you and examine it very closely. But I'm still waiting for your confession. Out with it!"

"Never mind about all that now," Ernest said, stroking Alice's hair and soundly kissing her yet once more before confessing he was starving. "It isn't important. Nothing is as important as you are, here with me right now, but exactly how cold do you think our dinner is ?" he asked, lying back and stretching his arms over his head. "Probably inedible? And of course you went to all that trouble dressing for the evening and doing your hair. Well, I wouldn't say it was a waste of time at all. As usual, you were enchanting."

Alice laughed. "All right. I can see its no use. I won't torture you any further or try to read your mind, but I must say that after all these years you should know Celeste is an expert at keeping food warm," she said, reaching for her robe on the nearby chair, "not for days, of course, but don't worry, my dear. You won't go hungry. There's a beautiful cassoulet for tonight. It's full of chicken and vegetables. All that holds for a while, especially with the wine Celeste knows you like her to add to almost everything. And there's always plenty of bread and cheese in the house. Let's have dinner here tonight, there on the table by the windows. I'll bring a tray up. I promise I won't be long."

He watched Alice fastening her robe and tying her hair back with a length of blue ribbon. As she reached the hallway door he took close notice of the room where every night she slept in his arms. Nothing must change this world she delighted in; this world filled with beautiful things; with fine furniture, draperies, carpets, everything of the highest quality. It took a substantial income to maintain the elegance of their lifestyle. Perhaps it was time to make a closer study of household expenses and find ways to cut a few monthly costs; nothing obvious of course, and nothing Alice would notice or worry about, but there had to be small things that could easily be eliminated, a decidedly concerned Ernest told himself as the bedroom door closed and Alice left him alone while his mind raced back to his meeting with Christophe Emmanuel.

"This could be the last of the lines of credit we can provide you, at least for the year's two remaining quarters," Emmanuel had said to him as the transaction was concluded. But things were going so well, Ernest reassured himself, remembering Emmanuel's remarks. There was no reason to worry. It was ridiculous. Sales at the store were good, employees were happy. Recession was just a word. Emmanuel was a banker. Bankers were always worried.

That same evening at the Café Guerbois, worry was taking on a similarly unsettling tone, the group of newly minted Impressionists gathered at their usual table although keenly aware of its remarkable achievement in actually having impacted the intellect of an entire city, was also in a state of uncertainty. It was true that people were talking. That much was good they concluded, but unfortunately most people were also aghast, shocked, and insulted. Many were laughing. The critics were the real challenge. With an influence second only to that of the Salon Jury, journalists had exercised their undeniable power to sway public opinion as no other group in Paris could. It was true that a few courageous fellow artists such as Edouard Manet and Fantin-Latour encouraged and comforted and that one influential Parisian named Hoschede and one supportive dealer named Durand-Ruel had fallen entirely into lockstep with them but it wasn't enough. In the shoddy confines of their Guerbois headquarters the newly named Impressionists decided to disband.

"We cannot continue this madness! If nothing else, we must at least restore our individual reputations. As a group we are being crucified!" Edgar Degas was first to admit, pounding his fist on the stack of newspapers carrying the latest discouraging assessments. "The Salon has a rope around our necks and so do these journalists!"

In his reliably cynical way, Degas knew as well as anyone that year after year a wide range of both well-established and lesser knowns submitted work to The Salon. He was also aware of the fact that there was no limit placed on the number of times an artist could submit and that no restrictions were placed on foreign entries. All of it annoyed him. Of course, it was not difficult to annoy Degas, but it annoyed him most to observe that some artists submitted year after year, subjecting themselves to feeding repeatedly at the trough of rejection and shrinking away from its poisonous venom in a veil of painful uncertainty, but be it struggling vie-boheme artist or one of established reputation, Monsieur Edgar Degas was forced to face facts. There was no higher honor for any artist than Salon Jury acceptance, and there was no more noteworthy tribute than the opportunity such acceptance provided for his work to be seen by the thousands who attended the annual Salon Exhibition.

Ratification of work submitted and approved was an artist's sine qua non. For a striving artist yearning for validation, the affirmative nod could be life-altering. The Salon's official red stamp applied to the back of a canvas, although not a guarantee, was by all standards a definitive act capable of transforming a life both financially and emotionally.

"I suppose each of us must simply continue to work on his own and hope for an occasional sale with Monsieur Durand-Ruel," Camille Pissarro added as the discussion continued, his natural optimism a sincere but lame attempt to affect the badly deflated egos of his daring colleagues whose first attempts at collaboration had not only failed but now had begun to engender bitter verbal exchanges as reasons for failure were explored with increasing exasperation.

"It was our name!" Renoir wailed from his chair. "It is too long, much too long! I cannot remember it myself. How could anyone else be expected to remember it? What was our Gustave Caillebotte thinking? He is so bright and so in touch with Paris. Claude tell me, what are we called in the catalogue?"

"In the catalogue and the advance notices we are Le Societe anonyme cooperative des artistes - peintres, sculpteurs, et graveurs," Claude replied, unable to suppress a smile, recalling young Gustave Caillebotte's brave leadership as time had grown short and no decision on a group name had been made.

"There you are!" Renoir declared, his fist pounding the table. "We are damned!"

That at the same time and on the same evening in the Hoschede apartment on Boulevard Haussmann a conversation related to the dilemma of the Impressionists was taking place seemed not only coincidental, but timely. "Who painted this Impression Sunrise?" Alice asked facing the Monet painting in Ernest's study after Celeste's delectable cassoulet accompanied by hearty slices of buttered bread and a bottle of fine Burgundy had been enjoyed.

"Claude Monet is the painter," Ernest answered. "He's one of the artists in the new group that's getting so much bad press."

"Well, they're taking quite a beating," Alice said, "and in a way I feel sorry for them, but people in Paris, including the critics and journalists must feel the way I do. We just don't know what to make of their work or of them. Clearly, they don't conform to the standards of the Paris art world in any relatable way and their non-conformity seems deliberate. Everything I saw at their exhibition looked amateurish and a little crude. Why would any artist want to publicly show such unpolished work? They've shown a good deal of courage though, and they're lucky to have you and Monsieur Durand-Ruel supporting them, but perhaps each artist would do better on his own. After such a bad showing their reputation as a group could be permanently damaged. Now the Salon may never accept any one of them and they will never make anything of themselves without Salon support, but don't worry, my dear. I'll do my best to get used to your Impression Sunrise. You must admit I'm doing better with each of your acquisitions. And so is Uncle Julian," she added with a wry, close-lipped smile. "I know how much you enjoy torturing him with these bewildering pictures," she concluded with another lighthearted laugh, rising from her chair, kissing Ernest one last time, and saying good-night as she turned toward the doorway.

Walking slowly along the hall toward the children's rooms to look in on them as they slept, Alice remembered that in the past month Ernest had told her about returning to the exhibition of Impressionists not once or twice, but again and again. He hadn't mentioned a painting titled Impression Sunrise, although for days he had talked to her of little more than the exhibition, describing how he had hurried into Durand-Ruel's gallery after one such return visit to confirm his reserve on two Marly paintings by Alfred Sisley and later to place reserves on several Camille Pissarro landscapes of which he had seemed particularly fond. What need had there been for such haste, Alice asked herself. No one else was interested in buying the new group's canvases. It was true that the prices Ernest had paid were attractively low, but there was nothing to the work, Alice had decided. It couldn't be taken seriously. These so-called Impressionists were merely creating one more brief drama on the Paris scene, and of course they were generating exactly the sort of careless phenomenon people loved to gossip about, but there was no need for her to make a fuss. Ernest would eventually get over this strange phase he was going through. Sooner or later he would straighten out and realize that these Impressionists were nothing but a temporary spark on the rich Paris horizon, one that would soon peter out and die. Thankfully, before too long, all these modern pictures he thought he loved would disappear. They would be sold for what few francs he could manage to get for them and replaced by the solid sorts of paintings Ernest deserved to have in his life, the sorts of important, relatable paintings that could be handed down to the children in years to come, the types of art they could be proud to own and hold on to. Thank goodness he wasn't spending too much money on this silly obsession.

Only vaguely interested in Ernest's collection of moderns and critical of the New Group's attempts to garner attention, Alice's assessment of her husband's enthusiasm for the new art, although generous in its loving indulgence, did not begin to touch on the true depth of his feelings. Fully absorbed in the myriad details of running two large household and the lives of her five young children, at the same time socially involved with her Raingo relatives, Alice had not for a moment considered the significant facts linked to her husband's obsession with the new painting and its protagonists, for not only had he attended the formal opening of their Boulevard des Capucines exhibition, he had returned again and again throughout its month-long run, with every visit and through conversations becoming ever more passionately allied with the basic Impressionist objective which lay grounded in the desire for change, and not simple, temporary, or casual change, but radical change within the powerful French art establishment and above all, persuasive change in the way the public looked at its pictures, particularly their pictures.

It would also be some time before Alice was aware of the fact that as more and more often Ernest was joining members of the struggling group at the Café Guerbois, his attachment to them was growing. As a result, he wanted to do all he could to support and encourage their efforts, especially now in the face of an economic downturn when purchases of art were not likely to be prioritized. In sharp contrast to his enthusiasm for new ideas and quite apart from his feeling of great personal triumph in having purchased Impression Sunrise, Alice was completely unaware of the financial risks accompanying her husband's unrestrained partiality to the band of renegades who, so like himself in a smug Paris priding itself on proven levels of established taste and style, were not only contentious, but belligerent, resentful of directives from a higher order, and above all, demanding to be accepted and successful on their own terms.

This culture clash, this social controversy which had set Paris buzzing in alternating waves of curiosity and scorn, was a condition very much to Ernest's liking. Alice understood that. She knew her husband loved the brashness, the insistence, the raw unbound freedom of it all. If he had developed a talent for painting himself, which she was convinced was languishing somewhere within him, he would have become one of them she had decided, perhaps their leader. Risky indulgence peppered with occasional dashes of irresponsibility lay at the heart of Ernest's personality and despite their dangers were part of his great charm. Unfortunately, his interpretations of indulgence and its commensurate risks were becoming seriously flawed, and although an uncommon man of uncommon means, by the spring of 1874 and unknown to Alice, Ernest had fallen into a common trap. He was overspending.

Although he seldom ever paid more than a thousand francs for a painting, the sheer number of Ernest's acquisitions in the last year alone had resulted in a considerable level of debt, but he was also overspending on a wide variety of things he could not resist, particularly on the expensive personal and decorative objects he felt his lifestyle demanded. He knew he was in arrears on his creditor accounts. He knew he owed money to banks and suppliers of goods for his store. He didn't care. In his pervasively optimistic way, he believed his money would hold out, and it really wasn't important for Alice to know he could be counted on to pay outstanding bills for an artist's rent and food. Didn't someone have to support these penniless talents? They had to survive. They had to be encouraged to continue working. He would manage it. He always had, for whenever spending exceeded income, a nasty inconvenience which of late seemed to have become more and more prevalent, Ernest showed himself to be the quintessentially creative provocateur.

True to his entrepreneurial character and with a fresh dimension of financial daring, he had recently found that now and then, in order to fund the opulent lifestyle and reputation for generosity he enjoyed, he was not at all opposed to selling a few of his prized paintings. His methods, like his taste in art, were new and innovative. To offset expenses when necessary and in order, at the same time, to meet the high costs of his highly acquisitive nature, he had begun to engage in an activity relatively new to Paris. Taking his cue from the famous Paris Opera singer and art collector, Jean Baptiste-Faure, who had made a half million francs on the well-attended public auction of his Corots, Delacroix, Dupres, and Rousseaus at the Hotel Drouot, the prestigious Paris auction house, but was perhaps best known for singing the Marseillaise wrapped in the French flag at the conclusion of each of his performances, Ernest had first looked to test the waters. Following Faure's example, he had auctioned off a few of his own Barbizons at the Drouot. He did well.

Without realizing the true reasons for his interest in auctioning off paintings, at first Alice was impressed by Ernest's success. Spurred on, he then occasionally and quite successfully began selling off a few of his Impressionist paintings at the Drout, essentially speculating in modern art. In a sophisticated city accustomed to handling its art purchases privately or through qualified, certified art dealers, this recent auctioning phenomenon had begun to raise some ire among the cognoscente and not just a few eyebrows among the bourgeoise. It wasn't long before Alice became embarrassed by the whole idea of publicly speculating on art.

"It looks as if we need money," she remarked to Ernest, which was of course, from time to time the case, a condition Ernest skillfully kept to himself. "No Ernest, you cannot continue with this," she stated in no uncertain terms. "Your store is a great success. You have a reputation for carrying high quality merchandise and you have a long list of distinguished customers. There is no need for this degrading business of selling paintings in an auction house!"

And as Alice continued to urge more elevated pursuits and Ernest assured her that auctioning was the modern method of selling art, he continued on with confidence, over time his speculative daring enabling him to buy back, sell, and again buy back many of the paintings he cared about most.

The Hotel Drouot, on Rue Grange-Bateliere, was the scene of the city's most important, high quality furniture and decorative arts sales. It became the setting for not one, but several of Ernest's carefully planned art auctions. His first having brought in a small but encouraging profit, the stage was set for two additional Hoschede auction events. With most of his Barbizons sold, both these sales focused almost exclusively on paintings by the Impressionists and in unrivaled Hoschede fashion were introduced to attendees not by a Drouot official attired in proper cravat and impeccably tailored morning coat, but by the jovial, celebratory remarks of the far more dapper, custom-booted Ernest Hoschede himself turned affable, articulate master of ceremonies and delightful, well-informed catalyst who ably assisted in the distribution of auction catalogues which, throughout the bidding process and much to the chagrin of the certified auctioneer, he readily autographed with flourish of pen and the infectious schoolboy smile for which he was becoming famous.

The most recent of these events had been held at the Drouot on January 13, 1874, three short months before the first Capucines exhibition. It had included paintings of the well-known Diaz and Vollon as well as a representation of the lesser known Impressionists Degas, Monet, Pissarro, and Sisley, whose paintings were among the first of the New Group's work Ernest had purchased at Durand-Ruel's urging and in an attempt to do little more than expand on his collection of traditional portraits and landscapes with a bit of contemporary work. Highly significant to the January of 1874 event was the fact that this was the first time the rebel artists had faced the test of a well-publicized public auction. On a personal level and yet more significant to the January event was the fact that Ernest had little affection for these paintings and that he was willing to part with them with no regret.

In the company of their colleagues as well as better-established painters, Pissarro's Grande Rue de village and Degas' La Tribune des courses a Longchamp proved most successful, bringing in 1100 francs ($220 U.S.) each. Monet's L'Ile de la Grande Jatte, Seine (Private Collection) brought 550 francs ($110 U.S.) and his La Seine a Argenteuil (Courtauld Museum, London) a disappointing 400 francs ($80 U.S.).

Unlike the earlier success Ernest had enjoyed with his Barbizons, this extensive January 1874 sale of his Impressionist works brought in less than thirty-five thousand francs ($7,000 U.S.) and did little to affect the debt-ridden side of his otherwise idyllic life. Interestingly enough to the band of renegades as well as to Ernest himself, Durand-Ruel bought back a number of the paintings he had sold to Ernest, but most fell under the auctioneer's hammer at a fraction of what Ernest had paid for them, embarrassing the artists and creating hard feelings, particularly on the part of consistently outspoken Edgar Degas who felt that if paintings of the new group were being sold, the artists themselves, since they were not yet dead and buried, should be receiving at least a part of the profit.

"Hoschede is whoring our work to the highest bidder!" he moaned. "Who does he think he is? He's making prostitutes of us! Pimping for us! And just like the pretty, painted Montmartre girls all we get out of it is a little pat on the behind! He makes all the money!"

"And what if someday one of our canvases brings a very high price at auction? How would the painter benefit? Perhaps we should insist on a commission from Hoschede," commented Renoir.

"It doesn't seem fair," I must admit, chimed in Caillebotte, the legal scholar, "but Monsieur Hoschede has no legal constraints whatsoever placed on the disposal of his property. And it must be said that his paintings, whether painted by Monsieurs Degas, Renoir, or Monet, are entirely his. He paid for them, he owns them, and he is free to do with them whatever he wishes. French law is quite clear on his rights as an owner."

So offended was Degas, despite the success of his own La Tribune des courses a Longchamps which had been purchased by Henri Rouart, himself a talented painter and one of the better-known artists who had participated in the Boulevard des Capucines exhibition, that after this auction he never again spoke to Ernest, not at the Guerbois, not at La Nouvelle Athenes, nor at any other time or place, and for the remainder of his life Degas refused to sell him any further paintings thus joining the ranks of Paul Cezanne whose work, for reasons of taste and style, remained likewise absent from Ernest's increasingly distinguished collection.

In light of such poor auction results, the speculating Ernest was left no choice but to beg for another loan from his mother. It was at times such as these that the senior Madame Hoschede sat in one of her straight-back chairs, delighting in reminding her only son of his rueful wife's "extravagances inexprimable," sublimely unaware, as in slow, painful detail she pointed out the ruinous consequences of a wife's overspending, that it was not Alice who was at fault at all, but the dear, devoted, overspending son upon whom the senior Madame Hoschede was convinced the French sun rose and set each and every day.

His relationship with his mother badly damaged in the hail of harsh maternal stabs aimed at his beloved Alice, Ernest did not dwell on his mother's stinging chagrin for long. On May 29th, two weeks after the closing of the Impressionist Exhibition and his purchase of Impression Sunrise, his father died, leaving him an inheritance sizeable enough to carry him through the remainder of 1874 and most of the New Year of 1875, an event which although saddening for many months, left Ernest feeling comfortably solvent and ever more confident in pursing his happiness.

CHAPTER 6

Eye of the Beholder

It was true that Ernest Hoschede bargained expertly and negotiated good prices for paintings that interested him, but there were other types of purchases, other challenging financial obligations which were not quite so easily managed. A large sum remained unpaid to Durand-Ruel who graciously made few demands, but a good deal more was owed to the Antiquarian Firm of Lacroix et cie, still more to the silver and porcelain purveyor, Villeaux, more yet to the prestigious firm of Simois et Delloite, dealers in fine furniture, carpets, and important decorative objects.

Not too surprisingly, for a tasteful man of inestimable pride and easily stirred passions, in addition to his obsession with modern paintings, Ernest had, in the years since Alice had inherited the Chateau Rottembourg, also become obsessed with the acquisition of fine decorative objects for the chateau's interiors. During their first year as its owners, he had begun a collection of signed French furniture, much of it post-revolution inventory removed from royal French houses and through a series of deceased or financially distressed owners, eventually left in the hands of Paris' most prestigious dealers in fine antiques. In a relatively short time

Ernest had managed to acquire beautifully inlaid desks, tables, and consoles from Lacroix, these treasures arranged on fine Savonnerie and Bellone carpets from Simois et Delloite, their surfaces covered with beautiful pieces of English silver, Austrian crystal, and porcelains from Villeaux, few if any of these luxuries sold to him at wholesale prices. It didn't matter. Following the spirited session of requisite bargaining, generous lines of credit were extended to the charming, sophisticated Paris emporium owner, collateral satisfied with a handshake, a signature, and the vague promise of a visit to the Hoschede country house "yes, perhaps sometime this summer."

Handshakes. Promises. Ernest's irresistible schoolboy smile. Brash, unbridled rebellion circling in the air. A small crack in the palace wall. The threat of recession. But always quality, style, taste, and the more prestigious the proprietor, the more appreciated Monsieur Ernest Hoschede's unfailing eye for quality seemed to be, but Ernest always understood the mood of the territory. He behaved accordingly and at the most opportune moment, shamelessly flattering proprietors and assistants, showering them with compliments and tokens of appreciation from his store: a box of exquisite lace bordered linen handkerchiefs for tall, flirty Mademoiselle Lourette who happened to be his favorite vendeuse at Villeaux. There were cigars for Monsieur Deloitte, the haughty proprietor of Belanger, also a fine Italian silk shawl for his even haughtier wife. The kindnesses were graciously returned. Before placing the latest arrivals in their showrooms, purveyors usually offered Ernest first choice, messengers sent all the way to the Chateau Rottembourg to alert their favorite client of expected summer shipments from Britain, Italy, and Spain. Unlimited credit was extended, on occasion an irresistible Louis XVI writing desk or flowered Aubusson carpet of absolutely perfect dimensions for one of Rottembourg's rooms made available in exchange for a daughter's lavish trousseau from Hoschede's, an engraved invitation to the elegant wedding festivities hand-delivered shortly thereafter.

Notwithstanding his discriminating eye and yearning for acclaim, Ernest began the Chateau Rottembourg's exterior beautification program out of necessity. In 1870, the Franco-Prussian War was at the French doorstep and many treasured country houses fell victim to considerable damage during the Prussian occupation. The Chateau Rottembourg was not spared. Troops camped in the estate park, trampling on plants and shrubbery. They hunted the readily available game in the adjacent Senart Forest, and although the house itself had not been occupied, the sheltering terraces and outbuildings were, as were the stables and barns. An uncontrolled campfire had burned a section of the north terrace and adjacent walls of the house. At the conclusion of the brief but costly war, Ernest engaged the prominent Paris architect, Paul Sedille, to make appropriate repairs. While Sedille was at the task, it seemed a convenient matter to have him design and build two pavilions and an orangerie and to alter several of the chateau's rooms, the sculptor, Eugene Delaplanche, brought in to add new fireplace facades, outdoor statuary, and to create indoor and outdoor decorative motifs for niches and overdoors.

Openly dissatisfied with the furnishings Alice's parents had placed in the rooms of the Chateau Rottembourg, as Sedille and Delaplanche were at work Ernest embarked on an interior redecorating program in room after room of the house he had come to love as much as Alice loved it, but for vastly different reasons. Having spent a number of happy family summers at Rottembourg with her eight siblings, by the time Alice had become Madame Hoschede and inherited her family's country house, she was deeply attached to Rottembourg and was familiar with every aspect of its livability. She knew which of the stairs creaked, where the roof leaked during summer storms, and she delighted in the elegance of terrace doors flung open to festive summer evenings of outdoor family dinners and candlelit garden parties. As she and Ernest took ownership, the well-established habits of her Raingo family's summers at Rottembourg became her own. To Alice the Chateau Rottembourg would always be a place of natural beauty and simple comforts and when it came to its interiors she liked things exactly as they were.

"There is nothing wrong with the furnishings in these rooms," she had insisted to Ernest when he began to voice his complaints, insisting that the fabrics were old-fashioned and worn out, the chairs awkward and uncomfortable, and just about everything else of poor quality.

"A few chairs may need to be reupholstered eventually, Alice admitted, "but the basic pieces are fine just as they are. I understand about the necessary outside repairs with Monsieur Sedille, but I would like, at some point soon, for us to concentrate our efforts on the landscape. I've thought about creating a new drive from the doors of the kitchens and root cellars to the kitchen gardens. This would make the coming and going with our carts of summer fruits and vegetables much easier. My father talked about doing it. I'd also like to replant the kitchen gardens themselves. They're getting too much shade. I'm sure you've noticed that the bordering trees have grown and matured all too well. They're beautiful and I love them, but our produce isn't thriving as it should. Everything needs more bright sun. I hate to cut down trees, so I'm thinking about leaving the trees and relocating the kitchen gardens farther back to the north of the property and starting them over. That would give us all the more reason to establish a new driveway."

Ernest, although raised in comfortable circumstances, had no memory of family discussions regarding extended driveways or plans for the relocation of kitchen gardens. His father's wholesale textile business was an important old company, but one in which the elder Hoschede had worked his way up from simple tradesman to owner. The household was capably attended to and adequately furnished, but the Hoschede family held no social position of importance. There were no beloved family heirlooms standing along portrait-lined hallways, no understanding of or solid attachment to the significance of such things, and certainly no lasting or respected sentiment associated with the reputations of distinguished ancestors. Once Alice inherited the Chateau Rottembourg, Ernest's views of the possibilities in his world were altered overnight. To him, ownership of Rottembourg epitomized the definitions of wealth and position with which he strongly identified, the property itself a powerful symbol of its owners' freedom to leave the demands of city life at a moment's notice and indulge in rarified country pursuits on a grand scale. Guests could be invited to visit and stay for weeks, their delicious meals prepared by talented cooks, their every need met by an army of attentive maids and housemen. Rottembourg employed more servants than any estate within a ten-kilometer radius and although its uncompromising day-to-day maintenance sustained its overall functioning to an outstanding degree, for Ernest, Rottembourg's greatest asset as a valued property lay in its access to a forest rich with wildlife. He marveled at the fact that on any given day, a man could ride and hunt. Conditions were superb. The Chateau Rottembourg property bordered the ancient Senart Forest, once the royal hunting preserve of a long line of French kings, its ring-necked pheasants and yellow-crested guinea fowl said to be descended from centuries of royal stock specimen. It was rumored that Louis XV had met Leonormand d'Etiolles, more famously known as Madame de Pompadour, during a Senart hunting party. Ernest liked that provenance. He liked all provenance. Background mattered to him as did his assumed role in its manifestations which at both the elegant Paris apartment and the beautiful

Chateau Rottembourg required a constant influx of funds. Never one to concern himself with shortfalls or lack of cash, Ernest proceeded to enjoy and enhance every aspect of Rottembourg's luxury to the fullest, but he insisted that the whole of it must please his discriminating eye. "It should appeal at any given moment, both night and day, to dignified tastes," he said to Alice as he set about making plans to redecorate.

Alice did agree that in her parents' time some minor redecorating had occasionally become necessary at Rottembourg, as for example when during one summer rainstorm all the old cane chair seats in the children's third floor hall were soaked and broken through by the leaks in the roof, but it took Ernest to make her painfully aware that the old dining room draperies had become so faded and tattered by the bright country sunlight that no one could remember their original color. Reluctant to dispose of Raingo family furniture under any circumstances but also eager to keep the peace, she finally agreed to have a few pieces of older furniture sent up to the attic storerooms. When her mother's oversized mohair daybed and massive pair of walnut wedding chests were among the first pieces to be banished she could not hold back her sincere dismay.

"Ernest, you must remember that Rottembourg is a country house," she said. "It's a home for rest and play. It's a lovely place, but it has never exuded the formalities of city life or city houses and I would never want it to. I like Rottembourg exactly the way it is and I thought you did too."

"Of course I love the mood of Rottembourg," Ernest had assured his concerned wife again and again through those early years, but under his assurances lay a driving desire to exercise his compulsive love of beautiful things and a conviction that his stylish tastes should set an inimitable personal stage for the legendary chateau life he envisioned as within easy reach.

Unlike her husband, Alice was realistic about the high cost of maintaining a country estate such as Rottembourg. She had observed her father's constant vigilance over expenditures and had heard him voice many an unguarded "Mon Dieu!" when it came to the ever-escalating cost of repairs and maintenance required of a large country house and its gardens. Diligent to a fault, he had kept careful track of expenses in his estate book, his detailed accounting notes and precisely written columns of figures left in the hands of Ernest and Alice shortly before his death. With appropriate ceremony and proper respect, Monsieur Denis

Raingo's son-in-law had taken possession of the estate book and promptly tossed it into a bottom desk drawer where it had remained unopened ever since. It was safe to say that Ernest's approach to handling Rottembourg's financial requirements differed dramatically from those of his vigilant father-in-law. Cautious Denis Lucien Raingo would have found Ernest's overall cavalier attitude toward money difficult to understand, his displays of economic nonchalance intolerable as when, contrary to Alice's clearly expressed wishes for budgetary discretion, he had set about ignoring the past as well as her wishes for the future and began disposing of Rottembourg's furnishings as he saw fit, his intention clearly to make a showplace of the Chateau Rottembourg, beginning with a stream of expensive purchases. This was an undertaking which tested Alice's patience as at the same time it seduced her heart and eye. Ernest's procedures and ruthless attitude toward disposal, if not immediately appreciated by her loyalties to the past, were, in time actually admired, for admittedly, she could plainly see that her husband's taste and unerring eye for scale, color, and proportion were gradually transforming Rottembourg into an absolutely enchanting country mansion of which she found herself immensely proud. Perhaps he was right after all. Perhaps the changes he was making were appropriate and perhaps it was exactly as he said, "expense be damned!"

Over time, little by little, and encouraged by her husband's enthusiasm and financial confidence, Alice began to change her mind about alterations to her family home as almost unnoticed, treasured old pieces of furniture disappeared, not all sent safely up to attic storerooms, but sold or given away. Well-worn curtains vanished overnight, promptly replaced by expertly fashioned and installed draperies of embroidered damask and silk. Priceless Savonnerie and Bellone silk and wool carpets enhanced the highly polished oak floors. In every room, expertly upholstered settees and chairs were artfully arranged, not one after the other in a dull succession along the walls of a room, but in the more modern fashion of grouping settees and chairs in the middle of a room or close to a fireplace, under a chandelier and near to one another, small tables and writing stands conveniently placed close by. Suddenly, color was everywhere. There were soft yellows, warm reds, deep blues, and the shades of green that magically brought Rottembourg's lush exterior landscape indoors. There was depth, perspective, new light, and there was no doubt that the Chateau Rottembourg's dark rooms were being shot up with new life. Despite her nagging doubt, Alice was delighted and increasingly proud. As the summers had quickly dissolved, one set of months, one admiring wave of visitors into the next, the old horse-hair salon suites and scarred family writing tables of an entire generation had disappeared. So had limp lace curtains, tattered bed hangings, and the collection of well-worn leather dog collars and chipped, scarred walking sticks that for as long as Alice could remember had always awaited by the front door. Familiar possessions were things of the past. Now there were extravagant purchases of important English and French furniture in pristine condition. Unscratched and unmarred, they glistened and gleamed. They came with provenance, pride, and hefty price tags. One July afternoon, several pairs of handsomely carved armchairs arrived from Leland. Four of them, upholstered in deep red floral linen, were immediately placed at the foot of the stairs by the piano in the rotunda where against freshly painted pale gray walls their scarlet drama was shown off to perfection. So pleased with this result was Ernest, that a week later, a collection of tall blue and white Japanese porcelain vases arrived from Poillot, immediately placed singly and in pairs on the floor of the room. At Christmastime that same year, exclusive Lepore provided Ernest with the perfect gift for Alice: a tea service for Rottembourg comprised of coffee and tea pots, cream pitchers and sugar boxes, salvers in four sizes, multiple sizes of serving spoons and forks, urns and vases, the entire suite in a pattern of ornate floral patterned silver engraved with the letters CR, the costs of these silver showpieces calmly added to the balance on Ernest's house account, additional arrays of furniture and decorative objects purchased at the best purveyor addresses in Paris, the various items casually selected on any given day happily and promptly delivered to popular, stylish Monsieur Hoschede who, over the course of many months, had neglected to pay a single franc on any one of his mounting debts.

"What is all this costing?" an alarmed Alice asked time and again as unexpected deliveries arrived at Rottembourg day after day, week after week, throughout the summer months of several years, her concern especially peaked when she knew Ernest had been alerted by messenger to the tempting arrival of a particularly interesting shipment of goods to the Paris shops he most frequented. "We don't need more chairs and tables! Ernest, please!"

It was at times such as these Ernest would laugh his impossibly engaging laugh, put his arms around Alice and hold her close, delighting in the beautiful surroundings he was creating with the wife he adored.

"My darling, this is a big house. Haven't you noticed how it absolutely swallows up furniture? Besides, it should be dressed as beautifully as you are," he would whisper against her cheek, "and I love surprising you. Don't worry. The money is there. I'm taking care of everything. Now, don't forget, the Martines arrive on Thursday. Let's have a party. They know the Caillebottes and the Carolus Durans. Let's be sure to invite them. And let's not forget DeLille."

If one personal quality successfully pervaded Ernest Hoschede's overall character, it was his enormous capacity for joy. As a young bride, Alice had delighted in the knowledge that her handsome husband was neither worrier nor naysayer, but a jovial, positive thinker who lived well, enjoyed his friends and family, and expected to die old, rich, and beloved. Fortunately for Ernest, it was the era of the self-made man, and although late Nineteenth-Century Paris may have been more favorably inclined than most European capitals of the time to adapt to and understand this new class of citizen, Ernest Hoschede was not the only man determined to continue to maintain his standing in a city facing the threat of immense socio-economic change, a very new free market system, and the overall looming threat of recession which was beginning to drive every aspect of European business and employment. On the heels of these worrisome conditions came the nasty but corresponding perils of serious market competition. By late spring of 1874 and exactly as Ernest had described to Jean DeLille, exclusive, high-priced E. Hoschede's was finding itself up against more than a few unexpected rivals.

'Les grand magasins des nouveautes,' the great novelty stores lining Rue de Rivoli and facing the Place de Chateau d'Eau and the archrival and largest of them all, La Samaritaine, were not only carrying a less expensive and more diversified array of merchandise than was Hoschede's, they were appealing to an enormous new class of shoppers. Much to Ernest's dismay, La Samaritaine's best customers were not the established upper crust Hoschede's catered to at all, but scores of former laborers who had suddenly become wealthy scrap and tar merchants, making fortunes in the Paris re-built under Baron Haussmann as the city's vast network of paved avenues, immaculate parks, and wide, tree-lined boulevards were built and savored, their constant utilization requiring a rigid schedule of maintenance and refurbishing.

Haussmann's brilliant sewer system, his web of urban railways, and the multitude of lavishly planted parks and elaborate municipal water features had become industries unto themselves, creating not only a new merchant class, new banks, and an influx of new wealth, but forcing a very new concept of supply and demand as the stage was set for a rapidly changing, ever-broadening base of employment and consumerism. Former shop-girls and artists models became well-to-do wives in need of more than one dress. Their children required school uniforms, winter coats, and party attire. Toys became a necessity. Painted rocking horses, toy trains, rubber balls, and porcelain-faced dolls were no longer playthings exclusive to the upper crust. Accordingly, the expanded fields of free enterprise along with increased ease in modes of transportation were enabling merchants and creative entrepreneurs alike to reach deep into the untapped outer reaches of Paris itself, creating valuable new alliances with scores of new candle and soap factories, perfume makers, glass blowers and factories for beer, grand pianos, matches, cigarettes, enamel, and freight cars, all at some distance from the center of the city.

Inevitably, with rapid economic development and soaring market profits came pockets of corruption which added considerably to the size of many fortunes. At first the tradeoffs were treated as simple barter, one small service, one small favor quietly exchanged for another of more or less equal value, but when large, secret financial transactions and outright theft were added to exchanges of ever more elaborate services and favors, the opportunity for fraud, graft, and extortion increased dramatically, trickling down and creating additional opportunities for further expanded bases of employment as police departments and regulatory ministries were, out of necessity, enlarged and equipped, the numbers of solicitors, tribunals, and arbiters increased, a vast array of new municipal offices created as rental fees for professional space with views across city domes and spires soared higher and higher.

The new Paris had come with a high price, but the accompanying expansive spirit of its citizens had sprung directly from their Prefect of the Seine, Baron Georges Haussmann and his titanic building and beautification program which had provided seventeen consecutive years of uninterrupted employment for much of the city's population as familiar old areas were rebuilt, re-oriented, and more often than not unceremoniously demolished. Quaint districts and distinctive old neighborhoods teeming with unique collections of colorful shops, cafes, and patisseries were dissolved, their occupants forced out of beloved, often dilapidated, rat-infested buildings. Good-bye ancient history and community mythology. Au revoir, dear dirty Saint Denis, tender little decrepit Saint Antoine and my precious, smelly Sainte-Genevieve. And good day to you, steep rents, running water, gentrification, and high density.

Remarkable things had happened to muddy old Paris, but much to the amazement of the complaining population of the Haussmann years, when all was said and done the city was transformed by whitewash and amnesia and most shocking of all, the Seine was suddenly no longer the city sewer. Sadly, many old community habits were hard to break, and just when it seemed the citizenry had forsaken its time-honored practices of urinating in the streets and tossing human waste into the Seine, new challenges arose, restoring a long list of heated complaints lodged against the busy Baron which although overlooked for a time, had not been forgotten at all. At first, and until orderly re-districting and the system of Arrondissements was designed, were the periods of sudden disorientation. Overnight the Boulevard Raspail and the Rue de Rennes had been cut through the Left Bank. "What has happened to the Reisemont?" the creatures of habit and lovers of ancient mud wailed. "Wasn't it here just yesterday? I must be dreaming, and it is not a good dream."

In prompt succession The Louvre was connected to the Tuileries Gardens, The Bois de Boulogne was annexed to the city, increasing the city's parklands from a paltry forty-five acres to an impressive four thousand. The Place de l'Etoile grew from five intersecting avenues to an amazing twelve, and everywhere, everyone overused the word "new." All was nouveau, transforme, nouvelle, and by the late 1860's a highly visible new set of internationals was falling love with New Paris. This attractive generation of wealthy young Russians, Spaniards, and Italians sharpened their accents, pomaded their hair, and crowded into the smart, gas-lighted cafes, twirling their gold cigarette holders, tweaking their mustaches, and ordering magnums of expensive champagne while focused on new plays, new fashion, new art, new anything.

The 1870 war with the Prussians although costly had been brief and despite the dark days of the Paris Seige, the spirit of the city had been quickly restored. Pride and patriotism returned along with new fervor and commitment. Life was good again, stable and secure. It was under these pleasant circumstances and during this period that Ernest and Alice were happiest and at the height of their success and popularity, their city home in one of the most beautiful of the Haussmann-designed apartment buildings, its address at Number 56 appropriately on none other than Boulevard Haussmann.

"People may criticize the expense, but Haussmann will be remembered as the most forward thinking man of the century," Ernest was known to remark to friends as from his Boulevard Haussmann balcony he scanned the Paris skyline and by January of 1875 pointed out that he lived mere minutes from Garnier's fantastic new Opera and amidst the great show of Prefect Haussmann's spectacular boulevards.

"He understood scale and balance the way a great artist understands scale and balance," Ernest was also known to say of Haussmann. "He saw Paris as his own blank canvas and what a great talent he had for looking into the future of that canvas and understanding what to apply to it."

The orderly rows of Haussmann-designed, six and seven-story luxury apartment houses lining both sides of countless new avenues and boulevards represented not only a forward thinking, modern version of an aging city, but served as shining examples of all that was latest and best. Smart shops were found on the ground floors of the elegant buildings, extravagant apartments occupied the several floors overhead, and warrens of servants' quarters were situated under the eaves. In their quiet, mullion-windowed grandeur, these buildings honored the money and lifestyles required to own and maintain them, the boulevards and avenues on which they were erected named to celebrate with strength of limestone, brick, and mortar, the skill of their innovative creator, the dynamic Prefect of the Seine, who, not unlike the entrepreneurial Ernest Hoschede, also paid little attention to costs and budgeting, preferring to remain first and foremost, a devotee of the very best.

The influence of a powerhouse such as Baron Georges Haussmann had not for a moment been lost on the young, ambitious Ernest Hoschede. Maturing against the emergence of Haussmann's exhilarating urban background, the young Ernest Hoschede had seen what was possible and well within the grasp of a man with ambition, good connections, and the determination to succeed, but there were also personal considerations to be made. To Ernest, position in society was everything. Respect and admiration were as important as money, at times far more important. Regardless of economics, a person of position behaved in a particular manner, dressed in a particular style, moved in particular circles, and above all, lived within the tested confines of only certain Paris Arrondissements. Of itself, the expensive Hoschede apartment in the privileged heart of the Ninth Arrondissement conformed to this personally satisfying and admittedly modern socio-economic statement, but not all Boulevard Haussmann's inhabitants were rich social lions or even members of the impoverished but titled French aristocracy whose associations Ernest actively sought. Certainly, and in order to meet the high costs of maintaining a Boulevard Haussmann apartment, a high degree of financial security was a requirement for residents, but among the cognoscenti, commensurate with the responsibilities of wealth, real or supposed, came the more subtle requirements inherent in cultured French interests common to every class, these refinements manifested by displays of consistently good manners and the exercise of a consistently agreeable personal demeanor regardless of the ebb and flow of personal circumstances. By socializing with many of the same groups in Paris, by patronizing the same city restaurants and shops, and by being of similar mindset, the Hoschedes and their circle ultimately encouraged a similar range of human effort. By spring of 1874, however, as the largely structured habits of the comfortable world around him grew increasingly ripe for change, Ernest Hoschede found himself inextricably linked to developments central to upsetting the order, his views of the delicate human failings which were about to emerge closely and forever connecting him to a quietly evolving series of personal scenarios neither he nor anyone around him could possibly have anticipated.

CHAPTER 7

A Family Affair

It was against this productive, well-hinged background that Ernest Hoschede had assumed his role as the most important, some said the only serious collector of French Impressionist paintings in Paris. No one, not even cutting-edge Ernest himself, could have foreseen the lasting impact of this role, but on a human scale, as early summer of 1874 settled in along the quays of the Seine, it was also against this background that like other young, prosperous men of his acquaintance, he contemplated an undamaged future. Julian Raingo's birthday morning dawned, and as the mood of celebration took over his household, no one could have imagined that Ernest's vision was flawed, or that his optimistic nature would resist that flaw, but under twilight skies, as well-dressed, well-connected guests began arriving to wish Julian Raingo well, Ernest Hoschede's thoughts and energies were directed more toward one painting than toward a family patriarch's milestone birthday. The weather matched his mood. It was warm and clear, the rain of earlier days now past.

At Number 56 Boulevard Haussmann, candles flickered, crystal chandeliers sparkled, and from behind the balustrade on the second floor landing the Hoschede children and their faithful spaniel, Igor, watched as guests began to arrive. The Deschamps and Poichettes were the first.

"Oh, Madame Deschamps is wearing my favorite color," whispered a delighted but pale nine-year-old Blanche. In her white, long-sleeved nightdress, she was barely recovered from the cold which had kept her in bed for most of the previous week. "I love green and I love the white flowers in Madame Poichette's hair."

Six-year-old Suzanne knelt on the flowered carpet next to Marthe. She peered through the balustrade, holding on with both hands, eagerly awaiting the arrival of Madame Potatchka who, when the moment finally did arrive, did not disappoint. As if witnessing a royal entourage, Suzanne watched in awe as the elegant widow of the former Polish attaché to Paris appeared to float along the hallway floor, the train of her creamy white lace dress drifting behind her in a cloud, the tall white feathers in her headpiece giving her the appearance of a magnificent, rare bird.

"Next to our Mama Madame Potachka is the most beautiful lady in the world," the clearly enchanted Suzanne stated to Marthe.

"No one is as beautiful as our Mama," Marthe whispered, watching her mother greeting and engaging her guests with ease. Alice was wearing one of the long, gray-blue dresses she was known to favor, a gleaming column of silvery satin tonight, a pair of diamond clips in her dark hair. She gazed up and smiled to her children with a quick assuring wink and a satisfying feeling of having accomplished all her self-imposed tasks with excellent results. Her satisfaction was not ill-conceived. The house glowed. Freshly polished floors welcomed a flurry of refined footsteps. Open doorways to well-proportioned rooms invited entry, pause, and admiration, and much to Ernest's delight, Impression Sunrise was attracting considerable attention.

After much deliberation and several changes of mind, it had been hung on the drawing room's north wall. Vibrant and alive against its pale green damask background, it squarely faced the entrance into the room and as a result was creating exactly the sort of stir Ernest had hoped for. Guests clustered. There were questions, remarks, opinions.

"Yes, it's the one. Impression Sunrise," he was quick to point out. "Gave the group its name. Claude Monet painted it. If you attended the exhibition you saw it. You didn't just walk past it, did you? I can't believe it! Are you quite sure you were there?"

"You say it is the harbor at Le Havre?"
"Yes."
"That must be the harbormaster in the boat."
"Did you read what Wolff had to say?"
"And Leroy?"
"And Castagnary in Le Rappel?"
"Have you met him, this Claude Monet?"
"Yes."
"And the others in the group?"
"Yes."
"I've heard they all live at the Café Guerbois. Tell me, do they really? And where is the Guerbois exactly? Is it as filthy and rat-infested as I've heard?"

Rustling taffeta on polished floors. Profiles in shadows. Safety. Calm. Ernest wears a new black satin vest under a black velvet frock coat. A small ruby set into a gold stud pierces his gray striped cravat. The soft folds of a red satin handkerchief peek out from a breast pocket. He watches Alice, proud of her, loving her, loving his undamaged, privileged world.

Julian Raingo savors the congenial good wishes of his friends and family, enjoying the company, the festive mood, and most of all the elaborate arrangements Alice has made in his honor. Against the soft, flattering light and in his dark evening clothes it is impossible not to admire the gleam of Julian Raingo's silver hair as he makes his way through clusters of attentive guests. Every now and then his eyes meet Alice's and he smiles. "A la belle France!" he toasts, raising his glass of champagne as he stands before the long reception table in the dining room and the assembled guests raise their glasses, returning the traditional tribute in one devoted voice. "A la belle France!"

"This apartment has never looked more beautiful," he remarks to Alice, clearly appreciative of his favorite niece's efforts in his behalf. Standing beside her, his gaze sweeps appreciatively over the gleam of silver, the masses of white flowers everywhere, the inviting arrangements of chairs, settees, and tables which, although unchanged over several years, have taken on the gentle, soft-hued patina that comes with time and wear and the pleasure of family and frequent guests.

"It is superb. All of it. Thank you, my dear, for your love and kindness. And this dining room with its splendid table must be the most bountiful in all Paris tonight. Thanks to you I shall never forget this evening."

Alice smiles, reaching over to affectionately straighten her uncle's white satin cravat, recalling how as a young girl she admired his elegant appearance whenever they attended afternoon plays or toured the art galleries together and later enjoyed macarons and tall glasses of sparkling apple juice at Adelard's or Corentine.

"I wanted it to be perfect for you," Alice adds, delighted by her uncle's compliments as she squeezes his arm.

How comfortable and secure she has always felt at Julian Raingo's side, his tall, courtly frame and gracious air perfect complements to his attentiveness. Ernest had that same imposing way about him. He would probably age just as well, Alice has thought to herself many times over during the passing years. Remarkable though, how handsome Julian Raingo still is at sixty, Alice further observes, watching him as he circles the room, the only outward signs of advancing years to be found in his blue eyes which lately are becoming a bit clouded, unlike his generous shock of white hair which remains an elegant asset he uses to great advantage as he nods appreciatively to every woman in the room, both young and old. Even at sixty he is attractive to the ladies, and those who chat and flirt with him at greatest length, Alice notices with a smile, are neither elderly nor in the slightest bit infirmed.

Yes, all the preparation has been worthwhile, but she is exhausted. Tomorrow she would sleep until noon or beyond, she tells herself, but right now, completely happy in the midst of people she loves and satisfied with all she had accomplished, Alice has to admit her efforts have been worthwhile. Things are going beautifully. The apartment is lending itself perfectly to an elegant evening entirely devoted to celebration and no one is enjoying the festivities more than Ernest. He thrives on the splendor around him. His pride takes over easily and aloud, but on this evening Ernest cannot be accused of overstating.

Every surface, every seating arrangement, every tray and serving piece is perfection. The linen is impeccably crisp to the touch, the food delicious, the household staff polite and attentive. Alice cares about such things. Her insistence on the maintenance of a refined household reflective of appropriate, traditional behavior pleases Ernest enormously, but Alice occasionally takes things a step further, insisting on nothing short of perfection. What Alice fails to understand is that her own overachieving personality and unintended shows of wealth are often too much for many of her Raingo relatives to bear.

"This is what makes the world interesting," Julian Raingo has confidently reassured her on those occasions when she confides in him, detailing a particular family eruption where she had been made to feel her efforts are not only unappreciated, but unnecessary. "If badly handled, though, these differences, these greedy jealousies, can destroy the closest family relationships," he was always quick to add, "and that should not be allowed to happen, not under any circumstances, and certainly not in our Raingo family. We must remain a strong, unified unit. It is the most important thing."

In her own case and in spite of periodic shows of competition and outright envy leveled against her, it is Alice's strong, unflinching sense of security as Ernest Hoschede's wife that regardless of the occasional criticism a family member might voice against her has allowed her to remain completely comfortable in the elegant personal settings which she and Ernest have created. Above all, though, Alice confidently recognizes the power and impact of her own personal strengths. She has never lost sight of her talent for staying the course, and regardless of behavior or perceived intent she has never turned her back on those she loves, even when those same loved ones have behaved in a manner quite undeserving of her loyalty. Through the years of marriage to an increasingly flamboyant entrepreneurial art collector husband and with the arrival of five babies, Alice has discovered reliable levels of patience and strength in herself. Those who know her best would agree that these stalwart qualities were inborn in her and that they would hold her in good stead all her life no matter what challenges might lie ahead. Ernest's background reflects somewhat less purposeful objectives. Since his parents have worked hard to achieve a level of financial success enabling them to indulge and happily spoil their only son, they have created opportunities for him instead of insisting he seek out a few of his own.

Securely employed in his father's dry goods business, by the age of twenty the young Ernest Hoschede was developing into an aggressive self-promoter and a highly narcissistic creature. Known to his friends as a fun-loving, endlessly charming companion, he was possessed not only of a careless nonchalance when it came to money, but he was possessed as well of a highly acquisitive nature, this side of him requiring, in addition to the salary his father paid him, a generous monthly allowance, an enviable luxury which earned him a reputation for having fine but extravagant tastes.

Happy to live with his parents rent-free, it was not until Ernest assumed complete control of the family business and married Alice that details of financial responsibility took on a degree of importance, but his attention to money matters at his department store was short lived. He soon found he preferred to spend his time on the creative challenges of marketing and the new innovations inherent in advertising, in particular the promotion of luxury goods. Before long, he was leaving bookkeeping to an accounting staff, priding himself on possessing the wisdom and money to hire trustworthy, competent individuals and assign to them the economic and budgetary tasks he found boring and unnecessarily repetitious.

By any measure, these conditions created a highly agreeable personal climate in which to live and as Ernest was assuming his role as host of Julian Raingo's sixtieth birthday, he was at the same time enjoying the same exhilarating level of security and confidence he had known all his life, so of course when the elegant mood of the evening planned for the distinguished elder Raingo with infinite care was suddenly shattered by the sound of a loud commotion in the hallway, there was cause for concern.

There were quick footsteps and loud voices. Something had crashed to the floor with an alarming clang. People were arguing. Daniel, the butler, entered the drawing room and raced to Ernest's side. "Pardon, Monsieur, but there is someone in the hall who wishes to speak to you," he whispered, gesturing Ernest to step away from his guests; a Monsieur Armel Ducasse who says he is here on a matter of some urgency. There is a gentleman with him. I told them you were entertaining this evening and could not be disturbed, but Monsieur Ducasse insists he will not leave without seeing you. He pounded at my arm and I dropped my tray. I apologize for the noise. Monsier Hoschede, I did my best to send them away, but I had to let you know."

"Of course," Ernest nodded, excusing himself from the circle of friends he was engaging in conversation, the warm, composed smile on his face suddenly dissolved as he reached the hall. Seconds later he could be heard shouting, "Never! No, never! You cannot do this! Not to me!" his voice booming canon-like across the hall and into the well-appointed drawing room where an uncomfortable silence quickly fell over the gentility of an evening so carefully planned and brilliantly executed.

"Have more champagne passed, Daniel," Alice calmly whispered to the wide-eyed butler as she made her way to the piano. "And quickly!"

A few guests made tactful attempts to fill the embarrassing hush in the room by taking up fresh topics of idle conversation as Alice sat at the piano, smiled, and played what she could remember of the Moonlight Sonata. The champagne was quickly poured and passed. The piano music diverted attention and filled a void, but neither a sonata inspired by moonlight nor the gallant conversational efforts made by those assembled under the Hoschede roof could overwhelm the continuing boom of angry voices in the hallway.

"By Saturday! And make no mistake, Monsieur Hoschede. Saturday is the absolute deadline!"

"No, not by Saturday! Not by Sunday or Monday and not at the time of your choosing, but at the time of my choosing!" Ernest was heard to retaliate.

Alice left the piano and quickly made her way to the hall, leaving her guests to draw their own conclusions, a frozen, half-smile pasted across her lips, Julian Raingo directly behind her. Reaching the hallway, the two found Ernest holding a thick sheaf of documents. They had been delivered by Armel Ducasse, a compliance officer appointed by the Auditor Generale of the French Tribunal of Commerce. Ducasse introduced the man with him as Etienne Ahron.

Directing his comments to Alice, Ahron said, "Madame Hoschede, I am accompanying Monsieur Ducasse in my capacity as a dealer in antiques and a certified appraiser. I have a particular fondness for clocks. I understand that here in Paris and at the Chateau Rottembourg in Montgeron there is a fine collection of timepieces made by the talented Raingo Brothers, ancestors of yours I believe. I see one of the spectacular Raingo clocks here on the mantel of this lovely hall. How fortunate you are to have enjoyed the collection for so long. Is it two, or three generations?"

"Madame Hoschede," Ducasse acknowledged further, nodding to Alice before placing his black hat on his balding head and turning to the door, "Your husband has underestimated his financial responsibilities. His creditors have engaged me to represent their interests and satisfy their legal demands in full. To satisfy those demands at least in part, Monsieur Ahron has come prepared to appraise the household goods at this address, their confiscation to follow at a later date. I have communicated with Monsieur Hoschede on these matters a number of times, but to no avail. I do not wish to bring distress to you or your fine family and I apologize for the intrusion tonight. Under the present circumstances and what I am told is an important family celebration, the contents of your home will not be appraised at this time, but Monsieur Hoschede's debtors can accept no further delays in being fully paid what is legally due them. These matters must be settled. Tonight I have delivered the necessary legal documents in which requirements, due dates, and the nature of consequences for failure to comply are clearly indicated. As you must know, right now times in Paris are not good for those in debt. As you must also know, France is on the brink of recession. I hope I make myself clear. People want to be paid what is owed them. It is as simple as that. I wish you well, Madame. Goodnight."

The pair of unexpected visitors left with no further word, but their intrusion and the questions raised by their presence left Alice and Julian Raingo speechless, their shock further intensified when Ernest voiced no particular dismay.

"I owe a bit of money here and there," he volunteered with surprising candor, "and I am being asked to pay it all back by Saturday. There is nothing to it, really. I'll take care of it tomorrow."

"How much money?" Alice blurted out, her bewildered expression mirroring Julian Raingo's.

"About a million francs." Ernest answered. "Yes, that must be close to the amount. One million francs," he called back from the doorway. I just need time to make arrangements with Monsieur Ducasse and a few others, that's all. Don't worry, my darling. It's nothing. I have it all under control."

"My apologies, everyone," he announced, returning to his drawing room. Remarkably jovial and childishly lighthearted, Ernest's witty demeanor was once again that of the imminently cordial host, his smile as engaging and warm as it had been at the start of the evening when the most pressing matter on his mind had been a controversial painting by a struggling Paris artist.

"There has been a simple misunderstanding, dear friends," he offered by way of explanation. "It's all cleared away now. I do apologize for the loud voices, though. We must have sounded like the generals shouting out orders at Quatre

Bras! Now please, let us continue with our celebration. More champagne, Daniel! Ah, dear Cousin Beatrice, have I mentioned how very beautiful you look this evening? And Countess Potatchka, I must tell you that Suzanne, one of our young daughters, believes you to be quite the loveliest woman in Paris, next to her own lovely mother, of course!"

"By Saturday!" a bewildered Alice repeated to herself as feeling glued to the hallway floor she struggled to grasp the impact what she had heard. By Saturday her husband was expected to pay one million francs to satisfy his debtors, but how had he incurred such an enormous debt? Through the years of their marriage and as one extravagance was heaped on another with a smile and a signature, he had insisted that expenses were always under control. She had believed that to be true, but how could that be if Armel Ducasse had taken it upon himself to come to their home unannounced and make his demands within earshot of their family and closest friends, and on this, of all nights? And what could Ernest possibly do to solve such a dilemma by Saturday? That was only four days away. How would be able to raise such an exorbitant amount of money in so short a time? She and Ernest lived well. Certainly there were expenses to meet, but how could he possibly owe so much money? Most distressing of all, the family clocks were in jeopardy. A number of them were at Rottembourg, but several of the more important Raingo pieces were here in the Paris apartment. It was a fine, valuable collection, but it was much more than that. Raingo clocks defined the Raingo family. They represented the remarkable rise of an important old company and its founder, Zacharie Joseph, born in Mons, Belgium in 1775 and linked to no consequential lineage but creator of the extraordinary Orrery Clocks, the innovative planetary timepieces so highly valued and admired for their intricacy and accuracy in motions of the Earth and Moon around the Sun and requiring winding only every four years, that they were ordered one after another by the rich and royal, one purchased in 1824 by King George IV of England for the Royal Library at Windsor Castle, another by his brother The Duke of York, another by the Duc du Chartres for Saint-Firman Castle at Chateau de Chantilly. In total, only twelve priceless Orrery Masterpieces had been produced and in their own inevitable way the family bonds that followed were solidified both by the intricate splendor of the rare Orrereys and the financial success that ensued.

By 1874, members of the Raingo family owed a large part of their annual incomes and certainly their social standing within the prestigious Paris Belgian Community to Zacharie's brilliant success and to the succession of Raingo brothers including Alice's father, Denis, who had gone on to grow the thriving family business by developing professional relationships with the most talented French bronziers, porcelain makers, and artistic gilders, skillfully creating in cooperation with them the superb three-piece porcelain and ormolu Raingo clock suites, the innovative eight-day pendulum case clocks, and the highly desirable Raingo mantel clocks whose fanciful casings of gilded bronze graced by mythological figures and animals became treasured possessions of the most distinguished families in France and across Europe.

For Alice, the mere suggestion that as a result of Ernest's indebtedness a number of treasured family clocks in her possession could be lost was a staggering blow. They had been placed in her care by verbal consent and through the successful partnership of her father and his two brothers, but as Alice quickly recalled and with no little remorse, there were no legal documents to verify ownership. All the Raingo clocks in her two houses could be at risk. Visibly upset and deeply embarrassed, she longed to be alone to be able to think and absorb the meaning of the devastating possibilities swarming unrestrained in her brain, but guests were still in her home and she was their hostess. From where she stood in the hall, Alice could not see the oddly aloof clusters of soft spoken people assembled in her drawing room, but she was aware of the distinctly quieted tone in the house. The evening's earlier festive mood had been shattered, but a few of the more gregarious guests made every attempt to do whatever they could to restore its earlier gaiety. Ernest's flamboyant Cousin Beatrice was doing her stalwart best to salvage what was left of the evening. Her head tilted back, her voice clear and loud, she tapped into her well-honed talent for making utterly useless conversation based on an astonishing variety of useless topics. Although noble, Beatrice's attempts did not succeed. The spirit of the evening had been dampened enough to drown out even her bold voice.

In the hall, Alice stared down at the gleaming floor underfoot and from somewhere deep inside, a bleak sadness took hold of her. Feeling a hard lump forming in her throat, she swallowed hard, forcing herself to keep the tears at bay. She was mortified, but this was no time for breaking down. She would indulge that part of herself later. Yes, that was it. She would fall apart later, when she and Ernest were alone and could talk. There had to be a reasonable explanation for all this, but right now there were too many people around. Ernest had made it seem as if a mere trivial interruption of no consequence had taken place, but Armel Ducasse's harsh warning rang in her ears.

"By Saturday!" she had heard him shout. "As you must know, Madame Hoschede, times in Paris are not good for those in debt. We are on the brink of recession! People want to be paid what is owed them!"

Ducasse had succeeded in shocking her with his revelations, but there was Etienne Ahron's threatening reference to the family clocks. "Is it two or three generations?" he had asked with a familiarity that spoke of careful study and investigation.

Julian Raingo stood alone by the drawing room fireplace, his celebratory mood destroyed. Arms folded across his chest, his cynical jaw thrust forward as guests formed small awkward groups around the room and did their best to resume the festive mood of the occasion, he observed Ernest's every remarkable move and confident gesture, his sixty-year-old clouded blue eyes entirely receptive to the life around the matter, to heroic manifestations, to ill-advised concepts of selfish dreams, and most of all, to unavoidable destiny. Watching dear Beatrice, he too decided to salvage some shred of family dignity and carry on, but in spite of stalwart determination and a generous dose of natural grace, his mind was a vast open sea of hopeless contention, his mood not too far away at all from thoughts of catastrophic possibility

CHAPTER 8

Habits Respect, Tradition

By midnight the last guests had left and the house was quiet. Alice sat in one of the ivory brocade wing chairs by the fireplace in the drawing room, her hands folded in her lap, the glow of candlelight casting a silvery luster across her gray satin dress. She stared straight ahead, her dark eyes expressionless, her face pale and drawn. Ernest stood at one of the windows looking out across the boulevard and its gas lighted street lanterns. "How did this happen?" Alice asked, her voice bland and colorless. "Ernest, you must know I'm in shock to learn you've allowed yourself to be put into a position where you owe so much money."

"Alice, there is no need for you to be shocked," Ernest responded, turning from window to stride across the carpet and toward the chair opposite Alice. "I've told you I have everything under control. My dear, there is no reason for you to be concerned," he said, seating himself and leaning forward, intent on assuring his anxious wife. "Armel Ducasse is a minor public servant and a bureaucrat's pawn," he emphasized. "You mustn't give him another thought. And you must understand my love, that he has no authority and he certainly has nothing to do with my financial affairs. You must believe that. Some of these minor so-called officials assume an importance they simply do not possess. They thrive on their power to intimidate. I'll straighten Ducasse out in minutes tomorrow."

"But Ernest," Alice pressed. "A million francs is a lot of money! And Ducasse made a terrible scene! It was humiliating, and on this of all nights. How can you sit there and tell me there's nothing to discuss. I want to understand this!"

"Alice, I am not humiliated, nor should you be. My dear, this really is not your affair and I don't want you concerned. You've overtired. Everything looks worse than it really is when you're overtired. You need a good night's sleep. You'll feel better in the morning. Go to bed!"

"Not my affair? Ernest, how can you say such a thing?" Alice snapped back. "Of course it's my affair! We share a life, or have you forgotten that? I want to know how you have incurred the debts Ducasse was talking about. Tell me. I need to know!"

Ernest's patience with Alice's insistence was wearing thin. He had explained Ducasse's unannounced visit as well as he thought necessary, but Alice was demanding a full accounting. "Alice, you're making far too much of this," he blurted out, but alright! Have it your way!" he said, his voice tense with exasperation. "I admit Ducasse may have made a mistake in coming here tonight and stirring things up a bit, but I'll tell you this: it's true that I owe a little money here and there. Many people do right now, and exactly as Ducasse said, the country really is on the brink of recession. Alice, there's a great deal of financial uncertainty out there and people across this city are assessing their situations. You must understand. If recession does come, we will all be affected in one way or another. And if you were embarrassed, I'm sorry, but people make mistakes and unpleasantness does come up now and then. I said I'm taking care of it. Now forget all this and go to bed! I'm going out for a walk!"

Alice didn't move, convinced that Ernest wasn't being honest or forthright with her. He was too eager to attribute Ducasse's visit to a simple set of circumstances and send her off to bed with thoughts of a looming recession. He was insisting she forget all about what had happened with Ducasse, but how could she? Ernest was keeping something from her. She was sure of it, but he was right about one thing. She really was overtired. "We'll take this up in the morning," she said.

Much against her better judgement but acknowledging her exhaustion, Alice made her way upstairs to the bedroom, welcoming the chance to be alone and rest, but try as she might, sleep eluded her. Ernest didn't come to bed at all. Leaving a trail of anxiety in her thoughts was his insistence on passing off Ducasse's visit as something she was to ignore. She couldn't. Her eyes wide open in the darkened bedroom, Alice re-lived image after image of Armel Ducasse as she had seen him standing in the hallway. Her head buried in her pillow, she could not escape the memory of his shining yellowish scalp dimmed only by the few thin strands of dark hair drawn straight across his balding head. She remembered the oddly crooked black-rimmed spectacles perched on his nose as he had spoken to her, but most memorable of all, she heard the cruelty in Ducasse's voice and the grim urgency in his directives as over and over again she saw Ernest standing unflinching in the hallway, his face a remarkable study in human composure. To pass off the evening's embarrassing intrusion with talk of recession was unacceptable. There had to be more.

Lying awake in the dark, she tried to think back to any hint of trouble she might have overlooked. Of course she could have been distracted by preparations for the birthday celebration, but surely if Ernest had said he was worried about something she would remember what he had said. They shared every concern, every care. Again and again, she relentlessly re-lived events of the past few weeks, but all she could remember was the unusual anxiety that seemed to have surrounded Ernest the day Impression Sunrise had been delivered; that, and then at dinner several days later, when he admitted to being "under pressure" at the store. At the time she had placed no particular significance on his remarks. Ernest always handled issues at the store with great ease. Somehow, though, she did remember that he had not wanted to talk about whatever it was that seemed to be gnawing at him, but an issue at the store was no reason for evasiveness. As for the million franc debt Ducasse had specified, Ernest had said he was taking care of it, and surely he would. But how? A million francs was a lot of money. No matter. Ernest was a responsible husband and father. He took care of his family. He must have money saved somewhere; funds she didn't know about. Yes, that was it. She was overreacting. She must try to sleep. Everything would feel better in the morning. Pulling the quilt up over her shoulders one last time, she convinced herself that Ernest was right. Problems always did seem worst at night. It would all be better in the morning. Tomorrow she and Ernest would settle the matter of his debt to her satisfaction. The air would be cleared between them and with Uncle Julian's birthday celebration over, she would finally look ahead to the summer at Rottembourg, able to concentrate on its annual promise of great blocks of time in which to enjoy the company of her young children and her beautiful house at her leisure. Disregarding the evening's embarrassing interruption, it was with calming thoughts of the pleasures lying ahead that at last Alice fell into an exhausted sleep.

The change of pace Ernest and Alice would enjoy in the country in that summer of 1874 and the leisurely days to which Alice looked forward would serve the Hoschede family well. It had been a busy year. The older girls, Marthe and Blanche, had completed their terms at school and were making elaborate plans for all the things they wanted to do at Rottembourg. Alice encouraged such planning and was especially focused on finding activities that would please five-year-old Jacques. He was now old enough to learn to ride a horse. He would like that. Yes, it would be good for him to have something for himself, Alice felt, something that didn't involve his four sisters, and the girls would be busy enough on their own. This year they would have a small garden of their own to plant and tend. They were being allowed to put in whatever flowers they wished and had already decided on dahlias and gladiolas. Suzanne had wanted to raise vegetables. "Potatoes!" she had suggested, and "green beans! Also carrots, yes carrots!"

Reminded by Blanche that every summer the kitchen gardens at Rottembourg provided a plentiful supply of produce for the household, Suzanne's wishes for a vegetable garden were overruled. Satisfying at least for the time being, what her father good-naturedly called her "interest in domestic farming," he decided it would be a good idea to assign precocious Suzanne the task of helping the gardeners lay the cloches (domes) which protected row after row of freshly planted tender plants from the annual onslaught of nibbling rabbits, hungry squirrels, and noisy crows.

Alice had arranged for the older girls, Marthe and Blanche, to assist the Abbess Mother Catherine, at the Abbey de Notre Dame in the adjacent village of

Yerres. For a few hours each week, they would be helping the young novice nuns plant and gather produce from the Abbey's own kitchen gardens and they would be responsible for collecting eggs from the hen house. Most important of all to Alice, under Mother Catherine's guidance the girls would work on their religious studies and prayers. Alice was a devout Catholic and was raising her children with the same religious beliefs she had practiced all her life. In Paris, she attended Mass every Sunday morning at La Madeleine, and at Montgeron she loyally attended daily Mass at the Church of Saint Jacques which had been built on Rottembourg estate land adjacent to the chateau, the church a short walk along a garden path not far from Rottembourg's driveway gates and on property donated by the estate's longtime previous owner, Baron Henri du Rottembourg.

In the country, Alice often visited with Mother Catherine at Yerres, one or two of the children at her side. Mother Catherine took a special interest in Alice and her children. Over the years she had known all the members of the Raingo family who had homes at Montgeron. They were a respected Catholic family, loyal to church traditions and generous to its causes. Although acquainted with Mother Catherine, Ernest was not a churchgoer. He did, however, admit to believing in God, which was satisfaction enough for Alice. She had never insisted he accompany her to Mass in the city, or to Abbey prayers and occasionally to Sunday evening vespers in the country, but Ernest had been a willing participant in all the children's christenings as well as in Marthe's First Communion which, following family tradition, was a highly celebratory event conducted at La Madeleine and followed by a reception at home. At the tender age of six, Suzanne Hoschede had no intention of being excluded from preparations for her own First Communion which was still several years away. Already reciting short prayers, learning responses, and working on the Rosary, Suzanne was known to close her eyes and offer up a hasty Hail Mary whenever conditions warranted, as for example when her brother Jacques grew particularly annoying, which she insisted was all the time.

Ernest was godfather to his Cousin Beatrice's son James and had, during his christening, surprised the entire family by actually joining in the prayers and responses which he recited both emphatically and with a respectable degree of practiced knowledge. Later, enjoying Alice's compliments as well as those of Beatrice he said, "You see, some of the things you are forced to learn in childhood stay with you all your life. That, and of course the respectful fear they manage to instill in you from your first day at religious classes," he announced with a knowing smile. "As a little child you quickly learn that you don't want to be on Sister Mary Louise's bad side, so you had best memorize the Psalm on walking in the valley of the shadow of death and fearing no evil. And as you grow a little older, Heaven forbid you are an overly energetic or inquisitive child and do some terrible thing to offend Mother Mark Marie Helene, like forgetting to take off your hat when she enters the room or asking her what a womb is, as I did one Christmas when she was telling the story of the Nativity. You just know in your heart that the potential consequences are not pleasant. It's all a powerful motivation. Nothing in the world like it!"

Of course, Alice knew that at times such as these, Ernest was not only recalling a few schoolboy experiences, but that he was also remembering his mother's dogged insistence on a tightly structured Catholic education not only for her son, but for all the world's children, regardless of national origin. This universal structure, according to Madame Honorine Hoschede, was inflexible and should consist of two simple elements: first, of a strict Catholic School education and second, of corresponding and faithful attendance at the school's daily morning Mass. Over the years, the elder Madame Hoschede's many attempts at re-directing her own son's lack of religious and academic commitment having failed, she had turned to criticism, a weapon she first used against him first in matters of academics, religion, money, and girlfriends, then against Alice, who even after eleven years as her daughter-in-law and mother of her five grandchildren Honorine still referred to as "The Belgian."

"My Ernest had the pick of Paris!" Honorine was known to go on at the family gatherings she reluctantly attended and within clear earshot of Alice and members of her Raingo family. "All of them were beautiful girls, rich too. But he chose the Belgian. Pretty enough, and nice enough I suppose if you like opinionated, extravagant girls. Those clothes! Where could my Ernest have met such a girl?"

At the beginning, such cutting remarks had shocked the Raingo family and hurt Alice, but over time and with Ernest's unfailing encouragement, she and the Raingos had built up a powerful resistance to Honorine's overbearing, rude behavior and had learned how best to handle the woman. They remained polite and civil, but for the most part, they simply ignored tactless Honorine.

It was different with Julian Raingo. He hosted Alice and Ernest's engagement reception to which Ernest's parents were invited and he wasted little time in taking Honorine aside with typical charm. More than equal to engaging her at the reception planned to introduce members of both families, Julian Raingo was well aware of Honorine's outspoken reluctance to accept the marriage Alice and Ernest wanted so desperately. Not at all pleased by the show of rejection she quite openly aimed at the young couple, the Raingo family, and Alice in particular, and armed with a ready store of family ammunition, Julian Raingo wasted no time in letting Alice's future mother-in-law know exactly what the Belgian Raingos and their famous clocks were all about. Full of complimentary remarks and taking her firmly by the arm with a broad gracious smile, he led her to the Raingo clock on the mantelpiece of his elegant drawing room, his full, flushed cheeks growing pinker and increasingly cherubic as they both faced the clock and he launched into his favorite verbal essay, supremely confident and immensely proud of the high regard in which Raingo timepieces were held, not only in Paris, but around the globe.

"Madame Hoschede, I do hope you are enjoying the beautiful Raingo clock you received from Alice's parents once the betrothal was announced," he began. "As I recall, the timepiece you received is set into a large gilded lyre, quite like this one. I am sorry to say that today we Raingos have ended our clock making days as such. It became a very profitable business and many important prizes were won at International Exhibitions, but we no longer create our masterpieces of the clockmaker's art. No, instead of toiling away in dusty, cramped quarters on Vielle du Temple and dealing with renowned bronze artists and supremely talented porcelain painters, we must now toil at dull, time-consuming financial matters in spacious offices at the Bourse," he stated. "As I am sure you are aware, boring matters having to do with real estate investments, international commerce, and related financial activities require great diligence and enormous amounts of time. As you might imagine, such activity can be challenging to say the least, but now look here at the fine workmanship of this clock. Is it not remarkable? Flawless, I'd say. And do you see that beautiful gold-lettered Raingo family signature across the porcelain face? Alice has that same style of handwriting. Have you noticed? I understand she has written many invitations to you. As a matter of fact, at my request she wrote the invitations to today's festivities."

Honorine Hoschede was not possessed of the natural poise and engaging largesse she was finding in sophisticated Julian Raingo. Her roots modest, but her adult lifestyle made comfortable through her husband's intelligence and hard work in establishing the dry goods business Ernest was expanding into a prestigious Paris department store, she was ill at ease in social situations with people like Julian Raingo who lived more opulently that she. Unsure of herself, yet skilled in hiding her discomfort, she could take on a protective mood of stern negativity when threatened and intimidated as she was by Julian Raingo's articulate summation of Raingo family accomplishments and financial superiority, her face a rigid mask of opposition as the family patriarch made it abundantly clear that Raingos were of a particular class and rank and that Alice was their golden child.

Alice was aware of her uncle's defensive position toward Honorine Hoschede in her behalf. They had often talked about it at length. She was grateful for his support, and as the years had passed and Honorine made little effort to display affection or concern for her son's family, all parties concerned marginalized her in much the same way Julian Raingo managed to do, all agreeing that for Alice's sake and to preserve the peace they would remain respectful but distant, kind but measured.

For reasons she would never fully understand, on the morning following Armel Ducasse's untimely visit with news of Ernest's indebtedness, Alice's first thoughts when she awakened were of her mother-in-law and the fresh ammunition she would now be able to add to her weaponry. Once Honorine learned of the situation, Alice was certain she would be blamed for Ernest's financial predicament and it was with a return to the prior evening's pressing concerns regarding the enormity of his debt and reasons for it that she quickly dressed and joined Ernest at the breakfast table. She was not at all prepared for his buoyant mood. It was as if nothing had happened.

"I knew there would be lots of questions about Impression Sunrise," a delighted Ernest remarked as Alice appeared and the coffee was poured. "Did you hear Didier Martine ask if the group lived at the Guerbois? I tried my best not to laugh, but I couldn't help myself."

"You seemed to be enjoying the remarks being made about the painting," Alice offered, relieved and at the same time uneasy, "but I'm afraid Monsieur Ducasse's untimely visit overshadowed its debut. Surely you know I'll be writing notes of apology all afternoon."

"Alice, for goodness sake, stop this nonsense!" Ernest suddenly lashed out. "Last night there wasn't a person here who hasn't experienced a financial shortfall at one time or another. They will appreciate your notes, but I have no doubt that by this morning they understand completely and even sympathize. I do agree, though, that Ducasse was overstepping by coming here and making a scene, but that's the sort of behavior these people rely on to intimidate and force an issue. Everybody knows it's the game they play."

"Well, I don't like the game. I can't imagine that most people do, and Ernest I would still like to know who your creditors are."

An unusual gray shadow crossed Ernest's face. He looked away and took a deep impatient breath. Finally turning to Alice he said, "My banker is one of my creditors. That should interest you. For some time I've had a generous line of credit at Union Generale, the interest on which I've been informed I must pay soon," he added calmly. "That will amount to roughly two hundred thousand francs. Now let me think. Oh yes, other debtors you might be interested in include vendors I deal with to stock the store. That shouldn't surprise you, or does it? And of course there are my personal accounts; my tailor, my bootmaker, my barber. And Alice, let us not forget expenses for two large households, salaries for the staff, the best schools, a mademoiselle, and clothes for the children, and may I mention your lavish lifestyle, your flower-filled dinners and receptions, and your own abundance of lovely clothes?"

"Overlooking Ernest's sarcastic tone, Alice asked, "What about the paintings you've been buying from Monsieur Durand-Ruel? Are they paid for?"

"Alice, you know I've had an account with Durand-Ruel since I started collecting years ago," Ernest quickly hurled back, his voice growing louder with every word. "Prices on the new group's paintings I'm buying are shall we say, decent, and Durand-Ruel knows I support the group as a whole which sometimes allows me a little flexibility. Now please, let's end this inquisition! I have appointments at the store and I'm already late. I hope you're in a better mood when I come home!"

Watching him leave the table Alice was not satisfied with Ernest's vague explanations, but upset as she was, she finished her breakfast and proceeded through the morning, self-possessed and with her usual attention to the children and the housekeeping staff. With the birthday celebration over there was silver to be cleaned and stored away, bottles of unopened wine and champagne to be returned to the cellars, and a resumption of the normal daily housekeeping routine. Anticipating an afternoon of rest, Alice's best intentions were interrupted by her Uncle Julian's unexpected arrival just before noon. Clearly perplexed by events of the previous evening, he demanded an explanation. With Ernest gone, Alice was left to offer what words of explanation she could.

"Uncle Julian, there really is nothing to worry about," she calmly said over a hastily assembled tray of tea. "I apologize for what happened here last night, but please be assured. Ernest has everything under control. I know you were offended. I certainly was, but I'm not at all worried about the debt Monsieur Ducasse alleges Ernest has incurred and I hope you aren't worried about it either."

"My dear, I do not offend easily," the autocratic Julian Raingo interrupted, taking the cup of tea Alice handed him. "You should know that by now. You should also know that it takes more than a minor municipal auditor's representative breaking into any gathering I am attending to make my face red, no matter how distinguished the occasion. What does concern me is any financial dilemma your husband may be swirling in right now, and I have concerns only because such circumstances could negatively affect the reputation of our Raingo family. First and foremost, though, it is your interests, Alice, and the interests of those dear children of yours that I have at heart and feel obligated to oversee. With no wife or children of my own, perhaps I compensate for my bachelorhood by loving you and your children as much as I do, but there's something else. You may not know this, but just before your father died he asked me to promise I would look after you when he was gone. He knew his time was short and I knew exactly what he meant by his words. Of course I did promise, fully intending to keep my promise to that wonderful man, which I will continue to do until all breath leaves me. Your father knew you well, Alice. He knew your strengths and capabilities, and of all his surviving children, it was you he named to be owner and guardian of the Chateau Rottembourg property he and your mother cared about so very much. Nothing must jeopardize that legacy or any other aspect of our Raingo family's continuity, and as long as I live, nothing will. Alice, you must remember that continuity is the most important thing for the Raingos. We have a great deal to be proud of."

Alice was profoundly touched by her uncle's disclosures. Her eyes glistened with tears when she said, "Uncle Julian, all my life it's been wonderful to have the security of your love and care. When I was growing up, you were the one who made time for me. I had eight brothers and sisters. It wasn't easy for my parents to spread their attention around to nine children. I felt very fortunate to have you in my life and I appreciated every moment of your devotion through those years. You planned wonderful Paris outings for the two of us. I haven't forgotten. There were those afternoons at new plays and luncheons at Gaulois or Le Polidor where you encouraged me to try foods I had never tasted and grew to love. There were visits to the Louvre and walks in the Luxembourg Gatdens. I want you to know that in one way or another, I'm often reminded of those happy times and I treasure them. I am also reminded of my father's faith in me. Thanks to both of you, I know what a secure, happy life is and that is exactly what I am able to enjoy with my children every day. I also understand what you mean by continuity in our family. Over a long period of time the Raingos firmly established themselves in Paris and of course in light of what happened last night, none of our security and happiness could possibly be at risk. That would be impossible. Uncle Julian, you know as well as I do that Ernest is a capable business man and that like my father he is the responsible head of his family. If he isn't concerned about the likes of Armel Ducasse and his demands, then you and I shouldn't be either. Uncle Julian, I hope you can forget what happened last night. I certainly intend to. Now tell me, when will be you coming to Montgeron? July? August?"

Julian Raingo appreciated his favorite niece's loving acknowledgements, but he was not satisfied by her feeble attempts to brush off the prior evening's implications. Fourteen years before, when she had brought her new beau to meet him, he had liked the ambitious Ernest Hoschede who made no secret of having fallen head over heels in love with the young woman he had favored since earliest childhood. Young Hoschede had plans to turn his family's modest dry goods business into a successful Paris emporium specializing in luxury goods. He had seemed determined to succeed and Julian Raingo was convinced that with his drive and optimism he most certainly would. Now, overnight and with a financial disclosure he found intolerable, that certainty had faded into doubt and disappointment. With a fond farewell to Alice, Julian Raingo called for his carriage and in a short time was looking up to the gold-lettered sign reading Le Grand Magasin Hoschede, determined not to mince words with its proprietor.

Ignoring the stylishly dressed reception clerk who insisted that Monsieur Hoschede saw visitors by appointment only, he climbed the stairs and walked directly into Ernest's office where he found him seated at his desk, pouring over a stack of paper. Ernest looked up and immediately rose to his feet.

"Why, Uncle Julian, what a pleasant surprise!" he said coming forward from behind the desk, his hand extended, his ready smile broad and welcoming. "What brings you to the store? We can fulfill any request."

Unmoved by gestures of cordiality, Julian Raingo was in no mood for wasting time over handshakes and niceties. "Ernest, what is it all about?" he demanded of the man who had been entrusted with his precious niece's future. "What was Armel Ducasse talking about last night and how have you incurred a million franc debt?"

The smile left Ernest's face and in an instant he was no longer the polite relative. "Uncle, I suppose I should have expected you," he said. "First let me say that I understand your concern. I appreciate it. With Alice's father gone, you are the family's mainstay, but with all due respect, I cannot imagine why you would come out of your way and here to my place of business with questions regarding my private affairs. I do hope you do not mean to say that you expect me to explain myself to you. And again, with all due respect, I do not believe an explanation is necessary. I apologize for the interruption last night, but I am perfectly capable of handling my own financial affairs."

"Young man, Julian Raingo stated dryly, "if you have incurred a one-million franc debt at a time when the Paris economy is faltering and banks all over Europe are failing, then it seems to me you are not at all capable of handling your own financial affairs. Have you talked to your banker or to Marc Pirole about all this? They would be your best advisors. And tell me one more thing. Is it really one million francs, or is it more?"

Julian Raingo stood waiting, but Ernest refused to answer his question, the contentious silent air suspended between them fueling a heretofore unthinkable breach. "I thought so," he retaliated. "Ernest, you are behaving exactly like those irresponsible incendiary artists you associate with! Get hold of yourself for God's sake! Look around! This is no time to be incurring huge debt. Exercise some discipline. You've fallen into the trap of radical ideas and easy money. It's a dangerous place, and about that painting you were showing off last night! What is it called? Impression Sunrise or some such nonsense? It's not worthy of you Ernest. You would do well to turn yourself around and rid yourself of such trash, and soon! It's clouding your thinking!"

Julian Raingo turned on his heel and left Ernest's office without a further word. Outside, he quickly stepped into his waiting carriage and before signaling his driver to move on, he paused to look up to the imposing black-lettered sign at Number 35 Rue de Poissonniere, vowing he would not spend another centime in Ernest Hoschede's pretentious emporium until this matter of debt was explained to his satisfaction. Young Hoschede was obviously insulted by the visit to his store, the silver-haired senior Raingo concluded, comfortably settling himself into the lustrous brown leather seat and directing his driver to the Parc Monceau. Too bad! He should be! And Hoschede had seemed prepared for confrontation. That was good. But, admirable as it was on the surface, confrontational strength could be an impractical gift for a man whose life could be careening at the edge of a precipice, Raingo told himself as he lit a cigar and his carriage halted at the gates of the Parc Monceau where he had decided to walk for a while and think things over. Commendable at the onset of matters, confrontation in families invited useless debate and long-standing hard feelings, serving only to test the resolve of both parties and the superiority of one, he considered. When all was said and done, people held grudges and allowed resentment to fester. Confrontation by itself illuminated the scene but it solved nothing. Hoschede would learn that the hard way. Too bad he hadn't explained himself or even tried to, the way a man in business should, Julian Raingo concluded, sitting back on one of the benches by the Monceau's bucolic pond, watching the fountain and puffing at his cigar. He would have offered to help, and he could even have found it in his heart to be generous, but Hoschede had probably felt he needed to stand his ground and exhibit strength to one of his elders. It was a childish response, but at least there was that about him. The greater concern now that Hoschede had made his stand clear, was Alice. Clearly, she was refusing to face reality. It also seemed she was unaware of the gravity of the situation and its potential implications for anyone named Raingo, but whatever the reason, Alice's refusal to discuss the underlying reason for Armel Ducasse's demands was troubling. It was entirely possible that Ernest hadn't told his wife the truth or that he himself was in a state of denial. Be that as it may, sooner or later Alice would be forced to face reality, whatever it was, and deal with it. For now, though, it looked as if things had caught up with high-living Hoschede, and at the worst possible time. Well, as the old French saying went, the mustard was on the baguette. By itself, it would look good and seem tempting, but unless promptly eaten and swallowed up with meat and cheese, it would soon turn crusty, change color, and become unappetizing. Hoschede's debt was due paid on Saturday. That was just a few days away, Julian Raingo considered further, purchasing a paper cone of bread crumbs from a vendor to feed a flock of young spring ducklings. Hoschede would show his true colors by then. Either that, or denial would become his staunchest ally and Alice would fall victim to his dismissiveness.

* * *

    The dreaded Saturday came and went. Sunday and Monday too. In the Hoschede household there was no discussion of financial obligations and no sign of Armel Ducasse. Ernest went about his normal routine. He displayed no sign of worry and he discussed no aspect of a million franc debt. Although it was on her mind, Alice did not broach the subject herself. At this point it was best avoided she thought, and besides, Ernest was ebullient and full of good humor. Obviously he had settled things with Armel Ducasse. Days passed, and in the Hoschede household the normal daily routine continued.
    Every morning Ernest and Alice sat at breakfast and every evening by eight o'clock they were at dinner, elegantly dressed, carrying on the conversations they never seemed to tire of. They laughed. They made love. The sun shone. The city warmed. Borders of jonquils bloomed in the parks. Life, like spring itself, was being lived at its wonderful best. A full week passed, and another, and as the days dissolved one into the next and the full bloom of spring settled on Paris, Alice was caught up in final preparations for departing the city and installing her family at the Chateau Rottembourg for the summer ahead. It was as if Armel Ducasse's visit had never taken place, and as she busily packed personal items and organized the family's departure for the country, she managed to put all such unpleasant matters completely out of her mind. Folding the children's clothes, pairing their socks and shoes, and helping them to decide which of their favorite toys and books they would take to the country this year, her thoughts were quite completely absorbed by these simple tasks as above all such personal considerations she anxiously anticipated the sight of her cherished Chateau Rottembourg.

As for Ernest, he continued in his usual role as a man conducting business in the city, at the same time finding ample hours on any given day to pursue far more appealing personal activity once he stepped out of E. Hoschede's elegant doors, which now was more often than in the past. The store was being managed by a newly expanded executive staff which allowed him greater freedom. He had hired a new accountant and he had snared the manager away from his most serious competitor, La Samartaine, doubling his salary and as a final temptation offering him the newly re-decorated office on the second floor. The summer ahead would be leisurely and pleasant, he promised himself. With his business in reliable hands, he would be returning to the city far less frequently than in the past. He would shoot pheasant and wild hare in the Senart Forest. There would be festive evening dinners with friends. He would plan treasure hunts for the children. How they loved pretending they were a band of adventurous explorers in a new land, unearthing buried treasure comprised of the vividly colored glass jewels and coins he piled into small wooden crates and buried under the boxwood and willows for them to find.

That winter, one of his purveyors had provided him with sparkling toy crowns and dozens of play rings set with pieces of brightly colored glass which he added to the treasure trove. As a father, Ernest took great pleasure in the knowledge that for months each summer his children were free to roam Rottembourg's grounds at will, healthy and safe in fresh country air, their lives enriched by the background against which they thrived. In the mornings he watched them run and shout and play their hoop games on pristine squares of grass. Later, following a check on the geese in the pond, they reported back to him, filled with excited descriptions of small, downy goslings taken out by their mother for a morning swim and then a stroll beside patches of the long meadow grass. After an early lunch in their third floor playroom, they turned to their books or made paper dolls and animals, but most often they ran down the stairs and played statues in the garden with their mother, which was their favorite game, she, as always, their favorite playmate. And later, after naps and baths and as the clocks in the house struck four, they would gather at their third floor children's table for tea, a daily ritual supervised by their mademoiselle, Gabrielle, and one upon which Alice insisted. In the nurturing environment where they played and read and slept and dreamed, tea was poured at four for the Hoschede siblings gathered together, one child assigned each day to cut carefully and equally into a freshly baked fruit tart or warm lemon cake, exactly as their mother had taught them.

Habits. Respect. Tradition. Lessons learned in seasons. Summer of 1874 unfurled, full-bodied. Rich. Playful. Alice at her most beautiful. White gauze dresses by day. Barefoot on an emerald green lawn. Playing statues with her children on afternoons of endless warm sunshine. Smiling in doorways. Laughing in candlelit hallways. Seated with guests in Rottembourg's beautiful rooms. Ernest, hunting in the Senart Forest, the wild summer game more abundant than ever a mere short walk away from the ambling meadow border of the Chateau Rottembourg.

Early in June of that year, during one of his forays into Lenoir's, the smart antiquary on the Champs-Elysees, Ernest had purchased a pair of large iron garden urns which were installed to either side of Rottembourg's black iron entrance gates. Alice had them immediately planted with huge bursts of trailing red roses. Through early July the plants were pampered, carefully watered and fussed over, presenting by mid-summer a lush show of brilliant red blossoms tumbling onto the chateau's carriage entrance on the Concy Road. In a short time, Rottembourg's rose-filled urns became a landmark at the hilltop curve, their bright show of red an annual tradition planned for and executed with increasingly impressive results.

Of the many pleasures at Rottembourg and apart from the chateau's inviting interiors, it was the mood of country life that Alice loved best. She and Ernest were different people in the Brie Valley; simpler, more approachable, informal with guests and staff, more engaged with their children, Ernest seldom happier in the summer of 1874 than during long nights when the country rain pounded down on his roof and Alice lay warm in his arms. The fullness of the love they shared, the contentment and joy they found in one another had matured and settled, and far from having become commonplace, were more vividly apparent than ever, even to the most casual observer.

Many friends who visited at Rottembourg that summer said the Hoschedes' closeness must be due to the luxury of time spent captive together in the romantic splendor of a country summer. Others said it was the sorcery of an old French house at it lovely peak, but whatever the reason, 1874 summer visitors to Rottembourg took notice. In evening candlelight, they caught the intimacy of sheltered smiles their hosts exchanged across the dining room table, the intended ardor of those smiles captured later when hands were held and whispers quickly exchanged on terraces bathed in moonlight. And later yet, as under midnight skies showers of gentle rain fell over the Brie Valley fields, nourishing and sustaining its ancient hillsides, the sound of a woman's light, lovely laughter could be heard echoing like soft, lilting music along Rottembourg's stairway and upstairs halls. It was no wonder they had all those children, many had thought to themselves at the time.

It was true that the Hoschedes were often mesmerizing to watch and Jean DeLille may have put it best when he wrote, "They were not at all unlike the beautiful introspective people to be seen on the summer beaches at Biarritz and Trouville in those rapidly vanishing years; those unreachable, enchanting figures promenading aimlessly along the boardwalks without a single bothersome care to intrude on the preservation of their glamorous allure, the women serene and inscrutable under white, ruffled parasols, their long, elaborate pastel-colored dresses billowing up in the sea breeze, the leisurely steps of the men walking beside them taken in a steady, idle rhythm. Occasionally they paused to look out to the sea; pensive, mildly bored, and endlessly intriguing as they stared out from their mysterious, touch-me-not worlds."

And so the summer passed. An avalanche of guests arrived, accompanied by piles of luggage filled with elegant day and evening attire specifically selected for visiting the Chateau Rottembourg. Julian Raingo stayed for the month of July at La Lethumiere, his small rustic lodge at the river's willow-bordered edge nearby. Raingo family members visiting from Paris along with Montgeron neighbors were invited to dine. Dinner conversation was always animated. Laughter abounded. Food was delicious and beautifully served. Champagne and wine flowed. After dinner Jean DeLille often played the piano in the rotunda and sang a few of the admittedly raucous songs he had recently heard at the Folies Bergeres, his performances reliably entertaining and frequently generating outbursts of whistles and cheering. At times the men played billiards and smoked cigars while the women gathered in the drawing room and enjoyed chocolates, card games, and whatever news one or another of the ladies had received from Paris or from more distant parts of the world.

On the surface, the summers of those years may have seemed serene and carefree, but the realities of life continued on in bucolic villages such as Montgeron and they were worthy of conversation. Illnesses developed. People died. Babies were born. Love affairs were suspected. Age took its toll on the elderly, but at the Chateau Rottembourg no such dilemmas disturbed the exquisite balance. On sunny afternoons cool lemon tea was served under the copper beeches. Along with puffs of strawberry-filled meringues, trays of flaky apple and peach tarts were set out on tables under the towering old trees. Everyone sat in wicker chairs and talked until twilight. The children thrived. Igor ran alongside the littlest ones, Jacques and Suzanne, as together they chased rabbits and squirrels and somehow found the hollows under the boathouse and beside the old grotto where communities of frog families had taken up residence.

And so it went, neighbor amusing neighbor, guest engaging guest in the sweet shade of ancient trees, children at play, a house in the country accommodating every human wish, its inhabitants sated and happy, the hours of the summer of 1874 vanishing flawlessly into the fragrant Brie Valley air. Alfred Sisley came to visit. He spent two weeks. He painted the garden. The Manets also came that summer. Edouard painted a portrait of Alice in the garden. He tried his hand at plein-air painting but much to Ernest's amusement said he found no inspiration whatsoever for it. Late August came, and with it the last of summer's visitors. In September the garden roses began to fade and dry, the red trailing blossoms in their urns on the Concy Road too, and by late October, when the Chateau Rottembourg's espaliered peach trees had been wrapped in burlap for the winter and the silent white haze of an early hoar frost blanketed the gardens of Montgeron, the Hoschede family had returned to Paris for another hectic social season of life in a city they now found immersed not in mere idle café talk of possible economic downturn, but in a serious financial struggle, one that throughout the bucolic summer had begun to hold a number of Central European capitol cities in a grip of economic fear and uncertainty.

Recession was fully underway. Now it was abundantly clear that the unprecedented number of new banks and lending institutions sprouting up across Europe during the prosperous mid-century building boon inspired by the Paris success of the Baron Haussmann era were failing. Following the end of the Franco-Prussian War and during the early part of the decade of the 1870's, from Russia and west across Central Europe to Britain, mortgages were easy to obtain as building after building rose in city after city. Land values soared across Europe. More and more credit was extended. Blocks of unfinished commercial buildings, vast roofless municipal structures and miles of only partially constructed new roadways were acceptable collateral, but at the same time, prosperous European importers from Russia to Great Britain accustomed to successful continental trade in everything from cattle and tin to indigo and wheat, found they could no longer compete with American Midwestern Farmers whose export livestock and wheat prices were far below any in Europe and whose production volume and efficient shipping schedules overwhelmed their own. The import-export game had changed.

For British millers, American wheat was much cheaper than the grain they had been buying from sources in Central Europe. So was kerosene, the marvelous new American lighting product which was quickly replacing rapeseed oil and was lower in price and better in quality. In a short time, Black Sea traders accustomed to purchasing wheat, cattle, rapeseed oil, wool, coal, and tin from Northern Germany, France, and Britain found themselves in shrinking markets. The great fortunes of Central European importers and exporters were toppling, the unprecedented building boom in great cities had ended, and most shocking of all, the Vienna Stock Exchange had crashed.

In rapid succession, scores of continental banks failed, and uncertain of which institutions could be trusted, powerful British banks in control of vast reserves withheld all capital as stock markets across Europe crumbled. Britain's hard, inflexible stand was even felt across the Atlantic. America's ambitious interstate railway system was heavily dependent on British construction-issued bonds. Railroad financiers had borrowed heavily from American banks which themselves depended almost totally on British banks for cash, but once the dominant British refused to issue further credit or loans, a finely honed system which had worked so well for a highly profitable time collapsed. A series of American banks succumbed. Across the United States, thousands of once thriving businesses were failing. Wealthy railway magnates and ambitious financiers were losing fortunes, unemployment in America was soaring, and in a final stinging blow the New York Stock Exchange closed. As winter arrived and the year of 1874 came to an end, the global financial picture was indeed grim.

What of art? What of its practitioners? What of music and poetry in such a dismal climate? What of philosophy, friendship, and beauty and the survival of love? What of anguish and pity and paralyzing fear?

Remarkably, in the face of financial chaos, the resilient population of Paris did more than survive. It thrived, continuing to practice its arts, enjoy its reputation, and maintain its unique genius for hauteur as it always had, aware of the fragility of the times but in no way intimidated by them. Exemplary of the prevailing Paris attitude, his financial optimism secured by the generosity of his recent inheritance, Ernest Hoschede kept company with what journalists were calling the constant bright arc of hope. Encouraged by the smallest ray of light, Ernest had no time for naysayers or prophets of doom and into 1875 he and Alice and their circle of friends confidently maintained the sophisticated lifestyles they had always known.

Seeming oblivious to the economic crisis unfolding around him and choosing to ignore his own financial vulnerabilities, Ernest continued to make purchases. He bought paintings and furniture in greater quantity than ever before. In January of 1875 Durand-Ruel sold him twenty-three paintings: Pissarros, Sisleys, Monets, Morisots. He saw his tailor regularly. He and Alice dined in the finest restaurants: Laperous, Le Polidor, and Le Grand Vefour. He went so far as to lease a train, a gleaming dark blue, elegantly appointed private saloon car garaged at the Gare de Lyon and pressed into service for private travel to Montgeron as he required. The children adored the blue train journeys. Parties of guests invited to the Chateau Rottembourg met at the Gare de Lyon and joined the Hoschedes for the "blue" journey to Montgeron. Champagne was poured. Delicious pastries and individually wrapped baskets of fruit and chocolates were presented. Countryside landmarks were pointed out along the way as anticipation grew for the first sightings of the Brie Valley's rolling wheatlands and soon after, the spires of the Abbaye de Notre Dame, and finally the tall chimneys of the Chateau Rottembourg.

Sharing in her husband's infectious optimism, Alice also continued secure in her personal habits. She entertained and dressed as beautifully as always. By 1875 she was one of the fashion designer, Charles Worth's, best customers. Throughout 1875, the elegant Hoschede dinners, formal receptions, and family celebrations continued, but at the opposite pole of life, The Street of Pictures and its painters were being hit hard. Some artists became desperate, others didn't notice a change in their lives at all, but most Street of Pictures dealers lived in a prevailing climate of fear. Sales plummeted to almost nothing. It was unquestionably a buyer's market and some buyers took advantage of both desperation and emaciation. Remarkably, creative work continued, in some cases reaching unimaginable heights. Claude

IMPRESSION SUNRISE — 165

Monet, along with Pierre Renoir, Edgar Degas, Camille Pissarro, Berthe Morisot, Alfred Sisley, Paul Cezanne, and now young Gustave Caillebotte continued to work tirelessly, their output from summer of 1875 into spring of 1876 nothing short of dazzling.

The weather in winter of 1875 bore witness to the frigid financial times. In January the Seine froze more solidly than any living soul could remember. Making matters worse, in February fierce, icy cold winds tore through Paris and the surrounding countryside, damaging hundreds of houses and destroying vast, ancient stands of sturdy oaks, poplars, and pines. Remarkably, through the dark turbulence of the times, the insistent light of creativity continues to shine warm and bright and it is an absolutely stunning period for the now disbanded group of Impressionists.

Claude and Alfred Sisley use the winter weather to advantage, content to stand outdoors for hours in freezing cold and paint ice flows and shorelines rimmed in patches of frozen snowfields, their hands encased in fingerless gloves, their beards iced white, their work unparalleled. Perfecting his talent for simple form and ever simpler subjects, in his studio Sisley completes The Terrace at Saint-Germaine-Spring and Flood at Port Marly. In addition to more than seven paintings depicting snow and winter scenes at Argenteuil, Claude paints La Mere, effet de neige (The Pond, Snow Effect).

In late 1875, Paul Cezanne spends a few months in Paris, but by February of 1876 he is at his family's estate at Aix-en-Provence, soaking up the sunlight, painting tirelessly, and enduring the frequent tirades of his wealthy father who continues to do everything he can to discourage his son's artistic aspirations. Nonetheless, on the heels of his 1873 House of Suicide come The Sea at L'Estaque, Paysage:Etude d'apres nature, also known as La mer a L'Estaque and Head of a Man, Tete d'homme: Etude.

Into 1876, Edgar Degas concentrates on promoting the harsh, abrasive side of his charm-free personality, at the same time embarking on a period of spectacular work. He creates The Portrait of Monsieur H.R. (Henri Rouart), Ballet Rehearsal on Stage, Place de la Concorde, and in breathtaking succession come Henri Des Gas: Uncle Henri and Niece Lucie, Song of the Dog, The Ballet Class, Portrait of Jerome Ottoz, and The Absinthe Drinker.

Forced overnight to abandon his Louveciennes home by occupying Prussian soldiers at the onset of the France Prussian War in 1870, Camille Pissarro's huge volume of paintings is left behind and eventually found to have been used to collect horse manure and create dry paths over muddy stretches of the property to protect Prussian boots. Undaunted, at his new home at Pontoise, Pissarro finishes the first of his many Pontoise paintings, among their startling number The Saint-Antoine Road at l'Hermitage, The Meadow of Les Mathurins, Snow Effect at L'Hermitage, La Cote du Jallais, The Little Bridge, Peasant Untangling Wool, March Sun, and later in 1875, Winter at Montfoucault and Autumn; Montfoucault Pond. Pissarro is, at forty-six, the oldest member of what more and more often now is, by journalists, being called The New Group.

In 1875, Caillebotte, at twenty-eight, youngest of the lions, emerges from the tall, protective grass and in winter prepares a painting he titles The Floor Scrapers, centering ever more fully on the unpretentious subject matter of his colleagues. He spends the summer of 1876 painting The Park of the Caillebotte Estate, The Banks of the Yerres, and most of the eighty additional landscapes he will complete depicting his wealthy family's country life at their Yerres estate, as well as the surrounding areas of the River Yerres and Mont Griffon as he has known them since childhood.

In this same period Claude paints Train in the Snow; The Locomotive, and La Promenade, also called Woman with a Parasol. La Seine a Argenteuil is completed that summer as are Interieur d'appartement, Family Strolling in the Fields at Argenteuil, and The Poppy Fields in Summer.

The Monet family has moved from Rue Pierre Guienne to another house in Argenteuil-sur-Seine, this residence on the Boulevard Saint-Denis just across from the railroad station. A small, sturdy boat Claude has cleverly equipped as a floating studio takes him into the remote, narrow inlets and shadowy marshes he has only been able to see at a distance from the Argenteuil riverbank. Visiting Argenteuil in the summer of 1874, Pierre Renoir has painted a portrait of his good friend, Claude. A short time later he completes Dance at Le Moulin de la Galette and in 1876 comes The Swing. In that same summer, Edouard Manet is visiting his family at Gennevilliers and comes to nearby Argenteuil to paint with Monet and Renoir, the ease of their friendship a source of great pleasure to all three. Manet paints Claude in his studio boat and the immensely productive period continues, taking on historic proportions. In 1875, Berthe Morisot paints Laundresses Hanging Out the Wash, Figure of a Woman, and At the Ball, also known as Young Woman at the Dance. She spends the summer of 1875 working on the Isle of Wight. The year before she has married Edouard Manet's brother, Eugene, but in Paris it continues to be rumored that it is really Edouard with whom she remains in love. Berthe Morisot shares the same haute bourgeoise status of the Edouard Manets and their mutual friends, the Henri Rouarts. Their families travel in the same privileged circles and pursue the same genteel quality of life. The century's gender issues and social mores prevent the very feminine Morisot from joining her male colleagues at their Café Guerbois meetings, but she does frequently join Edouard Manet and Henri Rouart at the more dignified Café Nouvelle Athene and at times for dinners at the Café Riche or Polidor, both these locations possessed of a mood and intellect preferred by both Edouard Manet and his equally discriminating brother, Eugene. As time passes and life takes on its inevitable patina, Berthe and Eugene's beautiful daughter, Julie, will marry Henri Rouart's son, Denis.

Two leaders of the Barbizon School die in 1875, a third, two years later. In quick succession Corot, Millet, and Courbet fade from the active painting scene and in doing so lay claim to their greatness. At the same time, the sum and substance of the work of the collective Barbizons falls into significant historic perspective, the influence of their movement on the early development of Impressionism becoming increasingly clear if not intensely conspicuous.

As in all periods of history, prosperous or adverse, people everywhere, of every grade and station, have courageously carried on with the responsibilities and routines of their lives. Throughout Europe, in the face of increasingly severe economic decline, not only business owners and shopkeepers, but creative artists of all disciplines moved stoically forward and with ever more remarkable results. In music, Saint-Saens and Bizet are composing in Paris; Brahms and Wagner in Germany. Verdi is at work in Italy, Tchaikovsky in Russia, Gilbert and Sullivan in Britain. At this same time, unable, or perhaps unwilling to resist the opportunity available to them, the British buy more than 100,000 shares in the Suez Canal from Egypt, and very much taken with Baron Haussmann's remarkably effective new Paris sewer system, they complete their own similar system in London. The Impressionists do not hold an exhibition in 1875, but everyone works. Electing to match Ernest Hoschede's successes in selling their work at public auction and to meet their own financial emergencies, in March of that year, three of the more destitute members of the group, Monet, Renoir, and Sisley are joined by a reluctant and less needy Berthe Morisot who may be using the invitation of her colleagues to hold a sale not so much for profit, but to publicly promote her work in lieu of an exhibition that year.

Likely with Ernest's encouragement, the four courageously stage their auction-led sale of seventy-three of their paintings at the distinguished Hotel Drouot, an event to which the Paris police are summoned when the crowd suddenly becomes unruly, shouting profane insults and calling the artists, especially Monet and Renoir, shocking names. Paul Durand-Ruel is the official certifier and has presented the work in superb frames, but even this noble precaution does nothing to affect the crowd's malicious behavior or the auction's dismal results. Some paintings bring as little as 50 francs ($10 US Dollars) and Durand-Ruel maintains that is only because of the frames. Morisot, who does not attend the event, fares better than her three colleagues who do. For 480 francs ($96) Ernest buys her Interior. Morisot's brother-in-law, Gustave Manet, buys the pastel, On the Lawn as well as a view of Petites Dalles. Morisot's good friend, Henri Rouart, buys In a Villa at the Seaside, and the naturalist, Ernest Duez, buys Chasing Butterflies.

Claude shows Camille Embroidering, which is listed as Number 12 in the catalogue and is a portrait of his wife, Camille, engaged in her needlework while sitting on the veranda of their house at Argenteuil. It brings 290 francs, ($58 U.S.) His Les Dechargeurs de Charbon, Catalogue Number 16, brings 225 francs, ($45 U.S.). Through Durand-Ruel, Monet buys back his Un Coin d'Appartement (Apartment Interior), Number 14 in the catalogue, for 325 francs ($65 U.S.) It is at this sale that Claude's winter scene of Argenteuil: La Mare, effet de neige (The Pond, Snow Effect), Catalogue #15, is purchased by Paul Durand-Ruel. He will hold it until 1879 and its public showing in the Impressionist Exhibition of that year. Of the seventy-three paintings shown at The Drouot sale, the stalwart and instinctively blessed Paul Durand-Ruel purchases eighteen.

Through the course of this difficult year, the disheveled group, scattered and discouraged, has not only continued to work, but has communicated with dependable regularity, exchanging a great volume of notes and letters. Monet writes to Renoir, Caillebotte to Monet and Renoir, Sisley to Pissarro, Pissarro to

Renoir and Cezanne. Whenever possible, they leave their painting and various homes to meet in Paris at the Guerbois, but their unity and aspirations continue to be out of step with well-established Salon principles. Most offensive to those loyally supportive of the strict Salon system, is their insistence on independence which is essentially expressed in their desire to be accepted for who they are, what they paint, and how they paint it. Perhaps as a protective measure taken in its own defense, the Salon's standards now grow stricter, offering the rebel band further fuel for its Guerbois discussions and quite successfully discouraging any plans they may have had for future group exhibitions. There is no escaping the facts. Interest in them is waning and day by day through the mid 1870's the worsening French economy is playing its part in discouraging any hope of support from the private sector.

CHAPTER 9

Turning Points
1876

Jean DeLille, the portrait painter and Ernest's closest friend, wisely observed that now and again in art as in life, there are those unusual periods dictated by circumstance when the appearance of failure masks the quiet underbelly of steady progress. Later in life, and with the convenient gift of hindsight, DeLille accurately saw 1875 and much of 1876 as a highly significant period for the Impressionists; "a silent turning point," as he called it, "of great importance and a time in which the introspective arrows could very easily have pointed quickly downward," for difficult as it may have become for some to buy the most basic art supplies, persevere, and finish work in the negative face of overwhelmingly frail economic conditions, productivity continued at a splendid pace, among the most prolific of all the stalwarts the chronically impoverished but eternally optimistic Pierre-Auguste Renoir.

"It is becoming quite fashionable to be poor in Paris, I notice" he observed in the confines of the increasingly derelict Guerbois, his well-worn brown boots shabby, his black wool hat cocked to one side of his head. "At last I am relevant!

The poorer the better! Look at me. I am truly one of the people. It is a good feeling."

Included in a long list of works attributed to him in this challenging period and on the heels of his 1874 works which included La Loge, Dancer, and The Parisenne come Nude in Sunlight and The Lovers. Also into 1875 has come his Portrait of Claude Monet. In 1876, The Swing appears, also Ball at the Moulin de la Galette, Woman at the Piano, At the Café, and Young Woman Braiding Her Hair.

It is in this period that Ernest Hoschede purchases three Renoir works through Durand-Ruel: Woman with a Cat, Le Pont de Chatou, and Jeune Fille dans un jardin. At decade's end and four years after the Impressionists' first disastrous exhibition, in 1878 Renoir will triumph with The Portrait of Madame Charpentier and her Children, a large work which is accepted and exhibited by the Salon of that year and although not critically acclaimed, the painting that turns his personal tide while at the same time its Salon acceptance dramatically breaks with the Impressionist Group's primary objective which, as Degas continues to insist, is to resist the Salon at all costs.

The financial climate of the 1870's may have been presenting a number of serious challenges but it was also slowing the urban pace enough to allow for novel pockets of awareness and adaptability and as Alice and Ernest Hoschede celebrated the arrival of the New Year of 1876 with customary festivities and toasts and much of La Belle France once again looked to its illustrious past for comfort and inspiration, for the rejected Impressionist lions the emerging stage of the century's final quarter was being set for a very new way of life.

Reversing their earlier decision to disband, the rebels are re-grouping, re-charging, and against all odds have agreed to hold a Second Exhibition in the spring of 1876. Although immensely pleased by this news, Ernest Hoschede, has reason to look over his shoulder. Another collector is patronizing the Durand-Ruel Galleries on a regular basis and he is purchasing Impressionist paintings. The opera singer and speculator, Jean-Baptiste Faure, once exclusively devoted to Renaissance paintings and more recently to the Barbizons, has entered the world of brash Independents in a significant way and by 1876 is buying their paintings in a quantity that Ernest is finding threatening.

It was good to be known in one's personal and social circles as a courageous, daring visionary. It was much better, however, when one's taste and courage enjoyed an enviable degree of exclusivity. A few anonymous sales here and there were one thing and admittedly necessary to support struggling artists, but a seriously competing collector with a successful record as a speculator was quite something else.

"Is it that Faure has given up on the Barbizons because their leaders are beginning to die off?" Ernest inquired of Durand-Ruel during one visit to Rue Laffitte, unable to resist arriving at some assessment of his competitor's stand. "I should think now, with the deaths of Corot and Millet that Monsieur Faure would appreciate the Barbizons all the more, especially since Corot frequently served as a Salon judge and values of his work are soaring. I understand Faure cares about such things; the Salon, the Academy, their ceremonies and honors. Of course, thanks to his involvement with the Commune, our aging Courbet remains persona non grata with the Third Republic, so I expect you would be advising Monsieur Faure to hold on to his Courbets for a while or at least until French amnesia sets in. Tell me Monsieur, now that he has discovered the new group, whose work is Monsieur Faure favoring these days?"

Durand-Ruel hesitated in answering, finding himself in delicate territory, but true to his character and consistent with the unwavering beliefs of his professional position, he handled his client's inquiry with diplomatic tact.

"Monsieur Hoschede, please understand. I cannot allow myself to discuss Monsieur Faure's preferences or purchases with you any more than I can allow myself to discuss yours with him. You, of all my clients, know how very much I love talking about my painters, but my clients are another thing. If they, themselves, wish to divulge the details of transactions, that is fine, but as for myself, I work very hard at maintaining only the most confidential relationships with my clients and I like to think my loyalty is returned and appreciated."

"Oh, I meant for no disrespect or for any indiscretion to occur between us," Ernest quickly injected, realizing the impact made by his impudence, but I do care about that rebel group, as you know, Monsieur Durand-Ruel. I simply thought that with news of a Second Exhibition, Monsieur Faure might be searching for a bit of added fame. I heard about the planned exhibition just yesterday and thought our opera star might be interested in lending a few paintings to it, something of that nature. Please take no offense."

"I take no offense, Monsieur Hoschede, none at all," Durand-Ruel graciously offered. "I will tell you this, however: The exhibition the group is planning for the spring is being held here, in these rooms. It will likely be in March and they will officially be named Impressionists in all posters and newspaper announcements."

"Marvelous!" Ernest exclaimed, genuinely pleased at the prospect. "This is the best and most natural location for them and of course, I shall be your most frequent and avid attendee! And who knows? Perhaps there will be something to tempt me."

Pictures at an Exhibition, 1876

On opening day, Thursday, March thirtieth, Ernest's gleaming black carriage was among the first to arrive, the freshly polished silver bridles and braided manes of his chestnut mares as they came to a slow halt once again altogether in keeping with the indulgent spirit of a man who made no excuses for his narcissism. Stepping out at Durand-Ruel's alternate entrance on Rue le Peletier, Ernest made his customary striking appearance. A fresh white rosebud in his impeccable lapel, his every movement was typically fluent and affirmative as he approached the freshly lacquered green doors, his top hat and elegant afternoon attire entirely appropriate to the arrival of the stylish, pace-setting proprietor of the most fashionable emporium in Paris.

For its second round of tactical maneuvers, the embattled Impressionist regiment had cleverly decided to close ranks by employing Durand-Ruel's Rue le Peletier entrance rather than the doors on Rue Laffitte. It was determined that although known as "Durand-Ruel's back door," this distinctively windowed Rue le Peletier entrance would better attract the Boulevard des Italiens and Boulevard des Capucines crowds who, in spite of shrinking francs, seemed unrelenting in their wish to explore at their leisure the delights of bright, nouveau Paris. Additionally, it was also felt that from the entrance at Number 11 Rue le Peletier, Durand-

Ruel's three gallery rooms flowed in better sequence for the planned exhibition. The decision was brilliant on both counts.

Thoughtfully displayed and well-organized, at Durand-Ruel's insistence the assembled two hundred fifty-two works, ninety-five by the core group, were arranged by artist and, once again, there was the addition of work by the same better recognized painters and sculptors who had exhibited in 1874. Cezanne did not show, nor did Guillaumin, but popular Beliard, Bureau, Lepic, Ottin, and Rouart, Cals, and de Nittis took a deep breath and signed on for a second round of fire, their courage in doing so duly noted by their beleaguered colleagues.

In the first room, paintings of what one critic called "the more aggressive" Impressionists were nowhere to be seen, but Berthe Morisot's works on paper were. The well-known Jean-Francois Millet exhibited his sepia drawings and ten watercolors in this room, as did the even better-known Desboutin who showed six dry-point engravings and seven paintings, one a portrait of none other than Monsieur Jean-Camille Faure himself, the famous baritone of the Paris opera grandly costumed as de Nevers in Meyerebeer's Les Huguenots.

It was in the second room, or Grand Salon, that Ernest saw the "aggressive" work, as the critics put it, of Renoir, Monet, Sisley, and Gustave Caillebotte, who was exhibiting for the first time, officially increasing the number of core group members to eight. It was also in this second room, in the midst of its fifteen Renoirs, nine Sisleys, eight Caillebottes, and eighteen Monets that Ernest realized his nemesis, Monsieur Faure, was not only the subject of the dominating Desboutin painting introducing the exhibition in its first room, but that he was more than a convenient catalyst. Unnerving Ernest to some considerable degree was the disturbing fact that Monsieur Jean–Baptiste Faure was the exhibition's biggest lender of Impressionist paintings. Of the seventeen Monet landscapes in the Grand Salon, Faure had loaned nine. In the third room, where the twenty-two Degas, twelve Pissarros, and fourteen Morisot paintings prevailed, Faure had loaned Degas' Examen de danse. Annoyed by Faure's competitive edge and having completed his survey of the entire exhibition, Ernest decided to take matters into his own hands. He had not loaned paintings, but he would buy, and he would buy the biggest and the best.

Ernest's taste once again, was impeccable, his eye drawn to what critics would soon call the sensations of the exhibition. They were Monet's La Japonnerie, a large figure painting of a blonde-wigged Camille Monet in a bright red embroidered kimono shown to great advantage along with Monet's seventeen landscapes in the Durand-Ruel Galleries Grand Salon and at 91x56 inches the largest piece in the second room, and attracting Ernest's added attention in the third room was Degas' Nouvelle Portraits dans un bureau-Orleans, (Portraits in an Office, New Orleans), a 28 X 36-inch painting later purchased by the City of Paris in 1878, depicting figures in the American New Orleans Cotton Exchange. Born in New Orleans, Louisiana, Edgar Degas had visited cotton exchange related family members there in 1875. In his scene of the Cotton Exchange his brother, Achille, his back to an open window, watches relatives and associates reading the newspaper and showing cotton to customers at a center table. These two paintings admired and placed on reserve by Ernest, both Monet's Japonniere and Degas' Portraits dans un bureau-Orleans garnered the most favorable critical attention and were, much to his delight, heralded by critics in print the undisputed stars of the show.

Days later, taking great pride in his artistic judgment, his confidence as a serious collector elevated to a high degree once he found professional critics in complete agreement with him, Ernest took on a fresh challenge. He decided he would begin to write critical articles on the Paris art world himself. And why not? Did he not have an eye for all that was newest and best? Durand-Ruel said he did, now the critics did, and did he not frequent the city's literary and art cafes, acquainting himself with the modern art world's true movers and shakers? The Guerbois may not have qualified as the café of choice to the inner circles of snobbish, silk-gloved art critics, but the most interesting artists of the day gathered there and he knew them all. He interacted with them, heard their voices and saw their faces in unguarded moments. He felt their struggle as if it was his own, and in ways unnoticed by the most closely followed critics, Ernest Hoschede alone seemed to have understood the great significance of their collective human presence at Durand-Ruel's on that opening day of 1876. In meetings at the Guerbois, he had witnessed several preliminary conversations regarding matters of preparation.

"We should dress well and look our best," Degas had announced to the group prior to opening day during a Guerbois meeting at which, as usual, his piece being stated, he stayed for only a short time. "I myself, shall wear a cloak, top hat, waistcoat, and silk cravat."

"I have neither cloak nor cravat," moaned Renoir. "I have no money to buy a top hat, and why should we dress so formally on opening day?"

"Pierre, look like an artist. Dress as you would to paint," Caillebotte suggested, ignoring Degas' plan for personal formality. "Even the black wool hat. Yes don't forget your hat!"

"Renoir, at least comb your hair!" Degas retorted at the door. "And Gustave, please loan him a decent shirt!"

No longer seen in print as "Le Societe anonyme cooperative des peintres, sculpteurs et graveurs," but as the artists of "La deuxieme exposition" (Artists of the Second Exhibition), the group was stunned to see itself as the subject of an unusual essay and review by the widely respected Edmond Duranty who took it upon himself to publish at his own expense a thirty-eight-page pamphlet in which he titled the Second Exhibition: "La nouvelle peinteur: A propos du groupe d'artistes qui expose dans le Galeries Durand-Ruel" (The New Painting: About the group of artists exhibiting at the Galeries Durand-Ruel.)

Duranty avoided the term, "Impressionism," altogether, focusing instead on what he chose to call "The New Painting," and realizing that for the first time that "the partition separating the artist's studio from everyday life was being eliminated, everything arranged as if the world had been created expressly for the delight of the eye, for the railways and notion shops, for construction scaffolds, lines of gaslights, benches on boulevards, newspaper kiosks, and restaurants with their tables set and ready. It goes without saying that some of these subjects have not been painted (by any artist)."

On opening day Durand-Ruel was pleased and excited, but openings always excited him. As far as he was concerned, few things in life compared to having planned hard and worked harder to mount an exhibition, especially in one's own galleries. To think about it, to weigh its attributes and faults, and finally to watch it coming together was a process unlike any other. "Fantastic!" he called it. "You hope for the best, expect the worst, remain open to all surprises, and suddenly there it is. Ready or not. Doors open. Good afternoon ladies and gentlemen! Welcome to the Durand-Ruel Galleries."

It was at times such as these and on days such as this that for all its unknowns and vagaries the devoted Street of Pictures dealer knew he loved his work passionately and that there was no other career in the world at which he could possibly have been happier. It was a difficult way to make a living he had to admit, and he did so often and aloud, but like the young lions he handled, struggles and difficulties aside, he had come this far and like them, was still standing. It was enough. For now. Always the well-turned out gentleman, he had dressed with particular care for this event in his own gallery rooms, a new black silk vest under his well-cut dark gray frock coat, a softly tied black grosgrain cravat at his pristine white collar, his pocket watch and its hallmark gold chain draped across his vest completing his grand toilette. By mid-afternoon he stood in a corner of the middle room and observed the proceedings, his thumb flicking at his watch chain, a small smile on his distinguished face. He looked pleased, and why not? It was going well.

From the moment the doors had opened attendance had been good. The unusually wide range of public response did not go unnoticed or unappreciated. Overall, people were curious, but many did appear confused. Some quickly grew unsettled and left displeased and uncertain, but regardless of their reactions, people were there. By four o'clock, about 200 bodies had come through the door, Durand-Ruel calculated. No sales and except for Ernest Hoschede no reserves, not yet, but people were more interested than they had been two years before. They lingered a bit longer, looked a bit more closely, and when they left a bit later and new clusters of the curious and uncertain took their places, the scene was repeated. It was enough. For now.

Except for Cezanne, the young lions had all turned out. Durand-Ruel had wondered about Degas and Morisot, but there they were, the two standing before Morisot's Laundresses Hanging Out the Wash. In black from head to toe, the stately Madame Morisot stood a head taller than Degas. She wore a stiff black hat shaped in a severe straight band across her forehead. In one hand she held a black lace fan which she dramatically and repeatedly snapped opened and closed, waving it across the planes and hollows of her beautifully chiseled face. Degas appeared pleasantly animated in his conversation with her, but Madame Morisot soon left his side to join her husband, Eugene, who arrived late in the day. Oddly enough and co-incidental to this Impressionist exhibition, Eugene's brother, Edouard Manet, was holding a Studio Exhibition of his own and Eugene had spent the earlier part of the day with him, doing his best to engage attendees and promote sales. Ernest did not understand the reason for this obviously conflicting event and apart from his regard for Edouard Manet as a friend of Impressionism, it's implication as a competing event would remain a memorable thorn in his side.

Durand-Ruel watched the young lions, intrigued by their mood and behavior, sensitive to their nervousness and need, hopeful yet ambivalent about their futures. As a group they would not succeed he soberly presumed, but individually some would. With repeated exposure, sooner or later the public would come around. He felt it, but as success came to some, others would tread the choppy water all their lives. Sisley, the confessed lover of generic atmosphere, would remain thematic and reserved, his work like his personality timid and pale overall, his life quietly, perhaps even monotonously lived. There was Gustave Caillebotte, talking to his elegantly dressed mother who had come to see her son's paintings, pride and a degree of uncertainty etched across every inch of her patrician face. Caillebotte wasn't hungry enough, Durand-Ruel observed. He had great talent. His work was precise and well-finished, but he didn't need anything. His father had left the family a fortune in excess of two million francs and right now, unlike his colleagues, Gustave lived with the great privilege of choice. Surprisingly simple in his tastes and thrifty in lifestyle, he was generous to his colleagues, buying their paintings whenever they needed financial assistance and paying their bills, but sooner or later the erratic play of life would require something more of Caillebotte, Durand-Ruel determined, and once and for all he would be forced to define his life circumstances. Edgar Degas was another story. Nothing would stop him. He was bitter and angry, difficult, and abundantly rude. Best of all, he was despicably arrogant and hatefully confident of his own artistic ability, which was immense. Degas was pushy, unlikable, and friendless, and just complicated enough to stay glued to the lonely course and win, but his dark side, his growing predisposition to pornography and prostitution was becoming too well known. He would have to watch that, but perhaps it was this dark side that in some secret way fueled his talent. Time alone would tell.

Pissarro had joined Monet and Renoir in conversation with Hoschede. Now there was a man who lived with no great rush toward greatness, but it would most certainly come to him. Pissarro was gentle and sensitive, the superb colorist who cared so much about the frames surrounding his pictures, much more about this detail than the others. Above all things in life, Camille Pissarro simply wanted to be left alone to paint at his home in Pointoise. Peace and a modest living would do, but those two talking to Ernest Hoschede, Monet and Renoir, they were the ones who had the great hunger to achieve, and on a big scale. Disarming and affable when they chose to be, both were enormously talented and tenacious, but of the two, Monet had developed attitude and posture and seemed to have made a steely pact with destiny. Yes, those two were driven and tireless. They would crawl on their bellies if need be, to be able to paint and do nothing else for the rest of their lives, but they were determined to succeed with their art and make a good living at it. Of them all, it was Monet, though, Durand-Ruel observed, who was the most solidly determined to stand his ground and carve out a successful career based on nothing more than his own merit and without Salon assistance. And it would happen. Of this Durand-Ruel had little doubt, and it would happen for Monet with or without support of his colleagues.

Overall, by exhibition's end, little had changed. Although the Second Exhibition attracted more attention in the Paris press than the First and a few distinguished literary figures such as Emil Zola were writing about the group, sales remained "cold" as Durand-Ruel summarily put it, and sales were what this was all about. Monet and Caillebotte received most of what little praise there was.

In Le Messager de l'Europe, Zola wrote, "One cannot doubt that we are witnessing the birth of a new school, (one that) in twenty years will transform The Salon from which today the innovators are excluded." Zola praised Monet's Japonnerie and La Prairie, but he found Caillebotte "too precise and as a result "anti-artistic. He likened Degas' New Orleans cotton exchange painting to an illustration intended for newspapers.

Emile Blemont, also known as Emile Petitdidier, writing for Le Rappel on April 9 differs with Zola, naming Caillebotte "a newcomer who will be given a warm welcome……full of truth, life, and a simple, frank intimacy. One of his paintings shown us here was not admitted by the (Salon) jury last year……a very bad mark for the official jury!"

Calling the exhibition "a cruel spectacle," Albert Wolff, writing for Le Figaro says the work "betrays a complete lack of artistic education and…..in no way represents aspects of the real world. The Rue Le Peletier is doomed to misfortune. First there was the terrible fire and now an exhibition of so-called paintings has opened at the Durand-Ruel Galleries. The innocent passer-by, attracted by the flags which adorn the face of the building may go in, and if he does, finds displayed to his affrighted eyes, a horrifying spectacle. "Five or six lunatics, of whom one is a woman; a group of unfortunates afflicted with the madness of ambition, have got together there to exhibit their works. ……… Pissarro has no understanding of color and Degas has no understanding of drawing or color."

In La Gazette of April eighth, Marius Chaumelin writes about Degas: "…he has an unfortunate weakness for pink-skirted dancers and yawning laundresses."

Two days later, also on Degas, Arthur Baigneres writes for L'Echo Universel: "Edgar Degas is perhaps one of the most intransigent of this Intransient Company."

"They depart from sacred formulas," writes Alexandre Pothey in La Presse, praising "the self-starting exhibition policy that merits encouragement by all interested in the modern movement of the Beaux-Arts."

A colleague of Blemont, Ernest d'Hervilly, writes on April first, also in Le Rappel which is known as an intransigent paper: "The Intransigents of Art are joining hands with the Intransigents of Politics. How completely natural!"

This from Emile Porcheron in Le Soleil on April fourth: "Morisot cannot draw and stops painting before she has finished. Pissarro's work is laughable because everything is blue. Caillebotte martyrs perspective. Monet's landscapes are unintelligible, and his Japonnerie merely plays a juggling game with screens." This also from Porcheron: "Pick out any motif and render what you see in any fashion whatever, and Impressionism will count one more follower."

Phillippe Burty, art editor for La Republique Francaise, praises the exhibition and for the first time there is at least one encouraging sign from a respected source. "The public are fired with a kind of tender interest in this group of honest, hard-working, original young artists," Burty writes, "men yearly victimized by the majority who bear tyrannous rule over the Salon, its entrance, and its rewards."

Ernest purchased paintings by Sisley and Pissarro. He very much wanted Monet's Japonnerie, the painting also called La Japonnaise but he waited too long and his time-restricted reserve with Durand-Ruel expired. For 2,000 francs ($400 U.S.) it went to yet another budding Paris collector of French Impressionist paintings, Arsene Houssaye, a novelist and poet.

Distressed by the reviews garnered by the Second Exhibition and seeing little hope of future success, Jean-Camille Faure surprised Ernest and much of art-loving Paris by promptly abandoning the Impressionists and turning his full collector attention to Edouard Manet, in a short time becoming his most important patron. In the following year, Manet would paint Faure's portrait as Hamlet. Change was coming, but slowly, painfully, and with great effort. "The days had yet to come when a picture (by any one of the young lions) could be sold in Berlin, bought back in Paris, and sold again in New York, all in the space of a few weeks," as Ambroise Vollard would write, reflecting on this 1876 period of pedantic uncertainty during a visit with the widowed Suzanne Manet many years later.

A Commission

As was her habit every year, before departing Paris for the summer months of 1876 Alice paid courtesy calls on close family members. First, and in an attempt to have it over and done with as quickly as possible, she dutifully called on Ernest's mother who, during these visits made no attempt whatsoever to inquire about her daughter-in-law's summer plans at Montgeron or those of her five grandchildren. The elder Madame Hoschede cared not at all about visiting at the Chateau Rottembourg and although invited repeatedly, she had never been there. Aspects of life at a chateau in the countryside were challenges to her imagination and in fact intimidated her, but she did find in in her heart to end each of her daughter-in-law's polite visits with a kiss on each of her cheeks and her usual request.

"When you return to Paris in the autumn do bring me some of that wonderful lemon curd you make out there in the country. It is delicious with our petites croissants at breakfast! You won't forget now, will you my dear? Au revoir."

Her first obligation completed, the next afternoon Alice called on Ernest's Cousin Beatrice, now well-established as Madame Marc Pirole. After the tiresome visit with Ernest's mother, Alice looked forward to Beatrice's far more amusing company. The two women had developed a close friendship and visited with one another on a regular basis. They attended plays and browsed the shops together, and although their tastes could be at opposite extremes, Beatrice did occasionally succeeded in impressing Alice with her originality.

"I have been married to Marc for more than ten years and I am trying very hard to understand his newly discovered love of simplicity," she moaned to Alice as in the drawing room of her newly decorated house she poured champagne and confided: "The darling man insists he loves me and the way I dress, which I am first to admit is far from simple, but Alice, lately when we are out at dinners or at the theater, he will notice an attractive woman and tell me how much he likes the understated style of her hair or the soft, delicate colors she's wearing. It's happening more and more often and I don't understand. I want Marc to be proud of me, but he knew when he married me that I was a little eccentric. Now look at this dress I'm wearing today. Don't you think the purple and pink stripes are flattering with my red hair?"

"The colors you're wearing look perfect in this house," Alice responded honestly and with typical tact, "and you must remember that Marc loves you exactly as you are. Beatrice, I'm a little more conservative than you are, but there are times when I can tell that Ernest isn't entirely thrilled with what I'm wearing. And let's be honest. We do make mistakes now and then, but we really are fortunate to be married to husbands who care about us and how we look."

Although a longtime friend to Alice and a highly agreeable companion, to the world at large, Beatrice Pirole was seen as a woman of more than mildly unconventional tastes, especially when it came to her wardrobe. She favored tight, low-cut bodices on brightly colored dresses and the largest, most outrageously feathered hats she could find, creations to which she was quick to add further enhancements: a contrasting colored feather or length of tulle here, a knot of lace there. Long ago, the fact that she rouged her cheeks and lips and never left home without one of her gold lorgnettes which dangled from a long chain around her neck and swung rhythmically from side to side across her ample breasts as she walked, had become accepted and generally overlooked by those who loved her and knew her best. To the casual observer, however, Beatrice Pirole could appear shocking and forward, even vulgar, but under all her gaudy charm and audacity, Alice understood and loved Beatrice as the kind, nurturing soul she truly was. She was sure Marc Pirole saw that same kindness and nurturing spirit in his wife and that he loved her for those qualities which showed themselves to greatest effect in the spirit with which she approached what she saw as her civic duties.

Every winter, Beatrice took part in a number of Paris charity events. Following Alice's example, she participated both generously and happily, her outlandish dresses, long, flaring coats, massive hats, and strong perfume the personal hallmarks which endeared her to all the prostitutes and assorted painted ladies of the evening who eagerly attended the city's charity rummage functions and with Beatrice's eager assistance found cheap, attractive cast-offs and not just a few opportunities for stealing the occasional red feathered boa or irresistible length of purple silk. With her bright smile and engaging manner, Beatrice could be counted on to look the other way and ignore a bit of stealing and pilfering, readily engaging the attention of her fellow ladies-bountiful as a remnant of blue satin or a yellow plume was quickly whisked away under a long billowing skirt or deftly tucked into a bodice or sleeve. That winter, however, Beatrice had been noticeably absent from the charity bazaar circuit. Returning to Paris following an extended trip to London and Italy, she and Marc had moved into their new house on Rue de Rome and since then, supervising its furnishing and decoration had been occupying much of Beatrice's time and energy. As the months had passed and installations in room after room of the Piroles' grand, three-story hotel particuleur were rumored to be complete, everyone who knew Beatrice even vaguely was eager for an invitation to Rue de Rome and the opportunity to see exactly what Marc Pirole's inherited fortune had purchased for his provocative wife's personal environment. Just days before departing Paris for Montgeron, Alice was among the first to be offered just such an opportunity, delighted to see not only the home her friend was creating with inimitable ostentation and dubious taste, but highly impressed by the painted wall panels which only the day before had been installed in Beatrice's dining room. Alice could talk of little else at dinner with Ernest that evening.

"You must see them, Ernest!" she remarked with unusual enthusiasm as she unfolded her napkin. "They're set beautifully into the dining room walls," she continued from the familiar comfort of her chair across the table from Ernest, "and the moldings around them make it seem they are truly part of the room. There are four. And you, my dear, are in for a surprise. I know you will find it hard to believe, but with these panels your cousin has managed to create a beautiful room even you will appreciate. All four panels are painted in flowers; colorful flowers in lovely urns; brilliant reds, vivid yellows and purples against bright green leaves and long, trailing dark brown and black branches. The compositions are wonderful. Ernest, I couldn't wait to tell you about them. I loved them."

Ernest listened attentively to his wife describe the most recent additions to his cousin's new home, in particular the painted wall panels in her dining room. He readily admitted to being curious, for although like Ernest, his Cousin Beatrice was also interested in all that was new and most cutting edge in Paris, she was not particularly interested in painting or art in general, nor was she interested in the people who created it. Much to Ernest's frequent amazement and considering her traditional upbringing, when it came to his Cousin Beatrice, the smallest modicum of sophisticated taste could be in short supply. Rooms overcrowded with dark, ornately carved furniture, persistently outrageous clothes, and the latest racy novels and plays were more to Cousin Beatrice's liking than were developments in the Paris world of art and culture. The addition of elegantly painted wall panels to the décor of her Paris residence seemed a distinct departure from what, over time, Ernest had come to call his dear Cousin Beatrice's "tortured taste."

"Marc arranged for them," Alice went on, taking a sip of wine. "Zolany painted them. It took four months. I told Beatrice I thought it was well worth the wait. She thinks so too. She said the compositions were inspired by Monsieur Furber's Twelve Months of Flowers and that Zolany probably took so long with them because, like Furber, he was probably on a twelve-month cycle. That made me laugh. You know Beatrice. She may have a few faults, but she does have a good sense of humor. Of course, Zolany did all the work at his studio. Beatrice says that from time to time, once she and Marc returned from London, she dropped in to check on Zolany's progress, but for some reason she was always made to feel she had interrupted a far more important project than her wall panels. She thinks it was probably a female nude Zolany was working on, a beautiful specimen who was quickly hidden behind the studio screen."

Alice laughed, her dark brown eyes soft and playful in the candlelight's warm glow, her thick chestnut hair drawn softly back and held with a black velvet band.

"Beatrice says Zolany is arrogant, self-promoting, the usual," she went on, capturing with her every word her husband's affectionate attention. "I remember meeting him at one of the Soutierres' dinner parties last winter. The man talked of nothing but himself. Now that I think of it, though, I remember Beatrice mentioning to me that Marc was commissioning "that marvelous Zolany" as she called him, to do some paintings for the new house, but at the time I took her to mean portraits, perhaps of her son James or Marc. Whatever the intention, I would never have expected to see what I saw today, not this sort of lovely thing. What would you think of painted wall panels for Rottembourg, perhaps in the drawing room rotunda? I've never really liked the mirrors we have on those four walls."

Ernest smiled and reached across the table for Alice's hand in the way he usually did when one of her ideas struck him as entirely within the realm of possibility. His mood was playful, his tone warm and loving. "Ah, my dearest, now I do believe there was a secret motive behind this especially delicious dinner," he said, leaning forward in his chair. "I know how you do these things when you decide to place another of your well-laid plans in the works. You tempt me with something like this perfection of turbot in delicate beurre blanc and for dessert the apple pudding you know I love. You're an expert, Alice, but of course I am always your willing victim. With no contest I'll make it easy and surrender immediately. I'll gladly pay my cousin a visit and have a look at those panels, but I must say it's hard to believe they're as well done as you say. If you liked them, though, my love, your wish is my command. I'll talk to Durand-Ruel about the feasibility of a similar project for Rottembourg. It's a good idea, though. Yes, for the rotunda, and I agree with you about the mirrors we have in there now. I've never really liked them either. Durand-Ruel will recommend a suitable painter. But we won't be dealing with Zolany. He's a good copyist, but we don't need copies of seventeenth-century flowers in urns. We should have original landscapes depicting views of our own country property. Durand-Ruel will suggest someone, perhaps Sisley or Caillebotte. I have an appointment with him tomorrow. We'll see. I wonder how much Marc paid Zolany? I suppose my darling, you were too polite to ask? Of course. Too bourgeois, too non-Raingo. Mustn't discuss anything as tawdry as money. I hate to admit it, darling, but I do understand."

As had been the case from the moment of their first meeting and throughout their courtship and twelve-year marriage, it was often Alice's suggestions that mollified Ernest's most extreme thinking, especially when it came to his innovations at the store. The two were a good match, he a forward thinking, risk-taking man, she more traditional and seriously grounded. His tastes and interests seldom languished in the past. Hers were built on the strengths of proven history and visual experience. He remained constantly alert to all that was new and different around him and he adored Alice, but of the two, Ernest himself realized that Alice was the more practical and the imminently more tactful. He also realized that Alice ran her two houses with efficiency and a sense of order, but that with her children, her guard was often down. With them she was the innovative, spontaneous parent. She allowed them the run of the house, she played noisy games with them and was their best, most attentive audience. She laughed at their antics, often joined in the fun, and on a stormy day was first to pull out the play chests filled with assorted out- of-fashion adult clothing and hats which turned into costumes for the plays they wrote and enacted together as rain or snow pelted against the windows. She encouraged them to make up rhymes and songs for one another and they were taught to read and love books at early ages. Alice relished card games and taught the children to play Whist and Lanterlu. She gave them piano lessons and encouraged their creativity, inventiveness a quality she admired in others but one with which despite her Raingo family's highly creative accomplishments, she often struggled herself. The idea for painted panels at the Chateau Rottembourg had not come about as a departure from Alice's normally conservative approach to matters of art, nor had the idea grown out of her indulgent patience with Beatrice Pirole. The idea had come from her admiration of ingenuity, not so much in herself, but in others. That over time she had come to observe this distinct quality of ingenuity in everything about Beatrice Pirole however objectionable, was entirely consistent with Alice's personality. She often looked to the examples of others upon which to embellish and call her own. Enthusiastic admiration for Beatrice's painted wall panels being a rare departure from Alice's quietly dismissive position when it came to all matters Beatrice Pirole and well aware of his wife's attitudes, the very next day a typically curious Ernest paid his respects to Cousin Beatrice. Carefully making his way through the complicated maze of furniture and piles of bric-a-brac she had managed to squeeze into every available corner of her new home and politely commenting most favorably as he went, he complimented her on the Zolany panels in the dining room, paintings which sincerely impressed him, so much so, that following an unusually affectionate good-bye, he headed directly to see Paul Durand-Ruel, this time prepared not to purchase a painting, but to offer a commission.

"Perhaps you would be good enough to recommend someone from the New Group to paint views of the property at Montgeron," he proposed to Durand-Ruel, his enthusiasm for the project growing. "The gardens, the lawns, perhaps the pond or the view from the meadow. Yes, my wife loves that view of the house. Four panels for the rotunda drawing room should suffice, each one about six feet high, I'd say. And two or three weeks in August would be my preference for the studies, a bit longer and into autumn if necessary to complete the panels, and as you know, Monsieur, everything in the Brie is at its best in August, the trees, the flowers, the whole of the Brie Valley. I have been considering Alfred Sisley, who has been out to Montgeron and loves the property, or even Edouard Manet who has also visited us. I would ask my country neighbor Jean DeLille, but he makes a very good living with portraits and confesses to having no feeling whatsoever for landscape painting. What do you think?"

"This is a wonderful idea and of course I would be delighted to assist you in such an interesting project," Durand-Ruel responded, "but Monsieur Hoschede, forgive me for saying this, but I feel I must. Monsieur Edouard Manet would never entertain a commission. There is no need for him to do so. He could feel insulted. If I were you, I would ask for a personal favor and approach him as a friend. That would be the better way. As for Monsieur Sisley, he is off to England for the summer. He was here a few days ago, very much looking forward to painting in the British countryside. I do not think he plans to return to France much before October if you could wait until then. I'm expecting some good work from him by autumn."

"You're right about Edouard Manet," Ernest said. "I was far too presumptuous to suggest he accept a commission from me, but he is a friend and I do have five of his paintings. He did some amusing painting for Carolus Duran during visits with us at Rottembourg last summer; parrots on several drawing room doors, but in that instance it was just as you say, friend to friend. I won't bother him with this. And of course, by October, we are back in Paris, so Alfred Sisley is not a consideration. That's it then. Monsieur Durand-Ruel, I will leave it to you. You know me and my tastes well enough to find the right painter. Scenes of the property do seem appropriate. Please let me know what you are able to arrange."

"And what will you pay, Monsieur Hoschede?" Durand-Ruel inquired.

"Four thousand francs," Ernest answered, "one thousand francs per panel, and we will provide a place to stay, of course. There's a small lodge by the river. It belongs to Alice's uncle. Charming place, but he uses it only in July before going up to Trouville for August and most of September. Of course we'll take care of food and all the rest, and Alice will send our houseman, Bernard, to help look after things every day. He'll take care of bed linen and laundry, and tidying up, all that sort of thing. Yes, August is the best time, and I'll be spending more time in the country myself this summer, especially in August. The hunting is very good then. And whoever you recommend Monsieur, do tell him that we take good care of our guests."

"Very good, Monsieur Hoschede. I shall let you know what I've been able to arrange," Durand-Ruel confirmed, accompanying Ernest to the door. "Give me a few days. Everyone is scattering at this time of the year. Can you come in on Thursday of next week? I should have someone to suggest to you by then and who knows, perhaps a painting or two for you to consider."

The next day, Claude Monet traveled to Paris by train from his home at Argenteuil. He carried with him two paintings he desperately hoped Durand-Ruel would accept for an advance of three hundred francs. He was behind in the rent. Three months this time.

CHAPTER 10

The Dawn Lover
June 9, 1876

Through much of April and May, skies over towns and villages west of Paris had dawned dismal and gray, but now in June, after weeks of warm sunshine, the countryside from Val d'Oise and south to Montmagny and Seine-en-Marne was a blanket of tender green. The flourishing landscape rushing past just outside his window in the course of the short train ride from Argenteuil into the city should have lifted his spirits, but as verdant woodlands and moss-covered riverbanks were left farther and farther behind, Claude Monet remained stone-faced and silent. The pressures of everyday life were interfering and distracting him......again. His rent unpaid for three months, his landlady was threatening eviction. Formidable Madame Aubrey-Vitet had given her delinquent tenant twenty-four hours to comply with the terms of his lease which clearly required payment of 100 francs ($20 U.S.) by the tenth day of every month.

Earlier on that June morning, oblivious to the slightest sign of urgency and fully concentrated on his painting, thirty-five-year-old Claude Monet was quite unprepared for confrontations and their potential consequences. Anticipating nothing more than another precious set of hours at his easel, his day had begun as it would every day of his life. At dawn.

A disciplined working painter driven by encounters with color and contrast, the child born Oscar-Claude Monet in 1840 was diligent and curious by nature. Now, in his mid-thirties, he was also a creature of habit, but it was not the creature of habit in Claude Monet that awakened him every morning to the marvel of breaking dawn. It was the sensory anticipation of beholding nature at work as in one instant a fiery blaze ignited a not quite blackened sky and in the next an aimless phantom mist toyed endlessly with the confounding twists and turns of the eternal mystery called weather. In all its fickle incarnations, dawn was a sorcerer's tale to Claude Monet, for in the half-light birthing of each new day it embodied the marvels of nature and the tantalizing promise of absorbing hours locked in his palette world of tint and texture.

June Ninth's dawn did not disappoint. Nature's great diva stepped onto her waiting stage in a burst of golden brilliance untouched by dulling gray mists or threatening banks of clouds. Encouraged by wondrous flashes of gilded amber and lucent pinks streaking across the muted sky, by six he was at his easel in the makeshift studio he had created in the smallest room of his house. By seven, his encounters with floating veils of color were going well, very well in fact, that is until about eight when Madame Aubrey-Vitet barged into the silent voyage across his imperceptible universe. If her intention was to terminate his journey and embarrass him she could not have managed her intrusion much better.

"Monsieur Monet, by this time tomorrow morning you and your family will be out on the street!" she barked from the doorway, abruptly cutting into the fragile prospect of composition developing on his canvas. "And don't try to pass off another of those strange paintings of yours in exchange for the rent you owe me! Keep them! Monsieur Monet, I want my three hundred francs! You have twenty-four hours!"

Six short months before, a very different Madame Aubrey-Vitet had cordially welcomed Monsieur Monet, his pretty wife Camille and their young son Jean to the brown-shingled house on Boulevard Saint-Denis in the picturesque village of Argenteuil, enthusiastically pointing out its garden, its fine view to the river and convenient proximity to the railroad station directly across the boulevard, clearly proud of the manner in which she maintained the property and those nearby which had been left to her by her late husband, a former mayor of Argenteuil.

A rural village perched on a gentle bend in the Seine just twelve kilometers west of Paris, Argenteuil was a popular Sunday destination for city dwellers attracted to its riverside setting. It was also an ideal home for a working painter like Claude Monet who, in every season of the year, found inspiration along its riverbanks, inlets, and marshes, attempting to earn his livelihood by applying their unassuming themes and infuriating variations of light and shade to canvas.

At first Madame had shown great interest in the paintings neatly lining the pale green walls of the small room Monsieur Monet had quickly converted into a studio. Gushing with compliments and suggesting she would like very much to own one or two of his paintings, she had gladly accepted one of the landscapes Claude offered as payment for two months' rent. Now, Madame was neither gushing nor glad. Her threatening notices slipped under the Monet door with annoying regularity having been completely ignored, a third consecutive month's rent unpaid, Madame had had quite enough of this Monsieur Claude Monet and his failure to abide by the terms of his lease. Wagging her finger as she stood in the doorway to his improvised haven there was no mistaking the nature of consequences she was prepared to enact. Unquestionably, the woman was no one to trifle with, but as she launched into a humiliating tongue-lashing Madame Aubrey-Vitet also managed to suggest a practical remedy.

"Monsieur Monet, do not misunderstand," she stated in her icy tone. "I do not want to evict you and your family, but you leave me no choice. Yes, I want my three-hundred francs and that amount must be paid by this time tomorrow, but you must face facts, and soon. Your wife and son are suffering. It's pitiful! Your little boy is so thin! He needs shoes and a hot meal and I have never seen your wife with a smile on her face. She looks so pale and tired. Monsieur, you are living in a dream world. You cannot continue with this ridiculous painting. No one wants your pictures. Take my advice. The new match factory right here in Argenteuil is hiring. Why don't you apply for employment there? Its steady work. The world will always need matches."

An hour later and muttering, "damn that evil woman!" and "match factory indeed!" a furious Claude Monet hurried from the brown-shingled house on Boulevard Saint-Denis to the railroad station across the street where, with only seconds to spare, he boarded the nine o'clock train to Paris. With him, wrapped in brown paper fastened with string, he carried two of his paintings. It was year-old work, two scenes of Argenteuil railway bridges he hoped his dealer, Paul Durand-Ruel, would accept for the desperately needed advance of three-hundred francs.

Searching for a seat on the crowded train, he was breathing hard. His landlady's assessment of him as an artist had so unnerved him that once she had said her piece and left him to confront the very real prospect of being put out on the street, he had immediately abandoned his easel to quickly change his clothes and wrap the two paintings he had carried on his race to the nine o'clock train. And it was not only the hateful woman's humiliating opinion of him as an artist that had incensed him. Her mortifying assessment of him as a negligent husband and father continued to ring in his ears, the offensive suggestion that he give up painting altogether and seek employment at the local match factory a blistering insult that for the fifty-one years of life remaining to him he would never find in his heart to forgive.

As in blasts of whistles and puffs of steam the train inched slowly away from the Argenteuil station, he sat back, lit a cigarette and blew a slow, languid cloud of smoke into the air. His paintings placed on the floor beside him set firmly against one knee, he ignored the talkative young man seated next to him and stared straight ahead, immobile and indifferent. His ego badly bruised, on a train speeding toward Paris, Claude Monet remained angry and deeply offended, yet he had taken great care with two things that mattered to him: his paintings and his appearance.

The dark brown leather boots he had worn the day before to tie up the young clematis vines in his muddy garden had been quickly polished to a high gleam. His lighter brown worsted jacket and yellow flannel vest, although far from new, were immaculate and of a stylish, almost rakish cut. His dense black beard and mustache were neatly trimmed and under the narrow-brimmed brown hat he had quickly placed well back on his head, his short, curly hair, also thick and black, had not been left to its unruly devices. It was neatly parted and combed. But for his stony expression and complete silence, not one of his fellow passengers would have guessed that the man in the yellow vest sitting by the window was in one of his darker moods.

It was after ten o'clock when after routine stops at Chailly-en-Beuces and a long delay at La Garenne-Columbes he stepped off the train and joined the crowds swirling through the Saint-Lazare station. Arriving from his home in bucolic Argenteuil, the jarring sights and sounds of urban Paris always startled him, but he loved the startling; loved the crowds, the colors, the noise. Making his way to the Rue d'Amsterdam exit, he set out on foot toward his destination which was the central district of grand avenues and boulevards marked by The Louvre, The Tuileries Gardens, and the glittering new Paris Opera. He had some distance to go, but Claude Monet was a man who walked a lot and for long distances. Sometimes, lacking the ten centimes for train fare and carrying a painting or two, he walked the twelve kilometers from Argenteuil to Paris, returning home before nightfall, also on foot.

Transferring his packages from one hand to the other, he set his typically brisk pace, his uncompromising eye sweeping over the cityscape, his entire being delighting in the beauty of nouveau Paris. He admired the uniformity of its rooflines, the charm of its romantic balconies, and at every turn the delightful punctuation of splashing fountains, monuments, and colorful borders of flowers. Reaching tree-lined Boulevard des Italiens, he turned onto the Street of Pictures. Entering the green doors at Number 16 he found Paul Durand-Ruel seated at his desk, He was reading the latest edition of Le Figaro.

"Ah, Claude! What a nice surprise," the habitually cordial dealer said, rising from his chair with a smile. "I'm catching up on the London art news. Have you read the series of articles Le Figaro is running on the Elgin Marbles? It's an interesting fight. Greece wants the Parthenon sculptures returned and the British Museum says absolutely not! Looks like a war between museum directors. I wouldn't want to be part of that! And what do you have for me in those packages? Something more palatable than a museum war I hope."

"I'm behind on the rent," Claude stated in a near whisper as with great care he slowly unwrapped his packages, revealing the two paintings of Argenteuil, "and my landlady is threatening eviction. She will not allow another grace period. Monsieur, please take these paintings and say you will advance me three-hundred francs on them. I know my sales have not been good lately, but if I don't pay the landlady three hundred francs by tomorrow morning, Camille, and I will be out on the street with young Jean."

It was a familiar tale. Paul Durand-Ruel had heard it dozens of times from dozens of artists, but on this particular morning the resourceful dealer found himself in a position not only to provide an immediate solution to the pressing financial problem at hand, he also found himself in a position to present an attractive offer.

"Don't worry, Claude. Everything will be fine," the seasoned dealer said with a reassuring nod, examining the two scenes of Seine railway bridges. "I will take these paintings and advance you three-hundred francs, but today I also have an attractive proposition for you, one that will mean a good sum of money which could hold you for a while. Your patron, Monsieur Ernest Hoschede, wishes to have four large wall panels painted for a rotunda in his country house at Montgeron. He has asked me to recommend someone from your group to go out to the property in August as artist in residence to paint them. He wants scenes of the property, four landscapes. Claude, I thought of you immediately. Landscapes are what you're becoming known for. It's a perfect situation for you and conditions couldn't be more suitable. The Hoschede property is rich in the natural beauty you interpret so easily. Your eye will quickly find its focus. Beyond that, Ernest Hoschede is no stranger to you. You will be comfortable in his home environment and with his family. But here is the best part: he is offering four thousand francs for the four panels."

The long pause before Claude responded was hardly what Durand-Ruel had expected. More vexing were the excuses that followed.

"Monsieur Durand, since we met in London during the war you have encouraged my work," Claude finally began to explain, "and I appreciate your faith in me, but no, no commissions. Not now. I am very sorry, but I must decline the offer. I have a number of Argenteuil subjects to complete and in August, Pierre Renoir and I will be off to paint together at Bougival. Added to this, Camille has not been feeling well. I'm worried about her. If her health does not improve by August even Renoir and Bougival will have to wait."

Paul Durand-Ruel had not achieved his distinguished reputation by taking every opposing view he heard from a contentious artist at face value. As the professional he was, of course he wanted to sell and make money, but he also knew the value of exercising his gift for recognizing raw talent and fostering its potential with more than a little conviction.

"Claude, I understand the pressure you must be under right now," he began, choosing his words carefully. "The threat of being put out of one's home is terrible, but that problem is solved. Now, though, you have the responsibility of thinking ahead. I needn't remind you that rent will be due again next month and the month after. At the same time there will be the normal expenses that any family must meet. Claude, Ernest Hoschede's offer is the answer to fulfilling a number of your needs. I know how committed you are to completing work at home in Argenteuil. I also know how much you must be looking forward to painting alongside your friend, Pierre Renoir. All true artists would want to do those same things, but you cannot step away from this opportunity. Think of it! Ernest Hoschede is a passionate collector of your work and a strong supporter of your group. When I show him these two paintings of Argenteuil bridges I feel confident he will buy them, but how shall I tell him that when I presented his offer of four-thousand francs to paint four panels for him that you refused, preferring to pursue work both on your own and with a friend, and work I might add, that cannot guarantee the immediate amount of four-thousand francs in the palm of your hand. Claude, you must be practical! Think of it! A few weeks in the heart of the French countryside while you're paid to paint! The Brie Valley at the peak of its summer beauty, and did I fail to mention your own cottage by the river, food, and whatever else you may need? Frankly, I don't understand this reluctance of yours. If I could paint the way you do, I'd accept the Hoschede commission myself."

"But why must I travel out to Montgeron to paint the panels? I can paint them at home. And what exactly are the subjects Monsieur Hoschede has in mind?"

"It is as I said," Durand-Ruel quickly replied. "Four views of the property. He will likely leave it to you to find your subjects and you will have no difficulty there. First of all, the grounds of the Chateau Rottembourg will inspire you. There is a grotto and a pond, acres of lawns, beautiful gardens, and then there are the roses the Brie Valley is famous for. Madame Alice Hoschede grows at least a dozen varieties. She would, of course, be your hostess. I have met her on several occasions. She is a lovely woman, devoted to her husband and their five children. It may not have come up in your conversations with Monsieur Hoschede, but Madame Hoschede is a descendant of the Raingo family. I'm sure you've heard of them. The Raingo Brothers were, and to some degree still are, the famous Paris clockmakers known across Europe for creating beautiful, high quality pieces. And a lot of money. The current generation owns blocks of Paris real estate and a string of country houses. Claude, the entire situation with the Hoschedes is positive on every level. They could be so influential, so helpful to you. As to a reason for painting the panels at the chateau and not at your home, there is the matter of size. I understand each panel is to be about six feet in height. Transport of such completed canvases from where you live at Argenteuil to the Chateau Rottembourg would be costly and risky at best. The work should be done there, on site, the studies, even the finished work completed at Montgeron where it will stay. I am willing to send the canvas you will need and Monsieur Hoschede has said he will provide whatever supplies you may require. Anything at all. He is prepared to set up an account for you at Amalie's. You will be able to go there and buy paint, charcoal, sketch paper, everything you need. Claude, take this on. Do it."

Silent in the subdued light of the Street of Pictures gallery he knew well, Claude appeared composed and thoughtful. Not at all ready to concede and submit to his dealer's reasoning, he was not finding the idea of a painting project at a rich man's country retreat particularly appealing, but as befitting a contentious, controversial artist who had declared war on the establishment, his mind was racing, his imagination hard at work. He argued back and forth with himself. He liked Hoschede. He appreciated his patronage, but how could he consider the proposed commission? What good would it do him? Four six-foot panels hidden away in a remote country house would do nothing to promote his career. Who would see them? It was ridiculous. And wall panels? Renoir would split his sides with laughter. On the other hand, Durand-Ruel was right to point out the cold realities of life. He thought of the paleness and fatigue Madame Aubry-Vitet had noticed in Camille. He was well-aware of them himself. Clearly, Camille was not well. She needed a doctor and medicine, but there was no money for such things, neither was there money for the butcher or the green grocer or the fish monger, and there was nine-year-old Jean. He needed shoes and proper clothes for the school year ahead and that was another worry. Tuition had to be paid and the headmaster had said he would no longer accept paintings in exchange for tuition payments. Then of course, there was always the matter of painting supplies. It was endless. Rent, food, school, clothes, art supplies, a doctor, medicine. He alone was responsible for his wife Camille and their son Jean and his only source of income came from his paintings which weren't selling. As a family how could they live without money? He couldn't keep asking Durand-Ruel for advances. There were limits to the man's generosity. Finally, against all his firmly set principles he concluded that in this instance he should forget his pride and indulge a patron. Perhaps it was as Durand-Ruel had said and Hoschede did indeed hold a key to the future.

"It is not as you say, an opportunity, Monsieur Durand. It is a necessity," he finally managed to say. "I have no choice. Yes, please let Monsieur Hoschede know I accept his commission. Four thousand francs for four panels. I can be at Montgeron in early August. Two weeks for the studies, two or three more for the finished work, and I would like one thousand francs as a first step in solidifying our agreement."

"Wonderful! Durand-Ruel quickly said. "I'm sure there will be no problem with the thousand francs, "and Claude, you are making the right decision. I'm very happy for you, and of course I'm delighted for Monsieur Hoschede. I'll make all the arrangements. Come back to the gallery in a week or so. By then I'll have your train tickets and travel information. As I think about it, perhaps you'd like to come into Paris a day or so early and meet with a few of your friends. If you like, you can stay here overnight. There's a cot in the back room. It's not Le Manoir or Le Raphael, but it's free."

From that day forward, through what remained of June and into the month of July, thoughts of the journey to the Chateau Rottembourg nagged at him relentlessly. In a rush of distracting moments when he was painting in the garden or aboard his studio boat lazily exploring the river's inlets and sheltered coves, he questioned the wisdom of his decision in accepting Ernest Hoschede's commission. He had agreed too readily, he told himself again and again. He had been too needy. The four-thousand franc fee Durand-Ruel had dangled before him had seduced him. But he needed the money. There was no question of that, but he had also needed time to think through what the money required of him. He would be away from home for at least four weeks, depending on how long the studies would take. He would miss Jean, and he would worry about Camille. She didn't complain, but lately she was not herself. She seemed tired so much of the time. A number of household tasks she normally attended to with prompt attention went ignored. For the past week or so, the day's used plates and cups were left unwashed and haphazardly stacked by the wash basin. She was just not the same vivacious Camille he had loved for years. She needed his watchful care and for the better part of a month he would be at a country chateau in the company of wealthy, selective people and their circle of family and friends who very likely looked down on struggling artists, pitying their condition, assessing their need, and smugly evaluating their own superiority. He would feel compromised and alone. It would be difficult to work under such circumstances. He wouldn't do his best. The four wall panels would fail. They would fail to please him and they would fail to please Ernest Hoschede.

As the summer sped away, his feelings of regret were endless. He endured long periods of self-doubt and moments of genuine trepidation, and as the August departure date loomed ever closer, apprehension remained a constant companion; unabated, dark, and tolerated in complete secret. On the surface and on occasion to Camille, it seemed a simple act to say that he had not wanted to change his summer plans at all, but that in a weak moment he had given in to the powerful allure of money. He reprimanded himself for not setting his own agenda and naming his own terms. He told himself that four thousand francs was not enough for four large paintings. Ernest Hoschede could afford to pay much more. Besides, all through the cold winter, he had looked forward to summer at Argenteuil. It was the best time of year for painting. The natural landscape provided a generous array of subject matter. The full-leafed oaks and tall silver maples, the emerald green grasses, the dense mossy riverbanks, the early morning sunlight dappled in shaded hues of purple, green, and burnished gold strewn across the river, all nature's richness awaited his brush and palette. Why was it that summer passed so quickly, so effortlessly and thoughtlessly into a season of chilled meadowlands and cloistered hillsides? He should have declined Hoschede's offer. It was all wrong. In agreeing to its terms as he had so quickly with Durand-Ruel, he should have insisted on bringing Camille and Jean with him. He should have insisted on greater clarity regarding subject matter. He should have insisted on more money. He should have insisted on painting the panels at home in Argenteuil. And so, the quandary went on and on until the very last minute.

CHAPTER 11

The Gare de Lyon
August 1876

An amber dawn was breaking over Argenteuil's rooftops as he sat at the edge of the bed to say goodbye to Camille. He kissed her cheek.

"Au revoir, my dearest love," he whispered, stroking her hair. "The time we are apart will pass quickly and when I return our lives will be so much better. You must remember that and you must remember how much I love you."

Ignoring Claude and his endearments, Camille stirred under the blue quilt and turned away. She hadn't wanted him to go.

"Three weeks is too long for you to be gone," she had insisted the night before as she stood watching him pack two suitcases, one with clothes, the other with supplies. "Jean and I need you here. By the time you come back, summer will be over and Jean will be starting school. The boy needs his father. You've spent too little time with him this summer and Claude, surely you know you're not leaving me enough money for food. These few francs won't last a week. I worry that Jean isn't getting enough to eat as it is. Please don't go. You could bring Monsieur

Durand-Ruel another painting or two for another advance. He likes your work."

Claude understood Camille's personal concerns and he shared them. At the same time he also felt the desperate need for money, but he couldn't go to Paul Durand-Ruel again as Camille was suggesting. In just a matter of a few weeks between May and July, the Street of Pictures dealer had advanced him more than a thousand francs. Enough was enough.

"Camille, my darling, Monsieur Durand-Ruel's gallery is not a bank. I cannot continue to take an endless stream of advances from him," Claude had said, closing the two suitcases with a firm snap. "He's generous and kind to me, but right now my paintings aren't selling and he is making no money on me. In a short time Monsieur Hoschede's four thousand francs will be mine with no strings attached. My darling, please be patient. It's only three or four weeks. I will receive a thousand francs when I arrive at the Chateau Rottembourg and I will send it to you immediately through Gustave Caillebotte. Your worries will be over. You will be able to buy all the food you and Jean need, even a few of those beautiful chouquettes you love. Gustave is spending the summer with his family at Yerres which is the village closest to Montgeron but he comes into Paris every two weeks or so. I have talked to him and he promises to bring you the money as promptly as possible. I trust him and you should too."

"But you will be leaving me alone again," Camille insisted, facing her husband squarely. "Claude, I want us to live like a normal family. The way things are now you leave me alone here all the time. When you aren't painting in the barn or on the studio boat, you're either painting at Bougival or Fountainbleau or you're in Paris meeting with your friends and visiting with Monsieur Durand-Ruel. When you come home you're tired and need rest. There's no time for Jean and me. Now, you're disappearing again. I know we need money, but this is not the way I want us to live!"

"My dearest, I wish it could be different, and one day it will be," Claude said, taking Camille in his arms and holding her close, "but you must remember that Monsieur Hoschede is a loyal patron of mine and a well-connected man. He could be very helpful in promoting me. When I return, how would you like to go up to Trouville for a few days? The weather will still be good in September and there are places near the beaches that by then we'll be able to afford. I remember how much you liked Trouville when we were there just after our wedding. Of course we'll take Jean. He'll miss a few days of school, but the headmaster will understand. I'll pay the tuition and tell him that due to unforeseen circumstances our summer plans were delayed. Please think of Trouville while I'm gone."

The next morning he hesitated twice at the door, each time leaving his suitcases and returning to the bedroom to sit at the edge of the bed and again assure his beloved Camille that he was doing the right thing for them; that the painting project at Montgeron would solve their financial problems; that very soon there would be enough money to pay for adequate food, and that once the Hoschede panels were completed they would enjoy a fine holiday at Trouville.

"Four thousand francs will change everything," he said as Camille remained sulking and motionless under the blue quilt. "Please remember that, but I must go now. Au revoir, my love," Claude repeated for what seemed the hundredth time.

Heavy-hearted but convinced he was doing the right thing, he finally returned to the front door, grasped the handles of his two suitcases, and in long, firm strides made his way across the street to the train station and the start of a journey that would take him into Paris and from the Gare de Lyon to the country village of Montgeron.

Someday it would be about summer fruit, he thought as he waited to board. Someday it would be about apricots. Or green apples. Simple things. A few bananas ripening in a bowl. Someday it wouldn't be about money and all its complications, he promised himself as forty minutes later he stepped off the train from Argenteuil and into the swirling Paris crowd.

"Your train will depart the Gare de Lyon for Montgeron at one-fifteen on the afternoon of August fourth," Durand-Ruel had told him in July when another advance was granted on two paintings of the Seine and the Paris-Montgeron travel schedule was discussed, "and Claude, there will be no need for you to purchase a ticket," the well-satisfied dealer announced with a smile. "I'm happy to tell you that Monsieur Hoschede will be there to meet you under the clock at the Gare de Lyon at one o'clock. He'll take care of everything. He wants to accompany you to Montgeron as his guest. It's a good idea. I'm so glad he suggested it. On the train you'll have the opportunity to relax with one another and discuss subject matter for the panels. Claude, by the time your train arrives at the Montgeron station I predict you'll have the four panels well thought through. And Claude, one more thing: Monsieur Hoschede may be a bit a few minutes late, but don't let that bother you. He has a tendency to squeeze too much into one day. Of course you know what he looks like, but if there is any confusion, which I strongly doubt there will be, just look for the best-dressed gentleman in the station. He'll have a white rosebud in his lapel and will likely be carrying one of those beautiful blue boxes from the Dore. His youngest daughter, Germaine, loves the Dore's Peach Croustades and he never disappoints her. You'll find each other. I have no doubt of it," Durand-Ruel assured Claude further, making a seemingly extraordinary effort to explain the arrangements with crystal-clear clarity. Pleased with what he saw as Claude's improved attitude and pleased as well with himself for having successfully arranged this encouraging turn of events for both a struggling painter and a supportive client he smiled once again as from his money clip he counted out not the three-hundred francs Claude had expected, but five-hundred, handing the generous advance to the impoverished leader of the beleaguered renegade independents whose recent Second Exhibition had gone only slightly better than its first and whose fortunes showed absolutely no sign of improvement.

It was during this same July meeting with Durand-Ruel that Claude had agreed to the suggestion that he come into Paris a day early and meet with friends for dinner, acceptance of his dealer's invitation to spend the night on the cot in the back room one that waiting for Ernest Hoschede in the Gare de Lyon the next afternoon he deeply regretted. It was true that despite the city's soaring temperatures he had enjoyed meeting with Edouard Manet and Francis Sartorious at the Nouvelle Athenee, even finding he could laugh with them at the ridiculous state of la vie boheme and the notorious goings-on in La Ruche, the Montparnasse oasis which could always be counted on to provide tasty news of the most recent Paris debauchery, but Manet and Sartorious had not spent the night on a narrow cot in the sweltering back room of Durand-Ruel's gallery. Now, after enduring an inhumanely high degree of overheated, sleepless misery in hours of utter darkness and thoroughly convinced his dealer kept that relic of an army cot on hand to purposely discourage long-term boarders, the sturdily built but aching Claude

Monet decided it was a far more desirable torment to suffer the pain in one's back and stand upright on one's own two feet in the stifling heat of the crowded Gare de Lyon.

He thought of his soft bed at home and the cool refreshing breezes billowing up from the river through the open windows on warm summer nights. He pictured his studio boat peacefully afloat at its mooring, rocking to and fro in the deep, lazy basin of the Seine. Leaning against the wall supporting the Lyon's clock and closing his eyes, he imagined the sunlit shoreline he had explored time and again at Argenteuil's Porte Saint-Denis, it's every detail as clear and colorful as if he were actually there, the fleets of yawls, skiffs, dinghies and ketches of every shape and size crisscrossing the dancing water in a panorama of which he never tired. He stepped back, looked up to the clock, lit a cigarette, and loosened his collar. Twelve-fifteen. He had a little less than an hour to wait. Pacing back and forth once again, he blew smoke into the steaming air. He tried to concentrate on thoughts of colors and textures, shadings and patterns, but overwhelming his every thought, try as he might, he could not put the image of Camille out of his mind. Her cheek had felt waxy and oddly hot by the time he had finally succeeded in kissing her good-bye, but she would be fine. Of course. He was sure of it. Jean was a responsible boy. He loved his mother. He would look after her.

It was good of Durand-Ruel to have encouraged the Hoschede commission, he thought to himself as still pacing up and down under the Gare de Lyon's impressive clock he watched an attractive young woman pushing a baby pram, but having a patron like Ernest Hoschede occasionally join his group around the table at a rundown café in Montmartre was one thing. At least at the Café Guerbois there were other people around. There was talking and plenty of noise and just outside the windows there were the distractions of busy workaday Avenue de Clichy. People walked by. The pretty girls could be admired. Traveling out to the countryside alone in the company of someone like Ernest Hoschede was quite something else. What would they talk about? Durand-Ruel had said something about a cottage by the river being available to him. What would that be like? It was probably a derelict old boathouse, dust everywhere and rats running around. People like Hoschede meant well, but under their agreeable facades they thought all artists lived like vagrants, knowing nothing of good living and high style.

He looked up to the clock again. Durand-Ruel had said Hoschede would meet him at one o'clock. Only fifteen minutes had passed. He hated the waiting. He heard puffs of steam, whistles, and a rumbling sound in the distance. There were sudden blasts of heat, a reverberation underfoot. Bells. He took a deep breath. The heat was becoming unbearable. His whole body felt damp. He could feel the perspiration slowly trickling down from his face to his neck and further down to his chest. He shouldn't have accepted Hoschede's offer, he told himself, wiping his face with his handkerchief. It was the wrong time. He should have written to say he'd meet up with him later. Yes, sometime in the autumn when it was cooler. That would be better. Right now it would be best to turn around and return to Argenteuil and all its familiarity. Yes, that's what he would do. He would wait to meet up with Hoschede, quickly explain his change of mind, and be off. With a bit of luck he would be able to get back to the Saint-Lazare and catch the train to Argenteuil at three. But no. Wait. The Hoschedes wouldn't be in the country by autumn. Summer would be over and they would be back in Paris. What foolishness! Yes, foolishness, but the journey could have waited until another mutually convenient time and with careful budgeting he and Camille could manage. They had been managing all along, hadn't they? And if absolutely necessary, he could always resort to his friendships with Manet and Caillebotte. Those two never failed him. They bought his paintings when he needed money, even some they probably didn't like very much. He shouldn't have listened to Durand-Ruel. So what if his paintings weren't selling? He felt too rushed. Camille was not well. Jean was too young to look after his mother. It was all wrong. It was too hot. The crowds were too hurried, and where were all these people going? Of course. Why hadn't he thought of it? In the perfect lives of perfect people living in perfect worlds it was August, the idyllic month of holiday annually given over to carefree summer hours spent in a delightful series of long walks by the seashore and new books read in the cool shade of old willows. Ah, for such a perfect world! Once again he turned his attention to the passing scene, the seriously pre-occupied rushing here, the solemn-faced hurrying there. Why all this movement in a confusion of guises? It was a simple matter to understand the moods of those setting out on family holiday. Prepared for their annual month of pause and rest, they were the amusing groups who had dressed for their departures with great care, demanding to be noticed. There they were, the city-costumed bourgeoisie departing stifling Paris for impeccable country domiciles and enviable beachfront lodgings. He was tempted to remove a sketch pad from his suitcase and capture their splendid arrogance. He had not forgotten the caricature days of his youth in Le Havre and the speed with which he had learned to capture likenesses under the supervision of his teacher at the municipal drawing school. Claude's talent for creating swift likenesses with charcoal had not only made him popular with his friends at school, a condition which had fostered confidence in the developing views and habits of the young, sensitive Claude, but the success of his caricatures had also set a lasting path for the detailed manner in which he saw his world and observed the people in it. Now, years later, tired, hot, and anxiously awaiting Ernest Hoschede, the Gare de Lyon in all its hectic persistence provided a plentiful feast for candid study.

The anonymous, restless-eyed captivated him with their unasked questions and provoking isolation. A tall, long-haired man wearing a shabby brown coat hurried past clutching a dead cat. People stared. Most shook their heads in disbelief. Others looked away and pretended not to notice. A large spotted dog sniffed at a woman's suitcase and urinated on it. The smell of burning coal in the air was upsetting his stomach, making the Gare de Lyon seem hotter and more crowded than it really was.

Where was Hoschede? It was now a few minutes after one and there was no sign of the man. Wasn't it best to be at the station early when traveling by train? Didn't everyone know that? According to the posted schedule, the southbound train was due for departure as Durand-Ruel had said, at one-fifteen, but it hadn't even arrived at the station yet. Oh, well, today it must be as late as the train from Argenteuil had been the day before, Claude surmised, growing more impatient than ever. He checked with a uniformed timekeeper.

"Oui, bientot!" (Yes, any minute now!) came the optimistic response and an accompanying bright smile. Claude shook his head. Hoschede had better appear soon.

He took another deep breath and looked up to the immense metal and glass roof overhead, focusing on its vast vertical view and the sunlit transparency which fascinated him. How wonderful to turn one's gaze upward and watch the light reflecting into the station through that magnificent expanse of glass, all its angular iron beams flung out and effused as if through a lucid natural canopy. He searched for other diversions, turning to watch the uniformed timekeepers performing their dutiful ceremonies, pocket watches efficiently in hand, smiles pasted on their faces as people stopped to inquire about times of arrival and departure, their responses invariably polite and succinct, their excuses and exaggerations when it came to explaining delays, marvels of practiced tact and unquestionable authority.

He made a guessing game of identifying the prosperous men of the city, assigning to them a wide range of important professions. This one was a physician, that one a lawyer. This one wearing the gold lapel pin must be a ministry official. He noted the various cuts of fashionable vests and trousers, deciding which he liked best and which he would buy when money ceased to loom as the most pressing issue in life. He counted the groups of noisy children. He noticed so many smiles, so many peals of laughter. People were happy again. How good it was to see and hear joy in the air. A city so recently recovered from the devastation and siege of the Franco-Prussian War had, at least on the outside, succeeded in dismissing its own unpleasant memories of Otto von Bismarck's stringent demands. Of course, the problem inside still lay in the embarrassing sacrifice of all Alsace and part of Lorraine. In truth, Parisians had not yet recovered from the audacity of that outrageous sacrifice and perhaps they never would. Fact was, Parisians didn't take well to being embarrassed. They weren't good at accepting austerity programs or occupation, nor had they a particular talent for ignoring the insulting acts of invading foreign chancellors and their pompous emperors. Certain things in life were simply unforgivable. No, Parisians really hadn't known how to behave at all when just a few years before, column after audacious column of Prussian soldiers had come marching through the Arc de Triomphe du Carrousel, Bismarck at their head more resplendent than his own emperor in a flash of gold epaulets and a chest full of medals, a flurry of tall white plumes waving in the brisk wind from atop his gleaming silver helmet.

At the beginning, when the first menacing voices were heard from across the Rhine, Claude remembered how he, like most Parisians, pretended nothing too important was happening; a little saber-rattling, a few temper tantrums perhaps, but nothing that would prevent life from going on as normal. It was France. What could possibly go wrong? The "how dare they" attitude was everywhere, in every café and along every avenue and boulevard. But when Paris was indeed occupied, cut off from the rest of Europe, a Seige declared, curfews abruptly enforced, and as a result of food shortages people resorted to eating their pets, reality set in and the disbelieving French watched in horror as a Prussian conqueror clicked his heels across delectable France, halted by nothing but the final, expensive demands of an arrogantly presented treaty. Now, thankfully, all that was over and the mood was very different. It wasn't that people had forgotten, not at all, but they had found a place to store away their painful memories. The city itself bore testament to their optimism. It was true that piles of rubble remained on the Rue Saint-Martine and along Avenue Victoria and that repairs to a number of buildings across the city were ongoing, but most of the beautiful monuments and municipal structures were still standing, and even in the oppressive summer heat, Parisians were in the mood for displays of their famous light-heartedness. For many, war was an old, thin shadow barely visible on the French horizon. The blessed gift of amnesia had set in and along with the return of daily bread and plentiful wine, quintessential French pride had been gainfully restored to a re-energized populace eager to dust itself off and look ahead.

Despite his own dire straits and the personal disappointments of the past few years, Claude found the look and mood of this Paris of 1876 very much to his liking. Even in the face of serious financial decline, the city remained alive and vibrant. Its fearless fighting spirit felt very much like his own, its confidence close to the surface, the air breathed by its citizens stubbornly perfumed with the scent of irrepressible pride. Claude liked that pride. He identified with its gratification. Most of all, he liked the people, the look of the crowds strolling along on the wide public streets in the fascinating central district formed near the Opera, but there was also an encouraging flurry of reconstruction activity. The Rue de la Chaussee d'Antin, at one time a warren of dark alleyways, had become the elegant new center of fashion, and just a short distance away, lining both sides of the Boulevard des Italiens, stood the venerable cafes, The Riche, The Anglais, Tortoni's, The Grand, Santini, and now the brand new Americain. There were new roofs on the Palace of Justice and the Palace of Industry. At the Louvre, workmen continued to swarm over the Galerie des Tuileries in the Pavillon de Flore which had been burned when the Versailles Army took over the city. Amazingly, the Arc de Triomphe was being cleaned. It was covered in an intricate net of scaffolding, as was the Vendome Column, but most impressive of all, in the aftermath of the war remained the inescapable fact that France had been able to pay the Germans the five-billion franc indemnity incurred in two and a half years. Remarkably, the money had come from all Frenchmen in response to bond issues floated by the government before the threat of recession, the first in the summer of 1871, the second the following spring, the first over-subscribed by two and one half times, the second by thirteen times.

Ten minutes after one, according to the Lyon's massive clock. He had been waiting for almost an hour. Where was Hoschede? Perhaps the clock was wrong. Again he checked with a uniformed timekeeper. "Mais non!" (But no!) came the shocked response with a sharp shake of the head and a look of disbelief. "Ridicule!" (Ridiculous!) "Our trains may occasionally be a bit late, but our clocks are never wrong!"

The acrid smell of burning coal was making him nauseous. He wanted to take the deep breaths that usually helped when his stomach acted up, but he was afraid the foul-smelling air would make him feel worse. Why was it that in the sweltering heat things smelled stronger and time passed so much more slowly? He began to pace up and down again, this time counting the number of footsteps required to cover the distance between two platforms. Three pretty girls linked arm in arm passed by in a rustle of pastel-colored summer dresses, interrupting his count. The astonishing smell of starch and rosewater drifted after them. It reminded him of Camille. She used rosewater. He smiled, watching the trio as they gaily laughed and whispered to one another. Ten years before, on a cold winter day threatening snow, Camille had walked past the Café de Duc exactly like the slim, dark-haired girl in the middle. She had been just as animated with two of her Left Bank girlfriends in that same appealing, high-spirited way, hoping to attract the attention of at least one Montmartre painter in search of a model as above her long red woolen scarf she had tossed her pretty head back and laughed and chatted in those few moments before his eyes met hers and through a pane of café glass, life had instantly changed.

Inside the Duc they had talked. He bought her some coffee and two hot beignets stuffed with potatoes which she devoured like a starving kitten. Later that afternoon, she had posed for him, her naked, full-breasted body flushed and opalescent in the sheer fireplace light of the studio loaned to him by his good friend, Frederick Bazille, the tall, handsome southerner from Montpelier who, with Renoir and Sisley, had worked alongside him in Gleyre's Academie, all four sharing in the strict Gleyre process which allowed not a drop of paint applied to a canvas until drawing was mastered. The thought of those harsh, unyielding Ecole des Beaux Arts methods could still infuriate him. Gleyre had charged only ten francs a month for his drawing class and ten centimes for a pig bladder of color, but who was he, or anyone, to decide when it was time to paint or when drawing was mastered? Of course, it was true that Claude had enjoyed the summer months when Gleyre students were encouraged to draw and paint from nature, doing outdoor landscape work which, once again, was part of the prescribed Ecole tradition and considered essential even for students primarily interested in figure painting. By contrast and unlike Renoir, he had not particularly enjoyed the requirement of copying engravings and lithographs or making copies of Old Masters at The Louvre. He preferred to study the work of the past on his own, fascinated to compare Old Master uses and subtleties of color, especially the enigmatic vagaries of Rembrandt's white, but how he had delighted in setting up easels with Renoir, Bazille, and Sisley in the forests near Paris where in complete opposition to Gleyre's instruction and strict insistence that they conform to the technical formula requiring repetitious mosaic application of half-tones, highlights at full strength, and shadows thinly painted, they freed themselves and began to develop their own techniques of "loading" the canvas, even in the shadows their fluid brushmarks balanced by dry, dragged paint and impasted dabs of color. Painting under a canopy of ancient trees at Fountainbleau the three had laughed and mocked Gleyre's edicts concerning rules. What wonderful times!

"You must know the rules before you can break the rules!" Renoir would shout out from under a silver maple, mimicking Gleyre's high pitched voice. "And you must live with the rules and if need be, die by the rules!" Bazille would shout back with a laugh.

The thought of his dear, talented friend, Frederick Bazille, caused Claude to return to that earlier time with memories so fond that a lump could quickly form in his throat when he re-lived those treasured, careless moments of the past. Long parted from Gleyre, Claude still painted in the forests with Renoir who, like Claude himself, had spent the war years in London, unlike Bazille who had eagerly welcomed the adventure of French military life at the front, his youthful exuberance for the trumpeting thrill of battle forever silenced by the thrust of a Prussian bayonet at the Battle of Beaune-la-Rolande.

By nightfall in Bazille's studio as snow blanketed the rooftops of Paris, Claude and Camille had shared a bowl of cold potatoes, a bottle of wine, and a warm bed.

Had it really been an entire decade since he had first held that small naked waist in his hands, enchanted by the delicate smell of soft-scented rosewater on warm silken breasts? He had probably forgotten a few things in the course of the passing years, but he had never forgotten the delicate spell cast by skin fragrant with rosewater one winter night when he had fallen passionately in love with Camille Doncieux.

"Let me stay here with you," she had whispered to him that night, in her unrestrained, candid way. He could not resist. She had stayed, and she had remained with him and in love with him throughout the ten years since then, the meaning of "I love you" defined and re-defined between them in countless intimate ways, most often, "I love you" a phrase suspended in silence but clearly etched across both their faces when he left her for weeks at a time to paint at one location or another. Whispered to him as she kissed him good-bye, it meant, "I'll miss you," but murmured to him under a vague, urgent smile by dark-haired, sensual Camille, it was the ancient, provocative invitation extended to an eager lover. Now, as he waited for Hoschede and worried and paced, every slender, dark-haired woman in the Gare de Lyon, every rustling skirt, every smile above a soft, chalk-white bodice reminded him of Camille and more than ever he regretted having left her alone with Jean at Argenteuil.

Where was Hoschede? It was well after one o'clock and neither the train for points south and east nor Hoschede had arrived. Once again he wiped the perspiration on his face with his handkerchief, his mind a swirl of thudding images.

"A few weeks in the country! Think of it! Paid to paint! Durand-Ruel had insisted. "The best food! A charming riverside cottage of your own! You will be invited to dinners, luncheons. The Hoschedes are wonderful hosts! They will introduce you to new people including members of the Raingo family who could become interested in your work. Claude, you cannot refuse. Ernest Hoschede is an aggressive collector. He is young, like you, and his tastes are still developing but they are there. He could be a force. These things are inborn. He bought your Impression Sunrise, didn't he? Claude, right now he is your most important patron. There is no artistic sacrifice in admitting that."

He looked down at his clothes. They were no longer crisp, not the way he liked them, but in spite of the debilitating heat and the constraints of his poverty there remained a remarkably stylish look about him. Some of his colleagues thought him to be a bit of a dandy, a penniless one to be sure, but a man who could appear quite dapper in the striped vests and long dark jackets he chose to wear with all but the top button undone, as was the case with his attire in the Gare de Lyon. He lit another cigarette. He noticed a smudge of dust on his sleeve. He held the cigarette between his lips and brushed it away with one hand. Again he checked with a timekeeper, this time clearly inquiring as to the exact status of the train bound for Montgeron on the Compagnie de Paris a Lyon et a la Mediterranee. Given no satisfactory answer he began to admonish the bewildered man for being party to so inefficient a scheduling system.

"C'est idiot de la part de quie de faire! Stupide! Mal organize!" (What you do is idiotic! Stupid! Badly organized!)

Much to the relief of both exasperated men who appeared close to blows, within seconds the station master announced the arrival of the train bound for points south and east, and just as suddenly, the man Claude awaited appeared before him. There he was, Ernest Hoschede, prosperous man of the city, resplendent in summer attire: pale beige suit, soft yellow vest, composed and remarkably free of perspiration, white rosebud in his lapel, and just as Durand-Ruel had predicted, a large blue box tied with a silver ribbon in his hands, a piercing whistle from the track announcing his arrival with uncanny ceremony.

"How good to see you, Claude! Mes excuses," the well-modulated Hoschede voice offered, but my littlest daughter, Germaine, asked for Peach Croustades from the Dore and I couldn't disappoint her. Everything looked so wonderful in there today that I added an assortment of macarons and madeleines to my order. There was a big crowd and it all took a bit longer than usual to put together. So sorry."

Claude smiled politely and shook Ernest's free hand. His head was pounding.

"This way," Hoschede directed. "No, Claude, not there, this way. Have you been waiting long?"

"About forty minutes," Claude replied stiffly, making every effort to maintain a reasonable demeanor, "but I arrived at the station a little too early."

"I'm so sorry, but we're here together now and we'll be off in a few minutes. Look at all these children! Have you ever seen so many families in the Lyon? Oh well. It's August."

With Claude close behind, Ernest was leading the way through a confusing myriad of arriving and departing passengers and toward a platform where a gleaming, dark blue traincar awaited, outstanding centerpiece of several connecting coaches of the Compagnie de Paris a Lyon arriving late at the Gare de Lyon but now, its additional dark blue car being connected, preparing to depart for points south and east.

"My traincar!" Ernest announced with unrestrained pride, pointing to the gleaming blue passenger coach. "Today we two are its only passengers. We can discuss the rotunda painting project without interruption. We'll also sample a few of these pastries, just to be sure they live up to expectations," he added with a broad smile.

Hoschede's private train. Of course. His magic carpet to destinations of his own choosing," Claude surmised, the mere concept of a private train surely impressive to all his glamorous guests and wealthy friends. As impressed as he himself was, his patience had worn thin and in these moments of submissive weariness he was far beyond indented views of personal grandeur and gleaming blue examples of high living. He didn't particularly care where Hoschede was leading him. The noise, the heat, his concern for conditions at home, all of it had collected in a muddle of confusion that had exhausted him. He wanted to sit down. He was hungry and more than anything else, he wanted to escape that sea of overheated faces and be headed off toward his destination, wherever that might be, but as he followed Ernest Hoschede toward the waiting railcar and slowly boarded, he paused and slowly turned to glance over his shoulder the way people do when they have a premonition that upon their return nothing will be the same.

CHAPTER 12

The Company We Keep

The waiting steward greeted the train's two passengers with a cordial smile. "Ah, for Mademoiselle Germaine! Monsieur Hoschede, you never forget. I have come to expect these beautiful blue boxes whenever we leave for Montgeron."

Ernest smiled back. "Paul, I dare not forget. The child has a remarkable memory. She will be looking for this blue box as soon as I arrive at Rottembourg. In a while, though, my guest, Monsieur Monet and I, will want to sample a few of these delicacies ourselves. We must make sure the Dore continues to live up to its reputation, for Germaine's sake, of course."

Hoschede's words were clipped, but pleasant enough as he engaged Paul and motioned Claude to a seat by a window, soon coming to sit directly opposite him. Within minutes, the train bound for points south and east began its slow departure from the Gare de Lyon, inching slowly away in whistles and bells and puffs of steam and a sea of overheated faces, gradually building up speed and at last racing farther and farther away from rent that was overdue and Camille ill at Argenteuil and paintings that weren't selling and the quickly spent five hundred francs Durand-Ruel had advanced the struggling Claude Monet.

In a matter of seconds Ernest excused himself and walked to the train's small holding area where he chatted with Paul. Claude was grateful for the solitude. He was exhausted. Sitting back and trying to relax he closed his eyes, and tried to make sense of things. Camille would be fine, he told himself. Hadn't he been away on painting expeditions in the past? Camille was accustomed to his frequent absences, and wasn't young Jean a devoted son? Didn't he adore his mother? And what landlord would evict a woman with a young child? Certainly not Madame Aubrey. It was just a few weeks and Caillebotte would be bringing the one thousand francs Camille was expecting. Of course. It would be fine. The time would pass quickly. He opened his eyes and yawned. Through the window he could see thin clouds mottled chalklike against the bright blue August sky. The train was picking up speed. He could feel the acceleration. Soon they would be streaming full throttle into the Brie Valley. Yes, before too long he would see the Brie's iconic grasslands. Thankfully, it was growing cooler. He hadn't felt this comfortable since leaving home, but his thoughts continued in a swirling specter of concern. Durand-Ruel was right, he repeatedly told himself. Yes, a good commission like this would pay the rent for a few months and provide Camille and Jean with some comfort. Yes, for their sakes he would put all his reservations aside and try not to feel cheapened or compromised by taking on a patron's commission. The money would change so many things. Renoir himself said he was thinking about taking on a commission from the publisher, Georges Chapentier, and hadn't Durand-Ruel confirmed that Ernest Hoschede was a modern, forward-thinking man? If he liked the finished wall panels he would surely buy more paintings, perhaps introduce the new style of work to his rich friends who might be willing to do the same. But, maybe not. Why was there always another rational side to the argument? Durand-Ruel had also told him repeatedly that the public was too madly in love with portraiture and historic scenes to readily accept the remote simplicity of landscapes, the uncomplicated view of trees and boats and detonating strands of pure, elusive color. It was true. Things would not be changing as quickly as he wanted them to. Tradition ruled. The general public, the Salon Jury, and all Street of Pictures gallery dealers other than the innovative Durand-Ruel, still responded best to somber depravities of Spanish Inquisition-type pictures, the bigger the canvas, the more tortured and bloodied the naked, long-haired female, the better. Yes, it would take a man like this, a man like this Monsieur Ernest Hoschede to turn the tide. Yes, a man so rich and secure in his own thinking that he traveled to his country house in his own private train car without worrying about the expense. Why was it always about money? Would it ever be about simple things? Would it ever be about meadows and haystacks and one single fallow field?

The train had begun its eastward curve into the lush rural countryside. In the distance, he could see purple vineyards gleaming in the golden sunshine. The scene streaming past in ribbons of brilliant color delighted him, high summer flaunting long, dense stretches of flourishing dark green pines and the occasional deep grove of peeling white birches. Argenteuil had looked this way when he had moved there five years before. The waterside setting along the Seine and the tranquil mood of the community not too far away from the bustling city had attracted him, but now it was different. In a burst of industrialization the pines and birches had disappeared and the new factories were taking over, their smoke stacks and graceless facades quickly changing so much of the natural, untouched beauty he had found there. At the beginning and until recently, he had painted the endless treasure trove of subjects he found on the river; the sailboats, skiffs, and yawls, but through these past summer months he had been more and more comfortable painting in his own small garden. Perhaps he needed a change.

The ever-widening ribbons of purple, green, and gold he watched through the window were fascinating, but the array of lenient color and effortless fusing textures did nothing to hold his interest for very long. Again he thought of Camille. How she would have loved this mood of affluence and the appointments of this luxurious private traincar, its beautifully upholstered chairs as comfortable as a bed, its brass window frames and door fittings polished and gleaming. He thought of her at Trouville, just after their wedding when he had set up his easel on the boardwalk and painted the American flag at the Hotel des Roches Noires while she enjoyed the seashore with baby Jean, the newly developed Trouville resort a showcase for the glittering array of international resort guests who fascinated her, their constant changes of clothes and endless promenading from hotel to boardwalk to casino a parade more glamorous than any Camille had ever seen. They had not been able to afford the luxuries or prices of the grand Roches Noires and had stayed at the modest Tivoli, well away from the beachfront's high society but for Camille, daily glimpses of a sun-splashed world so out of reach were precious balm and for several memorable weeks she had slept and awakened content to live on its fringes.

"This is the France I love best," Ernest suddenly boomed, breaking into Claude's reminiscence as returning to his seat across from Claude he pointed to the passing scene viewed through the window. "It's so full of life out here, especially at this time of year, full of surprises, filled with color, like a beautiful, fascinating woman. It's no wonder our French royals chose to spend so much time here."

He pointed to the passing landscape as if the trees and fields and all the clouds were his; his alone to be flushed in golden sunlight in one second, shaded the next against an attentive blue August sky. All of it belonged to him: the gilded rush of beryl-blue above, the precious sweep of verdigris beneath, the rippling labyrinth of tangled roots and aged ash bound up by time, present and future commingled and unraveled for him alone, its pleasures and pastimes streaming past at his command, fragile outcomes streaked tall and dark on far horizons by columns of royal old poplars and the not quite faded splendor of a few French kings.

And there was that smile again, engaging, forthright, and well-integrated into the Hoschede composition, but exactly what could such a man really know of the French countryside or the substance of its engendered life? What did he understand about a country morning's fleeting images of color or the mystique of vague transparencies shadowed and harnessed in graying hours of afternoon? Hoschede spent his summers in country loveliness but what had he seen of its surprises and mysteries, of its extremes and endless miracles, Claude wondered, watching his host closely as he was offered a cigar, lit one for himself, and like Claude, quietly smoked and enjoyed the view. He studied Hoschede's hands. They were city hands; too clean, too correct, too big for the rest of his body. He wore a narrow gold band on his left hand. His fingernails were clipped very short and straight, the immaculate white crescent-moons at the base of the thumbnails prominent as he smoked and waved his cigar in the air like a conductor leading his orchestra with a baton. But there was something maddening about that smile. It was easy and gifted, and yes, infuriatingly hopeful.

Paul brought champagne. Claude took a glass from the tray and thanked his host.

"A la belle France!" Hoschede toasted, lifting his glass with a smile. "A la belle France!" Claude returned as just outside the windows la belle France sped by in summer clothes, soft-hued and shining, dancing into the self-absorbed grandeur of her verdant countryside. He envisioning the radiant swift beacons of sheer light flashing hot against the mass of iron speeding toward a small Brie Valley village and a chateau called Rottembourg. Although acquainted with Hoschede, he was becoming intrigued by this man who appeared to be in total control of every aspect of his life, but what could a man like this know of sparkling beacons of light trailing overhead in their wake as they did in these moments? People like Ernest Hoschede lived in coddled worlds of endless summer where skin and air and human bones shared equally and for all time in warm protected spectacles.

Cloudless blue skies. Sun moving slowly westward. Claude pictured the puffs of smoke ascending higher and higher in a trailing white funnel; spiraling, constricting, finally evaporating helplessly against the sky. He loved the motion, the incessant movement forward through the sheer, uncompromising air. He sipped his champagne, leaned further back into his seat, and breathed deeply of Hoschede's undamaged world. How peaceful the seclusion, how insular the quiet atmosphere. What must it be like to live in such a luxurious world day after day, year after year, a world effortlessly suspended between city and country in a life free of timetables, schedules, and common public encounters, an exclusive champagne world where time and endless summer itself must stand powerfully still?

They talked; polite, idle banter at first, the innocuous type of conversation intended to test the disposition and assess the mood. Ernest remarked on the surprising surge in summer business at his store but complained that it was becoming difficult to find reliable employees. Claude remarked on the crowds and the noise in the Gare de Lyon and by contrast, the serene views just outside the window. Yes, he answered in response to Ernest's question, he had indeed started out early in the morning from Argenteuil the day before. Yes, he had seen friends while in Paris and yes, the city was restoring itself after the war and would eventually emerge more beautiful than ever.

Hoschede's accent was clearly that of Paris, Claude noticed, but now and then he lapsed into country phrases and curses rarely heard in the city. "Un goujat" (a clumsy man), he exclaimed, or "Je me vois au pied du mur sans echelle" (I see myself at the foot of the wall without a ladder). With great emphasis he occasionally used the term "fils de pute" (son-of-a-bitch), but Claude was no stranger to the idiosyncrasies of Parisian speech patterns. Born thirty-six years before in the Paris of King Louis Phillippe, his youth spent in Le Havre, the young man christened Oscar-Claude Monet had returned to the city of his birth at the tender age of seventeen to paint at the Academie Suisse, no small thanks to the efforts of dear, rotund Madame Lecadre, his art-loving aunt Sophie whose own artistic ambitions had been repeatedly smashed and finally expunged by family opinion, most vehemently that of Claude's father Adolphe, who disapproved of all artists and their lifestyles, assigning to them a rather large portion of blame for the decline in French national character, many painters and their kind "singlehandedly responsible," Adolphe vehemently maintained, "for the alarming spread of syphilis."

"No son of mine will become an artist; not a painter, not a sculptor, no, never!" he warned his son when at the age of sixteen the boy displayed an unusual talent for caricature and exhibited a collection of his charcoal drawings in the window of a Le Havre art supply shop, meeting the landscape artist, Eugene Boudin, whose paintings were displayed in the same window. Boudin encouraged the boy to try his hand at landscape painting and invited him to join him for a few days on an outdoor painting expedition. Aunt Sophie had secretly applauded the invitation, ably assuring the stubborn, single-minded Papa Adolphe that it was a mere experiment.

"Nothing will come of it, Adolphe. Let the boy go," she urged. "He will hate the woods. He will be at the mercy of nature's elements with which he has no real experience. It will be cold at night. It could rain. Don't worry. In a few days Claude will return home with a change of heart, a bad cold, and perhaps you will have the great physician or lawyer you have dreamed of having in the family."

Ernest Hoschede reminded Claude of Sophie Lecadre. He was that same type of affable mentor, that same type of engaging being. He studied Hoschede's profile reflected in the window. They must be about the same age, he determined, but of course, Hoschede's shorter, well-trimmed beard and impeccably well-tailored clothes gave him the look of pampered elegance. There was something inquisitive in that face though, as if it conducted an incessant search. It was in his eyes. Yes, that was it. His questioning eyes were like Aunt Sophie Lecadre's; never still, but constantly surveying, judging, weighing. Paul poured more champagne. Claude thought about the beautiful Normandy coast in August and Madame Lecadre in her billowing black and white striped summer dresses on the terrace at Saint-Addresse, sipping lemon tea. How he had adored her. He placed his champagne glass down on the folding table Paul had placed at his side, suddenly reminded of her death six years before, her faith in his talent unwavering, her expectations for his future optimistic to the end of her life. He wanted to enjoy his champagne, but the rhythmic clacking on the tracks was making him sleepy. He could hardly keep his eyes open. He longed for a nap, but his host had other ideas. Ernest Hoschede hadn't spent a sleepless night on the narrow cot in Durand-Ruel's stifling back room. He was in the mood to talk.

"You will enjoy spending time with Monsieur Hoschede on the train," Durand-Ruel had said during Claude's last visit to his gallery. "He is a very interesting, very charming human being, but be prepared. He is a successful merchant who, by his own admission, sees himself as a pacesetter in his own exclusive world. He likes to take over a conversation, make his opinions known, and have them mean something, which somehow they always manage to do. Once you arrive at the Chateau Rottembourg you will see the private Hoschede world at first hand and the dynamics will change. There you will meet Madame Alice Hoschede. She manages to reach her husband's softer side. He is a different person with her, but like her husband, Madame Alice is also strong-minded and will surely share her specific ideas for the wall panels with you," Durand-Ruel had also told him. "Rest assured, very little happens at the Chateau Rottembourg that Madame, herself, does not approve and supervise, but it is all done in a most charming, most pleasant way. You will get on well with her."

Ernest sipped his champagne and assessed his guest's appearance as he had never quite managed to do at the Guerbois, conditions there always demanding more of his intellect than of his visual assessments. Claude's suit was rumpled, but well-cut, he observed, and his shirt collar looked damp with perspiration, but even rumpled and damp there was something physically impressive about this Claude Monet. He was a solidly built, barrel-chested figure of a man, his generally pensive demeanor and the intensity of his overall appearance not at all compatible with the characteristics of a man who spent his time applying color to canvas, but more those of a man who built things with his hands like houses and barns and fences and bridges.

"I hope your family doesn't mind your being away like this, for a few weeks," Ernest offered. "I should have given that more thought. You could have brought them with you."

"Monsieur, thank you, but I will have work to do at the Chateau Rottembourg and I must remain focused on that. Perhaps when the panels are completed my wife and son could join me for a few days. Is that a possibility?"

"Yes, of course," Ernest responded. "We'll arrange it. I know they would enjoy our property and our little village. My wife will see to them. She is marvelous with people; kind, patient. You'll see that when you meet her. She enjoys having company at Rottembourg almost as much as I do, and she knows everybody in the village. Her family has been spending summers at Montgeron for years. They've served on village councils and are very supportive of the nearby Abbey in Yerres. Yes, Alice would have a grand time introducing you and your family around; having luncheons, picnics, that sort of thing, and my children always welcome a new playmate. I know my son, Jacques, would be glad to have another boy to play with. With four sisters, he is often left to his own devices. He's nine."

Hoschede's sentences were like hammers, most of them short exclamations; stringent, thrifty, not a word wasted. "My wife's family owns a good deal of property at Montgeron. At Yerres too," he went on. "You'll be staying at a Raingo house. It's just a short walk down from us. If you don't feel like walking the landau is always available. The place is called La Lethumiere. Alice's Uncle Julian owns it. He's seldom there. Says it's too small for his dog. You'll eventually meet that monster. This is the third or fourth Saint-Bernard Julian Raingo has had. He's the biggest, best fed beast I've ever seen. Charming place though, La Lethumiere. A quiet secluded little lodge on the riverbank. There's a small garden in front. I think you'll like it."

Paul brought a tray of the Dore's famous Peach Croustades. "What do you think?" Ernest asked, as the two quickly finished off servings of the fruit-laced flaky pastry. "Is the Dore's reputation safe?"

The two men laughed, each leaning slightly forward, in full agreement that the Dore had nothing to fear and that the Croustades for which it was duly famous were among the most delicious delicacies in Paris. Together, and with little reluctance they enjoyed another serving. His cravings for pastry and champagne well-satisfied, Ernest sat back and proceeded to engage his traveling companion not in a conversation focused on the four proposed wall panels as was expected, but on revelations which in their candor displayed a side of Claude Monet few people had ever seen or would ever see.

"Well, I am pleased to see you survived the spring exhibition," Ernest remarked.

"I haven't seen you since then. Once summer comes, my schedule changes and I'm not in Paris so much, but I've had time to think about the show at Durand-Ruel's and I must say that the entire thing was very different from what I remember two years ago; a "cause celebre" this year, I'd say. Attendance seemed much better and the press appeared in greater numbers, wouldn't you say?"

"Ah yes," Claude agreed. Reviews were better, as was attendance but as usual, sales were disappointing."

"I had intended to buy your Japonnerie," Ernest interrupted. "It's magnificent! Durand-Ruel was holding it for me but as he has probably told you, I waited too long to complete the transaction. As you know, it went to Monsieur Houssaye, but its brilliant color would have been wonderful at the Chateau Rottembourg. You'll see that for yourself."

"Well, Monsieur, I wish you could have prevailed with Japonnerie, but I was happy to have that sale under any circumstances. I'm sure you understand. Since then, except for Degas, not one of our group has sold much of anything. That really was our hope this time, to exhibit and make some money, but life goes on and Monsieur Durand remains optimistic that at least a few of the seventeen landscapes I showed will eventually find buyers. In the meantime, I go on living and painting. It is not a terrible life. It is only terribly difficult."

In his rapidly evolving role as a serious collector of what by now were being commonly referred to as Impressionist paintings, Ernest listened to Claude with great interest, finding himself both curious and sympathetic.

"I sometimes worry about the prospect of success for your group," he stated frankly. "As you well know, I'm an avid supporter, but it will take a large group of enthusiasts like me to reach the goals you've set for yourselves. Breaking the rules is never easy."

"Yes, absolutely," Claude responded without hesitation, his interest in the conversation quickly erasing any sign of fatigue, "and we know that many people believe we are out there only for the sake of breaking the rules," he added, facing Ernest squarely, "but there is much more to our battle than breaking rules. "I wish there was a better way to communicate that fact. Above all, though, we feel there must be a wider vision, a greater openness and freedom in the world of art. We want our work accepted not for what it is supposed to be, but for what it is, and we are under no illusions. Acceptance and an understanding of our beliefs will be slow to come and we must face the fact that it may never come. We know that we suffer from being new and that our newness is loathed by the old establishment which enjoys its loathing. When they are finished with loathing us they will find something new to loath. It is the way things are, and if we are to battle on, then the work we present to the public must be what we feel is our best, new or old, for at the end it will be they, the people, who decide our fate. And, if some of our best painting is, as Monsieur Durand-Ruel reminds us, so new that the paint is not yet dry on our canvases when we exhibit, so be it. One day it will be dry."

"It isn't that I see your mission as hopeless, far from it," Ernest mused aloud, his gaze out to the landscape speeding past then quickly back to Claude, "but as much as I admire the boundless determination of your battle, at the same time I see the constant rejection, the constant criticism. It's always there, and it must take a toll. I wouldn't like it happening to me. We all need a little praise now and then. Claude, I've seen a good deal of your work from the past. I'm sure you know I have enormous respect for your current landscapes, but you have great ability with figure painting. You could be making a fine living with both figure painting and portraiture, establishing your reputation very quickly and earning a lot of money. Lady in a Green Dress (Kunsthalle Bremen) for example, is magnificent, a truly stunning painting. I wish I had bought it, but there again, Monsieur Houssaye prevailed. How did you feel about the confusion over your signature on the canvas? Almost everyone who saw that beautiful painting thought that Manet, not Monet, was the artist."

Claude laughed. "Edouard Manet has told me it was such a good painting that he almost didn't mind having our names confused! Unfortunately, I know him well enough to know he did indeed mind, and very much, but it was a great compliment to me. I am not well known. He is. He's a fine man and a finer artist, and although, as you know he is not really one of us and will never exhibit with us, he supports our beliefs wholeheartedly. I'm sure he has noticed that since Lady in a Green Dress, I have learned to be as careful in forming the letter "o" in my signature as he is in forming the letter "a" in his. But, Monsieur Hoschede, to somehow explain the endurance required of our uphill battle, you must understand that through it all we go on growing as individuals and changing as artists. From canvas to canvas we learn, we explore, we change, and much of the time we think we are not good enough and never will be good enough. Now and then there is that rare moment of satisfaction. It's a wonderful feeling, but things can quickly change. Colors go wrong, textures are inappropriate, subject matter becomes boring. Individually and on our own we handle our discontent as best we can. As a group though, it is something else entirely and conditions are not always easily dismissed. Often the human difficulties, the struggles of merely living our erratic lives can frankly be too much. We all feel it, and as I believe you have witnessed at the Guerbois, most of the time these difficulties have nothing at all to do with our subject matter or style, not our work habits, not our discipline or lack thereof, none of that. Basically, it is that everyone has a different idea as to how, when, and where our work should be shown. That was at the heart of our discussions in preparation for the exhibition just this past spring. Quite frankly, it was exasperating. This one asked, "How many paintings are you showing? And you? And you? What is the order in the placement of paintings? Whose will be seen first? Last? "We should be exhibiting at the Relais Donat or the Palais Blanc," someone else said. "No," someone else chimed in. "No one will find us there! Monsieur Durand-Ruel's gallery is our best choice."

Claude's annoyance with the exploration of endless planning details was clear as he spoke, but the ability of his group to withstand its present and future difficulties remained uppermost in his mind.

"Over time, Monsieur Hoschede, there have been long heated debates and many private discussions as to whether or not our exhibitions should be taking place at all, and from time to time and in one way or another we have all voiced the opinion that each of us should go his own way and give up on the belief that there is strength in numbers. The long, painful arguments over whether or not our exhibitions should be taking place at all came to a head last year when things were so bad between us that before irreparable damage was done to our friendships we decided to disband altogether and go our separate ways. Some of us are still not sure it was a good idea to change our minds as we did. And then there is the matter of our identity. One day we are Independents, on another we are Intransigents, on another we are an Anonymous Society, and lately we are Impressionists. It is a tortuous labyrinth!"

"Does the group ever meet at a location other than the Guerbois, another café, another restaurant perhaps to discuss matters? Sometimes a change of scenery helps," Ernest said in an attempt to offer at least one viable suggestion and once again Claude laughed.

"Ah yes, Pierre Renoir and I meet in the woods of Fountainbleau!" Claude exclaimed with a hearty chortle. "We set up our easels under the trees, admire the views, and settle absolutely nothing of importance in our conversations. We just paint and talk and sing during the day and find a boarding house to eat at and sleep in at night. Pierre is a good friend. He is also a formidable worker, unrelenting really, and not only in his painting. Once he gets an idea into his head he cannot let it go. I believe he actually has it in him to become very successful one day."

The landscape rushing past grew increasingly lush, the mottled horizon no longer etched by stands of oak and pine, but by waving fields of tall, wild grass flung out and unwound across a yielding blue summer sky. Against its polished sweep, intimate details of Impressionism were being revealed in honest, open terms by its chief exponent who spoke frankly but occasionally fell silent and for long, pensive moments gazed out to the passing scene ever more thoughtful before he turned to his host to take up the discussion once again.

"Monsieur Hoschede, if our work is to be accepted and judged for what it is, on its own terms, and not by a handful of powerful elitists who believe they alone know what art should be, what do you think we should we do?" he asked. "You, thank God, know and understand what is happening to us and you are a man of Paris. What must we do to change the way our paintings are seen by others like you? What do you think it will take for people to truly understand, and not only see what is before them, but approve of it?"

"Claude, I have given that a good deal of thought," Ernest replied, "and I'm sorry to say that in spite of my best efforts I have no answers for you. I do believe though, as most collectors do, that taste in art is a very individual thing. The success side of it for artists, the idea of winning people over and the financial side of it, which matters very much to all of you right now, those are very different elements in which acceptance and support play a mighty role, but, Claude, facts are facts. Right now you and your group have established a level of curiosity, but no following. To put it bluntly, you are sorry prisoners of your own beliefs and your own tastes; just a group of revolutionary artists being tortured by your powerful captors. You cannot and will not alter your beliefs, nor can you ignore your inborn natures and talents simply to conform to stringent judgments and arrogant assumptions for the sake of recognition and the money that always seems to go with it. It is an admirable war to wage, but difficult as it is for all of you right now, it is a fact that each of you is a human being with a human life, most of you with families and the very real demands that accompany family responsibility. I only hope you can withstand the challenges you face until success comes knocking at the door, as I sincerely believe it will one day. It could take time, but what concerns me also is the question of what will happen if by some chance the Salon begins accepting paintings by members of your group."

"Degas insists he will leave the group if any one of us submits work to the Salon Jury," Claude quickly offered. "One of our members believes it would be a good idea for him to do so. But make no mistake, Monsieur, we are all free to do whatever we need to do, and that includes submitting work to the Salon regardless of Degas' opinions or those of anyone else, for that matter. So, we must cross such bridges as they come. Perhaps we will lose Degas one day, perhaps not. Edouard Manet keeps reminding him that more than forty-thousand people attend the Salon Exhibition every year. "It is a huge audience," he insists. He thinks we should try again and again. As you may know, my Lady in a Green Dress was accepted in 1868 and that acceptance shocked me, but even back then, my views as a painter were as opposed to the structured way of doing things as they are now, and strange as it seems, Lady in a Green Dress did nothing to spur on my success. I gained no loyal following because of it and apart from the money Monsieur Houssaye paid me for it, no financial support either. Of course, my attitude was no secret. It never has been, but the fact is that I would never paint like that again. That work is of my past. Both Lady in a Green Dress and The Luncheon Party which was also accepted by the Salon, came about because I did what I was supposed to do. I conformed, at least to some degree. They are good paintings and I remain proud of them, but I succeeded with them because I followed what I understood to be the form and balance of accepted norms. More than that, I may have needed to prove something to myself, perhaps that I really could conform and achieve that elusive prize of Salon acceptance, that red stamp at the back of the canvas that proved my worthiness. But what came of it? Nothing! The victory was quick and hollow and meant little to me. Shortly after, I vowed I would never submit to the Salon or compromise myself again. Things had changed. I had changed. I was seeing the world and my place in it differently. I saw that my work had to be my own. It had to reflect my intention, my grasp, my view and understanding of the world. My colleagues understand those views and to a very large extent they share them, but we cannot continue to be brutalized in the press and watch our reputations shredded to pieces. If we are to go on with our collaboration, how are we to withstand the pressure?"

"You need a plan, an ongoing plan of some sort," Ernest said. "You cannot continue to be seen merely as rebels ready for a fight. Surely you have looked ahead together and decided on a path of action."

Claude laughed. "Plan? Path of action? Monsieur Hoschede, we have no plan. We can barely plan to arrive at the same place at the same time on the same day. And as you know, our paint is often barely dry before an exhibition. You are expecting too much of us!" Both men broke into peals of laughter.

"Seriously though, Monsieur," Claude found himself admitting, "I suppose we are not as well-organized as we should be. You are right. We should have a plan. Right now I suppose it is fair to say we are just rebels ready for a fight. Our battleground stretches from the Guerbois to the nearest exhibition hall and our strategy is developed as we go, moment to moment. And now that I have said that aloud, I also suppose it is no wonder we are getting nowhere!"

Once again both men shook with laughter as Claude confessed to the group's assortment of shortcomings with wit and affection. His disquieting anxiety was fading. He felt more relaxed, more jovial. His jocular demeanor was adding a touch of youthful softness to his eyes which were no longer heavy-lidded with fatigue.

"Ah, but Monsieur Hoschede, as I think about it now, we do have our saving graces. That much must be said of us," Claude added. "First of all, like the leaders of any decent rebellion we do confer at the front on a regular basis, in our case, once a week or so, usually on Wednesday, as you know, around our table at the Guerbois, a rendezvous point we all agree is highly conducive to revolution. Monsieur Hoschede, our intentions when we meet are honorable, but we talk too much, and very often about nothing. I am the first to admit it. The baby took her first steps, the oldest boy will be starting school next month, or the weeds are overtaking the garden. It is our way to divulge such nonsense to one another. I think the sharing of such simple things comforts us, assures us we are human, but it will not surprise you to know that everyone has an opinion when it comes to political issues. You have witnessed that yourself. And then there is always

Edouard Manet to talk about. When all else fails, Degas sees to it we argue about him. He cannot stand Manet, but he brings his name up constantly. Renoir says that those two talents are much too enormous to be contained in the same room. That may be so, but more than that, I myself believe it is Edgar's bitterness about the whole world in general that is at the bottom of it. Something eats away at him. I don't know what it is, but if he is jealous of Manet, he is not alone. We are all a little jealous of Manet, and it has little to do with his acceptance and success in a world where we are outcasts. It is that his painting is just as he is himself: elegant, important, solid. Everything about him is genuine!"

"Yes," Ernest agreed. "I know Edouard Manet and I agree that he is all those things, but perhaps deep inside Degas sees his own talent as superior to that of Manet and perhaps he really is jealous of the recognition and financial success Manet enjoys in Paris."

"That could be Monsieur, but who knows? I will always maintain that Degas is an important talent. He has all the basics at his fingertips and they never fail him. His drawing and draftsmanship are superior to any drawing or draftsmanship of ours. His work is truly exquisite, but the unrelenting anger and hardness in him get in the way. In spite of that, I like and respect him, but I may just be better able than the others to tolerate him," Claude continued, chuckling as with noticeable pause and patience he talked about the most chronically abrasive of the Impressionists, a curious man whose talents Claude recognized fully as at the same time he made clear to Ernest that Edgar Degas was indeed, the group's most incendiary provocateur and perhaps a danger to its survival.

"The real trouble for Edgar came just before the first exhibition, when we had not yet decided what to call ourselves," Claude confided, doing his best to suppress another chuckle. "We had toyed with this idea and that idea, with this name and that name, but one Wednesday, with the exhibition scheduled to open in only two weeks, we were still exploring ideas. Nothing was working. Degas sat next to me at our usual table in the Guerbois. He really hates it there, you know, but he hates many things. He had been unusually quiet and offered no contribution as Gustave Caillebotte, in his organized way, made a list of all our suggestions on a tablet of paper. Degas lit his second or third cigar in about an hour and suddenly said, "It is more difficult than naming a baby!" Everyone laughed. He laughed too. Then, after another long puff, an enormously satisfied expression crossed his face and he blurted out, "Capucine! (Nasturtium!) That is it! Capucine! (Nasturtium!) We are Capucines! Capucines! Capucines! It is a stylish, showy name and if we are exhibiting on the Boulevard des Capucines are we not Capucines?"

"Well, this suggestion that we call ourselves Nasturtiums immediately sent Renoir into gales of laughter. He doubled over in his chair. His face turned bright red as he uttered one loud guffaw after another, but we all knew that in spite of his laughter, his humor masked a more serious side. Renoir, like many of us, has been very much afraid of our taking on any name that might label us as odd or worst, as radical subversives which of course, we are, but he was right to insist that a questionable or mystifying name was to be avoided.

I felt that the label of "Capucines" would make our cause so much more difficult to explain or understand and could even lead to the suspicion that our real intention is to create a strange new school of art or a social movement, a situation we must avoid. Of course, it is no secret that the government is wary of our rebellious type and I do not believe I could have been the only one of our group to recall that following the Prussian victory, Courbet was exiled to Switzerland due to his active part in the Commune and the destruction of the Vendome Column. Getting back to the challenge of naming ourselves at the Café Guerbois, we agreed we were being castigated enough as it was. Naming ourselves after a flower was unseemly, even a little too tender sounding, but through the exchange between Renoir and Degas it was interesting to see that Caillebotte quickly came to Renoir's defense. He is very protective of Renoir and was quick to point out to Degas, and quite diplomatically I might add, that our dear Pierre Auguste Renoir is not a man of great personal flair or showy style and that his greatest, most flamboyant talents lie not on his person or in his ideas, but on his canvases. I found myself in complete agreement. Do you know that after the First Exhibition, one of Renoir's harshest critics went so far as to call him a walking travesty under a hat? Renoir didn't care a bit about that remark. He likes himself as he is, which is unkempt and happy. Frankly, I like him that way too. I hope he never changes. Fortunately, since then Caillebotte has succeeded quite well in saving Renoir from other unpleasant encounters with Degas. He also succeeded in naming our group, very clear to suggest that our best name should describe exactly who we are and what we are doing. He also observed that eventually an even better name might come from outside our group, which, of course, has happened. By the time we said our good-byes at the Guerbois that day and all thanks to Caillebotte we were Le Societe anonyme des artistes, peintres, sculpteurs, graveurs, etc. (The anonymous Society of Artists, Painters, Sculptors, Engravers, Printmakers, and so forth…….) It was the best we could do."

Ernest nodded once again. The smile had not left his face.

"In spite of everything, you seem, all of you, to be good friends," he commented, enjoying Claude's descriptive views of his group as well as his sense of humor. "I mean, even beyond Caillebotte's close friendship with Renoir and apart from Degas' bad temper you all seem protective of one another and very supportive."

"Oh, we are friends Monsieur, some of us very close friends, but as in every life, some friends are closer than others. Is it not this way for you as well? Monsieur, in our group we each have our individual strengths and weaknesses. I believe we know what those are and that is where the unwavering respect between us lies. That respect, I believe, and very strongly, is what will keep us together. Eventually it may be the only thing. I also believe that from the beginning we have recognized talent and purpose in one another, and would you not agree that this is very important and that it is what we must continue to be about, regardless of outcome? Right now, after two dismal exhibitions there is, of course, as you rightly suggest, a need for a more intellectual side to our thinking. Yes, I suppose we must be smarter in the way we move forward if we are to move forward at all, and that is where our baby Impressionist, Gustave Caillebotte, will likely shine most brightly for us. He is a fine painter and he has a good mind. He's a leader, really. Fortunately, his wealth quietly supports some of us during the bad times. Do you know that he buys paintings directly from each of us, especially when he knows one of us is down to his last few francs? Soon he may have a collection to rival yours. And there is no sense of competition, no show of financial superiority, not with Gustave. I'm sure you know he was trained as a lawyer. And he would have made a very good one. It may amuse you to know that as a result of his fine education, he has the kind of extensive vocabulary and way of speaking that baffles many of us at times. One Wednesday, Renoir arrived at the Guerbois with a dictionary under his arm. "Now there will be no question in anyone's mind as to exactly what our great young sage is talking about!" he proclaimed, placing the dictionary on the table for all of us to see as he further announced, "I know all of you have long suspected that our Gustave frequently speaks in a tongue known only to himself and to God and perhaps to Monsieur Durand-Ruel, especially when he wants us to agree with his ideas for our future! Now at last and once and for all, we can be certain what that tongue is!"

"Yes, I've wondered about that dictionary, Ernest remarked with another broad smile. "I've noticed it sitting there on the table each time you are gathered together."

"The dictionary was left that day in the hands of Juno, the Guerbois waiter who cares for it as well as he cares for his ugly gray cat," Claude further revealed. "I don't know where he keeps it in our absence, probably in the stew pot with the potatoes and peas," Claude said, shrugging his shoulders, "but every Wednesday, when we gather, he brings it out on his dilapidated tray along with cigarettes, cigars, and wine glasses and places it before Renoir with great ceremony. I've noticed that he seems genuinely pleased, almost relieved, whenever Renoir turns to it and consults one of its pages. Unfortunately, the dictionary and Juno's efforts did nothing to assist us when it came to deciding on a suitable name for ourselves. I was worried, particularly as Degas grew more and more contentious over the whole thing and Caillebotte did not always succeed as peacekeeper. And there was something else to worry about. As the opening date for our exhibition at Monsieur-Durand Ruel's gallery loomed closer, we all knew perfectly well that we had procrastinated in too many important things, mostly in getting work finished in time. We were really forced, and at the very last minute, to settle on an acceptable label and at the end, like it or not, it was Caillebotte's suggestion upon which out of necessity we all more or less agreed, but Monsieur, as the owner of my painting Impression Sunrise, you know better than most that in a short time and as our young Caillebotte predicted, thanks to the outside world we were saved from that very long, unwieldy title and I believe now we are appropriately called Impressionists."

"Your reference to Gustave Caillebotte as the baby Impressionist is amusing," Ernest said, reminded of his close association with the Caillebotte family. "Gustave and his mother are our country neighbors. They have a lovely house at Yerres, not far at all from ours at Montgeron. As you must know, Yerres is the adjacent village to Montgeron. The Caillebottes often come to dinner. My wife, Alice, likes them very much. Their gardens are quite beautiful. In his lifetime, Gustave's father, Martial, took great pains with the property. He was devoted to it, really. It's still beautiful, called La Casin and it has everything; a chapel, a dairy, a boathouse, even a lily pond; all this amidst endless plantings of the most thoughtfully placed flowers and trees. Gustave paints there. You must see La Casin during your stay with us. I'll arrange something."

"Gustave has mentioned very little to me about his family. But there we are. Each of us has our human side and some of us reveal more of our humanity than others," Claude ventured slowly, pausing once again to gaze out reflectively toward the passing scene then turning to face Ernest. "We all have out individual dispositions, it is true, and yes, our moods. I do often think about our group of characters and how we differ one from the other, though. We truly are a disparate group. When I think about Renoir I don't worry too much, at least not about his work and his potential for success. He is tenacious and he does whatever must be done to complete his canvases, but he sees vignettes of life that others never do. He grasps the importance of subjects that completely elude others, so it is not surprising that he is the gentle, humorous one among us, by contrast to Degas, who we have all come to accept as he is and nothing more. I am not sure what will happen there. A man can be his own worst enemy, but then there is Pissarro, who is the most prolific one among us, a hard working, somewhat naïve man, overly trusting much of the time I believe, shocked as a schoolmaster with our foul language and yet adamant when we don't share in his genuine concern for something like the frames that surround our paintings, which like Monsieur Durand-Ruel he says are very important things."

"You have said nothing of Sisley," Ernest pointed out, "the transplanted Englishman. I have a number of his paintings, more of those than of any other member of your group."

"Ah, Monsieur Sisley is the calm, soft-spoken British gentleman among us, very well-mannered, very elegant and correct, but a little nervous, a little shy, his quiet strength shown in his work, which is scrupulous. And do you know that he loves the ladies? They love him back. Scoundrel!"

Ernest signaled Paul to remove the champagne glasses. "And Paul, please be sure to tie the Dore box with the silver ribbon so it looks as if nothing has been disturbed. Germaine, small as she is, notices such things."

"How old is Germaine?" Claude asked, feeling far more comfortable in Ernest Hoschede's company.

"Germaine is five years old and wise beyond those mere five years," came Ernest's ready reply. "You'll meet her today and see that for yourself. Of my five children, I believe Germaine is blest with the most common sense. She's a lot like her mother. She just knows things, notices things. Loves to be outdoors, love her books. Alice is responsible for that. She's a wonderful mother and cares very much that all the children have every opportunity. She spends a good deal of time with them, all five. Frankly, I don't know how she does it; the children, the houses, the big family, me."

Ernest excused himself and said he had some details to review with Paul. I hope you don't mind, but Paul sees to it that at Montgeron this coach is garaged in the barn I had built behind the station house and gave to the village. He supervises the disconnecting and storage procedures and I have a few things to go over with him."

Claude smiled and nodded, grateful for the quiet and now able to fully enjoy the Briard Plateau's faultless swaths of color unfolding before him. Demanding thoughts and a city's suctioning heat could easily be forgotten under such circumstances, worry and all its restrictions replaced by the palatable refinements of sloping hills and endless borders of trees strung out and outlining the views that delighted him. Soon, mile after mile of waving pale yellow fields began to blur and ripple against the blue sky. Now and then they mingled in exquisite horizontal design with spider-thin strips of calm, dappled meadows run over with patches of red, self-sown poppies and just when it seemed the low growing brammis and buckthorn had taken over, soft waves of grasses and tall, red-faced poppies reappeared, their bright ruby blossoms scattered here and there, now mounded against brilliant green fields then clumped together, taller, brighter than before against deep burnished grasses, pervasive and shocking in nature's vast, panoramic solarium.

For a while he was captivated by the spectacular sweep of summer color, but before too long, every fresh knoll, every small clearing reminded him that he was being taken farther and farther away from Argenteuil. Again and again he fought to reassure himself. After more than ten years hadn't Camille come to expect his absences? Of course she had. She was his wife. She had been his model. She knew all his habits. She was patient. She understood. She loved him. It would be fine. But after this, it would be different. He would try not to be away so much.

There were enough subjects to paint in and around Argenteuil. He would talk to Durand-Ruel about selling all the Argenteuil paintings. Surely he would find buyers for them, or buy them himself as he had bought paintings in the past. They could bring in at least a thousand francs each, and once he was paid for the Hoschede panels perhaps there would be enough money to move to a better house. Yes, perhaps it was time to leave Argenteuil. But they had moved so many times, first, after their marriage, to Fecamp where Claude's family was close by at Le Havre and yet refused to meet Camille who, in their eyes and with a child born out of wedlock embodied the irresponsible, bohemian lifestyle relentless Adolphe Monet continued to insist his son abandon. And after Fecamp, there was the charming little hamlet of Saint-Michel, where according to Claude, conditions improved enormously. "There is no heat and no fire," he wrote to Frederick Bazille, requesting financial aid, "but my painting has never been better." And Camille had liked Saint-Michel, Claude insisted. There was a small garden. She loved the flowers. And she had understood perfectly that it had been absolutely essential he join Renoir to set up easels at Marly, at La Grenouillere, at Louveciennes, and at Bougival where he was convinced he had at last become unified with color in new, harmonic contrasts of light and shadow and the resulting chromaticism that excited him as few things could. It was true that Camille liked the house he rented at Argenteuil best of all. She said so many times. It was close to the river and within view of the tugboats and pleasure crafts that moved with the currents. It was at Argenteuil, when painting human figures in landscapes, that Camille and Jean were his models. The work had gone well for a while, so well, that by the end of 1872 he had sold twenty-nine canvases to Durand-Ruel. The next year, sales doubled and the average price for one of his paintings in 1873 was seven hundred francs, many purchased by the department store tycoon who now sat opposite him. Conditions were dramatically different now. But for Hoschede and his purchases, Claude's sales were non-existent and Camille and Jean suffered most. He could still hear Camille calling out to him as he had left the garden and walked through the door for his lunch only days before.

"A few pieces of pain poilane and what little is left of the cheese is all we have today!" she had said. "Monsieur Brabant says no meat until we pay him. Madame Luce said the same thing when I tried for a few handfuls of beans and a bunch of carrots. I was lucky to get this half loaf of bread from the new baker who doesn't know everyone in Argenteuil yet. I suppose before too long he will be turning me away too."

Again he leaned back in his seat. There was no escaping the harsh impact of his poverty, but now there was an opportunity for change. With Hoschede's commission and the sale of his Argenteuil paintings he could envision a happier future. He thought about finding his new village, his new home, one to inspire and encourage a new phase in life. He enthusiastically considered any number of remote locations; towns and villages he had only heard of, small, picturesque enclaves discovered by chance, secluded houses hidden by walls and gardens. His imagination led him to consider potential and possibility and the likelihood that Camille might welcome a change too. How he loved her. Yes, a change would be good for her; for both of them. A new house in a new village would revitalize their view of the world and renew their love with fresh devotion and ardor. Unrestricted by patterns and routines worn thin by time, once again they would know the spontaneous hours of delighted passion they had known when night after night not so long ago their heated lovemaking had been filled with promises of constancy and tender whispers of undying devotion. Recently though, everything, including their lovemaking, had become tepid and indifferent. There was a sameness to life and an accompanying dissatisfaction with its predictable daily details. In a new, more stimulating environment surely they would be able to capture the magic of the past and those enchanting nights when Camille had curled her supple body tight against him, her fragrant skin a warm blanket of rose-perfumed satin strewn over his by morning. Yes, times were bad and things were not moving along as quickly as he wanted them to, but all that was about to change. Soon, with the Hoschede commission paid, and in a new village filled with new people, Camille would buy bottles of rosewater again. She would laugh again. She would spend time outdoors experimenting in the garden with a few shrubs and potted plants. On winter afternoons he would hold her close on the sofa by the fireplace in his studio. He would unbutton her dress and caress her breasts. He would reach down to her warm thighs and the waiting temptation between and she would respond to him and press herself against him, and locked together as one they would know the soaring ardor of breathless fulfillment in moments of rapture they would remember for the rest of their lives.

The train had slowed. Must be in the heart of the Brie Valley by now. Yes, there were the grasslands bordering the famous Senart Forest. Almost there. Another kilometer or two. He was feeling better. And why not? Forty kilometers out of Paris the woodlands had skirted themselves in a hundred hues of ever more indolent color, languid and lonely yellow one minute, complicit rose and consenting purple the next. His anxiety was abating. He felt the tenseness in his shoulders relaxing. He could see his own reflection in the window. Was that a small smile? Impossible.

"Almost there now," Ernest announced, his eyes bright with anticipation as he glanced out of the window. He sat tall in his seat, brushed a hand over each of his shoulders, pulled at his cuffs, then pointed to the widening panorama of mellow, unspoiled summer splendor.

"Look there, Claude. The Concy Hills. And see there, just beyond that hillside, the woodlands of the Grange Lemeil-Brevannes. Beautiful place. And now look there. Beyond those oaks and pines you can see the spires of the Benedictine Abbey of Notre Dame de Yerres. And now there, just over that range of poplars, those are the chimneys of the Chateau Rottembourg. We are crossing the eastern boundary of my property right now, he added. Soon we'll be at the station. You'll hear the whistles any second now. They let the family know I'm coming. Sometimes, I just walk up to the house from the station."

The smile had not left his face. He clasped his hands across his chest. His index fingers tapped impatiently one against the other. "Today, our houseman Bernard, will be there to meet us with the landau," he said, clearly delighted as in puffs of steam and a burst of shrieking whistles the train gradually slowed and in a fall of absolute silence, ground to a halt.

"Our summers here are always wonderful here," he remarked, standing and turning to the opposite side of the train car and the station, "but there's something unusual about this summer, something out of the ordinary about the way things are growing and looking, not just at Rottembourg, but throughout the entire countryside. Alice has noticed it. She says in all the years she has known the Brie Valley that the village gardens have never been more beautiful. I must say, I agree with her. The blossoms in our rose garden are more plentiful and last longer than ever before when she cut bouquets for the house. Wait until you see her arrangements. Alice has a way with flowers."

CHAPTER 13

Arrival at Montgeron

Stepping off the train, Claude was immediately struck by the surrounding landscape. So taken was he by the picturesque scene that not for a moment did it occur to him that he and his host had discussed nothing at all to do with subjects for the proposed wall panels. Now, though, having finally arrived at Montgeron, Claude did find himself feeling more comfortable with his benefactor and as a result far more confident in his ability to complete the four wall panels for the Chateau Rottembourg in a timely manner whatever their themes might turn out to be. These realizations pleased him enormously, but at the same time there was an additional consideration to be made. In a manner which permeated and drove his life, this added factor had everything to do with his constant awareness of the natural environment around him, namely its immediate perspective, its exacting colors, and defining content.

Here at Montgeron, while standing on the station platform waiting for his suitcases, Claude Monet was finding himself greeted by a mystery, one which characterized and permeating the aura and mood of his immediate surroundings. This of and by itself, was a highly unusual if not altogether unprecedented experience for such a close observer of nature's many moods. Well aware of his talent for quickly grasping the tone and temper of any rural setting in which he might find himself, Claude was likewise well-acquainted with the French countryside's tendencies to enchant. He had painted in its meadows and camped in its woodlands. He knew the sorcery of its humorless forests and the foolishness of its undulating, unmarked borders, but the unnamed magnetism greeting him upon his arrival at Montgeron was not mere country enchantment. It was not the undulating beauty of purple hills clearly seen in the distance. It was not the perfection of fully matured silver fir and oak trees nearby, and it was not the delight of sheer, undisturbed silence stirred only by the occasional breeze. It was something else entirely, something more complex than the undulation of purple hills, something more obscurely layered than veils of sheer silence. It was a playfully confounding condition with which he had no experience. He wanted to see it, touch it, know its source, but the exasperating nature of its origin was as elusive as the gently shifting breezes surrounding him.

A contemplative, sensitive man given to brooding periods of deep reflection, this lover of nature's power to overwhelm and confuse called upon his simplest natural instincts and soon solved the mystery. The answer had been there all along, taunting him, tempting him, and it lay in the all-encompassing air itself. In this corner of the Brie Valley a heady mix of fragrant roses, grasses, and burgeoning vegetation was being flung out and borne up on a carpet of summer breezes. It was August in the heart of France's great wheat producing Brie Valley and Claude Monet had arrived in its midst, at the peak of its annual powers, in the season of reapers and gleaners.

The annual mowing and gathering had begun to stir the spirit of the fertile Brie, and from Villecresnes to Crevecoeur-en-Auge and on to Coubert and Soisnolles, August's warm ritual winds rippled through vast yellow wheatfields, flowering meadows, and languorous glades. Grainstacks had begun to dot the bundled landscape of the Briard Plateau, reaffirming noble old connections to the land as freshly harvested expanses of farmland from Boussy-Saint-Antoine at the edge of the plain and west to sloping Mandres-les-Roses were garnered and laid bare, the lavish fragrances of freshly clipped field grasses, clover, and honeysuckle carried aloft and windborne for many miles from the distant, ripe ploughlands. This was the great ambrosial flourish of which Claude was suddenly and acutely aware; this, the yearly unbridled balm unique to the famous agricultural region of France which for centuries had been called its breadbasket, its indestructible bonds with cyclical nature and the formidable rhythms of its annual habits anticipated and well-known to every French citizen who, like Ernest Hoschede and Claude Monet, from early childhood and with the sweet pleasure derived from every bite of freshly baked brioche or pain poilane, were taught to respect the Briard's time-honored traditions and the people related to them, the country people who loved the land and lived out their lives as their fathers and grandfathers had lived them, in devoted agrarian families who faithfully tilled the soil and gratefully harvested its bounty and were born and died in the same houses on the same plots of ground their ancestors had known for untold generations before them.

Located south and east of cosmopolitan Paris, and although situated at the secluded northern fringes of the fertile Briard Plateau, Montgeron was no remote agrarian community. It was a quiescent residential village, its slow-paced elegance light years away from anything at all to do with crowded Paris boulevards and attachments to opera houses or art galleries, for central to its preferred way of life were the care and cultivation of its beautiful gardens and the privacy demanded by residents of its gracious houses.

Those properties closest to the train station, built before the marvel of railway travel, remained frozen in time, vestiges of inherited, somewhat faded splendor, the turreted structures of touching beauty at the end of their gravel drives benefitting from improvements only when absolutely necessary: a new roof every eighty years or so, a fresh coat of varnish on the oak floors only with the arrival of a new generation of occupants, the planting of young trees and hedges completed reluctantly and only in the event of a destructive storm. The gardens of these properties whose owners insisted they did not hear the intermittent sounds of noisy trains arriving and departing so close to their doors were the only tangible signs of change and even then, most clung to their spectacular old-fashioned parterres planted in the same pattern year after year and with exactly same range of color they had known through generations of owners. Farther from the station and along the Concy Road the houses were larger, the gardens unseen. Glimpses of velvet lawn sprang out and quickly vanished behind gates and tall hedges in company with clumps of wild orange daylilies flourishing untended along the roadside under canopies of oak trees and against the occasional length of stone wall swathed in pink roses no one could recall ever having been planted.

Central to the practicality of village life was the gray shingled stationmaster's depot at which Ernest and Claude had arrived. The depot was not only the arrival and departure point for Montgeron residents and visitors traveling to and from the countryside or to further points north and south, it was also the depository for village mail which arrived twice each week from Paris. In addition to its practical purposes, over time the depot had become the destination of choice for many a villager's daily walks and leisurely airings. In good weather, people set out from their houses and strolled along one of the two unpaved roads. Dogs at their side, they picked up their mail, met neighbors at the station, shared family news and chatted as they sat on one of three iron benches under the trees. Some chose to sit alone on one of the wooden benches attached to the station where they read their letters and the out-of-date newspapers readily available from the stack kept for countless days beside a green jardinière filled with cascading yellow roses. Throughout the summer months, many residents could be found waiting for the afternoon train bringing relatives and friends who could be spending several days or weeks as guests. Whatever their intention or disposition, all idly watched the general comings and goings before returning home to continue on in their privileged, insulated lives in houses that had stayed in the same family through countless years and remained dear to those born in their rooms.

The functioning and maintenance of the station was in the hands of the long-time stationmaster, Louis DeLage and his wife, Cecile, a somewhat mismatched, middle-aged couple who conducted their daily business in an orderly if rather imperious manner as from behind the narrow black iron bars of their turreted ticket booth and looking for all the world like a pair of country jailers, they could be counted on to manage the station with the deftness of a Les Halles butcher and the absolute authority of an emperor. While slim Monsieur de Lage offered warm welcomes, distributed the mail, kept the station clean, watered the roses, and for a small fee ran errands for village residents between scheduled train arrivals and departures, stout Madame de Lage handled the ticketing and kept track of the money. With a good deal of time on her hands, especially in winter and from Tuesdays to Thursdays in summer when few passengers arrived or departed, she also ate a delectable variety of the fruit and cream-filled pastries prepared by her housekeeper while specializing in her favorite activity which was gossip.

Although diligently inquisitive and talkative, Madame de Lage did have her more endearing habits, a few of which the more observant village children had learned to mimic quite ably, a particularly entertaining and repeated favorite being her reliably obnoxious manner when proceeding through the motions of transacting ordinary daily business. As with stern authority she handed the traveler an orange-colored ticket from the roll at her elbow and carefully counted the money passed to her not once but twice, in one remarkable swoop she also managed to take a quick bite of pastry, gulp it down, wipe the sugary crumbs away from the corners of her mouth, and lean forward to mention a little tidbit to you concerning one or another of the residents of Montgeron. Long-time resident or first-time visitor, it made no difference. Madame DeLage's practiced deftness in her rapid series of acts amazed the children whose parents were well aware that the information Madame distributed with a quick wink or smug smile was never so offensive as to cause alarm. Everyone did know, however, that Madame DeLage enjoyed her information and the odd power it seemed to provide her. It was also common knowledge that her readiness to share in everyone's comings and goings was not always met with polite or dismissive nonchalance. The essence of community concern lay in the fact that Montgeron property owners placed a high value on their privacy and simply did not wish to have the scope of their personal activities or the nature of their travel plans circulated. Whether or not Madame DeLage was aware of this concern was never clear and it was generally assumed that even if it had been, she would have remained unstoppable, continuing to watch and report on what she saw and heard with consistent reliability, great pleasure, and in the time-tested manner of a town crier.

This August afternoon was no different from any other summer afternoon of the past and although eager to politely welcome Monsieur Hoschede, Madame DeLage found herself with a juicy morsel to share. The day before, Monsieur Merian, owner of the magnificent Chateau des Nuages, had behaved "very badly" as in a loud voice Madame opined to Ernest from behind her iron bars. Along with two large trunks, a satchel, and a very new-looking portmanteau, Monsieur Merian had brought two huge, hairy black dogs on the train with him from Paris.

"He said they were his son's prized Briards," Madame DeLage called out with a look of disgust as she shook her head. "As far as I could see, those prizes needed proper baths and clippings, and perhaps a thorough delousing. I have never seen such filthy dogs!" she pronounced in no uncertain terms. "Upon arrival here at my beautiful little depot, one of the beastly creatures promptly urinated on the stack of newspapers there beside my jardinière. Can you imagine such a thing? And Monsieur Merion did not even seem to notice," she further announced to Ernest as he waved a polite but silent greeting to her, reluctant to get too close to Madame's iron bars and find himself required to engage her, absolutely certain as he sped past that the story of Monsieur Merian's offensive pair of Briards had, within, mere hours of its occurrence been told, re-told, and ultimately acted out by a few Montgeron children as if it were a practiced scene on the Paris stage.

"Look now at my newspapers!" Madame moaned in a loud, strident voice, pointing to the stack of two week-old, yellowed papers she had the nerve to call the news. "They are completely ruined and my next delivery will not arrive from Paris until next Monday afternoon!"

The behavior of Monsieur Merian's Briards being the extent of the day's pronouncements thus far, it was with some heightened interest that the ever watchful Madame DeLage greeted the ever well-groomed and handsome Monsieur Hoschede just arrived from Paris, and today not only with the familiar blue box from the Dore, but with a guest. Ah, and the guest is quite interesting, she observes. He is square and solid, strong-looking, like an outdoorsman of some sort. Yes, must be a new gardener from Paris, one with experience, perhaps a former supervisor at a grand city garden, she determines as she waves and smiles, hoping all the while that Monsieur Hoschede and his new gardener will come closer and at least pause for a brief word, providing a golden opportunity for questioning and for adding yet one more tasty tale to the day's rather slim roster of information.

"The next arriving passengers will be hearing all about you, Claude," Ernest laughed as he and Claude stepped into the waiting open landau. "I hope you passed Madame DeLage's inspection. The woman is harmless, but she does take great pleasure in knowing everything there is to know about the comings and goings around here. My wife says that although they would pray to die before admitting it, all the women in the village check in with Madame at one time or another throughout the summer to find out if they're missing out on some important happening. They pretend to come to the station for a lovely afternoon walk with the dogs, or they go so far as to say they were in the mood for a little ride in the pony cart with the children or grandchildren and must pick up a Paris newspaper. Seems to me its Madame DeLage's reporting they value far more than any city journalist's."

As anticipated, the landau from the Chateau Rottembourg drawn by its pair of black Landais ponies had awaited the train's arrival. They stood quietly in the shade while Bernard, Rottembourg's gloved steward, collected the suitcases and loaded them onto the landau's rear carrier rack. Watching the process, Ernest was clearly eager to be on his way. Impatiently shifting his weight from one foot to other, his thoughts were now focused entirely on Claude's painting project.

"Views of the property! That's it, Claude," he called out. "Yes, the pond or the north view of the house from the meadow at the edge of the forest. Alice loves that view. Or perhaps the rose garden. It's especially beautiful this year. Oh well, you'll see it all soon enough. The children will show you everything."

Madame DeLage couldn't quite hear the conversation, but she noticed how the new gardener smiled and nodded in affirmation, sharing Monsieur Hoschede's enthusiasm for whatever it was they discussed.

"Don't worry, Monsieur! We will find the right subjects," she heard the new gardener from Paris remark. "They are there, waiting," he added.

Climbing into the handsome open landau, his senses stirred, his energies renewed, his satisfaction with whatever stroke of good luck had brought Ernest Hoschede into his life at a high point, Claude began to look ahead with ever increasing confidence. It would be fine, he told himself. He was sure of it. The time would pass quickly in this lyrical pocket of the Brie Valley and he would be paid for doing what he loved. Camille and Jean would be well and waiting. Two weeks for the studies, another one or two for the paintings and it would be done.

"Don't get too comfortable, Claude. It won't be too long a drive," Ernest remarked as the two settled into the black leather seat and Bernard took up the reins. "Along the Concy Road which we'll be getting onto in a moment, the distance from the station to the gates of Rottembourg is little less than a single kilometer."

The horses' hooves clattered along the station's apron of gray cobblestones before turning sharply northward onto the narrow Concy Road lined to either side with a show of full-leafed poplar and locust trees. A farmer driving a cart full of melons passed, causing the landau to pull over and pause at the side of the road. The farmer waved. The landau's occupants waved back. Formations of black treeswifts flew overhead. The only sound came from the crunching of the carriage wheels against the gravel, the only sign of life the occasional gate left slightly ajar.

As the Concy Road curved it also ascended, its gentle contours gradually growing more deeply shaded by a profusion of spruce trees and thick masses of red columbine joined like shadowed shields at their roots. Suddenly, the road curved once again and directly ahead, under a wide, stone arch, an open pair of black iron gates stood silhouetted against the radiant blue sky. To each side, a pair of massive stone urns held a blaze of trailing red roses. Just under the arch and through the gate, the landau slowed and stopped at the side door of a brick cottage. Three spotted hounds came running out, barking and wagging their tails as Ernest called out, "Poston! Aleron! Theo! Get plenty of rest this afternoon! Tomorrow we go back into the forest! The guinea-hens are waiting for us!"

"I heard the train, Monsieur Hoschede," the gatekeeper called out, hurrying through the cottage door. "On her way to morning Mass, Madame Hoschede came to tell me you would be coming with a visitor this afternoon. She brought my wife the most beautiful bouquet of asters! She said they are at their best right now in the lower garden. I hope you will have time to see them today. Welcome home, Monsieur Hoschede."

"And welcome to the Chateau Rottembourg," Ernest said, smiling to Claude as through the quickly closed gates, village rusticity and all its wild lilies were left farther and farther behind in a pampered succession of gracefully trimmed plane trees, close-clipped emerald green lawns, and flower borders thick with bright yellow marigolds. The close proximity of a church steeple rising parallel to the drive a short distance from the gatekeeper's cottage attracted Claude's attention as did the short path leading toward it through a wooden gate.

"That's the Church of Saint-Jacques," Ernest explained. "Several years before my wife's father purchased the property, the land for the church was donated by Baron Henri du Rottembourg. In about 1850, the church you see there replaced a much older one somewhere to the north. There's a plaque inside commemorating the Baron's gift. Alice prays there at Saint Jacques' every day. She takes the children to Mass every Sunday. I've been told there's been a church somewhere on this land since 1150 or so. I'll tell you more about Baron Henri du Rottembourg once we're at the house. He was an interesting man. The villagers loved him. A few of them are old enough to remember how he appeared at all the summer festivals, turned out in his full military uniform, complete with gold epaulets, medals and ribbons, sword at his side."

Its gravel freshly raked, the drive stretched out ahead, long and straight, and like a waiting sentinel at its end stood the Chateau Rottembourg, its grand Italianate rose brick façade subdued by the gleam of climbing ivy. As the landau approached, it slowly circled a grassy oval before coming to a halt at the three broad steps leading to the paneled front door. A young woman in a gray dress and white apron stepped out to greet the carriage as it slowed and came to a halt. Behind her, in the open doorway, a small, dark-haired girl peered out, clutching a doll.

"Papa! Papa! I've been waiting for you all day!" the child cried out, running into the bright sunshine, her pale yellow dress billowing up around her. "Mademoiselle and I heard the train whistle and we came right away. Did you bring Peach Croustades from the Dore? Jacques said you would forget but Mama said you never forget."

The child appeared to be four or five years old, her delight apparent as her father bounded out of the carriage and raced toward her, lifting her into his arms and kissing her soundly on the cheek. "So, Jacques said I would forget, did he?" he remarked with a chuckle. "You must tell your brother to have more faith in his Papa! And you will be happy to know that I not only brought Peach Croustades, I also brought pink macaroons, madeleines, and those fancy chouquettes au chocolat all of you love so much. Bernard will bring everything in. Oh, I almost forgot There are also palmiers for all of us to enjoy tomorrow. Soon we'll all be as fat as those kittens in the barn!"

The child threw back her head and laughed, her doll left to dangle from one hand as her father put her down in the doorway and said, "Germaine, this gentleman is Monsieur Monet. He is the artist I told you would be coming from Paris to paint panels for the rotunda." The little girl curtsied and looked up to scrutinize the visitor's face.

"You rode in Papa's blue train, didn't you, Monsieur Monet," she remarked, clutching her doll tightly, her voice filled with admiration as she rocked back and forth. "I love to ride in Papa's train when we come from Paris," she continued. "I have wanted to watch the smoke going up into the sky behind us when we ride with Mama and Papa, but we are not allowed to open the windows and lean out. Did you see the smoke, Monsieur Monet? Did Papa allow you to open the windows and lean out?"

The child's expressive face was a fascinating study as she spoke, her vocabulary precise, her lips forming her words with unmistakable mindset.

"Yes, Germaine," her father interrupted as Claude smiled indulgently. "Monsieur Monet rode in the train, and no, he did not open a window or watch the smoke. As you have been told many times, it is dangerous to lean out of a train window and no one is allowed to do so, not even a sweet little daughter like you. Now my darling, let's step inside. I must take our guest on a tour of the house and I want him to meet the rest of the family before the afternoon disappears. Where is everyone?"

"Playing statues in the garden," Germaine responded. "When we heard the train, Mama told me I could come up to the house to meet you. I ran all the way and waited at the door with Mademoiselle Gabrielle the way I'm supposed to until the carriage stops and you come out. Everyone is still playing outside."

"Then we must join them," Ernest said with a wide smile. "You run on ahead and tell Mama we're here. We'll be right along and it would be very nice if there could be some cool lemon tea waiting for us."

Germaine threw back her head and laughed once again, clearly delighted with herself for having been first in the family to greet her Papa and the artist from Paris. Her doll once again dangling from one hand, she reached up to hug her father before running off. "Do you play statues, Monsieur Monet?" she suddenly called out, pausing to look back.

"No, I do not, but I suppose I could learn," Claude answered. "Is it a difficult game?"

"Oh, no, Monsieur Monet, the game of statues is not difficult at all. I have taught all Papa's old friends to play! I could teach you. Perhaps tomorrow," Germaine called over her shoulder as she ran ahead and into the house where Mademoiselle Gabrielle waited and standing on the gravel drive Claude laughed.

Stepping into Rottembourg's entrance hall with Claude at his side, Ernest was suddenly circumspect and surprisingly apologetic. "I hope the children won't be too distracting while you're working," he said hesitating. "They're used to having visitors, but they have great freedom here in the country and sometimes they can be quite a handful. I guess I haven't told you there are five of them. Yes, five little inquisitive, energetic souls: four talkative little girls and one mischievous little boy to keep us busy, worried, and very happy. I think, though, that my son, Jacques, has problems with his four sisters at times, especially with little Germaine who despite her age, can be a bit outspoken. Germaine thinks Jacques is too rough and she doesn't hesitate to tell him so, but he is the only boy and naturally he has a boy's interests. Having a young son of your own, you know how that is. Jacques likes climbing trees, skimming rocks across the pond, and capturing live frogs and snakes. He doesn't mind getting dirty or falling down and scraping his knees and elbows. The girls, on the other hand, like fancy dresses, bubbles in their baths, and wearing their mother's hats while having tea parties on the lawn."

Claude nodded. "My only experience with children is with my son, Jean. I'm sure daughters are a very different sort of challenge. Jean likes to do the same sorts of things Jacques does. He's probably running barefoot along the riverbank at Argenteuil right now, watching the sailboats or searching for anything that is slippery and crawls."

"Claude, once again, I'm so sorry I didn't think to suggest you bring Jean and your wife with you. I've been involved with business matters lately, a little preoccupied I'm afraid, financial conditions being what they are in Paris and all this talk of recession. I'm sure you've heard about it. Unusual things are happening. Many of my customers tell me they're quite worried. Haven't you noticed that many shops and family businesses all over Paris are being shuttered, more and more of them every day? I hope it all balances out soon. Some bankers I know tell me they're preparing for the worst, but out here in the country I put all that aside and enjoy life. And there's a lot to enjoy. In the future, though, perhaps you will arrange to bring your wife and son for a visit. They would love it here at

Rottembourg and my children always welcome a new playmate. But come now, let me show you around."

The Chateau Rottembourg's imposing tree-lined drive may have set a formal introduction to the lifestyle conducted within its walls but once inside its front door, signs of family comfort and the ease with which daily life was lived amid a wealth of treasures was immediately apparent. In the entrance hall Claude paused to examine the commanding military portrait over the fireplace which Ernest explained was that of steely-eyed Baron Henri du Rottembourg, resplendent in his red military tunic and a profusion of campaign medals.

"When the Baron's heirs sold the property to my wife's family and emptied the house of its contents, this portrait was left in place there over the fireplace. Except for the year Alice inherited and we had all the walls painted, it's never been moved. I like to picture the Baron in these rooms. I wish I'd known him. He was one of Napoleon's most highly decorated generals and a member of the general staff. As Alice will surely tell you, his name is set in stone on one of the columns under the Arc de Triomphe. "By order of the Emperor, if you please!" he mimicked with a great sweep of his arm. "My Alice does love the history of this house."

Claude quickly absorbed the impact of welcome just inside Rottembourg's door with no little admiration. He took notice of the logs piled high by the fireplace and the large green porcelain bowl filled with pink summer roses on the round center table, an assortment of children's books and small wooden animals collected in five matching baskets set around it, each basket bearing a name engraved on a brass plate: Marthe, Blanche, Suzanne, Jacques, Germaine. Savoring the comfort of family informality, his eye was repeatedly drawn to the simplicity of the center table's bowl of flawless roses, but stepping further inside and walking into the center hall beside Ernest, he found the mood very different, for it was here that Rottembourg became a classic French chateau, its long center hall a masterpiece of architectural provocation, its blue-gray damask-covered walls unfolding a series of double mahogany doors opening onto spacious rooms filled with collections of furnishings comfortably arranged on soft-colored carpets, paintings and ornately framed wall mirrors everywhere.

"This center hall organizes all the rooms to each side of the first floor," Ernest remarked, "and for now, as we go along you'll catch glimpses of the rooms we spend our time in. Later in the week we'll have plenty of time to explore them more fully, but my greatest aim this afternoon is to have you see the rotunda. That's the important thing, and of course I want you to meet the family."

Clearly, Ernest was eager to have Claude finally see the room where the four panels would be installed, but walking beside Claude in the chateau world he occupied with obvious contentment and authority, he could not resist pausing to make remarks on the furnishings and decorative pieces of which the collector in him seemed particularly proud.

"This house holds a number of treasures," he said, "some very good signed pieces of furniture and several collections of silver and rare porcelains, but Rottembourg is really a country house, a home for a family, and Alice deserves all the credit for maintaining its qualities of welcome and ease. She sees to it that our family and friends enjoy every inch of living space here, and we are all very much the better for her care."

Evidence of Ernest's complimentary comments were seen through every open door, assortments of books and vases of fresh flowers casually placed on gleaming tables and set alongside silver trays of brandy decanters. In one room, a dog's wicker bed waited in a sunny corner, beside it a stuffed toy bear with a missing ear, nearby a child's well-worn rocking horse. Through another set of doors, sofas and chairs were arranged close to one another suggesting invitation to conversation, cushions and pillows slightly compressed, some askew, their rumpled appearance indicating the recent presence of an occupant or two. Most personally significant to Claude as he proceeded along the hallway with Ernest were the four wall tables, two to each side, hanging over each a beautifully framed painting signed by one of his Impressionist colleagues. Against the gray-blue damask of one wall hung Camille Pissarro's *La Route*, against another Pierre Renoir's *Woman with a Cat*. Against the opposite wall were Alfred Sisley's *La Seine a Marly* and Berthe Morisot's *La Toilette*. Set onto each of the glistening marble-topped tables below the paintings was a magnificent clock, each ornately gilded, the horologist name of Raingo

Freres inscribed in florid gold lettering on each glistening white porcelain face.

"These paintings are so right here," Claude said, slowing his steps. "Monsieur Hoschede, I am most impressed to see these paintings here in this house. This is exactly how our work is intended to be seen and enjoyed," he said: in residential settings where people live out their lives and pursue their daily interests, and Monsieur, the clocks are wonderful companions for them, but do they all chime at the same time?"

"Oh, no!" Ernest laughed, pausing before one of the elaborately gilded timepieces. "That would require a talent for synchronization we do not possess! We can barely manage to keep them wound. All they do is tick, thank goodness! They're family pieces, part of the Raingo clock collection here at Rottembourg. The chimes have been disengaged for now. I should tell you that Alice is descended from the Raingo family. All the clocks in the house belong to her. Her Belgian ancestors began the family business in Brussels in the last century and thanks to the Duc de Chartres who brought Zacharie, the first of the Raingo clockmaker brothers to France, it continues to this day, but the family is not directly involved anymore. They're more concentrated on the acquisition and sale of valuable Paris real estate, but Raingo clockworks set into art bronzes continue to maintain the family's fine reputation as well as a good deal of its income. The Orrerys are truly spectacular. They're in some very important collections across Europe. I'm told there are only twelve. Alice's uncle, Julian Raingo has one at his Paris home. He enjoys telling anyone who will listen, all about it, how it works, how it was put together and when. He'll be at dinner tonight so be prepared for one of his Raingo family lectures. Don't worry. I'll do what I can to encourage brevity. Of course we expect you to join us. Eight o'clock. We'll send Bernard and the landau for you. My cousin, Beatrice and her husband, Marc Pirole, will be with us too, also a neighbor of ours, Jean DeLille. He's a fairly well-known portrait painter, interesting dinner guest too. Maybe you've heard of him. If not, he'll surely tell you all about himself. The Piroles are staying through next week. You'll see them on their daily walks around the property. And at dinner, don't pay any attention to Marc. He's a bore and expects to be ignored, but Beatrice is special and my favorite relative. She can be a little flamboyant and loud, so be prepared. Just so you know, Beatrice and Julian Raingo are old friends. A while back, word had it that they might be a little more than friends. I personally believe they still are. In any case,

Beatrice is respectably married now. You'll be staying in Julian Raingo's lodge. He seldom uses it these days. Says it too small for his dog. That beast is a monstrous Saint-Bernard. Last year, both uncle and dog moved into a big, beautiful house at Yerres. It's just down the Concy Road, not far from Gustave Caillebotte's family property."

"Oh yes," Claude commented as he absorbed Ernest's rapid use of short sentences. "Gustave has invited me to come to Yerres on several occasions but for one reason or another I've never been able to accept his invitations. His painting, *The Floor Scrapers*, added so much to our exhibition this past spring. He's doing fine work, and he's so young. There's a bright future ahead of him. I hope to see him while I'm here."

"You will see him," Ernest quickly affirmed. "Gustave and his parents are coming to dinner next week; Wednesday, I believe Alice said, but in the next few days I'll arrange for you to visit the Caillebotte estate. You must see it. We'll go together. Gustave's father lavishes his attention on the place. His gardens are truly beautiful; not a weed, not a wilted flower or leaf anywhere. He and Alice are always conferring on one thing or another: how their roses are doing or why the lawns are developing so much moss this year, and on and on."

Caught up in Rottembourg's all-encompassing aura and pleased to anticipate a visit to the Caillebotte estate, Claude was startled by the unexpected sight of *Impression Sunrise*. Enclosed in the same gilded frame chosen by Paul Durand-Ruel for its Boulevard Capucine Exhibition two years earlier, the painting had been hung on a prominent wall toward the end of the hall and to one side of an arched opening, the exquisite inlaid marquetry chest beneath it and another Raingo clock adding to its impact.

"It took me quite some time to decide on the best place for your *Impression Sunrise*," Ernest confessed with a broad smile. "I had it sent up from the Paris apartment for the summer. For days I wandered all over the house searching out exactly the right spot for hanging it. Alice thought I was losing my mind over the whole thing. I studied the walls and the light in every room and finally concluded that since I wanted it to be seen by every visitor to Rottembourg and enjoyed every day by the family, *Impression Sunrise* must hang in as conspicuous a location as possible. Here, on this wall, everyone in the house, from the children to the staff and every guest must pass it to get to the rotunda and the main stairway which we'll soon see. I hope you approve."

"Yes, of course I do," Claude immediately responded. "*Impression Sunrise* is perfect here, and just as our paintings are intended to be, it is comfortably at home in a residential setting where people come and go every day," Claude responded, deeply touched by the thoughtful care with which his painting had been handled.

"The longer I live with it the more I believe *Impression Sunrise* represents the spirit of innovation and freedom you and your group seek to project," Ernest commented further. "I love having it, and Claude, don't ever lose heart. One day others will understand what you and I understand. Be patient and don't stop working. And speaking of working, now you are about to see the reason for your visit to Rottembourg."

Through the wide arched opening to one side of *Impression Sunrise* and its companion Raingo clock, Ernest ushered Claude into a spacious room where a broad stream of sunlight beamed onto a bare oak floor. Against its provocative gleam, four large armchairs upholstered in a brightly flowered ruby-red fabric were arranged at the foot of a curving staircase. Adding to the clearly romantic atmosphere, a crystal chandelier sparkled from the ceiling over a black lacquered piano.

Bathed in its inviting afternoon glow, the room's architectural symmetry was at first its most impressive quality, but then Claude noticed the balance, the prevalence of order, the chamfered ceiling, and the four slightly protruding pearl-gray walls separated by a series of tall, glass-paned doors through which the columns of a terrace could be seen. Clearly, these were the walls intended for the four paintings. How exquisite an idea it had been to plan for painted panels to be set into this magnificent space, a space filled with natural light and sensual color by day. He couldn't wait to see it in evening candlelight.

"Well, here it is at last, the destination for your paintings," Ernest announced, folding his arms across his chest. "As you can see, although the rotunda and its stairway serve as access to the upper floors, the space is directly accessible from the hallway. As you can also see, the rotunda faces the columned main terrace and is an extension of the dining room. It really is my favorite part of the house, and now that I'm seeing it with you I'm more convinced than ever that views of the property are the appropriate themes for the four paintings here. I hope you agree."

Claude nodded, looking through the rotunda and toward the spacious formal dining room where the large painting over the fireplace caught his eye. "It's Corot's *Morning, Dance of the Nymphs*," Ernest said. "It bears the Salon's red stamp of 1851. I bought it at the art sale of my late and very prosperous tailor, Laurent-Richard."

"And you have a great prize there," Claude said with a decidedly respectful tone. "As I believe you know, I'm an admirer of Corot's work. I understand there were some outstanding paintings at Laurent-Richard's sale. I passed his shop at the corner of Rue Laffitte and Boulevard des Italiens many times on my way to see Monsieur Durand-Ruel. Until his sale I had absolutely no idea he was such an important collector."

"I've heard that same remark from a number of my friends," Ernest said. "I suppose people can be full of surprises. Of course right now with the financial picture as it is, some people in Paris may wish to maintain the same sort of anonymity. It's understandable, but it doesn't mean that anyone should put an end to pursing their interests."

Claude looked away, shook his head, and said, "Monsieur, this financial picture you speak of worries me. It is likely to have a devastating effect on my group's progress. We must be realistic and face that. We must also face the fact that it could be the end of us."

"No! You cannot let that happen!" Ernest quickly interjected. "However difficult it may be to continue, you and your group represent an important journey into the art world's future. You must keep that in mind and go on. Paris and perhaps all Europe needs that new brand of forward thinking. You cannot allow anything to stop you from proceeding and I will help wherever I can."

Despite Ernest's words of encouragement which were sincerely offered, and although Claude nodded and seemed to agree, on the inside he remained doubtful of his group's ability to stay the course and maneuver through its many difficulties, most significant among them the matter of money. There was no escaping the fact that with the exception of Gustave Caillebotte, they were all completely dependent on income from their paintings for their livelihoods. Even in the rarified air of a country house gracefully set into its landscape and miles from Paris, Claude's thoughts were realistic enough to consider that before too long and out of necessity the group of working artists with whom he had formed a loyal bond could be disbanding. With or without the dealer expertise of Paul Durand-Ruel, in the face of dire financial conditions each individual artist would be forced to independently embark on a search for buyers and patrons and hope for the best. For now, though, he had this Hoschede commission. It would provide a welcome level of security and a respite from the worry with which he had been living with little relief. It would be a productive, gratifying period of time, and whatever the future might hold, he would always appreciate Ernest Hoschede's generosity and support.

"Claude, before I get much further in acquainting you with the house," his host interrupted, re-focusing Claude's attention, "I want to be sure you know that while you're here at Rottembourg you are free to explore the grounds of the property at your leisure. You are a guest here as well as artist in residence and as I said at the station, the children will be helpful to you in pointing out possible subjects for the panels. They know the estate grounds better than my wife and I do. You'll find that out soon enough. By the way, do you play the piano?" he added, stepping closer to the gleaming Pleyel at the room's center.

"No, I do not," Claude responded with a broad smile, "but I enjoy music. My family is quite musical. My mother was a fine singer. She had a lovely voice. An uncle of mine played the flute. When I was living at home in Le Havre, there was always music in the house. Occasionally, after Sunday luncheon I joined in the singing. I loved the folk songs of the Auvergne. I learned a few of them from my Aunt Sophie."

"Alice plays the piano," Ernest remarked, "very well, as a matter of fact, and she's teaching the children. At least she's trying to teach the children. I think the girls like the lessons, but from the sound of his practicing, I've suggested that perhaps Jacques would do better with a triangle or a drum!"

Claude smiled again, suddenly considering yet another luxury this Rottembourg commission could bring into his family's life. "Monsieur, you lead me to think that when I return home I must talk to Camille about piano lessons for Jean. I think I will buy a piano. I would like my son to know the pleasure of music. There must be a good teacher somewhere in Argenteuil."

"That sounds like a very good idea," Ernest immediately responded. "I think it's important for children to know the joys and disciplines of music. Alice chose the piano for our children because she plays herself, but with your love of songs of the Auvergne, perhaps your Jean would take to singing in the church choir or some such thing. Our brood often sits on the stairway there when there's music in this room. They love it when our neighbor, Jean DeLille, plays the piano and sings his silly tunes, some which I must admit are not entirely suitable for children. Of course they've heard his songs so many times and know the words so well that they often join in singing the repetitious choruses. Its great fun for us to listen to them. They can be a little loud at times, but we don't mind. We've enjoyed many good times in this rotunda and we find it serves a multitude of purposes. Sometimes, instead of using the dining room, Alice sets a table there by the terrace doors for a small luncheon or dinner. I like that, especially when she and I are alone here on a summer night and we can watch the stars through the open doors. Right now though, let's find the family. The day is getting away from us. "Do you hunt, Claude?" Ernest casually asked, opening a pair of the rotunda's terrace doors. "Right now the deer are finding their way to the edge of the meadow and the carpophore and low-growing seedstalk there. Some of them are young enough never to have heard a rifle shot. Join me some afternoon, perhaps later this week. We could take horses and ride into the forest if you like."

As Ernest led him out onto the Chateau Rottembourg's broad terrace with practiced ease, Claude found himself well satisfied in the knowledge that when completed and installed, his four paintings would be assimilated into the routines of a beautiful house in the country and the activities of its intriguing occupants. The idea of riding into a forest on horseback and hunting deer, however, held absolutely no appeal and he responded accordingly.

"Thank you for the invitation, Monsieur, but I do not hunt," Claude answered, "and I do not ride. I have never taken to it. I was forced into riding lessons when I served in Algiers with my regiment at Mustafa and I hated every minute."

"Did you really? When were you in Algiers?"

"I was conscripted in March of 1861. Out of the 228 men on the list, the first 73 were assigned. I had drawn number 74. I knew what was coming. A few days later, after a dinner of roast duckling and a bottle of very nice wine, a friend of mine who was on leave from his regiment in French Algiers, regaled me with exciting tales of glamour and adventure with the Chasseurs in the African Desert. Facing military service at absolutely the lowest rung of the French military ladder, I was enthralled by his tales of magnificent uniforms and romantic moonlight rides across rippling desert sands. I'm afraid my youthful imagination, and perhaps the wine, got the better of me. The very next day I volunteered for the Chasseurs d'Afrique and proceeded to spend two of the most miserable years of my life on the

African desert, most of them on guard duty. I hated it. I hated the riding lessons. I hated the routine. I hated the heat. After a while I even hated the uniform. I have not been on a horse since."

Ernest chuckled. "Well, then," he said with a broad smile, "I suppose I shall be forced to rely on my neighbor, Jean DeLille, for company in the Senart, but I really shouldn't complain. Jean's a very good companion."

CHAPTER 14

Birds of Paradise

"You must be very happy here," Claude commented, standing beside Ernest on the sunlit terrace. "The house, the rotunda, these grounds; everything is a delight to the eye."

"You must be very happy here," Claude commented, standing beside Ernest on the sunlit terrace. "The house, the rotunda, these grounds; everything is a delight to the eye."

"Yes, we are happy here, very happy," Ernest readily admitted, looking out across the pristine lawns. "I suppose it's safe to say we love it here at Rottembourg," he added, his voice touched with unmistakable warmth. "It's a place where as a family and away from city life, we're able to spend a good deal of time together," he continued, seeming happy to reveal not only personal sentiment, but future plans as well. "Alice and I have decided that once the children are grown and into lives of their own, we'll live here the year round. The children, and hopefully our grandchildren can come whenever they wish, and of course by then I will have retired. I will have sold the store as well as the Paris apartment and Alice and I will be free to spend all our time together here. I doubt we'll be bored. Perfecting aspects of the house will always interest us and I expect I'll enjoy continuing to add to my art collection with occasional visits to Paris and Monsieur Durand-Ruel. Of course because of Alice's family connection to the property, she has a particularly close attachment to it. She looks after things with great dedication, keeps a close watch on the housekeeping, the overall maintenance, that sort of thing. She takes a special interest in the gardens. She's begun thinking toward eventually building a greenhouse and trying her hand at orchids, but all that is a long way off. For now we do all we can to simply maintain and enjoy the place and fortunately, through the course of its long history, the house and grounds have been well cared for. The people who have lived here over the years showered quite a bit of attention on the place. As you can see, the trees and particularly the boxwood hedges have matured to an impressive point, but over time the entire property has undergone a number of changes. When Alice's family came, the fragment of boundary wall overlooking the Concy Hills you see out there in the distance was all that remained of the original estate borders, but in the archives at Yerres, Alice's father found a marvelous drawing showing the entire estate as it had existed in 1800 which is about the time the Rottembourgs arrived. In the drawing, a park and terraces are faintly sketched out in pencil and it's clear that the entire property included much more land and many more ornamental touches than you see today. There were large fish ponds and countless acres of apple orchards and topiary gardens. I'm sorry that's all gone. It must have been quite grand, but the Yerres drawing served as a plan for the re-design of the gardens Alice's father began. Now she continues the work. There she is with the children. And they're playing statues just as Germaine told us. Let's wait here. They seem to be in the middle of things."

Under the mottled shade of copper beech trees a grouping of white wicker chairs could be seen. A short distance away, on the sloping lawn, five children laughed and shouted out to the woman standing before them. She wore a long white gauze dress and white slippers. Her eyes were closed. She stood absolutely motionless. A long, trailing mantle woven of willow branches drifted from her shoulders to the ground. Dried leaves and twigs were caught in her long, dark hair.

"Printemps! Printemps!" (Spring! Spring!) called out one of the children.

"Automne! Automne!" (Autumn! Autumn!) called out another.

"Mendiant! Mendiant!" (Beggar! Beggar!) interrupted still another.

"Ah, Claude, now you witness the famous game of statues which Germaine will be teaching you to play if you are not careful," Ernest whispered. "As you can see, the children are trying to guess what the statue represents. Looks like autumn to me: dried leaves, brittle twigs. Now, it is important to understand that when you play this game, you must remain absolutely still, say nothing, and remain as breathless as you can, as if you were a statue made of stone. When I give in and play statues with these little darlings, they deliberately take all the time in the world to decide who or what I am. My own children think I don't know how much they enjoy seeing me frozen in my tracks. Yes, those darlings out there can be cruel little things!" he added with a gentle laugh.

Germaine was first to spot her father as he and Claude came across the lawn. "Oh, there's Papa, and the gentleman with him is Monsieur Monet! He has come to paint pictures for us!" she shouted. "Ah, Monsieur Monet, please play statues with us!" she pleaded, putting an abrupt end to the game in progress, her chubby arms waving at each side of her yellow dress as she ran toward him. "Jacques is not a nice Jacques today," she said, looking up to Claude. "He has been pinching my arm, sticking out his tongue, and making dreadful, ugly faces at me. Please play the game with us Monsieur and stand between Jacques and me!"

"Now, now, Germaine," Ernest interrupted, "before Monsieur Monet plays statues with you, I want him to meet Mama and your brother and sisters. There will be plenty of time for games in the coming days."

Ernest and Claude came across the pristine carpet of lawn with Germaine in the lead, both men smiling as they watched the statue in the long white dress coming to life and struggling with both hands to free herself from her long, trailing mantle.

"I must be a sad tribute to mother nature right now," the voice above the mass of twisted branches laughed as she shook her head and stood removing the stray leaves she knew must be in her hair. "We started off with a very beautiful creation earlier this afternoon, but somehow it has fallen victim to a little too much tossing about. First it was a sorcerer's magic cape, then it was a tiny elf's woodland house. Finally it became the wilted crown of a cruel king and alas, this is what is left."

Ernest kissed the cheek of the creature in white, doing his best to set her free from the tangle of leaves and branches she wore. "Darling, meet Claude Monet," he said, unable to suppress a broad smile. "Claude, this is my wife, Alice Hoschede, today a vision of autumn. That is what you intended, isn't it, my love?"

"Yes, precisely, Alice said, her face gently flushed in the bright sunshine. "How nice it is to welcome you to the Chateau Rottembourg at last, Monsieur Monet. We have looked forward to your visit," the figure cloaked in vestiges of autumn added, entirely at ease in her disheveled state as she extended her hand. "And these are our five children: Marthe, Blanche, Suzanne, Jacques, and I believe you have already met Germaine."

"Enchante, Madame," Claude responded, politely kissing her hand, at the same time trying not to appear as intrigued as he really was by the remarkable sight of the fanciful woman standing before him. "It is a great pleasure to meet you and these five children," he managed, turning to the collection of Hoschede offspring. "I have but one child, a son. His name is Jean."

"You must tell us all about him," Alice urged, "and I do want to hear all the latest news from Paris," she added. "Ernest tells me about the goings-on in and around the Bourse and of course on Rue Laffitte, but I suspect your news could be a bit livelier. Please tell me it is," she added with another engaging smile, "and let's make our way to those chairs in the shade. I could use a rest. We've been out here in the sun for at least an hour. Yes, we'll go there, under the beech trees. Blanche, be Mama's darling. Go up to the house and ask Bernard to bring out some cold tea with lots of cut lemons and sugar; two or three pitchers please."

"Blanche, also ask Bernard to bring us a tray of the peach croustades I brought from the city!" Ernest called out as Blanche obediently headed for the terrace steps and he settled himself into one of the white wicker chairs under the beeches.

"Yes! Yes! Peach croustades! Thank you Papa!" Germaine called out, climbing onto her father's lap. "And do you see, Jacques?" she said, turning to her brother. "Papa did not forget to bring peach croustades. Mama was right. He never forgets. You must learn to have more faith in our Papa!"

A gentle breeze had blown up, filling the air with Montgeron's distinctive summer fragrance of wild roses and honeysuckle. Suzanne, the daughter who at eight years of age most resembled her mother, tilted her head back and took a slow, deep breath as her siblings gathered close to their parents and Germaine held on to her father's hand. "Monsieur Monet, tell us about riding in Papa's train today," she requested, her sweet young voice clear and decisive as she leaned back confidently against her father's chest and examined the Hoschede guest from head to toe, noticing in particular his sturdy brown boots and commenting accordingly.

"Papa has brown boots," she said without waiting for Claude's comments on the train. "Today, though, he's wearing his shiny black shoes that tie," she said, stroking her father's hand. "He wears his big brown boots for hunting in the forest. Do you have big brown boots for hunting, Monsieur?"

"I do hope the children won't be too much for you," Monsieur Monet," Alice interrupted as Claude seated himself and she turned to Germaine with an indulgent smile, her long, chestnut brown hair and the few leaves remaining in it catching the glinting sunlight. "I want them to have good manners, but I also encourage them to express themselves as they wish. I think my husband doesn't always approve, but this is the way I was raised."

"And well raised you were, my darling!" Ernest affirmed with a sharp nod. "Our children are fortunate indeed to have you for their mother."

Claude smiled the full, honest smile he needed in order to absorb this wonder that was the Hoschede family. Slowly settling themselves in the shade of sprawling copper beech trees, the composition they created was mesmerizing. Taking in the scene before him, he couldn't help but stare. As if in a painting precisely posed and anchored against the perfection of splendid old trees and emerald green lawns, the figures could not have been better arranged; a husband and father, the head of a family relaxed and at ease in his white wicker chair, a beautiful young daughter on his lap, his self-possessed wife seated nearby engaging their four older children, their beings a composition of summer incarnate, their clothes the soft colors of fresh sweet pastilles: creamy yellows, pale blues, snowy whites and soft pinks, the air around them still, the light gloriously radiant. He wanted to sit there without talking or moving, left to watch them in a long, precious fragment of time, but one he knew would vanish in an instant and never come again. In no time at all, it would be very different. They would be different. The whole of the universe would be different; the shadows and the light would change and the breeze would come to alter and stir everything and they would never sit together in this way or be this way again. How he wanted to paint them exactly as he saw them in those swiftly fleeting moments. He thought of his own family: his parents and Aunt Sophie as he had painted them on the terrace at Saint-Addresse. He had painted Camille and young Jean in similarly fragile, human moments at Argenteuil. Watching the Hoschede children it was impossible not to notice their poise and remarkable maturity. Clearly, like his Jean, they adored their parents, but these children expressed their devotion in unconstrained, candid ways and seemed to take every opportunity to do so.

Entirely comfortable against her background, Alice Hoschede was unaware of the fragile tenets of time her visitor found so startling. Safely at home in moments of which she took no particular note, she engaged her visitor in conversation and found him to be a man whose soft brown eyes met hers with calm, well-tempered ease. Here was the artist who had exhibited Impression Sunrise two years before at the exhibition of independent artists on Boulevard des Capucines which mainly out of curiosity she had attended with Ernest. But this visitor to Rottembourg was not fitting the image she had formed as a result of Ernest's frequent references to the artist he regarded as the leader of the new group of painters he supported with unusual enthusiasm.

Anticipating Claude Monet's August arrival at Rottembourg, Alice had been expecting an apprehensive, somewhat shy individual, not a man who appeared completely in control of himself and generally unaffected by the poor reception he and his colleagues were receiving in Paris. He wasn't pale and drawn, she observed sitting back in her chair; no, not at all, and he wasn't like other artists she knew who day after day confined themselves to city studios, but of course this was, as Ernest had told her, an artist who painted outdoors; in the woods, at the river's edge, in a garden, and the regimen appeared to agree with him. Claude Monet looked healthy and solid. Broad-shouldered and barrel-chested, his complexion was ruddy and freckled and although his beard could have used a trimming, he was otherwise impressively well-groomed. This Monsieur Monet had the look, Alice decided, while conversation idly touched on the fine weather and the charm of country villages such as Montgeron, not of an indolent painter of pictures, but of a rugged outdoorsman. Unlike an outdoorsman, however, he wore his clothes well. Seated as he was, in a white wicker chair under age-old trees, he could have been taken for a cultured explorer only recently returned from one more rigorous expedition, prepared to enjoy idle country pleasures for a brief while before setting out once again on a long, tedious mission of unique discovery. Quite unlike the restless adventurer however, as conversation ensued, this man of the outdoors showed himself to be articulate and composed, his French the city French of Paris, not the idiomatic, casual French of the remote countryside. His manner was direct, as might be expected of a man acquainted with disciplined work, but his hand had felt surprisingly smooth as he had taken hers she had noticed. In sharp contrast to his hardy appearance and in his effortless refinement he reminded her of Michel Nosante, the estate supervisor who had stayed on after the Rottembourg family had left Montgeron and her Raingo family purchased the property. Until Michel's recent death, he and his wife had lived in the cottage by the gates. Daniel, the present-day gatekeeper, was their son.

In her father's day, in addition to overseeing the maintenance of the Rottembourg estate, which by itself was a huge responsibility, there were hunting parties for Michel to organize each year. He had a talent for these assignments. In spring and early summer the small woodland game were hunted in the Senart by parties formed of invited family members and good friends, but by autumn the roe deer and elusive Elaphe or Red Deer were the deep forest prizes. Because over the years he came to know the Senart Forest so well, Michel became an expert stalker, his many tales of life in the forest endlessly intriguing to the Raingo family. Their favorites, as individually or in groups they walked the grounds with him, centered on his expertise in preparation for the hunting parties. A romantic figure, self-confident and bold, Michel was known to spend days at a time alone in the forest, spotting and following trails of foxes and deer. He tracked their every move and it was said that living like a woodland hermit he came to know the animal habitat as well as he knew his own. Most interesting to the young children was the fact that Michel had learned to walk in complete silence, listening for the signal sounds of unsuspecting animal life. Alone in the forest depths and undaunted by surprises in animal behavior or sudden changes in the weather, like this visitor, Michel had worn his clothes like a self-possessed forester accustomed to walking long distances by day and camping under trees by night. Alice had never quite forgotten how he had regaled not only adult family members and Raingo children, but also many of the Montgeron children and grandchildren with his adventurous tales, both true and some said, tall. More fascinated than the others by his close association with the forest and its moods, Alice had come to think of Michel Nosante as the most fearless human being she had ever known. At first meeting, Claude Monet was impressing her in that same way.

The refreshments arrived on silver trays. Bernard and a housemaid poured cool lemon tea from two white porcelain pitchers and passed trays of the much anticipated Peach Croustades. Cups of lemon tea in hand, like a flock of summer fireflies the three older children sat in the grass, enjoying their croustades and more than mildly interested in the gentleman visiting Rottembourg who, they soon discovered, knew all about fireflies and grasshoppers and glow worms and liked to watch clouds in the sky as they moved and changed from moment to moment. Jacques leaned protectively over his mother's shoulder, picking at the dried leaves remaining in her hair as he listened. Her examination of Claude Monet complete, little Germaine traded Ernest's lap for Alice's.

"What did you think of our train station, Monsieur Monet?" Jacques asked, his voice unusually authoritative. "I think it is the finest station in the world, apart from the Gare de Lyon in Paris, of course, which I think is very beautiful. Did you see Madame DeLage in her little green prison with her pastry box when you arrived? Were there little sugary crumbs around her mouth today?"

The children laughed, but the meaning they saw in their mother's raised eyebrows quickly put an end to their moment of amusement at Madame DeLage's expense.

"Now, Jacques," Ernest said, "Monsieur Monet is not here to be questioned. Let him enjoy his tea and a bit of rest. I would imagine the Gare de Lyon was very hot today and the heat can make old people like us very tired."

"It's all right," Claude reassured Ernest, turning to young Jacques with a smile, "and to answer your question, Jacques, I thought your train station to be quite the most charming I've ever seen. My house at Argenteuil is across the street from a train station. I often rush over there to catch the train to Paris. I must admit though, that your station is far more attractive than mine, and I must also say that I very much enjoyed the country scenery during the carriage drive from the station here to the Chateau Rottembourg. The houses I saw surrounded as they are by beautiful lawns made me think that there are likely to be many small flying insects hovering there. Of course living here in the country as you do, you must know that many flying insects such as fireflies like to make cozy homes in quiet grassy places. But do you also know that they choose those territories because the sun is warmest in open, untilled spaces on summer afternoons, which is when insects like to do most of their sleeping?"

The children laughed. Germaine again traded laps.

"Monsieur, is that what will you paint here at the Chateau Rottembourg?" Jacques asked. "Fireflies? Perhaps worms?" Again the laughter rang out.

Claude laughed with them. "Oh, no," he quickly responded. "Your father has invited me here to paint views of the property, not portraits of its insects, although I probably should give fireflies and worms some thought for the future, shouldn't I? Do you think they could be convinced to stay still long enough for me to sketch them?"

"Monsieur Monet," Germaine asked, pursing her lips. "If the insects sleep during the day, what do they do at night when we are sleeping?"

"They bite little girls who ask too many questions!" Ernest blurted out with a laugh, hugging Germaine close to his chest.

"Ah, then you will paint things growing in the gardens; the trees and flowers," Suzanne assumed in her lyrical voice which, like her mother's, was light as air. "I see. Monsieur Monet, we can take you to Rottembourg's most beautiful places. There are so many, and we each have our favorites. It could take some time for you to decide, but you are staying with us for a few days, are you not?"

At the tender age of eight, Suzanne was clearly the budding family beauty. Her features were delicate and well-proportioned. Her hair, which was many shades lighter than that of her siblings, framed her oval face in a thick topaz cloud and like each of her siblings, Suzanne was also possessed of the fine Hoschede posture, her shoulders admirably straight, her head held high and set in a decidedly patrician pose which, as Claude now observed, seemed to be a physical hallmark of the entire Hoschede family.

"Monsieur Monet will be with us for more than a few days," Ernest said to Suzanne. "He'll need a few weeks to complete his work and at the beginning he will be exploring the property to decide on his subject matter. He'll be staying at Uncle Julian's cottage and in the next few days I'm sure you can all be helpful in suggesting appropriate scenes for him to look at. But promise me you will not wear him out with your games and questions! He has work to do!"

"I love Uncle Julian's cottage," Blanche added, brightening up after only listening to the conversation around her. "The river runs right alongside and Uncle Julian keeps a little red boat tied up to one of the willows. I've sketched it many times."

"Blanche is our young artist," Alice announced, turning to Claude. "She draws quite well for an eleven-year-old. Lately she's been painting with water colors. Perhaps she will want to show you some of her work."

"Come to tea with us tomorrow, Monsieur Monet," twelve-year-old Marthe, the oldest of the children suggested, her profile, like her mother's, gently etched against the lengthening shadows, "and you'll see Blanche's watercolors. They're beautiful. Some of them are hanging on the walls. Mademoiselle Gabrielle has tea for us every afternoon at four o'clock. You'll meet her when you come. Mama, it would be all right, wouldn't it?"

"Of course it would," Alice answered, "It's a good idea, and between now and then all of you can be thinking of the most interesting places for Monsieur Monet to see. Be ready to share your ideas with him tomorrow, and Blanche, perhaps you will want to show our guest some of your drawings as well as the watercolors. I'll tell Gabrielle to expect Monsieur Monet at four."

"Yes, you must come. Four o'clock! That will be wonderful!" chimed in little Germaine, clapping her hands excitedly. "Yes, come up the stairs that are near the piano in the rotunda and walk all the way up to the top. That's the third floor and it's all ours. It belongs to us. Monsieur, you will love it there. Our mademoiselle allows running up and down the stairs and drawing on one of the walls, and we'll show you our parrot. Her name is Veronique. She's blue. She lives in a green cage. Sometimes we take her outside to watch us play. Papa brought her to us one day when I was still a little, tiny baby. Veronique is from a place called South America. Papa says it is very warm in South America and that there are deep woods there called jungles. Have you ever been to South America, Monsieur Monet? I will go there someday when I am all grown up and Mama allows me to travel. Perhaps I will even go into a jungle and find a husband for Veronique."

"Well, Claude, I don't imagine you were expecting so much information and expert travel guidance today," Ernest interrupted once again, this time with another hearty laugh and a hug for Germaine. "Now children, listen to me carefully," he announced. "Once Monsieur Monet has chosen his subjects and begins his work, you mustn't bother him, no matter how tempted you are. He has four large paintings to complete and he will need to concentrate without interference. Also, you must understand that he has a family of his own. They will be counting the days until he returns home. I hope I am making myself clear."

"Remember what your Papa has told you," Alice emphasized, "but to begin I'm sure Monsieur Monet will appreciate your ideas. Think and plan toward his visit to the third floor tomorrow," she said, her smile that of a caring, nurturing mother confident in the strength of her children's poise and collective imaginations.

Five children. Five young fledglings full of high spirits, bursting with robust good health, minute by minute the patterns of their mother's life dictated by them, by their spontaneous ideas and humblest observations, by their immediate needs and most basic concerns, and in their own disarming ways these precocious youngsters clearly thrived on her attention and returned her devotion. Even in the company of a stranger about whom they were immensely curious it was clear she was the one they wanted to be near. They wanted to see her, touch her, hear her voice, remain safely locked in her world.

Under lengthening afternoon shadows of an August afternoon, while delighting in the acquaintance of new companions, the visitor to the Chateau Rottembourg sat contentedly under a stand of ancient copper beeches enjoying simple things: fragrant country air, deliciously cool lemon tea, and members of a family caught in the act of being themselves. It was a portrait of amber-hued time he would recall many times in the coming weeks. An hour later, Ernest took up the reins of the gray landau and drove him to the lodge he was to occupy during his stay at Montgeron.

CHAPTER 15

A World Apart

The pitched-roof cottage Julian Raingo called La Lethumiere and rarely visited stood nestled into a copse of tall willows on the right bank of the gently flowing River Yerres. After the grandeur of the Chateau Rottembourg, the rustic fisherman's cottage looked lost in its own landscape, but to Claude its setting was a visual masterpiece. The land sloped gently downward, toward the river. A narrow path led to the water's edge, and exactly as Blanche had said, a small red boat was tied to one of the willows sweeping the riverbank. To each side of the arched front door and bordering the compact building, flower beds had been planted in a brilliant show of red begonias, pink mignonettes, and purple asters.

"You'll have plenty of light in here," Ernest said as he opened the unlocked door and led Claude inside. "This should work out as a fairly good studio for you, and although you might be working outside much of the time, you'll probably do at least a little painting in here. And, Claude, do feel free to spread out your things anywhere you like. Bernard will come in every day to look after things and tidy up. Tell him about anything you need. Most evenings we'd like to have you join us at dinner, but perhaps you'll want to look after yourself sometimes, even cook now and then. Just let Bernard know your plans. Alice will come down to check on you from time to time, but right now I'll leave you on your own to explore for a while and settle in. And don't forget about dinner tonight. Eight o'clock. A dark suit will be fine, and if you didn't bring one, come just as you are. I'll send Bernard in the landau to drive you. It's dark by eight and even though you're not too far from us, you don't know your way around just yet."

Claude watched Ernest returning to the landau. Still in his city attire, his vest, cravat, and trousers free of a single wrinkle, his long-legged walk was brisk and sure. It was the walk of a man in control of his world and well-aware of his place in it. Even out here, in the midst of simple country diversions, it was impossible to overlook Hoschede's sophisticated charm. More and more, Claude's view of his host was taking on the dimensions of genuine respect and likeability. The man who owned the painting representing the Impressionist flag was turning out to be everything Durand-Ruel had said he was. Further comforted by the charm of his pleasant surroundings Claude began to anticipate the work ahead in ways he had not expected at all.

Unpacking his things and settling into his little lodge, he found himself grateful as he looked forward to dinner that evening that at the last minute he had thought to pack his one good black suit. At the same time, in his own intelligent way, and perhaps in his sensitive heart, Claude was coming to understand many of the reasons for Ernest Hoschede's identity with the radical spirit of his Impressionist group. Like them, a restless part of him was constantly striving for recognition of something of his own making, something unique and exciting, but by odd contrast here at the Chateau Rottembourg another part of him remained the proper country gentleman who lived in his privileged world with time-honored tradition, the far from radical pursuits of hunting wild game and more than likely dressing for dinner in formal evening attire the refined habits ingrained in the nature of a man and not acquired over time purely for the sake of vanity.

In the fading light of afternoon, Claude found himself the occupant of a three-room cottage in excellent repair, its fine northern exposure, large windows, and fine view of the river providing a near idyllic setting for a painter. Like the Chateau Rottembourg, La Lethumiere was well maintained. The green wooden gate at the pathway entrance looked freshly painted. The arbor arching over it was covered in a burst of purple clematis, and like a responsible sentry a life-sized stone deer stood guard over the borders of flowers in full summer bloom.

The walls of the central room were painted pale yellow, the alcove kitchen to one end well stocked with wine, tins of butter cookies, tea, and a covered tray of sweet almond cakes. All the wide pine floorboards had been polished and left free of rugs. The furnishings were sparse but adequate and comfortable. The gently worn sofa and pair of armchairs in the central room were upholstered in a fabric of blue and white flowers. By one of the chairs, a table held a collection of Chinese wooden figures. They were exquisitely painted and had been arranged on a black wooden tray. Brass candlesticks and bundles of candles were everywhere. Freshly split logs were piled high by the fireplace and as a further welcoming gesture a basket of fresh apples and peaches had been placed on the room's round center table. The bedroom, which led to the riverbank through an arched door was also painted yellow, but a shade darker than the main room, its white, fringed bedcover arranged over white linen sheets. Simple white muslin curtains hung from thin brass rods at the two windows. A tall Chinese black lacquered clothes cabinet stood against one wall. On its bottom shelf were a stack of newspapers and a few books as well as a basket of cinnamon sticks covered in dried orange rinds and lemon peels. Fresh linen towels and a bar of soap had been neatly placed beside the wash basin in the small adjacent lavatory. No detail seemed to have been overlooked. "Views of the property," Hoschede had said to him. "Yes, that's it. Perhaps the pond or the view of the house from the north meadow. Alice loves that view of Rottembourg." Yes, it would all be fine, he told himself. He would sketch outdoors and paint here. The work would go well. Three weeks. Perhaps four.

That evening the Chateau Rottembourg glowed in soft candlelight, as did its occupants. Children were nowhere to be seen and the woman who just hours before had greeted the painter from Paris with dried leaves clinging to her hair had been transformed into a vision of well-groomed loveliness. Her dark hair was elegantly bushed away from her face and wound into a thick bun at the nape of her neck. She wore a long, pale blue-gray tulle dress, its low-cut neckline and short, lace-edged sleeves not at all like the high neckline and long sleeves of the white gauze dress she had worn that afternoon. As guests gathered, she engaged them in a warm, affectionate manner, each person clearly well-known to her. She was particularly attentive to her uncle, Julian Raingo, her fondness for the tall, silver-haired gentleman obvious from the moment of his arrival.

Attired in a black dinner jacket and gray striped cravat, Ernest introduced Claude with obvious pleasure as champagne was served in the long hall before dinner, Claude's Impression Sunrise on its prominent wall mere feet away from the talkative group which Claude found eager to engage him.

"I understand it's the harbor at Le Havre," Julian Raingo remarked to Claude, his manner cordial and surprisingly amicable, "and that must be the harbor master standing in the small boat. Monsieur Monet, I collect rare old books and Old Master paintings, rather nice ones I've been told, and you must forgive me, but frankly I do not understand new pictures like this Impression Sunrise of yours. With his interest in your group, these days Ernest is making every effort to change my point of view and I must say that meeting you makes a difference. I didn't expect you to look like such a normal human being wearing such a nice black suit. In the city I occasionally see those tawdry-looking Montmartre people who call themselves artists and think it perfectly acceptable to parade around with their bandanas and grimy hair. You don't look like one of them at all. We must arrange for a quiet visit together. With summer coming to an end, I'll soon be leaving for Trouville, but in autumn, when I return to Paris we should arrange to meet and talk. I'll send a messenger."

"So many people in Paris are talking about your group, Monsieur Monet," Ernest's cousin Beatrice broke in with her loud, typically overdone gaiety, the spray of blue feathers in her tightly curled red hair trembling with every dramatically uttered word. "I'm Beatrice Pirole, Ernest's cousin," she made abundantly clear, "and Monsieur Monet, I'm so very sorry the reviews on your spring exhibit were not as complimentary as I'm sure you would have liked," she said, "but Ernest is confident that better days are coming for your group. He has a feeling for these things."

Ernest had not overstated Beatrice's tendency to be more than slightly overdone in both personality and appearance. Claude was, in fact, clearly taken aback by Beatrice, draped as she was from head to toe in a mass of pale blue lace, her rouged cheeks as always a bit too pink, her heart-shaped lips typically too red, her Otto de Roses perfume more powerful than usual. Stepping back and quickly sipping his champagne, Claude was promptly told by Beatrice that at one point in life she had been left "financially unstable" by a handsome French lawyer with a good mind "who should never have tried to run a cognac business," as she put it. "He drank most of the inventory!" Beatrice further disclosed without a moment's hesitation. "Monsieur Monet," it turned his liver to pure vinegar," she added, lowering her voice as she stepped closer to him. "Too much of Napoleon's nectar will do that, you know," she further added with an authoritative toss of her head, "but at least my dear, handsome husband died with a smile on his beautiful face and me and my beautiful feathers at his side," she concluded with a hearty laugh and a flutter of her fan. "Oh, you mustn't mind me," Monsieur Monet," she said. "I just have a very clear view of life and what it does to people. Look at what it did to me!"

Uncertain as to how to react to such candid disclosures, Claude simply nodded his head, grateful for a second glass of champagne, but Beatrice had even more to say.

"Now I'm married to that wealthy banker talking to Ernest over there," she continued. "Dear Marc showers me with expensive gifts and provides me with a lifestyle far more elegant than my late, alcoholic husband was able to afford. Just last week he brought me this beautiful pearl and diamond necklace from Boucheron. Isn't it splendid? And it's worth a fortune! Lucky me!" she laughed once again raising her glass of champagne. "A la belle France! She toasted with a wink, clicking Claude's glass with her own as Alice joined the two and Jean DeLille arrived, kissing first Alice then Beatrice on the cheek.

"Ah, Claude Monet! I've looked forward to meeting you tonight!" DeLille announced extending his hand with a broad, friendly smile. "Ernest has told me all about you and the work you'll be doing in this wonderful house. He is very enthusiastic about the project for the rotunda. So am I, and just so you know, I'm the impoverished neighbor who is regularly invited to dine with the Hoschedes and that is only because I am a bachelor with a hearty appetite, readily available at a moment's notice on any night of the week. As you can see, I dress beautifully, and as you will also eventually see, I am very good with maiden aunts and sad, recently widowed cousins and the like. You understand. Of course, Ernest may have told you that Alice invites me only because I play the piano after dinner. Don't you believe it! I am a marvelous dinner guest. I have beautiful table manners. I will eat anything placed before me and Ernest wishes he could engage guests and play the piano half as well as I do. Isn't that so Alice?" he remarked with a wink to Alice.

"I hope I can hear you play sometime," Claude said, thankful for DeLille's rescue from Cousin Beatrice as he returned DeLille's smile.

"After dinner tonight we'll have a little musicale," Delille stated, "that is if Alice is agreeable to a performance of a couple of my witty ballads."

"On one condition," Alice said. "There's to be no profanity and no disrespect. I'm beginning to take a dim view of your visits to the Folies Bergere and its effects on your repertoire, Jean."

"Well then dear Alice, I shall confine my entertainment to When Love Holds You Fast in its Clutches and Come to the Bocage," Delille responded with a typical smile. "Ernest is likely to join in the chorus of Come to the Bocage, he said to Claude. "It's one of his favorites; a catchy tune I picked up over the course of a few, shall we say, exuberant evenings at the afore-mentioned Folies Bergere. Claude, you'll find Ernest to be a terrible singer, but I humor him, and we do play piano duets sometimes: a little Bach, a little Beethoven. We're not very good at the preludes and fugues but we try hard and we do laugh a lot when we make mistakes. What else is there to do out here at night? By August it can be unbearably dull if you don't take matters into your own hands. Monsieur Monet, don't let this get too far," DeLille added, lowering his voice, "but I can hardly wait for the summer to end. I'm starved for city nightlife and some loud noise. Oh, there's Bernard opening the dining room doors. It must be nine o 'clock. Dinner is served. Alice, my dear I'm starving, as usual!"

Seven chairs were arranged at the table. Wine was poured, Claude was welcomed with appropriate toasts, and the sounds of amiable conversational exchanges became lively accompaniment to platters of delicious melon drizzled with port, duckling roasted to perfection, and an assortment of tender vegetables gathered that afternoon from Rottembourg's kitchen gardens. Claude watched Julian Raingo who was seated directly across from him, Ernest's cousin Beatrice beside him. Between sips of wine she leaned over and whispered into his ear, her remarks leading the elder Raingo to chuckle, quickly square his shoulders and glance around the table, hoping no one had heard whatever she had said. As desserts of flaky cream puffs with chocolate sauce and cream were served and at Ernest's urging, Jean DeLille shared his tales of woe concerning the ongoing restoration of his Montgeron house, an entertaining litany which the assembled guests enjoyed with frequent bursts of hearty laughter.

"DeLille, tell us, how are you progressing on your gardens?" Ernest asked, baiting his friend, wine glass in hand. "Claude is new to this little world of ours and as a landscape painter I'm sure he'd like to hear all about your recent undertakings with Mother Nature. Any flowers yet?"

"How am I progressing on my gardens? Any flowers yet? Oh, Ernest, you are too hilarious," Delille stated with an unmistakable note of affected sarcasm. "I have barely had time to keep up with my leaking roof. If you had told me about the great tradition of the Brie Valley's frequent summer night rains, I would never have considered buying an old country house when you tempted me with your picturesque descriptions of the fine little former estate manager's house with the winding stairs and the delightful tower on the estate next to yours, so charming, so perfect for an artist. Claude, these lovely people gathered here tonight know all about my travails as the owner of a country house which due to years of neglect has needed every conceivable renovation known to man, but I must let you know from the start that my troubles have all been Ernest's fault. He is entirely to blame for these fresh wrinkles on my brow and the dramatic reduction in my bank balance."

Ernest laughed his deep resonant laugh as with high degrees of warmth and anticipation the dinner guests prepared themselves for what they knew was about to come. "Claude, the story is that a few years back, Delille bought the former property manager's house on the large Rue de Pres estate nearby," he said by way of introduction. "I had told him it was a beautiful property and that it might need a little work, but because he felt a country house did not fit into his financial picture, I said I thought that since it might need a little work, the price could be negotiated, which it was. Besides, I needed a hunting companion and Alice had said we should cultivate a circle of younger friends," he added with another of his throaty laughs."

"A little work? Younger friends?" DeLille commented leaning forward with a hearty guffaw. "Claude the truth is that until I met Ernest I was a perfectly happy young portrait painter with an enviable Paris clientele. After the nasty war with the Prussians when people who had managed to hold on to their money wanted to have their likenesses preserved just in case another disaster came down the Champs Elysees to put an end to them, I was making that wonderful thing called money. Once I had established a reputation for my Van Dyke-looking portraits; you know, those deliciously languid hand positions and all that gold satin and blue velvet people love, I found I could indulge in a few luxuries now and then: a new suit or smart looking top hat from Le Dienne, a fabulous eight-course dinner at Polidor or Grand Turk. I even had a lovely lady friend with baby-soft skin and the biggest....well, you know.... upper female torso you've ever seen. Ah, to think of it now! Pure heaven! With a bottle of half-decent Burgundy and a little kissy-kissy she could be convinced to spend the entire night tucked under the duvet with me. Sad to say, all that changed when Ernest came into my life to arrange for a portrait of himself as a birthday present for Alice and during our sittings enchanted me with bewitching talk of leisurely country life and the allure of a village in the beautiful Brie Valley. The cunning man took me like an innocent little lamb to slaughter and I foolishly succumbed to descriptions of a world I had only read about. As a result, for the past three years I have been in the process of restoring my baby chateau with the tower and the winding stairs and the leaking roof and I am growing old and poor doing so!"

Candlelight flickered and the sounds of joyous laughter resounded in Rottembourg's dining room as DeLille regaled the assembled group with his tales of woe and Ernest goaded him on. The gaiety echoed along the Chateau Rottembourg's wide center hall. It sped past the Raingo clocks, past Impression Sunrise, and past the dazzling array of Impressionist paintings hanging on blue-gray damask walls. How delightful it was after a long, worrisome day, Claude observed, to sit calmly and at peace as a guest at the Hoschede dining room table that evening and in the very house where his four wall panels would soon be installed. And how could anyone not feel at ease in such surroundings where every detail was attended to, every sense satisfied. Touch, smell, sight, sound, all of it was bound up in exquisite waves of perfection. The linen napkins were impossibly white and crisply starched. Red roses arranged in a Chinese blue and white porcelain bowl presided at the center of the table. At the sideboard, behind Ernest's chair, silver candlesticks and wine urns shone, and in the room's flattering long shadows, the strands of pearls encircling Alice Hoschede's neck gave her face a gentle gleam, her conversation, her gestures, her smiles, her entire demeanor that of a polished, elegant woman of means and intelligence, one well-practiced in the art of conversation and one born to her role as chatelaine of a fine country house. This was a self-disciplined, highly feminine creature who, as far as Claude was concerned, left no doubt in anyone's mind that every detail concerning the running of her household was left entirely in her capable hands. Further impressing him, as the evening progressed he found her engaging conversation as unpretentious as that of an old acquaintance.

"I hope you've enjoyed the melon with port," Monsieur Monet" she thoughtfully commented as the platters of roasted duckling and vegetables were passed. "The melons came from our garden just this afternoon. They really are at their best right now. I'll have Bernard bring you some tomorrow."

Claude smiled, amiably agreeing to the arrival of fresh melons the next day, at the same time aware of the ease with which the assembled company were engaging with one another.

"Claude, how did you find things in Paris?" DeLille asked as later Bernard poured calvados and the cream puffs and chocolate sauce were served. "Ernest told me you saw some of your artist friends a day or two before coming out to Montgeron. How are they surviving the summer heat?"

Claude smiled. "Yes, as I told Monsieur Hoschede on the train, I did see Edouard Manet, but no member of my group is in Paris right now. Manet and I had dinner together with Francis Sartorius. I had hoped to see Edgar Degas, but I was told he had left the city for the sea breezes of Trouville. Pierre Renoir was not in Paris either. He was planning to paint for a few weeks at Bougival and I understand that Alfred Sisley is in the cool British countryside for the summer. At this time of the year, everyone's painting somewhere in the countryside and simply living. It is what I like to do myself. What more is there? But Paris is always Paris and regardless of the season or the summer heat I do treasure any chance to be there. However, I am looking forward to seeing Gustave Caillebotte while I'm here at Montgeron. I understand he lives closeby."

"Yes, he does. He will be coming to dinner next week. Isn't that right, Alice?"

Ernest asked. "You must join us, Claude," he added as Alice nodded her head and Ernest's invitation was extended with the broad engaging smile to which Claude was becoming accustomed. "Wednesday, isn't it, darling? DeLille you must come too, and of course Uncle Julian and Beatrice and Marc will still be here. We'll be a fine group. Yes, a fine group. DeLille, sharpen up your pianistic skills for the occasion. After one of Alice's beautifully planned dinners we'll be ready for one of your more brilliantly executed entertainments."

"Well, thank you Ernest. I shall do my best to live up to your expectations, and Alice, I promise to keep everything up to your standard. No overly suggestive lyrics and no references to the Almighty or his close friends."

"Thank you, Jean. I shall keep you to that promise," Alice nodded with a light laugh, turning to Claude. "Monsieur Monet, I understand you are well-acquainted with Gustave Caillebotte. Ernest tells me he is a member of your group, but do you also know Carolus Duran? He and his wife Pauline have a lovely house nearby and are special friends of ours."

Claude nodded. "Ah, yes, Monsieur Duran is making quite a name for himself. His work is superb. He captures the interest of the Salon Jury on a regular basis."

Ernest ran his finger over the rim of his wine glass. "Sounds as if we're surrounded by painters out here, doesn't it, Claude? To some extent I suppose, we are, but we have a few writers too. Alphonse Daudet has a house at Mandres-les-Roses. I don't see much of him, but DeLille here does He's a good friend of his. Alice has read Lettres de Mon Moulin and Tartarin de Tarascon. Claude, let's try to see Daudet while you're here. DeLille, arrange things for one day next week. That would work out well. Right now though, I'm sure everyone here would like to know more about our artist in residence. Claude, tell us about your family."

There it was again, the Hoschede sentences striking out like hammers against a wall. Alice, familiar with her husband's habit of sharply issuing directives to those around him, glanced toward Ernest and came to the rescue with masterful poise as she graciously asked Claude if he had painted portraits of his wife and son.

"Oh, not portraits exactly," came Claude's answer, "but as I think of it I suppose you could call them that. On several occasions I've painted Jean with Camille in the garden."

"Is your son Jean your only child?" Alice asked.

"Yes, he is, and right now he has been assigned the task of caring for his mother. Since is he only nine years old, this concerns me because Camille has not been feeling well and I could be asking too much of my young son. I'm hoping Camille will be herself again once I return to Argenteuil."

The expressive brown eyes revealed nothing unusual, but as he spoke about Camille and Jean, Alice detected more than a slight touch of regret in his voice.

"Another time you must bring them with you to visit with us," she suggested.

"I would never have taken him for one of your Impressionist friends," Alice remarked later that evening when guests were gone and upstairs she and Ernest prepared for bed. "He just doesn't have the manner of an irresponsible person living a careless life."

"Yes, Claude is very polished, very polite," Ernest replied, watching his wife as she fastened her blue robe and began to brush out her hair at her dressing table. "I knew you'd like him."

"Does he play the piano? Hunt?"

"Neither, my darling. Claude Monet doesn't ride, doesn't hunt, doesn't play the piano. The man paints!"

Engaging as he had been at dinner earlier that evening, Alice had observed not only the touch of regret in Claude's voice when he talked about his family, but an overall restlessness in him as well. When not eating his food or drinking his wine, his hands had been in almost constant motion. She had never seen anything quite like it. He intertwined his fingers or placed one hand in his lap and clasped the other at his forearm. Again and again, he ran his fingers over his napkin. She had watched him as he sipped his wine. There was not a trace of fragility about him. He looked sturdy and strong. She pictured him in the hot, crowded Gare de Lyon waiting for Ernest who had probably not thought to write him about the likely train delay. An outdoorsman accustomed to nature's quiet spaces he would have hated the waiting and all those people crowded into one place in the heat; noisy children racing about, steam, whistles, and the rumbling underfoot that always unsettled her.

After dinner, appropriate expressions of gratitude expressed, Claude had insisted on walking back to La Lethumiere alone. Ernest offered him the use of the gray landau and Bernard to drive him but Claude insisted on walking.

"Claude, you don't know the way," he said. "You aren't familiar with the countryside here or the distance."

"Monsieur Hoschede, thank you very much, but I'm on good terms with Mother Nature. We have a fine relationship, a love affair my wife tells me, and tonight my lover has provided a bright full moon and a blaze of stars to light my way. I appreciate your concern, but please. I need a walk."

The night was clear. Not a leaf or branch stirred. The air seemed more deliciously fragrant than it had been in the bright sunshine of afternoon. Pensive and reflective as he started out on the moonlit path toward La Lethumiere, Claude's thoughts once again turned to Ernest Hoschede, his curiosity about this enigmatic figure piqued to a degree he could not have predicted. In Paris they had talked fairly often in the Guerbois, but it was different there. In the Guerbois, Hoschede was more often a listener, an interested observer, a man absorbed by the moment and incapable of being distracted from it. Here though, in this extraordinary place he left no doubt that he was master of his world. What was it in life that made it possible for some men to have so much and be so much? He thought of climates of the past, mountains of time he had wasted, measures of love he had ignored or overlooked. He thought of other men he had admired, first among them the painters Boudin and Daubigny, his early mentors and the two influential painters who had built up his confidence as an artist, directing his young, untried talents from caricatures to drawing and the painting of landscapes in the outdoors, pursuits to which he had taken immediately. And there was his unforgettable best friend, young handsome Frederic Bazille, the talented painter and delightful companion he had met in Gleyre's studio, Bazille's death at the battle of Beaune-la-Rolande the single heartbreaking event that had motivated his own firm decision to avoid a similar fate by taking up safe residence in London, far from the dangers and deprivations of Paris as the Franco Prussian War had loomed and trainloads of French citizens fearing the Prussian invasion had abandoned their city. Camille had joined him in London. Renoir and Pissarro too.

War, death, the bleakness of gray England, friends of the past, old attachments, old loyalties. Strange to think of such things in the radiant aftermath of a memorable evening. It was in gray London, Claude reminded himself, turning onto the path leading to the lodge that he was to occupy for the next weeks, that he had met Paul Durand-Ruel, the man who had directed him to this earthly paradise of Montgeron and a man who, for his own reasons, had also escaped the terrible Paris Siege, optimistically setting about preparing a London exhibition which featured Claude's work. Their meeting had marked a turning point for Claude and a year after returning to Paris he had sold more paintings than ever before, thirty-six canvases in total, twenty-nine of them to Durand-Ruel, the remaining seven to his friends Gustave Caillebotte, Henri Rouart, and Felix Braquemond for a total of 12,000 francs. It was with this solid encouragement that Claude had grown eager to produce more and more work and finally, by the end of 1873 to consider an exhibition with a group of like-minded independents. In preparation for such an event and at Durand-Ruel's urging, he had returned to Normandy to paint at Saint-Adresse, at Etretat, and finally at the Port of Le Havre where the canvas Ernest Hoschede had purchased for 800 francs, Impression Sunrise, had been painted, instigating what Durand-Ruel would thereafter refer to as "the perfect match" and the momentous personal transaction which, of itself, had ignited a freshly inflamed passion for collecting in Ernest Hoschede, a man full of contrasts, Claude was now beginning to understand, and a conflicted being who, on the outside espoused traditional French values, but one who on the inside saw himself as an integral part of the disruptive Paris avant-garde.

"Stupid to stand up in a small boat!" Durand-Ruel had told Claude that Hoschede had joked during their moments of bargaining over Impression Sunrise as he had skillfully jousted for a price less than the one thousand francs Durand-Ruel had set, "and especially in the middle of the harbor at Le Havre!" Hoschede had added, throwing his magnificent head back, his throaty laughter thundering along the carmine red walls of number 16 Rue Laffitte.

Reaching La Lethumiere's gate Claude smiled to himself, recalling the marvelous twinkle in Durand-Ruel's eyes as he had divulged a transaction's rare narrative detail. Like Durand-Ruel, Claude understood the classic veneers of French humor and their effective, though sometimes trivial uses all too well. And now, in the perfection of a moonlit summer night he also understood how Ernest Hoschede's interest in the Paris art world would have sprung out of his own demanding personality and the whims of any number of his ambivalent, untested tastes. However motivated Hoschede may have been as a novice collector even a short time ago, it was now abundantly clear that his decisions in choosing one painting over another were being consistently culled out of a rapidly expanding range of experience and a remarkably quick grasp. The man knew exactly what he wanted and he made excellent choices. That evening and apart from the paintings prominently displayed in the center hall, Claude had seen one example after another of his sharp decisiveness. At the conclusion of DeLille's after dinner entertainment, Ernest took Claude to the far end of the hall and invited him into a room where the walls were covered with an astonishing array of Impressionist paintings. He had seen the work of his Impressionist colleagues assembled in such numbers at only two other places: during the First Exhibition in 1874 at Nadar's, and during the second that past spring at Durand-Ruel's, but never had he seen so many examples assembled in one private place, not in this volume, not in one person's private hands. Opening the arched door to La Lethumiere, he could escape neither the impact of those images, nor the oddly disturbing enigma that was Ernest Hoschede.

"The children were very interested in you this afternoon, and you were so good with them out there in the garden," Hoschede had said to him, rising from his chair at the conclusion of dinner. "I had planned to show you part of my art collection here at Rottembourg this afternoon, but this is probably an even better time for you to see the paintings I've assembled here. Let's hear what DeLille has in store for us at the piano first and then we'll take a tour!"

DeLille had smiled, Claude recalled, taking his seat on the bench at the piano under the glistening chandelier, proceeding to regale his audience with renditions of When Love Gets You Fast in its Clutches, an English ditty he had learned at his British boarding school and which he had translated into French. Come to the Bocage, and I Touch My Harp and Dream Again followed, these also rousing tunes which required lusty group participation through all four of its rhythmic refrains.

A smiling Alice had excused herself immediately after DeLille's well-executed entertainment, the evening requirement of checking on the children in their third floor haven at the end of the day a ritual to which she explained to Claude she conformed without fail. DeLille expressed his thanks to her and said good-night.

"I have an appointment with my chimney sweep tomorrow morning," he announced. "Seems I'm badly clogged, and since on top of everything else I cannot possibly consider the expense resulting from a fire just now, I shall welcome him with open arms. Don't bother to see me out, my dear. I know the way. Merci, dear Alice and Ernest. Good night all, and it's nice to have you among us, Claude."

"I hope you will be comfortable at La Lethumiere, Monsieur Monet," Alice offered in parting. "Do let me know if there is anything you need. We want you to enjoy your stay with us. The children will be eager for your visit tomorrow. Four o'clock."

Guests having departed, Claude had accompanied Ernest along the center hall, admiring once again the Raingo clocks he had seen earlier in the day. He wanted to study them more closely, but Ernest urged him on toward a pair of open doors at the end of the hall where candlelight shone out from every surface. The room's two stately windows faced the drive. A marble fireplace stood prominently between the windows. Above it was DeLille's portrait of Ernest.

"There you have a sample of DeLille's portraiture," Ernest said, looking up to the gilt framed canvas. "As DeLille said at dinner, it was my Christmas present to Alice two years ago. She was delighted with it; said I look the way everyone should in a formal portrait. Of course she loves DeLille, and apart from his more tawdry Folies Bergeres tunes she enjoys his friendship and sense of humor just as much as I do. What do you think?"

"Well, he certainly has captured your likeness expertly," Claude remarked, "and his use of color is brilliant; very carefully mixed and applied. I must say the painting is wonderful here. Monsieur, you have a gift for placement and the arrangement of wonderful things. Not everyone does."

Here, in what appeared to be a family library, books prevailed in low, glass-enclosed cabinets surrounding the room, their uniformity broken only by the fireplace and the windows. Above the cabinets were paintings in a startling array of style and color, each canvas that of a member of the Impressionist group. Two large paintings by the supportive but Salon-loyal Edouard Manet had been hung at opposite ends of the room. Claude was fascinated.

"I see the question in your eyes, Claude, and I understand. Edouard Manet may not be one of your Impressionist colleagues, but I think he belongs here. He's a kindred spirit, completely at one with your cause. In 1872, I bought five of his paintings, all in one transaction with Durand-Ruel. This one is Woman with a Parrot. Since you're a good friend of Manet's and visit at his Rue Guyot studio, you could have seen it there," Ernest said, standing before the full length figure of a woman clad in a creamy yellow coat, a parrot at her side. Claude had indeed seen Woman with a Parrot at Manet's Rue Guyot studio more than three years before and Manet himself had told him about Durand-Ruel's 1872 visit where he had bought everything in the studio for thirty-five thousand francs."

"And this, Edouard calls The Ragpicker," Ernest went on, a satisfied smile crossing his face. "I love this old beggar," he added with a hearty laugh. "Professionally involved in a business related to textiles as I am, his rags appeal to me on every possible level. Beside, he looks like a fairly contented beggar, wouldn't you say? When Durand-Ruel showed this to me I knew I had to have it. And when Alice's uncle, Julian Raingo, saw it he took on one of his dour expressions and was quick to advise me that the old beggar should serve as a constant reminder to me of the consequences of extravagance. Of course, he takes a dim view of my choices in paintings."

The friendship between Claude Monet and Edouard Manet was closer than Ernest knew. There was enormous respect between the two painters and because Manet's studio was within easy walking distance of the Café Guerbois, Claude was offered frequent opportunities for the visits Manet encouraged.

Claude would learn that in total, there were five large Edouard Manet paintings in Ernest Hoschede's possession, three at the Paris apartment, two at Rottembourg, all five acquired from Durand-Ruel shortly after his purchases from Manet. In addition to Woman with a Parrot and The Ragpicker, they were The Street Singer, Young Man in the Costume of a Majo, and Embarkation at the Port of Boulogne. Claude's own paintings: In the Garden, The Beach at Trouville, and The Thames and the Houses of Parliament created an unforgettable image in his mind as he returned to La Lethumiere and lit several candles in the main room, settling into one of the blue flowered chairs to reflect more fully on what he had seen.

Much to his amazement he had counted at least eight works by Alfred Sisley including his Boat in a Flood, Autumn, and The Saint-Germaine Road near Bougival. On yet another accommodating wall were Camille Pissarro's Effects of Fog in November and La Route, and on and on it had gone, the stunning array of color, perspective, and viewpoint continuing with Renoir's Bridge of Chatou and Young Girl in a Garden, these two Renoir paintings added to his Woman with a Cat seen earlier in the day on the accommodating walls of Rottembourg's center hall, each and every piece comprising a personal collection of remarkable proportion.

"I've developed quite a fondness for all this," Ernest had confessed in the honeyed light of the large room, and I've paid fair prices for each piece you see here, but I will tell you that the first lot of Sisleys I bought came to barely forty francs for each picture. Hard to believe! It would probably never happen that way again, and of course that transaction was irresistible, but now you see it is all this that keeps my accounts active with Durand-Ruel, which he doesn't seem to mind at all. He's a very good businessman; always wants to make a sale, but he also knows I like to buy, and I do enjoy his company. Monsieur Durand-Ruel is a good friend and an excellent advisor."

And so it had continued. An unexpected wonder of paintings by Claude and his contemporaries to be viewed and enjoyed in the privacy of a gracious country house, all but Edouard Manet's by the embattled regiment of Impressionists gathered in one beautiful room and in such volume as to be stunning. And through it all there was the unmistakable domination of Ernest Hoschede's portrait above the fireplace, his expression pleasant but supremely authoritative, his entire demeanor that of the proud owner of the volume of artistic work he had gathered with infinite care and now presided over with the hazardous pleasure that comes effortlessly to the careless lover of risk and remote possibility.

"Durand-Ruel tells me I'm becoming his best customer," Hoschede had said. "As an artist's dealer though, he's your special champion, Claude. He thinks a great deal of you and I've told him I'm interested in acquiring more of your work. There's still a little space left in here and if necessary I can move things around a bit. Later on, let's talk about what you might have available by the time the panels are finished and we both get back to Paris."

Surely, Claude had to assume, in the two short years since the first exhibition, no one had acquired the sheer volume of Impressionist paintings Ernest Hoschede had collected, and although his acquisitions as a whole represented what could be considered the finest work to date of its core members, Claude now realized that Hoschede himself understood perfectly well how as a result of his advancing interest in Impressionism he was quite possibly becoming one of Durand-Ruel's most significant clients. And why not? Expert advice. Shared opinions. Confidences. Deep pockets. And Durand-Ruel understood the value of social exchanges between like-minded people. The Hoschedes were splendid hosts and excellent conversationalists. People must love being in their company; important, well-connected people, the best people transported to and from the Chateau Rottembourg on a private train. A picture book family. A privileged, art-filled life driven by an eager protagonist and a beautiful chatelaine. "Alfred Sisley came out to Rottembourg last summer," Ernest had told him. "He did some painting while he was here, but as I said on the train, I think he was much more interested in my cousin Beatrice even though I told him she was married to my banker. I don't know what it is about that woman. Men are attracted to her like bees to honey. I hope you weren't too offended by her."

That smile had been there again, secure and obstinate but open to mindless innuendo. Little did Claude know it was becoming the smile of a man in a mask, and that behind the mask there was little to smile about. Two weeks before Claude's arrival, a messenger from Paris had arrived at the Chateau Rottembourg. He had delivered a large envelope addressed to both Ernest and Alice. Opening the envelope, Alice was shocked to read through its contents. Armel Ducasse, the formidable compliance officer from the Tribunal of Commerce who had interrupted Julian Raingo's sixtieth birthday celebration two years before was now threatening a lawsuit. The list of Ernest's debtors was extensive. The generous extension Ernest had been able to arrange with Ducasse was about to expire. Alice was stunned.

"But I thought you had taken care of our debts long ago!" she insisted, her voice tense and determined when in the entrance hall she confronted Ernest upon his return from an afternoon of hunting. "Ernest, during Uncle Julian's birthday celebration two years ago you said your outstanding one-million-franc debt was nothing to worry about. You told me you had everything under control and that we had plenty of money to take care of any debtors Armel Ducasse represented. In all this time you've said nothing at all about ongoing financial problems. This letter is threatening a lawsuit! There is a long list of debtors. Your debt is no longer one million francs. It is two million! What has happened?"

Ernest said nothing. He slowly placed his rifle on the gun rack and turned to face Alice, thoughtful and silent for a moment, but then choosing his words with great care.

"Well, my darling, I hadn't counted on a number of developments," he began, realizing the time had come for full disclosure, "not the least of which is this nasty business of recession throughout France, but it does seem that a bit of vinegar has now been added to the pudding," he confessed, seating himself in one of the straight-backed chairs by the fireplace and taking a deep breath.

"I haven't wanted to tell you this, but the new people I hired at the store have not live up to expectation. Some months ago I was forced to face the fact that the manager I had trusted to take care of things was a complete failure. I dismissed him along with at least a dozen other employees. I admit that for a long time I wasn't paying enough attention. It was a mistake. As a result of my negligence and while employees I trusted were ignoring their responsibilities, the store was enduring substantial deficits. Needless to say, I wasn't prepared for that, so once the situation became clear, in addition to dipping into cash reserves, I've needed to borrow heavily to meet obligations. Fortunately, several friends at the Bourse helped me out with lines of credit and personal loans and I suspect it is this added indebtedness that has been called in and has prompted the threatening documents we have received. The truth of the matter is, my darling, that we have had no income for more than a year, and of course expenses both at the store and at home have continued. Right now I owe purveyors, importers, craftsmen, employee salaries, even the store's cleaning staff. And through it all, the usual household and personal expenses have continued. Our reputation for having the largest staff in Montgeron is well founded. It's also the most expensive. Here at Rottembourg alone it's the gardeners, the maids, the housemen and the butler, the children's mademoiselle, three cooks, their assistants, and a team of laundresses. Who have I left out? Ah, yes, Daniel at the gatehouse, the stable boys, and the man who comes to wind the clocks! And everybody has to be fed!"

Alice was speechless. This time, Ernest's view of the financial picture was not the optimistic scene it had been two years before when Armel Ducasse and Etienne Ahron had appeared on that all too memorable evening at the Paris apartment. She had noticed of course, that through the past two summers Ernest had returned to Paris more often than in the past, but what Alice did not know was that while in the city, he was meeting ever more anxiously with bankers and lawyers, and as the recession had deepened and worsened, that he was also in contact with the ever-increasing number of loan sharks populating the area of the Bourse. Over time he had successfully worked out several problems, some in a more clandestine manner than others, but expecting rapid improvements in the overall financial climate, from month to month a mountain of other difficulties had remained unresolved.

Through the year of 1875 and with funds from his inheritance, Ernest had managed to put off his creditors. He had even satisfied a few with small balances paid in full, but now, the money his father had left him was completely spent and neither the persistently dark financial picture in Paris nor Ernest's place in it appeared even remotely stable.

"You mustn't worry about any of this," he was quick to insist to Alice. "I will go on doing all I can to get back on solid ground. And I will succeed. Every day I'm meeting with qualified people in Paris who are advising and assisting me and it will be only a matter of time before I have everything straightened out. I'm sure of it. You are not to worry, my darling. Go on with life as usual. Promise me you will. Everything will be fine."

She had promised, but it was an empty promise intended to placate Ernest and she had worried ever since. Sleep eluded her, the boundless energy for which she was known began to fade, and only days after Claude Monet's arrival, she began to notice things missing from the house: a crystal vase one day, a pair of silver candlesticks another, small things at first, but eventually there was a vacant space on a wall where a gilded mirror had hung for years. Suddenly a cabinet was stripped bare of its collection of porcelains and finally, overnight, two Raingo clocks disappeared from the collection which had been in the Raingo family for generations. When she confronted Ernest, demanding an explanation, he admitted to having sold a few things in order to cover overdrafts on lines of credit.

"But the Raingo clocks will be back within the month," he had assured her with a confident smile. "I used them to secure a loan. Etienne Ahron loved them. He was full of accolades for the Raingo workmanship. You'll be happy to know they are paying more than just the interest due on a few of my loans, and don't you worry, my darling, your clocks are in safe hands. They'll be back very soon. Alice, smile! There's nothing to worry about. These choppy waters will be calmed. I promise. Before too long it will be nothing but smooth sailing along the River Yerres!"

Optimism. Rare stoicism. High summer of 1876. Claude Monet in residence. Ernest conveying absolutely no trace of the worry he carried with him every day. The pleasant homogeny of summer life and country pursuits continued unchanged. With no outward indication of anxiety, Ernest traveled back and forth between Paris and Montgeron, and as had become the established summer habit, visitors came to Rottembourg on the private train. Again and again champagne was poured, and friendships were nurtured. In Paris Ernest met with bankers and private lenders. At Montgeron he and Alice entertained almost constantly. It was a hectic schedule, but at his best and able to set aside his concerns in the midst of good company, at every hour of every day Ernest appeared confident. He was seldom still or at a loss for words. He laughed and joked and Alice made attempts at similar shows of optimism, but anxiety was a constant companion for them both.

It was summer at her Chateau Rottembourg, Alice told herself repeatedly. Yes, it was a beautiful summer in Rottembourg's gardens and it was a fragrant summer along the freshly raked gravel paths. It was a summer of daily delights with her children and it was a series of comforting summer evenings with the closest members of her Raingo family and visiting friends, one group after another. She had very much enjoyed Edouard and Suzanne Manet's company in early August. Edouard had painted a portrait of Ernest and Marthe seated together at a table under the dome in the garden pavilion. It was a painting which showed Ernest and his oldest daughter where they could be found on many a summer morning, but even in its subtle depiction of family life, Manet's portrait did nothing to convey the change in mood at the Chateau Rottembourg. A dark cloud was invading late summer's incarnate pleasures. Manifested in small, elusive ways, the cloud passed unnoticed over the heads of family and visitors but the grayness brought penalties with it. For the first time in their thirteen-year long marriage, Ernest and Alice were altering their lavish lifestyle. They were economizing.

During one of their afternoon hunts, Ernest confided in Jean DeLille, making details of his financial dilemma abundantly clear. Sworn to secrecy, the stoic, ever loyal DeLille continued to present himself at Rottembourg as always, remaining a pleasant distraction during dinners, the attention required by the ongoing restoration of his house a frequent and welcome source of humor, but there was a subtle change in him. He was not seated at the piano as often as in the past, entertaining after dinner with his flashy music hall melodies. He did, however, seem to be enjoying Rottembourg's dinners as in the past, dinners which now were smaller, quieter, served by a smaller staff, and held with neither a widowed cousin draped in black nor a haughty maiden aunt anywhere in sight.

This was the world into which Claude had arrived from Paris on an August afternoon. The golden summer of 1876 was rapidly coming to a close, but on a fine moonlit evening at a chateau deep in the French countryside a new chapter had begun and he had turned a page. His faith in the future had been renewed, and in the silence of a country night he slept soundly until the first light of another dawn awakened him.

CHAPTER 16

The Children's Hour

A raspy shriek of "Vite! Vite!" greeted Claude the next day as promptly at four o'clock he reached the third floor landing, welcomed at the top of the stairs first by the persistent screeching of Veronique, the blue Brazilian parrot, then by sedate Gabrielle, the saintly, red-headed mademoiselle who looked after the Hoschede brood and the activity of their third floor paradise.

"Pardonne, Monsieur Monet," Gabrielle apologized in a near-whisper, wringing her hands as she introduced herself and greeted Claude, "but 'vite' (quickly) is the only word Veronique knows right now, and some days she practices at it with an iron will. Of course she has chosen today, just in time for your visit, to work on her pronunciation. We had hoped that by now she would have added to her vocabulary, but thus far there has been no success there. Please do forgive her, and us," she said, shaking her head. "I shall collect the children. They have been looking forward to your visit. We won't be a moment."

Claude stood waiting in the light-filled central playroom where, arranged on a blue and yellow flowered carpet, two round tables held stacks of colored paper and books. Stuffed animals, boxes of color sticks, and more books filled the shelves in the cabinets against the walls. In one sunny corner a tall, gaily painted wooden soldier stood awaiting the next order, in another a row of long-haired dolls wearing beautiful dresses sat in small chairs, but those strewn on the floor were not quite as well groomed. Their faces were scratched and chipped and they had neither dresses nor hair. At the large center window facing the lawns, eight identical chairs were arranged around a long rectangular table which had been set with a white cloth, yellow plates, matching porcelain cups and saucers, and a vase filled with blue delphiniums.

It would not be long before Claude would discover that the same Gabrielle who managed to assemble all five freshly bathed, properly dressed Hoschede children for tea at the center window each afternoon at four o'clock also faithfully carried out the permissive philosophy of the third floor paradise. In addition to allowing running and shouting and writing on one of the walls, her pale gray service dress starched and crisp through it all, she also tolerated all manner of jokes and pranks, participating in many of them herself with the good humor and cleverness for which her five charges adored her. Quickly made aware of the flexibility of life on the third floor, Claude would also soon take as a matter of course the further knowledge that the same Gabrielle who spoke five languages and played the clavichord, the flute, and the harp, also allowed kittens in bed, collections of live worms and frogs squirming in jars set on window sills, the barking of Igor, the beloved family spaniel, and the screeching of Veronique who, the whole family knew perfectly well, had learned to repeat "vite! vite!" from none other than Mademoiselle Gabrielle Lenoir herself whose own most frequent directive to her young charges was "vite, vite, mon petits fils!" (Quickly! Quickly! My little children.")

With a gift for loving indulgence and stores of endless patience, good-natured Gabrielle clearly understood the demands of her employers. Having come from a noble but impoverished family of landowners and chateau dwellers herself, she was quite familiar with the indulgent range of Madame Alice Hoschede's maternal priorities. As a result, well-bred but permissive Gabrielle-Marie-Genevieve Lenoir heard neither banging doors along the third floor hallways nor sudden splashes of water from the direction of washstands. She ignored delectable, long slides along freshly waxed floors, secret rides in the dumb waiter, and she could be completely relied upon to look the other way during a heavenly glide down the smooth, freshly polished mahogany stairway banister which connected all three floors of the Chateau Rottembourg in one thrilling sweep. But, every afternoon, having taken the stairs two at a time, a stack of freshly ironed laundry in hand, Gabrielle managed to assemble all five of her immaculately turned out charges at the table by the window with its fine view across the lawns to the Concy Hills where they sipped milky tea or hot chocolate and ate beautiful little sandwiches and wedges of warm fruit tarts from fine yellow porcelain plates, engaging with Gabrielle, as their mother insisted, in topics of conversation suitable to the development and interests of haute-bourgeoise French children, which the Hoschede children were.

Auburn-haired Suzanne was first to step out to the center of the third floor oasis with Gabrielle. She greeted Claude with a welcoming smile, the ease of her poised gentility not at all unlike her mother's. The two oldest girls, Marthe and Blanche came next, Blanche a little shy and carrying a collection of her watercolors, pink-cheeked Marthe reserved and observant. Jacques burst in breathless, the buttoning of his shirt not quite complete and directly behind him came Germaine, holding tightly to her doll and immediately assuming the role of official hostess as she skillfully took the hand of the third floor visitor to lead him toward the chair with the best view to the hills through the center window.

"This is the chair Mama sits in when she comes up for tea with us," she announced with firm authority. "She says that from this chair she can see all of us as well as the gardens. She loves us and the gardens. She won't be coming for tea today, though. She's busy with the roses, so we have decided you will sit there in her place, Monsieur Monet."

Claude expressed abundant thanks for the privilege being extended to him and took his seat exactly as his miniature hostess directed, his view from the third floor center window providing a commanding panorama of Rottembourg's well-tended landscape, its trees shading carpets of lawn in late afternoon sun, its needle-shaped cypress meeting woodland hawthorn, its thickset background of green forest pines at the edge of the forest, and against the distant purple hills wrapped in the wonder of brilliant light and flickering shadows everywhere. He watched Gabrielle pouring tea then adding milk and sugar, carefully passing a cup and saucer first to him, then to her chattering charges as she assigned Blanche to pass the tray of small sandwiches and Marthe to cut deftly into a golden crusted apple tart, each well-trimmed sandwich and triangular slice of apple tart placed on a blue-bordered yellow plate with practiced skill.

Alice Hoschede had been raised this same way, with these same habits, Claude thought. Yes, she would have known afternoons exactly like this, perhaps at another window at another family country house, and at this same time of day. There would have been milky tea, fine porcelain plates, perhaps these same plates, and fruit tarts still warm from the oven made from the peaches, apples, or pears grown in the household gardens. He sipped his tea and enjoyed a wedge of apple tart, enclosed in the insulated third-floor world of pale yellow walls and beautifully framed pictures of animals, lakeside scenes, and a series of Blanche's watercolors upon which he commented favorably and with genuine admiration, all the while trying not to think too much about the marvel of unassuming autumn draped in her magnificent tangle of dry branches and summer grasses.

"This morning, we made a list of our ideas for your paintings, Monsieur Monet," Marthe announced, interrupting the reverie he knew must be interrupted. Jacques, you go first."

"Monsieur Monet, I think you should paint portraits of all five of us for the four rotunda panels," Jacques offered, quickly calculating aloud that if Marthe and Blanche sat together, which they usually did, and each of the remaining three children were depicted individually there could be as many painted wall panels in the rotunda as the four required by his father. "Mama would like that very much and even in winter, when we live in Paris, a part of us would be here in the country too."

Basking in the flurry of affirmative responses from his four siblings to such a novel plan for being in two places at once, Jacques smugly concentrated on another sandwich as Claude attempted to address the suggestion set before him.

"My young friends," he began, "although I do like to paint people in pictures and I would certainly like to paint each of you, your father's wishes are clear. As I said yesterday when we met under those wonderful trees out there, he invited me here to the Chateau Rottembourg to paint outdoor scenes. He will be expecting views of the grounds and I had best keep that in mind and not disappoint him. If time permits, though, during my stay I believe I could do a study of each of you. Right now, though, as we discussed yesterday, I could use your help in finding a few of the truly special places on the grounds. Tell me, what else do you have in mind for my consideration?"

"The edge of the pond near the rushes where Mama bundles the watercress!" offered Blanche first.

"No, no!" came Jacques' booming voice with a change of heart. "If Monsieur Monet is not to paint portraits of us for the rotunda, then he should paint the purple bank of the high meadow where the summer lavender grows and you can see all the way to the tall spires of the Abbey."

"The thick garden hedge where the robins build their nests in the spring," Germaine chimed in, hugging her doll close. "Their eggs are blue," she added. "I love the color blue."

"I think you should paint the path into the woods where Papa hunts," was Suzanne's thoughtful contribution, "by the tall grass at the edge of the forest where the wild white turkeys come to feed."

"I have seen watercress growing by a stream," the charmed third floor guest remarked, "and yesterday, from the train, I saw the tall spires of what your father pointed out to me was the Abbey of Notre Dame d'Yerres, but wild, white turkeys? Here at Rottembourg? Unheard of! There can be no such thing in this part of the Brie Valley!"

"Oh, yes, Monsieur Monet!" insisted Germaine quickly leaning forward in her chair, her doll suddenly dropped to face the flowered carpet. "The white turkeys live somewhere in the forest and in the morning they come to feed in our meadow. They are very large and very white and one of them bit Jacques last summer and he cried. His hand and arm were bleeding and Mama had to apply salves and ointments and make a tourniquet."

"I did not cry!" interrupted an insulted Jacques. "I was brave and Mama said so!"

"You were not brave, and yes, you did cry, Jacques Hoschede!" continued Germaine relentlessly, her unflinching certainty expressed as much by the honesty of her unblinking stare and assertive tone as by the merciless detail in which she described her brother's unfortunate encounter with the white turkey he had attempted to capture and hopefully keep in a cage.

"Mama said Jacques was lucky the turkey had not plucked his eyes out!" Germaine added, encouraged by the affirmative nods she had elicited from her sisters as the tale peaked. "I, myself, will take you to the north meadow where the turkeys come, Monsieur Monet," she concluded, once again with unquestionable authority. "But first I must ask Mama's permission," she hastily added as Jacques bristled. "After Jacques' "temp-de-grande-horreur," Mama made us promise we would never again go out to the meadow by ourselves, or at least without asking permission. Marthe, why don't you come too."

Early the next morning, permission granted, appropriate warnings issued, Germaine, Claude and a reluctant Marthe descended the terrace steps together and walked through the rose garden toward the north meadow, Claude smoking a cigarette and carrying a sketch pad, his small guide clutching the doll that seemed to be her constant companion. He watched her, clearly enchanted. She was the most engaging child he had ever known; observant, interested in everything around her, quick to comment on the sweet smell of honeysuckle, the formations of black treeswifts flying overhead, and as they neared the meadow, enthusiastic in her evaluation of the season's plentiful crop of wild berries.

"Mama says that the raspberries this year are the biggest and most delicious we have ever had and that later in September, before we return to the city, we will be making another batch of raspberry jam for the Christmas meringues. It smells so good in the kitchen when the berries get hot and Mama allows one of us to put in the spoons of sugar, but all the jam we made last week is almost gone. The gardeners got some and Monsieur DeLille got some, and we have been spreading quite a lot of it on our breakfast croissants every morning. It is delicious. If there's any left, I'll ask Mama to give you some."

As the three walked and talked, their path narrowed under cover of oak and elm. Germaine stopped and turned to look back at the house. "Mama says our house is prettiest from here," she stated to Claude, lifting her doll to sit atop her head and face the house. "I think it is too. I love it here at Rottembourg. I wish we could live here all the time, but Jacques and my sisters go to school in Paris and Mama says they must keep up their good attendance. I will be going to school with them, but not until next year. I hope I like it. Do you think I will, monsieur? Jacques doesn't like school very much."

Nodding affirmatively and assuring her that she would indeed like school and likely do very well, Claude delighted in sharing Germaine's view of the house. Seen through the branches of pine trees from the edge of the ambling meadow where gold-tipped wild grasses abutted the forest, the length of Rottembourg's graceful rose brick façade stood engraved against the cloudless morning sky, its mullioned windows glinting in the day's early sunshine, its chimneys solid and tall.

"I can understand why you and your family are so fond of the Chateau Rottembourg," Claude remarked, admiring the Italianate architecture of the house in its flawless setting, admiring as well Alice Hoschede's skill in having made of a large, imposing estate a home of informal comfort and delight for her husband and children. Turning to Germaine to comment further, he saw that she had run ahead. "The turkeys come here, to this spot," she verified to Claude in a secretive whisper as he and Marthe caught up with her. "We should wait for them, but closer to the trees so they won't see us," she directed, managing with one hand to expertly pluck at a few gold-tipped blades of wild grass clumped at the edge of the clearing, playfully waving them in the air like wands before sharing them with her companions.

Without a word exchanged, the three stood side by side in the cool shade. Scepter blades of meadow grass in hand, a beloved doll held tightly by one, three woodland observers were mystically partnered in the eloquent stillness known only to those who love the ways of the country and are practiced in its customs. Interminable minutes passed with no sign whatsoever of white turkey feathers or red wattles when Claude suggested they start back to the house. Impatiently tapping one foot then the other, Germaine was clearly disappointed and had tired of waiting, but her impatience and dismay were short-lived. As if purposely designed to fulfill a precious wish, the three had just reached the border of willows rounding the edge of the meadow path when Germaine glanced back, and there they were. Out of nowhere and at the exact spot where only moments before the three had waited in silence, a flock of eight magnificent white turkeys approached the sun-drenched clearing, their red wattles undulating from side to side as they slowly paraded their preserve in the tranquil peace of an August morning, picking at seeds, berries, and the piles of acorns that had begun to fall from the oak trees and littered the ground. "They were there in the brush all the time just waiting for us to leave," Germaine whispered to a pleasantly astonished Claude. "They have been watching us!"

Alice Hoschede had spent her summers this way Claude thought to himself, quickly taking up his sketch pad and realizing he had found the subject of the first panel. Yes, exactly like this remarkably observant child, from an early age she too would have discovered the wondrous world of nature flourishing in the tranquility of country life. Safe and accessible and revealed in scene after scene of natural splendor, she would have uncovered more than a few of nature's carefully guarded secrets and she would treasure them all her life. There would have been the wonder of dry, brown tubers asleep under the snow through winter, turned miraculously alive and suddenly flowering under silent vigil of spring's fist warm sunny rays. On a wet Monday morning in May the colors of familiar woodlands would have sparkled in crisp opalescent brilliance, and on a sun-drenched afternoon in August a tapestry of soft-hued pink and yellow blossoms would have taken over to welcome late summer's close scrutiny.

Deftly moving a waxy black crayon over his sketch paper in quick, efficient strokes, anxious to capture the delightfully improbable view of a flock of white turkeys at an imposing country chateau, Claude's curious mind was that of the vagrant wanderer dangerously adrift in foreign lands, his thoughts coursing through vast sanctuaries of polished summers and bronzing autumns. Yes, she had walked and read by the shady banks of a stream somewhere near here, at a treasured place, home to sparrows and shuttlecocks and gentle breezes from the distant plain; yes, a secret place near to this habitat of improbable white turkeys, a haven close to this vital, staunch domain safely framed by tall clumps of golden meadow grass and in the distance a fine show of summer's wildest roses. There it was again, the old, seductive glory of the French countryside stirring the waiting soul of him as nothing else could, igniting his rich imagination with its unfailing magic and reaching deep into his heart to touch the lonely, empty places that had never quite been filled.

Subject One: White Turkeys at a Country Chateau

In the next days he returned to the meadow again and again to observe the turkeys and sketch, fascinated from moment to moment by their grace and gentility as in the tender glimmers of early morning larger and larger flocks went about their foraging. Standing at an easel by La Lethumiere's north window, he worked on his painting of white turkeys, applying paint to canvas, secluded and alone in his sanctuary on the right bank of the River Yerres, standing back, judging, assessing, arguing with himself, cursing himself, remembering, and hour by hour and day by day, consumed by thoughts of a woman he didn't know at all.

While Claude worked at painting, Ernest worked at life, and now much harder than he had planned. Through June and July Armel Ducasse had become far more than a nuisance, intensifying his interference in Ernest's Paris life by making it abundantly clear through a barrage of legal documents and demand notices delivered to Ernest's office that within a short time there would be increasingly serious problems to solve, "and solve them Monsieur Hoschede must!"

In June of 1876 the list of creditors had filled two pages. By August, the pages had grown to three. Ducasse, for all his demands, pointed out that the many antiques dealers, importers, clothiers, jewelers, and silver dealers with whom Ernest had dealt over the years were out of patience, and not only with Ernest Hoschede, but with all their credit-loving clients, for the unthinkable truly was underway. Paris was reeling. Financial times had grown much worse than had been predicted and day by day throughout the summer of 1876 the picture had grown steadily bleak. Bankers and financiers were not entirely surprised, but now the man in the street was panicked. Where would it end? No one knew, but now, even as late summer's beauty peaked, the word recession was not only being defined by the attitudes and activities of a generation of sophisticated French citizens unaccustomed to financial hardship, it was being felt everywhere by everyone. The pain was palpable. Once prosperous businesses saw their profits tumble. Spending habits had been changing for months, but now café regulars disappeared from their usual tables. Restaurants, which through the summer had enjoyed the patronage of devoted customers and an endless stream of international visitors, were now faced with empty tables and early closures. Florists and bakers closed their doors. So did dressmakers and tailors. Retail establishments such as Hoschede's saw a shrinking clientele and those proprietors of businesses which for years had offered easy, unlimited credit, were demanding to be paid immediately.

"I'll hang on until the storm passes," Ernest told DeLille. "That's all there is to it. I'll stare it down. What else can I do? Life presents these challenges now and then and we must ride them out. It will be fine."

Basically unmoved by all he saw around him, particularly in the Second Arrondissement's financial district where he was spending most of his time, Ernest remained firmly convinced of his own distinct entrepreneurial ability to withstand the storm by somehow continuing to access small but adequate bank loans, establishing new financial resources wherever possible, and securing fresh lines of credit, however short-lived they might be. He must devote himself to two things, he decided. It would be difficult and it would require innovation, but first he must stabilize the operation of his store so that in spite of cuts in consumer spending his financial statements showed at least some profit. This, he hoped, would serve to solidify his position with bankers and allow him to open at least a few fresh lines of credit. Second, he must appeal to Ducasse's sympathy and convince him to somehow extend the due dates on his larger debts for as long as possible. The very idea of establishing a sympathetic friendship with Ahmet Ducasse was more than the gifted charmer in Ernest Hoschede could bear, but this was no time for snobbery. He was under too much pressure. He would swallow his pride, bare his soul, and prey on Ducasse's softer side, if indeed he had one lurking beneath that deathly pallor of his. Apart from dealing with Ducasse, what Ernest really needed was cash, and more than cash, he needed time. He must get Ducasse to agree to an extension not of additional weeks, but of many months. Beyond the problem of Ducasse, Ernest also knew he desperately needed good advice, not legal pen and paper advice, but sound, common sense financial advice from someone he trusted, someone who knew a thing or two about the way money worked. Reluctant to divulge the seriousness of his situation to anyone, much less a Raingo family member, Ernest decided to swallow his pride further and consult with Julian Raingo. He met with Ducasse on a Tuesday. He met with Julian Raingo on Wednesday.

"Ah, Monsieur Ducasse!" he began with the reliably broad smile that always served him well, "Thank you for seeing me on such short notice," he added, breezing through the door of Ducasse's third floor office in one of the rambling buildings of the Bourse. I thought you might have escaped Paris for Deauville by now. I understand you have a lovely summer home there. It certainly is a hot August in Paris this year."

"Monsieur Hoschede, I appreciate your pleasant manner but I have no time for idle conversation," Ducasse immediately retorted, gesturing to one of the two chairs facing his desk. "I'm a very busy man, especially today, so let's get down to business. What is it you have come to see me about? Are you prepared, at last, to satisfy your debtors? They grow more impatient by the day and so do I. As you know, I've done my best to prolong the inevitable but I'm sure you also know that legal action is just around the corner. Of that there is no question. Do spare me a lot of additional paper work and tell me there is a bank draft or better yet an abundance of francs in one of those well-tailored pockets of yours. I would like nothing more than to remove your name and those of your debtors from my very long list."

Ernest looked directly into Ducasse's stone-cold eyes. The man's facial pallor was starkly odious in the gray interior light of his small office, his grim expression emphasized further by his heavy-lidded bloodshot eyes and the few long dark hairs glistening with too much pomade arranged like dry twigs across his balding head. Ernest tried not to stare, but he was struck by this touch of pomaded vanity in such a callous man and he decided to play on that vanity.

"Ah, Monsieur Ducasse, you are very observant to notice my tailor's fine handiwork. He pays great attention to pockets. Yes, pockets and shoulders, and he recently put me in touch with a fine bootmaker. Here, you must have a close look at these boots of mine." Ernest stood and took several steps to make his point. "Are they not the most beautifully stitched and finished boots you have ever seen?"

Ducasse stared appreciatively at his visitor's polished leather boots, nodding his head in approval as Ernest deftly lifted first one custom booted foot, then the other. "Ah, but a man of your stature must have a fine tailor with an eye for detail, the best bootmaker as well!" he continued, returning to his chair. "And of course, you must travel to the continent for such things. Italy perhaps? Or London? Where in the world are there such fabrics and leathers as come from the Italians? And of course when it comes to style and fit, who compares to the British?" He lit a cigar. "Oh, do forgive me, Monsieur. May I offer you one of these marvelous Turkish cigars? I have begun to import them for the store. The tobacco grows on vast fields tended by Greek farmers in the Turkish countryside. I'm convinced it is the Turkish sun itself that brings out this wonderful flavor and aroma. You must tell me what you think. Have you seen the Golden Horn? Those sunsets there along the Bosporous are stunning. As a boy I visited Constantinople with my father several times."

Ducasse hesitated for a moment, but took the cigar Ernest offered him. He lit it, slowly puffed at it a few times, and leaned back in his chair while examining his visitor and assessing his demeanor. Good-looking man, this Hoschede. Impeccably groomed, and those boots! Never had he seen such fine leather boots.

"Things being as they are, this summer there is much to keep me in Paris, Monsieur Hoschede," he confessed in a somewhat more congenial manner. "My wife is not happy with my schedule, but there is nothing I can do about it. I am being absolutely suffocated by paper work. Our house in Deauville will have to wait until the end of this recession I'm afraid, and as far as custom made clothing and boots, I have no time for such indulgences, nor do I believe it wise to spend on such things, financial conditions being what they are. Now, tell me, what can I do for you today?"

A more approachable Ducasse now clearly within his grasp, Ernest was quick to make his point. "Monsieur, I came here today to enlist your help. My request is a simple one. All I am asking for is time. Alas, today I have neither francs nor bank drafts in my pocket. I wish I did, but I know I will be able to produce both within a few weeks if you can be good enough to offer me just a bit more time to see the profits from an auction I am holding at the Hotel Drouot at which I will be selling some of my very best paintings. I hate to part with them, but I know I must. I am expecting good returns. The income from that auction should take care of several of my larger obligations and I would very much appreciate your patient indulgence until then."

Ducassse leaned forward with a chuckle. "Monsieur Hoschede, if you mean to tell me that you are expecting good returns from the sale of a few pieces of the new radical art with which you have a reputation for surrounding yourself, I am afraid I cannot honor your request for more time. Today, no one in Paris is willing to pay big prices for the work of unknown painters, especially when it comes to that band of disparate illegitimates you patronize, and to judge from the amount of your indebtedness you will be requiring very big profits indeed. Now, if you happen to have a Leonardo DaVinci or two out there at the Chateau Rottembourg, or perhaps a lost Raphael Madonna and Child hidden in the attic that would be another matter. Even in this difficult financial period, investments and collateral on that level are sound and always will be, but Monsieur Hoschede, I am sorry to say that I cannot accommodate your request for more time. I know you are a strong supporter of the new group of, what are they called, Impressionists? But there is no real money to be made there. I would advise you to forget any further involvement with them and find another, more realistic way to raise the funds you need, and quickly. Now, unless there is something else, I have many pressing matters to which I must attend. Finally though, Monsieur Hoschede, I must inform you that if you do not resolve your serious matters of debt within two weeks, I shall have no choice but to administer final notices which will inform you of a number of legal penalties which I can guarantee you will not like. I hope I make myself clear. If there is nothing else our meeting is ended."

"Oh yes, there is just one more thing, Monsieur Ducasse," Ernest said, rising from his chair. "What is the size of your boot? And what about color? Black? Brown? Ah, you look to me to be a man for brown boots, but perhaps you should have a pair in each color in, oh, shall we say four to six weeks? And you appear to wear a size forty-six. Yes?"

On the following afternoon Ernest found Julian Raingo in his Rue Miromesnil drawing room, bent over his collection of carved Egyptian reguli exactly as he had seen him for the first time thirteen years before when Alice had brought him to meet her illustrious uncle. At sixty-two, Julian Raingo still lived at the same fashionable Paris address. He still enjoyed the loyal services of the same white-haired butler. His drawing room walls were still covered with Flemish paintings and he remained remarkably healthy. But for the addition and subtraction of several magnificent old master paintings and the comings and goings of several attractive ladies who were known to share the elegant Rue Miromesnil address with him from time to time, very little had changed in Julian Raingo's formidable domain. Time had, however, altered the elder Raingo's opinion of Ernest Hoschede, a man he now saw as chronically distracted by too much good living and a self-centered, free-spending lifestyle he could not possibly continue to support, especially in the tense financial climate which had cast its suffocating cloud over the entire city of Paris.

The year before, the strategist in Julian Raingo had found himself very much aware of what was coming. He had sold several valuable paintings and pieces of commercial property, closed all but one of his Paris bank accounts, and had transferred funds to London and Switzerland, placing a fair amount of cash into his library safe. Financial conditions as dire as they presently were, he was not at all surprised by Ernest's visit. His advice was simple and succinct. "Young man, forget about having a good time and enjoying yourself in the country with all that hunting and wining and dining. "Those days are over, at least for now. You must be in the city and working at your store every day! From morning to night you must involve yourself directly in its every operational aspect. Be there and sell, sell, sell! Turn that famous charm on your clients and don't let up. And no house accounts! Cash only! Cut down on your imports. Better yet, eliminate them altogether. Our French artisans are the best in the world. Why do you need to court the Italians, the Turks, and the British? Reduce your prices on everything, especially on books and clothing which are things people will always want to buy. Put signs up in the store that clearly let people know prices have been reduced. Do everything you can to bring people in. One day each week give something away to each person who makes a purchase: a linen handkerchief, a nicely wrapped chocolate bonbon, anything to encourage people to get into the store and buy something. Get your suppliers to give you free merchandise for those customer gifts. They owe that to you and they know it. Take anything they want to give and extend them a big thank you. This month cut your number of paid employees by half. Next month cut that number by half again. If you must assume all the responsibility and do all the work, so be it. Working hard is what good business is all about. Working hard is what staying afloat and making money is about. Working hard and seeing the results of your efforts, that's what makes the thrill of success worthwhile."

Ernest found Julian Raingo's advice more than depressing. The man was brutal in his approach to improving the financial picture, and there was more. "Start selling whatever personal property you can," was Raingo's final injurious salvo as he sat at his desk and prepared a bank draft for twenty-thousand francs. "Sell some of that nice furniture you've accumulated at Rottembourg. It's too crowded in there anyway. I can hardly walk around without bumping into something. And sell those silly modern paintings for whatever you can get. They're eye sores. And Ernest, use this bank draft to buy back those two Raingo clocks I know you sold to Ahron. I saw them in his shop a few days ago and I left a reserve on them in your name. And one more thing, Ernest, please understand this: Raingo family clocks are not among the things I am advising you to sell. They are to stay exactly where they are at Rottembourg. They are a Raingo family legacy. They belong to Alice, not to you. Do you understand?"

All prospects of leisure at the Chateau Rottembourg were set aside. His days no longer devoted to hunting and picnic luncheons, the successful operation of E. Hoschede's, as Julian Raingo had advised, did become Ernest's greatest and most time-consuming challenge, the elimination of his enormous accumulated business and personal debts his most demanding obstacle. Out of necessity and like many similarly distressed Paris merchants, he was spending long periods of time in the city. As time allowed, he was meeting with creditors individually, attempting to personally convince as many as he could to postpone legal action against him. He was in frequent contact with a long list of purveyors who, because they had not been paid in months, had stopped filling orders. He all but begged for their patience. Some were willing to cooperate and continued to ship to him. Others stopped communicating altogether. As Julian Raingo had suggested, he reduced prices and one day each week gave away toys, candy, or books to any customer who made a purchase. At first these items were taken from overstock. Customers were delighted. They came back. Sales improved, but as suppliers refused to replenish give-away merchandise for lack of payment on larger orders, the practice was abandoned and once devoted Hoschede customers looked to other merchants who had copied the clever gift-with-purchase idea and were able to continue the practice.

The days grew hectic and more worrisome, Ernest constantly tired, often short-tempered when he arrived at Rottembourg. "It's the store. There is so much to do right now, and I must be there," he explained to Alice when she remarked on his impatience. "So many businesses are closing their doors and I don't intend to join their ranks. Most of all I do not want to appear in a court of law and be sent to debtors' prison. If worst comes to worst, surely you know I could be facing that."

"Never!" Alice shouted. "Debtors prison is an impossibility! Ernest, don't you dare ever think of it or speak of it, not ever again! The store will survive and so will we, but we're at the point where I feel I should be doing more. Perhaps I could help at the store. I think I could function as well as any vendeuse in Paris. Perhaps in fragrances or hats, even lingerie. What do you think?"

"Oh, of course, that would be marvelous!" Ernest shot back. "Yes, Ernest Hoschede's wife serving the public from behind the counter showing corsets and the very latest styles of French pantalettes in an assortment of colors! Makes me proud just to picture it," he said, shaking his head, unable to suppress a chuckle. "My darling, do you think you could also handle several sizes of breast bandeaus decorated with pretty ribbons and bows?"

"Yes, I could," Alice retorted with a laugh, "and I could bring the children to help me." Can't you see Jacques parading around the store with a pink breast bandeau on his head? You know very well he would do that!"

They broke into gales of laughter. "It's all too ridiculous, all of it!" Ernest said taking Alice into his arms and holding her close. "We'll manage, though" he said, and I didn't mean to frighten you with talk of debtor's prison."

"Of course we'll manage," Alice said as tears began to stream down her face. "I just hate seeing you suffering this way," she managed to add.

"It will be fine, my darling. Just fine," Ernest assured her, "but right now we are going upstairs to take a rest from all this. You will fall asleep in my arms and I will close my eyes and keep telling myself that I am the luckiest man in the world to have you for my wife."

How patient she was, and how very loyal Ernest thought to himself, but it was a façade. Little did he know that under her mask of encouragement Alice dreaded what she feared could be coming. She knew the recent extension of time Ducasse had allowed was quickly running out and that now Ernest was scouring the city for relief from any source. At the same time, though, but to protect and placate Alice, Ernest had begun to initiate a wide range of exaggerated and false explanations. "Ducasse is willing to consider another extension," he said. Ducasse wasn't. "Ducasse is talking to my most pressing creditors about dramatically reducing the amounts of acceptable settlements." He wasn't. "Rumor has it that Ducasse is actually dismissing quite a few complaints." He wasn't. By law he couldn't.

"It will all be over by autumn, my darling," Ernest promised Alice. "By Christmas the hectic schedule and all this silliness over recession will be in the past. How would you like to spend the Christmas holidays right here in the country? The children would love it."

Ernest was too distressed, too beleaguered to share the truth of his deep concerns with Alice, and although the suggestion of Christmas at Rottembourg was appealing, soon he avoided discussing future plans or financial matters with her altogether. Everything was fine, he insisted. His darling Alice was not to worry, but she did, and as September drew closer, Ernest's schedule in Paris grew ever more demanding. So did Armel Ducasse, and as the beautiful days of August vanished one into the other and September's golden haze began to settle on Montgeron, Claude Monet's presence at Rottembourg and the prospect of enhancing its solid beauty with four painted panels for the rotunda was Ernest's most welcome distraction.

CHAPTER 17

Touches of Yellow Ochre

Yes, it might be a good idea to think ahead to Christmas, an excellent idea Alice decided looking into the mirror on her dressing table while brushing her hair the next morning. The present was riddled with too much worry, too much anxiety. It was much more pleasant to think about December sleigh rides and the gaiety of Christmas Day where at noon in the drawing room the long hickory logs were set ablaze in the fireplace and everyone was smiling and happy opening their presents. Yes, Christmas at Rottembourg was an excellent idea.

Yes, it might be a good idea to think ahead to Christmas, an excellent idea Alice decided looking into the mirror on her dressing table while brushing her hair the next morning. The present was riddled with too much worry, too much anxiety. It was much more pleasant to think about December sleigh rides and the gaiety of Christmas Day where at noon in the drawing room the long hickory logs were set ablaze in the fireplace and everyone was smiling and happy opening their presents. Yes, Christmas at Rottembourg was an excellent idea.

Despite her every attempt to overlook prevailing circumstances and anticipating the distraction of Christmas at Rottembourg, day by day Alice lived under a disturbing cloud of worry and confusion. Ernest's current position was unclear to her, his procedures in solving their financial crisis a mystery and now never discussed. When asked, he flatly refused to discuss finances. Everything would be fine, he insisted. Much to her dismay and with concern growing and festering, the informative details Alice sought were never provided. As a result, day by day, adding to the fear of what could be lying ahead, an uncomfortable wall of silence began to build between Alice and Ernest, causing Alice to feel increasingly isolated from Ernest and his Paris life, but remarkably, just as in the past and as if nothing of any consequence at all was happening, life at the Chateau Rottembourg continued on in all its familiar patterns. The one difference in the scheme of things was the presence of Claude Monet, and even there Alice found dissatisfaction.

Apart from evening dinners and the occasional afternoon picnics to which the children insisted he be invited, Alice didn't see much of him, but from what she could tell, Rottembourg's artist in residence appeared to be well-occupied. Every day, either from the terrace or one of the open doors she caught a glimpse of him strolling about the property, familiarizing himself with his surroundings, sketch pad in one hand, cigarette in the other. And as the last days of August quickly dissolved one into the next, she didn't see him at all. Of course not. He was painting steadily at La Lethumiere, working on studies, eager to complete the panels in as timely a fashion as possible, Ernest told her. He seemed pleased with his progress, Ernest also informed her. She really must find time to visit La Lethumiere and assess progress for herself, he was quick to add, but Alice was not eager to follow Ernest's advice.

At the Rottembourg activities to which Claude was invited, Alice was finding the painter from Argenteuil remote and not at all forthcoming about his progress with her wall panels. She told herself she certainly had a right to know how things were developing. Rottembourg belonged to her. Everything about it was important. In her state of constant anxiety Alice did not yet realize that her private concerns were beginning to overshadow the simplest of personal interactions and that in the case of Claude Monet, she was beginning to exceed the boundaries of her responsibilities as a hostess. She had yet to understand that Claude was an artist who chose not to discuss unfinished work and predict its hour of completion.

Somewhat put off by his ambivalence, at dinners he attended she resorted to asking long litanies of questions, her manner crisp and direct, as if she wished to exert her superiority and make her controlling position clear.

"How is your work progressing, Monsieur Monet?" she would ask. "Have you decided on subject matter? Are there studies in progress? Have the children been helpful? I see you walking the grounds here but do you also take walks to the village train station?"

Claude's responses were always polite but never thoroughly informative. Yes, he had decided on subject matter. Yes, the children were very helpful. Yes, he had enjoyed walks to the station. On more than one occasion Alice chided herself for having asked too many questions, aware that her inquiries were taking on a meddlesome tone. Ernest noticed her strange new tendency to prod.

"My darling, I'm sure Claude appreciates your efforts to engage him," he said to her. "I certainly do, but you needn't feel it necessary to force him into lengthy conversations. He's a very good guest in every way. He's pleasant, speaks when spoken to, and he eats everything on his plate. The terms of my commission, as I clearly recall, do not require he be a chatterbox. Remember, he is a painter, and we are paying him to paint. By the way, have you been down to La Lethumiere to check on things there? I think Claude has everything he needs, but I've told him to expect you. I know Bernard is looking after him, but Alice, you really must go. It's not like you to allow a guest to do without your famous fussing, and aren't you dying with curiosity to see if there's a painting in progress propped up on an easel somewhere there at La Lethumiere?"

Although she said nothing about it to Ernest, as far as Alice was concerned, Monsieur Claude Monet was behaving too oddly to inspire a visit to La Lethumiere. Apart from his acquaintance with the children and his alliance with Ernest, he gave off absolutely no indication that he was taking any genuine interest in life at Rottembourg at all, and as far as whatever her curiosity about his painting might or might not be, she would attend to that in due time. She would make her way to La Lethumiere on her own terms. After all, Monsieur Claude Monet was being paid to paint at Rottembourg. That was all. There was no need to fret over him. Besides, he would be gone in a few weeks, his work finished. Thank goodness he had at least one saving grace. He was polite. That much was true, as Ernest had correctly pointed out. Alice smiled, admitting to herself it was also true that the visiting artist really did eat everything on his dinner plate. But, he was a man of too few words and after his first evening at Rottembourg when he had been so gracious and complimentary, he had changed. Since then he hadn't responded to her general conversation in quite the engaging manner she had come to expect of her guests. His good, almost elegant manners could not be denied, but his responses to her questions seemed perfunctory and not at all the fluent, clever phrases one expected to hear at a polished dining room table on any given evening in the country over servings of well-prepared aiguillette de caneton and the always anticipated Brie plateau de fromages. Something had happened. The man was difficult to reach. In a word, he was exasperating. His forceful profile etched in the glow of evening candlelight, over dinner he occasionally did venture into a few details of his life as a painter, especially his friendship with Pierre Renoir and the pleasure of their painting excursions together, but apart from generalities and vague descriptions of his preferred daily routine, it was clear that Monsieur Monet was extremely guarded when it came to his work. When it came to his life at Argenteuil and his family, however, he was often of another mind, and at those times he was full of information which he seemed almost too eager to share, Alice observed. Ernest himself found this surprising since at the Guerbois he had become accustomed to Claude's tendency to reveal very little about his private life.

"I am living in my second house at Argenteuil," he related during one evening dinner. "We moved there five years ago. Our first home was near to the alms house at Porte Saint-Denis," he further explained. "The one we live in now stands at the corner of the Boulevard Saint-Denis, quite near the railroad station which is a convenience for me since I go into Paris often. It is a rose-colored house, quite attractive, with small shutters at the windows, about twelve kilometers from the city. We are also quite near the riverbank, where I enjoy painting. The views are lovely. I do wish the factories were not expanding so rapidly though, and spewing their smoke as they are doing these days, but I have been able to escape much of that in my small boat which I have outfitted as a floating studio. It is nothing grand or even very safe, Camille reminds me, but it allows me the luxury of studying inlet subjects more closely than I can at a distance from the riverbank. With so much changing in the character of Argenteuil, this summer and before coming to Montgeron I was working not on the river so much, but on landscapes in my garden. Camille, is in all of them. Young Jean is in a few."

"In all the paintings Camille is *"comme il faut,"* (appropriately, or as one should appear in public) he had said at the dinner table more than once of Camille, each time turning toward Alice with a gentle, thoughtful smile. "She is wearing a hat and, in most of the paintings, carrying her parasol," Claude had informed his hostess, his emphasis on the correctness of life and its polite public rituals of proper hats and parasols unexpectedly impressing Alice as at first she had listened to his brief descriptions of Camille Monet's gentle, unpretentious manner and then to his increasingly unabashed flattery as he expounded on her role as his favorite model.

"She was one of the great beauties of Montmartre," he said of Camille with obvious pride, "tall, curly-haired, magnificent! She was walking with her girlfriends when I saw her passing by the window of the Café du Duc. Our eyes met and that was the beginning. It was ten years ago."

Alice had listened to his descriptions and personal reminiscences with interest, but what was it about Claude Monet that disturbed her as seated at her dinner table he repeatedly spoke in glowing terms about his wife, Camille and their son, Jean? Was he missing them and regretting having left them at Argenteuil to complete a commission at the Chateau Rottembourg, or was he studying his hostess and comparing her and her children to Camille and his young son Jean? Nonsense! He didn't know anything about Alice Hoschede, and although the children had taken a great liking to him and spent time with him almost daily, he had little to say about exploring Rottembourg's grounds with them. Furthermore, he had never inquired about her interests and favorite pastimes the way people do in the course of normal friendly conversation, and there had been plenty of opportunity to do so. And why was that? Alice Hoschede was imminently approachable, she told herself. People always engaged her, attracted to her gracious manner and natural ability to draw them out. She asked questions. She had opinions. She led an interesting life. Everyone she met was curious about her. "What will you and those beautiful children of yours be doing at Rottembourg this summer?" she was invariably asked by the time the Paris lime trees took on their first tinges of spring green and summer plans were being made. "I imagine this year the gardens will be as glorious as in past summers there at Rottembourg," was an often repeated compliment, another being " Do tell me what's being planted in the kitchen gardens this year, and please, dear Alice, do bring me some of that delicious peach compote when you return to the city. It's so delicious, it could win a prize."

Coming from every corner, the accolades were known to fly non-stop, and of course, there was always Cousin Beatrice who couldn't resist the trivial, amusing inquiries and comments which came so easily to her. Valuing Alice's opinion above all others and long before recession had altered a few of her more extravagant habits she would ask her to comment on the new hat or dress she had recently purchased.

"I bought the most enormous hat at Hoschede's last Tuesday," she would wax on with her red-rouged smile. "It's the most wonderful shade of gold and loaded up with feathers. Alice, do you think gold is a good color for me? You have such splendid taste in hats. Do you think gold makes me look ill? Marc says it casts a dull, sickly shadow across my face. Oh, well, gold, red, green, what does it matter? Life is full of choices and they cannot all be flattering, can they? There is one place in Paris, though, where I shop very confidently and where I'm assured my choices are very good indeed, and Alice, you've known me long enough to know that for years I have made it a point to spend at least one entire afternoon each week at Hoschede's. There's always something new and wonderful to see there. It's heavenly really, a new collection of this, a stunning display of that. Ernest outdoes himself with every new item he adds to the store's fabulous inventory. I almost don't care what I buy there. I just know I'll love it when I get it home. Did he send you my regards on Thursday? I asked him to lunch on Wednesday but he declined; said he had an important business appointment."

No, there were no such trivial questions, no such light-hearted observations from Monsieur Monet. There was no running commentary to compare with Beatrice's trifling revelations, no personal show of curiosity, no inquiry, not at all the sort of sociable give and take to which Alice Hoschede was accustomed. Claude Monet was just passing the time at her chateau dinners until he finished his work, nothing more, she decided, and admittedly it was a fine way for a working artist to end a summer day. He did comment freely on the beauty of Rottembourg, though. That much pleased her, and he did express concern for completing the rotunda panels within a reasonable period of time, Alice reminded herself, but everything else was pure pastime.

"And where exactly is the Café du Duc?" she asked Ernest at breakfast one morning. "From what Monsieur Monet has occasionally said at dinner, I have the impression he spends a lot of time there."

"The Duc was on Rue Gueridon, almost at the top of the hill at Montparnasse. I understand it's closed now," Ernest replied. "These days, Claude and his group frequent the Café Guerbois, but I think he met Camille somewhere near the Duc. I think she was an artists' model at the time."

He had told her his age, that he was married, and where he lived. He was thirty-six, his wife's name was Camille, he came from Le Havre, and he had lived at Argenteuil for five years, but that was all. There was nothing more about himself, no candid observations on current events and life in Paris; not what had led him to be an artist or what his view of the future might be. Did he read novels? Attend plays? Concerts? What did he think of the lovely new parks and the commercial district growing around the Garnier Opera? Perhaps he thought she knew all about him. Perhaps he assumed that Ernest had gone into elaborate detail with her, praising Claude Monet and his work to the heavens, praising his Impressionist colleagues and everything related to their struggle. Yes, that had to be it.

One evening after dinner as good-nights were being said in the entrance hall, along with Alice and Ernest, Claude stood before the painting of Henri du Rottembourg. "Fine looking fellow, the Baron," Claude remarked pausing to study the painting and thank his hosts for yet another pleasant evening. "He would heartily approve of all you do for his house, Madame Hoschede," he remarked to Alice. "I can tell just from my short time here that it is a constant joy to you and your family. Not all houses are, you know. It takes a loving hand and a generous heart."

It was more of a personal observation than he had allowed himself to express since his arrival, and in a way she could not forget Alice had been aware of an all-knowing quality about the Argenteuil artist just then. It was as if he knew all about houses and all about the people in them; that he saw things in rooms and on the walls of those rooms that no one else understood or saw. In her hallway, in a few brief perceptive moments, his steady gaze into her eyes had been riveting. He spoke the words, but as they fell into the air it was as if he had been prying her open and peering inside so he could see things; personal, private things that no one else could see. She would avoid him, she decided. This Claude Monet was too complicated, too difficult to offer the pleasant, light-hearted summer companionship to which she was accustomed. He would never be cultivated as a personal friend. Ernest would have to deal with him on his own. This Monsieur Claude Monet simply didn't know how to enjoy himself. Ernest was right. Monsieur Monet had been commissioned to paint panels for the rotunda and that was the end of it. He didn't ride, didn't hunt. "The man paints!" Ernest had said. Yes, she would leave him to his work and be done with it. He certainly didn't need her worrying about him. Besides, the children would provide him companionship enough. They had been following him everywhere, chatting incessantly, asking question after question and occasionally tossing a ball with them. Soon all that would turn out to be a trial for him, Alice further determined, nodding her head with a smug smile, her five young chatterboxes walking the length and breadth of the estate with him every day, pointing out their favorite places as he regaled them with his tales of early morning painting expeditions in the forest at Fountainbleau.

"That is when the trees in the forest look like gray ghosts, eerie and awkward and frightening," he had told them, according to Blanche, "but then when dawn breaks and daylight flashes up very fast, everything changes. In bright white and pink light the trees become the friendly natural features of the woodland nature intended them to be. That is when the vast carpets of Fountainbleau's dried red and brown leaves underfoot appear to be polished to a high gloss in the full light of day," as he had put it, Blanche had further related, absolutely delighted, she had added, to be in the company of a true working artist who appreciated nature more fully than anyone who had ever visited Rottembourg before."

For now it was a satisfactory situation, Alice concluded. Claude Monet was completing his work and everyone was co-operating, but for a man with only one child, five siblings let loose in the country and demanding an enigmatic guest's daily attention would eventually prove challenging indeed.

Quite contrary to Alice's conclusions, not only was the companionship and spontaneity of the five energetic Hoschede children amusing and immensely helpful to Claude, his stay at the Chateau Rottembourg was turning out to be a far more stimulating experience overall than he had expected when only weeks after the Second Impressionist Exhibition's closing and in the wake of its dismal aftermath he had reluctantly accepted Ernest Hoschede's commission in Paul Durand-Ruel's gallery. From the beginning, the estate's natural setting had lifted his sagging spirits. Finding comfort in Rottembourg's undemanding environment he was engaging himself more closely with nature than ever before, finding new dispositions of color in studying the well-ordered gardens and by sharp contrast the irregular borders of the adjacent dense forest. He was discovering fresh inspiration in the ever-changing moods of the ornamental pond and he was finding fresh perspective in the mystery of the grotto. For most of his adult life he had spoken the language of nature, but here was a very new communication. In the past he had acquainted himself with the wonders of clouds and rivers and hillsides and fields. He had found he could endure all types of weather and under the most negative climactic circumstances search out the endless functions of light and shadow, but now, with no constraints placed on his time, his mind and eye refreshed and exploring his surroundings either alone or in the company of five fertile young minds, he could analyze nature's myriad abstractions during any hour of the day and in observing their selective form and natural function he could watch for subtle changes in light, moment to moment variations in its reflection, and the ever-intriguing influence of the sky on all the earth's activity. Sometimes he wished he could see the night at Rottembourg and paint it.

During this period of intense observation, a new alliance with his young Impressionist colleague, Gustave Caillebotte, was proving not only enjoyable and sustaining artist to artist, but also highly informative gardener to gardener. At the proposed Chateau Rottembourg dinner which was to include the Caillebotte family and as a result of Ernest's urging that Claude see the grounds of Gustave's nearby family estate, a significant professional alliance begun in Paris and nurtured at the Café Guerbois soon developed into a warm and close personal friendship, Claude's interest in horticulture piqued and greatly expanded as a result of his experiences with his young Impressionist colleague at La Casin, the beautiful Caillebotte estate which Claude found was all Ernest Hoschede had said it was, and much more

"I was twelve when my parents acquired the property," Gustave related to him as the two strolled the grounds following a Sunday luncheon with Gustave's widowed mother. "They bought the place from the heirs of a Madame Biennais.

Now there's a story! Monsieur Biennais, was a jeweler and executed nothing less than the imperial insignias Napoleon wore for his coronation ceremony, including the gold laurel wreath which became so famous in David's painting. Biennais also designed the great gold necklace of the Order of the Legion d'Honneur. Needless to say, after all this acclaim and Napoleon's stamp of approval, clients flocked to him. I've been told that at one point his workshops on the Rue Saint-Honore employed six-hundred workers! The history of the Yerres property captivated my father, and of course the beauty of the entire estate here was a wonder to us. What freedom a boy from the city and his two brothers enjoyed prowling their own country woodlands at will and exploring the Yerrres Valley's grasslands, the forest of the Senart, and the beautiful shadowed knolls and pine groves of the Chateau la Grange du Milieu. Every year we started coming out from Paris at Easter. We stayed until October when my brothers and I returned to school. I hated leaving La Casin at the end of the summer. I still do, but soon I will be leaving it forever, I'm sorry to say. The property is for sale and we have an interested party. My mother can no longer be here alone and I want to spend my time in other ways. She understands as I do that a property of this size is too much to maintain now. With my father's death on Christmas Day two years ago, and my brother, Rene's illness, this lovely place has become a great burden. My mother is strong and realistic, but I know it will be difficult for her to go on without all this. On a personal level, losing my father was difficult enough, but she sees his hand and heart in everything here: in the house, in the gardens, in every corner. I do too. He worked tirelessly on the gardens here and loved every minute. La Casin was a splendid place for him and for all of us. I want my mother to remember it that way, but giving it up will change her life, mine too, I suspect."

    La Casin was a splendid place indeed, attention lavished on every path and flower-filled border. In addition to the impeccably maintained white stucco Italianate manor house and an array of well-tended surrounding lawns and gardens, there were a number of outbuildings including a greenhouse, an orangerie, a Swiss chalet, a collection of cottages, and an aviary for peacocks. Martial Caillebotte had seen to it that La Casin's many paths led to many different destinations, each ending with a well planned focus of his design: a view, a building, a bench, and always the surprise of seasonal color waiting to hold the eye: masses of white impatiens, red begonias, and purple pelargonium in summer, groupings of yellow and bronze Swedish chrysanthemums in autumn, and a perennial population of clumped purple crocus and pink eupatorium in bloom from early spring until June's magnificent peonies and roses took over the show. There was a perimeter road, an icehouse, a belvedere, a chapel, fruit and vegetable gardens, and there was the rosarium Alice had long admired, and at Martial Caillebotte's urging planned to duplicate for Rottembourg as a lengthy structure composed of a series of metal arches created to form an arbor for climbing roses. Thoughtful, meaningful details were everywhere, a fanciful piece of statuary here, a fountain there. At the river's edge, a pair of benches had been set into a rustic pavilion. They served as a resting place for scenic outlooks and were constructed of chestnut wood, the chestnut tree native to the Yerres region. Not far away, a narrow bridge built of rustic timbers led to the opposite riverbank and a small cabin and dock where boats were moored. La Casin's entire landscape fascinated Claude, but two of its components intrigued him most of all: the lily pond and the element of shade.

 La Casin's lily pond was planted with the two French species of water lily: the yellow pond lily called "lutheum" and the white water lily, or "nymphae" whose large snowy flowers completely enchanted Claude with their great beauty. He loved watching them afloat in the gently rippling water and no visit to La Casin was complete without a long, studied view of the nymphae. Gustave painted the theme of La Casin's water lilies in a work he called *Yerres, on the Pond*. As for the aspects of shade, Claude saw that the deepest, most impressive variations of light and shade at La Casin were to be found not in the formal gardens nearest to the house. The fascination of elusive shade was most profound to him at the undulating borders of the woodland, where under branches of tall, multi-shadowed forest oaks left to nature's care, the fern and moss were allowed to crowd at the base of ivy-clad trunks and the unexpected spurts of sagittaria and wild iris were entirely at home in the nearby sun-drenched company of more elegantly massed dahlias and low-growing primrose. A number of lessons were learned from long periods of observation at La Casin, not the least of which had to do with the successful cultivation of grasses. Because of its close proximity to the river and related levels of humidity, Claude learned that the lawns at La Casin required a watchful eye and careful maintenance.

 "What is happening to the lawns?" he asked of Gustave one afternoon, alarmed at the sight of large patches of grass being torn up by a team of gardeners.

"Oh, they are just raking away the moss," Gustave explained with a laugh. "Don't worry. It looks terrible I know, but it is absolutely necessary. Every summer we have a problem with creeping moss, which can be fatal to a lawn. Today, after raking it all away, the gardeners will spread a layer of coal ash which not only kills the moss, but is very good fertilizer for the grass. In a week or so, the cover of dull gray ash will disappear and the lawn should look fine again. My father insisted on planting English meadow grass here at La Casin, which is the most resistant to moss, but after particularly rainy springs, such as the one we've had this year, even that precaution can prove futile."

As at the Chateau Rottembourg, it was also at La Casin that Claude saw fine examples of the potential inherent in privately owned, privately maintained residential gardens. Both these properties and their impact would strongly influence the choices both he and Gustave Caillebotte were to make for their own future gardens, and from the summer of 1876 forward, through the exchange over subsequent years of seed catalogues, bulbs, tubers, shoots, and saplings, the friendship between Gustave Caillebotte and Claude Monet would remain deeply bound not only by their lifelong work as painters, but by the studied attention and great love they lavished on their own private gardens.

The large painting Claude had titled *White Turkeys at a Country Chateau*, was in progress at La Lethumiere. Six feet in height, it depicted the scene of white turkeys he had witnessed with Marthe and Germaine. Preliminary work had also begun on studies of the pond and rose garden. Still another painting but one not intended as a panel was also in progress. Ernest had introduced Claude to one of his neighbors who, along with Jean DeLille, was a frequent hunting companion, a Monsieur Debatise. With Ernest's encouragement Claude began a painting of the Debatise house which he titled *The House at Yerres*. In 1871, Debatise had been Ernest's staunchest supporter when he had actively campaigned for the position of Mayor of Montgeron, but a popular, lifelong Montgeron resident, Edouard Bonfils had served as Montgeron's mayor since 1841. He had remained in this office for thirty years, through the Second Empire, and into the early days of the Second Republic. The local council of April 1871, of which Ernest was a member, was appointed by action of the Prefect of the larger Essonne district, the mayor periodically elected by vote taken within the membership of the town council. Although appointed in 1871 to a six-year term on the council and actively involved with its members, in two attempts Ernest had failed to unseat Mayor Bonfils, a disappointment Monsieur Debatis had continued to share with him in conversations conducted on the terrace of his charming Montgeron house.

Before too long, the days fell into a pleasant pattern, Claude's close observance of nature's cyclical habits seldom far from the basic substance of his days and nights in a manner that for years had guided the progress of his nomadic life. At Rottembourg, however, the outdoor subjects with which his painter's palate were so familiar continued to take on new meaning and direction, the elusive vagaries of light, air, and color gradually weaving themselves ever more closely into his unwavering desire to live for all his life within the fascinating confines of nature's simplest, most intrinsic schemes.

Each day took on its own natural rhythm, each hour its opportunities for spontaneity and at Rottembourg, Claude began to see himself anew. He could stand away at some distance from the problems at Argenteuil. He could forget that his paintings weren't selling, that the rent and the butcher weren't paid, that Jean needed closer supervision, and with a defensive, almost helpless view, he could also tell himself that Camille was not as ill as he had thought on that sweltering afternoon in Paris as he had worried and fretted about her and against his will departed the Gare de Lyon in puffs of steam and smoke for this hidden paradise that was the Chateau Rottembourg. In what seemed no time at all, his natural optimism returned. He refused to be unhappy. In the first week of September he wrote to Camille to tell her that his work was going well and that his energy was high, his hosts thoughtful and kind. A few days later he wrote, "In a week Monsieur Hoschede will be advancing me another portion of my commission which as was done shortly after my arrival here, I shall immediately forward to you through Gustave Caillebotte. The amount should cover rent with enough left over for the butcher and other remaining expenses." Immensely pleased with himself for fulfilling at least a portion of his personal responsibilities, privately and at the same time Claude was experiencing the exciting rush inherent in all freshly advancing points of view, and in the secluded charm of the setting provided him at La Lethumiere, he came to a greater understanding of his relentless hunger for an ever closer and more meaningful connection with nature.

Day by day, the grounds of the Chateau Rottembourg and the picturesque villages of Montgeron and Yerres were opening themselves to his eager senses. He walked and watched the river, the sky, and the clouds, but he was also developing important new human alliances, his friendships with Ernest Hoschede and Gustave Caillebotte among the most significant he would form. The freedom Ernest had allowed him to explore the grounds of the Chateau Rottembourg and those Gustave offered at La Casin came with no constraints, and with access allowed to few outsiders Claude also became a frequent visitor to the first-floor studio in a corner of the main house at La Casin where Gustave worked on paintings depicting his family's privileged country life. There, the two discussed favorite selected themes. They shared in a mutual understanding of the pleasure and sustenance they derived from painting and it was while walking and surveying La Casin's magnificent landscape and in studying the color and organizational scope of its borders and plantings carefully laid out and exquisitely maintained, that over and over again Claude saw there was much to learn and admire, much to discuss, and much to remember about the possibilities in the natural world around him.

He became attuned to the smallest detail in the landscape and in particular to the manner in which human thought and attitude affected the creation and nurturing of a garden. Thoughtfully planned and tended, at La Casin, nothing jarred or shocked the eye, he observed. Nothing appeared forced or contrived, yet on the sloping grounds closest to the house there was a great sense of order and sensibility. Every circular flowerbed and linear border was a fine study in form and color, the smallest plants always graduating toward the viewer and away from the tallest ones, the harmony and hues of the gardens consistent and refined. At some distance from the house, roses flourished in their own lavish beds, not in a wildly inopportune riot, but in carefully planted compositions of harmonious, singularly graduating shades of red and pink. The creamy white water lilies Claude constantly admired floated like carefully chosen, perfectly formed wafers across the pond, but again and by contrast, the errant clumps of wild orchids were left to casually litter the pond's mossy willow-lined edges. In a short time it was this private, prosperous human climate that touched Claude deeply in an advancing wave of receptive thought and inspiration and in its own unavoidable way it was this rare and private visual climate, this fresh encounter with peace that was methodically constructing the setting of his ultimate future stage.

At Argenteuil, in Claude's absence and not yet in receipt of the money Claude had promised, Camille Monet was confronting a somewhat different visual and emotional climate. It came in the person of her landlady, Madame Aubrey, whose well-tested patience had once again worn painfully thin.

"I cannot allow this house to remain in your hands much longer," Madame Aubrey announced, arriving at Camille's door on a chilly mid-September morning. "You must let your husband know that you and your son will be out in the street within the month if the rent continues to go unpaid for one more week!"

"Please," Camille pleaded, "Madame Aubrey, my husband is completing a commission at a fine chateau in Montgeron. It will pay him very well. It is just taking a little longer than we expected. Please, Madame, be patient with me."

"Madame Monet, I have been extremely patient," the exasperated landlady expressed, stepping into the small hallway of the tidy Monet house. "I have waited for my money and have done my best to understand your situation," she continued, noticing Camille's pallor, "but your husband is an irresponsible man to leave you in this condition, alone and without money for weeks, sometimes months at a time. What kind of life is this? I don't understand why you wait for him. Why don't you and the boy go to your family? Winter is coming. You would be so much better off with your own people. Where are they? I will write to them for you if you wish."

"No, please!" Camille quickly insisted, tears welling up in her soft brown eyes. "I must be here when my husband returns. I cannot leave our home. An advance on his commission will be arriving any day now. He promised me. I will bring you the rent money as soon as it arrives."

"As you wish," Madame, but if Claude Monet were my husband I would take matters into my own hands and go to my family immediately."

It was with an uncharacteristically heavy heart that the demanding owner of the house on Rue Saint-Denis left Camille and Jean Monet. Camille was much too thin and pale, the boy as well. Where was their food coming from if it was coming at all? It was a pathetic situation. Monsieur Monet was indeed a negligent, irresponsible husband and father!

Miles away from Argentueil and all its deprivations, Claude continued to paint, pleased with his progress, delighted by the freshness of the natural world in which he lived, content with the daily wonders that met his eye and touched his heart. He awakened every day just as the last traces of night hung suspended dim and silent over the gentle gray river and the first timid rays of daylight glazed the horizon. Following the morning ritual of coffee, rolls, and fruit, he painted for a few hours and then he walked along the riverbank. When later he returned to concentrate on his work, the mid-morning light was gentle and sheer, the air floating through the open door invariably cool. By mid-day everything changed as a flash of golden hues danced across the no longer gray but suddenly transparent river and the Brie Valley sunshine glazed warm and bright against its rippling current. When he wasn't painting, he liked to sit on the wooden bench he had found by the river, amused by the antics of sunlight casting about the unsuspecting water, sparking here and there against the surrounding landscape. Most afternoons, after a lunch of cold meat, bread, and cheese, he returned to his painting. At twilight, he grew pensive. It was always this way at day's end. For a long while he would stand, not outside in the garden, but inside, at the window overlooking the river, where he could watch the stippled pink blush of summer afternoons linger and tease and fade gently into fragrant country nights as black as pitch.

Whenever Ernest was at Rottembourg, Claude was invited to dine and usually, despite worrisome financial conditions, in the company of a flurry of guests: neighbors, visitors from Paris, relatives, or visiting relatives of neighbors as well as one or two of the artists and writers who lived in the area. Ernest enjoyed this mix of personalities immensely and quiet and reserved as he was, Claude did as well, but he never stayed later than ten o'clock, his habit of rising at dawn to begin work one he would steadfastly maintain throughout his lifetime.

The well-known painter, Carolus Duran, was a favorite Hoschede companion and a man whose company Claude also came to enjoy during Rottembourg evenings. Handsome and dapper, Duran was every inch the image of the cloaked, ready-at-the-sword romantic French hero. Duran and his wife lived closeby in a lovely old house they called Le Moutier, a property they were restoring and a project which provided the Durans and Jean DeLille countless opportunities for sharing the many woes of dealing with the needs of a long neglected house and its gardens. Left to his own devices during the day and apart from working on his own painting, Claude's exploratory walks became the best part of every day. By the end of his first several weeks at Montgeron, he had fully grasped not only every detail of the Chateau Rottembourg's landscape, but much of the local color as well. Intrigued by the profusion of clumped wild lilies and the clusters of ancient oak trees along the old Concy Road, it was inevitable that he would find his way to the train station. Much to Madame DeLage's delight, he introduced himself one afternoon, providing the keeper of village news with fresh information and exactly the sort of personal revelation upon which she thrived.

"Ah, so you, Monsieur Monet, are a painter and not the gardener from Paris I thought you might be!" Pardonne! Pardonne! It is just that Madame Hoschede is so particular about the gardens at the Chateau Rottembourg that when you arrived with Monsieur Hoschede it seemed to me you were examining all that met your eye very carefully, the way a gardener does. So, you are an artist! Ah, gardener. Artist. It is the same thing, no? A little dab here, a little dab there! Ah, monsieur, perhaps you will paint a picture of my beautiful little Montgeron station."

More and more, his eye was being irresistibly drawn to nature's simplest forms, to its shapes and inevitable ranges of color, shade, and shadow, and now more and more often to its interaction with human activity. One morning, returning to the meadow and the edge of the forest where with Germaine and Marthe he had watched the white turkeys, he turned onto the well-trodden path leading into the forest and there he spotted a group of hunters. They stood silent and watchful along the forest border in the early morning light, the tallest among them Ernest Hoschede. He wore his hunting clothes and boots. Felled pheasant and hare lay on the ground beside him. This scene was developing into the painting Claude was calling Hunting at the Edge of the Senart Forest. It would depict Ernest Hoschede engaged in his beloved sport of hunting and as September cooled it was, along with White Turkeys at a Country Chateau, the ambitious work in progress at La Lethumiere.

CHAPTER 18

Striations in Color

Increasingly irritable, he was consumed by his problems at the store, he said, but they barely spoke. Alice tried to be patient, but the entire mood at Rottembourg had changed. The happy, carefree hours to which she was accustomed had vanished. Ernest was hard to reach. No longer enamored of the Brie's Valley's unleashed beauty, he was inundated instead by the mountains of paper he brought with him from Paris. Adding to the worrisome mood, heavy brown envelopes sent from Paris with the weekly mail had begun arriving at Rottembourg's train station, left in Madame DeLage's care until they were delivered to Ernest by her husband as had been arranged. The heavy brown envelopes from Paris came on a regular basis, their curious frequency arousing Madame DeLage's curiosity and once delivered, Ernest's careful scrutiny. There was no time for casual conversations or leisurely walks with Alice as Ernest isolated himself in his study or left for Paris without a word being said about his plans or when he could be expected to return. Most disappointing of all to Alice and the circle of local friends she treasured, by late September the elegant evenings for which the Chateau Rottembourg had become famous, were being cut short when Ernest insisted on returning to his desk to attend to pressing business matters immediately after dinner. There was no impromptu piano playing by Jean DeLille, there were no naughty backroom ballads, and no laughter echoed through the hallways of the Chateau Rottembourg. Ernest became ever more solemn and grave. His warm, easy smile had vanished and Alice began to notice that the handsome face she had fallen in love with was taking on a pattern of lines and shadows that had never been there before. Deeply moved by Ernest's appearance, her anger subsided and she attempted to offer whatever encouragement she could. She told herself she must be more patient, more affectionate, more understanding.

"I don't like seeing you this way, my darling," she often whispered, stroking his cheek. "Where is my old Ernest, the smiling, happy husband I used to know, the handsome Ernest who was never bothered by much of anything? The children are beginning to notice something very different in their father. Let's all go up to Trouville next week," she suggested one evening at dinner. "Beatrice wrote to me and suggested we join her at the new Roches Noires. The weather is still good. The Allaires and their children will be there, the Bolandes too. You like them. We would have a wonderful time together just relaxing and enjoying the sea air. The children would have new playmates on the beach and it would be so good for you, darling. Beatrice says the new hotel is beautiful and that even you would approve of the food and decor."

"No, not just now," Ernest had said. "I simply cannot leave. I'm too busy. I have Armel Ducasse and his mountains of paper to deal with and right now the store needs my complete attention, especially with the August holidays over and autumn coming in. The competition in Paris is becoming fierce. We have lost a great deal of money this year and now we seem to be losing good customers too. People aren't as loyal as they used to be. Times may be bad, but somehow attractive new stores carrying cheap merchandise are sprouting up overnight. The world is becoming too accessible, too difficult to deal with on the old terms. Things are simply not the way they used to be. I honestly don't know what to make of it."

It would pass, she told herself. Armel Ducasse was one thing, but all businesses experienced financial problems from time to time and now it was Hoschede's turn. It was true that increasingly intense competition and a market for inexpensive goods were quickly changing many of the public's purchasing habits. Alice understood that. People had less money to spend but they also had more and more choices to make and the ever-increasing variety of shops being opened presented a long, more modestly priced offering of novel experiences for a new crop of Paris shoppers. But Hoschede's stood for high quality merchandise and the very best standards in service, Alice insisted. It always had. It catered to the best people in Paris. There was simply no comparison to be made with those new, cheap bazaar-type stores opening along the Rue de Rivoli facing Place de Chateau d'Eau. No, it would be just fine. People might not be as loyal to their old habits when a little new shine and gloss came along, but the right people would always want high quality merchandise and the service that went with it. Could it be that just a brief change would get her through this tiresome period? Trouville began to sound like just the sort of diversion she needed. Understanding the strain in the household and sensitive to Alice's feelings, Ernest generously encouraged her to take the children and join Beatrice at Trouville.

"Why don't you go without me, my darling," he said to her wearily. "Go to Trouville. Join Beatrice. I want you and the children to go and have a wonderful time by the sea. I'll miss all of you terribly, but I have so much to attend to. Besides, I'd be a terrible bore to you all right now. By the time you return, things will be better. I promise." Hesitant to travel without Ernest, Alice said she would think about Trouville a bit longer.

Her daily walks were solitary and grew longer. For a while the gates, trellises, fences and hedges on the property captured her attention as she noted the necessity for repairs and alterations before winter set in. She met with the gardeners more frequently, laying out her ideas and plans for the new rosarium she planned to install the following summer and which she now spent time describing to them in detail. It was to be a structure made up of several securely set metal arches which would serve as arbors for the fragrant climbing roses she loved. Shortly before he died, Martial Caillebotte had shown her how in just two growing seasons his climbing white roses had completely overtaken and entwined his own rosarium arches like a magnificent curving mass, the metal structures completely invisible under their aggressive, rapid growth. "Through the winter you will have time to ready the arches and we'll begin planting the roses early in the spring," she had told Jacob Nosante, the head gardener. "I'll come out to Rottembourg a little earlier than usual next year, April perhaps."

Distracted by her expanding plans for the estate landscape and grateful for the diversion as Ernest spent more and more time in Paris, Alice decided against traveling to Trouville. Instead, she would proceed with planning one further ambitious project at the Chateau Rottembourg. It would be time consuming enough to hold her interest as few things could.

In his lifetime, Alice's father had replaced the estate's old wooden gates with the pair of sturdy black iron gates marking the entrance to Rottembourg at the Concy Road, adding a row of linden trees to each side of the drive. Alice had added the statuary along the drive and now she intended to make an additional statement by expanding the garden pond and re-orienting the kitchen gardens. Over passing years, the trees bordering the walled kitchen gardens had grown so large, their branches spread so widely, that now there was too much shade being cast across the orderly rows of annually planted vegetables. The espaliered Doyenne plum and Saint-Germaine pear trees bordering the rows of vegetables, although adequately sheltered from harsh winter winds by the capped stone walls surrounding the solid structure that was the adjacent gardener's cottage, were also in need of more generous doses of sunlight. A lover of trees, Alice had no intention of removing a single one of the sturdy old maples and oaks, but she did spend a good deal of time with Jacob Nosante exploring possibilities for establishing newly located kitchen gardens nearer the stables where the land could be divided into orderly partitions and provided with paths. There would be no tall shade trees planted, sunshine would be bright, and the project would begin the following summer by planting persimmons, quinces, broad beans, fennel, tomatoes, and spinach in longer, wider beds than before. Alice was delighted by the prospect of lavishing yet more attention on the property she loved, but her ambitious plans, although sensible and practical, were not to be realized. Returning to the house one Monday afternoon, her head full of fresh ideas for the landscape, her enthusiasm high, she discovered the true extent of Ernest's financial problems. She also discovered the extent of her own involvement in them.

On a September day designed for thoughts of sunlit kitchen gardens and the planning of rose covered rosariums, and just as she set her wide-brimmed yellow straw hat on the hall's center table, two of the heavy brown envelopes from Paris were delivered by Monsieur DeLage. They were addressed to Ernest. He was in Paris and not expected back at Rottembourg until the following Saturday afternoon. More than slightly curious and in a rare breach of the privacy she normally observed with mail addressed to Ernest, Alice opened both envelopes. The first revealed unthinkable news.

Liens had been placed on the Chateau Rottembourg for non-payment of debts. Alice dropped into a chair. Her heart was pounding. Reading quickly, she discovered that without her knowledge or permission, Ernest had been using the Chateau Rottembourg as collateral against his loans. He had also used her collection of Raingo clocks to secure several substantial lines of credit. Like an addicted gambler, he had borrowed heavily against the values of the house and the clocks, the chateau at more than five-hundred thousand francs, the clocks at over one-hundred thousand. Worst yet, from what she could tell from the contents of the second envelope, advances on personal lines of credit had been used not to pay off suppliers and purveyors, but to incur additional debt. In just over two years, not only had Ernest's 1874 one-million-franc debt grown to more than two million francs, but due dates on most loans had expired long ago.

Any thoughts of new gardens were forgotten and instead of contemplating the prospect of expanded country landscapes or a few distracting weeks with Beatrice and the children at the seaside, Alice began to seethe, able to think of little more than Ernest's Saturday arrival from the city and what she would say to him. Why had he done this to her beloved house? How could he have used Rottembourg in such a dangerous way? Her anger grew daily. Her fears too. She thought of returning to the city the very next day to confront Ernest immediately and demand he do something, but as if her sheer physical presence would ensure protection for all she loved at Rottembourg, she waited possessively in its precious isolation. By day she walked the grounds. Unable to sleep, in the dark of night she lit candles and wandered slowly through the rooms she loved, running her hands along walls and plumping up cushions and pillows. Every morning she threw open the draperies and let the light flood into all the rooms through which she had wandered the night before. No, nothing was at risk. "It couldn't be!" she told herself, looking across the terrace to the perfection of the rose garden in bright sunlight. How foolish she was. It would be fine. Full daylight had a way of diminishing nightly worry and besides, Ernest would make it fine. He always did. There had to be a rational explanation. It was a mistake. She had misinterpreted or misread the information in the documents. She was overreacting. The language in legal documents was always difficult to understand and they had probably been sent out only hours, or even minutes before Ernest had taken care of things. It was alright. The beautiful Chateau Rottembourg was hers. It always would be hers. There would never be encumbrances placed on it. Rottembourg was part of her. She knew its sounds and smells, its traditions and serenity. Its walls spoke of respect and love and the lives and adventures of its distinguished owners. Its future had been left in her capable hands. She was the keeper of its history, trusted guardian of its future, and every day, through a veil of stubborn apprehension, she found delight in recalling events and incidents that formed her fondest memories of life at Rottembourg.

There were the summer weddings on the great lawns, the birthday parties in the dining room, her mother's treasured settings of Sevres biscuitware waiting at each place, the gold-rimmed goblets filled with wine, admiring murmurs from congenial company; men in satin vests, women in clouds of silk taffeta, flames dancing in every fireplace, the texture of old Belgian tapestries hanging on walls, the piano covered with silk damask where the champagne glasses were set out on silver trays, conversation hinged by events of the day, fond reminiscences, hunting stories, anecdotes, music, laughter, her father's hundredth stag.

"We mustn't disturb the roe deer in the park," Denis Raingo had repeated to all nine of his children time and again as Rottembourg summers cooled into autumns and the hunts were planned. What excitement once the leaves began to fall and the house filled with guests! There were the men from the village chosen to paunch the game as soon as it was killed, the luncheons outdoors with everyone gathered around a fire in a clearing, the dogs, the horses, the rich smells of leather and wool, the crackle of rifle-fire. There had been rules for the children; expectations, safety precautions, and as always, there were compensations, the most prized of these being inclusion at the adult dinner table for as many as twenty guests if you were ten years of age or older and promised, on the blessed souls of your most rancorous Raingo ancestors, to speak only when spoken to and sit still at table for more than an hour while fantastic adventure stories flew back and forth and hunting tales of wild chases, swift, long rides, and great victories over creatures of the deep hillside woodlands were told. At such times, on the third floor, the younger children could run and shout, eat warm biscuits dripping with butter, and fall sleep with the family's enormous sheepdogs at the foot of their beds. How clearly she remembered those haunting sounds of childish laughter, of little running feet, a door banging shut at the end of the nursery hall, a shout, a barking dog, a call.

She thought Saturday would never come. She worried that something would delay Ernest, keeping him from the confrontation she knew must take place. Walking the length of the drive every morning and turning onto the short path to the Church of Saint Jacques to attend Mass, her ardent prayers for assurance and certainty were tearful as she sat in one of the rush-seated chairs or fell onto one of the kneelers, her hands clasped around rosary beads, her heart racing. The wait for Ernest seemed interminable.

Through these anxious days, the children provided much needed solace, even humor as they played their games and continued in their normal summer pursuits. They were as active and happy as ever, but the change in their mother's mood did not go unnoticed. Lacking adequate sleep, on most afternoons Alice was too tired to play at statues, to read to them, or play the piano. Leaving her to rest, they took to seeking out the interesting painter from Argenteuil who they usually found walking the grounds, examining the landscape. They knew he painted in the morning but that he continued to search for subject matter most afternoons. Unaware that he had begun two large canvases intended for the rotunda panels, they had grown curious about the final choices he would make for the four proposed panels.

As a group of five, they very much liked the fact that Claude shared his observations with them and that he seemed genuinely pleased to be in their company, their interest in Monsieur Claude Monet's project at the Chateau Rottembourg greatly heightened when seated on the ground under the silver oak trees and following much guessing he revealed to them that he had begun a painting of the white turkeys he had seen feeding at the edge of the meadow. Germaine was overjoyed and it was she who quite unwittingly applied a fresh, hot ember to Alice's smoldering disposition, thus adding immeasurably to the mounting anxiety which was consuming her.

"Monsieur Monet has begun his painting," Germaine proudly announced to her mother at the four o'clock third floor tea to which she had begged her to come. "Today he told us that for one of the panels he has decided on a painting of the white turkeys Marthe and I took him to see! Mama, isn't it wonderful to know that I was the one to think it a good idea that he watch the turkeys feeding at the edge of our meadow? He said he had never seen such beautiful birds!"

Patient as she always was in listening to her precocious children's revelations, Alice could not hide her dismay.

"Turkeys? No, no, you must be mistaken, my darling," Alice said with a laugh. "Certainly there is to be no painting of turkeys in our beautiful rotunda! Are you sure Monsieur Monet said he was painting turkeys? I do not understand. Papa has made it very clear that Monsieur Monet is to paint scenes of the property; the pond, the rose garden, pretty things."

The train from Paris arrived at the Montgeron station on Saturday at three-fifteen. Monsieur DeLage took note of its time of arrival in his logbook. Madame DeLage took note of the private Hoschede traincar's single passenger. Monsieur Hoschede looked tired, but he kept his distance as for some reason he was doing lately, but always the gentleman, he smiled and waved.

As usual, Bernard met Ernest in the gray landau and drove him along the tree-lined Concy Road, turning at its wide hilltop curve through the Chateau Rottembourg's open gates. All the old habits were in place: the dogs barking their welcome, the drive freshly raked, Germaine holding her doll, waiting for her father at the door, the carriage crunching to its familiar slow halt on the gravel, Ernest stepping out, carrying the anticipated blue box from the Dore. On this Saturday, handing the box to Bernard, he hugged Germaine and stepped into the hall where he found Alice waiting. Her expression immediately told him something was wrong. She held the incriminating documents in her hand. Germaine was quickly excused and sent to the third floor while Alice calmly suggested she and Ernest talk in the sitting room.

"Ernest, it seems you have been using my house as collateral against your impossible debts," she began, slowly closing the sitting room door behind her. "If what I read in these documents is true," she said, facing him, "you have been relying on creditors over a long period of time, years really, to support a lifestyle that would embarrass a prince! As a result, it looks as if the Chateau Rottembourg could actually be at risk. Liens have been placed against it! How has this happened?"

Ernest glanced away for an agonizing moment and then with an unmistakably determined tone in his voice he looked into Alice's eyes and calmly began to explain. "Alice, I never expected this to happen. I love Rottembourg as much as you do, but we're in the middle of a storm. Quite frankly, I thought that by now I would have raised enough capital to cover my debts and protect you. I didn't want you to worry. I have never wanted you to worry. I also thought the financial situation in Paris would have improved by now."

Alice dropped into a chair in disbelief as Ernest walked toward the fireplace and stood staring at the flames. "Alice, I have been working very hard to hold everything together," he finally said, his voice faltering in the middle of his sentences. "I'm sure that eventually I'll be able to do that," he went on, "but you know how things are in the financial markets these days. You read the newspapers. You talk to people. Guests here at Rottembourg always comment on current financial conditions. We aren't the only people suffering through this crisis. My darling, I fought the liens off as best I could and for as long as possible. I didn't want you to know anything about them. I knew how you would feel and how you would worry, but there could be a happy ending for us. According to Armel Ducasse the Chateau Rottembourg has enough value to extend my credit lines and make it possible for me to function for a while longer. This property really is the best collateral we have. I was delighted to hear it."

Alice couldn't contain herself. "You have been using the Chateau Rottembourg as collateral so that you can function for a while longer and all this delights you? How long Ernest, will you delude yourself into thinking that your creditors are providing the carefree lifestyle you demand free of encumbrances, and for what? So that among other frivolities you can continue to support that silly band of artists and their laughable paintings? Wake up, Ernest! No one wants those so-called Impressionist paintings you find so irresistible! You are devoting yourself to a disgusting folly! You fool! You incredibly selfish fool!" Alice shouted, bolting up from her chair and forcing herself into Ernest's direct view.

"How do you expect to solve a financial crisis that has gone this far and is this huge by continuing to "function?" she raged, waving the intimidating documents in his face, her eyes ablaze, her angry voice filled with a rancor Ernest had never heard from her before. "You have risked everything I care about; this life, this house, our children's future. You know how much I love Rottembourg. You know what it means to me and to them and you have compromised it! Not only have you compromised my house, you have done so behind my back! How could you let this happen without my permission? And why?" Alice's voice cracked. She was shaking, fighting back tears, feeling as if she was breaking into a million small pieces. "According to what I read here, the debt has been building and building while your spending has just gone on and on," she continued, unfazed by her own crushing anger. "Ernest, creditors have been lining up, demanding their money for at least two years and you've virtually ignored them, putting them off by overwhelming them with your charm, your fine taste, your insistence on quality above all! This situation has been festering for too long. Worse than that, you've gone on as if nothing at all was happening and you've led me to believe you had everything under control. Now liens have been place against this property. What comes next? Liens on everything we own?"

"Alice, I'm afraid something like that has already happened," Ernest confessed. "Ducasse is placing liens on just about everything. Not only will Rottembourg be affected, but so will the Paris apartment. The contents of both houses too. Everything. I had to tell you. I'm so sorry."

Alice would remember these agonizing moments for the rest of her life. Even years later, in her final days, she would remember the searing pain that had surged through her, and in ways she would never quite understand she would also remember the bright sunlight streaming down onto Rottembourg's broad terrace as she had gazed out through one of the windows and at least for a fraction of time escaped the dark reality engulfing her. Through it all she would remember the sound of Ernest's voice, resigned and direct as he had detailed terms of the pending arrangements.

"If Ducasse goes ahead with full legal authority there will be appraisals, a public auction, every worldly possession carted off, our houses and their rooms emptied of their contents."

Most of all, in rare episodes of retrospection Alice would remember the scream she had felt rising up in her throat that day, a hot fiery entity filled with swirling spumes of hate and malice, the likes of which she had not known before or would ever come to know in future years. Clearly though, her thoughts and behavior were not too far removed from the levels of solid common sense inbred into her and remarkably, Alice was more stoic and more logical than she would ever give herself credit for.

Controlling herself and clasping her hands together tightly as if in prayer, she had gazed out to the lawns and beyond to the farthest distant hills. The vineyards wrapping the hillsides were beginning to turn bright yellow and orange, she noticed. Of course, the grape-gathering season was underway, she reminded herself. Entire families would be taking part in the annual garnering and crushing, and as happened every year the quality of this year's wine would optimistically be predicted to be absolutely the best in memory.

Summer was waning, slowly releasing its seductive grip on the Brie Valley, Alice reluctantly admitted to herself. Soon the air would bristle with the first chill of autumn. There would be thick morning mists and in mid-October the first hoar frost would lace the valley in shimmers of white, then one morning the smell of wood fires crackling in the fireplaces of Montgeron's beautiful houses would replace the delicate scent of roses and meadow grasses no longer warmed by the sun.

"Ernest, when were you planning to tell me about this terrible upheaval very likely coming into our lives?" she asked with surprising calm. "Next week? Next month? Next year? Ernest, I am your wife and I have a right to know about everything that affects us. Why haven't you been open and honest with me?"

"I wanted to protect you!" Ernest snapped. "It was the most important thing. I wanted to straighten everything out without your knowing anything about it. I wish I had been here when those documents arrived. We wouldn't be having this dreadful conversation right now."

"Ernest, hiding the truth of the matter was not the best approach, but I suppose as the head of our family you felt a great responsibility. I understand that, but what I cannot understand is why nothing has changed since Armel Ducasse barged into our house in Paris two years ago and shocked me and my Uncle Julian as well as our guests with the news of your million franc debt. You said you were taking care of everything. Ernest, I believed you were doing exactly that, but it looks to me as if since then you have done nothing but incur more debt so that you can continue to "function!" Ernest, now the amount exceeds two million francs!"

"I know," he said quietly as he turned to the door. I am very well aware of the amount. I live with that knowledge every day."

"Oh, no!" Alice shouted as he turned away from her. "You'll not be leaving this matter hanging in mid-air the way you did two years ago! I won't have it!" she went on, reaching for Ernest's arm and pulling at it with a strength she didn't know she possessed. "What do you plan to do? Tell me right now, Ernest! There must be a way to avoid this looming disaster. Your Paris contacts do not seem to be helping you. Have you spoken to Uncle Julian? He can help us."

"Alice, earlier in the summer I discussed the situation with Uncle Julian. At the time he advised me to pay close attention to business at the store, which as you know, I did. Things went well for a while, but Paris is not the city it was even at the start of summer. People are holding on to their money and when they do spend, they patronize stores and shops with lower prices than I can afford to offer at Hoschede's. For now I intend to continue dealing with my own circle of advisors at the Bourse, but quite frankly, it doesn't look good. Alice, my dear, we could be approaching dangerous waters. Ducasse seems to have set his sights on us. We can discuss this further later on, tomorrow perhaps. Right now I'm very tired. I've been fighting and arguing for days."

No, Ernest! These are serious matters and we'll discuss them here and now,"

Alice insisted. "You will not leave this room until you tell me exactly what I can expect to happen. Ernest, I need to know. Could I really lose Rottembourg? Everything in it? Tell me the truth!"

Ernest took a deep, slow breath and looked into Alice's unblinking eyes. "Yes, the way things stand today, the Chateau Rottembourg is at great risk," he said quietly, "the Paris apartment too, and yes, the contents of both houses. Alice, I'm so sorry. I'll continue to do all I can. I just need rest right now. I'm very tired. Please."

She blocked the doorway, her body a firm unyielding barrier, her eyes flashing a red hot anger. "No, Ernest, you're not leaving this room, not yet, because there is one more thing! Before you climb the stairs and nestle your weary self under the bedcovers, there is the matter of your Monsieur Claude Monet. Germaine tells me that for one of the rotunda panels he is planning to paint a scene of the wild white turkeys that come to feed at our meadow. Turkeys! How foolish! Please see him first thing in the morning and let him know there will be no turkeys parading across the walls of the Chateau Rottembourg; not white turkeys, not blue turkeys, not yellow turkeys, not ever! This is my house and in spite of our ridiculous French laws which allow husbands to claim full ownership of a wife's inherited property, I will not allow either of you to forget that fact!"

CHAPTER 19

The White Turkeys

The threat to her beloved Chateau Rottembourg foremost on her mind, Ernest's maddening ambivalence a torture, the next morning at breakfast Alice again addressed Claude Monet's painting of Rottembourg's white turkeys. Clearly annoyed at the prospect of coming into possession of a painting of mundane turkeys and similarly annoyed by the painter who seemed determined to depict them, her intemperate tone was nothing less than that of a woman bent on total opposition.

"Ernest, it's a ridiculous idea! I will not have turkeys on my walls! It's as simple as that. Turkeys! And you told him exactly what to look for on the property. These artists! Your dazzling group of so-called Impressionists! Ernest, I expect you to do something!"

The night's rest Ernest had sought in the tranquility of the countryside had eluded him. Consumed by the now well-established condition of worry, he had barely slept at all and by morning he was in no mood for further confrontation. The previous afternoon's bitter exchange with Alice remained very much on his mind. Hurtful things had been said and now, unrecovered from one battle, Alice was sparring with him once again.

"My dear, it isn't as if the man opposed my instructions," he offered, his tone more than mildly conciliatory. "I said I wanted views of the property, and the turkeys do come onto the property. You've seen them. I've seen them, and you must admit they do put on quite a show."

It was no use. Alice was determined to have her way.

"Ernest, you are putting too fine a point on this. No, there are to be no turkeys on the walls of the Chateau Rottembourg, no white turkeys, no brown turkeys, no purple turkeys, and that's final! Now, talk to your Monsieur Claude Monet this morning and straighten this out!"

"Oh, I think perhaps you should take this one on by yourself, my dearest," Ernest said slowly, sitting back in his chair, his arms folded across his chest, his voice dripping with sarcasm. "You do these things so well, I mean convincing people to do exactly what you want them to without so much as a little catch in your voice."

He leaned closer toward Alice, taking her hand in his. "Remember this my dear. I've seen you in action with our children and that Raingo crowd you call a family for quite a few years now. And look at how well you have done with me!" he concluded with a terse smile as he tossed his white napkin onto the table and rose from his chair, eager to be off and leave issues of turkeys and artists and paintings that should or should not appear on chateau walls to Alice and get on with the hunting outing he had planned with Jacques for that morning. It would be Jacques' first experience in the Senart and in spite of prevailing domestic circumstances, Ernest intended to see that all went well. The week before, while searching the red oaks for roosting pheasants, he had spotted a covey of partridge not far from the thickly clumped fern at the north end of the forest's edge. He had watched to see the birds scurry and quickly take cover under the dense, overgrown spears of green. For a boy beginning to hunt, that would be a fine place to start, but before embarking on this highly anticipated adventure with his son, Ernest stood in the dining room doorway with a final word.

"I seek merely to inspire and provide options," he called out to Alice, and today my dear, in that capacity I am appointing you commissaire des dindons! (Turkey Commissioner!) "Toutes mes felicitations!" (All my congratulations!) "And one more thing, Alice. I'll be returning to Paris tomorrow. It seems best for me to be in the city just now. I'm sure you agree."

Shortly before noon and smarting not only from her confrontation with Ernest but incensed by his readiness to escape to Paris with absolutely no intention of discussing either pressing financial matters or Monsieur Monet's painting of turkeys, Alice decided to take matters into her own hands once again. Ernest could be as sarcastic and as irresponsible as he wished, but she was still in control of life at Rottembourg. She would make her way to La Lethumiere and set the errant Monsieur Monet straight. More irritated than ever by the prospect of indolent, dull turkeys parading across the beautiful pearl gray walls of her chateau rotunda and spurred on by a heightened resolve, she set out for La Lethumiere at a brisk pace, her shoulders set firmly back, her dark blue skirt trailing behind her along the gravel path, the black streamers on her yellow straw hat waving gaily in the gentle breeze as with every furious step she recalled the floral beauty of Cousin Beatrice's lovely painted wall panels. The same Monsieur Zolany who had painted Beatrice's panels should have been commissioned for the Chateau Rottembourg, she told herself. It was maddening to think that Ernest had placed such confidence in an unknown, inexperienced artist. Rottembourg deserved the very best. Thankfully, it wasn't too late to bring all this Impressionist nonsense to a halt once and for all and engage a proper artist.

In a small basket she carried an assortment of peaches and apricots which, at the last minute, she had hastily gathered from the plentiful supply kept in the porcelain tubs just outside the shaded kitchen door. The ripening late summer fruit was intended as no peace offering nor must it appear to be one, she told herself with a huff, but after all, unlike some people who had no idea at all how to behave as one's guest in the countryside, she, at least, would maintain considerable grace and behave like a proper hostess.

The day was sunny, the air warmly fragrant with the inescapable scent of roses and honeysuckle, such pleasure seldom surprising to residents of Montgeron who, like Alice Hoschede, understood only too well that by August all of Montgeron was one huge garden.

Everyone grew roses. Some were planted in small, tidy gardens, others in long, sweeping rows of dazzling color, the Brie area long famous not only as the revered wheat-producing area of France, but famous also for its cultivation of what by the Mid-Nineteenth Century had become the known world over as the flower of France. The rapid growth of the French rose's popularity could still be traced to Grisy-Suisnes and attributed to one Admiral de Bougainville who, in the eighteenth-century, being a man of leisure and having nothing of any importance to do at his divine Chateau de Suisnes, devoted himself, together with a team of gardeners, to rose cultivation, studying its Chinese origins and diligently experimenting with Rosa Gigantea and China's hardy Rosa Chinensis, the red or pink climber from which all roses are descended. By the last quarter of the Nineteenth Century, many residents of the Brie had continued to cultivate species of the ancient Rosa Gigantea, whose enormous ruffles smelled like tea. The proud owners of these beauties enjoyed telling their visitors all about Admiral de Bougainville at the Chateau de Suisnes, proud of the pedigree borne by their prized specimen. Overall, there were at least seventy varieties of roses in cultivation in the Brie by 1876, and from Rosas Gigantea and Chinensis to Gallica, Alba, Virginiana, Borboniana, Damascena, and Sombreuil, the rose gardens throughout Montgeron provided not only pleasure and vistas of unequalled beauty, but numerous opportunities for employment as well.

Rose gardens require constant tending, but so do vast lawns, gravel drives, swaths of thick hedges, and assorted varieties of domestically grown fruits, vegetables, flowers, and trees. By the time Alice inherited the Chateau Rottembourg there were so many gardeners at work in the area that they had formed a benevolent society called The Society of St. Fiacre. The organization was initially formed to benefit and support widows and orphans of deceased local gardeners, but frequent picnics, Sunday boating parties, and other special events such as the annual September parade on the Feast Day of St. Fiacre had made membership highly desirable.

St. Fiacre had long been known as the Patron Saint of Gardeners and every year on his Feast Day, a village parade was held to celebrate and show off the best of the Montgeron area gardeners' handiwork. The event was blessed at dawn by the Abbess of the local Benedictine Abbey, enthusiastic participants at the reigns of horse-drawn wagons decorated in flowers of every variety formed at the Montgeron train station and at the sound of a morning trumpet call began a procession along the old Concy Road. Prizes were awarded for the best floral displays. Alice was a judge every year, her affection for the country village she loved seldom more in evidence than on the first Saturday in September when everyone for miles around turned out for the parade of St. Fiacre.

Alice found it immensely satisfying to watch every participating horse-drawn wagon displaying the best examples of its freshly cut blossoms and greens in well-designed presentations of every shape and size, each display impressively provocative and distinctive. Some were designed to be formal, flowers and leafy greenery precisely arranged and organized by color. Other displays were loosely structured in magnificent profusions of brilliantly colored floral bouquets. There were huge baskets formed entirely of roses. There were hand painted trellises drawn across wagon beds to show off hardy climbers. Garlands of flowers decorated the horses. Some wore flower-trimmed hats with holes poked out for their ears. Children and dogs were everywhere.

The boundaries of the old properties nearest to the station were marked by stone walls and by the time the gardeners' parade was held they were completely blanketed in small, yellow rose blooms the color of citron and wheat. Originally planted behind the walls and directly on their owners' properties for private pleasure, over the years the roses had been allowed to spill over and drift down onto the roadside for passersby to admire at festival time. Farther from the station, bolder red roses trailed in brilliant swaths across stone estate markers and as the road widened at the curving hilltop and the black iron gates and red rose-filled urns of the Chateau Rottembourg came into view, even the lowly honeysuckle seemed to take pride in itself, having somehow grown noticeably fuller and more fragrant for the occasion.

This year's parade would be taking place in a few days time, Alice reminded herself, somewhat comforted by that thought as La Lethumiere's roof and chimney came into view and she paused to admire the clumps of lavender clustered under the maples and elms lining the turn in the path leading to the front door.

The gate stood open. Passing through, she saw that the front door was open as well. Pausing at the threshold and peering inside she called out. "Monsieur! Monsieur Monet! I have come to see you on an urgent matter. It is Madame Hoschede!"

There was no answer. She stepped inside and called out again, this time a bit louder. Still, there was no answer.

The room was filled with bright light. It smelled of spicy roasted sausages, likely cooked on the fire for a late morning or mid-day meal. She glanced towards the fireplace. Its embers burned low. On the table she saw a yellow plate and the remains of a meal: a few slices of sausage, a piece of bread, slices of cold potatoes, and beside the plate a half empty glass of wine. She called out again, and looking straight across the room to the large window facing the river she saw the figure of a man standing outside with his arms stretched up to the sky. He was naked from the waist up. He faced the river, so she could not see his face, but she knew it had to be Monsieur Monet. What was he doing? She looked away, embarrassed to have intruded on his privacy. She turned to face the door, her back to the window and the shirtless gentleman just outside, and as loudly as she could she called out, "Monsieur Monet! Please come inside! I must speak to you! It is Madame Hoschede!"

She heard footsteps behind her and a man's loud laughter. "Ah!" came his loud voice. "Pardonne! Madame, pardonne! Un moment, un moment, s'il vouz plait!" (One moment, one moment if you please!)

In what seemed mere seconds Claude came to face her, a shirt quickly pulled on and buttoned, a thin, long cotton jacket hastily placed over his shoulders, one of his hands quickly patting at his hair, the expression on his face one of complete bewilderment.

"Ah, Madame Hoschede, quelle plaisir! (What a pleasure!) How wonderful to see you, but I must apologize for my appearance," he quickly uttered, adding, "What you must think of me! But please understand. At times when I paint for long periods of time my arms and hands tire. I'm told reversing the circulation of blood in them will help. It does, and when a river is as beautiful and gentle as this one just outside my window and the day so lovely, so much the better." Continuing to talk, he deftly placed his arms in the sleeves of his jacket and buttoned the top button. "I don't know when you were last here at La Lethumiere, Madame, but do come and see the river," he said, doing all he could to appear completely composed. "At this time of day it is so beautiful. Had I known you were coming I would have been at the door to greet you. I'm so sorry. I hope you have not been waiting long."

"Monsieur Monet, we are enjoying an unusual abundance of fruit this year," Alice said flatly, placing the basket of peaches and apricots on the round table in the middle of the room, revealing no interest whatsoever in the river or whether or not she had been expected. "I'm told it has much to do with all the rain we had in the spring. I hope you enjoy these."

"But of course, of course I will," Claude replied quickly, clearly delighted. "They are beautiful. Perhaps I should paint them before I eat them. What do you think?"

He laughed again, looking directly into her brown eyes. In return, she looked into his brown eyes, unmoved by his laughter and his overdone attempt at lightheartedness which remained in clear contrast to her own icy solemnity.

"Yes, Monsieur Monet, perhaps a painting of our fruit would result in a very good still life," came the terse response. "Rottembourg's fruit is grown in the vicinity of our gardener's cottage where it can be easily tended. I'm very proud of it. Last year, at the Feast of Saint Fiacre we won a prize for our pears. The peach and pear trees are espaliered every autumn and covered in burlap for the winter. Perhaps you should see them as right now there is still a good deal of fruit left on the branches. I am very fond of peaches. And apricots."

"May I offer you some tea, Madame?" Claude suggested, continuing to make every attempt to relieve the human chill in the air. "I make a very good pot from the Belgian tea provided for me here," he added. "Thank you very much, not only for the fine tea, but for everything else as well. At times I think I really am too comfortable. This house is delightful and a fine place to paint. And the river! Do come and see."

He turned and crossed the room, stepping toward the window. Against her will and without taking a step she watched him and for a moment gazed through the window herself, drawn to the view of bright sunlight glistening on the rippling tide. A small sailboat bobbed up and down in the graceful current, making its way toward Yerres. She had to admit, even if it was only to herself, that the view of the gentle, unassuming river was as lovely as he had said it was. Her attention only momentarily diverted, it was large canvas propped up against the wall nearby that captured Alice's greater attention. So, it was true. He did have something to show for the time he was spending at Rottembourg. This must be one of the four panels he was preparing. Curiosity getting the better of her, she completely ignored the view of the river and turned to examine the canvas instead. It was taller than she was. She could make out the rose brick outline of a house and faint streaks of white paint in against it. The blue sky behind and above the house was filled with clouds. Two tall trees had been partially painted, pines she thought, but the curly wild grass of Rottembourg's lower meadow in the foreground was clearly depicted. The painting was far from finished but Alice recognized her own house in its own setting. Its rose brick color and the center pediment facing the lawns and lower meadow were clearly there. The tall windows and terrace doors were in all the right places, and yes, those two trees had to be the two pines at the center of the grassy park. It was her favorite view of the house. The morning sun had just begun to light the sky. Streaked gold and pink and pale yellow, here was the early morning sun in the view of sky she knew so well. She immediately recognized the look of it, the mood of it. It was the Brie Valley's sky caught just as the eager, streaking sun broke through the clouds of morning, its colors racing past and disappearing only to be replaced by new cloud formations that lingered and teased but soon performed the same ritual dance with the sun and just as quickly, vanished.

Before her marriage to Ernest, she had watched the clouds on many a summer morning. From the windows of her room, from Rottembourg's wide sweeping terraces, and from the secret knoll she had discovered just inside the forest border and made her own secret haven she had cherished the magical rhythms of the sky in all its moods. Alone, she would lie on the cool curly grass there and look up to the sky, happy to escape just for one precious hour, the incessant turmoil in a bustling household of nine children preparing for the activity of a new summer day. In peaceful quiet she dreamed the dreams that young girls dream as the continuity of sun and clouds overhead provided suitable accompaniment to thoughts adrift in beauty and silence. It was her knoll, her 'bocage,' hers alone. When she took Ernest there for the first time she had made him promise never to tell anyone about it. Again and again during their courtship, they had met and kissed and made promises there. Even now, after more than a dozen years of marriage, they occasionally escaped to the secret knoll to be alone at daybreak, to kiss and make love and lie back on the grass to watch the sky coming gloriously alive with color.

"It's a start for the first panel," Claude said, standing back from the window and stepping toward the canvas Alice examined. "Monsieur Hoschede tells me you very much like the view of the Chateau Rottembourg from the angle of the meadow and I must agree with you, Madame. It is a very beautiful sight, and I'm sure Marthe and little Germaine have told you all about our adventure with the white turkeys there. It was a delightful experience. There were so many of those magnificent creatures, at least a dozen, and they were very much at home in their setting. They are so beautiful here in this environment, so appropriate."

He was making no definitive statement about painting a collection of white turkeys parading before the favored view of her beloved house, but surely those few streaks of white paint she saw on the canvas were being planned as creatures likely to end up with feathers and a wattle. Alice had not intended to blurt out her objections, but the words tumbled out.

"Monsieur Monet, I do hope the white lines I see in the foreground of your canvas are not intended to be turkeys in the finished painting of my house."

"But yes they are. Madame, the turkeys you have here at Rottembourg are wonders of nature! Have you seen them recently? They are stunningly beautiful, spirited and proud, especially when the early morning sun reflects on their white feathers as they strut out of the woods on their long spindly legs."

Somewhat taken aback by Madame Alice Hoschede's implied disdain of his intended painting subjects, Claude took no immediate offense, but the woman's attitude was baffling.

"The flocks of white turkeys here at Rottembourg were begun with a pair of specimen birds my father was given as a gift when he purchased the estate," Alice was quick to inform the painter from Argenteuil. "No one expected them to survive the predators of the forest, but they succeeded not only in surviving but thriving and multiplying over and over again, generation after generation as they obviously have every year since. We never paid too much attention to them and my parents tolerated their noisy gobbling only because along with the few sheep we had, they kept the meadow mowed and the privet trimmed. They are not an important part of the Chateau Rottembourg and as a matter of fact, I have asked my husband to winnow the flock later in autumn this year. I understand the Americans find turkey an appetizing menu item. I have never eaten it myself, but my husband's cousin, Beatrice, was in America last year and was served an American turkey dinner which she told me was quite delicious. Perhaps in a week or two we will be cooking turkey at Rottembourg. I hope you will join us."

Claude was aghast. "Ah, but Madame, please. The white turkeys at Rottembourg are superb creature parts of the whole of life that is here. They are the continuity, the vitality, the silent strength of nature going forward here. Madame, during dinner on my first night here, I clearly saw there was 'un beaucoup d'estime' (a high regard) for all that was established around you; the comfort, the ease, the grace. These are qualities that do not come easily or overnight in a home or in a family and I have seldom, if ever, experienced anything at all like the "sout ambiance" (special ambience) you have created at the Chateau Rottembourg, but it does not come of or by itself. It is developed and nurtured over time not only by its human inhabitants, but also by its natural occupants. Perhaps you have just forgotten."

"Monsieur Monet," Alice interrupted, "I appreciate your compliments and to be quite honest with you, I am somewhat surprised. You are very quiet when you come to dinner, but you obviously notice everything, and yes, you are right. I do work hard at seeing to details others might ignore. I care deeply for Rottembourg and everything it stands for, but you must understand that the turkeys of which you speak so highly, however noble to you, hold no great significance for me and represent nothing of the Chateau Rottembourg that is important to me. There are, however, many other themes, very beautiful themes, that do. Having had time to examine our grounds, I believe by now you must know what those are. I urge you to concentrate on them as you pursue your work here. It will more than likely make our association the pleasant one I am sure we would both like it to be."

Claude could not believe his ears. Why was this spoiled, over-indulged society woman being so rude and overbearing? He wanted to tell her what he thought of her high-toned demands, but for reasons he would never quite understand he quickly decided to control himself.

"Madame Hoschede, I very much want to please you and Monsieur Hoschede with my work, but you must understand my point of view as an artist. Those white turkeys I watched with your daughters at the edge of the meadow are, to me, important symbols of this fine property. They are as important to the character and meaning of the Chateau Rottembourg as are the people who dwell inside its walls. Like you, they are safe here, and free, and in some small way, I believe they know it. I have watched them every morning since I was introduced to them. What elegance! What arrogance! Uninvited, they go about their daily foraging. They mingle with the shrubbery and the bushes. They pick and choose. They take their time. They inspect and peck at berries. They know they are beautiful. They admire one another. They preen themselves. The males show off and alert the females to the slightest hint of danger by fanning out their magnificent tail feathers. They stand guard like watchmen and the silly females pretend not to notice. Male and female, they all appear complacent and a little too slow, a little ignorant and unworldly, the way we humans can be when caught up in the glories of the countryside. But I am rambling on unnecessarily. You must forgive me, Madame."

He turned his eyes away from the tall canvas and returned his gaze to the river.

"I would hate being an artist!" Alice said, breaking the silence as standing beside Claude and as if she had heard nothing he had said, she too gazed out to the river. "I would much prefer writing poems or being a gardener."

Claude laughed. "Then you already are an artist, Madame."

Alice smiled a slow, unusually tight-lipped smile. "No, Monsieur Monet, I am no artist. I am the mother of five children who are not always well behaved and the wife of a man who takes a unique view of life. We have two houses, a dog, a parrot, servants, and gardeners. My work is to take care of them, to keep them all happy, to affect their mood and their imprint in positive ways. I feel I am reasonably successful at doing that. I also feel I am reasonably successful in looking after this property and seeing to it that its future is protected. As you might understand, I fully expect my children and their children's children to enjoy life here at Rottembourg as I have. Obviously, the way you see it, Monsieur Monet, I am not succeeding in promoting Rottembourg's finest natural assets for the future however subtle and significant they may be."

Claude gaze remained fixed on the river. Another sailboat appeared in the calm wind of afternoon.

"Is it that you see yourself in your paintings, Monsieur Monet?" Alice suddenly asked. "I mean, parts of yourself, "votre humeur, votre empreinte?" (your mood, your imprint?)

Claude faced her, exasperated by her lack of understanding. It had started out as such a pleasant afternoon. His work had been going well and at first he had welcomed her surprise visit. Now, though, he resented her brash intrusion. Beyond that infraction, Alice Hoschede's attempt to impact his work with shallow comment and selfish observation was ridiculous and rude. "Madame, I am a man struggling in a nightmarish world," he snapped. "It is a world you have never known and never will know."

"Then you are unhappy as an artist?" Alice continued, her invasion into the substance of his creative thinking one more maddening violation.

"No, Madame Hoschede, I am not unhappy as an artist, but perhaps I am unhappy as a man. I am resigned to living with my choices, but there are times when I am not happy with them."

"What is it then, that makes you truly happy? I'd like to know," Alice asked, her tone softened, almost fragile.

"The sky makes me happy, and the river, and those peaches and apricots you brought."

He had not taken his eyes away from sailboats on the horizon.

"What do you see out there, Monsieur Monet? What are you watching?"

"Do you see that point, that dot at the top of the last sailboat on the right? I am watching that."

Alice squinted and tried as hard as she could to find said point and dot.

"You must have extraordinary eyesight, Monsieur Monet. I cannot see your dot," she confessed looking toward him."

They faced one another. He said nothing. There was a faraway, lonely look in his eyes just then. A strange, dark shadow had crossed his face. She wanted to ask more questions about his dot but something told her she had said enough.

"Thank you for coming to visit," Claude said, turning away, his tone unmistakably dismissive. "I must get back to my work now."

"Monsieur Monet, Saturday is St. Fiacre's Feast Day," Alice said brightly before turning to the door. "Every year at this time we hold a parade in St. Fiacre's honor. The village gardeners decorate their wagons with the very best of their flowers and vegetables. They compete for prizes and make quite a day of it with the parade and music and all sorts of festivities. Everyone attends. My husband is very busy these days and may not be there this year, but the children are looking forward to it and I am a judge every year. Do come."

"Thank you Madame," Claude responded politely. "I will try."

"Everyone meets at the train station at eight. I'll send the landau for you."

"Madame, if I decide to attend, I shall walk to the train station. I know the way and I am accustomed to walking. Merci."

Without another word, Alice stepped away from Claude. She walked across the sitting room's polished floor and at La Lethumiere's door she set out on the path. Claude stood in the open doorway watching her. He watched her dark blue skirt combing the gravel in the sunshine as she walked. He watched the ribbons on her straw hat trailing in the breeze. He watched her until she had become a dot on the horizon, unaware that as she returned home she was hating herself for having failed to make a friend of Claude Monet. She had a genuine talent for making friends. People were drawn to her. She had a gift for dealing with people, she told herself. She knew she had been overbearing, perhaps too demanding, but during the walk back to the house she changed her mind and told herself she had been right to insist. She knew what she wanted and what she wanted for her wall panels was not what Claude Monet had in mind. And what lofty thoughts he had about white turkeys! "Elegant! Arrogant!" he had said of them. Nonsense! And what was that silliness about a dot?'

"Well, my dearest, have you solved the turkey dilemma?" Ernest asked at dinner later that evening, his voice strained and tired. "Yes, I believe I have," Alice exaggerated, unwilling to confess her utter failure in having convinced the visiting artist to confine his subject matter to her preferred themes. "Monsieur Monet understands what we have in mind for the wall panels, but of course he has a particular philosophy about his art. He seems to place great emphasis on relationships with nature."

"Well, of course he does," Ernest remarked. "He paints outdoors, in the woods, in the fields, by the rivers. He is not like us, my dear. While we fuss about wearing our fine clothes in our fine houses, he stands outdoors for hours at a time watching the changing light, the clouds, the air."

"The air? How does one watch the air? Oh, Ernest, really! What nonsense! I don't understand him at all, but I did feel a bit sorry for him, all by himself out there at La Lethumiere. I invited him to the Saint-Fiacre parade on Saturday. Why don't you come and keep him company while I review the afternoon entries?"

"Oh no you don't!" Ernest answered quickly with a tense laugh. "I have stacks of accounts to go over and a number of important matters to attend to at my desk. The house will be blessedly quiet with everyone away for a few hours. You are taking the children, aren't you? Say you are. Gabrielle and Celeste too? Wonderful!"

Later that night as she sat at her dressing table brushing her hair, Alice regretted having left Monsieur Claude Monet at La Lethumiere without holding him to a clear decision on his themes for all four of her panels. How could she have allowed that to happen? Now she would be having another discussion with him. And why had she been so gracious in extending an invitation to Saturday's parade? It wasn't at all necessary. He had work to do!

Following Alice's unsettling visit, Claude returned to the riverbank. His jaw was tightly clenched as he paced up and down. The sailboats had disappeared and the water was turning its afternoon gray. He watched the graceful willows skirting the water's edge and he wondered about strange, presumptuous women who ran great houses and raised fine children and judged entries in country parades. What was it that set them apart from women he knew? What went on in their lives that was so different from what went on in the lives of women like Camille? Why did they have so much to say and do, and who on earth was this Saint Fiacre?

CHAPTER 20

A Primed Canvas

On Saturday morning a still gray mist shrouded the river, clouding his customary view to the hills over the sultry willows. It would be a somber day, he predicted, slowly sipping at a cup of the coffee he had made shortly after sunrise, a day better suited to naps and writing letters than to attendance at a country village festival celebrating an obscure saint.

Standing at the window, he debated with himself as to the wisdom of a walk to the train station on such a morning. No, he wouldn't go, he decided. There could be too many people, too much noise. It might rain. He enjoyed La Lethumiere's peace and quiet and there was always work to do. Besides, he should write a long letter to Camille and Jean. Yes, he would tell Jean all about the flock of white turkeys at the Chateau Rottembourg and he would describe Alice Hoschede and each of the Hoschede children. Camille would like that.

La Lethumiere was feeling familiar to him now. The door handles, the soft bed, the smell of fresh linen delivered promptly at ten every Tuesday morning, the milled soap at the wash stand, the way the front door needed a push to close tightly, all of it felt comfortable to him. There was nothing that belonged to him in the rooms of La Lethumiere, no furniture he had brought, no books or plates or cups he had selected, no soap or plants or candles he had placed at washstands or tables, yet he felt safely sheltered and content within those walls, free to enjoy, at least for a time, the essence of belonging in a place apart, a peaceful place where he could come and go at will and work unrestricted by the nagging boundaries of worry and concern, always securely mindful that whenever he returned from one of his forays across Rottembourg's grounds and beyond, that the small, friendly lodge at the bend in the river awaited him.

He had never really loved a house. He had fond thoughts of his childhood home in Le Havre and the pleasant family activity he remembered there as a boy, especially the music on Sunday afternoons in summer when his mother sang folk songs from the Auvergne while his uncle played the flute and afterwards tea was set out on the sunlit terrace, but once his father had begun to attack his interest in art and later relentlessly criticize the friends he was making, his feelings for home had changed. The final blow was struck when shortly after their wedding, Claude had brought Camille and their baby, Jean, to Le Havre and Adolphe Monet had flatly refused to meet his daughter-in-law and grandson, forcing the young family to stay at an inn and not at the family residence. And later at Fecamp, when there was no money, no food, and Jean had been sick, Adolphe Monet had remained unrelenting. It had been the same later yet, at Saint-Michel on the Seine, west of Paris, Claude's pathetic appeals to Frederic Bazille and Arsene Houssaye who ran the magazine, LArtiste and had purchased his painting, Woman in a Green Dress, those of a disfavored, disenfranchised son. No, to Claude, houses could be difficult places. They weren't always friendly. They made demands, required attention. Their owners could be selfish and thoughtless. Thank God there were gardens. Gardens were good houses, perhaps the best houses in the world.

It was after eight o'clock when he pulled a thin, dark blue jacket over his shirt and reached for his soft black cap before closing the door behind him. Curiosity had gotten the better of him and by nine o'clock he decided he would take a walk to the train station and simply observe what it was all about, this great hoop-la over a saint, a flower parade, and what appeared to have been an entire summer of preparation. He wouldn't stay long. He would remain a mere bystander, but he'd have a look at the people and the overall activity and then quickly return to his riverbank.

In spite of the gray start to the morning, the sky held some promise for sun, he noticed, walking along in his crisp, decisive cadence. The clouds were moving swiftly overhead and the light against the hills had grown brighter every quarter hour since dawn. Branches of the tall oak and maple trees along the roadside swayed in a gentle rhythmic breeze, but there was no sound along the gravel road. Where was everyone? There were no barking dogs to be heard, no music, no excited children running out to join a celebration, no one to be seen. When the station came into view, he understood and was surprised to see the size of the crowd. It was enormous and utterly silent. Drawing nearer, he found he had arrived at the start of a blessing and the entire village was taking part.

A huge green and white banner flared out into the air fragrant with Montgeron's country roses and just behind it a priest wearing a large silver cross over his black cassock stood, raised his hand, and bowed his head in prayer. In one sweeping motion, the people fell to their knees on the gravel surrounding the station house. Some knelt on the small, cobblestone carriage pavilion where under normal circumstances, arriving passengers were met and driven home. The priest's black robe billowed up in the breeze as he slowly recited the words of prayer and received the time-honored responses of the crowd. At the conclusion of his final blessing a trumpet was sounded and a beating drum set the rhythm for two clarinet players, three flutists, and a dozen or so trumpeters who moved forward and joined in playing a slow march. Once they passed, all in the crowd stepped back to watch a glass-enclosed casque being carried on a red velvet pillow by a young man in formal black morning coat and tall top hat. The young man carrying the casque passed in silence, but once he had reached the foot of the Concy Road, the crowd burst into loud cheers and the procession of wagons began.

Claude moved into the crowd to get a better view, only to find himself standing beside a tall, imposing nun, her stiffly starched white wimple framing a gently lined, rosy-cheeked face, her lilting voice surprisingly girlish as with neither question nor invitation she obligingly shared the expected order of the traditional Saint Fiacre Feast Day Procession with the stranger who had come up beside her.

"Do step in closer, Monsieur. But on this other side," she directed, leaning out from the crowd, a corner of her stiff wimple almost stabbing him in the eye as she motioned Claude to move to her right. "First comes the banner and behind it the Saint's relics," she whispered to him. "You will see them better from here.

That's the serious part of things; the casque and Saint Fiacre's relics. It's the same every year," the rosy-cheeked face smiled to him with a decisive nod. "It's all very respectful. And terribly old. You'll see. The crowd is very quiet until Saint Fiacre passes, but then they break into a cheer. In past years the cheering has gotten out of hand. I don't like that at all and I've said so, but it is a festival, isn't it?" the talkative nun continued, standing on tip-toe. "The flower girls will come next, and finally we will see what we really came for: the wagons covered in their wonderful creations of flowers, vegetables, and foliage of all sorts, one after the other. Isn't it exciting? And I think the weather will hold. What do you think? You must be a visitor, Monsieur. I've not seen you in our village before. I am Mother Catherine, Abbess of the Benedictine Abbey of Notre Dame d'Yerres. Have you come especially to see our parade? Many people come all the way from Paris every year. Several of my own cousins and nieces are here today. That little blonde angel in the blue dress across the way there is my sister's daughter."

Sixty-five-year-old Mother Catherine had succeeded more than fifty abbesses at the medieval, twelfth-century Benedictine Abbey of Notre Dame d'Yerres where Fiacre's saintly relics were safely enshrined in a glass-covered case, and although known for a stern demeanor and haughty, some thought overly assertive presence, few of her predecessors enjoyed Fiacre's annual festival more than she.

"I am visiting Madame and Monsieur Hoschede at the Chateau Rottembourg," Claude replied, now wary of Mother Catherine's unusually large white wimple and her dangerous tendency to turn her head quite rapidly from one side to the other. "Madame Hoschede invited me to the day's festivities. My name is Claude Monet."

"Ah, yes. Dear Alice Hoschede is one of our special children," Mother Catherine nodded decisively. "She has been attending this feast day since her family purchased the Chateau Rottembourg. She loves it as much as I do. Members of her family have owned property here at Montgeron for years, but Alice has probably told you all about that. Fine people, the Raingos. They raised their children in the Church. Of course, you must also know that Alice judges the Master Gardener entries every year. She is so good at it, conscientious too. Now there's a woman who knows how to do things! The young girls here in the village could take a lesson or two from her. Monsieur Monet, perhaps you will come to Sunday Vespers at the Abbey tomorrow. Our chapel is open to all and our music is beautiful. I shall look for you. Five o'clock."

He could see Alice. She stood chatting with the group gathered on the cobblestone walk rimming the turreted stone station house. She wore a long, pale green dress and the same wide-brimmed yellow straw hat she had worn to La Lethumiere when the issue of white turkeys had proven so annoying a few days before. She held an unopened white parasol in one hand and as she talked she toyed with the small embroidered purse dangling playfully from her wrist on a metal chain. If her appearance and demeanor were to be taken as any indication of her mood on this September morning, Alice Hoschede would be seen by any observer as a genteel country woman incapable of issuing pointed reprimands concerning white turkeys or for that matter incapable of issuing edicts on any negative aspect of life at all. She smiled and laughed happily, the tilt of her head delicate, her every movement graceful and refined. Her two oldest daughters, Marthe and Blanche stood nearby, chatting between themselves, both girls dressed in white and carrying baskets overflowing with flower petals.

"Marthe and Blanche Hoschede are flower girls this year," Mother Catherine continued to Claude. "You no doubt know them of course if you are visiting at the Chateau Rottembourg. They will toss flower petals out over the spectators. Be sure you are touched by a few petals, Monsieur Monet. We have blessed them in the chapel and they in turn will bless you."

Claude smiled and nodded appreciatively as the procession began, his eyes riveted not on Mother Catherine and not on the approaching flurry of blessed flower petals at all, but on Alice Hoschede. She was beautiful in the country environment she knew so well. She glanced over her shoulder and caught his eye with a nod. He waved a silly, awkward wave, surprised to see her coming directly toward him.

"I am so happy you came, Monsieur Monet," she said to him with the same dazzling smile he had seen lighting her face when he met her shortly after arriving at Rottembourg. "And good morning, Mother Catherine. Mother, this gentleman is Claude Monet. He is an artist and is painting wall panels for the rotunda at the Chateau Rottembourg. Monsieur Monet is staying at Uncle Julian's cottage. I thought he would enjoy our festival today. Have you seen Marthe and Blanche? They are so happy. As you know, they have wanted to be flower girls since they were very small."

"Monsieur Monet and I have been getting acquainted," the Abbess said. "I've been explaining details of the procession to him, and yes, Marthe and Blanche do look very happy, but this is always such an exciting day for the children. I think I enjoy it as much as they do."

Alice stood between Claude and the Abbess, her wide-brimmed straw hat as much an impediment to Claude's view as the Abbess' threatening wimple. Alice watched him leaning out, straining his neck to catch a glimpse of the proceedings. She laughed. "I once thought about becoming a nun," she whispered to him, "but when I realized the wardrobe had its drawbacks, I changed my mind and married Ernest Hoschede and his department store instead."

They both laughed. "I would say, Madame, that you made an excellent decision there," Claude returned with a chuckle.

How different she was from the difficult woman who had stormed at him a few days before. Today, her gaiety and good humor seemed so natural and came so easily.

"How is your work progressing?" she asked with a bright smile as the first of the wagons appeared. "Am I to have white turkeys on my walls or did I manage to sway your thoughts toward other subjects, Monsieur Monet?"

Suddenly there was so much going on. He couldn't answer. The crowd had grown very noisy. Children shouted. Some ran in circles, carrying balloons. A riot of colorful flower blossoms fluttered in the breeze. The music grew louder and the approaching succession of flower-decked horse-drawn wagons captivated his attention as the floral work Mother Catherine quickly informed him was called "The Bouquet" began the entire, carefully staged production.

By tradition, every year The Bouquet was created, she told him, on one of the larger wagons by arranging fresh flowers, vegetables, moss, and foliage on a horizontal shaft in such a way that all the elements made up an intricately woven tapestry-like design. Such work was extremely popular in the Brie Valley and required the most competent gardeners and skillfully run greenhouses to produce. On this carpet, a statue of Saint Fiacre was displayed against a vertical armature on which more flowers, foliage, and vegetables were attached topiary-fashion, all in keeping with whatever possibilities the weather patterns of the gardening year had afforded. In a similar manner, on the armatures of the wagons following The Bouquet there came a pageant of rose-covered millwheels followed by artichoke and meadowgrass waterfalls, gigantic vases formed of blue delphinium, sailboats fashioned of late summer's white asters, and one after another of hot-air balloon baskets playfully fashioned of red poppies and yellow sunflowers, each creation formed entirely of flowers and vegetables.

Claude took in the remarkable passing display with a delighted, irrepressible smile. Swept up in the color and motion he scanned the crowd and standing at Alice's side he congratulated himself for having made the decision to attend an event that was exceeding his expectations by some considerable measure. When he expressed his great pleasure and complimented the quality of the proceedings, Alice laughed.

"Oh, and did you expect we would be little country know-nothings showing off our weeds and compost today, Monsieur Monet? The gardeners of Mongeron and Yerres are among the finest and most productive in the entire Brie valley."

Earlier that morning, before Claude's arrival, observers and parade participants had assembled for the Blessing of The Bouquet. The initial procession had begun with the arrival of The Bouquet in the chapel courtyard at the Abbey as Saint Fiacre's glass-enclosed relics were removed from the side altar. It was concluded at the train station with a priestly blessing of the people and it was this ceremony that Claude had seen in progress as he had approached the station.

"I saw you watching us from the foot of the road as you arrived just before the blessing," Alice said to him. "I wish you could have seen your own face. You looked absolutely shocked to see so many people in one place so early in the day. This is only a suggestion, Monsieur Monet, but since you seem to be a lover of nature you may be interested to know that the afternoon will be devoted to the Master Gardeners Competitions which I judge every year. Perhaps you will stay to see how that turns out. We've added more categories and products this year. Do look at the fritillaria persica. They're very dark blue and I'm told the cultivation of those dear, thirty-inch tall stems dates back to the time of Shakespeare. They're powerful enough to repel deer and rodents."

"Handy items for a garden, and for the world!" Claude returned with a chuckle.

The morning passed quickly and as Alice had said, the afternoon was devoted to a horticultural exhibition and competition in which individual gardeners entered plants and products which they had grown or developed and of which they were most proud. Many products derived from local plantings were for sale. There was a variety of jams and fruit butters artfully arranged in jars of every size and shape. Bowls of tomato and cucumber ragouts and an endless variety of stewed fruits and vegetable purees in small tins were packed into baskets and decorated with fresh flowers. The judges' prizes were awarded based on uniqueness, difficulty of cultivation, and presentation.

Each year the highly respected Corporation of Master Gardeners was carefully organized into categories according to special skills such as those comprised of individuals in charge of large estate gardens and those responsible for the care of small, enclosed family gardens. Additionally, those caring for fields and small meadows, the keepers of orchards or Officers of the Inland Waters and the Brie Valley Forestry Commission were likewise assigned to special categories and exhibited a wide variety of artfully presented grapes, fish, and game. Exhibits of the men skilled at trellis work, training plants into hedges and on arbors, or those skilled as espaliers or market gardeners responsible for the wholesale cultivation of vegetables were quite popular. Prizes were awarded in those categories as well. These were engraved silver medals set onto red and blue satin ribbons. Past winners proudly wore their medals every year. Some proud chests were bedecked with as many as five or six.

"You may be interested to know that at nearby Yerres, where the Caillebottes live, the path of the trellis workers which begins at the boundary of Limeil near the Chateau Brevannes and ends at Etoile de Bellevue, near the Chateaux de la Grange du Milieu and Grosbois, keeps the memory of deceased trellis workers alive and is so marked," Alice informed him. "Do you think you can remember all that, Monsieur Monet? It took me a very long time to get all of it right. It takes a little practice. Perhaps you will do better than I did." She laughed again, the flattering sunlight soft against her face. "I'm sure Gustave Caillebotte would be happy to take you along the path. It is a beautiful walk, especially in early autumn when the leaves are turning color which should be very soon. I highly recommend it."

At their invitation, Claude joined Alice and the children at their picnic luncheon. Obviously well experienced in the annual procedure, Marthe and Blanche deftly spread a fringed white cloth under a stand of oak trees where, young as they were, they said they had picnicked "for years." Wicker baskets containing generous portions of sliced cold chicken, perfectly ripened peaches and pears, bread, cold tea, and chocolates seemed to appear out of nowhere and were shared in the shade of ancient trees, the delights of a day in late summer captured not only in the happy faces of the five Hoschede children completely at home in the open air, but also reflected in the face of their visiting companion, an artist sated and content as he found himself in the relaxed, charming company of a gracious, happy woman whom he could not for a moment have begun to suspect was excelling magnificently at concealing her deepest fears and darkest forebodings.

Jacques was unusually talkative. That summer he had become a boy growing happily into his natural element, delighted to have been allowed to hunt quail and partridge with his father in the Senart, and as a result feeling more a part of Rottembourg and, as his father was often telling him now, as the male heir, the destined keeper of its future. Feeling more importantly connected to Montgeron and its village life, Jacques, who like his sister, Germaine, had been born at Rottembourg, was also becoming familiar with the local legends that passed from one generation to the next.

"Mother Catherine says that once, hundreds of years ago, when Satan came to tempt Saint Fiacre, he planted a peach stone," Jacques shared with Claude. "The Mother Abbess says the small seed in the stone grew into a tree bursting with flowers and fruit and that we must eat peaches at our picnic every year to keep Satan away," Jacques informed the contented artist, biting into a juicy specimen as he concluded his revelation. "I suppose that means eating peaches will protect us from Satan, at least until next summer's feast day. Do you think peaches could really do such a thing, Monsieur Monet?"

"If Mother Catherine endorses such a belief, then so do I," Claude promptly answered with a thoughtful nod as he closely examined the flawless ripe peach he held in his hand. "Besides, what have we to lose? A year isn't really so long, and isn't it a delicious precaution?"

The two continued to enjoy their tasty insurance against touches of Satan, both thoughtful, both contemplating the implications of Mother Catherine's admonition. Claude leaned back against an accommodating tree trunk reviewing the day's events in his mind, finding that in one day he had been blessed not once but twice, first by an avalanche of flower petals tossed by Saint Fiacre's pretty flower girls and now, according to a sensitive boy and a persevering Abbess, by ingesting a few delicious peaches. He was not a religious man, but if the gifts of nature could be taken as the generous symbols of a higher being, then this dwelling place of peace and plenty must surely be likened to a church, he concluded.

"Have you begun to paint the panels for the rotunda, Monsieur Monet?" Suzanne asked, beginning to collect the picnic baskets as Marthe folded the fringed white cloth. "Germaine says that for one of them you may be painting a picture of the white turkeys. Will you, Monsieur?"

"I have some sketches and studies and I am working out a few details with your parents right now," Claude tactfully replied, glancing toward Alice. "There are so many beautiful sites at Rottembourg and I hope all of you continue as my guides."

"Of course, we will," Alice commented, quickly adding, "Monsieur, have you seen our rose garden in the afternoon when the sunlight is bright and radiant? All along I have thought the roses would be wonderful subjects for you. The blooms are lovelier than ever this year and the surrounding foliage, the hedges and trees, are at their best right now. The children and I could meet you there when I finish here and you and I could discuss your project further. Would that suit you?"

"Of course it would, Madame," Claude quickly agreed. "I know the area you speak of and on the train from Paris Monsieur Hoschede commented on the special beauty of the roses this year. I could meet you there. Shall we say near four o'clock?"

"Yes, four should be fine. If we are a bit late it is only because I like to say good-bye to as many of the gardeners who have come today as I can. Not every one of them can win a prize, but that doesn't mean their work is not noticed and appreciated."

"How right you are, Madame," Claude responded. "It is the same with me and my colleagues."

Alice looked him directly in the eye, catching his meaning. "Yes, it is the same, isn't it?" she said to him slowly.

At four he admired the roses. Yes, of course he saw the potential for a fine composition, he said. Suzanne walked closest to her mother on the walkway gravel.

"I think the turkeys would make a much better painting for our house!" Germaine suddenly called out, doll in hand. "To me they are as beautiful as

Mama's roses and they are at Rottembourg all the time. They just stay there and live there and no one has to worry about them or wash the little bugs off."

"I quite agree with you," Claude acknowledged with a barely suppressed laugh.

Alice looked over to Germaine, the child's candid assessment of Rottembourg's wild white turkeys so natural; so like Claude Monet's own, but as charming as the turkey bantering was, she told herself it was time she handled the matter of large birds parading in her meadow in a definitive manner, making her wishes abundantly clear.

"Monsieur Monet, I would like to see how your work on the panel I saw progresses," she said. "May we come, the children and I, tomorrow afternoon to La Lethumiere? We don't want to intrude or inconvenience you in any way and I promise we won't stay long."

"But of course, Madame. It would be a pleasure to see you and the children at La Lethumiere. I shall expect you tomorrow."

"Let's say five o'clock," Alice added. By that time the children will have had their tea and the light is still good at that hour. We'll take one of the larger pony carts."

The house was quiet that night. The children were tired after a long, festive day in the outdoor air and when bedtime came there were no complaints. Alone downstairs, Alice lit candles in the hall and the rotunda. In the flickering light she sat in one of the red flowered chairs nearest to the piano, imagining how paintings of turkeys and scenes of rose gardens would look on the walls. Monsieur Monet had seemed more agreeable today, she thought. Yes, and perhaps she should have seemed more agreeable to him too. Could it be that she was making entirely too much of a fuss with a struggling artist who just wanted to work and do his best? If his painting of Rottembourg's turkeys didn't please, it wouldn't be the end of the world. He would be paid regardless, and right now there certainly were more pressing issues on her mind. And what did wall panels matter at all if at the end Ernest failed in his efforts and the Chateau Rottembourg was indeed sacrificed?

Yes, there were always thoughts of Ernest. He would have arrived in Paris by now. He would be totally absorbed in his fight to prevail in the financial crisis he had brought about all by himself. Poor man, he was probably happy to be away from her right now, yes, very happy to avoid realities he wouldn't face and the truth of his overspending which she forced him to confront every time they were together. She felt her blood boiling up every time she thought of it. Her house, her beloved Chateau Rottembourg was actually at risk and her own husband's behavior had caused its vulnerability. How would she continue to deal with the threat of losing Rottembourg and how would its loss be explained to the children and her Raingo family?

Ernest's indebtedness was hurting her more than he would ever know. Exhausted by the day's activities and at the same time riddled with a flood of anxiety, by nine o'clock she had climbed the stairs to the bedroom she and Ernest shared. Convinced that sleep would not elude her on this night, she gathered the bedcoverings around her, placed her head on her pillow, and lay still. She closed her eyes and breathed deeply, but alone in the quiet darkness sleep did not come, and once again her mind was seized by a hundred thoughts of Ernest and what had led to the conditions with which they now lived. Again and again she thought of his relentless quest for status, for being the best and doing the best and having the best. She thought of his insatiable appetite for the acquisition of beautiful things: for works of art, for beautiful furniture and beautiful clothes and the finest decorative objects he could find; for an impressive private train and for an army of servants, and most of all she thought of his cavalier attitude in acquiring and maintaining these refinements, money recklessly spent and seldom a genuine concern until now. With tears soaking her pillow, a deeply saddened Alice also thought of the handsome young man she had fallen passionately in love with and married, the tender lover and thoughtful companion with the wonderful throaty laugh and the mischievous schoolboy smile which had never entirely left him and likely never would.

The next morning it was clear that as pleasant as Saint Fiacre's Feast Day had been, it was not without its casualties. Overnight, Marthe and Suzanne had broken out in rashes. Their hands and arms were red and itchy. "They must have touched a poisoned plant, perhaps a patch of water hemlock. They said they were near the river," Gabrielle diagnosed, ignoring her own susceptibility as she applied salves and ointments to the red bumps.

"Yes," Jacques remembered as Alice tried to understand how and where the children could have been exposed, possibly to water hemlock. "After lunch, we played "cache-cache" (hide and seek) with the Bonfils grandchildren near the trees on the riverbank," Jacques recalled. "Suzanne and Marthe hid behind some tall wild bushes," Jacques related, "but Didier Bonfils and I found them. Some of the poisoned hemlock could have been growing near where they were hiding."

"Perhaps that's what happened," Alice replied, "but we have talked repeatedly about the dangers of playing in areas you are not familiar with, especially near shaded riverbanks where all sorts of plants can grow in the moist shade. In the country we must always be on our guard against unrecognizable plants or flowers. Well, the salves should help with the itching."

"I don't feel well either," Germaine complained, listening to her mother's admonitions and examining her small hands. "I think I have a headache. Feel my forehead, Mamma. Is it hot and red? I think it feels itchy inside."

Blanche and Jacques teased the wounded warriors, but Alice could see signs of rash developing on them as well. Their arms and hands were turning pink. Germaine and Blanche had worn short-sleeved summer dresses the day before. Jacques had sported a short-sleeved striped shirt. Alice suspected the worst.

"Let me have a good look at those hands and arms, all of you," she ordered. "Put them out. Ah! Well, there will be no outings for us today," she promptly announced, the red bumps on all five pairs of hands and arms clear indications that not one of her five country-bred children had noticed or even recognized the poisoned hemlock or any other poisonous plant growing somewhere along the shady riverbank where they had all spent time the day before. "The rashes will pass," Alice assured her five sensitive, "but I hope all of you have learned to be more cautious in the future."

The children remained on the third floor with watchful Gabrielle for the rest of the day. Alice used the time to meet with the cook, the butler, and the head gardener. She checked on the children at mid-day, noticing a mild improvement in their rashes. Later in the afternoon she busied herself with the day to day functioning of her well-organized household. There were meals to plan, guest rooms to refresh, and instructions to prepare for the gardeners who would be attending to approaching autumn's garden chores. The pear trees would be pruned and espaliered no later than the second week in September. By October, as the family prepared for its return to Paris for the winter, the orange trees in their painted white boxes with the knobs on the corners would be brought indoors. The floors would be cleaned and waxed, the wall moldings thoroughly dusted, the carpets taken outside and beaten. Alice loved days like this, a series of hours which were hers alone, hours in which she could luxuriate in looking after her beloved country property. So concentrated on Rottembourg's needs was she, that by four o'clock she had decided she would not meet with Monsieur Monet at La Lethumiere as planned the day before. The children would not be leaving the house and there was too much to do. She rang for Bernard.

"Please go to La Lethumiere and tell Monsieur Monet that I cannot meet with him this afternoon," she instructed. "Tell him the children have contracted rashes and that we'll plan to visit another time."

"But Madame Hoschede," Bernard said to her in his gentle voice, "a short walk would do you so much good today. It is a lovely afternoon and the dahlias and asters are beautiful in the little garden at La Lethumiere. I couldn't help but admire them when I brought the fresh linen on Tuesday. The gardeners are always very thorough, of course, but I think Monsieur Monet himself has been doing some work in that little garden. Some people just have way with gardens. You certainly do. But, Madame, I do hope you will go to see the dahlias. They will be fading soon."

A few minutes before five o'clock Alice walked along the gravel path to La Lethumiere, Ernest's massive debt and the fate of the Chateau Rottembourg continuing to flood her thoughts. The day's earlier bright sunshine was rapidly dissolving into cool lengthening shadows. She gathered her shawl close to her shoulders and slowed her step as the small lodge came into view. How charming it looked in its uncomplicated setting, safe and unpretentious, a place for quiet thoughts, an attractive little haven of peace untouched by pain or worry, and Bernard had not exaggerated. La Lethumiere's picturesque garden was as delightful as he had described, the heads of the dahlias enormous, the clumped pink and lavender asters a soft play of pastel against the pale exterior of the house, the stone deer who stood in the midst of his pampered setting appearing to be a proud participant in the memorable summer scene.

Anticipating the Hoschede family visit and although known to be meticulous with his personal effects, particularly fastidious about the care of his paints and supplies, Claude had taken time to tidy the main room in which he painted and where he spent much of his time. He fluffed the chair cushions, readied a tray of tea, and with the children in mind arranged a plate of the meringue cookies he had purchased at one of the previous afternoon's product displays. Realizing that the sunlight was rapidly fading, he quickly replaced the worn down candles on several of the small tables. All meeting with his approval, he left the front door open in a gesture of welcome which, as Alice approached and for no known reason, touched her deeply. In the few moments it took to reach La Lethumiere's arched door, a surge of emotion swept over her and meeting Claude, who appeared in the doorway, she fought back a flood of tears.

"I do believe these dahlias could have won a prize this afternoon day," she said brightly, swallowing hard. "You must be casting some magic spell over them, Monsieur Monet. This garden has never looked lovelier. Bernard paid it very high compliments today and he knows a good deal about flower gardens. His father and mother are known in Montgeron for their own beautiful borders of asters and dahlias. They live in one of the houses close to the station."

Claude stepped outside, onto the slightly raised landing where he joined Alice in admiring the small garden on which he admittedly enjoyed having lavished some time. Facing her directly, though, he could see something was wrong. He couldn't know that the weight of worry so absent the day before had returned to consume her, but the face so unclouded in the joy of celebration the day before now looked tired and pale. The lips were set in a tight line and the eyes were too serious, too sad, too strained. "Madame Hoschede, I do enjoy tending the flowers," he remarked pleasantly. "It is no trouble at all. But where are the children? I thought they were coming with you today."

"Monsieur, they are down with rashes from what we believe is water hemlock. Poor Marthe has the worst rash of all along her hands and arms. Playing in the hollow by the river yesterday after lunch was not a good idea. There must have been some nasty clump of plants growing there. Of course I wouldn't have come to visit you without them this afternoon, but Bernard convinced me. He wanted me to see the asters and dahlias and now I see why."

"Well, Madame! You are most kind and I'm glad the little garden pleases you, but it is no trouble at all to spend time on flowers. They repay us generously. I am disappointed, though, that the children can't be with you today. Please tell them how sorry I am about the rashes. I myself, am constantly on the lookout for poisonous plants when I am painting outdoors in unfamiliar surroundings. Let them know that in spite of my diligence I have suffered with rashes a time or two, the worst in the beautiful forests at Fountainbleau. All should be well in a day or two, though. With salves and white kitchen powder the itching and red bumps will dry and go away as quickly as they came, but I'm sure you know all about that. Will you come inside? I know you are curious about the paintings in progress but I did prepare some lemon tea for you and the children, and there is a plate of lovely meringues. I bought them yesterday from one of the product carts. It was difficult to choose something. Everything looked so delicious. After yesterday's activity I imagine you must be tired. It was a very long day for you, but you must feel gratified by its success

Alice said nothing in response, but looking into Claude's brown eyes, she was grateful for his kind words, aware that somehow with his thoughtful remarks, especially those focused on the children, he had softened the hard edges of dread with which she had lived for weeks. Feelings of disappointment and dissatisfaction had welled up in her at the door, but somehow his calm, simple words had managed to settle the torment of emptiness she felt deep inside.

Claude attempted pleasant conversation as Alice stood and glanced around the room where he worked. He was awkward, unsure of what he should say, but a comment or two on the pleasures of the Chateau Rottembourg would surely improve what he correctly interpreted as Madame's somber mood. He stumbled a bit and repeated himself, reiterating the same appreciative words he had spoken during her last visit, but Alice did not miss his good intentions.

"I feel I may not have taken enough opportunity, Madame, to tell you how much I admire what you have created here at the Chateau Rottembourg and the generosity you and your family have shown me, especially with this little lodge," he began, standing beside Alice. "Rottembourg truly is a special place, and I see your hand everywhere: in the gardens, in the house, in the way your family enjoys every moment it spends here. It is one thing to own a chateau. It is quite another to live in one and nurture it as you and Monsieur Hoschede do, and so well.

"Stop! Please stop!" Alice suddenly called out, tears flooding her eyes. "The Chateau Rottembourg you know and admire with all your pleasantries could belong to someone else soon!" she blurted out, dissolving into tears, her brave defenses lost to emotions she could no longer control. "Monsieur Monet, you might as well know the truth," she sobbed. "Soon, everyone will. The Rottembourg property is at great risk. My husband's debts are immense. He has used the Chateau Rottembourg as collateral against loans and lines of credit. He has promised things he should not have promised and has said things he should not have said. I am helpless to do anything at all about the situation, and if you've wondered why he is away from Montgeron and in Paris so much this summer, it is because he is dealing with creditors, bankers, and vicious solicitors."

"There must be some mistake!" Claude interrupted, shocked by Alice's disclosure. "This cannot be! "Monsieur Hoschede would never allow anything to happen to the Chateau Rottembourg. He loves it here, loves everything about it, just as you do. No, perhaps you have overheard a conversation and have misunderstood its meaning. Anyone can do that."

"No, there's no mistake," Alice insisted. "I've seen the documents. I know what is happening."

"Sometimes financial difficulties arise. They can come to any of us," Claude likewise insisted, facing her. "It is no secret that I live with them every day of my life, but Monsieur Hoschede will surely manage his, whatever they are. He is a capable, dependable man. You mustn't let yourself believe otherwise."

Suddenly, life had turned cold, indifferent, and he could see that the carefree Alice Hoschede of the white dress in high summer struggled for composure. She carried a wounded heart under a shadow of fear now so palpable that Claude felt completely defeated in his efforts to sympathize. "Surely, there is an explanation for this," he said, "and a solution."

"I very much doubt it," Alice quickly replied. "Ernest tells me that because of the impact of the recession the loans and lines of credit he once so easily obtained are running dry and that soon there may be no money at all for anyone to borrow in Paris, and if we are to survive, borrow we must. I don't know why I'm telling you this, Monsieur Monet. It really isn't any of your concern. I haven't spoken about it to another soul. I try so hard to keep up appearances. It's just that I could lose this place I love, this place my children love."

"Oh, but no, that won't happen. It can't, and even if it does, you are brave, braver I think than you yourself know. You will manage it." He took her hand and kissed it.

"Come, he said with a smile, "let's watch the river. You'll be surprised to see how river-watching can quiet the heart and soul. It does splendid things for me."

"This is so unlike me," Alice whispered, her tears subsiding as they stepped out to face the riverbank. "I'm the strong one in the family. Everyone says so, but this has come at me very hard. All you've come to know at the Rottembourg property means so much to me, even this little lodge and this gentle river, and today, before I came here, I was planning for the autumn chores as every year we prepare for winter. I love seeing to all that, but this year it may be useless. And it's silly of me to think of such things right now. I do love the planning every year though, and the satisfaction that comes with completing the picture I have in my mind, even the worrying and the waiting."

"It shows," he assured her once again, helpless to know what to say or do next, "but for now let's just stand here and watch the river. Look there, at those two little skiffs bouncing up and down out there like little elves."

How terrible he thought, gazing out to the rippling water, doing his best to hide his shock. Ernest Hoschede hadn't let out so much as a clue that he was experiencing serious financial difficulties. He had advanced Claude a thousand francs on the commission for the four panels. He was always affable and good humored and endlessly enthusiastic about the project for the rotunda, but Alice's façade was apparently more fragile. He looked over to her and saw she was trembling.

"You're cold. Let me take you inside," he said, glancing to the open door. "At day's end there can be a chill out here. I'll light the fire."

"Oh, no, don't bother, monsieur. I really must go. The children will be waiting for me. I'll come another time to study the paintings with you. We can talk then."

He took her hand again and as they turned away from the riverbank he did not release it. He held it tightly. She didn't pull away. His hand was warm and protective in its clasp over hers.

"You must think me to be a very foolish woman," she said, glancing up into his eyes. "I don't expect you to understand my deep attachment to Rottembourg. It's only a house on a plot of land. Such things are not important to you. I know that. You care about the world out there, that world on the river, that dot above it, that place beneath it, on the other side of it. You care about painting. I care about Rottembourg in the same way. It is my pride, my heart, my life. All my fondest memories are here, memories of my family, many of the firsts in my life. Monsieur, you are another kind of being, able to live anywhere and be happy just to walk outdoors in sunlight, along rivers, under clouds. It's the rivers and the clouds, isn't it? Rivers make you happy, don't they? Perhaps those are your houses. Right now I wish they were mine. But I shouldn't be burdening you with this," she said, taking a deep breath. "You have your work to do and I must go home."

He had still not released her hand and she had still not pulled away. He led her inside and looked into her pale, tear-stained face and somewhere in those generous, sad brown eyes he saw the thousands of little aching stings and hundreds of little bruising hurts that come to reflect a lovely woman's fears. He could only imagine the depth of her loneliness and anxiety as others were taking control of her future. She was so unfamiliar with adversity and its trials, but how quickly things had changed. Only hours before, as she had smiled at a country festival, her life had seemed a celebration in itself, its perfect pieces well-ordered and dressed in summer color, all its heartbeats rhythmic and in perfect harmony with the style and spirit of a day designed for pleasure and the rewards of hard work. He, himself, had been caught up in the joy of it all, seduced at first only by the simple, visual beauty of a colorful country ritual but soon moved by the sincerity of its participants, country people devoted to their labors who found great happiness in what the sophisticated city world might see as tedious country things: modest wagons festooned with nature's handiwork, the memory of an ancient saint whose selfless dedication to the cultivation of gardens had been kept alive over centuries, and at the root of it all, the unwavering dedication of a generational succession of gardeners and farmers devoted to upholding a beloved annual tradition. Now that mood of happiness and gaiety was gone. He felt sad, disappointed too, that this lovely creature beside him who was more attached to the land, more in tune with the patterns of nature than she herself realized, had been suffering under a terrible, painful mask.

It was growing dark and it was quiet. It was the quiet that comes to surround uncertainty and uneasiness and the hesitancy of unwanted goodbyes. It was the quiet that comes to confront an intensely restless man only mildly aware of his own vulnerabilities. It was the quiet that descends upon a defenseless woman who has found that silence is all there is. Nothing was said, no words of encouragement, no compliments, but he stroked her cheek. He kissed it gently, not once but twice, and suddenly every fiber in him was scorched by need, but also by fear. He held her close, hesitant, unsure. She did not pull away. Her nearness seared through him. The faint scent of tuberose was in her hair. He felt her long, slender fingers clasped at the back of his neck. In the lonely gray twilight it was as if she was desperately holding on to the only moments of comfort she had known in days, but she was wrong to be here, wrong to be sharing details of her confusing, complicated life. He was wrong to want her here. There were old loves, old habits, old worlds, loyalties, vows and promises, but in the fading light, dangerous raging desire overtook concern and caring. Images, shapes, and colors streamed through his brain. It was too much. It was all wrong. She was an illusion, a mistake, but with another kiss, another caress, more than anything else he wanted her there, safely wrapped in his arms. He wanted to erase her fear, destroy her worry and he told her so, whispering that he would be her shelter, her shield, her cloak, her cover. He drew her closer and closer until she seemed part of him, part of his beating heart, part of his hungering soul, essential to the deepest requisites of his nature. His strong hands slid across her back. He pressed her against his broad chest. His lips brushed along her cheek. He sealed her mouth with his. All that mattered was her nearness. All he cared about was this enveloping ambrosial dream from which he never wanted to awaken, the urgency, the intense need blazing up in him blending light and darkness, ardor and tenderness into a dissolving sweetness he had never before known. He had made love to his share of Montmartre girls and as a younger man had been no stranger to the Paris demimonde of the notorious Café de Martyrs, but no woman had been like this, not this tender, not this vulnerable, and he had not made love to Camille in months. No, even when she was well and healthy it had never been like this with Camille, not with this burning fever, not with this passion and hunger.

Lost in secrecy and chased by their own discordant lives they streamed away together, off into that lovers world untouched by time, where past and future hang suspended and the present hovers isolated, invisible, and still. She murmured softly as he led her to his bed and unbuttoned her dress, her full-breasted body warm and yielding against him, her closeness intoxicating. It was all wrong, a delusion, a mistake. He knew it, but she was too close, too real. He was too tender, too alien to her world, but with a flood of kisses and warm caresses he erased her fear and worry.

"I have loved you since the day I arrived at Rottembourg and saw you standing on the lawn in the white dress. Dried leaves were caught in your hair," he whispered. "You were completely disheveled and you knew it, but you laughed and made light of your appearance and you were the most beautiful woman I had ever seen. Since that day I haven't been able to get those images of you in the white dress and the tangle of leaves in your beautiful hair out of my mind. They have been seared across my heart and I have been at war with myself, fighting off thoughts of you, telling myself I was being as foolish and idiotic as a besotted schoolboy. I haven't understood it at all, but on any given day, at any given hour, I've wondered what you were doing or thinking or saying. Were you on the lawn laughing and playing at statues with the children? Were you sitting quietly, reading in some corner of the house? Were you welcoming a visitor in the hall? It was the sorcery of the countryside I kept telling myself. Yes, that was it. I was allowing myself to be seduced by a country village and the charm of a lovely house set into the perfection of summer, but I have never forgotten the sight of you standing there on the sunlit lawn and I never will," he whispered again. "You were so beautiful, so exquisite. You are even more beautiful, more exquisite here with me now." And again and again he kissed her, promising to be her shelter, her shield, her cloak, her cover.

Twilight blanketed the river, and as the infant evening breeze stirred the skirted green willows across its ashen banks and nightfall shrouded the distant purple hills, all fear, all loneliness, all regret vanished, and they did nothing to stop the rippling tide of secrecy and isolation that came to overtake and own them with all its ravenous impossibilities.

Throughout the following week Ernest remained in Paris and Alice lived in a guilt-ridden chasm of self-loathing. "What have I done?" she repeatedly asked herself day after day. "He is an impoverished, unknown painter, a man I hardly know at all. I love my husband. We have five children."

Alice had never strayed from her marriage vows the way many of her Paris friends had, those idle, lonely women married to arrogant, self-absorbed men who indulged in occasional, always passionate, always brief love affairs. But in the midst of endless self-recrimination she could think of nothing but Claude. She wanted to see him, be near him again. What must he be doing, thinking, feeling? Was he out on the riverbank searching for the dot on the horizon? Was he painting, mixing color, thinking of her?

It was no different for Claude. He despised himself for having betrayed Camille. What had happened to his understanding of devotion, of obligation? Occasional dalliances were one thing, a flirtatious encounter, a harmless trifling hour with an attractive dark haired coquette in the shadowed corner of a Paris café; a brief kiss, an invitation, an unfulfilled suggestion. They meant nothing, but this, this passionate entanglement with a married woman who lived in a world dramatically apart from his was something else. It was true that she was elegant and proud, but she was also troubled and disenchanted and in many ways she was like him, struggling to survive through disappointment and the dim prospects of an unknown future. In ways he did not understand or want to understand he felt connected to her, responsible for her, and he knew he wanted her in ways he had never wanted a woman before, not even lovely, unassuming Camille, but it was all wrong. He had to set all this aside. He had to put a stop to this ridiculous infatuation with a woman who belonged to someone else. He struggled to fight off images of reckless kisses, intimate whispers, and the moments of tenderness and soaring passion he had known in the enchantment of a twilight hour, but in spite of good intentions and only a short distance away, Alice Hoschede was ruling his every thought. He told himself that in the magic of an idyllic country summer he had made love to a dream, but now he hated the dream and he hated himself. He had foolishly lost himself in waves of temptation and lust and he had risked too much. The dream in the white dress was just that: a dream. He wanted to help her, but he had to leave her and soon.

He threw himself into his work but he made time to write to Camille every day, his sentences filled with words of love and caring. He told her he missed her, missed their closeness, missed their nights together. He apologized for the delay in completing the four panels. Settling on subject matter had been difficult, he explained. They would take the promised Trouville holiday the following summer, he promised, and they would stay longer.

In the next week he worked feverishly and hardly slept, his intention to finish the Hoschede commission as quickly as possible, collect his money, and return to his life at Argenteuil with Camille and Jean, but his work was not pleasing him. He was rushed and distracted and embarrassed. He wanted to go home.

Alice did all she could think of to divert her attention. Every morning she attended Mass. In the nearby Church of Saint Jacques, rosary beads in hand, she knelt and cried and prayed for forgiveness and courage. At home she polished silver that didn't need polishing. She straightened contents of cupboards that didn't need straightening. She re-organized larders that were kept as well-organized as any in the military. She worked on the estate grounds relentlessly, like one of the hired gardeners, anything to keep herself busy and free from thoughts of the Argenteuil painter ensconced at the riverside lodge only minutes away.

In the mornings after attending Mass, she weeded, pruned, clipped, and carted away. In the afternoons she played statues with the children. When it rained they played cards together indoors and made up stories for one another. Alice was the consummate mother. With their father in Paris for long periods, she insisted the children dine with her every evening in the dining room. They loved the idea and made a great show of dressing for dinner in their best clothes, descending the stairs and entering the dining room with great ceremony. At the long dining room table they ate consommé, chicken and wild guinea hen roasted with tender carrots and slender green beans brought to the kitchen just that morning from the ice house and kitchen gardens. There were warm braided breads, custards and fruit tarts, trays of chocolates, and pitchers of lemon tea. After dinner, Alice played the piano and they all sang in the rotunda. On the terrace as darkness fell they held hands and watched the stars begin to sparkle in purple night skies. The children loved the attention their mother was showering on them. Alice's energy and relentless drive were intended to distract and heal, but her attempts failed miserably, and in the way that fresh new love affairs take hold and grip mercilessly at the heart, she became painfully aware of her helpless infatuation with a married man she barely knew.

Ernest arrived at Montgeron the following Saturday. It was the last week in September, the time of year when pheasant and hare are searching for stores of winter food and growing careless in their foraging. The best of the hunting season was at hand and he had planned to take advantage of every opportunity to scour the Senart Forest.

"How are things going in Paris?" Alice asked over dinner that evening. "I hope you've been able to solve at least a few financial problems."

"Right now things are better than I could possibly have imagined," Ernest answered, leaning back in his chair. "My mother advanced me fifty thousand francs and with that handy amount I've managed to put off a few creditors. There are others, though, my love, waiting to pounce, but for now I am alive and comfortable enough."

She watched him and heard what he said, his unflinching nonchalance and selfishness in the face of financial instability and pending doom an unsettling, hateful marvel to her, his callous disregard for her feelings causing her to see him not as a beloved husband but as an adversary.

"And how is Claude Monet doing?" Ernest asked, sipping his wine. "Did you resolve the turkey dilemma to your satisfaction my dear? I think I'll see him myself tomorrow. Perhaps he will share the extent of your admonitions with me."

"Ernest, please, this sarcasm must stop."

"Sarcasm? I wasn't aware that a man's wife could accuse him of sarcasm when she is insistent, meddlesome, and judgmental when it comes to his every effort."

"Ernest, how can you say such things to me?" Alice blurted out. "Your management of our finances is as much my business as it is yours! And when such an enormous debt as the one you have incurred is putting everything we own at risk, especially the Chateau Rottembourg, then yes, I will be meddlesome and insistent and judgmental! And perhaps I should add that I will also be worried and afraid and disappointed, or doesn't any of that matter to you?"

"Alice, I know that right now things are a bit confusing, but I have given you a wonderful life. You have had everything you want. I admit we're experiencing a little difficulty right now but I see no reason for you to feel worried or afraid or disappointed. You have lived in two beautiful houses filled with beautiful things. You have gorgeous clothes. Your dresses have come from Worth, the finest couturier in Paris, perhaps the finest in the world. You are the envy of all your lady friends, and I will point out to you that this is only because of my taste and my judgment, not yours!"

"How dare you!" Alice pounced back, rising from her chair, her eyes blazing fury. "Ernest, how dare you take credit for the advantages and level of taste provided me not by you, but by my Raingo family! And the Chateau Rottembourg was never yours! It is mine! All you have done is to make it your playground, your showcase! And you have squandered a fortune on creating a façade for yourself, not only here at Rottembourg, but everywhere you can. You wouldn't know taste and judgment if it struck you down! Things have come too easily to you, Ernest. You are a spoiled, arrogant man."

Alice did not intend to tolerate her husband's childish lack of concern over the staggering debt he had incurred. Outward appearances seemed to be his greatest worry. She would be able to forgive him a great deal, even his ridiculous insistence on having guided her taste and judgement, but his lack of responsibility when it came to Rottembourg was unforgivable. Worst of all, he had shown no regard whatsoever for her feelings, and he had said not a word to comfort her or allay her fears as the threat of losing the home she loved became an ominous burden.

In the course of the following week the weather cooled dramatically and autumn settled in. The trees turned golden and began to shed their leaves and there were no attempts at reconciliation. The fireplaces roared every morning and evening, breakfast, luncheon, and dinner were served as always, but the strain and tension grew and in spite of these less than favorable emotional conditions, Ernest seemed to be in no hurry to return to Paris.

The hunting was good, the best in years. He was delighted. Every day, felled pheasant, hare, quail, and guinea hen came into the ice house to be dressed, wrapped, and stored in the larders. Jean DeLille was spending more and more time at his own Montgeron home. Temporarily departing from the formal portraiture for which he was known, he had begun painting still life in the tower of his country house. Encouraged by several sales to Paris collectors, he seemed to be enjoying the experience immensely. He also became a welcome and frequent hunting companion for Ernest. Young Jacques often accompanied the two men along the well-worn paths of the Senart, his enthusiasm for being first to spot and silently signal the presence of small, feathered game a talent for which he was more and more often being complimented.

Adding to Claude's personal discomfort, Ernest visited regularly with him at La Lethumiere, seeming to enjoy his company, his approval of turkeys as a suitable theme for one of the four rotunda paintings noticeably enthusiastic, Claude's studies for the pond and rose garden subjects although incomplete, also satisfactory, Ernest's mere presence at La Lethumiere adding enormously to the overwhelming guilt with which Claude lived every day.

DeLille often accompanied Ernest on these visits, enjoying the conversations centered on painting, its modern proponents, and the unpredictable vagaries of the world in which artists lived, DeLille amusing Ernest and at the same time unknowingly rescuing Claude from ever deeper discomfort with his continuing complaints over the persistently high cost of renovating his country house.

The three lunched with the Caillebottes at La Casin. Caillebotte was suggesting a Third Impressionist Exhibition for the following spring. Claude wasn't sure. He felt the group had dissolved, its cooperative spirit irretrievable. Ernest loved the idea.

"I will be happy to loan whichever of my paintings you wish," he offered. "Claude, the four panels you are working on would make fine inclusions."

"If we are to proceed with this idea of another exhibition it will be left to you, Gustave, to reorganize us," Claude said flatly. "No one else from the group will take it on, and I am not at all sure that even you can do anything at all to restore our old alliance. There has been far too much negativity and disappointment. The vision and cohesiveness may not be what it once was. I know for a fact that Renoir and Degas are determined to work independently, but our Pissarro may very well entertain the idea of another exhibition."

Later, Claude would recall that as September had quickly faded into early October and the idea of a Third Impressionist Exhibition took hold, Ernest had taken greater and greater interest in acquiring more of Claude's paintings with thoughts toward lending them to the proposed exhibition. He had gone so far as to purchase a number of Claude's existing canvases, some directly from him, most through Durand-Ruel, the question of cost or payment never raised. At the same time, Claude announced he would be leaving Montgeron to spend a week at home at Argenteuil. He had been away from Camille and Jean not for the three or four weeks he had planned, but for six.

Alice was tormented when Ernest finally left for Paris. Alone through the early days of October she felt abandoned and ignored. She had expected him to apologize, or at least to comfort and reassure her and put an end to their estrangement. She desperately wanted him to. Reconciliation would bring finality to her thoughts of another man's arms. She was sure of it. Most of all, reconciliation would put an end to her overwhelming guilt. It would be over. It must end, she told herself. She cried and worried and argued with herself. Anticipating Ernest's return she rehearsed a number of likely scenarios, but she knew she would never bring herself to act on them. When Ernest did arrive at Rottembourg, the chill in the air remained palpable, putting an end to her best intentions, but in spite of the widening gulf between them, the dinner hour remained a civilized affair. Every evening she and Ernest sat at the dining room table together, the candlelit evening ritual as consistently bone-chilling as advancing autumn itself.

The vibrant color of waning October gave way to a gray November. Claude had returned to La Lethumiere. He worked furiously, but again his work was not pleasing him. He felt rushed and uninspired. Ernest remained at the Chateau Rottembourg for two weeks, the late autumn hunting in the Senart more attractive than ever, he said. During this time it was decided to prolong the family's stay at Montgeron beyond Christmas and at least until spring. The mood in Paris was too serious right now, too grim and uncertain Ernest maintained, and to further emphasize his personal need to present as positive a public image as possible, he added that many owners of country properties were also extending their stays at country retreats. "Yes, in this winter of 1876 everyone is better off away from financially challenged Paris," he insisted.

Once the decision was made to remain at Rottembourg through the winter, Ernest's mood was dramatically improved. In conversation with Alice he insisted he was in control of everything. She was not to worry.

November brought the annual arrival of the first hoar frost which signaled that nighttime temperatures were dropping low enough to form ice crystals on tree branches and create patches of ground frost across woodlands and open fields. In the chill of gray afternoons, Ernest donned thick wool sweaters and warm gloves and now and then was perfectly happy to simply watch the activity at the edge of the Senart where beautiful large groups of brilliantly feathered male pheasants and their dull, brown mates scoured streaks of icy ground under the trees for wild berries and seeds. All seemed to be well at the Chateau Rottembourg, but the views of country beauty and its natural surrounding peace did not last. Called away to Paris by an urgent message, Ernest left Montgeron on the eighteenth of the month, announcing that he would be gone for at least a week. Alice appeared at La Lethumiere on the nineteenth. She didn't knock at the door or call out Claude's name. She simply walked into the main room where she found him sitting in a chair, not painting, but reading. He looked up, stunned to see her, hesitant and uncertain, but once she was in his arms and he held her close all the urgency returned, all the ardor, all the helpless need, all the melting calm.

The hours they spent together in the following days dissolved into a rapturous haze. But for the week he had spent at Argenteuil, Claude had now been at Rottembourg for more than two months. Apart from the large painting of white turkeys which did not entirely please him and which he continued to re-work, the remaining three studies and related panels were progressing more to his liking, their themes focused on the rose garden, the pond, and Ernest in his hunting clothes at the edge of the forest. In the meantime, additional distracting projects had been found. He had begun a small portrait of Germaine holding her doll. He sketched the five children. He completed a painting of the arriving train at the station as well as several subjects of Montgeron and Yerres houses. His work continued daily through November, interrupted only by the sound of a woman's footsteps hurrying across La Lethumiere's threshold. There were moments of great private anguish. There were hours of great passion. There was laughter and tranquility and a mountain of uncertainty. Stories were told, treasured childhood memories, yearnings and dreams shared.

Ernest returned to Montgeron on the twenty-fifth of November, greatly encouraged, he told Alice, by his last meeting with Armel Ducasse, who he said was, at least for the time being, succeeding in holding the most obstinate of Ernest's creditors at bay. It appeared that Ernest's creditors themselves were being pursued by their own creditors, creating an unusually sympathetic attitude on the part of many who found themselves closely allied in an erratic swirl of insurmountable debt.

Although delighted to remain at Rottembourg for an extended period, in an effort to keep her children progressing in in reading, writing, and French history now that they were away from their city school schedules, Alice insisted that the children maintain their studies in daily lessons with Mademoiselle Gabrielle. They took well to this approach to their schooling. Every morning they patiently applied themselves to Gabrielle's masterful grasp of French literature, history, sentence structure, and word usage, but as well as they took to dear Gabrielle's clever word games and funny stories about historic French characters, all the children missed their father when he was away in Paris.

Each time he returned, they told him of their feelings, and always aware of the important and loving place his children held in his heart, Ernest put his creative talents to work and among other delightful projects he concocted during the periods he did spend at Rottembourg, he suggested the occasional treasure hunt in the piles of dry leaves left to nature's will along the lower borders of the chilled meadow.

The very idea of this type of outing with their father was met with shouts of delight and a sense of anticipation which Alice herself found endearing. Wearing their warmest gloves and scarves in the cold, often cloudy afternoons, under accumulated clumps of brown oak and maple leaves they uncovered the brass crowns decorated with colorful glass jewels their father had hidden. Deeper down into the piles of leaves there were silver whistles, black pirate eye patches, toy rubber swords, yards of red satin ribbon and small pirate treasure chests filled with more colorful glass jewels decorating chains, rings, and bracelets. One afternoon from behind a tree, a kite appeared in Ernest's hand. Three attempted launches failed, but on the fourth, he managed to hoist the big red triangle aloft. Thoroughly thrilled by their father's success and delighting in his company, the children took turns holding the tightly wound string board in the stiff cold breeze. They were happy, robustly healthy children at their best in the environment they loved most in the world, quite unaware, under their father's easy autumn smiles and encouraging cheers, that resignation was settling in. Money was running out. So was time. It was true that Armel Ducasse was doing what he could for Ernest. The fine Italian leather boots and easy banter had helped the relationship with Ducasse, but now there were legal deadlines to meet.

Alice had never kept anything from Ernest. He knew when she had a headache or an upset stomach. He could tell in a moment when she was tired or anxious, but now she had a great secret, something to hide from him. It was agony. She was afraid, and her fear began to show. She was pale and drawn. Ernest attributed her anxiety and general malaise to the stressful financial crisis facing them. As a result, Alice's secret guilt remained well hidden from Ernest as into late November life continued on at the Chateau Rottembourg and the first snow blanketed the gardens, the meadow, and the pitched roof at La Lethumiere. Logs were split every day. Fireplaces roared. Once again, the wintry smell of burning hickory was in the air replacing the summer fragrance of Montgeron's famous summer roses. Upstairs, on Rottembourg's rambling third floor, the children wore warm socks and thick sweaters, gathering at their own blazing fireside to read books such as Les Ennuis de mon Petit Chien (The Troubles of my Little Dog), and the somewhat less beloved Geographie de monde (Geography of the World). In lighter moments they played cards and games with Gabrielle, while into November's final days, alone in Paris, their father continued to secure whatever assets he could and at La Lethumiere their mother found solace in the arms of the man who was fulfilling his promise to be her shelter, her shield, her cloak, her cover.

One afternoon in the last days of November Ernest returned to Montgeron, his spirits never lower. In Paris, Ducasse was now threatening the severe legal action Ernest had been hoping to avoid. It was imminent. If successfully prosecuted, Ernest could face a prison term. The likelihood of a declaration of bankruptcy was being discussed. It would satisfy his creditors and might help Ernest to avoid a term in debtors' prison, but it would also mean enormous personal losses. Everything he and Alice owned would be auctioned off to the highest bidder. It would all be sold: the Boulevard Haussmann apartment and all its furnishings, the Chateau Rottembourg and all its contents. Distraught by such pending debacles, Ernest wanted only to be with his family. He abruptly abandoned the city, his thoughts as the train made its way out of the Gare de Lyon and into the bleak November countryside focused on his children's lives and what they could be facing in the near future. What would they think of him?

At Rottembourg, Ernest and Alice found themselves confronting the same personal dilemma they had endured for months, Ernest determined to make as little as possible of the looming disaster, Alice equally determined to hold him accountable for the facts as she understood them. Wearied by the lonely, opposing pressure they both felt, their defenses worn to the barest thread, one afternoon they sat side by side in the pair of chairs by the fireside in the drawing room. Their attempts at civil conversation failing miserably, Ernest resentful of Alice's lack of patience and understanding, Alice accusing, angry, and hostile, it was Ernest who broke through the wall of resistance between them.

"Alice, please let's try to make the best of all this together," he blurted out in desperation after yet one more fiery exchange. "Please, let's get through this together, both of us bearing the same burden. Alice, I cannot go on this way. I love you. Yes, I love you, perhaps more than I ever have, but we live like strangers. We must do something!" He looked into her eyes, his face reflecting a crushing mass of unhappiness and pain, his sudden declaration of devotion and love the words Alice had long hoped to hear.

"I need you so much right now," he said in a bare whisper, his head falling into his hands. "Alice, hear me out. "Please, let's put all this bitterness about money and houses and the threat of loss behind us," he pleaded, lifting his head to face the wife he had never stopped loving and tried to protect. "All that really matters is our love and our children's love. What more is there? I'm tired of being alone. I know you are too. We'll manage. I will take care of you and the children. You know I will. You must trust me. Say it. Say you trust me. Say you love me."

Alice leaned back in her chair. She had heard what she had desperately wanted to hear. Her head dropped back and with an exhausted sigh she closed her eyes. When she opened them, Ernest was there, leaning over her, taking her hand in his, stroking her cheek, and managing a small, hopeful smile.

"Help me, my dearest. I need you so," he whispered "I have never loved you more and I'm so terribly sorry for all the worry and suffering I'm putting you through. I know perfectly well how you feel about Rottembourg, but somehow I know it will be alright, all of it. For a long time I thought I could solve everything, do it alone, quickly and easily, but it isn't happening that way. I know that somehow I can manage it all for us, but what I need most of all right now is to know you are with me, on my side. Say it. Say you are there for me. Say it to me. I can do anything if I know you are there for me."

"I know you're doing all you can. Of course I do," Alice whispered back, her tears released in a stream of endearments. "I love you, and I will always be there for you, Ernest, always. It's just been too much for me to think of losing everything in the only world I've ever known. Please understand. This place, this life, it's who I am, who we are. I need your help as much as you need mine."

It was over. The strain, the sleepless nights, the worry, the lonely, secret exile. Everything would be set right. They both felt it. The bewildering pain would fade and disappear and like a cold, gray shadow racing past the winter moon a secret episode would be forgotten as if it had never been. Life would begin anew and it would fill to overflowing with fresh, unthreatened promise.

On a cold night in late November, in the bedroom overlooking the fallow winter gardens of the Chateau Rottembourg, a delicate barrier was lifted between two people adrift in a troubled universe. Disenchantment and illusion had hurt them. So had separation and harsh words, but alone together and newly confident in their trust of one another they found that the love and constancy once so strong between them had endured. They would try again, they promised. Nothing would change between them, they pledged. The passion they remembered had not lain dormant at some distant door. It was warmed by faith and loyalty. It was heated and fired by loneliness and hopeful renewal. It was complete.

Further unifying their reconciliation and now, as intensifying conditions demanded Ernest's constant presence in Paris, it was decided that the family would not remain at Rottembourg until spring, but that after the Christmas and New Year holidays they would return to the city. There would be no further separations, no lonely hours, no travel between Paris and Montgeron.

In the following days Alice did not meet Claude at La Lethumiere. He waited for the sound of her hurried footsteps. He watched for her. She did not come. There were no dinner invitations and no words of explanation exchanged between them, but in the first week of December, his work on the panels nearing completion, Claude left for Argenteuil. Apologizing for the length of time it had taken to complete the rotunda project, he assured Ernest that he would return before the end of the month and that the paintings would all be finished by Christmas Day, even the troublesome white turkeys.

At Argenteuil he found Camille looking remarkably well. She had gained a little weight and her energy had improved. Jean was happy at his school. Apparently, the money Ernest had advanced and which Claude had sent through Gustave Caillebotte, had provided thrifty Camille with the desperately needed funds she needed to pay the overdue rent to Madame Aubrey and to buy adequate food for herself and Jean. Claude spent a week with Camille and Jean and once again promised a leisurely summer stay at Trouville. Before leaving Argenteuil, he packed warm clothes and met with Durand-Ruel in Paris to discuss Caillebotte's plans for a Third Exhibition as well as prices on the paintings Ernest had promised to buy and pay for. On the same day he returned to Montgeron and La Lethumiere.

But for the painting of white turkeys which was presentable but remained unfinished, all four paintings for Rottembourg's rotunda were completed by mid-December. At that time Claude expected to be paid the balance of what was due him in full, but now Ernest found himself able to pay for only two paintings: the white turkeys which he accepted as unfinished, and the hunting scene depicting him in his favorite pastime at the edge of the Senart Forest. He was completely honest with Claude, apologizing for financial conditions over which, at least for the time being, he insisted he had no control. It was agreed that the two remaining paintings: *The Garden at Montgeron* and *The Pond at Montgeron*, as well as the two studies for those works, would remain at Rottembourg until March, at which time Ernest said he fully expected to establish a fresh line of credit with a private lender and complete his transaction with Claude. In the meantime, he somehow managed to advance Claude five hundred francs and with typical largesse invited him to stay on at La Lethumiere through the Christmas Holidays which he made clear the Hoschede family was planning to spend at Rottembourg.

"Let's send for Camille and Jean," Ernest suggested. "Write them today."

Claude graciously declined the invitation, but by December 20th when he departed Montgeron, the panels for Rottembourg's rotunda accepted as complete, he had formally sold the studies for two panels: *The Garden at Montgeron* and

The Pond at Montgeron, to Ernest together with the portrait of young Germaine holding her doll. On Christmas Eve by the drawing room fireside at the Chateau Rottembourg, Ernest gave Alice Claude's portrait of Germaine as well as Claude's sketch of the five Hoschede children. Alice gave Ernest a pair of gold and lapis lazuli cuff links which had belonged to her father.

The long December holiday spent at Rottembourg was unusually festive for all seven Hoschedes who enjoyed spirited family games played in deep snow and hot chocolate served every afternoon by the roaring library fire. The New Year of 1877 was being anticipated with unusual optimism, but as it approached and preparations were underway for the family's return to the Paris apartment on Boulevard Haussmann, Alice found herself with yet one more nagging concern. By New Years Eve she suspected she was pregnant with her sixth child.

CHAPTER 21

One Brief Shining Moment
January 1877

When he was feeling pensive and sorry for himself, one of Ernest's favorite destinations was an area not too far from the center of Paris where age-old yew trees marked the site of the abandoned palace of Saint-Cloud and its magnificent garden staircase overlooking the city. The financial situation was at a catastrophic stage. The eternally optimistic man who had convinced himself that nothing as ridiculous as a financial crisis could possibly affect him was adrift and floundering in an alien, confrontational world and now Armel Ducasse was not his only adversary. Shop proprietors he had befriended over the course of years, many having once accepted gracious invitations to the Chateau Rottembourg, were now bursting unannounced into his office at the store, shouting and swearing at him and insisting on being paid. He was called a cheat, a scoundrel, a filthy fraudster who deserved nothing less than a long prison term. Burdened by feelings of shame and utter failure, the man who to the outside world appeared as affable as ever, was bearing his deep humiliation secretly and quite alone.

Cigar in hand and grateful for the solitude, he liked to lean against the balustrade at the top of Saint-Cloud's flight of garden stairs where in the cold breeze he could turn up the brown beaver collar of his coat and imagine the tragic figures linked to Saint-Cloud's long, colorful history standing alone in that same spot under similarly distressing circumstances. Oddly enough, unlike those figures frozen in the haze of history, the man so at ease in a wide variety of circumstances could never bring himself to descend St. Cloud's abandoned stairs and walk the ruins of its abandoned lower gardens. Instead, like a rare bird safely poised at a secret perch, he remained content to look down from the top step and survey the Paris profile from its loftiest, most advantageous point.

A short distance west of Paris at Hauts-de-Seine and once the glittering suburban palace of a long list of French royals, Saint-Cloud had graced its superbly elevated site in quiet splendor for centuries. Ernest knew its colorful history well and in the early months of 1877, from his "point d'appui" at the top of its haunting stairs he reflected on Saint-Cloud's many historic ironies, finding more than a few parallels to his own.

Queen Marie Antointette, Emperor Napoleon Bonaparte, and several Ducs d'Orleans had, each in their own time, taken great pleasure in the palace of Saint-Cloud's beauty and peerless setting once formal court life became overly demanding at Versailles. Marie Antoinette had painstakingly re-decorated room after room, upon their completion, arranging for lavish entertainments to which she invited only a handful of the most prominent members of the French court. Little more than a quarter century later, it was in the chapel of Saint-Cloud that in 1810 Napoleon married Marie Louise and it was there, at his beloved Saint-Cloud that later, his conquerors dishonored him most severely. Enemy troops camped in the gardens he was known to have loved. Cavalry horses were watered in the famous fanning fountains he had ordered "soaring to heaven." Hounds were kenneled in the queen's opulent bedchamber and soldiers took turns lying in the Emperor's bed, amusing themselves by tearing down the heavy blue velvet bed hangings with swords and daggers, piece by priceless piece. Later, it was at Saint-Cloud in December of 1852, that the Empire had been restored, and on July 28, 1870 it was also at Saint-Cloud that Louis-Napoleon declared war on Prussia. Badly burned during the ensuing Prussian occupation and Siege of 1870-71, now seven years later as from its finest vantage point Ernest Hoschede pondered the dilemma that had become his life, Saint-Cloud's once magnificent center palace pediment remained an ironic burned out shell in his background, its windows opened to the sky, its once beautiful façade entirely blackened and scarred, not by time, but by the chasms of war and human folly.

Ernest's mood when he was at Saint-Cloud, took on a deep melancholy he almost enjoyed, and through the early months of 1877 he returned to Saint-Cloud many times, standing alone at the top of its sweeping garden stairs in the icy winds of January and February, enduring the pain and loss of its tragic past as if they were his own.

Conditions in the City of Paris were worsening dramatically, the larger financial picture darkening more drastically day by day. The circle of affluence was shrinking and many once prosperous Paris citizens were not only seriously affected by debt, but also by the alarming reality of rapidly dwindling cash reserves. Worried Parisians could talk of little else but the succession of bank failures and their increasingly frustrating inability to access funds as well as the most rudimentary lines of credit. Vanished were the casual concern and frivolous indecision of the previous year. Obvious now was the fact that the hard gristle of affirmation had been grudgingly transformed into an unappetizing confrontation with cold reality.

The French economy may have been in tatters, it foundations shaken and unnerved, but with touches of both irony and humor, an exclusive number of securely wealthy Paris residents continued to go about their lives unaffected by the times, the dilemma unfolding everywhere around them sympathetically discussed but virtually unnoticed as they moved forward with no lack of grace or funds. In mid-January, elements of such grace and security were exemplified in the elegant invitation extended by the safely affluent Gustave Caillebotte to his Impressionist colleagues. Fully determined to convince the disbanded, now scattered group to exhibit in Paris yet a third time, he invited the seven primary painters to dinner at his family's elegant Rue Miromesnil home, carefully laying out, in his own well-organized mind, the strategies and arguments he knew would be necessary to convince them to mount a fresh assault at the well-guarded gates of the opposition. The letters of invitation were perfection, the menu a work of art, Gustave Caillebotte's own confidence as an artist never higher. He knew he was painting well and now at last, he had work to show, very good work.

To Pissarro he wrote a singularly personal note: "My dear Pissarro, please come to dinner at my house next Monday. I am recently returned from London and would like to discuss certain matters with you relative to a possible exhibition this spring. Degas, Monet, Renoir, Sisley, and Edouard Manet will be there. Madame Morisot is unable to attend, but I count absolutely on you. Monday at seven o'clock. All my best, G. Caillebotte."

"Pissarro will never exhibit with us," Monet quickly wrote back to Caillibotte after receiving the news that members of the group were in favor of attending the dinner. "He is the most disenchanted of us all and with his friends, Cezanne and Guillaumin, is part of that anti-bourgeois union of artists who are planning an exhibition of their own. If Pissarro does not exhibit, neither will Cezanne, and without those two, we will appear dangerously fragmented."

"I am doing all I can to urge Pissarro to join us," Caillebotte quickly replied, "and I think I am succeeding, but you will be happy to know that I am also doing all I can to convince Edouard Manet to show with us. He will be at our dinner and I know you will agree that his participation will encourage our colleagues as little else can. If Fantin-Latour can also be convinced to come over to our side with Manet, so much the better. I am meeting with him tomorrow. Wish me well."

"Gustave Caillebotte could be the great logistician this time," Durand-Ruel observed to Ernest who, in spite of the monumental monetary crisis confronting him, continued to shop for paintings almost daily and in the five-day period between January 19 and January 23, astonishingly purchased twenty-nine Impressionist paintings from Durand-Ruel, most by Monet, eight by Sisley, including *Bridge with Ducks* and *The Machine de Marly*, all credited to his house account with the promise of timely payment in full. "This sale could represent more than half Monet's income for the entire year," Durand-Ruel had delightedly shared with Ernest, as yet unaware of the Hoschede debacle in progress.

"Caillebotte has the time and money to lead," Durand-Ruel observed further, entering the Hoschede transaction into his ledger, the true extent of his own financial concerns left unspoken. Rent on the eighteen-year lease he had signed in 1869 for the premises at 16 Rue Laffitte and the connecting space at 11 Rue Le Peletier had increased substantially over the years, the annual 30,000 franc fee he had paid in 1870 now an obligation approaching 50,000 francs.

"Because the banking crisis doesn't affect Caillebotte," Durand-Ruel went on in his now familiar declaratory tone of voice, "his solid position will encourage the others. Even in these unsettled times, he has been buying quite a few of his colleagues' paintings and paying fair prices for them. At first I thought he was doing this only because he knew most of his fellow painters were in dire straits and needed the money. By nature he's a generous person and a loyal friend, but now I'm beginning to believe Caillebotte purchases only what he sincerely likes. Odd situation there, isn't it: a painter, a patron, and a collector all wrapped up in one body? Frankly, I don't believe young Caillebotte will be able to convince Edouard Manet to show. Manet is an enigma. He approves of the Impressionist spirit, but that is where his support ends. The Salon is everything to him. Who knows, though? Right now, Manet's sales are, shall we say slim at best, and he could need more exposure than he lets on. You know how he can be about keeping things close to his chest. Claude Monet tells me that you, Monsieur Hoschede, are agreeable to lending this spring. If the exhibition does indeed come together, what do you think of loaning the panel paintings Claude did for your country house? I haven't seen them yet, but Monet seems pleased with the results he achieved and I've advised him he should show only the work with which he is most satisfied."

"Ah, Monsieur Hoschede!" Gustave Caillebotte called out to Ernest who once again was at Durand-Ruel's looking at paintings a few days later. The youngest of the lions was wisely reaching out to the group's most significant advocates, assuring them, few as they were, that he counted "absolutely," as he had written to Pissarro, on their support and friendship and that without them there could be no chance of success. His visit to Durand-Ruel's gallery was seen as highly important to the range of support he was seeking.

"I do hope, Monsieur Hoschede, that you have not forgotten the details of our conversation with Claude Monet in the country this summer and the idea I proposed regarding a Third Exhibition of our group's work," the enthusiastic, fresh-faced Caillebotte ventured. "We will be meeting soon to begin our discussions, but I want you to know, Monsieur, that your encouragement meant so much to me during those luncheons with Claude in the country this summer. Your positive view of things truly propelled me forward. If we can put it together, would you still be willing to lend paintings? I'm sure you feel as I do that we must try once more."

Ernest smiled to the aspiring young architect of the proposed Third Exhibition, struggling to conceal his excitement. Had he forgotten about his conversations with Claude Monet and Gustave Caillebotte in the country that past summer and the idea of another exhibition of the group's work? Hardly. Would he lend paintings to such an exhibition and could he somehow find himself central to an exhibition at which his treasured paintings could be seen and admired? When not involved in holding his creditors at bay, comforting Alice, or meeting with a constant stream of uncooperative bankers and solicitors, Ernest had thought of little else. The diversion helped to keep his anxiety at bay. Frequently recalling the country conversations with Monet and Caillebotte, by the time Caillebotte asked at Durand-Ruel's if he would be willing to lend, Ernest had already decided he would not only lend if an exhibition were planned, he would be the exhibition's biggest lender, loaning the greatest number of paintings and at the same time enjoying a prominent position at the spotlighted center of what would surely turn out to be the Impressionists' finest moment.

"Gustave, if you can assure me that my paintings will represent the largest number of works loaned by a private collector for your proposed exhibition, then yes, I'm agreeable to lend, Ernest stated emphatically. "When you are ready and plans are solidified we should discuss my participation in greater detail."

With enthusiasm for a Third Exhibition of Impressionist paintings growing and as Ernest eagerly anticipated his prominence as its most important lender, Claude decided to spend more time in Paris where he felt he would find inspiration for new work suitable to exhibit.

On one of the coldest evenings in January of 1877 and one by one, except for Pissarro and Sisley who had met at the Guerbois and arrived together, by seven-thirty, five of the seven invited artists had arrived at Gustave Caillebotte's Rue Miromesnil door. At the last minute, Cezanne had decided against traveling to Paris from Aix and Madame Morisot was clear to say that she was not favorably inclined to accepting dinner invitations which did not include her husband. Edouard Manet and Fantin-Latour had sent regrets more than a week before. Knowing Caillebotte quite well by now and aware of his intentions, each of the five had come prepared to enjoy a fine dinner served in elegant surroundings, but each had also come prepared with solid, well-founded arguments against the proposal they suspected would be presented by the youngest member of their dispirited group. They felt they had suffered enough. In two rounds of public scrutiny they had been chastised, embarrassed, and rebuked not once, but twice. There was no denying that their work and their purpose had been soundly rejected and that their reputations were in tatters, but remarkably and by some miracle, one distinct quality remained common to them all and Caillebotte saw and understood this linking thread very clearly.

Each member of the core group had remained completely true to his, and in Madame Berthe Morisot's case her, individual talent. Each was a hard-working, diligent artist, doing whatever must be done in order to survive and continue on in the only endeavor that uniformly mattered regardless of economic conditions, and that was painting.

Their fortitude and relentless perseverance under the worst possible circumstances well known to their astute young host, Gustave wisely used their astonishing mettle to great advantage. He also used the simplest human approach in order to reach them, and like the talented young lieutenant eager for promotion he was, Gustave Caillebotte had decided that his battalion's uncommon valor and sheer stamina were the only ammunition needed in order to proceed to the next skirmish. The potential for renewal and victory loomed, and he intended to explore its possibilities fully.

Pissarro didn't smile. Degas was late. Sisley admired the interior decorating and the profusion of orchids which Caillebotte expertly cultivated. Renoir picked at his food. Monet dreaded the confrontational debate he knew would be coming once dessert and cognac had been served. He felt sorry for poor Caillebotte.

"I thank each of you for coming," the skillful, young catalyst began, standing and raising his glass of champagne for the initial toast once all were seated at the rectangular table in his dining room. "It has been much too long since we have spent an evening together and since that is indeed the admitted case, I propose we begin our evening in talk of what we care about most: our lives, our families, our gardens, and our friends. A la belle France!"

"A la belle France!" the chorus of voices returned in unison, raising their glasses, their hearts and minds at odds, their bonds so badly broken that any situation in which future collaboration could be discussed and planned seemed quite impossible.

"What is the news from Pontoise?" Monet gingerly asked of Pissarro, first to break the ice with the most obviously disillusioned guest at the table who sat directly across from him.

"There is no news in Pontoise," Pissarro uttered dryly, slowly fingering his beard as the first course, brochet au beurre blanc (pike in butter sauce), was served.

"Unless there is a flood or a war, there is nothing," he commented further. "Is it not the same at Argenteuil? What goes on there? Is there something I haven't heard? I see almost no one outside my family so it was good to come to Paris even in this bitter cold. I was truly grateful for the sight of people breathing in and out. I went to the Guerbois yesterday, and with Sisley again today. Everyone there looked all right to me."

"Who was at the Guerbois? It's been condemned again! Haven't you heard?" Renoir quickly broke in, seated next to Monet" his tone nervous but surprisingly confrontational, his true intention far from audacious. "Camille, you could not have seen too many familiar faces at the Guerbois. Everyone is moving to the Athenes. I think it is because of the mirrors along all the walls. They are so flattering. I look at myself all the time when I am there. I watch myself drinking coffee or chewing on a crusty bit of pain poilane. Sometimes I adjust the angle of my hat or the tilt of my head. At times I find myself irresistible. Camille, you must go. I can meet you there tomorrow. Edgar, you like the Athenes, don't you?"

"As long as Edouard Manet is not there I like it," the surly Degas replied in his acidic tone, reaching for his wine glass as the fish course was cleared and the entrée was served. "I get very tired of watching him walk around all puffed up and souffled as if he discharges francs right out of that tight bottom of his!"

He took a bite of the blanquette of veal. "Gustave, my compliments to your cook! This longe de veau is the best I have ever tasted. Not too many people in Paris are eating such tender veal these days, or enjoying such fine béchamel for that matter. What lovely cream! Delicious! And where does one find pike at this time of year? You must have a secret source. I must tell my cook, Zoe, all about this wonderful dinner."

His mood improved by the delectable elegance of the cuisine being placed before him, Degas raised his glass in appreciation and continued to concentrate quite totally on the meat course which was served with a fan of tender carrots, tiny white onions, and Claude's favorite steamed chestnuts in cream, the artfully arranged entree presented to each guest by a butler and served from a simple Creil porcelain platter.

"How long did it take you to come to Paris from Argenteuil?" Sisley asked of Monet. "I thought my train would never leave Sevres. The ice delayed everything."

"I did not have far to come. I have taken a flat here in Paris," Claude responded, "quite near the Gare Saint-Lazare. I'm painting there."

"Wonderful!" Sisley exclaimed. "Is Camille staying with you? And Jean?' he asked. "I remember Camille once telling me how very much she loved being in Paris. And what woman wouldn't? Is it that you are moving back to Paris? I know it inspires you."

"No, we still live at Argenteuil, and Camille and Jean are there," Claude quickly clarified. "Jean goes to the Fayette School now, so of course it is best for Camille to be at home. We cannot afford to board Jean at his school."

"Then the flat is your studio?"

"Yes, my studio."

Claude's first floor Paris flat was at 17 Rue de la Moncey, quite close to the Gare de Saint-Lazare. It consisted of a small sitting room, a bedroom, and a storage closet. In early January it had been quietly leased for Claude in the name of Gustave Caillebotte who generously paid the 175 franc rent each month. Where the Gare de Lyon serviced passengers bound for points south and east, the Saint-Lazare station provided passenger service for points north and west and as far as the Normandy towns of Rouen, Bougival, Louveciennes, and the villages of Veheuil, Pointose, and Giverny. Ernest had learned about Claude's newly leased Paris studio during a luncheon with Caillebotte who admitted to having encouraged the idea when the likelihood of a Third Exhibition had been presented to Claude.

"Claude immediately anticipated the need to complete more work for a proposed exhibition and said his interest in Argenteuil subjects had waned," Caillebotte had confided to Ernest. "I really think he was worried that he would have nothing new to show. Of course, you and I both know he has probably exhausted Argenteuil subjects by now. He has, after all, lived there for five years and works constantly. I suggested he spend more time in the city where he has always found inspiration of one sort or another. Paris life is so rich in its endless panorama of wonderful subjects and that eye of Monet's misses nothing. He told me he had been thinking about the railway stations."

As was the case with both Edouard Manet and Gustave Caillebotte, the subject of Paris railroad stations had intrigued Claude for years and as further discussions for an exhibition took place in the early days of January, both Caillebotte and Durand-Ruel had encouraged his interest in painting either the Gare de Lyon or the Saint-Lazare. The small flat Caillebotte leased for him close to the Lazare station had determined his decision to paint there. By early February, Alice was well acquainted with the address and the inspiration Claude found in it. Now in the city, miles away from the Brie Valley's summer enchantment, she and Claude had resumed their secret meetings.

"Ernest and I were afraid the children were getting too far behind in their schoolwork," she explained to friends, "and of course they missed their city friends and the winter activities they're used to. Overall, it seemed best for us to leave the Chateau Rottembourg and come back to Paris."

The explanation seemed believable enough, but of course their reconciliation having successfully reunited them in a concerted effort, Alice and Ernest had returned to Paris so that Ernest could attend to financial affairs without enduring long absences from his family at the Chateau Rottembourg.

Both having left Montgeron, Claude for the last time in December, Alice and her family just after the arrival of the New Year, the two had met in Paris quite by chance on a cold, rainy day in January, just outside La Madeleine, where Alice had attended the eleven o'clock Sunday Mass with Julian Raingo. Claude had arranged to meet with Gustave Caillebotte on that same day, Caillebotte suggesting they meet near noon at the Gabriel, his favorite restaurant located at the end of the Eighth Arrondissement's square, Place Louis XV. On his way just before noon and turning from Place de la Concorde onto Rue Royale, Claude spotted Alice descending the Madeleine's wide, sweeping steps, arm in arm with her uncle Julian Raingo. Even in the mid-day throng departing the Madeleine there was no mistaking them. In his signature top hat and a fur-collared coat, the tall, elder Raingo had snapped open his big, black umbrella, sharing its shelter against the rain with his gray-cloaked niece who descended La Madeleine's stairs like a sure-footed city sparrow. Claude quickly debated with himself as to the wisdom of extending even the briefest greeting, but watching Alice, he had stood frozen in place. She was a vision. Her long gray woolen cloak billowed up around her in the sudden gusts of wind, its deep folds extended like wings out to the Madeleine's famous temple-like stairs as she chatted with her uncle and in moments came face to face with the summer lover who once again found magic in the uncontrived appearance of the woman he remembered wearing the white dress of August, the woman who had played at statues in summer's sun-kissed grass and now wore winter's warm, gray cloak, quickly gathering it close around her when she saw him.

With not the slightest hint of the genuine awkwardness being felt on both sides, pleasant greetings were exchanged, Alice smiling, Julian Raingo politely inquiring as to the progress of Claude's work, the address of the recently acquired Paris studio discussed as casually as one discusses the acquisition of a new pet.

"I am working in Paris now, a mere two blocks from Rue Fessart, at 17 Rue de la Moncey. It's a small flat, but since my wife and son are at Argenteuil, it is adequate for my needs right now. I am painting scenes of the Gare Saint-Lazare, which is conveniently located closeby, Claude revealed. The work goes fairly well."

Alice had argued with herself for days following the encounter, hating the inescapable thought of Claude in Paris, hating herself for thinking about him constantly, hating the idea of wanting to be with him, at the same time feeling lonely and abandoned by her pre-occupied husband who, contrary to the original return-to-Paris-plan which was intended to provide him adequate time with Alice and the children, except for observing the obligatory ritual of evening dinner and calling her "darling" whenever he addressed her, was seldom at home.

"I have news, darling" he announced during one such dinner and on the same January evening as at Caillebotte's table on Rue Miromesnil potential was being explored and the strength of old relationships was being tested. "Our friend, Claude Monet, has taken a studio here in Paris, on Rue de la Moncey, quite near the Saint-de-Lazare station. There's some talk about the possibility of another exhibition of his group's work and I understand he's preparing some paintings of the Lazare in anticipation of such a project. I've been asked to consider lending some of my paintings to the event."

Alice could feel her jaw stiffen. She clenched her fists under her napkin.

"Claude Monet? Here in Paris? But he lives at Argenteuil with his wife and son."

"It's a temporary arrangement, just until he finishes some new work which he hopes will be ready in time for the proposed Spring exhibition, but what he's doing is really quite a marvel. I understand that with a little help from Gustave Caillebotte, the man has actually received official permission to set up his easel right there inside the Lazare. He can't finish paintings there what with trains and people coming and going, but Gustave says his studies are progressing extremely well. You'll remember, darling, that as a member of the French Tribunal of Justice, Gustave's father had connections in all the city's municipal offices. I'm sure that has helped. Martial Caillebotte may be gone, but the Caillebotte name is still known and respected in many Paris corridors. Claude is fortunate to have such a good, influential friend in Gustave. I'm thinking about paying Claude a visit, perhaps tomorrow sometime. I'd like to see how he's getting along."

Alice watched Ernest fingering the rim of his wine glass, the hard knot in her stomach tightening.

"I have an idea," he said suddenly, "why don't you come with me, darling? Claude would love seeing you. We could make a day of it, just you and I. We could lunch at Laperouse, take a table with a view of the river, and enjoy some of that bouillabaisse you like so much. It would be wonderful. We could take our time, linger over a fancy dessert and a little champagne and then head to Claude's by late afternoon. What do you say?"

"Oh, Ernest, that sounds like an expensive day," Alice was quick to respond. "We really shouldn't be that extravagant, not just now with everything up in the air as it is."

"No, it isn't extravagant at all. We need a day to ourselves away from all the tension and anxiety," Ernest quickly interrupted. "I'll send Bernard to reserve at Laperouse. I know just the table I want."

Delighted by prospects for a day spent alone with Alice and eager to make plans for the exactly sort of elegant luncheon they had not enjoyed together in months, Ernest saw no sign of his wife's alarm. He couldn't know that seated at the dinner table, her food untouched as his enthusiasm grew, she felt her stomach churning. How could she possibly entertain the idea of a face to face visit with Claude Monet? And with Ernest at her side! By Christmastime, when he had left Montgeron, she had hoped never to see the Argenteuil painter again. His work at the Chateau Rottembourg had been completed. Any further encounter with him was unthinkable. She had worked hard at forgetting everything about the indiscretions of the summer months. Yes, and she had succeeded very well in putting it all aside once and for all. Until the unexpected meeting at La Madeleine she had been sure her feelings for him had dimmed and that the painter who found beauty in white turkeys and looked for dots on horizons had provided a mere dalliance during a particularly trying time, nothing more. Until their chance encounter at the Paris church dedicated to Mary Magdalene, she had managed her guilt, convinced that her own self-discipline would sustain her. It hadn't. Seeing Claude after several months and succumbing to feelings she could not control, she was in his studio and in his arms the next day. Now, at her own dinner table with her husband at her side, it was entirely different. The old guilt and feelings of self-loathing returned. For days, confusion and pangs of regret were persistent companions. There was so much at stake, so much to lose.

For almost two months she hadn't allowed herself to be overwhelmed by indiscretions of the past and with an altruistic view of circumstances she had repeatedly told herself that although life might be dealing her an unfair blow, it was foolish, no, reckless to remain emotionally involved with anyone but Ernest. She wasn't at all sure what he was doing to resolve their overwhelming financial problems, but since that night in late November when they had rekindling old feelings and made passionate love at the Chateau Rottembourg they had begun to mend the breaches in their marriage and life had gone on, not altogether smoothly, but there were noticeable improvements every day. Wasn't their life together important? Wasn't it really the most important thing, especially now when Ernest was confronted by so many challenges. In the dining room, from her chair beside him, she looked at Ernest closely. He needed her. He loved her. Yes, somehow she must move beyond this terrible period, she told herself. And yes, it would happen. Somehow Ernest would solve their problems and life's pendulum would steady and regulate itself once again. Yes, everything would be fine. It had to be fine. She mustn't see Claude ever again. Looking into her husband's eyes, she could plainly see that he was happy. In the glowing candlelight he was smiling the old smile she loved. It had been missing for so long. With a fresh smile of her own, Alice agreed to spend the following day exactly as Ernest was planning. She would do her best, she adamantly promised herself, to be the companion he needed her to be. She would rise to the occasion as a brand new person. Yes, she would turn an old page and begin a fresh new chapter. Tomorrow she would enjoy a long luncheon with her husband. She would dress attractively and make charming, intimate conversation with him at Laperouse. They would flirt with one another again and hold hands under the table. She would admire his handsome profile. He would tell her she was still the most beautiful woman in any room, and while dessert was being served she would think of something to say to avoid seeing Claude Monet: a headache, a chill, a cold coming on. Yes, Ernest was always so sensitive to how she was feeling and now there was a good excuse. Yes, a perfect excuse. She had waited to be absolutely sure, and now she was, and perhaps tomorrow, over luncheon at a table with a fine view of the Seine, she would tell Ernest she was pregnant. Yes, wasn't it wonderful news? By late summer sometime, late in August, Dr. Rimaldi believes, she would say. Yes, I'm fine. Everything seems quite normal, the good doctor says, but today, my darling, I'm beginning to feel a bit too tired for a late afternoon visit anywhere. Goodness, I must be needing a nap! You go on to Claude Monet's without me. Bernard will take me home. I'll send him back to wait for you at Claude Monet's studio. Yes, it would be a celebration lunch and Ernest would be thrilled to anticipate the birth of his sixth child.

The January evening wore on, the mood in the Hoschede apartment at 56 Boulevard Haussmann was warm and resonant, Ernest relaxed and calm. His smile came often as he and Alice managed the sort of idle conversation they had found difficult to share for many weeks. All the short-temperedness and resentment were magically gone and suddenly there was so much to talk about. Long into the night they put all concern aside and let themselves laugh, recalling years of children's antics, family celebrations, and memories of winters past. It was as if the anger and disillusionment of the past months had never come between them and that once again their life together was all that mattered. It was well after midnight when two despairing lovers found peace in affirmation and passion in one another's arms, their hearts and minds of one persuasion, one compelling hope.

On this same evening, not far away from Boulevard Haussmann and with an air of similarly sated satisfaction, on Rue Miromesnil the old, unbridled camaraderie returned. Times outside the elegant boundaries of Gustave Caillebotte's well-appointed dining room were not good, but inside, on that splendidly clear, cold January night there was renewed courage, a fresh view, and best of all, the reassurance that in two years no one had changed. Sisley was still the cooperative, soft-spoken British aesthete, Renoir the playful, hesitant advocate, Pissarro the direct, prodigious workman, Degas the brash, reliably offensive goat, Monet the unflinching, solid catalyst whose ambition was set in stone.

Their respect and affection for one another went unspoken but it was all there, manifested in a friendly glance, a knowing smile, a reluctant nod, a familiar chuckle. Yes, they would exhibit a third time. Gustave Caillebotte would choose the location, make all the necessary arrangements, and as Paul Durand-Ruel had predicted, would take it upon himself to become the great logistician of the Third Impressionist Exhibition. A date was set for April.

"I'm glad I sent Bernard to reserve our table," Ernest remarked to Alice as just inside the door the Perouse maitre welcomed them from beside his imposing escritoire and showed them to their table, the refined din of voices above the inviting aromas of menu items for which the Rouse was famous elegantly fused with the fragrances of expensive perfumes and strong black coffee.

Every day but Sunday, the Rouse was busy by one o'clock, its loyal patrons not always hungry but emotionally tied to its handsomely mirrored, clock-free world, its leisurely rhythms those defined by Paris residents such as Ernest and Alice who by their mere presence defined 'l'entente de la vie' (the art of living). Under the gilded ceiling and through the columned arches people were seated at tables draped in ivory damask. There being few fresh flowers available in January, lush arrangements of dried lavender, spiraea, and thick branches of winter spruce decorated each table. Her pregnancy far from obvious as yet, Alice wore a cobalt blue wool dress, its long slim skirt and the sleeves of its short, fur-lined matching jacket trimmed in her favorite ornate black passementerie, the distinctive embellishment which required hours of an experienced dressmaker's beading and braiding skills. A small brimmed black hat, black gloves, and a muff also in cobalt blue completed her ensemble which, as the Hoschedes were shown to their table, was met with more than a few admiring glances.

"A new baby? A child for us in late summer?" Ernest was thrilled. "Alice, this is wonderful news and it comes at a time when we really do need good news. Oh, my darling. When? Late August? Perfect! Yes, perfect!"

He sat back in his chair, clearly stunned but at the same time delighted by the unexpected news that another child was about to be added to the Hoschede household.

"And you're absolutely sure?" he asked, his broad smile concealing his quick mental calculation as he counted the months back from August and remembered the night in late November when at Rottembourg he and Alice had found each other again after a long, painful period of isolation and loneliness.

"Oh, yes," Alice reassured him. "I've seen Doctor Rimaldi. He confirmed my suspicions. He says he expects all to progress as well as it has with all five of our previous babies. Ernest, let's hope for another son. It would be so good for Jacques to have a brother."

CHAPTER 22

The Third Exhibition

"**B**lue again!" Louis Leroy exclaimed loudly upon surveying the contents of one after another of the gallery rooms carefully chosen and arranged for the Third Exhibition of what many critics insisted on calling "The Batignolles Group."

Functioning as the capable logistician Durand-Ruel had predicted he would become, Gustave Caillebotte had, at his own expense, rented a five-room apartment on the second floor of Number 6 Rue Le Peletier, almost directly across the street from Durand-Ruel's Le Peletier entrance at Number 11 and just off the intersection with Boulevard des Italiens. Several of the rooms thus enjoyed splendid views of the sumptuous boulevard and the smart swirling pedestrian traffic of Nouveau Paris. Mere minutes away from Garnier's elegant new Opera and in a highly attractive area of shops and apartments, the location was intended to draw, as it had at Durand-Ruel's galleries the year before, an audience in touch with a capitalist economy. Unfortunately, the reality of the times may have eluded Caillebotte and the painters whose unity and camaraderie he had so successfully restored.

Given the strains of Second Empire inflation, the costs of Baron Haussmann's expensive urban plan, the Franco-Prussian War reparations, and the Commune rebuilding debt, the group, although harshly realistic in the most basic matters affecting their personal lives, was highly optimistic about selling their work at a time when they knew French confidence in spending during a recession was at a particularly low point. Again however, public curiosity reigned, and although sales of paintings were weak, attendance was excellent throughout the month- long April exhibition of 1877 and in the fifty or more critical reviews written there was considerable discussion surrounding the true meaning of Impressionism as it was now being depicted and implemented by the artists who had decided to officially adopt the title. Commensurately, so often were the terms, Impressionism and Impressionists seen in reviews, that there remained little further question of the group's identity by the public. Whether the critic hated the painters and their paintings or was in sympathy with them, he was finally grasping just what their movement was about and that what linked its members was not merely a reaction against the establishment, but a mutual respect for the independent spirit. Finally, the new rebel group of nose-thumbers had its label, its "sobriquet," its brand, and hopefully, its saleable product.

Admission was fifty centimes. At Caillebotte's insistence, both the selection of the location as well as the installation had been approved by the artists themselves, "so there will be no one to blame for either success or failure," as he put it.

Opening day of April Fifth was something of a cause-celebre. Well-attended by the public and press alike, the event was met with the expected mix of strong, conflicting, often hot-tempered opinion, unlike the private reception and viewing Caillebotte had hosted in the exhibition rooms the night before, an occasion which, due to his careful preparation, was met with great enthusiasm and the sort of polite tolerance displayed when one invites only one's closest friends and the emotionally obligated members of one's family.

In addition to all the participating artists, Caillebotte's guest list had been culled mainly from the social milieu of haute bourgeoisie Parisians his family had known for countless years and the fashionable society in which he had been raised. His young, privileged friends from the Paris Sailing Club where he was particularly active and where later he would serve as president attended, as did his late father's closest friends, the Marquis de Saens et Danvere, a fellow justice at the Tribunal of Commerce and Monsieur Didier DuClair, professor of art history at The Sorbonne. The blonde, magnificently tall Comtesse Diana d'Auvers, wife of the Danish ambassador and a friend of his mother was present, as was Madame Louisa Brabant, newly widowed, fabulously wealthy, and on the arm of the dashing, dramatically mustachioed Comte DeVilliers known to be down to his last franc, but still considered the best ballroom dancing partner in all Paris. The highly decorated General Montresant, his left arm severed at the same bloody battle of Beaune-la-Rolande at which Claude's good friend, Frederick Bazille, had been killed, attended, as did, and rather ironically, Monsieur Thors, Director of the Bank of Paris.

"Leave it to our Gustave to think of everything, even the Bank of Paris!" Degas commented in a dry whisper.

"Well, that is, after all, where the money is," an approving Renoir returned.

Apart from his younger Paris Sailing Club contemporaries, Caillebotte's guests were, as a group, the older Paris haut establishment figures and family friends who had watched the sensitive, young Gustave growing up. As a whole, they supported the edicts and established practices of the Salon. They also subscribed to a mutual regard for tradition and, as in a neatly closed circle of like-minded people, the bonds formed in this group had solidified over the years. These were people who encouraged the efforts of one another's children and grandchildren at every stage of life, and whether or not in step with the activities, tastes, or accomplishments of those offspring, when it mattered most their loyalty and support were unshakable.

Choosing yet again not to exhibit with the Impressionists in spite of Caillebotte's repeated efforts, Edouard Manet and Fantin-Latour attended opening day together and returned once or twice throughout the course of the four-week exhibition to support their contemporary colleagues, most of their attention focused on Madame Morisot's work. Friendly and enthusiastic in their praise and, as was expected, turned out in the most fashionable finery of the day, Manet and Fantin-Latour nonetheless maintained their public distance from the disavowed group, privately and publicly convinced of the far greater career benefits Salon approval could mean to them.

As the most generous lender to the exhibition, Ernest Hoschede had needed no encouragement when Gustave suggested he and Alice attend his reception and invite a number of their friends and family members to the evening reception. Not to be outdone by Caillebotte's title bearing and prestigious guests, Ernest drew up his own distinguished guest list, using the opportunity to impress. First on his list was the dazzling Polish Comtesse Potachka, a woman he knew would appear opulently dressed, feathered, and bejeweled. A number of his more prominent department store customers were invited, including the Marquess Antoinette D'Aubry, the Baron and Baroness Robout, the Comtesse Thalouet, and the British art critic, James Craig, who was a Boulevard Haussmann neighbor and spent most of his time in Paris wandering about the Louvre, comparing shades of the color white in the paintings of Rembrandt to those in paintings of Vermeer. Ernest's widowed mother attended, as did his Cousin Beatrice and her husband, Marc Pirole, Beatrice bedecked in clouds of yellow tulle and yards of glistening pearls. Present also, was Julian Raingo, now walking with a decided limp and sporting an ebony cane. He arrived with the jeweler, Auguste Blaiche and assorted members of the Raingo family. Alice attended under considerable duress. This then, was the small, select audience introduced to the private showing of the Impressionists' third attempt at piercing the establishment's thick skin. Overall, it was a polite, if at times awkward encounter with change, Gustave Caillebotte's large, remarkably smooth-surfaced paintings met not only with fondly issued encouragements by those who knew him best, but all six of his exhibited canvases enjoyed the same high degrees of well-deserved flattery and praise which many critics would soon attach to him in articles published during the exhibition. At the end of the evening reception, the work of his colleagues was, on the whole, quietly regarded as "interesting," or "colorful," Renoir's *Bal du Moulin de la Galette* a delightful surprise to Cousin Beatrice.

"Oh, Marc, let's buy it!" she whispered to her husband. "Those people look so happy!"

"We'll see," Marc replied casually, hardly interested in spending a single franc on Renoir's "happy" people, his personal taste in art directed more towards the silvery, secretive landscapes of Corot and Courbet which he found far more compatible with the introspections of his own life.

Clearly emerging as Monet's patron that evening, Ernest wore an expression of triumph. "Isn't it marvelous?" he commented to whoever stood beside him. "I have loaned this painting, and yes, also these. Yes, they are all Impressionists. No, these painters are not really interested in submitting to the Salon and probably never will. What do you think of this one?"

If Ernest Hoschede clearly emerged as Claude Monet's patron, Victor Chocquet emerged as Renoir's, and the banker, Gustave Aroso, as Pissarro's. By the end of the year 1877 and through the efforts of Monsieur Aroso, Pissarro would meet Paul Gaugin, who was Aroso's godson. Gaugin, twenty-nine at this time, was a successful stockbroker, well regarded in the confines of the Bourse, and a mere fledgling amateur painter. Through his godfather and during the course of the 1877 exhibition, Gaugin was introduced to Pissarro who would become his teacher and introduce him to Paul Cezanne, the Impressionist painter who would influence him most.

As uncomfortable as the mere thought of seeing Claude in public made her feel, Alice was left no choice but to attend Caillebotte's evening reception as well as the exhibition's public opening the following day, Wednesday, April 4th. Her husband was, after all, the exhibition's most important lender and of course she would be expected to be at his side. Knowing that an encounter with Claude was unavoidable, she had faced both occasions with feelings of dread, but at Caillebotte's reception, once she began to circulate in the exhibition rooms with Ernest, viewing paintings, voicing comments, meeting up with family members and a number of surprisingly complimentary friends, her confidence re-emerged without a trace of clumsiness, allowing for surprisingly cordial conversation when she eventually did face Claude.

"I see you have been working very hard," she said to him from Ernest's side in a practiced tone as she shared a great overabundance of comment and information.

"Congratulations! Monsieur Monet, you have produced a great deal of work, and in a short time, my husband tells me!" she said, her voice suddenly emphatic, her sentences somewhat disjointed, "and I see that the Chateau Rottembourg's white turkeys occupy a place of honor! Well, I never thought I would say this, but the painting is wonderful here. Do you think you will finish it sometime soon? Ernest is very proud of it, proud also, of course, of all your work on the Montgeron paintings. Right now, though, his greatest interest in this exhibition revolves around the pieces he has loaned, and how odd it is to see my own garden and pond on public display through your paintings, my little Germaine too. I must bring her one afternoon to admire herself and her doll. I'm sure you know that another of my daughters is also being seen by the public this spring. Paul Baudry's beautiful portrait of Blanche was accepted by the Salon. He painted it during one of his recent visits to the Chateau Rottembourg, but surely Ernest has told you about meeting Monsieur Baudry just after he finished his wonderful paintings at the Opera for Charles Garnier."

Despite the stress he heard in her voice, she laughed the easy, gentle laugh Claude knew so well. Somehow the sound of it calmed his own feelings of discomfort in seeing her in public with her husband, Ernest Hoschede, the man now so clearly and so publicly his most enthusiastic supporter and the man he knew was anticipating fatherhood for a sixth time. Alice had told Claude about her pregnancy in January, shortly after she had made her announcement to Ernest. Seeing her now, at Ernest's side, he tried not to think about the duplicity of their meetings, the betrayal and secrecy, but it was impossible. He also felt his pulses quicken as he attempted to curb his swiftly elevated feelings of jealousy toward Paul Baudry who had apparently been a guest at Rottembourg and like him, had painted there, likely invited to dinners followed by Jean DeLille's entertaining musicales. His distress aside, he took particular notice of the elegant, very full-skirted black taffeta dress Alice wore, noting the sapphire blue satin lining of its long matching cape which could be glimpsed only when she walked, the intense jewel-like color tone flaring out and swaying in gentle rhythm with her every move. Her dark hair was drawn back just as he remembered she had arranged it for summer dinners at Montgeron. It gleamed in the soft candlelight of Caillebotte's reception just as it had at Rottembourg. Alice's approaching motherhood was most becoming, he decided.

"I understand you have a Paris studio now," Alice bravely remarked, standing before the portrait of Germaine, Ernest beside her.

"Yes, once this exhibition was firmly decided upon I needed to explore new subject material," came the quick response. "The Gare de Saint-Lazare paintings loaned by Monsieur Hoschede were finished there in the Rue de la Moncey studio."

Of course they were, Alice thought to herself. She had seen them at every stage of development, the series of seven finished in a remarkably few weeks and despite the distraction created by her presence, Claude having remained gripped by a dogged determination to complete as much work as possible before the April exhibition.

The conversational farce continued on, the banter almost too easy, Ernest paying no attention at all to Alice or Claude, distracted instead by his own prominence at an event where it seemed everyone wanted to talk to him. Walking slowly side by side and from room to room, the lovers occasionally faced each other in tense silence and quickly looked away, their feigned attention directed to the well-organized display of pictures, their minds diverted by memories with which neither of them knew how to deal.

"The five rooms are divided by panels which cleverly conceal some of the windows," wrote Georges Riviere, the most enthusiastic of the critics. Riviere was Renoir's friend and later would author a book on the artist. He was also a frequent companion on those idyllic Sunday afternoons spent in the small suburban open-air taverns such as that at the base of the old windmill on the Butte Montmartre with views to the river which Renoir had depicted in his painting and where in no time at all the cheap wine tasted like champagne and one could waltz away the afternoon with all the pretty shop girls. Riviere was the one critic who called the arrangement of the Third Exhibition paintings "exquisite."

"The first of the five galleries is hung with several paintings by Messrs. Renoir, Monet, and Caillebotte," Riviere accurately described. "The second focuses on a splendid large painting of white turkeys by Claude Monet, Catalogue Number 53, and landscapes by Sisley, Monet, Guillaumin, Cordey, and Lamy."

The middle room, as Ernest's Cousin Beatrice had discovered and much to her delight, was dominated by Renoir's *Bal du Moulin de la Galette*, Catalogue Number 186, a painting which was, as the tulle and pearl-bedecked Beatrice herself, impossible to ignore, situated as it was, in the central place of honor, Georges Riviere one of its depicted figures. Unwilling to appear unfairly partial to Renoir, in his glowing review of *Bal du Moulin*, Riviere failed to identify himself and the assembled group of figures who were all friends well known to him.

"Oh, Marc, please let's buy it! Please!" Beatrice burst out to her husband once again, both her yellow lace-gloved hands raised in sheer delight. "It would be wonderful in our dining room."

"I don't think so," the monocled, chronically bored Marc Pirole responded, eager to leave the tiresome event and with absolutely no intention of encouraging the purchase of an avante-garde painting of a badly dressed bohemian crowd wasting away a day on the river.

Pierre Renoir's painting of the hapless crowd garnered a good deal of attention and was purchased not by Beatrice and Marc Pirole, but by Gustave Caillebotte who promptly installed it in his Paris sitting room.

The remainder of the middle room was devoted to a large vertical Pissarro peasant landscape: *Le Verger, cote Saint-Denis a Pointoise*, Catalogue Number 163, owned and loaned, according to the catalogue, by M.C. (Monsieur Caillebotte) and later titled *La cote des boeufs, Pontoise*. The remainder of the room was devoted on two separate walls to what one critic called "the dramatically opposite sensibilities of Paul Cezanne and Berthe Morisot." Of the four Cezanne landscapes, two had been painted near Pointoise and Auvers where Cezanne had worked with Pissarro, the remaining two in Provence where he painted in the splendid isolation he was coming to prefer. His *Les baigneurs; Etude, projet de tableau*, Catalogue number 26, later titled *Baigneurs en repose*, received much positive comment. Of Berthe Morisot's *Head of a Girl*, Roger Bally wrote in La Chronique des Arts et de la Curiosite: "Too bad Berthe Morisot has strayed among the Impressionists! Her initial studies miss, the drawing is off, but among her works the tact and feeling for color cannot be denied."

The fourth and largest gallery room contained the work of Monet, Pissarro, and Sisley but in every sense it was Gustave Caillebotte's room. Dominated by his two immense paintings of the *place de l'Europe* in which he showed the new bridge spanning the installations of the Gare Saint Lazare, it also held Monet's seven versions of the Gare Saint-Lazare. Movement and modern urban relationships were everywhere. In sharp contrast to the pastoral landscapes of the second room, this third gallery was alive with exactly those elements Caillebotte's circle of admirers would come to recognize and admire, and not only in his work, but in that of Monet: urban promenaders unhampered by inclement weather, clouds rushing by, winds whipping the Seine, boats at full sail, and trains steaming and puffing in city stations. Caillebotte's *Rue de Paris, Temps de pluie*, and *Le Pont de l'Europe* would be remembered for their size and smooth, silken surfaces. The room in which these paintings were exhibited was the same room in which the public first encountered the white frames for which the Impressionists would become famous, their pale chalkiness long preferred by both Pissarro and Degas to gilded frames.

The last room was filled with Degas and in a short time was called "The Degas Gallery." Several watercolors and drawings by Morisot were included here but all Degas' entries were confined to this area. Degas and Morisot seem to have appealed to the most hardened of critics, but for a time this was difficult for the public to understand since Degas' fat women getting in and out of bathtubs vied with his prostitutes making obscene gestures and contended further with the popular singers he portrayed performing their ditties to a variety of lecherous admirers in depictions of ribald nighttime Paris. These sensitive subjects however distasteful to some viewers were however, brilliantly well-tempered by the presence of *Ecole de danse*, the *Portrait of Henri Rouart*, as well as a number of pastels hanging over monotypes of ballet dancers. Exploring matters of class status and behavior, Degas was now paying attention to clothing, behavior, even posture, the critics noted.

"Degas is a true artist," wrote Paul Chillot in Le Bien Public of April 7. "He is often very imperfect, but occasionally exhibits the signs of a master." Paul Mantz in Le Temps of 22 April wrote, "It is hard to understand exactly why Edgar Degas categorized himself as an Impressionist. He has a distinct personality and stands apart from the group of innovators......."

Overall, the works in the exhibition ranged from enormous paintings to slight watercolors and monotypes. There were landscapes, genre scenes, portraits, and still life, each area represented sufficiently to make its presence felt. With Caillebotte's masterful approach to arrangement and sequence, the viewer was able to compare flowers of Renoir with those of Cezanne and Monet, to do the same with portraits by Monet, Cezanne, Renoir, and Degas, and again the same with the domestic interiors of Morisot, Monet, and Caillebotte. Balance was everywhere: in the city, the suburbs, and the country, each almost equally represented. There were interiors and exteriors, figures and landscapes. There were large and small paintings, all arranged not in a series of traditionally formal gallery settings, but in the rooms of an apartment, a brilliantly innovative ploy which allowed the viewer to easily imagine these works of art at home.

If not entirely convinced they were in the presence of seriously valid art, in the two hundred forty-one framed works shown, critics noticed a new focus and many commented favorably on the reduction in the number of artists represented.

There were only eighteen participants in 1877, compared to the confusing thirty in 1874 and the nineteen of 1876. Monet was the largest exhibitor, represented by thirty paintings, most of which he had painted in the past year. Degas was second, with twenty-five, Pissarro third with twenty-two, Renoir fourth with twenty-one. Sisley came next at seventeen, Cezanne at sixteen, and Morisot at nine. In addition to his Monet paintings and the three Sisleys he had loaned, Ernest also loaned four Pissarros, including the much favored *La pleine d'Epluches*, also titled, *Arc-en-ciel*.

In attendance almost every day and extolling Claude Monet's virtues as if he and not Paul Durand-Ruel functioned as his dealer, Ernest was in his glory. He was, however, competing for audience attention with Renoir's equally enthusiastic patron, Victor Chocquet, an official with the French Customs Service and a staunchly vocal proponent of Renoir. Ernest had met his match with Chocquet who, much like Ernest himself, liked nothing more than to regale an audience with his enthusiastic support of the artists he cared about most, in Chocquet's case, Renoir and Cezanne, but as Ernest was quick to point out to individual attendees and groups alike in rather cringe-worthy moments, "Monsieur Chocquet has loaned a mere handful of paintings to the exhibition while I have loaned more than sixteen, most of them by Claude Monet. There is Monet, standing over there. Have you met him? No? Then let me introduce you. By the way, the woman standing beside him is Berthe Morisot. You know who she is, don't you? An accomplished artist, yes, but she is also Edouard Manet's sister-in-law. Surely you know who he is. Wait until you get to the last room and see Madame Morisot's watercolors and pastels! I own some of her work too. I also own the painting that has named this group of Impressionists, Claude Monet's *Impression Sunrise*. It is my prized possession," Ernest frequently added in addressing whomever he felt appeared only mildly interested in absorbing his freely distributed information. "*Impression Sunrise* was exhibited in the new group's First Exhibition and named them Impressionists," he made it a point to add. "I would like to have seen that fine Le Havre harbor scene by Monet included here, but it seems to be an unspoken rule that these Impressionist paintings are to be exhibited only once. I can't say I fully understand that reasoning. It is not for sale, of course, but if I had my way, *Impression Sunrise* would be exhibited at each and every Impressionist exhibition ever held!"

Ernest's moment in the Impressionist sun of 1877 brought him more personal satisfaction than even he had imagined it could, and when several critics referred to his generosity and artistic taste in print, some by name, most by complimentary inference, he felt he had played an important part in successfully promoting the group of painters in whom he had placed great confidence, particularly his friend, Claude Monet, from whom he had purchased three of the *Gare Saint-Lazare* paintings.

Ernest's euphoric feelings in the days and weeks following the exhibition's closing were not entirely without merit. His contemporaries could now look at him with fresh admiration as in April's wake and in spite of poor sales the Impressionist movement appeared substantially established, its existence if not accepted, openly discussed, its mysterious, elusive style, its common, natural subjects less and less unfavorably regarded, but more than the opinions of Parisians who knew him or only knew of him, history itself was waiting to commend Ernest Hoschede for having purchased and loaned to public exhibition more than a mere few of Impressionism's grandest examples, a total of eleven by Claude Monet. Presently and for the time being, though, the man with a variety of pressing matters on his mind was absolutely devouring the reviews.

"I congratulate its lucky owner," Charles Bigot said in April 28th's La Revue Politique et Literaire of *Arrivee du train de Normandie, Gare Saint-Lazare* (Arrival of the Normandy Train at the Gare Saint-Lazare which Ernest had purchased that past winter. "Among the twenty-nine paintings Monet is exhibiting, seven or eight are dedicated to showing us every aspect of the Gare Saint-Lazare," Bigot went on. "These studies are certainly not uninteresting, and one of them seems excellent. It is the one exhibited closest to the window, at the bottom, that shows an interior of the train station. The number is missing from the frame, but I am told it is Number 97, and belonging to M. Hoschede. This piece gives an accurate, clear impression, is unpretentious, well done."

"About the panel with the white turkeys clucking around on the loud green grass, I will say nothing, not knowing too well what to say," wrote Louis de Fourcaud in Le Gaulois on April 10[th.] "Monet's decorative sense canned be denied, but the painter admits that this panel is not yet finished, and I agree completely."

In Le Charivari of April 11th the irrepressible Louis Leroy wrote, "I come now to the *Dindon blancs*, No. 101. I am not afraid to announce that this is the last word in Impressionist art. These fowl have exquisitely irresolute form. Do not look at them from close up! One breath might send them floating away like feathers. Those fools who convulse with laughter at the sight of them obviously are unaware of the amount of courage it took for the artist to dare to throw to the wolves these creatures so completely outside the order of gallinaceous birds!"

"Great Gods! What will it be when the last brushstroke has been added?" Le Moniteur Universel asked of unfinished *White Turkeys at a Chateau*.

Sadly, Ernest's dearly sought personal validation would not, could not hold. Sadder yet, Caillebotte's well-planned, well-executed and glorious personal success was equally brief, its multitude of commendations collapsed and forgotten well before the warm touches of summer settled into Paris and the city realized it had far more pressing matters on its collective mind than a few examples of Impressionist art.

In May of 1877, the month directly following the Third Exhibition's closing, the French economy succumbed. In the unvarnished face of cash shortages and non-existent sales of paintings, the rebels disbanded once again, each artist going his own way, working independently once again, disillusioned and disheartened, and struggling with greater difficulty than ever to survive. Caillebotte's noble attempt had been destroyed by the times and no further Rue Miromesnil dinner parties were planned to restore the old bravado.

Bankruptcy loomed as the next very real step in Ernest's life and through the remainder of 1877 his difficulties worsened, the euphoria of the Third Impressionist exhibition soon left to memory and those few occasional, private reminiscences of glory on which he called when he stood alone at the top of Saint Cloud's magnificent ruined garden stairs.

"We may have to prepare for the worst," he finally revealed to Alice one afternoon in mid-May where, in the Boulevard Haussmann apartment, preparations were underway for the annual departure from the city, pending doom hardly considerations of a wife and mother whose daily efforts were centered on a long list of family details and whose pregnancy had begun to make itself obvious. The children were excited, Alice herself appeared happy, and in the midst of optimistic plans and anticipation Ernest knew the time had come when he must present the dreadful news and face the consequences before his family was settled for the summer at the Chateau Rottembourg.

"My darling, I have no choice but to tell you that I'm against a brick wall," he began, seated with Alice in his study on a May morning, his voice strained, a pained, anxious expression on his pale face. "I must finally admit to you that the opportunity for recovery just isn't there for us. There is no easy way to say this and I have hesitated to tell you, especially now, when your condition is so delicate, so I'll be as direct as I can."

He stood and walked toward the window. He turned and looked at Alice then glanced away. "I've done all I can do," he stated, his voice unsteady. "Alice, you know that in the past year profits at the store have dwindled, but more than that, now our personal cash reserves are almost gone and in his uniquely pervasive way, Armel Ducasse has worn me down. I have no lines of credit with banks and no further access to private lenders. There is no way to avoid the inevitable. I'm so sorry to tell you this, my darling, but bankruptcy is the next step. I'm afraid this means that the Chateau Rottembourg will be sold within the next months, this apartment too. Everything must go: the furniture, the carpets, the carriages, all of it. Ducasse is arranging for a court date. I've told him about the new baby coming and I have virtually begged him to try to put it off at least until the child arrives, but he remains stone-hearted and blames the inflexible court calendar which is apparently set in stone. I'm so sorry but those are the consequences we must face."

Alice jumped to her feet, her eyes wide with disbelief. It couldn't be. She had not heard those deadly words from her husband. It was a bad dream, a nightmare from which she would awaken. Overwhelmed and completely caught off guard, in an explosive flash of time, like a paper doll crushed and twisted by a reckless hand, she crumbled to the floor. It was as if all breath had gone out of her. Ernest ran to her side. Her eyes were open, but she was pale and very still lying on the dark floor. She looked up at him, took a few shallow breaths, gasped and quickly turned away, stroking at the gleaming dark wood under her with her long, slender fingers and making circles on the floor; slow, perfect circles. After a short while she lay motionless and it was then that she began sobbing and moaning.

"Alice, it's all right," Ernest said to her gently, kneeling beside her. "Cry it out, my darling, but do it here, in my arms. Think of the baby. Please try to calm yourself. I'll send Celeste for the doctor. I can't bear to see you like this, my darling. Oh, I hope you haven't been hurt. Please, God! I'm so sorry my darling, but I had to tell you. Surely you understand that. Alice, please. I need you. Our children need you. Our unborn child needs you."

He forced her to stand and tried to lead her to the nearest chair. She pulled away. He tried to draw her close to him, but she fought him off, her fists beating wildly at his chest, her anger let loose in a tirade of accusations.

"You have ruined us!" she shouted between huge wrenching sobs. "Where are we to go? What are we to do? And don't dare to say you need me, Ernest Hoschede! You need no one but your pathetic, arrogant self!" she blurted out. "Don't touch me! Don't come near me!" she continued to shout, her fists clenched tight, her eyes blazing, her energy suddenly restored. "I hate you! And your children will hate you too!"

"Well, isn't that wonderful!" Ernest lashed out, taking a step back, his own temper flaring. "Now you hate me! For what? For single handedly trying to solve our financial dilemma? For having no control over conditions around me? And what exactly do you think I have been doing with myself these past months? Alice, day and night I have tried my best to save you and the children from harm, but nothing has worked. I have met with bankers, with solicitors, and with every scoundrel and low-life lender known to frequent parts of Paris I didn't know existed before this! The bankruptcy is being forced on me! I have no choice. Do you realize I may spend time in prison? And what, may I ask, have you done to alter your lifestyle and make this easier for me? You have everything you want and so do our children! They can't even tell anything is wrong! No one can! And in the face of it all what do you do? You do what you always do! You think about yourself and your precious Chateau Rottembourg and how your life will change if you lose it. Oh dear, oh dear! What will people say? Alice, I am not the only one in this house who wishes this was not happening, but I face it squarely every day! Every morning I wake up to the conscious dread of what the hours will bring and every night I fall asleep exhausted by my futile efforts. It's a losing battle, but I go on hoping. I go on thinking. I have even taken to what you do so well. I pray! Yes, I ask God to handle this! I beg him to deliver a miracle! As you can plainly see, so far He hasn't listened! It must be too late for me to develop a working relationship with the Almighty! Put in a good word for me next time you're on your knees in that church next door you love so much. My dear, I may not talk about our dilemma here in this house, but you sweep it under the rug where you don't have to look at it or bother about it! Don't you think I've always known that about you Alice? Don't you think I've always known you cannot bear the slightest unpleasantness in your life? And why should you? That Raingo tribe you call a family has trained you very well! But now they can't protect you, not from this, and mark my words, once they know what's going on, they'll turn on you. They'll criticize and find fault. They'll say ugly things about you behind your back. But don't worry. I'll be there to hold your hand and defend you the way I always have!"

Doctor Rinaldi came, and after careful examination determined that Alice was in fine health, the baby also well and developing normally. "There has been no injury to mother or child," he announced to Ernest who waited anxiously just outside the bedroom door. "Fortunately, your wife is a very strong, very healthy woman, but she mustn't fall again. At this point, things are too far along. Take care of her."

A potential tragedy had been avoided, but through that long night there was nothing in the rooms of the elegant Hoschede apartment on Boulevard Haussmann but silence, blame, and the searing pain of emptiness and loss.

Ernest had been denied at every turn. With generous touches of his natural charm and loans provided by his mother and a few friends, Jean DeLille, Julian Raingo, and Marc Pirole among them, he had managed to keep his creditors at bay for an admirable length of time, but now he was cornered and feelings of defeat manifested themselves in conflicting ways. He stopped going to the store, but almost daily his carriage was left waiting outside Durand-Ruel's gallery for longer and longer periods, his one diversion continuing to center on his art collection and the world of art in general. At 17 Rue de Moncey, Alice had found a diversion of her own. Feeling completely estranged from Ernest and embarrassed by the dire financial situation about to narrow her world, with no one else to confide in she had continued to meet Claude in his Paris studio.

At first, in January, they had talked for hours. That was all. They discussed the direction of Claude's painting which more and more often he told Alice was expressing his vision, not so much of art, but of life. He felt he was changing, that he was seeing the world through a wider lens, with a shaper eye, a clearer mindset. Increasingly receptive to his views, Alice began to take greater interest in his work with a new understanding of his connection to natural themes and as never before she began to respect those connections. She complimented his stores of self-discipline and stood in awe of the demands he made of himself. Most often though, they exhausted the nagging topic of the financial dilemma Alice faced, the fate of her beloved Chateau Rottembourg, and what the future might or might not hold for her children and the coming baby. There were tears and shared remembrances and in spite of worrisome times there were generous doses of laughter in those moments when aspects of their respective situations seemed too absurd for serious discussion.

Through winter, their trysts at the Rue de Moncey flat became those of intimate friends, Alice's pregnancy keeping their deeper passions at bay, but the sheer pleasure they found in one another's company and the simple joy they found in the ease of relaxed hours spent together became more and more essential. By late spring, the memory of a chance meeting in Paris at the foot of La Madeleine's sweeping steps in gusts of winter wind had grown to mean much more to each of them than they had thought possible during the previous year's summer months of scented roses, country festivals, and panels being painted for a country house.

"I knew if I saw you after the summer that I would weaken and find a way to come to you," Alice confessed. "I struggled with that thought. I wanted so much to push it away. What happened at La Lethumiere seemed like a dream to me, but it was a dream I knew I had to put aside, out of my head, out of my heart. If only I had succeeded. I've been so afraid, afraid of you, Claude, afraid of myself. What we had last summer was wonderful, but it was far from wonderful for the people we care about most and who care about us. It was wrong then and it's just as wrong now. Claude, we both know it. We must admit it, but here we are, helpless and pathetic in our helplessness.

She knew she shouldn't laugh at their dilemma, but she did, in that easy, soft lyrical way Claude now knew he loved more than any other sound in the world. "And Claude, there's something else. When I'm not with you I don't know what to do with myself," she confessed. "Right now, in my condition and with things as confused as they are, the details of my domestic life are too embarrassing to discuss openly and I don't know what to talk about anymore, even to the people closest to me. "How are you feeling, Alice?" someone will ask. "How am I? Well, I am not very well at all, thank you, I want to say truthfully. I am pregnant, often tired, desperately worried, estranged from my husband, and I stand to lose everything that matters to me. Why, you ask? Because my husband has squandered all our money and is begging complete strangers to help him find a way out of a massive financial dilemma he has brought on himself. And did I mention that I cry myself to sleep at night? Claude, sometimes I think I must be losing my mind. It isn't that I'm not busy enough with the children or that time doesn't pass, but because I don't or can't talk about what is happening, no one understands what all this is doing to me. You're the only person I have. Ernest is living in another world. Sometimes I think he doesn't even see me. Oh, I know he's worried and desperate, but even the prospect of a new baby seems to mean very little to him now. The novelty of an addition to the family has worn off. At this point, maybe he sees it as just one more mouth to feed."

"I know you worry," Claude was always quick to respond, sensitive to the growing despair in the proud eyes that now and then went blank and then lit up again when he came close to hold her in his arms, "but I'm here and I will be here for you always," he assured her time and time again, "but, mon cher, you have a child on the way and you mustn't give in to despair. "It can't be good for you or the baby." Claude's concern for the pregnant Alice's well-being was well-intended, but it was not without its inner conflict. He remembered the passionate hours of late November when after weeks of staying away she had come to him at La Lethumiere. He had counted the months to August when the baby was thought to be due and he had wondered.

Through the weeks of early spring and in hours of candor and inclusion they began to trust one another implicitly. They discussed events of daily life with relaxed honesty. They were entirely themselves, completely at ease together in a world of their own making, Claude's small studio their haven, its modest walls enclosing the tender words of love and devotion that now came often and with little effort. The confinement of the small studio too much to bear at times, they risked discovery by meeting at a remote Left Bank church, a secluded bench in a small, little-known park, anything to reassure themselves that all was well.

Ernest was increasingly distant, Alice often told Claude at these times. He was constantly preoccupied, cold and unreachable, she said, and she was more frightened than ever, haunted now not only by what lay ahead, but by their secret rendezvous and the disquieting anxiety that accompanies all secrets.

Claude was fighting off demons of his own. He tried not to think about his betrayal of Camille and Jean, and although he knew he had fallen hopelessly in love with Alice, his concern for his wife and child and conditions at Argenteuil did not abate. Not too surprisingly, his confusion over these personal circumstances had begun to gnaw away at him. He needed to go home for an extended period of time, he announced one afternoon in May. Soon Alice would be off to Montgeron for the summer with the children he reasoned, and perhaps it was best that neither of them come to Paris for a while. They both needed time to decide what was best for all concerned. Alice said she agreed and that of course she understood, but she really didn't. She had come to depend on her cover, her cloak, her shield. Alone at Rottembourg through the coming summer, alienated from Ernest and without Claude's strength and reassuring presence how would she manage to deal with the upheaval ahead?

The month of May had given way to early June and predictable plans for another summer at the Chateau Rottembourg went unchanged. Unaware of the delicate condition of their lives and excited by the prospect of a new brother or sister, the five Hoschede children eagerly anticipated another long, happy country summer as Alice forced herself to go through the motions required of preparation, but as her pregnancy advanced and plans her confinement were made, she remained fearfully anxious. It was decided that as with the births of Jacques and Germaine, the baby due in August would also be born at Rottembourg. Doctor Cremont, an associate of Doctor Rinaldi, took care of his Montgeron patients very well, Alice assured Ernest.

As always, the trunks had come down from the attic, and on the second floor hall of the Boulevard Haussmann apartment Alice had dutifully folded playsuits, dresses, sweaters, and socks. She had sorted through stacks of outgrown baby clothes and boxes of toys, and she had made her annual round of visits to family members, calling first on Ernest's mother.

"Oh, my dear, you will have a boy, this time. Look at the size of you!" remarked the senior Madame Hoschede, examining Alice from head to toe and air-kissing her from a distance as if pregnancy was contagious. "Now, do be sure to send me a message once the baby comes. Six grandchildren! My goodness! Do you think you'll be up to making the lemon curd this year? I certainly hope so! Of course, you have your babies so easily and recover so quickly. I was in bed for more than a month after Ernest was born. It was a terribly difficult birth. There are days when I still feel the after affects."

Cousin Beatrice was not as irritating. "Alice, are you sure everything is all right? You're out of sorts and look worried about something, and you shouldn't be, not for a minute and not with the baby coming soon," she said, studying Alice closely as the two sat in Beatrice's paneled drawing room and Beatrice poured tea.

"Oh, it's nothing," Alice remarked. "Business at Hoschede's is not as good as it was last year. Ernest is feeling a bit of pressure. It will be all right."

"Financial pressure?" Beatrice asked, her gentle voice touching and reaching Alice in the penetrating way Beatrice had of conveying her affectionate concern.

It was too much. Her nerves raw, her energies exhausted, Alice could not continue the charade, not with Beatrice. Biting her lip and breaking into great, heaving sobs as she felt Beatrice's arms coming around her shoulders, Alice dissolved into a tender, vulnerable woman who had no experience whatsoever with reversals. Beatrice immediately grasped the seriousness of her circumstances and held her close.

"It's a terrible time!" Alice sobbed, "Beatrice we are about to lose everything! It isn't only the store. Everything we own is at risk; the houses, their contents, everything. Your cousin Ernest, has spent us into bankruptcy! We are waiting for an official court date. Beatrice, this isn't the world I want to bring a new baby into!"

"Oh, Alice dear," Beatrice sympathized. "Can't Julian Raingo or your other relatives help? You come from a big family. Surely Ernest has talked to Marc, but I must say that from what he tells me, the bank loans and generous lines of credits he extended with ease not so long ago are now impossible to grant, but I'll talk to him. There must be a way. There simply must!"

"I'm not sure anything can be done at this point, and it's just too embarrassing for me to go to my relatives," Alice sobbed. "You know how they are. They would jump at the chance to gossip and stew like witches over my fall from grace. In no time at all they would exaggerate the details of Ernest's demise and our dilemma would appear even worst than it is. People thrive on that sort of thing, as Ernest has reminded me on more occasions than I care to remember. As for my Uncle Julian, he and Ernest no longer get on well. They barely speak, and my uncle's coolness toward Ernest has affected my own relationship with him. That too has hurt me very much. You know how close my Uncle Julian and I have been. But surely you're aware that Uncle Julian and Ernest have been at odds ever since the birthday celebration when Armel Ducasse interrupted things and ruined the evening. I'm also sure Uncle has told you about his disenchantment with Ernest.

He confides in you." Alice nervously dabbed at her eyes with her handkerchief and sighed.

"Then there's Ernest's mother. Need I say more? You know what she's like. She's not about to provide her son with further loans. He has gone to her too many times as it is and after all these years she still sees me as an irresponsible, extravagant woman. She'd love to see me suffer."

The pressure was building for Alice, but Ernest was also feeling it every day; the frenzied demands, the incessant worry, the exhaustion. He was gaining weight. After climbing a flight of stairs he was short of breath and perspiring. At night he was sleeping for shorter and shorter periods of time and by afternoon he was usually dozing off seated in his chair or slumped over the desk in his study. His clothes were not fitting him the way he liked. He was eating too many rich desserts and smoking too many cigars. Worst of all, with dwindling cash reserves it was difficult now to maintain appearances and continue in his preferred role of free-spending confident man-about-town. At the same time he was becoming irresponsible, now relying totally on staff to conduct every aspect of what was rapidly becoming a waning business base at the store. He avoided certain places, certain people. Jean DeLille became his most frequent, most trusted companion. They often sat in one of the dark cafes on the Left Bank where they knew no one and no one knew them and where DeLille paid for meals and wine.

"Fine state of affairs, isn't it?" Ernest commented to DeLille again and again. "There you are, a great, successful painter with plenty of money in your pocket and here I am, falling apart before your eyes."

His laughter was brittle and bitter, his rancorous tone unbecoming and unfamiliar, the boisterous, irrepressible Ernest Hoschede no longer the pleasant, engaging man DeLille had met three summers before when he had appeared one warm spring day in the studio doorway; handsome, fit, the whole world in the palm of his hand, his easy, charming conversation centered on the delights of houses in the country and the joys of extensive gardens filled with an abundance of specimen roses. Now DeLille was a patient, sympathetic friend to a very different Ernest Hoschede, his own sensitivities deeply affected by the pain and desperation he saw in a man he had come to admire above all others. DeLille's work suffered as a result of his close association with Ernest. Functioning as a near full time companion, he turned down attractive portrait commissions he very much wanted and yet, ironically, he was in greater demand than ever before, offered unheard of sums for his portraiture, the increasingly impoverished Paris nobility more eager then ever to have the most in-demand portrait painter in Paris preserve its grandeur in oil and canvas before all was lost, waiting lists and cost be damned.

"Ernest, pull yourself together!" DeLille repeatedly urged in the Café Pascal, its décor and the quality of its food on a disparaging par with that of the once-again condemned Guerbois. "Your health will fail and what good will that do you or anyone, especially Alice and the children? And there's a new baby coming. You're not the only man in Paris being hurt by this recession. Ernest, wake up! There are hundreds like you!"

"Jean, I have never counted myself among the masses and even in the throes of my declining circumstances I have no intention of declaring, much less considering such a common affiliation. My problems are mine, exclusively mine. I don't care about the others, those anonymous numbers out there. Let them live with their worries. I will live with mine."

He was drinking too much and worst yet, settling for cheap wine. DeLille was appalled. The seamy Café Pascal was one thing, but a sharp decline in personal values was totally unacceptable for a refined man who had traveled to his country house by private train, entertained lavishly, and spared no expense on the best of everything. Soon, wherever they went together, DeLille took to ordering the food and wine before Ernest had a chance to engage the waiter and cajole him into preferential treatment, convinced just after the closing of the Third Impressionist Exhibition and Ernest's triumph as its biggest lender, that the boyish light around him had begun to dim and that Impressionism's great champion, unlike its seven brave combatants, was facing the genuine prospect of personal failure without so much as a hint of the formidable valor that was their trademark.

Undaunted, DeLille faithfully took it upon himself to watch over his increasingly desperate and disgruntled friend, and as summer arrived and the two settled into their respective Montgeron houses, the loyal oversight continued, DeLille's one diversion, the attention continually required of his country house.

Although the tower roof leaked, its windows were in need of repair, and the vegetable garden DeLille had planned with great enthusiasm had yet to materialize, in three summers the Montgeron house he had acquired at Ernest's urging had undergone admirable transformation. Enchanted by the rambling old property which, when he had purchased it was in dire need of countless repairs, many of them more costly and extensive than had been anticipated, three years later the roof of the main house and its extended gables no longer leaked, all the rooms had been painted, the floors had been scraped, sanded and waxed, salvageable old furniture had been reupholstered and refinished, the flower garden had been garnered and re-planted, and the old shrubbery and trees had been pruned and fertilized. Fortunately, the sturdy stone exterior of the house had required few repairs and by the time DeLille's eccentric cousin "Emile, The Banker," as he was addressed by the family arrived for a two-week visit in the summer of 1877, DeLille's baby estate, as he liked to call it, was finally flourishing. A profusion of healthy roses and asters bloomed in the garden, gravel paths and walkways were immaculate and bordered with leafy hostas and red salvia, and shutters and exterior doors were freshly painted in DeLille's favorite cobalt blue. All appeared well maintained and impressively substantial to the fussy bachelor banker, Emile Lamant, who was proud to say he lived in 'nouveau Paris' and upon entering the hallway of his cousin's beautifully paneled country house remarked, "All this on a few portraits! Amazing!"

In late May, Claude said good-bye to Alice and returned to Argenteuil, intending to stay for the summer. He would work at home for a while, he told her in parting. There would be no summer painting excursions and no invitations to Montgeron to take him away, he insisted to Camille and more fervently to himself. Camille made no effort to conceal her delight. Every day, by noon, she listened for his footsteps coming along the path from the garden where he was painting, doing her best as she set out the meager basics of a mid-day meal to smile and ignore the periodic feelings of malaise which had never left her following the loss of the child she had miscarried more than two years before.

The routine and quality of life in the house on Rue Saint-Denis seldom varied when Claude was at home. Each day near noon, settling himself into the chair it was his habit to occupy at the center of the square table in the larger of the two first-floor rooms, he was at ease and comfortably dressed, the blue linen shirt he wore for painting predictably clean but wrinkled, his black trousers neatly tucked into his boots, a strip of brown leather tied at the waist. "Where is Jean?" he frequently asked, reaching for the bread basket.

"Oh, probably out where he always is, by the riverbank," Camille invariably answered, seating herself in the chair across from her husband, her flowered apron covering the long gray skirt she wore every day. "Claude, you always ask the same question. You know Jean loves watching the skiffs and yawls on the river almost as much as you do. This summer, though, he does have two or three friends who come to join him there. They fish for a while and then practice skimming rocks on the water. I'm glad he's with other children. I worry that he's alone with me too much."

"What has he eaten today?" was often Claude's next question.

The answer was as unpredictable as the weather, but on a sun-filled day in mid June, Camille pursed her pale lips and slowly patted the wisps of hair at her temples, her faint smile quickly vanished into an all too serious expression of maternal concern. Her vulnerability touched Claude.

"He had a few potatoes left from yesterday and the last of the milk," she said slowly and in a near whisper. "That was early this morning. He'll be hungry when he comes home. I've saved him what was left of the soup from last night and if you aren't too hungry yourself right now, there should be enough bread left in the basket to fill him up. Claude, we cannot go on like this. Hunger haunts this house. Jean is suffering. He's only a boy!"

Claude closed his eyes, the sparse serving of cold sausages and colder potatoes that had been set before him a stark reminder of the difficulties he was facing. He was out of money again, Ernest Hoschede's only partial December commission payment having vanished into the usual basic expenses of modest living: rent, food, shoes and clothes for Jean, and supplies for himself. Now, six months later, the remainder of the commission Hoschede had promised had not appeared and Claude feared it never would. Making matters worse, results of the sale he and several of his Impressionist colleagues had held at the Drouot following the disappointments of the Third Exhibition had been dismal and once again, woefully embarrassing. Here he was, at the start of another summer and following the hard work of preparing for three unsuccessful exhibitions he faced the same state of affairs with which he'd lived for years. Nothing had changed. The same demands continued. It was exasperating. He was running out of painting supplies again, Jean was growing out of his clothes again, now running barefoot along the riverbank because he had grown out of his shoes, and in spite of visits to a doctor, consultations with a specialist, bottles of expensive tonics, and an endless variety of purgatives and herbal concoctions, his thirty-one-year-old wife was still rail thin and pale as a ghost. Something had to be done. He thought of Alice and her children at the Chateau Rottembourg. He couldn't help himself. He thought of La Lethumiere and its insulating, dreamlike charm. He pictured Jean untying the small red boat from its mooring and taking it out onto the tranquil river. How tempting it was to entertain the thought of a peaceful stay at La Lethumiere with Camille and Jean. And how utterly ridiculous! He forced the thought from his mind and in the following days made the decision to end his affair with Alice once and for all. It was an impossible situation. Nothing but pain and agony would ever come of it for either of them, and after her baby came how would they find the strength to remain merely friends? Here at Argenteuil, Camille and Jean needed him. The summer would heal everything. Yes, he would forget his feelings. He would find a way to force Alice Hoschede out of his thoughts and out of his life. He would be at home with his family where he belonged. Yes, he would paint in the garden. He would produce good work, his best work. He would restore his devotion to Camille and assume the responsibilities of a good husband and father.

In June the grape fern and pink gentian sprouted up along the wide riverbanks at Argenteuil. In July, the myrtle and colorful cineraria shaded the sunny arbors where Sunday visitors escaping the Paris heat paused to watch the regattas. The young couples held hands, enjoying fine, romantic views of the Seine. They talked and laughed and kissed and fell in love, and throughout that summer, in the house on Rue Saint-Denis with its view to the Seine and disregarding the dire conditions of life, Claude and Camille restored the passions of the past. They too talked and laughed and kissed and promised, and every night as the cool breeze drifted in through the open windows facing the river, they whispered and caressed and made love. Camille had never been happier.

The summer months raced past in an idyllic set of hours. Edouard Manet came to Argenteuil to visit and paint, as did Pierre Renoir. Daily life fell into a satisfying pattern. Claude painted and tended the garden, Camille kept house, and Jean fished and played with his friends along the riverbank. The deception of the past was set aside, its secrets hidden, every day its memories driven further and further away with a kiss, an embrace, a promise, a pledge.

In late July, Ernest wrote to Claude. "…….I must delay yet again my payment to you on the sum remaining due on the panels for the Chateau Rottembourg's rotunda. I don't know why you should continue your patience in this matter but since we are friends, I can only hope you do. I am sorry to say that my financial situation has not improved since we last met and discussed our agreement. In fact, conditions have so deteriorated that the Paris apartment on Boulevard Haussmann is being sold from under us. I fully intend to fulfill my obligation to you, but for now friendship is as much as I can offer. I write this so you will know how much I appreciate your splendid work."

In early August Claude wrote back, "……Monsieur Hoschede, I understand how difficult your situation must be. I myself am struggling to survive, but whenever it is at all possible I would appreciate at least partial payment on the sum to which we agreed more than a year ago. You must know that at times it is difficult for me to continue on, especially when I have no sales and nothing about my work satisfies me. I am thinking about moving away from Argenteuil and finding a new place where my work, and as a result my sales, might improve. If I am to move, it must be soon, since Camille and I are to be parents once again. A baby is due sometime in March of the New Year."

Camille pregnant, her fragile health further compromised by shortages of nourishing food, Claude faced the demands of a growing family. With not a single painting sold in months and supplies running out, Gustave Caillebotte was called upon to rescue him once again, which with typical generosity he did. Caillebotte was spending the summer at nearby Petit Gennevilliers. His family's property at Yerres had been sold and he was growing quite fond of the pleasant house he had found at Petit Gennevilliers close to Argenteuil. Its row of lime trees and close proximity to the Seine reminded him of Yerres. It helped that Monet was closeby, that Renoir visited often, and that industrialization had not encroached on Gennevilliers' bucolic riverside setting. Most appealing of all, Gustave was able to keep his sailboats within sight of his garden which he had begun to plant with dahlias, lilacs, peonies, and fruit trees. As the boats he named Whitetail, Roastbeef, and especially The Condor, whose mainsail made of white silk decorated with a heraldic cat were more and more frequently anchored within steps of the flourishing garden, he began to consider residing at Petit Gennevilliers permanently.

At this same time Ernest Hoschede was experiencing no such security, nor was he anticipating any such pleasant residential prospect. The official declaration of bankruptcy looming, the Hoschede world of luxurious apartments in Paris and magnificent houses in the country was turning not only upside down, but inside out. Prior to announcement of formal bankruptcy proceedings which were expected to begin in in August, massive lawsuits demanding substantial and prompt satisfaction had been filed by several claimants whose lawyers prevailed in their pleadings. To satisfy their demands and by order of the court, the Boulevard Haussmann apartment was put up for sale. Its furniture was removed and headed to public auction, the rooms at Number 56 judiciously emptied of their elegant contents, Ernest's favorite chair, the desk in his study, the Raingo clocks, and the bust of Cardinal Richelieu still wearing his green woolen scarf unceremoniously stacked outside on the pedestrian walk and loaded onto open wagons, the beloved possessions of a family awash in debt left unattended and fully exposed to the sunny summer obeisance of all Paris, readily available for any passerby to examine at close hand.

Alice was devastated by news of the pending sale of the Boulevard Haussmann apartment and the loss of its contents. Perhaps as a shield against his own disappointment, Ernest took on a philosophic position, asserting that there was no shortage of luxurious Paris apartments for sale and that when the time came, they would take up residence in one of the best of them. Julian Raingo was appalled, not only by the ensuing loss of Alice's Paris home, but by Ernest's cavalier attitude and utter disregard for the affectionate feelings she associated with it.

"You must divorce this thoughtless wastrel!" he insisted to Alice. "The time has come! He is hurting you, hurting your children, and creating a hellish atmosphere to exist in your lives. It cannot continue!"

"Uncle Julian, I can't divorce Ernest and you know why," Alice interrupted. "I will be excommunicated by The Church and my children will hate me. Besides that, people will ridicule me and look on me with disgust. You know how divorced women are treated. No, there has to be a way for me to maintain my marriage to Ernest with both sanity and a sense of propriety. I don't know how to accomplish that right now, but I'll find a way. Somehow, I will maintain a respectable semblance of family life and preserve my dignity. I simply must!"

Hardly knowing what to expect next or how what the future would hold, at the Chateau Rottembourg, Alice filled her time with the same familiar tasks she had known through all the summers she had spent there. With a heavy heart she routinely met with the gardeners, walked the grounds, examined the flower beds, and played at statues with the children, all the while realizing that the end of life as she had known it at Rottembourg, was coming to an end. Ambitious plans for a new kitchen garden and an avenue of young fruit trees were abandoned. The iron arches she had planned for a colonnade of climbing roses were made and ready for installation just as she had requested the previous summer, but now they waited in the warm sunshine of another summer, leaning against a stone wall and forgotten behind the tool house. Contrary to her every attempt at dismissing Claude from her mind and forgetting their secret past, he was in her thoughts at every turn. What was he doing at Argenteuil? What subjects was he painting? Was he working in his garden? What of Camille? Jean? No, she must stop this, she admonished herself. She had a husband and children. A new baby was coming and soon she would have a myriad of details to attend to.

Throughout early July, a stream of Paris friends visited, none aware of the Hoschedes' expanding difficulties. No longer was a private train provided for their pleasure and convenience, but there were afternoon picnics to be enjoyed at Rottembourg. They were smaller and less luxurious, but memorable and still held in the shade of the stately stand of copper beeches. Dinners, less formal and less bountiful, were now served at a circular table in the rotunda where Claude's panel painting of Ernest standing at the edge of the Senart stood leaning against one wall, the white turkeys leaning on another, the paintings of the pond and the rose garden side by side, close to the stairway.

"We'll be installing them next month," Ernest explained to inquiring guests. "The carpenters I want can't come from Paris until then and I want the molding work done perfectly. You know how I am."

Champagne culled from the shrinking supply in the cellars was poured. Amiable toasts to "la Belle France" were exchanged. DeLille played the piano and sang. Ernest's extensive collection of Impressionist paintings still lined the walls of the center hall and those of the library, but nothing was the same. The gaiety was becoming forced, the conversation hollow and meaningless. Pressure mounted, and under increasingly unpleasant circumstances Alice's final weeks of pregnancy became Ernest's greatest concern. He remained at odds with her and she with him, but under all the harsh exchanges and continuing anxiety, their mutual devotion to the welfare of the coming child was paramount. That devotion, however well-intended, did nothing to alter the legal circumstances overwhelming their lives. During this same time, they were informed that the bankruptcy would be formally declared in August.

By mid-July, it was mutually decided that the family would leave Montgeron and that for a time Ernest would remain in Paris at his mother's house. Alice would take the children and accept Cousin Beatrice's invitation to join her at Biarritz where she would have her baby not at the Chateau Rottembourg as had formerly been planned, but far away from the oppressive mood overtaking the most beloved of her environments. There was no thought of returning to Paris. It was impossible. The Boulevard Haussmann apartment was no longer a viable home. It had been quickly sold, its prestigious location and pristine condition making it highly attractive to several interested parties, its final prevailing buyer a wealthy Paris jeweler. Despite crushing disappointment, one bright factor did emerge. Beatrice and Marc Pirole had bought a large airy summer house at Biarritz, and as one of the only people in the family to sympathize or know the true seriousness of her Cousin Ernest's circumstances, Beatrice had, at Ernest's request, extended an invitation to Alice and the children with typical candor and affection, urging Alice to have her baby there at Biarritz.

"Do come to keep me company," she wrote to Alice from her seaside aerie. "My neighbors are great snobs, and now that the British Royal Family has discovered our beautiful Biarritz, there is no end to the boring receptions, dinners, and ghastly dresses one sees at the Hotel de Palais. I am invited everywhere, but I shall welcome your friendly company and that of those darling children. Do be sure to tell them that they may bring Igor and even take him onto the beach. Rest assured, there are plenty of bedrooms for everyone, including Mademoiselle Gabrielle whose presence will be essential to you and to the children at this delicate time. Alice, dear, I have taken the liberty of speaking to a doctor here who has delivered many infants. He tells me he has contacts with two midwives who assist him, so you and the new arrival can be assured of excellent care. Besides, you will have me to fuss over you. I owe at least that to you dear Alice, for all the patience and kindness you have shown to me over these many years and, I might add, when others have chosen to ignore me. Do write as soon as you can and say you are packing up and preparing to come."

Although the children were reluctant to leave Rottembourg, a stay at the seaside appealed to them and once settled in Aunt Beatrice spacious house with its sunny rooms and views to the sea, their reluctance turned to enthusiasm. Now aware of the disagreements occasionally erupting between their parents and troubled by them, they knew nothing of the true scope of the mounting crisis swirling around them and Alice intended to protect them from news of pending disaster for as long as possible.

Providentially, but in fact because he was worried about Alice and missed his family terribly, Ernest arrived in Biarritz on August seventeenth, four days before Alice showed signs of labor. As he nervously waited with Beatrice and the children in the plant-filled sunroom, the healthy baby named Jean-Pierre was born in one of his Aunt Beatrice's magnificent hand-painted canopied beds on the morning of August 22nd. The very next day, Ernest returned to Paris by train, his bankruptcy formally declared in the French court just one day later, on August 24th. It was only the beginning. As required by law, all his assets were immediately frozen, Armel Ducasse appointed as legal conservator, the disposal of the Chateau Rottembourg and its contents assigned to Ducasse. Ernest was on the train to Montgeron on the afternoon of August 25th.

A few days later and under Ducasse's direction, an army of court-appointed officials swept across the summer lawns and into the rooms of the Chateau Rottembourg, itemizing in their registers and assigning a number to every piece of furniture, every mirror, sofa, chair and desk and bed and table; every clock and book and basket, pot and pan; every tray and bowl, carpet and candlestick; every garden statue, decorative planter, and garden tool.

Ernest insisted on being present during every moment of the time required to complete the Chateau Rottembourg inventories. Cordial and patient as he appeared on the outside, he despised the invasion of strange hands on his possessions. He heard the snickering, the joking, the laughing, the sarcasm. He walked through the slowly disassembled rooms he loved like a dying man, the breathless pain he felt unlike any he had expected to experience ever in his life.

Large cardboard tags were pinned to Rottembourg's beautiful chairs and carpets and to the draperies whose fabrics he had selected with care, the numbers hanging on them scrawled in large black numerals. He wanted to tear them off and shred them to bits. He wanted to shout at the offending intruders and force them out of his Chateau Rottembourg. He wanted to be left alone in the rooms he loved, the rooms Alice loved, the rooms his children had been born to.

Ernest was not a man given to tears, but he had never been faced with a personal ordeal of such overwhelming gravity. Assets confiscated, the Paris apartment sold, the fate of the Chateau Rottembourg left in the hands of a certified auctioneer, the sale of its contents now scheduled to be held on the grounds at Rottembourg over three days, it was cause for grief, and like a man mourning the death of his greatest love, Ernest began to mourn. He wept and lamented and hated himself. He stormed angrily along the garden walks. He cursed and shouted and spat and wept again. Everything would go. Alice would never forgive him. His children would grow up disappointed in their father. They would always think so little of him and he had wanted so much for them. Where had he gone so horribly wrong? What had happened to his undamaged world? He was sure he could feel his heart breaking. Each new morning arrived with a fresh stab of pain that never quite vanished. Each night ended in a throbbing sleepless fog of raging anger and a swirl of haunting questions that found no answers. What could have changed the course of these matters? What could have steered his thinking and led him not to this, but to a positive outcome? What steps could he have taken to prevent this terrible catastrophe? There were no answers. There were no steps, no explanations, no trite, commonplace redundancies. Worst of all, Ernest could see no way to stop the inevitable. When Ducasse and his team of associates left Montgeron for Paris, their reports were formally submitted to the French Court. Along with the completed inventories, Ducasse's precise accounting named all claimants who had filed petitions. It was a long, detailed list of more than two hundred names, all familiar to Ernest, his total indebtedness found to be in excess of two million francs. Confiscated and temporarily deposited into Durand-Ruel's hands, Ernest's entire art collection was to be sold at a future date, also at public auction. Each of his Impressionist paintings along with all other acquired artworks were to be catalogued and offered at public sale, sold to the highest bidder with the crashing slam of an auctioneer's gavel. Adding great insult to greater injury, before the year of 1877 was out Ernest also faced the very real prospect of serving a month-long prison term.

The penalty for declaring bankruptcy in Ancient Rome was slavery or being cut to pieces, the uneasy choice left to the creditor. In medieval France, bankrupt debtors were required to wear a green cap at all times and anyone could throw stones at the offending party. In England, bankrupt debtors were thrown into prison, often pilloried. Occasionally, one ear was cut off. In Ernest Hoschede's France of 1877 imprisonment was a common punishment for a legal declaration of bankruptcy which in itself was seen as a sensible means to liquidate financially distressed companies or individuals and efficiently distribute assets among creditors. Under certain conditions, a French citizen who was a friend or relative of the debtor could meet the debtor's bail, which, depending on the mood of the Justice Tribunal, was not always set. Luckily, in Ernest's case the Tribunal's mood was good and his bail was set at 50,000 francs ($10,000 U.S.), the sum immediately paid by a sullen, but consistently judicious Julian Raingo for whom public family embarrassment such as imprisonment of one of its members was to be avoided at all cost.

Not too surprisingly, no detail of Ernest's debacle had been overlooked by the financially solvent senior Raingo, but since the first incident with Armel Ducasse and as knowledge of Ernest's increasing financial recklessness became apparent, his personal involvement with Ernest remained cold and perfunctory, his readiness with occasional cash advances and bail money accompanied by a resounding lecture as well as a personal reassessment of his niece's marriage to Ernest Hoschede, which he saw as disastrous. More significantly, the elder Raingo's unrelenting insistence on what he saw as the necessity of a divorce between Alice and Ernest was creating a dramatic and disappointing change in his relationship with Alice.

"Take the children and move in with me, or with Beatrice. We would be happy to look after you until some acceptable decision for the future can be reached," he insisted in frequent letters to her as she recuperated at Biarritz. "And the future should be foremost in your mind. Alice, take your beautiful children and leave that irresponsible, wastrel husband of yours. You have invested far too much of your time and yourself on him. How he fooled us! And forget the Church and that Mother Catherine out there in the country. Alice, Ernest Hoschede is not worthy of you! God knows it and I know it. Mother Catherine probably knows it too. Put that scoundrel and all his slobbering about behind you. Divorce him! It wouldn't be the end of the world. Together we can arrive at some satisfactory answer to your future. Forget Ernest Hoschede. Your children and that new baby son deserve more from a father. You deserve far more from a husband."

Alice and her newborn infant together with Beatrice and the five older children left Biarritz for Paris by train on the first Saturday in October. It was decided that for the time being, the five older children and loyal Igor would remain in Beatrice's care at her house on Rue de Rome. When the children asked why they could not return to the family apartment on Boulevard Haussmann which they had no idea was now a home owned by others and emptied of its contents, Alice told them that their building was undergoing a few renovations.

"I will be leaving for Montgeron in a few days," she also announced. "Papa and I have matters to attend to at the Chateau Rottembourg before winter sets in, matters that may require a week or more of our time. I don't know how long I will be away, but Aunt Beatrice will be looking after you in my absence. I'm sure you understand it's best for all of you to stay with her while I'm gone. Besides, she tells me she has planned a few exciting city excursions for you while your Mama is away."

A week after arriving in Paris, Alice and her nursing baby, Jean-Pierre, left from the Gare de Lyon for a final return to the Chateau Rottembourg where with Ernest and prior to the final auction she would see to removing the family's personal belongings as the court had allowed. At the Lyon there were tearful goodbyes and long, loving hugs from all the children. Alice had never felt so torn. Knowing what lay ahead for her children, she could not control her tears.

"Take us with you, Mama! Please!" Germaine cried out at the last minute, reaching up to brush at her mother's tears with her small hand as she kissed her. "We will be very, very good, Mama. We promise! And I can take care of baby Jean-Pierre for you! You know I would be very good at that, but I wish you were taking us to Rottembourg with you! You know we love being there with you! Please Mama!"

Except for schooling, the children and their mother had never been separated. "My darlings, as I told you there is serious family business to attend to right now," Alice responded as brightly as she could, sickened by the realization that her children would likely never see the Chateau Rottembourg again, "but soon we will be all together. Papa and I will come for you soon. I promise we will. Have I not always told you the truth? Now, you must all be on your best behavior for Aunt Beatrice. She loves you and is very good to you, but she is not accustomed to having children around her all day every day, so please, be on your best behavior and try not to make too much noise when Uncle Marc is at home. Eat everything on your plates at mealtime and go to bed on time. Gabrielle will be there with you. You know she loves all of you very much. The time will fly and Jean-Pierre and I will be with you again very soon. I will write letters to you as often as possible."

The children unaware of the true extent of their family's difficulties, Beatrice, true to her promise to Alice, gave off no hint whatsoever that anything at all could be wrong in their lives, but the two older girls, Marthe and Blanche, had heard their parents' arguments. They had felt the strain in the household. They knew something was very wrong and that money was at the root of it, but like the younger ones they had no idea of their mother's true purpose in leaving them with Beatrice. Arriving in Paris, Alice had realized it would be left to her to prepare them for the days ahead. She must do it, and soon. They would be told about everything when she returned to Paris from Montgeron, she decided. Ernest could not possibly oppose such a decision.

He waited at the Montgeron station, relieved, under the circumstances, to see his wife and infant son looking so well. As had been the case with all five Hoschede babies, Jean-Pierre, or Bebe Jean as he was soon called, was a robust, healthy baby with a lusty cry and a good appetite. In the September sunshine and crisp sea air of northern France, Alice had recovered from childbirth quickly and as circumstances now demanded, her energies were quickly tested. There was a great deal to do.

The black iron gates at the curve in the Concy Road stood open wide against the blue October sky. The rows of plane trees along the drive had begun to turn golden. The house stood waiting. She closed her eyes as the carriage approached, afraid to look, afraid of the pain beginning to surge through her.

"They're things, only things, meaningless, small things," she told herself again and again during the last days she spent at Rottemboug, but at every turn, in rooms she had known and loved, while packing the personal items she was being allowed by the court to remove into trunks and suitcases, a terrible guilt swept over her. The feeling that she had failed her beloved mother and father was overwhelming. She had been a daughter of this house. She knew everything about it. Its future had been left in her capable hands. The continuity of family tradition had been left to her. Yes, family most of all. There was so much to remember. Birthday parties in the dining room, wedding celebrations on the lawns, laughter, smiles, profiles in cool summer shade, conversations, hunting stories, events of the day. She thought of Ernest. His hunting, his paintings, his country world of woodlands and moss-covered paths winding between ancient oaks to the beautiful hollow where as young lovers they had kissed. She thought of Ernest standing at the edge of the forest to watch his children flying kites in the fallow winter meadow.

Dismantling the third floor was the most difficult of all the tasks. Beautifully clothed, long-haired dolls seldom disturbed gazed out from beside the dearly loved hairless, chip-faced dolls lined up in a row on the floor, ready to be packed into boxes and stored in Jean DeLille's basement as had been arranged in advance. Their contents removed and also packed in boxes destined for Jean DeLille's basement, cabinets stacked with colored paper, watercolor paints, and color sticks were closed for the last time. A heartbreaking stillness and a silence so alien, so distressing, was left to hang over sun filled rooms once bursting with only laughter and joy. The third floor tasks complete, Alice escaped to her room, flung herself on the bed, and wept.

For a time her one consolation came with the knowledge that Paul Durand-Ruel had been appointed as custodian of Ernest's paintings. They would be stored at his Paris gallery where they would remain until an auction date was set at the Hotel Drouot. It was not so much the collection as a whole that she cared about, but included were the panels intended for the rotunda drawing room which Alice promised herself she would somehow find a way to own again one day. She hadn't thought much of them at all as Claude had begun to create them in August the year before, but now they were scenes of life as she had loved it at Rottembourg and as she wanted to remember it always: the pond, the gardens, and the view of the house in its grassy park where the white turkeys roamed.

"Views of the property!" she remembered Ernest had said he suggested to Claude as they had stepped off the train at the Montgeron station, "perhaps the pond, the rose garden, the view of the house from the meadow. Yes, Alice loves that view."

Drained of energy at the end of every day, the hours she spent dismantling cupboard after cupboard and shelf after shelf dissolved one into the next in a muddle of resentment and exhaustion. Adding to the emotional upheaval she was dealing with, she learned of Camille Monet's pregnancy from Ernest.

"I had a letter from Claude Monet," he remarked, surrounded by the growing assortment of trunks and boxes collecting in the upstairs hall. "Shortly after Jean-Pierre was born I wrote to him to be sure he understood why I couldn't pay what was due for the rotunda panels just yet. He answered promptly. Claude's very good about answering his letters. He was very nice, very understanding in his reply. Things are not going very well for him I'm sorry to say. His paintings aren't selling, buyers are in short supply overall, the usual, but he seemed very happy to let me know that Camille is expecting a baby. Sometime early next year, March he thinks according to his letter. Alice, we should send something. It doesn't have to be anything as grand as a complete layette, but perhaps a christening gown and a nice bonnet from the store."

CHAPTER 23

The Unthinkable

It was over. Clearly, now that Camille was pregnant the affair had come to an end. Without a word being said, the summer of 1877 had changed everything. In August, at Biarritz, Alice had given birth to a son and at some point in the final months of Alice's pregnancy Claude had fathered his second child with Camille. The inescapable fact that he had made love to his wife barely weeks after saying fond good-byes to her in springtime Paris was shattering and for a time forced Alice to question Claude's sincerity, but now, in October, as by order of the French court the ominous consequences of bankruptcy loomed, Alice knew she must take herself in hand, shake off haunting romantic notions, and once and for all set out on a path of firm resistance.

At Rottembourg, she nursed her baby and every day wrote letters to the children. She confined her letters to pleasantries, failing to mention that there was a mountain of work to be done and that she had little help in dealing with the re-organization of a life she now fully grasped would never be hers again. Without the small army of servants she had once commanded, Alice was left quite alone to attend to the final details of gathering and packing her family's personal possessions. In their own complicated way the tension, resentment, and confusion saved her.

Allowed by the court to retain specifically designated personal and household items, she awakened in the early morning and proceeded every day to carefully sort and pack clothing, personal household items, toiletries, photographs, and the children's belongings. Ernest took over the packing of books and the family's collection of table silver including a myriad of forks, spoons, knives, trays and serving pieces of all shapes and sizes. Alice's repeated requests for retention of the Raingo clocks and the beautifully crafted Pleyel piano were denied, but Jean DeLille had generously offered the storage space in his basement for whatever items, boxes, and trunks could not be moved until permanent housing arrangements were made.

Physically and for the most part, Ernest and Alice worked side by side, but the emotional distance between them remained. Together, and chipping away at remnants of a faded life by day, they slept in separate rooms by night, but out of habit, each evening they dined together, seated at the dining room table across from one another in what they both knew was a ridiculous but sincere attempt at preserving some small degree of human civility in a beloved house they both felt was deserving of one last encounter with the grace and dignity it had known throughout the years.

Prior to Alice's arrival at Montgeron, Ernest had sent for Celeste, the Hoschedes' long-time Paris cook-housekeeper and her butler husband, Adolphe who, following the sale of the Boulevard Haussmann apartment, had found themselves both unemployed and homeless. Over the years they had been sent to Rottembourg when additional help was required for special fetes. Familiar with the house and devoted to the Hoschedes, now they were happy to be helpful, agreeing to remain in service for as long as they were needed and without being paid their customary wages.

"You have been very good to us for many years, Monsieur Hoschede," Adolphe had said to Ernest. "You have paid us well and have seen us through illnesses and family emergencies. Now all we want is a room with a bed and a little food every day. We will stay on with you and Madame Hoschede for as long as we are needed. Celeste and I want to help and we can be paid later on when life returns to normal for you."

Now at Rottembourg, Celeste cooked and Adolphe served meals as they always had in the city, but during the dinner hour, even as indulgent smiles and perfunctory remarks were exchanged at the dining room table, Adolphe found it impossible not to notice the ugly shadows of hostility festering between his employers. His demeanor reflected nothing of the disappointment he felt and shared with good-natured Celeste, but day by day, through an entire week, it became increasingly clear that the Hoschedes were walking on tenterhooks with one another, wordless one day, tempers flaring the next, accusations flying back and forth in a steady sweep of anger which by week's end they did nothing to conceal. Throughout the week, from hour to hour, the tension had grown. Again and again, cruel things were said. Two people who had known years of great joy together were becoming strangers. They were hurting each other and taunting each other and as the last of their personal possessions were packed into trunks and suitcases, no attempt was being made at reconciliation. Blame took center stage and at times its assignment grew fierce.

"This is all your fault!" Alice shouted when late in the day the dismantling became too much.

"No, it's because of your indifference!" Ernest shouted back. "You're impossible to reason with! It's the way you were raised! Mustn't talk about matters as mundane and tasteless as money or what things cost; mustn't cut corners on clothes or luxuries for the children. God forbid!"

"You hid the truth from me!" Alice accused. "You sacrificed everything I care about and you allowed my house to be compromised!"

"I protected you!" Ernest blared. "And may I remind you that all thanks to this bankruptcy action, to one degree or another our debts will be paid? I may have to leave the country for a while to save my skin, but doesn't the idea of a clean slate matter to you?"

"Not if it means losing my house! The things in it are just that: things! They can all be replaced, and Ernest, in all honesty I'm glad to see some of them go; yes, very glad, but even with nothing in it the Chateau Rottembourg is my home. It is who I am, who my children are, and as I remember, you, Ernest Hoschede, seemed to find the stage my house provided you pleasant enough."

It was his wild spending and damnable good taste. It was her maddening demand for perfection, her over-privileged background, her disdain for unpleasantness. It was too many guests and it was too much champagne. It was Julian Raingo and it was that vile band of Impressionists. It was Jean DeLille and it was the never-ending renovations at that house of his. The alienation took its toll. Ernest was hurt but Alice suffered most. In the week it took to complete the task of packing and removing the last of their personal possessions from Rottembourg, they both endured painful headaches and bouts of complete exhaustion, but the strain was most apparent in Alice. Her face took on an anxious pallor. Dark circles formed under her sad eyes, and every day the stressful hours grew longer and darker and like a death knell, as the full picture of what lay ahead became clearer and time dragged on, life fell into a desperate pattern of inescapable dread.

The unknown distant future was worrisome enough, but the state of present conditions loomed more ominously than Alice had really taken the time to understand during the past anxious months. Now, judicial calendars having been formally settled, official notices arrived by messenger almost daily, one of particular concern to Ernest. By order of the court, he learned that his art collection was to be disposed of at a public auction to be held at the Hotel Drouot the following June. The news struck him hard. The auction date was eight months away. Although humiliating and painful enough to anticipate for Ernest, it was not the inevitable loss of the art collection that hurt Alice in the rock solid way it did Ernest. It was the additional official notice informing the Hoschedes that in seven months, on May 15th of the following year, the Chateau Rottembourg and its furnishings were to be sold at a public auction to be held on the grounds of the estate itself. With its sale and the final disbursement of its contents just seven months away, Rottembourg would fall into the hands of a new owner and the Hoschede family would have no home at all. The realization was unbearable. The city apartment on Boulevard Haussmann was gone. The store on Rue Poissonniere was being liquidated. Where would they live? How would they manage? Where would they find money for basic essentials? What would the future hold for the children?

Once again, astute, forward thinking Beatrice stepped in. Well aware, through Ernest, of the losses he and Alice and their children were about to endure, on the return from Biarritz she had suggested that Alice think about remaining with her in Paris on Rue de Rome until suitable arrangements for the family's permanent residence could be made. The children would be comfortable, she reasoned. The older ones could continue at school, and she would see to it that the city's many distractions would keep them occupied on the weekends. Beatrice's kind invitation once again gratefully accepted, Alice planned to leave Montgeron for the last time in mid-October and to immediately return to Paris to take up an extended period of residence in the Pirole household on Rue de Rome. There she would join the children and dear Gabrielle who remained an unwavering mainstay, her reliability a great comfort to Alice. Ernest insisted on remaining at Rottembourg through the winter and until the chateau was officially auctioned and sold in May and the public auction of his art collection was over in June. He would see every miserable detail of the debacle through to the end, alone if need be, but more than once he asked Alice to join him and to bring the children for one last season at Rottembourg.

"We could spend Christmas together and enjoy a wonderful winter here," he urged at one point in a rare moment of rancor free air. "Alice, just one last time, all of us together at Rottembourg."

"How ridiculous!" Alice said responded without hesitation. "No! Absolutely not!" she emphasized, her eyes aflame. Once she left, it would be over she insisted, and neither she nor the children would ever return to Montgeron or the Chateau du Rottembourg, not at Christmastime, not at Easter, not ever and not at any time or for any reason!

The physical act of leaving the house she loved was wrenching. Alice had tried to prepare herself for her final departure and she had worked very hard at accepting the fact that she would never return to Rottembourg or the village of Montgeron, but when the last day she would spend in the house at the bend of the Concy Road finally dawned, she awakened hollowed out and desperately sad, her limbs numb, her skin feeling like a mere shell supported by nothing but sheer will. She spent the day dry-eyed and walking; walking through rooms soon to be emptied of their familiar contents, walking through gardens burnished in a blaze of autumn glory, walking under oaks and maples turning bronze and golden in the cooling shade.

Late in the afternoon, as the last of the trunks and suitcases were packed onto the carriage, ready to take her along the tree-lined drive and to the village train station for the last time, there were no tears. She felt nothing. She insisted that Ernest not accompany her to the station, but in Rottembourg's hall and at the last minute, he spoke to her of reconciliation and a new beginning.

"Alice, right now we're going through a terrible time in our lives," he said as they faced each other in tense, adversarial moments. "We're angry and sad and we say things to each other that we really don't mean, but when everything is over, and one day it will be over, we'll begin a new chapter. Once all this nasty business of official notices and public auctions is in the past, I intend to re-establish myself and put things back together. We'll be happy again. I promise you that will happen. You and the children will be fine with Beatrice for the time being, but you must understand that your stay with her is temporary. While you're waiting I'll be organizing my affairs and pursuing new projects. I may open another store or an art gallery, or both. I'll also be looking for a house, a large, lovely property in the country where we'll be able to forget all this pain and take up our lives as a happy family again. You probably should assure the children of those prospects. They may be feeling anxious and disoriented right now. They need to know there is a happy future to look forward to. You need to know that too. Say you do, or at least say you'll try to look ahead with optimism. Alice, you and I can be happy again."

Seated alone in the carriage, her baby wrapped in a blue wool shawl as Adolphe drove her along the gravel drive and toward the gates, she was like one of the motionless statues she had enacted with the children on the lawn in summer sunshine, a pale mask drawn across her face. She had heard the words Ernest had spoken in Rottembourg's once welcoming hallway but she had offered no response. There was no good-bye to him, no fond thank you to loyal Celeste, but from the front doorway both Ernest and Celeste stood to watch the carriage moving slowly down the drive. It paused and halted twice. The first time it came to a slow halt Alice could be seen stepping out to stand in the cool autumn breeze, her baby son in her arms. She looked up to the sky, the way we look up to the sky at a cemetery when a loved one has died. The second time, the carriage stopped at the short path to the Church of Saint Jacques where holding Jean-Pierre close to her heart, Alice walked along the path, entered the church, and knelt to pray before saying her last good-byes to the golden chapter in her life which was now nothing more than a young memory.

Through November, Ernest wrote to Alice and the children, but he was not seen until Christmas Day when he appeared at Beatrice's door. Full of smiles and cheerful holiday greetings, he carried an armful of presents. There were games, puzzles, and books for the children and a box of lace-edged white linen handkerchiefs for Alice. For Beatrice there was a box of the cherry-filled chocolate candies he knew she loved. Although brief, the holiday visit with his family was pleasant. Alice was polite but distant. She had no gift for him, but in the hopes that their father would come, the children had made a booklet of pencil drawings for him. Held together with a length of thick red yarn, it was a collection of sketches they had made of the fanciful benches and statuary they knew he admired in the Parc Monceau. Alice could not help but notice the great fuss they made over him. They missed having their father in their daily lives. Germaine and Marthe broke into sobs when he left. Blanche, Suzanne, and Jacques quickly escaped to their rooms. The older children sulked for days, a clearer picture of what the future might hold forming in their minds.

Having postponed the inevitable for too long, her excuses increasingly feeble, since leaving Biarritz Alice had made only vague references to her bewildered youngsters regarding the dire financial circumstances the family was facing and the reasons for their stay with their Aunt Beatrice. In past months they had noticed instances of thrift and had overheard discussions regarding money, but the time had come for honesty, and in January of the New Year Alice called the children together in Beatrice's library. With frequent catches in her voice, she revealed that the family's money was gone, that there were large debts to pay, and that in order to do so the Chateau Rottembourg and everything in it was to be sold the following spring. Summers would no longer be spent there. As expected, her simply stated announcement was met with shocked disbelief by five trusting youngsters who immediately broke into tears, some angry, some deeply crushed, all broken-hearted.

"But why? What has happened to our money? Mama, you must be mistaken! Rottembourg is our home! We love it there! You love it there! No! No!" were the tearful cries ringing loud in Alice's ears as she made every effort to comfort her children and calm them. Struggling to find the right words when she needed them most, she tearfully gathered her beloved children as close to her as she could, and in long, despairing moments she would remember for the rest of her life, she hated Ernest as she had never hated another human being.

"Papa has had a bad year at the store. Business has not been good and there are many big bills to pay," she explained, wiping away her tears and trying to soften the blow. "There is great value to the Chateau Rottembourg and it must be sold in order to pay those big bills. Right now, Papa is very busy attending to all the things that must be done to finalize things, so we will be staying on with Aunt Beatrice until he straightens everything out. It will be just fine. Blanche, Marthe, Suzanne, and Jacques will continue at school and the little ones will be here with Gabrielle and me."

"But where will we live in the summer now?" Germaine demanded, her dear, tear-stained face a mask of uncertainty. "Will we stay in our house in Paris all the time now?"

"No, my darling, we will find a new house to stay at in summer, and I'm afraid I must also tell you that the apartment in Paris isn't ours anymore. It has been sold."

"Then we have no home at all!" Suzanne cried out. "Everyone has a home!" she went on in disbelief, her lovely young face filled with an anguish Alice had never imagined she would see there. "What about our things, our clothes and toys and books, our furniture and pictures?"

"We will have a home!" Alice quickly interrupted. "We will always have a home! You are not to worry yourselves about that for a single minute! We are a family! These arrangements with Aunt Beatrice and Uncle Marc are temporary. Papa is looking for a wonderful house for us right now. It could be in the country or it could be in the city. I don't know where it will be, but it won't be long before he comes to tell us all about it. He will work everything out. He has promised, and you know that Papa will not disappoint us. And as for your things, I have taken care of all that. I went to Rottembourg to pack up all our personal belongings; the clothes, toys, and books, even the linens and some of the china and kitchen utensils. For now it's all being stored in the basement at Monsieur DeLille's house, but I did bring what I thought would be most important to you. The furniture and carpets and pictures are another matter. Those must be sold too. For now I think you have everything you need and if you find you are without something important to you, please remember that we cannot expect Aunt Beatrice to take all our things as well as all of us into her house, but make no mistake. We will have all our personal things as soon as we have a new home. Don't worry. Papa will find a fine house for us with lots of room. He's working on that right now. You know that Papa loves us very much and that he will always take care of us. You must remember that. We must be patient and pray for him every day. Promise me you will pray, even when I don't remind you. Now, let's put aside all our worry and concern aside and live only with light and love in our lives. I have always believed that unpleasantness puts limitations on us and everything we want to do, so we must do all we can to be happy and productive every day no matter what comes our way."

Alice had provided her children with the ray of hope each of them would hold close to their hearts. At the same time, her choice of words in explaining the family's misfortunes echoed Ernest's understanding of his wife's disdain for unpleasantness. Clearly, Alice was possessed of a talent for looking the other way when facing life's trials, and although with her children she had succeeded in calming their fears as she explained family circumstances and emphasized the happiness they would know in brighter days ahead, her own level of hopefulness was another matter.

Alice realized that she and her six children could not continue to live with Beatrice and Marc for an indefinite period of time, but if they left the Pirole house on Rue de Rome, where would they go? Where would the money it took to support them come from? Would she be able to rent a house and buy food and clothes for six growing children, or could it possibly be that as Ernest had said, he would indeed be able to put things back together and restore his family's lives to what they were? But how would he finance a new business venture, a new family home and all related expenses? Private bankers and lenders were not granting loans or lines of credit and even if they were, Ernest's reputation was in tatters, but just as he had said to her, perhaps he really was determined to somehow reorganize himself and establish a new, lucrative career. It was true that ownership and management of another department store and perhaps an art gallery would be perfect projects for him. They could provide substantial incomes, but what of the personal issues between them? In past months had they gone too far with hurtful accusations and unrestrained hostilities to restore the devotion and intimacy of the past? Were their wounds too deep, too raw, and how could the rancor and deception they had lived with for so long be set aside as if it had never happened? A new house and a new career did not guarantee happiness.

But for occasional visits with Alice and the children in Paris, Ernest remained at the Chateau Rottembourg throughout the winter months and into spring of 1878. As the weather warmed and spring returned, the children begged to go to their father at Rottembourg, just for a 'little visit,' as Germaine put it. Alice wouldn't hear of it. The ties to Rottembourg had been permanently severed.

The hoar frost came late that winter. The gardens at Rottembourg were strangely green well into mid-November. So was the Senart where Ernest hunted every day. It was only when the days grew bitterly cold and snow fell that he stayed indoors reading, enjoying his art collection, and writing to the children from the library fireside. His letters to them were cheerful and reassuring, and exactly as he and Alice had agreed they must be, they were also candid and honest. Alice, herself, remained equally straightforward with the children, her repetitive explanation of personal circumstances constantly tinted with the same hopeful optimism Ernest readily displayed. Her attitude now, as in the past, served as a steadying influence and with her careful guidance and steely determination, her children were led through a painfully difficult period in their young lives, accepting worrisome circumstances as best they could, but always anticipating what they wanted most: the happy day when they would be told that a new family home awaited them and that their lives with their parents would return to the well-remembered, happy days of the past.

In his letters to them, Ernest openly expressed great regret at the loss of the Chateau Rottembourg, but their lives as a family would soon improve, he insisted. "There will be another house in the country and another set of happy years," he assured them. In the meantime they must continue with their school work, obey their mother, and they must always remember how very much he loved them, each and every one.

During lonely winter afternoons his defeat and the impact of his losses an accepted reality, Ernest turned to his art collection as never before. Awaiting the inevitable fifteenth of May when Rottembourg would slip out of his hands and the subsequent June dates during which every piece of his art work would finally be sold, an obsessive study of his Impressionist paintings ensued. Long, soothing hours were spent admiring the remarkable strength of color and subtle delicacy of extremes evident in the admirable scope of creative talent he had assembled. There were periods of deep introspection and brooding and always, elements of surprise.

Examples of mood and style were closely noted. Comparisons were made. The intimate warmth of Morisot's interior studies stood in sharp contrast to Pissarro's complex hints at landscaped loneliness. Sisley's detailed, cool reserve in portraying the industrial environs of Paris became increasingly profound, particularly in the paintings of the great machination at Marly which had made possible the complex water system feeding the great soaring fountains miles away at Versailles. He felt Renoir's great human reach in faces and figures caught in unsuspecting personal moments, and try as he might to grasp its source, he remained baffled by Monet's startling appetite for the physical world and his ability to paint its air. Not for a moment did Ernest's Impressionist paintings lose their hold on him. Every day, they fed his wilted spirit, their mysterious impact seductively unresolved.

Through the early months of the New Year of 1878, he sank into an isolated, largely predictable existence but unlike most prisoners, he was not unhappy. He reveled in his solitary entrapment, locked as he was, in Rottembourg's splendid hold, Celeste and her husband, Adolphe, his only human companions and the only servants left to tend the house, their two cats the last remnants of Rottembourg's once extensive household menagerie of four dogs, five cats, an assortment of short-lived singing canaries, and the aging parrot, Veronique who, at Jacques' repeated urging, had been taken to Paris on the train in her green cage by indulgent Adolphe and deposited into endlessly tolerant Beatrice's hands, Veronique's vocabulary soon appreciably extended to include a frequent 'Mon Dieu! Mon Dieu!'

The Montgeron house that not so long ago had employed more servants than any other in the village was now left in the care of two devoted custodians. Unpaid, but having no home of their own and very much wishing to remain in at least one of the two Hoschede houses they had known and lived in for years, Celeste and Adolphe, continued to do their best in maintaining the high household standards upon which Alice had insisted. They knew that a long period of difficultly had begun for the family they loved and had faithfully served for years, but they managed to fulfill the requirements of their remaining months at Rottembourg with typically high spirits and uncompromising levels of professional service. Every day Celeste cooked and Adolphe served Ernest's meals at the dining room table. Economy remaining paramount, Celeste baked bread, prepared simple soups, and once weekly managed to gather the ingredients for enough chicken and vegetable stew to last for three days. Together, she and Adolphe attended to

Ernest's personal and domestic needs. They washed his clothes, starched his shirts and attended to bed linen. They swept floors and kept the furniture polished. In February they nursed Ernest through a nasty cold and in March they endured his two long episodes of intestinal upsets.

Comfortable in his small house near the river and doing what he could to deal with the entire Rottembourg landscape without assistance, the head gardener had stayed on for reasons similar to those of Celeste and Adolphe, but the houseman, Bernard, and Daniel, the gatekeeper, had been let go, the friendly welcome of his barking dogs a thing of the past, Rottembourg's impressive black iron gates now left unattended and open to the sky, its immediate roadside landscape sadly unkempt.

There had been no ritual raking of fallen leaves that past autumn. By the time May arrived and the ancient oaks along the roadside were bursting in tall columns of fresh, spring promise, at the open gates of the Chateau Rottembourg and all along the drive the red squirrels scampered and played in neglected mounds of dull, clustered leaves, enjoying the absence of annoying barking spaniels and daily human interference into their hitherto forbidden springtime antics. Life was not quite as playful for the Monets.

Debt piling up by January of 1878, forced to leave the house at Argenteuil by their out of patience landlady, and rescued once again by Gustave Caillebotte, Claude quickly and out of necessity moved his family to the Quartier de l'Europe in Paris. The address at 26 Rue d'Edimbourg was to be temporary, he insisted to Camille and Jean. They would be there only until a more suitable country village could be found, but it was in the house on Rue d'Edimbourg that on March 17th Camille gave birth to her second son, Michel. It was a long, difficult birth and Camille was not recovering well, but in the weeks just prior to Michel's arrival a suitable country village had indeed been found and shortly after the baby's birth the Monets moved yet again. The upheaval of two moves in a short time and adjustment to a completely unknown area took a further toll on Camille's already seriously compromised health, but Claude had found his village. It was Vetheuil. Much farther from Paris than Argenteuil, it was situated on the narrow road to La Roche-Guyon, but in its remote setting it was providing an invigorating procession of fresh subject matter for a newly inspired Claude Monet.

At first he painted every day, enthusiastically attracted by the panorama of the picturesque village and the Lavacourt riverbank, but he also worried and fretted. Camille was failing before his eyes and there was no money for a doctor. He needed help and advice. He had to sell some work. In the hope that Durand-Ruel would once again advance him at least a thousand francs, carrying three paintings he boarded the early morning train at Mantes and arrived in Paris on the last day of April.

For some reason, he always felt better on The Street of Pictures. Its personality inspired hope, mainly due to the sight of pedestrians walking in and out of the galleries and shops, which in spite of the economic hardships of the times, was encouraging. Leaving the Gare de Lazare he had reached crowded Boulevard des Capucines and turned at the odd jog in the pavement onto Boulevard des Italiens, increasingly optimistic with every step. Durand-Ruel would like the work he had brought. He was sure of it, he told himself, turning onto Rue Laffitte and its unforgettable view to the columned Cathedral of Notre Dame de Lorette in the distance. Yes, it had been a good idea to move to Vetheuil. These paintings he carried would prove that. Occupied with more positive thoughts than he had experienced since baby Michel's arrival, much to his surprise, upon entering Number 16's gallery door, he saw Ernest Hoschede engaged in conversation with Monsieur Durand-Ruel. He paused at the threshold. Perhaps he would return later. He was in no mood to see Hoschede. The unexpected sight of him stirred old feelings, old regrets he had sworn to put aside and forget. But no, it was inevitable that they would meet up sooner or later and it was probably best here, in an environment where he felt comfortable and where his work could divert personal conversation.

Hoschede was animated and almost jovial, Claude noticed as he approached. His smile was broad and cheerful, his voice as resonant as Claude remembered, but profiled against the carmine red walls and as Claude drew closer, Hoschede appeared tired. He had gained weight, but his face, although fuller, had not changed much at all in the course of the difficult past months, news of which had begun to filter into insider café conversations. Hoschede's well-proportioned features were still impressively dramatic and the added strands of silver hair only added to his distinguished good looks, but in the subtle interior light Claude noticed the old brightness was missing from his brown eyes. The strain of his debacle was taking its toll.

"This is remarkable!" Durand-Ruel said with a warm handshake. "We were just talking about you, Claude. Congratulations on the new baby!'

"A fine son, we hear!" Ernest added. "Good news travels very fast in Paris these days. There's so much of the bad."

"It looks as if you've brought me some paintings," Durand-Ruel noticed. "Good, and yes," he added. "I will be happy to take them. You'll be needing a few extra francs for that addition to the family, but first tell us, how are Camille and the new baby?"

"He is a fine boy, my new son," Claude said smiling, an unmistakable note of fatherly pride in his voice. "We have named him Michel. He is doing well, but his mother is recovering slowly. We moved to Paris in January and then to Vetheuil shortly after he was born in March. All of it may have been too much for Camille during a delicate time. On most days, even the smallest tasks with the baby or the house require great effort and exhaust her. Our neighbors and landlady do what they can, but they have families and homes of their own to look after. I do what I can, but like most men I am not always sure it is the right thing."

"Can you write to a relative?" Ernest suggested, eager to be helpful and carrying more than a touch of guilt for delaying the payment he owed Claude. "Perhaps a niece or cousin in Le Havre could come to stay with you and Camille and help for a few weeks? Surely there is someone."

"Monsieur, my Le Havre relatives were not at all receptive to our marriage," Claude admitted. "I doubt any of them would come to help with its fruits."

"I'll talk to my cousin," Ernest offered. "I'm seeing her later today. She may know of someone. Beatrice Pirole has friends all over Paris. I'll let you know. We'll try to work something out for you."

Later that same day, Ernest visited with the children in Beatrice's drawing room. Marthe and Blanche were quiet and withdrawn, but Suzanne, Jacques, and Germaine were as talkative as ever. They had been to a marionette play at Teatro Niele and acted out several humorous scenes for their father. Alice was on her way from her room on the second floor when she overheard Ernest telling Beatrice about Camille and Claude's baby son. "I saw Claude Monet today," she heard him say from the stairway landing where she paused. "He has a new studio on Rue de Vintimille, just around the corner from Rue de Moncey. Says it gives him a good place to finish new work and see his friends. He also has a new baby son. They named him Michel. He's doing fine, but it sounds as if Claude's wife, Camille, is not recovering as well as she should. They moved to Paris at the first of the year and then, almost immediately after the baby was born in March, they moved again, to Vetheuil I think he said. It could be that the two moves so close together were too much for her. Beatrice, do you know of a woman who could stay with them and help with the baby for a while, perhaps one of the ladies who buys those feathered boas and outrageous hats from you at charity bazaars? One of them might need the money, especially now. Of course, we want someone kind and reliable and I'm afraid you'll have to take on the monetary arrangements, but I promise I will settle with you as soon as I can. I haven't paid Claude in full for the panels he did at Rottembourg and I feel obligated. If you could find someone and pay her for a while it would be a great help to me in setting things right with him until I'm on my feet again."

"I'll see what I can do," Beatrice said to him with a light chuckle. "I don't know exactly why, but I've always had a soft spot in my heart for you, my dear Ernest. I'll find someone. Don't worry."

Alice returned to her room without seeing Ernest. Her heart was racing. When Jacques came up to tell her Papa was waiting to see her, she said she had a bad headache and needed to lie down.

A baby boy. They had named him Michel. Claude had deliberately created a new life. He had found a new village, a new home. He had seen a brave new dot on the horizon as only he could see it. He had said good-bye to her that past spring and he had found secrets in colors and redemption in an untouched land and it was far away, far away from places they had known together. He had been searching for something new. He had needed an anthem, a song, a cathedral bathed in winter moonlight. She understood what he had done and in mere minutes the quietude and peace she had demanded of herself were no match for her inner turmoil. Claude had fought off his own images and haunting memories of the past just as she had. He too had searched for ways to look ahead to the future, but he had succeeded where she had failed. He may have triumphed over his guilt by creating a new life and finding a new home, but how could he have triumphed over the power of their bond? He couldn't have forgotten. She hadn't.

She was a stupid, foolish woman, she told herself. Claude Monet had inflicted great pain on her by fathering a son with Camille while like a caged bird she had remained prisoner of their precious, dangerous moments. But he was in Paris that very day. Ernest had seen him, had talked to him. He had brought work to Durand-Ruel. Why else would he have been in Paris? He was working and the work must be to his liking. He would never have come to The Street of Pictures otherwise. His new home must be providing the new subject matter, the fresh interest he had sought. She was a mass of contradictions. Anger and disillusionment returned, as did emptiness and an inescapable longing for the half-heard music of an afternoon when poignancy and pride walked hand in hand and twilight came to blanket fear and destiny. In an instant the categories of hard won peace and benediction were blurred by excuses and forgiveness and the luster of vanished hours. She had to go to him, had to see him, watch him, listen to his voice, listen to him telling her about his new world.

The first-floor studio at 20 Rue de Vintimille was not far from the former Rue de Moncey studio address and once again the rent was paid by Gustave Caillebotte. Carrying a basket of coconut macaroons baked that morning by Beatrice's cook, Alice appeared at the door on a warm, sunny afternoon. Claude was caught completely off guard.

"Un pendaison de cremaillere," (a housewarming present) Alice announced brightly in the voice that could still sear through him. "I wanted to be among the first to congratulate you on your new studio. I trust your work goes well here."

"Merci, Madame," Claude responded cautiously, "but I wasn't expecting anyone today. I'm working and things here are in a state of great disarray."

He was afraid to allow her beyond the threshold. The studio was in the same pristine order upon which he always insisted, but he feared his own weakness. He feared what the sight of her stirred in him, feared what he knew her beautiful nearness forced him to want so desperately. He even feared the beautiful white cape that cascaded from her shoulders in deep, sheltering folds. It reminded him of the cloak she had worn when he had seen her descending the steps of La Madeleine the year before. The becoming silhouette was just as spellbinding. Defenseless and sustained by their mutual resistance to the troubling events of life around them, in seconds they were in each others arms. Nothing had changed. It was as if no time had passed, but there was much to say, much to discuss and remember. Amid tears and laughter and the joy of reunion, in the following days they trusted and talked and ignored the danger. In forgiving, re-awakening hours and awkward as it was, Claude felt he must say something, however feebly, to Alice about the past year's events: his new life, his new home, his new son.

"I was forced, as a result of unpaid rent and other failed monetary obligations, to move out of my Argenteuil house in January," he explained, "and much sooner than I could prepare for. I had no choice but to bring Camille and Jean to Paris. We were about to be put out on the street. The Rue de Moncey studio was much too small for a family expecting an addition in March to live in, so on a snowy January day and with Gustave Caillebotte's financial help we moved into a rather nice third floor flat he found for us at 26 Rue d'Edimbourg in the Quartier de l'Europe where Michel was born on March 17th. Two witnesses signed the certificate of Michel's birth at the Town Hall of the Eighth Arrondissement, my good friends Edouard Manet and Emmanuel Chabrier. As a result of my friendship with Manet, Chabrier has started an art collection and at Manet's suggestion he purchased three of my paintings shortly after Michel's birth for three hundred much needed francs."

There would be a number of sharply contrasting events in the lives of Alice and Claude as spring turned to summer, but the strength of their secret love would remain an anchor. Claude continued to paint and to wait for sales that never came. The Grand Paris Exposition Universelle of 1878 had discouraged efforts to mount an Impressionist Exhibition that spring and without an exhibition venue and the opportunity to sell, Claude's sales were suffering badly, as were those of his colleagues. Attracting vast crowds to the Champs de Mar and the Trocadero Palace, the Grand Exposition forced even The Salon to postpone its annual exhibition, a tantalizing detail of life that absolutely delighted Edgar Degas.

"At last, justice!" he harped in the mirrored Athenee. "Not the complete justice I seek, but justice nonetheless. If only postponement could lead to cancellation!"

Living in Paris during the early winter months of 1878 and as Ernest had faced his demons alone at Montgeron, Claude had found new subject matter not only at Vetheuil, but at L'Ille de la Grande Jatte, a charming island he had often admired from the train out of Paris to Argenteuil as it crossed the Asnieres Bridge. Close to his Rue d'Edimbourg address, la Grand Jatte had been handily reached over the Neuilly bridge. Setting up his easel at the eastern end of the island, one of the views he had painted in several canvases depicted the area surrounding the Courbevoie bank through the woodland. He was distracted only by the Grand Exposition and its immense success.

To celebrate that success, General MacMahon, the French President, decided to make June 30th a National Festival Day. There would be parades and street festivals and to motivate citizen support, residents of Paris were encouraged to decorate their windows and doorways with flags and bunting for the occasion. Their enthusiasm resulted in an unprecedented city-wide display of the red, white, and blue French national colors. Huge, happy crowds took to the streets, proclaiming with immense pride the solid state of the Republic, its flag proudly unfurled from countless flagpoles and adorning countless neighborhood windows and doorways in swags, pleats, and fans. Claude loved it. He loved the purpose and passion. He loved the color and the pride. How wonderful it was to live in Belle France!

The narrow streets between Les Halles and the grand Paris boulevards were home to the cloth trade. Claude knew that most of the red, white, and blue bunting had been made there, in the warrens of shops employing hundreds of workers where Rue Mandar connected with Rue Montorgueil. He painted the joyous Rue Montorgueil scene he witnessed on the 30th of June 1878. Intrigued by the same celebratory spectacle on Rue Saint Denis, he created *The Rue Saint Dennis, 30th of June, 1878*.

Somehow, later in the summer, Ernest Hoschede would find one-hundred francs to purchase Claude's Rue Saint Denis painting. A few days later, he would sell it to Emmanuel Chabrier for two- hundred francs, his one hundred percent profit a small, but personally rewarding triumph over an event that was about to change his life.

As in the past at Rue de Moncey, Alice and Claude met at the Rue de Vintimille studio, their affair continuing through long, passionate winter afternoons and into spring, their comfort with one another, their need for one another so routine, so natural, that they grew careless.

Ernest arrived at Claude's studio door unexpectedly one afternoon in late April, his intention in coming to Paris to see Alice and his children, and then to let Claude know that his cousin Beatrice had indeed succeeded in finding a capable young woman who was willing to look after Camille and the new baby at Vetheuil. Her name was Lisette. The details of wages and requirements having been worked out between Beatrice and Lisette, all that remained was for word to be sent to the young woman as to the expected date of her arrival at Vetheuil. Ernest was immensely pleased by his role in this helpful development and even in the face of the approaching auction date of May 15th which was little more than two weeks away, boarding the train for Paris at the Montgeron station he looked forward to presenting his good news to Claude.

In anticipation of an increase in summer travel, the April train schedule had changed, allowing for greater flexibility in Ernest's plan to travel into the city and extending the length of his one-day visit to Paris by more than two hours. By leaving Montgeron at eight in the morning instead of ten, he could now plan to arrive in Paris earlier in the day and if the trains were even close to being on time he could spend at least two additional hours with the children. Pleased by this prospect, he decided he would take them to the Parc Monceau for the afternoon. They would sit together in the sun on a facing pair of the fanciful lion-legged benches by the fountain and there they would enjoy a simple vendor's lunch of ham and hard cooked eggs wrapped in cornets of brown bread with perhaps a chocolate savoyarde and a sugar stick or two afterwards. They would listen to the strolling musicians as they lunched and later they would watch the baby ducklings embarking on their first outings across the lake. Returning the children to Alice and Beatrice by four, Ernest estimated he would have just enough time for a brief visit with Claude before racing to the Gare de Lyon to board the day's last train back to Montgeron.

He arrived at 20 Rue de Vintimille shortly before four. There was no answer to his repeated knock, but when he turned the knob, he found the door unlocked. Calling out Claude's name, he slowly opened the door and walked into a scene for which he could not possibly have been prepared.

The room was small. It smelled of freshly made coffee. A few canvases were randomly scattered about the walls and under the two windows. Two easels held paintings in progress. Neatly arranged on a table were several stained palates, brushes of all sizes, and numerous bladders of color. Alice sat cross-legged close and barefoot beside Claude on a wine colored sofa. She wore a blue robe loosely fastened at her waist. Her hair was tousled and fell in long cascades around her face. Claude immediately jumped to his feet.

"What is this? What are you doing here, Alice?" Ernest asked in a shocked dull voice. There was no reply, only deadly, wide-eyed silence.

"I cannot believe what I'm seeing," Ernest said flatly, suddenly desperate to escape, to turn and run away from the unbelievable scene as fast as he could.

"I wondered why you weren't at Beatrice's when I arrived today," he called out over his shoulder as he blindly reached for the doorknob. "She said you'd been away the entire afternoon. The children are waiting for you, Alice. The baby needs you. Surely you know that!"

Standing alone outside on Rue de Vintimille he was a man attacked as if by the blows of a thousand hammers. He felt a scream welling up inside him. He swallowed hard. His head was pounding. Tears stung at his eyes. He had no sensation in his legs. When he did begin to move, he staggered, his steps stiff and labored. At the corner of Place de Rigaud he hailed a carriage and directed the driver to his mother's house on Rue de Courcelles. Unable to discuss the truth of the day's events, he told her he needed a glass of cognac.

"Is it money again?" his mother asked, pouring the cognac from a decanter on the sitting room's sideboard. "My son, you look terrible."

"Yes," Ernest lied. "Yes, Mamma, it's about money. And it's about bankruptcy and bad friendships and my inability to control anything at all in my life anymore, not even my own wife."

"What did you expect?" the elder Madame Hoschede emphatically asked. "That Belgian was born to a bottomless pit of money. She has no stomach for the problems that come with difficult times. She has spent you into the poorhouse, hasn't she."

The reasons for her dear, long-suffering son's agonizing financial failure revealed to her only weeks before, the elder Madame Hoschede was now gloriously consoled by the convenience of blame. She assigned a blizzard of condemnation not only to Alice and any living human being so unfortunate as to bear the name,

Raingo, but also to anyone and any thing she could name as having had the slightest negative influence on the hideously embarrassing events her son now faced. It was Armel Ducasse and it was Beatrice Pirole. It was Paul Durand-Ruel and it was Alice. It was the store on Rue Poissoniere and it was the Chateau Rottembourg, but it was also the times, the economy, the politics, the newspapers, the cafes, even the Church, and in particular, the Archbishop. Alice's affair with Claude was as yet unknown to Honorine Hoschede, but like his mother, on that night when crushing secrets of his personal world weighed on him and overtook all other concerns, Ernest too fell into the infected realm of blame. Through a sleepless few hours, lying on his bed in the darkened room he had known since boyhood, blame and its assignment became his noxious basis of perception. Blame protected him from himself. It comforted him and soothed the raw edges of his bleeding heart as with his reliable talent for personal solace he decided that Claude Monet bore the greatest blame of all. He was a thief! He should be arrested and jailed for the rest of his life! He had stolen what was most precious from the man who had worked hardest at buying his work and securing his reputation. He had betrayed his own wife and son. Seething with anger, Ernest left his mother's house and returned to Rue de Moncey well before midnight. Alice had left Claude's studio immediately after Ernest's unexpected appearance and having fallen into a fitful sleep on the sofa, Claude was shaken awake by the loud pounding at his door.

"Is Alice here?" Ernest blared into the darkened room as he crossed the threshold and slammed the door behind him.

"No, she left shortly after you did. She was very upset," came a voice from out of the dark. "Please, let me light a few candles."

Illuminated in candlelight, Claude could see Ernest's face masked in ashen anger, his eyes ablaze with sheer hatred. "Alice was upset you say? Was she now? "Was she really? And what about you, Monsieur Claude Monet? How upset are you? And who do you think you are to come into my life and conduct a relationship with my wife?" Ernest shouted, his voice dripping sarcasm and bitter accusation as mere inches away from Claude's face he blared. "It began at Rottembourg, didn't it? Of course, it had to have begun there. Yes, in the beauty of the countryside you profess to love and along the gardens and paths and riverbanks you so admired. Yes, there in Mother Nature's bountiful lap where you found a lovely woman often alone, feeling vulnerable and uncertain, friendless perhaps, and abandoned, the beautiful chateau she loved at risk. Oh, I see it all too clearly now! I hired you to work, to paint, that's all! But you came into my home and plunged into the center of my beautiful life. You took advantage of my hospitality! You befriended my children! And like an immoral, penniless thug without an ounce of decency, you deceived me in the most hateful way! Monet, I willingly supported you. I encouraged your every pitiful effort. I gave you money and stood by your side when no one else would, and this is the way you thank me? I swear, if I had a sword with me right now, I would have you pinned against the wall and I would be taking pleasure, yes pleasure in watching you die. Understand this, Claude Monet: you are never to see Alice again! Do you understand? Never! Whatever has happened between the two of you is over and so is my association with you!"

With no argument to make, Claude endured the tirade he had fully expected would come. Ernest Hoschede was behaving exactly as he should, he told himself. He was a husband shocked and deeply insulted, but he was also a man in a wild rage of hurt and anger.

"I agree completely with everything you have said to me," Claude stated quietly in the dim light of the studio where hours before he had made love to the woman who was married to this raging man. "You are right to condemn me. You are also right to say that I have behaved in the worst possible manner toward you. I have deceived you and I have betrayed my own wife, and children. I am well aware of my great fault in this matter. You can condemn me no more than I have condemned myself, but you must believe that I did not go to the Chateau du Rottembourg to create anything at all like this terrible breach. Monsieur, you have been kind and more than generous to me, but what happened came about in the most unexpected way. Neither Alice nor I understood what was happening. She was a friend, the wife of a respected patron, but she was a woman needing support and affection during a very difficult time in her life. I was there and I wanted to help, but our friendship and my regard for Alice quickly developed into a closeness neither one of us has really known how to handle. I'm almost glad to have it out in the open with you. Alice must feel the same way. Will you see her later?"

"That is none of your business!" Ernest exploded. "My dealings with my wife are my concern and my concern alone. Just remember what I have told you, Claude Monet! Stay away from Alice. She is my wife and the mother of my six children! Yes, my six children!"

Having said to Claude what he had wanted to say, what needed to be said, Ernest suddenly assumed a surprising level of self-control. Perhaps the great dilemma he had lived with for so long had prepared him for yet one more terrible layer. Now he had to see Alice, but it was very late. He returned to his mother's house where he sat alone in the dark on a drawing room sofa while his mother slept soundly in her room, fortifying himself with several glasses of mellow brandy. Stepping out of the hired carriage onto Rue de Rome early the next morning he paid the driver and looked up to the rooms he knew Alice and the children occupied. Nothing was about to stop him from holding his family together, not an affair with a pitiful impoverished painter, not a bankruptcy, not an auction or any court action in the world. Alice was his wife and the mother of his children. She had lost her place for a brief time and had taken up with a struggling renegade artist, but he loved her and it was over. He would forgive and forget. So would she.

"Claude Monet won't be needing anyone to help at Vetheuil after all," he announced to his cousin Beatrice as in a bright blue dressing gown she poured steaming hot coffee into two cups and avoided asking what the reason for his sudden visit could possibly be at what she considered to be this absolutely primitive hour of the morning.

"I very much appreciate the arrangements you have made, my dear, but he tells me Camille won't be needing anyone now. She is feeling much better, but thank you Beatrice, and please thank the young woman for me," he said, heading toward the stairs. "You never disappoint. I don't know what I would do without you. Of course, to tidy things up you'll cross the girl's palm with a little silver, won't you? I'll make it up to you."

"No, I won't be dismissing the girl, Ernest," Beatrice interrupted. "Alice needs more help with the children, especially now with the new baby. She and Gabrielle have their hands full. Poor Gabrielle is running up and down the stairs from morning to night and getting thin as a rail. I'll hire Lisette to help her, and I'll take care of her wages. You and I can work things out later. Go on upstairs. You want to see Alice. Frankly, I want you to see her too. She looked terrible when she came back from wherever she went this afternoon."

Alice sat by one of the windows in the second floor sitting room. Looking up to Ernest as he approached, she said, "Sitting here I watched you paying the carriage driver. I heard your footsteps on the stairs and I was sure I would be able to find the words to explain things when you walked through the door. Now that you're here in this room with me I'm afraid I don't have the explanation I know you've come for. Ernest, I truly don't know what to say to you."

"What was the allure? Tell me that!" Ernest demanded, his voice a block of ice. "I need to know. That will be explanation enough. Was it loneliness or boredom or the dwindling cash reserves? Was it too much time on your lovely hands at magnificent Rottembourg while I was away in Paris, racing through the city every day, dealing with lawyers and bankers and doing all I could to hold life as we've known it together?"

He walked to the window and turned to face Alice squarely, his voice a stream of acid as he leaned close and looked into her eyes. Silent tears rolled down her cheeks as she looked up at him, but for the first time in all their years together he didn't care about Alice's sadness or pain. "Or was it the thrill of making love to a man so far beneath you, a man so in need of elevating himself and his station that you took it upon yourself to become his entrée into a better world, perhaps introduce him to finer things, better people, an elevated view of life as you, yourself, have seen it and lived it with me?" he fumed at her, his rage intensifying with every acidic word. "What did you think would come of all this? Alice, I've always though you to be a responsible, intelligent person! You have children! A newborn child! I don't understand. Help me to understand!"

Alice looked away and gazed to the clouded gray sky outside the window. When she turned to face Ernest once again, her voice was filled not with the remorse and tearful pleas for forgiveness he had expected and wanted to hear, but with an element of secure acceptance and a calm reserve for which he was completely unprepared. "I know what you must think of me," she said, "and Ernest, I'm so sorry to have hurt you this way. I really don't know quite how to put it, but I suppose the simple truth is that you were never there when I felt more alone than I have ever felt in my life. There at Rottembourg, alone with the children, I was terrified and felt isolated when words like bankruptcy and court action and auctions came into my life. You thought nothing of those words, and when you were at Rottembourg you refused to talk to me about what they could mean to us until it was too late. As a result I had no way of telling you that I didn't know how to handle what I saw coming. From day to day I didn't know what was happening to the world we had known and especially to the secure world I had lived in and loved all my life. That must sound very spoiled and selfish to you right now, but Ernest, everything was falling to pieces around me. I didn't know what the future would hold. If worse came to worse, where would we go? Where would we take the children? How would we live? So much went unspoken between us. So much went wrong. Oh, you came and went, Paris to Montgeron and back again, and of course I knew why, but you didn't seem to care that I was frightened and worried. You ignored me when I needed comforting. I begged for your attention, but you shared nothing with me. You didn't trust me to listen or try to understand. You didn't make me part of things. I had to learn the truth by reading documents. I know I've always seemed to you to be a strong, confident woman, capable of handling any crisis, but for the first time in my life I wasn't that way at all. I was alone with the children, hiding the truth from them and tortured by worry every day. Claude became a friend, someone to talk to and confide in. From the beginning, he understood that part of me that needed simple companionship. Please believe me, that's all I expected it to be, nothing more. But, Claude listened and didn't judge. He didn't criticize or ask questions. He is a decent, thoughtful man, Ernest. He lives in a world very different from the one you and I have known, but you are wrong to think I encouraged him to elevate himself to meet higher standards. His standards are higher than mine, perhaps higher than yours. He has nothing; he owns no fine house, no private train, he has no money, often no food, and yet he is rich beyond words. Under circumstances you and I have never known until now he not only survives, he thrives. Of course he struggles and doubts himself at times, but he is equal to the struggle. He believes in himself and every day the components of his world revolve inside him like the steady workings of a clock. Yes, exactly like one of the clocks I've loved and am about to lose thanks to the ruses of folly and carelessness. And Ernest, right now I don't blame you for any of that loss. I certainly played my part in spending too much and caring too little and running away from unpleasantness just as you've said. Unfortunately, as a woman who was well taken care of all her life, I now understand that I have a lot to learn about the real world, but I'm not afraid, not anymore. Claude has made me see things I've never seen before; simple, uncomplicated, very ordinary things that don't require elaborate explanations and that make me happier than I have been in a long time. He also understands the part of me that will always need protecting, not materially and not with useless material things, but here, in my heart, where the most important part of me lives. Someday he will find the success and satisfaction he craves. I'm convinced of it. He has all the tools at his fingertips."

The color had drained from Ernest's face. "You talk about this man as if you love him, as if you admire him, as if he has cast a fantastic spell over you, as if I am less than he is, as if I have been completely insensitive to your feelings and failed in the most important aspect of my life! Alice, this is ridiculous! Claude Monet has a wife! Two children! You're overwrought. You don't know what you're doing or saying. I think all this trouble in our lives has been too much for you. It's been too much for me! And you're right. I see that now. I shouldn't have protected you the way I did, but I didn't want you involved in all the terrible turmoil I was facing every day. I have too much pride. I wanted you and the children to go on with your happy lives, nothing changed, nothing lost until I found a solution, and I was absolutely sure I would. You must believe that. Now I see I was wrong. It went on for too long. It's been too much of a strain, too much of a burden, and I suppose because I was so busy, so frantic, I didn't realize how deeply you were being affected, but my darling, the worst is almost over. Just a little longer and we can put this behind us. We're strong enough to do it. I want to. I know you want to. Alice, you are my wife, for God's sake! Nothing and no one can come between us!"

Alice rose slowly from her chair, her tear-stained face pale and drawn, the tone of resignation in her voice impossible to ignore. "Ernest, can't you see what has happened? It isn't only that we are losing money and houses and everything in them. It isn't even the humiliation and embarrassment anymore. Ernest, somewhere in the middle of all this I have lost myself. Every day when I look in the mirror I see a stranger, a woman I don't know. She wears my clothes and brushes my hair. She eats my food and takes my baths and sleeps in my bed and I have lost heart for holding on to that woman. She doesn't exist anymore. She died somewhere along the way, perhaps on that terrible day when I was the one to tell the children the truth. It was a dreadful day Ernest, and you have never asked me about it, not what I said or how the children I love more than anything in the world reacted to the news that both their homes were gone and that our lives would change. Suzanne summed it up best when through heartbreaking tears she said, "But everybody has a home!" Ernest, right now the children may not understand why life has turned on us this way, but they're strong and bright and I intend to help them handle the difficult days ahead. I do envy you, though. You manage the unknowns in life better than I do. I just don't sail the choppy water as skillfully as you do. I don't know how. I never learned to let myself float while the uncertain tide takes me with it. Ernest, I need to go away. I want to be able to breathe again. I want to recognize that woman in the mirror again. I want to be free of all this confusion and dark dread. Claude tells me there is a house available near his at Vetheuil. I would like you to lease it for me. He says it is not what I'm used to, but he assures me that it will comfortably accommodate the children and me, at least for a while. Ernest, I want to be away from Paris and Montgeron and all the uncertainty around me. It's getting much too difficult for me to be here, facing people. There's already too much gossip about us in Paris. No one knows me at Vetheuil. It's a small village. Please understand."

"Understand? No, I do not understand! I will never understand and I will not agree to this ridiculous suggestion of yours!' Ernest shouted, his face suddenly red with fury. "A house near Claude's? At Vetheuil? With my children? It's out of the question! No, you and the children will not be living anywhere but in Paris with me! We'll manage somehow. This is insanity! What has happened to you, Alice? I'm beginning to think I should call for a doctor."

Alice stared directly into Ernest's face. "I'm saving myself! Can't you see that? I'm saving my children! That's what is happening, and I'm begging you to help me. Please, Ernest!"

He wanted to vanish, to disappear like a thin vapor of smoke rushing up into the soft faraway clouds, never to be seen again. He closed his eyes. He saw rapid images. They streamed in a straight line, one unrelated frame of life fading into another. The children played with their dog. Alice danced in her wedding dress. Alice played the piano. Alice walked in the garden. Alice lay warm in his arms.

"Do you love him?" he asked in a hushed whisper.

Alice didn't answer. She returned to her chair by the window and began to sob.

"Answer me, Alice! Do you love him?"

He stood at the window, looking out. It had begun to rain. He gazed down to the wet pavement below. The corner flower vendor had taken shelter under her green and white striped canopy and had begun to cover the bright yellow jonquils bunched into its corners with a length of canvas.

"I stood at the window of our apartment on Boulevard Haussmann waiting for *Impression Sunrise* to be delivered on an afternoon exactly like this, almost at this same time of year," Ernest said quietly. "It was raining very hard, but there was a flower vendor across the street with bunches of bright yellow jonquils just like those poking out from the corners of that cart across the street. It was too early in the spring, really still too cold for street vendors and flower carts, and yet the sight of those yellow flowers made me think of the coming summer at Rottembourg and all the wonderful things waiting for us there. Our life was good then, wasn't it Alice?"

Before eight o'clock on the sunny morning of May 15th, from one of the Chateau Rottembourg's third floor windows, Ernest watched the first waves of curious spectators making their way up the gravel drive. He recognized many of the faces. There was the thief disguised as a collector, Jean Rouillard, and at his side the famous international antiquarian, grizzle-bearded Charles Bourdon, who like many of the serious bidders eager to walk away with his treasures, had traveled from Paris to the Chateau Rottembourg by train or carriage with the sole intention of vying for the Raingo clocks. Scores of eager Paris agents, dealers, and shopkeepers followed in the next hour, but the early morning crowd was mainly made up of strangers who arrived as if prepared for a country festival. They came in family groups, armed with picnic baskets and small, shouting children. How he hated them all, those dealers and agents and anonymous legions of early morning descending like vultures to look and leer and rob him of his furniture and carpets and the collection of Raingo clocks of which his Alice was so proud. He hated the husbands in striped shirts. He hated the wives with flowers on their hats and smiles on their faces. He hated the children most of all; hated the way they gaily tossed their red and yellow striped balls back and forth across his children's lawns. They set balloons adrift and played noisy games of hide and seek while their parents reclined in the springtime shade under his magnificent beech trees, awaiting the official bell that would signal their first opportunity to enter the rooms of his fine house, inspect his fine things, make their comments, pass their judgments, and before returning outside for the start of the first auction session, perhaps catch just a glimpse of the bankrupt man-about-town, Ernest Hoschede, himself.

Contrary to expectation, if people expected to see a broken man, they were severely disappointed. Promptly at ten, as the warning bell sounded and the public bidding began, a handsome, a smiling Ernest Hoschede dressed in hunting clothes and freshly polished boots left the privacy of the children's third floor, descended the two flights of stairs, flung open the three sets of drawing room doors, and strode down the wide steps of his terrace, assuming the role of amiable, celebrated host. He moved slowly through the crowd, greeting and joking with avid bidders and casual observers as every tangible shred of his life with Alice and their children at the Chateau Rottembourg began to slip away, one precious piece at a time.

His eyes attentive to watching one after another of the treasures of his entire household placed on the sacrificial altar that was the auctioneer's red brocade-draped block, no one could have suspected the true degree of his suffering, but under Ernest's gallant façade surged the most scorching pain he had ever known. He thought of Alice and Claude as now, outdoors, in unforgiving sunlight and first to be set onto the auctioneer's crimson damask-covered guillotine was the small inlaid table at which, after a late night, he and Alice had often shared a mid-morning breakfast. Next to be executed on the auctioneer's guillotine was the spectacular silver tea service he had given Alice one Christmas when life was perfect. Not trusting its care to one of the housemaids, Celeste herself had taken particular pleasure in keeping it's every piece gleaming. Charles Bourdon, the dealer who had sold it to Ernest, succeeded in buying it back, and for a higher price than Ernest had paid. Next to go were the Bellone carpets, the piano, and the three-tiered serving console from the dining room, a particularly treasured possession because at meal times it's six intricately carved legs had been used to teach the youngest, smallest of the children to count. Thereafter, there came a parade of assorted chairs, settees, desks, tables, and at the end of the morning session, the children's nursery furniture, their finely hand-carved walnut beds, their gaily painted wooden soldier, their rocking horse and yellow banded nursery plates, their pictures of mountains and lakes, and finally, the five, hand-woven willow play baskets from the hall's long center table which Alice had refused to take, each one labeled with a name. Marthe. Blanche. Suzanne. Jacques. Germaine.

The dispersal of the Raingo clocks was the most painful loss of all, twelve examples of the Raingo brothers' clockmaker art quickly sold at the end of the afternoon session, the bidding spirited, the final bids predictably high. Individually, each of the clocks was a work of art but as a collection of twelve pieces they were magnificent, displayed as they were one after the other against a long length of blue damask on the bare, green grass like fabulous jewels. Again, Bourdon prevailed, acquiring, in rapid succession and in a matter of highly spirited minutes, eight clocks. But for the nature of items, the same wrenching scene was repeated relentlessly through the course of May 15th, a day during which not a drop of rain fell, not a shred of curiosity waned, and although from hour to hour the faces changed, not a fraction of the crowd seemed to thin.

Until the very last moment, Ernest prayed for a miracle. It never came. Only heartless memory and painful doses of remorse were left to haunt him. So much was being sacrificed, but most difficult of all to face was the dreaded suspicion that after this demanding experience certain things might never be. What had happened to the bright arc of hope that had followed him all his life? Where was his place in the world now? What was left for him? Permission? Refusal? Courage? A succession of failed attempts to reinvent the past? Would he really find a way back? That was the fiery torment. Right now it was the end of life as Ernest had dreamed it and lived it, but could it also be the end of future dreams, future desires?

"Jean DeLille!" he called out in a decidedly booming voice during the first morning session to the Montgeron friend and neighbor he recognized as the only man in a sea of ladies in large hats gathered to examine and assess the quality of his garden statuary. "I thought all my neighbors were politely staying away," Ernest remarked with a broad smile. "I hear that some of you are referring to this auspicious event as an art auction. Considerate of you, and kind, but Jean, I know you entirely too well. You have come to provoke bidding wars over Alice's clocks. Or is it one of my red chairs you're after?"

"Guilty on both counts!" DeLille confessed, striding briskly towards Ernest, greatly disturbed by the day's events and at the same time hoping his own smile would conceal the mounting sadness that had begun to churn at him. It was difficult to see the Chateau Rottembourg's idyllic privacy being overrun, sacrificed, and destroyed so mercilessly.

"I want at least two clocks, and I also want at least one of our chairs!" DeLille further confessed, his smile becoming a great pressing weight forced against his face. "And once they are mine, I shall be delivering them back to you free of charge. It is the only reason I am here, but Ernest, I really want to know that you, my friend, are bearing up under all this," he added with a great warmth that did not escape Ernest's notice. "You really shouldn't be here. You should be miles away, with Alice and the children."

"No, Jean, this is exactly where I belong right now. I deserve every bit of this torture. Alice certainly thinks I do," came Ernest's admission, a vague smile on his face as looking into his friend's eyes he searched his own heart for answers. "Today, DeLille, I am a hated man in my family! Alice blames me for everything, and she should. I am an ass and a bungler of the worst sort!"

"I cannot imagine such a thing!" DeLille quickly asserted. "Alice can't possibly wish you any more blame than you've piled onto yourself. Both of you have loved this place too much for that."

"We've had quite a time here, haven't we Jean?" Ernest mused, looking toward the house. "I wish we had it to do over."

"So do I," DeLille returned, his eyes sadly clouded. "I feel privileged to have been a part of those good times. It was like a dream to me, but I'm concerned about you, Ernest. I want you to get through this and go on to a new chapter in your life. Perhaps you don't see it right now, but that chapter is there. Concerned as I am about you, though, I hope you know I couldn't live with myself knowing that a perfect stranger could be in possession of our historic chairs! How many chairs in all France have had such a grand time holding such distinguished posteriors? None! I'm certain of it! You are too!"

"I wish I could give you the chairs myself," Ernest said hesitantly, "but right now the court seems to be in control of my distinguished posterior. "Jean, you must promise me that you'll keep my wonderful chairs somewhere in that charming house of yours if you prevail in the bidding, which I have a feeling you will. I won't be needing them. God knows where I'll be living, probably in some cold, cheap garret somewhere. All this is of the past, but I'm coming to terms with it. Truth be told, I may miss the piano most of all. The Pleyel is a prize. And weren't we getting rather good at the German masters, especially Beethoven? Our mistakes were almost unnoticeable last time. I don't believe old Ludwig would have been too offended. Must have been the wine and that great brandy! By the way, that too has been confiscated. Can you believe it? I should have taken all the alcohol I could carry out of there to your house! I should probably have consumed most of it with you too, but there was so much to do. DeLille, bankruptcy is exhausting! I don't recommend it at all."

Both men laughed once again, recalling the happy hours they had spent at the Pleyel and that seated side by side at the gleaming ebony piano in the rotunda drawing room they had played duets; Beethoven and Beginners Basic Bach, but after generously poured glasses of wine at dinner and several brandies following dessert, they remembered how they had also danced and pirouetted up and down the polished rotunda floor, singing bawdy ballads and dancing like stars at the Folies Bergeres. DeLille had always provided the finish to their complex choreography, rushing to the piano to play an appropriately loud and highly spirited finale of chords while watching Ernest spinning himself into the seat of one of the red flowered chairs closest to the piano, both his arms extended in mid-air.

Ernest had doubled over with laughter at these times, shaking his head in disbelief at the simple perfection of his partner's pianistic skill and his own graceful ballet dancer finale. Simplicity had always been difficult for Ernest, a small fact to which Jean DeLille gave considerable thought as the next day, when the Chateau Rottembourg's final auction session was over and he was alone at home, proudly seated by his fireside in one of the hard-won Hoschede chairs for which he had gladly bid too much and examining with great pleasure the porcelain dials and bronze mounts on each of the two Raingo clocks he now owned, not at all surprised to see close up that they were of precisely the exquisite quality and fine workmanship for which Alice Hoschede's Raingo family had become duly famous. How he wished that Alice had been there to see Ernest during those two terrible days. Painful as it would have been, and in spite of her embarrassment and resentment, she would have seen her husband at his best, a man broken in spirit, disappointed in life, hating himself, but outwardly in control of an impossibly difficult situation and committed to seeing it through to its bitter end with his famous schoolboy smile.

By mid-afternoon on that final day at Rottembourg, once the last wagonload of unsold carpets and trunks full of unsold porcelain and glassware had disappeared into the indifferent horizon and everyone had gone, Ernest closed the Chateau

Rottembourg's heavy front door behind him and walked slowly through the empty, silent rooms of the house which not so long ago had been filled with a daily cacophony of marvelous noise; with children's laughter and a barking dog, with footsteps on the stairs, a call here, a shout there, the screech of a parrot, and the thousands of daily clangs and peals and blares that feed the soul of a family and speak of its loyalty and love.

His footsteps echoed along the naked spaces. His slow pace resounded against the bare walls. Even freed of furnishings and in the unforgiving light streaming through windows shorn of all their draperies, every room was immaculate, he noted, as if an invisible team of capable hands bearing brooms and mops and beeswax had just that morning swarmed through. Celeste and Adolphe had indeed managed well. Just days before, tears in their eyes, they had left Rottembourg to take up new employment in a household at Chalandry, but their years of care and attention could be seen everywhere. The floors shone and the windows gleamed. Not a single smudge or scuffmark was to be seen. So well-maintained was the Chateau Rottembourg under their care that now, completely emptied of its contents, its only blemishes were to be found on the walls, in the many small gaping holes tracing the places where his paintings had hung.

His eyes swept up to the ceilings and across the emptiness of rooms now freed of their spectacular contents. He leaned against one of the dining room walls and everywhere, he saw Alice. Alice in her beautiful gray tulle dresses. Alice coming toward him in the hall. Alice chatting with guests at the dining room table. Alice in candlelight, on the terrace, on the stairs, Alice in sunlight, Alice in his arms. It was in their bedroom at the end of the second floor hall where the final, searing magnitude of Rottembourg's loss struck him hardest. Left on the floor in a forgotten heap was the fringed green shawl Alice had often gathered around herself for naps on summer afternoons. Ernest gathered it up, kissed it, and falling to his knees, sobbed uncontrollably into its generous folds.

The embroidered Hoschede world of springtime lilacs and summer roses was gone. For just over 120,000 francs the Chateau Rottembourg had been sold, passed callously and in a chilling instant, like so much ash and fallow meadow grass, to a new owner who would soon come to know its every splendor; its fine rooms and halls, its wide sweeping terraces and spectacular views, its September brake fern turned yellow and bronze against purple shadows of cooling hillside vineyards, its flocks of nesting starlings, sparrows, and white turkeys scouring the stubbled woods of the Senart, its vast summer skies suffused at twilight with sparkling bursts of warm pink sunrays, its loyal heart broken and forever scarred by memories Ernest had convinced himself would forever remain untouched by time. Like him, the spirit of the Chateau du Rottembourg would remain frozen in its idyllic past; in his past, in Alice's past, in their children's past, he told himself. The old property would withstand the onslaught of new faces and new voices, but as if it lived and breathed and listened, it would remember the roses just in from the garden waiting in a basket on the table in the hall. It would recall reflections of beloved faces in the mirrors and the ticking of clocks on mantelpieces and little things, meaningless, shallow things: a dog's favorite napping place on the stairs, the satchels and trunks piled high in the attic, the cords and tassels on the draperies, the worn steps on the ladder in the library.

Jean DeLille was pouring himself a glass of brandy when he heard the clang of the brass doorknocker and footsteps crossing his hall. It was Ernest. He carried Alice's green shawl over his arm. Well-acquainted with the neighbor at the Chateau Rottembourg, Marie, De Lille's housekeeper, had shown Ernest in immediately.

Without a word, DeLille poured another glass of brandy from the decanter and handed it to Ernest whose bloodshot eyes were riveted on the clocks. Ernest took the glass, walked toward the clocks standing side by side on the mantel, and stared at each glistening dial. He turned, and with one hand carefully placed Alice's shawl across the back of the familiar rotunda chair which DeLille now owned. Standing absolutely still, he sipped at his brandy and swallowed hard.

"Jean, I've changed my mind. When the last of this is over and life is back to normal, I want to buy these clocks back from you," he announced, "so don't get too attached to them. I'll buy Bourdon's clocks too. And I'll buy Alice another house in the country. And it will be better and grander than any Raingo house has ever been. You'll see. They will all see."

His voice was strained and hoarse. Oddly silent in one moment, he was intensely talkative in the next. His eyes darted from one end of the room to the other.

"Somewhere in the country you and I, Jean DeLille, will play our terrible duets on a gleaming Pleyel again. We'll eat too much pheasant and we'll drink too much wine. We'll sing and dance and I will fall into this red flowered linen again and we will laugh and curse and gossip about as many people as we can think of and Alice will pretend she's upset with us for being too noisy and waking the children. Yes, we'll hunt and ride again and all the torture will end. Alice will forget. No more deception. She will never again accuse me of neglect and failing to protect her, and she will never again pretend she doesn't love me. I will start a new career and make a great new fortune and Alice will adore me, the way she did at the beginning, the way she did before she took her lover. Yes, her lover. Didn't you know, Jean? Don't look so surprised. Of course. Surely you know. Claude Monet and Alice!"

"He has such a kind face," Ernest mocked, imitating Alice's lyrical voice, his cheeks aflame, his lips grimly white, "and he has such a nice way with the children. I'm sure you see it Ernest dear, don't you? They like him so very, very much. And he seems perfectly comfortable at La Lethumiere. I'm so pleased he's using that house. Did you know that he works in the little garden there? DeLille, this is her shawl! I found it in a forgotten heap on the floor in our bedroom! In her great rush to leave me at Rottembourg and return to her lover in Paris, my careless wife left it behind. I brought it to her from the store about two years ago along with some Italian figurines that arrived in a shipment from Milan. She said she wasn't fond of the figurines, but she loved the shawl. The figurines went to my mother that Christmas!" Ernest couldn't stop himself. DeLille grasped his shoulders and forced him into the infamous chair. He poured another glass of brandy.

"He stayed on, didn't he, perhaps a bit too long," DeLille offered, unprepared for Ernest's unbridled sarcasm and the avalanche to follow.

"Too long? Too long, from August to December? Is that too long?" Ernest shouted. "Let me see. Yes, that's it! Why didn't I think of it? You are correct, DeLille! The lover stayed on too long!" He laughed. "Oh, yes, of course, that must be it! He stayed on through those August luncheons under my pines and copper beeches, through country festivals, and crisp, cool September evenings when the fireplaces begin to roar and the air is pungent with burning hickory and pine. He stayed on through the chill of October, watching my orange trees in their white lattice planters being moved indoors and my pear trees wrapped in winter burlap as if they belonged to him and not to me! The panels were taking longer to complete than he had expected he told me, and by the time November came and Alice and the children were still at Montgeron he was part of the household! He walked around at Rottembourg like a member of the family."

Still shouting, Ernest was on his feet. "I saw them together in his studio in Paris about two weeks ago. Kind, reliable Caillebotte took out a lease for him again. I didn't mean to walk in on them but I did. I didn't suspect a thing. No one answered my knock so I tried the doorknob. So eager were they for each other's arms, they hadn't even taken the time to lock the door! Alice was sitting beside him on a sofa. She was barefoot and wearing her blue robe and had that look on her face, that look I thought I alone would ever know! The breath fell out of me. I felt as if I'd been stabbed a hundred times. Question after question raged in my brain. I wanted to scream! When did it all begin? Why? Where? Was it at La Lethumiere or was it in one of the rooms of the Chateau Rottembourg? And the most pressing question of all. Is Jean-Pierre really my son? DeLille, I can't remember how I got there, but I spent part of that terrible night at my mother's house. I know I didn't sleep. I wanted to die and I thought I would die thinking about them together and the way it must have been between them; the laughter, the whispering, the touching, his hands on her skin, the bed sheets a mass of wrinkles by morning. Before midnight I went back to Rue de Vintimille. I wanted to kill him with my bare hands. Who would blame me? Instead, I was a French gentleman and like a stupid fool I simply demanded that he not see Alice, not ever again! DeLille, by then I was so tired of fighting and arguing and constantly pressing the point. I told him not to see her ever again, but he will see her. I know it. She will want him to. DeLille, things between them may have gone too far for me to do much of anything now."

"Views of the property! Those were my instructions!" the ranting went on, Ernest pacing up and down. "Yes, Claude, perhaps the garden, the view of the house from the meadow at the edge of the forest! Yes, Alice loves that view!"

Watching Ernest, DeLille was making every attempt to process the words he was hearing. He recalled having noticed vague evening smiles occasionally exchanged between Alice and Claude amid the stream of summertime guests at Rottembourg, but Claude was a guest and Alice was doing all she could to make him feel comfortable. It was what she always did for guests at Rottembourg. At the time, he had thought those smiles to be expressing nothing more than friendship on Alice's part and appreciation on Claude's, but now their memory carried meaning. He remembered having watched two indulgent profiles often paired at the table in the candlelit dining room; yes, seated beside one another or across from one another, talking, laughing, and always Claude's admiring murmurs for every unappreciated detail Ernest took for granted and to which Alice attended with ease. The veal blanquette served from a silver tray was "magnificent," he was heard to tell her with a flurry of generous compliments. The apples pureed with meringue presented in tall, slim crystal compotes were "perfection". The wine was expertly decanted, the calvados just tart enough, and all the while conversation was linked by Ernest's hunting stories, by the Senart's royal history, the kill of the day, the thrill of the chase, and always Ernest's beloved Rottembourg world, his dogs, his horses, his paintings, and again and again the agreeable nod, the polite smile, and at evening's end at the front door the reluctant good-night.

"The lover liked fresh game, the hare well hung and bled lean, my wine-drenched pheasant served with pureed chestnuts and a touch of cream," Ernest went on in a hoarse whisper. "He liked my Portuguese Madeira too. Do you ride horses?' I asked him at the beginning, on the train out to Rottembourg.

"No, Monsieur, I do not ride and I do not hunt."

"That was his answer! That comment alone should have alerted me. Jean, he wasn't one of us. He was never one of us! Never! I let him into my world. I brought him to it on a private train!"

"Alice has just been flirting," DeLille interrupted. "Ernest, it's not love. Maybe it's an affair, but it's not serious. It can't be. It's just a passing dalliance," he said, intending to do all he could to calm the friend and neighbor whose face was still aflame. "Women do that sometimes, especially our pretty French women. It's nothing new. Ernest, you can forgive whatever has gone on in the past. I know you can. You and Alice are meant to be together, but married or not, I've seen what can happen with you yourself and a pretty girl in a café: a little compliment, a little smile. Nothing ever comes of it except a boost to your ego. But come now, Alice couldn't possibly care for anyone but you, not really, especially a struggling artist with no money and no future. She has certain requirements. And there are the children. Think of it. Six now!"

"Jean, I have thought of that. Yes, there are six Hoschede children and now, more and more often I've wondered if baby Jean-Pierre is really my child. The idea has been haunting me. Given his birth date of August 22nd and knowing that all five of Alice's previous pregnancies have been perfectly normal and without exception covered the full nine month term, she would have conceived in November, sometime around the 20th. In November of '76 the lover was still there, alone with her at Rottembourg, while I was busy putting off my creditors in Paris. He didn't leave for Argenteuil until later in November, sometime at the end of the third week of the month or the beginning of the fourth. I returned to Rottembourg around the twenty-seventh or twenty-eighth as I remember. It was then that Alice and I came to an understanding and made love for the first time in weeks. It had been terrible between us for so long; the alienation, the hurt and pain, but in one afternoon of complete honesty we discovered that in spite of the turmoil swirling around us we truly loved one another. We became the old Ernest and Alice again. We talked and laughed. We remembered old stories. We made love again and again. We were happy. It felt as if we were ten years younger and falling in love all over again. It was wonderful. In the next weeks, we were at each other's side almost constantly. We were touching, watching, promising, and living, really living. The lovemaking was beyond description. It was late in January when she told me she was pregnant and when I thought back to how we had spent the weeks leading up to Christmas, I thought I knew exactly when our sixth child had been conceived. Funny though, I never mentioned that to her. I suppose I liked knowing it myself and taking it for granted. Why wouldn't I? It was such a happy time for us and as you know, last April, by the time the Impressionists exhibited for the third time I was in my glory. Of course I was proud to have loaned so many paintings. The limelight was irresistible, but knowing that Alice was at my side, on my side, made the real difference. The whole world was mine again. I felt I could solve all our problems. I should have told her that but I never did. DeLille, you saw Alice on that opening day at Rue Laffitte. She was radiant, smiling, happy, truly beautiful. And I thought all that was because of me and the baby that was on the way. How could I know she had been seeing Monet all the while he was painting the Gare Saint-Lazare paintings that I had bought and loaned to the exhibition?" DeLille shook his head. Ernest fell silent. He sipped at his brandy.

"We spent that Christmas at Rottembourg," he reminisced in a measured tone. "Alice had planned one of her beautiful Christmas Eve dinners. You know how she does things: the starched white linen napkins, the sparkling silver, the china, everything just so. We were alone with the children. The fireplaces and the candles glowed. There were small, exquisitely wrapped presents at all the places at the dining room table. Each of the girls received gold bracelets, even little Germaine. They were thrilled. Jacques smiled from ear to ear when he unwrapped his present and found a pair of binoculars. They came in a brown leather carrying case stamped with his initials. There was a fine gold pocket watch for me, my initials engraved across it in a florid script. I don't know where Alice got the money for such expensive gifts. I didn't ask. I was too happy, too content really, to care, but now that I think about it, Julian Raingo probably came to the yuletide rescue."

Silent and pensive, DeLille placed a fresh log on the fireplace embers and dropped into the chair closest to Ernest.

"I remember the children had been playing in the snow that Christmas Eve afternoon," Ernest continued, the strain in his voice impossible to ignore. "I was in the reotunda when I heard them laughing outside. I opened one of the terrace doors to find they were making snow people close to the house, on the terrace. There were two such snow creatures. One was a man, and but for a scarf and hat he looked pretty well finished. The other creature was a woman. I could tell that because they were trying to attach breasts to this enormous white monster with a tiny little waist. They struggled and struggled, first on one side, then on the other, but the breasts refused to stay on and kept sliding away. Each time this happened, they erupted into gales of laughter and fell into the snow. I had to close the door and come inside so they wouldn't see me laughing too. I should have gone out there to play in the snow with them. I regret that. Do you have regrets, DeLille? Do you wish you had things in life to do over, meaningless, little things that somehow you didn't make time for and that now mean so much when you remember them? I do, and I remember that later, at dinner on that Christmas Eve, their cheeks were still rosy from the cold, but from the dining room windows in the starry evening light, we could enjoy the results of our children's handiwork. Monsieur Snow Creature wore one of my old black top hats and a red scarf. Madame wore one of Alice's yellow straw garden hats with trailing ribbons. She also wore a red scarf. It was tied around her breasts and from what I could see, it held things together quite nicely. The children had planned our entertaining Christmas Eve dinnertime view of snow creatures just perfectly. I wish you could have seen it. I wish you could have seen my family then."

He rambled on and on about the tall pines in the park at Rottembourg. Tears in his eyes, he described the summer roses and the gardens and he dwelt on his feelings of great happiness whenever he was leaving Paris for Montgeron to be with Alice and the children. Occasionally he put his head back and closed his eyes. He smiled as he described the beautifully tended lawns where his children had safely played. He remembered every detail of the overstuffed sofas and bands of embroidery on silk and damask which had become the settings for his much loved evening rituals of spare, unhurried country pleasure. Throughout the evening with DeLille, the Chateau Rottembourg's long tradition of rotunda candlelight, conversations linked by news from Paris, the galleries, the theater, the music, pervaded Ernest's every memory with poignantly haunting power.

"It was all for them, you know, all of it," the injured voice declared. "It was all intended for them, for my children and their children. We gave him, Claude that is, Uncle Julian's cottage. Every day he came walking along the drive or through the meadow, smoking a cigarette and pausing as he sketched and surveyed and began the studies for my painted wall panels. The children were incessantly curious about him and what he might be doing that day. They asked endless questions. He, in turn, was endlessly patient. What subjects would he paint for their rotunda dining room? Would there be pictures of them, of me, of their mother? Each of them volunteered suggestions. They made lists of their favorite places on the property for him to see. They invited him to the third floor for tea. He played their games and read their books. He talked to their parrot. They followed him around like a flock of devoted sheep. Now I realize they were responding to his approachability. How intrigued they were by the fact that he seemed to have all the time in the world for them as well as his painting, quite satisfied to live as an impoverished artist, happiest of all when busy outdoors in the world of nature. DeLille, the adults my children know are well-to-do and pursue busy lives either as well-paid, hard-working professionals or wealthy do-nothings who make great careers of being very grand and simply decorating life's auspicious occasions. DeLille, you know who they are. You've met the most offensive of them, and in my own house. I suppose in many ways Claude was a very sharp contrast to all that, a fellow child to my own children who were eternally charmed and fascinated by the simplicity of what he pointed out to them in nature. "Oh, look here! And oh, see there!" And now they are all in Paris, my children, my wife, and of course, Claude. It's really quite unbelievable, isn't it? People we know see Claude as my good friend, a struggling painter I've supported and from whom I have purchased countless canvases. Ernest Hoschede, the great collector! And Jean, you've seen those paintings on my walls: *Le Village, Saint-Germain-l'Auxerrois, Jeunes Filles dans un Massif de Dahlias*, and the painting that started all this, the great 800-franc bargain I struck with Durand-Ruel for *l'Impression, Soleil Couchant*. Funny, isn't it, that I have actually been supporting him while all this betrayal has been going on? Friends caring for friends! Monet's patron!"

The logs flamed up and Ernest's red-rimmed eyes blazed in the flickering firelight as he ended his reverie and one by one, named the twelve paintings by Claude that in a few weeks would be auctioned off at the Hotel Drouot. DeLille could see tears welling up in his eyes again. He looked away and shook his head in utter disbelief, immensely unsettled in the knowledge that the man Ernest had called The Lover had come into the resonant, undamaged Hoschede world an invited, welcome guest, paid to paint while he spent a few weeks in the country, not paid to charm the entire household, not paid to play with the children and gain their trust, not paid to fall in love with Alice.

"She wants to take the children and move to Vetheuil," Ernest stated flatly. "He's living there now. Apparently he needed a change, new subject matter to inspire him so he moved. Argenteuil had lost all its charm and Alice needs to breathe, she tells me. Oh, it's all to be very civilized. Two houses, in one the Monet family, in the other the Hoschedes, and it's just a temporary arrangement. Just until Monsieur Hoschede attends to his affairs in Paris and Madame Monet's health improves. And of course, the Monets and the Hoschedes are such good friends! Monsieur Hoschede is Monet's great patron, and isn't Madame Hoschede kind to be looking after Madame Monet? The poor woman is having difficulty recovering from the birth of her last child."

"DeLille, he's taking her away from me and right now I don't know what to do about it, but if it takes twenty-four hours a day, seven days a week, I will put things back the way they were. Right now my family needs a place to live. They can't impose on my cousin, Beatrice much longer, but I swear I will buy my country house back. I'll make such an irresistible offer for the Chateau Rottembourg that we'll be moving in that very day. You and I will be neighbors again. Alice will come back to me. She will love me. My children will be mine again. It will all happen. I swear it! And don't forget what I've said!"

"Ernest, you're exhausted. You need rest," DeLille said. "Most of all you need to forgive yourself. Stop imposing all this remorse on yourself because of a few human mistakes. We all make them. Alice has been through a very difficult time. She's never had adversity staring her in the face. Stay here with me as long as you like," DeLille offered. "It's quiet and peaceful. No one has to know you're here. You can rest and take your time to figure things out. The bed linen gets changed regularly and the dogs don't bark much before sunrise."

"My paintings were good weren't they?" Ernest abruptly asked, his tone aggressive once again. "I've always thought they were the very best of what Durand-Ruel had to offer from that group he supported," he went on without waiting for the encouraging response De Lille was prepared to offer. "I wonder what will happen to them and where they'll go. Truth be told, I've had enough time to realize how attached I've become to them. I spent last winter alone with them. It was like living underground with candor and bare bones for companions, but it felt very good. It will be difficult to see them go, even the Monets. Imagine that! In the middle of all this I still admire his painting. Perhaps he is the better man after all. And thank you, DeLille. You are a good friend. Yes, I'd like to stay here with you for a while."

"Good, I'm glad you'll stay, but Ernest, if you don't stop torturing yourself this way I'll be forced to toss you out. You cannot allow what has happened to make you ill. I'm a terrible nurse, and it will all straighten away, all of it. And yes, your paintings are very fine. You have an eye, an unusual eye," the caring country neighbor assured his weary friend. "I've always thought that you and the new group were made for each other, but now so much still lies ahead of you. There will be other paintings, other opportunities. You're a young man, Ernest. The Street of Pictures will always be there but now you should think about starting something new, something you can breathe life into. Unfortunately, you must make a living."

"I should be starting something new, you say? And what exactly is it that will content me do you think? Stabs at mediocrity? Less? De Lille, I'm forty years old and I have lost my store. It was a huge success. As I see it, I could live for another thirty years. What do you think I should do with myself during that time? How shall I make a living?"

De Lille hesitated, but offered a suggestion. "Ernest, this may sound silly to you right now, but why don't you think about covering the modern art scene in Paris and becoming an art critic? You know the artists, the dealers, the way things work in the Paris art world. You'd be a great critic."

"There's no money in it," Ernest said, shaking his head. "I tried my hand at it a few years back. Writing criticism is more difficult than it looks. And if I'm to put my life back together the way I want to, I'll be needing a substantial income. In years to come there will be daughters to marry off to wealthy husbands and sons to educate and send out into the world confident of success."

"But Ernest, you could be the best of them! Think of it! You could become the most widely respected art critic in all Paris, someone the public relies on, an expert they can look up to. You could present lectures. People love listening to you talk. They believe everything you tell them, even though they probably shouldn't." Ernest laughed. "Ernest, you could write books. It could be the same way the store was before all this. Don't you remember that people said if it came from Hoschede's and Ernest Hoschede had stocked it in his store, it was the best Paris had to offer?

EXPOSITION PUBLIQUE, COLLECTION HOSCHEDE
Hotel Drouot, Salon Eight; June 5 and 6, 1878; One until Five O'Clock
Maitre Dubourg, presiding

"Sold! Lot Number 49, *Les Rives de la Tamise et le Parlement, effet de brouillard, a Claude Monet*; Merci, Monsieur May! Ladies and gentlemen, Lot Number 50, *Saint-Germaine-l'Auxerrois a Claude Monet*! Do I have one-hundred francs? Yes!" Two hundred francs! Merci! Merci! And so it went. Merci! Merci! For two days Georges Petit's expert-valuer voice rang out in Salon Eight at the Drouot. One hundred eight lots relegated to the auctioneer's gavel. Sold! Sold! Sold!

He should have stayed away. He tried. Everyone he knew, including the ever-present Armel Ducasse, had discouraged him from attending. It was useless. He had to be there, but it was worst than he thought it would be. The houses and furnishings sold to partially pay off the crush of creditors had been humiliating and bewildering enough, but this was very different. This was about his great personal passion. These were the paintings he had thoughtfully gathered carefully and over time. He had studied and loved them and now they were being disposed of in mere minutes, the painful pounding of Petit's relentless gavel beating at him with every lot, the aching wound cutting across his heart one that even during those two dreadful days Ernest knew would never heal.

He had wanted to shout out and stop it, end it. "It's all a terrible mistake!" he wanted to cry out into the crowded room's sea of black top hats and crisp frock coats. At one point he had wanted to beg. "Please, no! You mustn't! You don't understand! Everything I care about is gone! This is all I have left!" But until the last agonizing moment and with a wrenching regret from which Jean DeLille himself predicted his friend would never recover, Ernest stood quietly alone at the back of Salon Eight until the final wretched pounding of Georges Petit's gavel had finally stripped away every last remnant of life as he had known it.

Over the course of two days, Wednesday June 5th and Thursday June 6th of 1878 and along with a considerable number of paintings by a long list of popular, at the time well-known Paris painters such as Bonvin, Chaplin, Leclair, and Diaz, more than forty of Ernest's Impressionist paintings were sold. There were the twelve by Claude Monet and also the five by Edouard Manet. There were nine Pissarros, three Renoirs, thirteen Sisleys, and one Morisot. All fell under the hammer at embarrassingly low prices. Ernest was deeply offended. The painting that had named Impressionism, his 800-franc *Impression Sunrise* brought a shocking 210 francs. The five Manets combined brought less than 3,000 francs. The highest price paid for a Pissarro was 100 francs and that was for his *Saint-Ouen-l'Aumone (Oise)*. Sisley's *L'Aqueduc de Marly* sold for a paltry 21 francs. His *Piece d'eau dans Pelouse et un parc* and *Les Hauteurs de Montretout, Effet de neige* did only slightly better, each at 40 francs. Renoir's *Woman and Her Cat* brought an outrageous 84 francs. His *Jeune Fille dans un jardin* brought a horrifying 21 francs and *Le Pont de Chatou* brought a depressing 42 francs.

Thanks to Edouard Manet's best patron, two of his five paintings did better than the combined work of the Impressionists. "Sold! Lot Number 42, *Edouard Manet:La Femme aux cerises*; 450 francs, Monsieur Faure. Merci. "Sold! Lot Number 43, *Edouard Manet: Le Torreador*; 650 francs; Merci, Monsieur Faure."

"Sold! Lot Number 47, *Claude Monet: La Plage au Trouville*; 200 francs, Merci, Madame Cassat."

"Sold! Lot Number 55, *Claude Monet: L'Impression, soleil couchant*; 210 francs, Merci, Monsieur de Bellio."

The Aquarelles. Sold! Two Boudin watercolors, two by Lalanne, and *Un Port* by Morisot. Sold!

It was the paintings by the wildly popular, well-known Paris establishment-oriented artists which Ernest had also owned for some time and which much of the world would soon forget such as Bonvin, Diaz, Chaplin, Hereau, and the Rousseau brothers that were the stars. Theodore Rousseau's *Marais dans le Berri* brought a solid 10,000 francs. His brother, Philippe's, *Les Prunes* brought 2,000 francs. Sold! Sold! Sold! It was relentless, humiliating, heartbreaking.

At the end of the second day and in the auction's final minutes, the eleven lots of furniture and decorative pieces from the Chateau Rottembourg which had gone unsold and were taken in wagons from Montgeron in May were brought to the stand. Now, in Salon Eight's prevailing mood of bargain-basement prices, all eleven lots were sold in quick succession, among them the suite of four pearl-gray, gilded settees which had stood against four walls of the rotunda. The large faience vases, also from the rotunda, went under the hammer, followed by spirited bidding for the Louis XVI marble topped tables, consoles, and cabinets which in short order had been summarily stripped from the Chateau Rottembourg's drawing room, library, and halls.

From the small, modestly furnished apartment he took at 64 Rue de Lisbonne when it was over and he was alone, Ernest withdrew, wondering both day and night what he must do to restore his broken marriage and what life might have been like if he had never heard of Impressionists and Impressionism and Claude Monet and a painting called *Impression Sunrise*. He questioned the wisdom of his most innocuous personal decisions and like a condemned man he re-lived every action of the past nightmarish months, also wondering what he could have done to avoid the terrible day in his life when the certified auctioneer had arrived at the Chateau Rottembourg appropriately dressed as an undertaker in black morning coat and black cravat, the empty black wagons following behind him in the bright sunshine lined up behind the ice house like hearses prepared to cart off to Paris whatever went unsold in the two unspeakably painful days for which he knew Alice would never forgive him.

"Hold on to it for a while," Durand-Ruel had said to him of *Impression Sunrise*, he recalled. "It could be worth something some day."

"The perfect match, Paris' most notorious collector acquiring Paris' most notorious painting," Durand-Ruel had also said of the transaction.

"Tell me, Claude, is that you standing in the boat in the middle of the harbor at Le Havre?" Ernest had joked four years earlier with the impoverished artist who now held sway over his life.

"I come from Le Havre. I know the harbor and it knows me," came the gentle, introspective reply.

On the evening of June 6th at seven o'clock, Ernest walked away from the Hotel Drouot alone, his life in shambles, his spirit broken. He was thirty-nine years old and the genial, natural spark of optimism in him had died. He took to his bed and did not leave it for three days. When he finally found the strength to open his eyes and stand, he was ravenously hungry. Dressing quickly and paying no attention to his appearance, he walked to the nearby Alsatian Café Evy where he ordered a bottle of wine and a bowl of German Baeckeoffe, the popular hearty lamb and potato soup that had found its way onto Paris menus with the loss of Alsace and Lorraine to the Prussians. He sat alone, oblivious to the clatter and noise and not particularly pleased with his food, his thoughts rambling and at odds with any semblance of rational order. When he returned to his Rue de Lisbonne address, he found Jean DeLille waiting for him under the building's streetside marquee.

"I've been worried about you. I checked your rooms and you weren't there," DeLille said to him. "I thought we could have dinner together, you and I."

"Thank you, Jean, but I've just left the Evy," Ernest replied, his voice hoarse, his eyes red and sad. "The soup wasn't too bad, but the wine was really terrible. I'll be poor company for you tonight, DeLille, but if it is mere company you're suggesting, I'll sit with you and nurse along a glass or two of decent wine while you have your dinner or whatever you have at this hour. Sebastiani's is just a block away."

DeLille was shocked to see Ernest so disheveled. His clothes were rumpled, he was unshaven, and his hair was barely combed. He looked lost and haggard and very lonely.

"What are your plans now, Ernest?" DeLille asked him pointedly in the simple white-walled setting where Giorgio Sebastiani conducted a lively business and served his delicious Mediterranean dishes to patrons at all hours of the day and night. "You can't spend the next months wallowing in self-pity. I expect more of you. And Ernest, you should expect more of yourself!"

"Ah, Jean DeLille, you are the industrious one, aren't you, everything in order, everything tidy and working out according to plan," Ernest said to him, leaning back in his chair across the table. "I was like that once, and not too long ago. Remember? Every spring, every summer, every autumn, Monday through Thursday at the store and then eager to be off to lovely Rottembourg to join my wife and children for a few days in a house that was all happiness and gaiety. DeLille, it was a wonderfully well-ordered life I thought would just go on and on unchanged until I was an old man and stopped breathing in my bed one night. I didn't make plans for all this chaos, so to answer your question the simple truth is I have no plans. The future lies ahead of me like a stark sheet of white paper torn out of a tablet, no writing on it, no instructions, nothing."

"Have you thought of doing more writing for Voltaire and Le Monde? You have a genuine talent for expressing what goes on in the city. I've liked everything of yours I've read. Do it, Ernest!"

"My articles could get me through, I suppose, but I have no idea what expenses will turn out to be once Alice and the children are at Vetheuil. I'll find the money somewhere, but the income from writing is unpredictable. Just ask the Goncourts. They're successful and famous and even they can't count on much security. Everything is so different for me now, DeLille, my life, my family. You understand it all better than just about anyone else. In a few weeks I'm going out to Vetheuil with Alice and the children to see them settled and so forth, but I won't stay. I'll visit them there when I can, but I'll have to come back to Paris and take up my life's blank page. Do you think I really can write something on it?"

"Let's go away for a while when you finish all that Vetheuil business and before you start that new career," DeLille suggested with a smile. "I have a little money set aside for travel this year. It's enough for two. I haven't been to Spain since art school. We could critique the contents of the Prado; a little Velazquez, a little El Greco. What do you say? We might even consider Florence for a while; a little Botticelli; Venus being born; a little Caravaggio, a ton of saintly blood? What do you say?"

CHAPTER 24

Vetheuil
1878

It was over. Clearly, now that Camille was pregnant the affair had come to an end. Without a word being said, the summer of 1877 had changed everything. In August, at Biarritz, Alice had given birth to a son and at some point in the final months of Alice's pregnancy Claude had fathered his second child with Camille. The inescapable fact that he had made love to his wife barely weeks after saying fond good-byes to her in springtime Paris was shattering and for a time forced Alice to question Claude's sincerity, but now, in October, as by order of the French court the ominous consequences of bankruptcy loomed, Alice knew she must take herself in hand, shake off haunting romantic notions, and once and for all set out on a path of firm resistance.

Anticipating the journey north and as excited as the Hoschede children, Mademoiselle Gabrielle assembled her young charges in the hall, counting aloud to be sure that they and every piece of luggage had been collected and brought downstairs. Veronique was Marthe's responsibility, the children's pet parrot in her green cage despite the December temperatures, added at the last minute to the traveling party departing that morning for Vetheuil.

"Alice, are you sure about all this?" Beatrice hesitantly asked Alice, watching Veronique's cage being carefully covered and added to the collection of baggage in the hall. "Moving is such a big step, especially a move from a city like Paris, and I still don't know where this Vetheuil is. I may want to come to visit you there, wherever on God's earth it may be. I hope there's a good restaurant! It is in France, isn't it?"

Alice hugged her friend with a hearty laugh. "Yes, Vetheuil is in France, and Beatrice, you should be glad to be getting rid of us. We've been with you for much too long, and too many of our things have been cluttering up your lovely house. It's taking two carriages to move us out! But Beatrice dear, I will never forget what you've done for us and how kind you've been. I can't imagine how we would have managed without you. I'm not sure there is any way to repay you, but I thank you with all my heart. It may take me a while to get settled so you mustn't worry if you don't hear from me right away, but everything will be fine. I'll write. Beatrice, please be happy for me."

"The house will be much too quiet without you, my darlings," Beatrice confessed, tears in her eyes as she hugged each of the children. "And Igor, do watch out for these little ones," she added, patting the head of the loyal, tail-wagging spaniel who was collared and leashed and ready to accompany the traveling party on its journey. Beatrice fell silent as the door pull rang and Ernest arrived, prepared to accompany his family into a new stage in their lives.

"I'm very excited today!" Germaine announced to her father. "Mama says we are to be farmers for the summer. Isn't it wonderful? She says that at Vetheuil we will be planting a garden and raising vegetables. We'll be close to the river too, which I think is also wonderful. We will have a boat and Mamma says we can all help with Madame Monet's garden. She is ill, you know, and cannot take care of the garden by herself right now. Papa, did you know that she has a tiny baby? His name is Michel. Mama will be taking care of him and I am going to help. I think I'll sing to him."

"Well, it sounds as if you will be very busy my sweet one," but you will be farming and helping with Madame Monet's baby for just a little while, only until Papa settles things and finds a fine new house for all of us to live in." He looked at Alice and smiled. "It won't be long. I promise you."

Not for a moment did the underlying message in Ernest's optimistic words fool Beatrice. Plans for the move away from Paris well underway, Alice had confided in her a few days earlier when deftly opening a celebratory bottle of champagne Beatrice had said, "Well, here we are. Bon voyage, my dear Alice. You know I want you to be happy, but I must ask you why this Vetheuil, of all places?"

"Because I've been seeing Claude Monet and he's living there." Alice had stated simply. "He has asked me to come."

"Asked you to come?" Beatrice repeated, not at all sure she understood. "Why on earth would Claude Monet ask you to come anywhere?"

"Claude and I began a friendship at Montgeron two years ago when he came to paint the panels for the rotunda," Alice explained. "I went to see him one day at La Lethumiere because the children had told me he was planning to paint white turkeys for one of the panels. I thought such mundane subject matter was completely wrong for Rottembourg and I told him so. Frankly, I was furious. We didn't exactly argue, but I made myself very clear. I suggested other, more acceptable subjects to him. I pointed out the pond and the rose garden which you must admit are beautiful. He was very polite and didn't respond one way or the other except to say that the white turkeys who freely roamed our meadow were entirely natural to life at Rottembourg, part of the spirit of things, as he put it. He went on and on about loving the sky and the movement of clouds and how one can never fight and win with nature. At first I thought he was a bit strange in the way he rambled on, but Beatrice, there was something about his sincerity, his awareness of time and place, and his very clear understanding of the natural world at Rottembourg which I love."

Beatrice had to sit down, the story she was hearing too remarkable, its implications too far removed from the conduct of the impeccably self-disciplined Alice she had known and admired for years.

"We are poles apart, he and I," Alice went on, her face suddenly flushed. "I knew that then and I know it now," she added with a self-conscious glance away, "but Beatrice, I found peace and safety with him when I needed it most. He's poor and he doesn't own a thing, but he has confidence in his talent and his ability to succeed, and with a little more time I believe he will. Beatrice, I don't expect you to understand and you have every right to disapprove, but what has happened between Claude and me has seemed perfectly right and natural, as if it was intended to be. Once the panels were finished and we were back in Paris, I began seeing him at his studio here in the city. He recently moved to Vetheuil with his wife and two sons but he comes into the city regularly."

Sitting back in her chair, Beatrice's champagne glass became unsteady in her hand, its contents dangerously close to flowing onto the skirt of the green satin dress she was wearing as appalled and quite totally bewildered she listened to Alice's astonishing tale. "So that's where you've been running off to every afternoon!" she blurted out. "Oh, Alice! Oh, my dear Alice! And now you're running off to this Vetheuil place to be with him? An affair! Oh, Alice, it will ruin you! Oh, Alice! Ernest doesn't know, does he? Do the children? Alice, this is terrible! We must do something immediately!"

"Beatrice there is nothing to do and yes, Ernest knows everything," Alice's confession went on, her message resolute yet agonizing to Beatrice, "but the children know Claude only as a family friend and someone who is helping us through a difficult time. Of course they know about our losses and they understand our need for a home, however temporary. I've told them we are going to Vetheuil to be near Monsieur Monet and his family for a while because right now their father is attending to necessary business almost every minute of the day and he wants us to be near good friends while he works things out. Beatrice, I'm not at all sure they understand but I've really had no choice. Think about it. The children and I have no home. The Paris apartment is gone and Rottembourg is gone. If it weren't for your generous hospitality only God knows where or how we would have lived through these past months. To add to that, except for my Uncle Julian, my relatives have distanced themselves. They all despise Ernest now and I want to get the children away from all the chaos. The worst sort of gossip could reach their ears before too long. The little ones wouldn't understand or care but the two older girls are at an age where they could be hurt. They're beginning to attend events and parties. At their age girls can be terrible to one another. I certainly had my share of that sort of thing. You did too. I suppose at some point I'll have to find a way to explain the truth about Claude and me to them. When that time comes, I hope I can. In any case, Claude is good to my children and to me and at Vetheuil at least we'll be in a safe place where no one knows us or cares about us. "

"I can't imagine how Ernest is handling this," Beatrice whispered, shaking her head, tears welling up in her dark, sensitive eyes. "He loves you and the children so much, but he's been under so much pressure. Of course, you have too, but it seems to me this is a very dangerous step you're taking. Alice, I hope you know what you're doing. It all sounds very complicated to me. Maybe you're just having a little breakdown. You could be a little confused. It happens. You've been under a terrible strain. Why don't you postpone the journey to Vetheuil and stay here with me a while longer?"

"No, Beatrice, no postponements," Alice replied with her light laugh. "I've explained my feelings to Ernest and I've told him what I want to do. Of course he doesn't approve, but at the same time he knows the children and I desperately need a change and he does agree that we should leave Paris for a time. He'll visit us when he can. He tells me he wants to put things back together, but I don't know if that's possible. He keeps talking about a clean slate and the new beginning we'll have when everything is back to normal, whatever that means. We'll see what happens. For now, he wants to take us to Vetheuil, and see us settled, but he won't stay. Beatrice, Ernest and I have an understanding."

"An understanding? Oh, Alice! Once you're away and you've had a chance to clear your head you could feel quite differently about this so-called understanding," Beatrice warned, fearful of unforeseen consequences she felt Alice had not taken the time to consider. "You may want to forget all about a passionate little romance with an artist and come straight back to Paris to take up your real life with Ernest and the children again, no matter how reduced the circumstances are. I just don't want you to do anything you'll regret, and Alice, you can't possibly care for a penniless painter. If he were a rich and famous artist, I might understand, but Claude Monet has nothing to offer you. Alice, Ernest has told me he's married and has two children! End it. You and Ernest have built a solid life and a lovely family. It's the kind of life and family I wish I had."

On departure morning Beatrice said her final good-byes with a heavy heart. Except for Claude Monet and the children, Alice wouldn't know a living soul at Vetheuil, she told herself. She would be a total stranger in a remote village. For now the simplicity sounded appealing and as romantic as the poetry of Andre Chenier which Beatrice adored, but she wouldn't like it for long. Not Alice. No, soon she would begin to miss her luncheons with the elegant Paris crowd at Laperouse. Oh yes, for a while she would enjoy the luxury of reading quietly for an afternoon and playing card games with the children, but she certainly wouldn't be wearing dresses from Worth and chatting away at elegant evening dinners. And the children! They would be a little afraid, completely disoriented, and totally dependent on one another for companionship. Alice's children were accustomed to city life and country privilege. They had their elegant little friends and their elegant little habits. They had their four o'clock teas and their third floor paradise. Anticipating her new life, little Germaine had developed storybook illusions of farming as a delightful pastime. Farmers indeed! The Hoschede children didn't understand what farming entailed. Their idea of farming was a pristine, weed-free estate kitchen garden behind the Chateau Rottembourg planted and tended by hired help and poked at now and then with their brand new little spades, rakes, and hoes whenever the spirit moved their little lacey white socks in that direction. Right now Vetheuil sounded like good summer fun, but Alice's children were sophisticated, quick, clever children, accustomed to dressed-up urban beauty and well-groomed country living. Soon, fashionable Alice herself would see that all too clearly.

During a luncheon with Julian Raingo, Beatrice had learned that Vetheuil's only link to Paris was by train from the Gare de Lazare, a journey which did not take passengers directly into the village of Vetheuil at all, but only as far as Mantes, which after the lengthy rail journey, still required a twelve-kilometer carriage ride. This alarming information prompted a visibly stunned Beatrice to ask questions of Julian Raingo she had dared not ask before.

"Julian, this is terrible. Why haven't you done something? Alice and the children cannot be expected to live in a place so difficult to get to from Paris. Why haven't you helped them through all this? You practically raised Alice. It was you who introduced her to the theater, to the smart cafes and restaurants she loves, and it was you who taught her to love books and music. For goodness sake, it was due to your encouragement that she married Ernest. Julian, they've needed money so badly for so long and this terrible move so far away from Paris wouldn't be taking place if you would support them for a while, just until Ernest establishes himself again. Won't you please do it for me? It's not too late."

Raising his eyebrows across from Beatrice at the Polidor's center table, the silver-haired Julian Raingo did not hesitate to respond. "Beatrice, I won't give Ernest Hoschede another penny, not even for you. I've helped him in the past and I kept him out of debtor's prison. My dear, I know he is your cousin and that you love him, but the man is a wastrel! Do you know what he does with my loans? He immediately runs out to buy another fine chair or another irresistible signed French desk or worst yet, more of those worthless Impressionist paintings he so loves. He thinks they're good investments! No, I cannot have him squandering Raingo money on such nonsense. The family worked too hard for it. I love Alice very much. I always will, but what I do plan to do is to convince her to divorce that scoundrel and begin a new life. She'll eventually get over this Monet person, and once she does she must forget the Church and her Catholicism and think of her future and her children's future. So she'll be excommunicated! So what! There are worst things. God will understand. And don't worry about Alice being penniless at Vetheuil. I've established a Paris bank account in her name. She'll receive an allowance every month. Between what little is left of her inheritance and my help she'll be fine, but I've told her that Ernest mustn't, under any circumstances, know about the allowance. That scoundrel is capable of finding a way to take it over. She'll have enough to last for a year or more, depending on how desperate conditions become. You don't think I'd let her go off with six children to a God-forsaken place with no money, do you? Oh, and Beatrice, one more thing. You'll be interested to know that all six-hundred of Vetheuil's inhabitants make their living off the land. Doesn't it sound like the perfect place for our glamorous Alice?"

Standing outside the entrance doors to her Rue de Rome residence, Beatrice waved and smiled watching the departure of two carriages stuffed with passengers, a mountain of luggage, a barking dog, and a screeching parrot. They would be at the Gare de Saint-Lazare in half an hour. It would be fine. She took a deep breath and patted the wisps of hair at her temples. There was no need to worry, no need at all. Very soon, glamorous Alice would see that life at rustic Vetheuil was too difficult and too plain and that she had expected too much of a casual dalliance with a penniless, married artist. Soon all would be forgiven and in no time at all Alice Hoschede would be returning to her husband and her real life. Confident of her assessment, Beatrice could not know that settling into the carriage headed for the Saint-Lazare, Alice was also reassuring herself that all would be well. Weren't there positive signs everywhere? The Saint-Lazare was the train station Claude had painted in his series of seven canvases the year before, she reminded herself. And he had promised her a safe haven, a secluded home near him, a tranquil refuge in a world he knew and understood. On a sunny morning in early July, the train bound for Mantes took on its Hoschede passengers, their baggage, their dog and their parrot, and moments later, in puffs of steam and shrieking whistles, Alice and her family began their journey northward into the unknown.

Bordering the vast, sweeping curve in the River Seine, and although lacking in the views of bridges and boats that had served Claude's interests at Argenteuil, the river vistas at Vetheuil were far more picturesque. Small islands dotted the channel and upstream the undulating Ile Saint-Martine was outlined in the distance by tall poplars. Across the river lay the village of Lavacourt which immediately after arriving at Vetheuil with Camille, infant Michel, and young Jean, Claude had begun painting.

The Monet house was one of three set in a row at the edge of the village, on the road parallel to the river. Across the road were steps leading down to the riverbank where Claude's bateau atelier, the floating studio boat he had brought from Argenteuil was moored. The gently undulating hills of Garenne rose beyond the river and Vetheuil's charming village Twelfth Century Church highlighted the scene. Lavacourt had provided the background for studies from the riverbank and from his floating studio Claude was painting scenes of both Vetheuil and Lavacourt at close range.

The furnished house awaiting Alice and her new world was next door to that of the Monets. Camille had taken it upon herself to prepare it for the Hoschede family's arrival. Making a great effort to fight off her chronic exhaustion, she had dusted the furniture and mopped the floors, eager at last to meet the family about whom Claude seemed unable to say enough. She had even gone so far as to convince the green grocer to extend her enough credit for the luxury of peaches and apricots sufficient to fill the basket she proudly placed on the center of the table in the sitting room.

Ernest was quiet during the train ride to Mantes. The relationship between Alice and Claude continued to hurt and distress him but he had at last agreed that a brief stay at rural Vetheuil, however difficult the separation from Alice and his children might be, would suit the situation for now, but only until he was on his feet once again he emphasized. Alice was right he told himself. She should be away from Paris with the children for a while and Vetheuil was far enough away to provide the refuge and opportunity for renewal she said she needed, but things would right themselves by autumn, he had promised himself. It would all come together. He would make it come together. There was nothing to worry about. For the remaining summer months he would swallow his pride and put up with Claude Monet, but soon enough the quality of life with which Monet contented himself would yield a fatal blow and cut away for all time the thinnest chord of affection that might lie in Alice's heart. Ernest had accepted Jean DeLille's invitation to travel in Spain and Italy for a month or two. Everything would be different when he returned and somehow, before year's end and just as he had told Jean DeLille, he would succeed in buying back the Chateau Rottembourg. Life would be wonderful again, better than before. He would fill Rottembourg with lovely things again; with beautiful furniture and yards of damask and he would recover many of the same paintings he had loved. If necessary, he would pay more for them than he had the first time. Best of all, the betrayal would be forgiven and forgotten and the name of Claude Monet would never be spoken again.

Arriving at Mantes, the travelers terminated their train journey and boarded the two horse-drawn land coaches that would take them the remaining twelve kilometers to Vetheuil. With Gabrielle's help Ernest supervised the older children and Igor in one carriage. Alice took the younger ones and Veronique in the other. Lisette, the young woman Beatrice had engaged to assist Gabrielle with the children, was included in Alice's coach. The children could barely contain their excitement. It showed on all their faces. First, crossing a narrow bridge traversing the Seine, the coaches slowly climbed the sloping hill of Saint-Marin-le-Garenne. The terrain was rocky, the surrounding landscape dull and uninteresting but once at the top of the hill Alice understood why Claude had come to this part of the Viennes Valley. The view was spectacular, the landscape bright and vivid with summer color, the rippling blue-gray river sprinkled with islands, the chalk-white cliffs on the pristine right bank running on jagged and sun-drenched and as far as La Roche-Guyon.

"It's beautiful!" Alice exclaimed, tears of relief springing to her eyes. "Oh, yes, Mama!" added Suzanne, who had been the most apprehensive of the children. "It's like a picture," she added, "a very beautiful picture. I'm so glad!" Germaine stared out at the scene. "We will be farming in a beautiful place."

"Oh, look at the church!" exclaimed Marthe, delighted by the charm of the old village centerpiece. "It looks like a cake!" added Jacques with his indulgent smile, "a very large, very fancy cake!"

Brown tile-roofed houses were clustered around Vetheuil's centerpiece church, its ornate Renaissance façade a great source of pride to generations of inhabitants. Claude had begun work on this irresistible theme immediately upon his arrival and it was serving as constant inspiration. Convinced of his wisdom in having chosen to live and work at Vetheuil, he anticipated success with his continuing exploration of the tantalizing new subject matter surrounding him, the prospect of Alice's arrival adding a further positive dimension to his fresh spirit of optimism. Anticipating a bright new chapter in life, he and Camille welcomed the large Hoschede entourage with warm smiles. Claude was friendly and hospitable, but Camille was visibly overwhelmed. She had been led to expect a large family at the doorstep, but once the Hoschedes had actually arrived, the traveling party of ten accompanied by their mountain of luggage, their dog, and their parrot swallowed up every inch of available space in the modest, low-ceilinged house neighboring hers. She went through the motions of welcome, but the noise and the crowding were not at all to her liking. Alice Hoschede was not much to Camille's liking either. She smiled to her and politely expressed hope for the Hoschede family's happiness at Vetheuil, but Alice Hoschede was unlike any woman Camille Monet had ever met. Dressed in a finely tailored dark blue traveling ensemble complete with matching veiled hat, Alice's bearing was that of a sophisticated city woman, a woman whose experiences were worlds apart from hers, everything about Alice Hoschede from her hair style to her elegantly pointed shoes quite out of keeping with Vetheuil's simple way of life.

The two-story house Alice was to occupy with her six children was on the Mantes Road, next door to Claude's house and across the street from the river.

Although she was pleased by the visual riverside beauty of Vetheuil, she also saw that the house itself presented a number of challenges. It was small and compact. The garden at its back door was also small and compact. The few trees were mature and lovely, but of no particular pedigree. Alice did her best to hide her disappointment. Jacques was not as polite. "We cannot possibly be expected to live in such a small house!" he announced to his mother in disbelief. "There isn't enough room here for all of us! And it smells! Papa, please take us back to Paris. Tonight!"

"Now Jacques, you know these arrangements are temporary and that you will be here at Vetheuil only until I settle our affairs," Ernest said to his agitated young son, taking him aside and urging him to lower his voice. "Yes, I admit the house is a bit small, and yes, it does smell damp, but please do your best to set a good example for your sisters. You can manage here. The Monets are doing a fine thing in being good friends during this unusual time and I expect you and your sisters to show your gratitude and respect."

The housing arrangement required Ernest to sign the lease, pay the monthly rent of six-hundred francs, and to send Alice funds enough each month for food and miscellaneous expenses. With no solid career to provide him with income Alice had no idea how Ernest would meet these responsibilities. As advised, she said nothing of the financial arrangements Julian Raingo had made in her behalf, but she took great comfort in the security her uncle was providing. If Ernest failed to meet his family obligations at least she would be able to hold things together. Unknown to her, however, and in yet one more unrevealed set of circumstances, Ernest was now receiving five-hundred francs each month from his mother, most of which he intended to apply to the monthly support of his family. Now, seeing Vetheuil for himself and what little it offered, he was confident it wouldn't be at all necessary to send Alice as much as he had planned on. By summer's end, once he had returned from Spain and Italy with arms full of lovely gifts, the little house at Vetheuil, inadequate and modest, would have served its purpose and Alice and the children would be grateful to him for rescuing them. Before leaving for his return to Paris it was with no small sense of satisfaction that he inspected the humble house his family was to occupy.

He found the furnishings adequate and plain, the rooms running into one another without the grace of connecting hallways. In the prevailing French style of similar houses, on the first floor there was a sitting room connected to a dining room alcove. A kitchen and two small bedrooms completed the first-floor plan. Four bedrooms completed the second floor and upon arrival Alice immediately set about assigning the children to these rooms. Jacques was assigned the smallest of the second-floor rooms. Marthe and Blanche were told they would share one of the corner rooms. Suzanne and Germaine were assigned the room across the narrow hallway from Jacques. Alice and the baby, Jean-Pierre, would occupy the largest of the second-floor bedrooms, while Gabrielle and Lisette were to share one of the two downstairs rooms behind the kitchen. Once settled, Alice planned to hire a cook who would be occupying the remaining bedroom behind the kitchen.

Assuring himself of his family's overall safety, he kissed his children good-bye and leaving three hundred francs with Alice, he returned by carriage to Mantes where, arriving late at night, he took lodging at the boarding house near the station. Early the next morning, he was on the train back to Paris, his thoughts rapidly turning to Spain and the Prado, to Florence and Botticelli and the journey with Jean DeLille that promised exactly the diversion he needed. Now he would travel on the continent with a clear conscience. There was nothing to worry about. All would be well upon his return. Looking forward to his holiday, Ernest did not consider for a moment the fact that at Vetheuil Alice and Claude would be alone together and that as far as they were concerned being together was all that mattered. Yes, they were to live in separate houses, but they were free of time constraints and like the forbidden lovers they were, from the moment of Alice's arrival they both felt the euphoria of freedom. No longer must they part at day's end. No longer must they pretend not to notice each other in flickering candlelight across a dinner table. Like the close friends they had truly become, they could talk at length, especially at mealtimes which in a matter of days were shared, both families crowded at a table in one or another of their houses. From the beginning and in a completely alien world, Alice set about seeking her personal renewal. It was a formidable task, but in Claude's company she was confident she would find her center on solid ground. As for Claude, in this society woman, this paragon of bourgeois Paris who was exactly the type of indulgent female the Impressionists as a group had sworn to avoid, he had found precisely the intelligent, well-organized, and loving companion he had not known he needed or wanted.

Apart from the pleasure she and Claude took in their new found personal freedom, Alice's first weeks at Vetheuil were difficult in the extreme. With six children, two governesses, a cook, a dog and a parrot, her small house quickly became, as Ernest had predicted, unbearably cramped and noisy. Outdoors, even the garden was crowded. When the children wanted to play their familiar games of hoops and tag they complained there was not enough room. They sulked and cried, and every afternoon Alice escaped to her room where sitting at the edge of the bed she sobbed into her hands and questioned her decision. More than once in those first trying weeks she considered a return to Paris. But how would she explain to Claude, to Ernest, to the children, even to herself that she had run away from too demanding a challenge? She would appear weak and stupid. She loved Claude and she wanted to remain near him, but if she was to succeed in adjusting to life at Vetheuil she had no choice but to find a way to make the situation tolerable. All she really knew was how to run houses, look after children, and supervise gardeners. But she did that very well. She enjoyed doing it. The village of Vetheuil certainly was not Montgeron and her Vetheuil house was hardly a chateau, but there had to be some way to create a reasonably happy, acceptable home on the Mantes Road.

In a manner that for the rest of her life she would never fully understand, from the very beginning Alice faced her reduced Vetheuil circumstances with stores of resolve and reserves of energy she had no idea she possessed. Within two short weeks she had methodically set about the efficient running of not one, but two households. Asking no questions and unaccustomed to interference, she took charge of Claude's daily life as well as her own. She may have been an alien in an alien land but she understood the realities of her territory and true to her natural inclinations she rose to every occasion with grace and dignity. Camille made no secret of resenting Alice's overreaching interference. She complained to Claude repeatedly, but he minimized her concerns, pointing out that they should be grateful for Alice's help at a time when Camille's health was fragile and that caring for Jean as well as baby Michel was often too much for her. Agreeing with him that her energies were often depleted and that she was indeed neglecting many household duties, Camille was left no choice but to accept the radical changes in her household. She certainly could not deny that Alice Hoschede was consistently pleasant and more than capable in managing her assumed matriarchal role, her boundless energy as she moved back and forth from one house to the other several times a day a source of complete wonder to the young wife and mother who herself required care. So compromised was Camille that before long she not only encouraged Alice to organize the Monet household exactly as she saw fit, she also encouraged her to befriend young Jean who was clearly confused by the onslaught of so many noisy and over-active Hoschedes into his life. Alice treated Jean with great kindness. She cut his hair, read to him, and concerned by his paleness and bony frame, she insisted he finish every last morsel of food on his plate at every meal. In no time at all she and the girls had assumed full responsibility for looking after Jean, Camille, and baby Michel. His household in good hands, his wife and children well cared for, Claude was freer than ever before to do what he did best. His work reflected his contentment. Paintings were soon bursting with fresh color, with lively vitality, and a new luminosity. One was a view of the village church's splendid façade. Alice was particularly fond of it. Called the Church of Notre Dame, the notable centuries-old structure not only served as Vetheuil's religious and social center, it dominated Claude's creative view of the world. At the same time, it filled a great void in Alice's religious life as at seven o'clock Mass every morning she privately coped with her own personal moral issues which, despite all outward appearances, continued to haunt her.

The days became long and demanding and soon Alice realized that she had taken on a gargantuan task. Every day she looked after an extended family totaling fifteen needy individuals. There were meals to prepare for eight children, two of them infants requiring attention day and night. In addition to three adults, one of them chronically ill and not always able to keep food down, there was also Alice's small household staff of four to consider and feed. These included the governesses Gabrielle and Lisette, Marie the newly hired cook, and now Annette the laundress, a woman from the village also newly hired, her daily services quickly found to be absolutely essential to the functioning of the large, combined Monet-Hoschede household. With the financial freedom to which she had been accustomed at Rottembourg, Alice's assumed role would have presented no challenge, but at Vetheuil there was neither a large staff of servants nor funds adequate enough to pay one reduced out of necessity. Reluctant to spend her Uncle Julian's monthly allowance too rapidly, she cut corners and made do, determined to hold on to every franc for as long as possible. Before leaving for the Mediterranean coast, Ernest had sent the August rent and a small, inadequate amount for food. Unwilling to jeopardize the children's health, Alice refused to cut corners when it came to meals, spending whatever it took to see to it that food was of good quality and well-prepared. Household conditions otherwise reduced to mere basics, Claude barely able to provide for his own family and busy painting every day, Alice was left to shoulder all the responsibility and direct all the traffic, but a bar of Souler soap in hand at the scrub board, her hair hastily pinned up at the top of her head as she assisted the new laundress, she somehow found the courage to smile, remembering with no small degree of nostalgia and the occasional tear the small army of servants she had commanded at the Chateau Rottembourg which in spite of her every effort, was never far from her thoughts.

She often wondered about Rottembourg's new owners. Were they meeting with the gardeners twice each week as she had? "The ice house vines always need tying up by July," she told the laundress. "The roses will need pruning soon, and I hope the new people remember that the gravel on the drive is to be raked every morning." Looking back, as she so often did before drifting into an exhausted sleep, the past was reflected in a set of recurring dreams, Rottembourg's black iron gates flung open, the house at the end of its drive seeming to reach out to her from its mullioned windows and forever welcoming front door. How life had changed. Her rented house was at the side of a well-traveled road. Her backyard garden was unworthy of attention. Each and every day there were hungry mouths to feed, a mountain of laundry to wash and iron, and a myriad of little hurts and childhood offenses to deal with, but the man at the head of her extended family was painting with a fresh vigor and when he was pleased with his work there was laughter in the house and flowers on the table and lovemaking during a stolen midnight hour when it could magically seem unimportant that for another week the butcher would go unpaid and that by early autumn the basic task of providing adequate food for all those hungry mouths would become a constant worry.

Into the days of 1878's late summer, it bothered Alice not at all that Claude spent long hours painting every day. It was his work, like going to the office or tending the store, and although she did not fully understand his process or his intended schedule, she talked herself into believing that he could not possibly be pursuing any other career. Locked into these terms and although confronted with a barrage of overwhelming daily issues, Alice felt cared for. Having neither to concern herself with measuring her words or accounting for her time, she very much liked the idea that her children were her own exclusive responsibility now and that she was free to care for them on her terms and without Ernest's interference. They missed their father and discussed at length what he must be seeing and doing in Italy and Spain, but they were also eager to explore the village and acquaint themselves with their Mantes Road neighbors. Before too long, however, the village of Vetheuil itself seemed as small as the house they lived in, their neighbors as dull and uninteresting. But it was only until Papa returned to Paris and made his arrangements, they reassured themselves. Their hopeful, young optimism overshadowing their disappointment, they all seemed quite oblivious to the true nature of the housing arrangements.

Outwardly and to neighbors, it appeared that the Monets and the Hoschedes were two families living in separate houses. The Hoschede house was the home in which Madame Hoschede and her six children lived. The Monet house next door was the home where an artist and his wife and their two children lived. The Hoschedes and Monet were close friends. As such, Madame Hoschede was looking after Monsieur Monet's sickly wife and her baby. This was the intended perception, and although effective, it was a pretense. The barn, close to his house was where Claude painted and the location where for a time he and Alice continued to conduct their love affair, their encounters occurring as time and privacy allowed, discretion proving a great challenge, for on any given day the children were allowed access to both residences, free to come and go at will, this unpredictable coming and going resulting in a constant flurry of activity. Neither house was ever calm for long, this unavoidable situation creating a level of chaos Camille found most annoying, her health by September clearly in decline. Alice recognized the symptoms of ovarian cancer. Several of her friends had suffered with the disease. She discussed her suspicions with Claude who agreed that out of respect their rendezvous should be curtailed. Considerate of Camille's condition and now very much aware that Jean had taken on a highly protective role with his ailing mother, both Alice and Claude bore levels of personal guilt and worried that the boy's attachment to Camille was taking over too much of his young life. Abandoning his friends on the riverbank for days at a time, the child who had been left alone with his mother so often as his father had left them to paint for weeks in the forests at Fountainbleau and along the borders of the Barbizon now withdrew into long periods of silence, keeping watch over his mother as she slept through an afternoon, his hand clasped tenderly over hers. Alice understood his loving devotion but she made every attempt to draw him into daily activities with her own children, hoping that her success in having made a friend of Camille would somehow influence young Jean.

The child, despite his protective behavior, could not help but notice that in the course of a few short weeks a warm alliance had developed between his mother and Madame Hoschede. Reassured at least somewhat by their relationship, Jean determined that Alice Hoschede and her family were valued friends, important to his father's career, and that their intrusion into the Monet world was to be brief. Jean also saw that weakened by her illness, his mother needed Madame Hoschede's commanding expertise. She purchased the food, planned the meals, and took charge of the housekeeping. She nursed and comforted his mother through bouts of nausea and lengthening episodes of pain and on more than one occasion Jean overheard her telling his father that Alice Hoschede was the kindest woman she had ever known. Before long, though, Camille had genuine reason to worry. She observed the easy informality that existed between her husband and Alice Hoschede. She also noticed that since Alice's arrival something about her husband had changed. He was lighthearted and more pleased by his work than he had been in months, but it was at mealtimes that she became aware of being ignored. She and Jean ate in silence as Claude directed his remarks almost exclusively to Alice and her children and not to them. Suspicious, threatened, and at the same time increasingly weakened, Camille could not find the strength to insist that Alice leave her house and take her noisy children with her. Instead, maintaining a gentle resolve, she stoically accepted what she understood to be a close relationship between her husband and the woman who had summarily taken over her life's every aspect. True to her meek, unassuming character and suspecting the worst, Camille went so far as to tell Claude that when her suffering finally ended as she knew it eventually would, she would rest easier knowing that Alice Hoschede would be looking after her family. Claude was appalled. "Camille, you mustn't say such things!" he insisted without hesitation. "Nothing will happen to you! You will get well and we will live a long, happy life together. We will turn white-haired together and watch our children grow to be accomplished men of importance."

"Alice can always find the right words to make me feel better," Camille said more than once to Claude from the chaise lounge he and Jean carried out to the riverbank for her on warm late summer afternoons, "and when the children and I are at our absolute worst, she can throw her head back and laugh. She tells funny stories, and Claude, she knows the words to all the popular songs. She has told me that one of her Montgeron neighbors played the piano and sang at her chateau. Did you meet the man who played the piano and sang at the Chateau Rottembourg?"

She bathed children, judged disagreements, nursed an ailing young mother, cared for two infants, bargained with the butcher and the green grocer, planned meals, and whenever she could find them, arranged flowers for two houses. In her spare time she laughed and joked and played the piano. Alice was very strong, very patient, and very decisive, Camille concluded as September's cooling breezes brushed at her bedroom windows. She was also a fine, pretty lady given to kind, thoughtful gestures and intelligent conversation about books and city life and the mysterious world of fashion. And as she grew weaker and the shadows around her lengthened and darkened, Camille Doncieux Monet understood with complete clarity why her husband had fallen in love with Alice Raingo Hoschede.

Established as an integral part of Claude's daily life and in the midst of children's repeated illnesses and concerns about money, it was at Vetheuil that Alice and Claude found a happiness greater than any they had known together either in Paris or at Montgeron. They became closer, more trusting, and more reliant upon one another. Until Camille's failing health became a daily issue they had treasured their stolen hours together. They had made love. They had laughed. They had learned so much more about each other; about childhood triumphs and adolescent disappointments; about horrid relatives, dear old friends and precious old times. In the process, Claude watched Alice go about her self-appointed tasks with growing admiration for her patience and tenacity. For her part, Alice was surprised to discover that in the face of constant financial struggle Claude insisted on maintaining a particularly high standard in his daily life, especially when it came to food. Altogether dependent on the sympathies of tradesmen for credit, he nonetheless insisted on the freshest produce, the best cuts of meat, and the choicest selections of fish from the monger's cart. The two lived under highly confusing and difficult circumstances, yet their respect and affection for one another continued to grow. They openly admired the abilities they saw in one another. At the same time, they saw the small flaws and vulnerabilities that form personalities and determine behavior. As autumn took over the landscape, Alice came to understand that Claude's work required long periods of seclusion and that the largest portion of his day did not include her. By October he was spending longer and longer hours painting. Every day, his easel was set up by the river, in the barn, or on the studio boat. For several weeks, except for appearances at evening meals he followed the same schedule: rising at dawn, away for the day, and returning by late afternoon. Through much of autumn of 1878 Alice was left to manage her myriad responsibilities without benefit of Claude's help, advice, or companionship and as autumn colored and cooled the hills surrounding Vetheuil, more and more of her time with Claude was confined to evening conversations with the children over dinner. It was not enough. Claude's newfound freedom at Vetheuil had come hand in hand with Alice's feelings of loneliness and isolation.

"Tell me what you expect of me!" she blurted out in one exasperated moment when they were alone in the barn and he was painting. She had brought hot coffee on a tray and he did not look up from his work. "Claude, where are the boundaries?" she asked pointedly. "Am I doing too much, too little? Tell me. You leave me completely alone day after day. I understand your devotion to your painting and I support it, but I didn't come here to become a slave to two families and content myself with an occasional stolen hour. You must tell me how it is to be between us."

Claude immediately arose from the bench at his easel, put down his brush, and took her in his arms. "What has brought this on?" he asked, his lips brushing against her cheek. "I thought things were going well and that you were happy here."

"Claude, you are blind. I'm beginning to thing it was a mistake for me to come to Vetheuil. Your work consumes so much more of you than I had imagined it would. It takes over and shuts me out!"

"My darling Alice, surely you know that your presence here every day has made it possible for me to work harder and better than I have in years. I thought that's what you wanted. We talked about it. At Rottembourg you told me repeatedly that you understood how important my work was to me."

"Claude, of course I realize your work matters, but our lives cannot continue to run in opposite directions all day every day. I had enough of that with Ernest. You promised me a safe refuge and I welcomed it, but even with two busy households to contend with, that refuge has turned out to be a lonely place."

"Alice my dearest, I didn't realize you were so troubled. Of course we can change things, but you can be a very strong distraction to my work. I'll have to discipline myself." His eyes met hers with the reassurance she had hoped for and in his arms she felt calm and safe again, grateful for his strength. Claude would never disappoint her. She was certain of that, but there were questions with no answers and worst of all a void in the future. What lay ahead? Were Vetheuil and her modest house to be more than temporary? Would there always be a shortage of money? Clearly disturbed by her uncertainty, Claude pulled her close and kissed her hard. "Listen to what I am telling you. I love you my darling and I want to make you happy, but our life here is complicated in the extreme and there are difficulties under both our roofs. I wish I could let my guard down and express myself exactly as I would like. I wish I had more time with you, but I wish for many things. I know it is the same for you."

Weeks passed before Alice understood with complete clarity that for all his solid declarations, Claude's attention to his work took precedence over all other aspects of his life. Nothing was more important to him than painting; not her presence and not her central role in his life, but through autumn afternoons when twilight fell early and time could be suspended in the magic of a few quiet minutes or hours, they did find an acceptable balance. At sunset they often walked together along the riverbank. For a precious hour they took time to enjoy a cup of tea or coffee seated side by side on the old oak bench in the barn. During these times Claude had no difficulty whatsoever in expressing himself. His hushed endearments came easily and with poetic clarity and he opened his heart to Alice not only with declarations of affection, but with revelations about his greatest hopes and fears.

It was in these delicate moments that Alice learned of Claude's concern with the prospect of change. Although he welcomed and expected dramatic modifications in the way his world and the people in it worked and grew, at the same time he wasn't at all sure that the modifications he sought for himself would come in time to affect the course of his career in a positive way. The old traditions of the Paris art establishment continued to stand in his way and he continued to resent their interference in his progress. Opinions of paintings such as his that in their unconventional style shocked and startled might never change he feared, and now his most passionate conversations with Alice were centering on a burning desire for acceptance by the same Paris establishment that was rejecting him, his accompanying hunger for its recognition of him as a superb, well-respected artist a demand Alice found touching and imminently revealing of this strong, solid man's vulnerability.

One afternoon, he confessed to her that he had never quite recovered from the accusation made by one Paris art critic who wrote that "in his painting Claude Monet denigrated every aesthetic value France held dear, disregarding all facets of professional decorum." He had gazed into her eyes and asked if she agreed. "Of course not," came the protective reply, but in one delicate moment Alice realized that stalwart and proud as Claude was, he actually expected the establishment base, that wall of stone, to re-invent itself, accommodate him, and soon. How could such a thing happen in Paris?" she asked herself. Claude was a determined man, unwavering in his beliefs, but he was facing a bloody battle and time was not on his side. He was nearing forty. Both the enormity of his challenge and his fear of failure suddenly became very real. They explained so much about his dark moods and frequent dissatisfaction. Oh, what a world of adversity lay ahead, Alice concluded. Things could go very badly. The battle he waged so diligently could be lost at any time, but one thing had changed. Now she was part of the battle. Yes, in coming to Vetheuil she had donned the armor and joined the fray and now she found herself more than willing to share in the challenges ahead. She would not stand by and watch him fail, she said to him. She would partner into his war and together they would win. She was strong. She was intelligent and resilient and she knew how the establishment worked. She had been part of it.

In moments she wished would stand still, she kissed him and rested her head on his chest. In a country barn far away from the dictates of influential Paris, Claude's arms closed her in and once again, despite their best intentions, the outside world faded into oblivion. Sweet desire and tenderness blanketed harsh reality and created new truth. All thoughts of defeat vanished. There were no boundaries. The vast sky and its cushion of clouds were within reach. A pair of freshly coined rebels escaped to the safety of wild dreams. Nothing was impossible. Time raced past unnoticed. Touch and nearness were all that mattered and released from the lonely isolating prison of haunting doubt, Claude was freed to embrace the narrow promise of renewed hope.

"It will be all right," Alice assured him. "We'll see it through. Somehow we'll manage it. I will be there at every step of the way." Once again she was facing an unknown world, but this time an indestructible bond had been formed with someone she trusted implicitly. It was the sort of protective bond between lovers that elevates caring. It was the sort of bond that makes a woman feel needed and included in a set of circumstances that demand something of her. It was the sort of bond that makes a man love that woman more deeply than he thought possible. The fight would be long and hard. They were well aware of its serious challenges and of the very real fact that all could be lost at any time, but at remote Vetheuil and secure in their love, the terms of a shared future were being securely defined.

Unfortunately, the euphoria and optimism vanished quickly. A few days later, Claude became indecisive and moody once again. Something had gone terribly wrong. In the confines of the same barn where days earlier nothing had seemed impossible, he reminded Alice that he had left Argenteuil because he had become bored with its themes. Now he said he was not at all sure of Vetheuil. It was too far from Paris, too isolated, too boring. It had outlived its usefulness. "Initially, I was seduced by the Renaissance church and the beauty of the surrounding hills," he said to her, "but now I'm not at all sure these elements can make a difference in my painting or in what I want for the future. It was a mistake for me to come here."

Of course he hungered for success and acceptance, but he also yearned for mastery, for triumph over the medium, over the use of color, for victory over the capriciousness of air and light. It had been his hope that at Vetheuil he would not only find fresh new subjects to paint, but that he would, at last, find his center. Like all great artists who struggle to explore the secrets of the universe and expect to succeed in having them fully revealed, Claude Monet was disappointed. "I could fail miserably here," he confided. "Who knows? Perhaps I should have stayed in Paris or even Argenteuil. In his letters, Gustave Caillebotte keeps reminding me that the city has always inspired me. I do love it there. But there's something else.

Alice my darling, I worry that our situation, yours and mine is too fragile. I know I am expecting a great deal of myself but perhaps I am expecting too much of you; too much of your patience, of your love. Perhaps I have already failed. Here I am nearing forty and I have made no mark at all. I struggle constantly just to scrape together enough money to survive. I don't know what else I could possibly do with my life, but as an artist I fear my time may never come. I go on searching for change, the right change at the right moment, in the right place, but at the same time I honestly fear it. Will I recognize it? Will it be what I want? I look for the balance I know must exist in life but in the end I'm afraid of making the wrong choices. It could all elude me. I could even lose you in the process and that would be the worst of all."

"Stop it!" Alice snapped. "I cannot and will not listen to this insanity! How can you be afraid of anything? Do you fear the sunshine and the river and the fields you paint with such freedom? Do you fear the rain pouring down on your head in summer and the cold boring through you in winter?" she shouted. "From dawn to dusk you paint the changes in nature and you paint them quickly and without fear. You paint the flight of seconds racing across a rippling river, the billowing clouds fleeing the sky, the effects of snow spilling out in a white winter haze over spires and domes! Claude Monet, this self-doubt, this negotiation you constantly conduct with yourself must end! We cannot live this way. You will not survive and neither will I. If I have learned anything at all in this past year it is that change comes whether we want it to or not. It's been a very difficult lesson for me to learn but it's one that has taught me that most of the time the change we get isn't the change we want. We make mistakes and we expect too much. I expected heaven to guide my life and I got a lot of hell thrown in. As I grew into womanhood I was very foolish to expect myself to remain suspended in the sublime world I'd know since childhood and as that world was spinning out of control I fought and cried and beat my fists and I asked why. "Why, God, are you doing this to poor me? Why are you so angry with me? What terrible thing have I done to deserve this punishment?" And at the same time I railed and cried and begged God for answers he sent me something of real value and it changed everything. I got my answer. It wasn't the answer I expected or recognized right away, but it was the right answer. It was you. You held me together in the face of great change. You brought an honest strength to my life. You showed me in simple, loving ways that it was possible to accept and live with the changes I had to make no matter how ugly and unmanageable they seemed. And there was something else, something even more important. Claude, you encouraged me to have what I have seen in you, and that is faith in myself. You say you doubt yourself right now but I've watched you cope with levels of public denial and discouragement that few men should be asked to endure. You may not know it, but you've built up a great reserve within you. Rely on it! Use it! The battle could go on for a long time! It could bite at your heels and knock you down again and again. Change? I welcome it and you should too. My need for change is what brought me here to you. And so be it if you have made a mistake by coming to Vetheuil! You'll move and I'll move with you. We'll find another village, another dot on the horizon. You will find the balance, and yes, you will find the acceptance you want. Claude, I have eight children, a sick woman, and two households to look after right now. If I cannot handle change and all the hell that comes with it then I will have failed quite miserably and I do not intend to fail, not as a mother or friend and not as your strongest ally. Claude, your time will come. I know it, and you must believe that every day."

Ernest came for a week in late September. He and Claude did not speak to one another and after two days of silent agony, Claude retreated to his studio boat. The children were delighted to see their father. Just returned from his travels in Spain and Italy and eager to distribute the presents he had brought them, he told them all about the Prado and the Medici Gardens and the delicious food in Italy, but they in turn later told Alice that their father had changed.

"He hardly smiled at all," Germaine complained. "He is sad," Blanche observed. "You must stay here with us," Suzanne said to her father during a walk along the riverbank. "We miss you very much, Papa, and I know you must miss us. Please say you'll stay. I know I shouldn't tell you this, but Germaine cries whenever one of us mentions your name. She loves you very much. We all do. You are our Papa."

The September visit and the strain he saw in his children pained Ernest greatly.

He returned in October and it was worse. It had rained for days and the time-consuming journey to Vetheuil was exhausting, the twelve-kilometer carriage ride from Mantes along the muddy, deeply rutted road taking twice as long as it did in good weather. When he finally did arrive, he found both households in turmoil. Claude was nowhere to be seen, Camille was in need of constant attention, the children were bickering, Veronique was screeching, Igor would not come out from under Germaine's bed, Gabrielle was threatening to leave, and Alice said she needed more money than he was providing. The predicted household turmoil at Vetheuil had developed much sooner than Ernest had expected. He could hardly conceal his delight, and now, adding to the precarious mix, he told Alice that although he had just begun to write an art column for Le Voltaire, it did not appear it would pay enough to cover both his Paris expenses as well as those of family's at Vetheuil.

Following Jean DeLille's suggestion, Ernest was indeed writing as a Paris journalist. Just after his return to Paris, the popular periodical, Le Voltaire, had engaged him as an art critic and observer of fashionable Paris life, but the position was paying him only two hundred francs per article and he was to write only two articles each month. The more expansive, highly profitable entrepreneurial opportunities he sought in Paris and which he felt were easily within reach were not developing as grandly or as rapidly as he had expected even though the financial picture in Paris was improving. Banks were lending again and lines of credit were available, but Ernest's bankruptcy was well-known. It had tarnished his reputation. He was considered a serious financial risk and prospects for another department store, a fashionable new art gallery, restaurant or hotel, and the financial backing to support such ambitious ventures were not presenting themselves.

Through November of 1878 he had proposed a variety of imaginative, viable projects to any number of land developers, architects, and commercial real estate investors who, although enthusiastic at first, ultimately turned their backs and walked away once his financial history became known. He was forced to re-evaluate. Perhaps the situation at Vetheuil was not so terrible after all, he told himself. Alice and the children were out of circulation in Paris and there was a strong man around to look after them. It was an acceptable temporary solution and easily explained to curious friends in Paris. And the children were fond of Claude. Like Alice, he indulged them at every turn, not materially, but intellectually, and for now that was fine. He knew about their favorite foods and favorite colors. Blanche was painting and drawing with him. She told her father that Monsieur Monet was teaching her to mix color and create charcoal likenesses on paper. The relationship between Alice and Claude would soon end Ernest also continued to tell himself. One day she would appear in Paris, ready to resume life with him. It would happen.

Ernest did not visit in November. He paid the rent but he did not write to Alice or the children. His life was at a standstill and he simply could not bring himself to face his family with the admission that as yet all had not returned to its former glory. Alice suspected this was the case, but it was just as well. Her two households were running smoothly, she and Claude were happy, and the children were adjusting, or so Alice thought. The presence of their father right now would only disturb the delicate balance, she told Claude.

The truth was that if Ernest had indeed come, the children would have shared a few of their more glaring disappointments with him. Just as Beatrice had predicted, they were finding life at Vetheuil confining to say the least. By October the riverbank held no attraction, nor did the garden, and the farming project to which Germaine had looked forward so eagerly had proven unsuccessful. "Farming is hard work!" she had announced tearfully one hot, humid day in late August after turning over a small section of soil in the garden with the hoe Claude had given her. "The ground is too hard and I'm too hot!" the child so rarely angered had complained in the bright sunshine, "and the carrots have been eaten up by rabbits! I don't see any of the cabbages we planted either! Gabrielle says we put them in too late," she cried to Alice, her little hands dry and dirty, her tears more frequent every day, her naturally bright disposition dulled by circumstances she did not understand, the afternoons of pleasant companionship she had expected with her mother and siblings in a pretty new home now altered every day by the demands of two seriously compromised families. Marthe and Blanche made no secret of their unhappiness. "We are too far away from the city," they complained.

"There is nothing to do here and we have no friends. The children who are our age work with their families every day. Everyone has a farm. We want to go to school! Please let us go back to Paris. We can live with Papa and begin learning things again."

"Please Mamma, please let's go back to Paris," begged Suzanne over and over. "We could go to live with Aunt Beatrice until Papa finds a house for us. You must want to go back to the city as much as we do."

At first Alice ignored the complaints, but as winter arrived and everyone was confined indoors, she understood the great new dilemma of her circumstances. She had wanted to keep her children happy, to see them as free, thoughtful individuals on good terms with their world and with each other. Now they argued, competed for attention, and stomped off sulking. They shouted insults in selfish fits of anger. They were too crowded. The house was too small. They must move to a larger home, Alice decided, but winter had come in quickly and by November no thought could be given to the ordeal of moving. It was too cold. Surviving and staying warm were the priorities. Christmas came. There were candies wrapped in silver paper and new warm socks for the children and there was snow on Christmas Eve. Ernest did not appear. He sent a large box of tea for Alice and books for each of the children.

The winter of 1878-1879 was one of the coldest anyone in Vetheuil could remember. Her children confined to the small house on the Mantes Road for days on end, Alice's energies and imagination were stretched to their limits. Unable to afford the required tuition at the nearby school, at first Gabrielle and Lisette tutored them in basic arithmetic, history and geography and Alice gave them piano lessons. Aware of their renewed interest in learning about the world, Alice also made a decision that would change everything. Dipping into funds from her bank account, she sent for a dictionary, an encyclopedia, and a variety of history books from Paris. Beatrice sent maps and the volumes of French classics she requested. The children began to read poetry. With Alice at the piano, they learned the folksongs of the Garenne. They had spelling contests and learned to bake bread. As New Years Day of 1879 dawned they were living on a rigid schedule and thriving on it.

Monday through Saturday there were three hours of reading, writing, history and geography in the morning. After luncheon there were two hours of drawing, singing, spelling, and reading aloud. On Sundays they attended church and following Mass returned home to as festive a meal as could be prepared under increasingly stringent financial circumstances. Sometimes a thin soup served with compatibly thin slices of bread was all that was available. Ernest came twice that winter, but he was neither corresponding regularly nor was he providing the financial support he had promised. Alice was keeping her large dysfunctional family together on less than five hundred francs each month, some months less, most of her income now coming from the account her Uncle Julian had provided. Fearing her bank balance would dwindle too quickly, she made withdrawals only when absolutely necessary. Claude provided what little he could, but there was a shortage of firewood and the two houses on the Mantes Road were icy cold. Alice contented herself with small victories. After countless invitations, in January of the New Year, Jean reluctantly left his mother for a few hours each day and joined the tightly organized group at work in the sitting room and dining room table. His attitude and demeanor slowly improved. Germaine, Alice noticed, was taking immense pride in her rapid progress with reading. By February she cried less and less, announcing one morning to the entire group that she was no longer interested in farming and that from now on she would devote herself exclusively to books. Suzanne was found to be the best speller, often consulted on matters related to proper use of the dictionary. Her sense of pride returned. Jacques was a good storyteller and once his grammar and vocabulary improved, he wrote some of his more humorous declarations on paper, enjoying immensely the reciting of his own comedic words to a laughing, applauding audience. Jean discovered his fine singing voice and with Claude's urging joined the church choir. Blanche pursued her talent for drawing and painting and Marthe, as the oldest of the children, was Gabrielle's teaching assistant, reading aloud, keeping books and paperwork in order, and capably supervising and encouraging the educational progress of her siblings in a manner that would earn her their lifelong respect. Sadly, Veronique did not survive the Vetheuil winter. Her food in short supply, the temperatures far too frigid for her delicate tropical constitution, she succumbed one night in mid-January, her demise a source of great sadness to the entire household, but especially to Jacques who had often set aside morsels of his own food to bring to her green cage. Veronique was gently enclosed in a shroud of white, placed in a wooden box, and with appropriate ceremony buried in the garden near the fence which through the frozen earth took an hour to dig, her name carved into the small wooden cross Jacques made and placed at the site.

In this period, Claude's prolific output included numerous paintings of the Lavacourt riverbank, a fine view of the belltower of Saint-Martin-le-Garenne, panoramas of Vetheuil, a painting of Jean-Pierre, who was now affectionately called Bebe Jean, and a portrait of baby Michel Monet. His sales, however, were negligible and his spirits sagged once again. In January, he met with Gustave Caillebotte in Paris. Caillebotte quietly passed him 200 francs and at the same time offered him 2,500 francs to participate in a fourth Impressionist exhibition. Yet again, Caillebotte intended to breathe life into the Impressionist group now so scattered and disparate that Pierre Auguste Renoir's successful entry into The Salon was met with surprising encouragement by all but Degas who regarded Renoir as a hateful traitor to the cause. Not only was Renoir's large *Portrait of Madame Charpentier and her Children* accepted by the Salon jury of 1879, it received high praise. Renoir encouraged Claude to try once again for Salon acceptance himself. Although tempted, Claude declined and instead accepted Caillebotte's 2,500-franc offer.

The Impressionist group now met at the Café Legrand where once again they explored the pitfalls of yet another trial by fire. Renoir, Sisley, Morisot, and Cezanne refused to show but due mainly to Alice's encouragement, Claude gathered his waning emotional reserves and through the early months of 1879 worked feverishly, preparing for what she referred to as "the Caillebotte exhibition." As before, Gustave attended to all details and paid for the exhibition's arrangements, but without Renoir, Sisley, Morisot, and Cezanne, the Fourth Impressionist

Exhibition lacked luster and dazzle. It also lacked Ernest Hoschede's colorful patronage and devoted support. He neither attended nor in his column for Le Voltaire did he mention a single word regarding its month-long run. His absence, however, was felt, his reputation again a factor. Well-remembered news of the disastrously low prices brought by his Impressionist paintings at his bankruptcy auction ten months before seriously impacted Fourth Exhibition prices, each participant receiving at its conclusion a mere 450 francs on over fifteen thousand visitors.

Held at 28 Avenue de l'Opera, its formal opening on the afternoon of April 10th, it was the biggest exhibition of Impressionist works to date. Two hundred forty-six works were listed in the catalogue and once again work of more popular artists of the day was included. The representations of the core group were remarkable in quality and staggering in quantity. Degas showed twenty-five paintings, Caillebotte also twenty-five. Claude showed an astonishing twenty nine, his number exceeded only by Pissarro's thirty-eight. True to form and never one to disappoint, as if on cue Albert Wolff resumed the critical hostilities. "…Monsieur Monet has sent landscapes that look as if they were done in a single afternoon. He is stuck in this mess and will never get out!"

Claude did not attend the exhibition, Caillebotte's letters providing his only accurate link to the event. At the close of the first day he wrote to Claude, "We are saved. By five o'clock this evening, receipts were more than 400 francs. Two years ago on opening day we had less than 350. And don't think that Degas sent the twenty-seven or thirty pictures you may have heard about. It is a rumor. This morning there were only eight. He says there is more to come, but as usual he is still putting things together at the last minute and as a result is very trying to all of us, but we must admit that when he does get ready and present, there are some truly marvelous pieces. I hope you will come to Paris between now and the close of the show. Do try."

Caillebotte had not exaggerated about Degas. In all respects and from the public's view, the 1879 exhibition was Edgar Degas' show. There were eight stunning portraits and seven dance and theater subjects, only one of which was dated before 1879. Even more recent were the one racetrack subject and a depiction of a café concert which was loaned by Camille Groult who, until his discovery of Degas, was a collector exclusively devoted to eighteenth-century French art.

Degas' seeming effortless touch to the charm and beauty of ballet dancers and sporting events, to horses and riders pulsating with movement and life in all twenty-five pieces he chose to exhibit, was said by many viewers to be dazzling. Additionally, three of his zealously loyal students exhibited. They were Mary Cassatt, Frederico Zandomeneghi, and Jean-Louis Forain. Not one of Pissarro's thirty-eight paintings enjoyed favorable acclaim, but Leroy was kinder to him than most, commenting dryly and with some effort on "some sincere Pissarro studies where the grey touches are marvelous." What was rather more marvelous to casual observers was Pissarro's inclusion of paintings of fans. His twelve competed with Degas five. They set the stage for a new approach to themes in exhibition, Degas going so far as to suggest an exhibition exclusive to the painting of fans. "Our profits amount to 439.50 francs for each of us," Caillebotte wrote to Claude on closing day. "Take heart. We enjoyed a success far greater than we obtained in previous years." It was an exaggeration. The exhibit had provoked the same type of public outrage of the past and individual artists were again brutally attacked, but unlike the critical success he had enjoyed as a talented young painter new to the scene two years before, now Gustave Caillebotte himself suffered the pain of critical slings and arrows. Overall, his work was seen as falling into the nasty Impressionist mold: too hasty to be considered finished and as a result entirely inappropriate for public exhibition.

Again unappreciated, unaccepted, and after four unsuccessful public exhibitions still impoverished, Claude fell into a deep depression. Alice was beside herself, doing all she could think of to stir him out of it, but he had concluded he was a consummate failure. He had worked hard and cared deeply. He had remained true to the purposes of his colleagues and their cooperative but nothing had come of all his devotion. Alice suggested he re-consider submitting to the Salon Jury for the following spring. Nothing else was working. Why not? He gave the matter serious thought. He set about preparing and planning. Alice encouraged his every effort, going so far as to rise with him at dawn every day to prepare the cold lunch he carried with him along with his folding easel and the ever present brown leather satchel containing his brushes, palettes, and bladders of color.

Through the winter of 1879 Ernest continued to live on Rue de Lisbonne. He occupied three small, sparsely furnished rooms facing the inner courtyard of a building with no garden and an austere view to rows of neighborhood windowsills. Occasionally he ventured out on afternoons that had once been spent at Durand-Ruel's or at the Café Riche. Haunted by faces he could not forget and a past he yearned to restore, he walked alone and for the first time noticed things about the city he had lived in all his life, many parts of which he had never before explored. Standing in the snow, he studied architectural details: intricate facades, magnificent staircases, the balustrades and passageways of a stone-clad city as beautiful dressed for a snowy winter as in sun drenched spring and summer glory. In the Parc Monceau he watched the small winter sparrows pecking at bits of seed and crusts of bread their admirers generously provided. He walked farther and farther and for longer and longer periods every day, pausing to admire the acanthus decorated pilasters on the galleries of the Palais-Royal, the design of the Cour d'Honneur, the grand buildings of the Bibliotheque Nationale, and always he paused by the Seine, intrigued by the secrets of its countless generations winding, twisting, and eternally melancholy along its quays and under its bridges. He wandered into neighborhoods he had not known existed; the small, intimate hollows of a secluded Paris untouched by Baron Haussmann's citywide renovations but home to the residents of a random block or two of old unpretentious buildings in the company of bakeries, blacksmiths and street bands. He sat in cafes he had never heard of, in small narrow spaces where napkins were unknown and coffees were served in cups free of saucers. He watched people he had never met engaged in animated conversations with friends they had known all their lives, drinking their coffees, smiling and laughing and living in nearby houses that seldom changed much except for a coat of paint every fifty years or so and a new roof every hundred. More melancholy by the day, as January vanished into colder February he assessed the many changes in the Paris skyline as he walked, remembering the days when a happy, laughing schoolboy ran out of the green doors at Saint Ignatius with his friends at the stroke of three every day when classes were dismissed and he could scamper freely along city streets unchanged by the sights and sounds of modernization. Winter passed and in April, when the rows of lime trees in the Luxembourg gardens were fully budded, he saw more of Jean DeLille. DeLille was encouraging another trip, this time to the Netherlands, but Ernest was in no mood to travel.

1879

Spring turned to summer and at Vetheuil the village covered in deep snow all through the long winter sprang to colorful life. The apple trees of the countryside served as subjects for Claude's paintings and the Lavacourt shoreline provided inspiration but still, his work wasn't selling. Expenses for the large combined Monet-Hoschede families continued and support for his own wife and children was not forthcoming from Ernest. A furious Alice wrote to him demanding he assume responsibility for his family. She insisted he travel to Vetheuil to face her and establish a workable plan for resolving what had become a most pressing financial situation. Ernest arrived in late August only to find the entire Monet-Hoschede household thrown into complete chaos. Camille was dying.

On Tuesday, September fourth, the Abbe Amaury from the Vetheuil church came to administer the last sacraments and on the morning of Friday, September fifth, Camille passed away. The end was terrible. For weeks Camille had suffered in agonizing pain and when she did escape into an exhausted, hallucinatory sleep with the aid of laudanum, it was only for minutes at a time. In the final days, Alice was at her side day and night, administering carefully measured doses of what little laudanum they could afford to buy. She held Camille's hand and offered words of encouragement. Towards the end, episodes of vomiting came at frequent intervals With the help of the laundress, bed linen was changed morning, afternoon, and night, Camille's basic human body functions attended to as they arose, which toward the end were unpredictable. Claude blamed himself. "She should never have had the baby," he said to Alice. "By last summer she was doing well. The color had returned to her cheeks and her energy was restored. I had decided I must leave my memories of Montgeron and you behind me for good, and at home at Argenteuil, I wanted my family back. I wanted to live a better, more stable life with them. Now I know that what I really wanted was the same sort of family life I saw you had at Rottembourg, a warm, loving home where everyone thrived and was happy just to be together. For a while it was good. Every day we still struggled, but there were moments of tender closeness and some of the old feelings returned. When Camille became pregnant, everything changed. She was constantly sick and after the baby was born, her health deteriorated rapidly. Again and again I called on Doctor Dionne, but it was hopeless. The medicine he left us did nothing for her. Camille never recovered her strength. While the weather was still good I had wanted to do a portrait of her, a pose in our garden here. I never did it. Now I wish I had."

Alice took charge of death's necessities. She bathed Camille's lifeless face and body, brushed her hair, and dressed her in the white robe Camille had only days before told her was folded in the bottom drawer of the armoire. She sent Gabrielle for the Abbe Amaury and while waiting for him she wrapped Camille's face in the thin veil of white tulle which Camille had also placed in the armoire in anticipation of what she knew was coming. Alice remained with Claude at Camille's bedside until the Abbe arrived to begin the prayers for the dead. The children cried at the bedroom door. A short time later the Brothers of Charity, Vetheuil's undertakers, placed Camille in her coffin and by that evening the document of death had been submitted to the town magistrate.

"She looks so beautiful," Claude had whispered before the Abbe had arrived, his tear-filled gaze riveted on his young wife now still and blessedly quiet. Her final hours had tormented him. "She is at peace now, resting and free of all that raging pain at last," he said. "Now her face is just as I remember it when we met, when there was light and happiness all around her. It's the face I wanted to paint last summer, that tender, innocent, delicate face."

"Paint it now," Alice suggested. Claude turned to her, his expression one of immediate grasp. He quickly left the bedside, gathered the sketch pad and charcoal he kept in the nearby sitting room, and from beside Camille's deathbed began a study of the beautiful, young Camille asleep for eternity, her face wrapped in a thin cloud of white. Beginning the next day, the traditional two-day vigil followed, after which, on the afternoon of September Seventh, Camille Doncieux Monet was buried close to the enclosing wall in the Vetheuil churchyard. Ernest would never forget the heartbreaking sight of young Jean Monet standing by his mother's open coffin before it left for the church, reaching out to touch her lifeless body, stroking her hands and whispering to her through his tears as her coffin was closed and locked and she was taken away from him forever.

Ernest reluctantly joined the mourners, uttering no word of sympathy whatsoever to Claude. With no other appropriate choice for mourning, Alice wore the exquisite black taffeta dress designed by Charles Worth she had brought with her from Paris. All the children wore black armbands over their left sleeves and at the last minute Alice quickly fastened one around Ernest's sleeve. A bouquet of purple asters cut from the garden adorned Camille's coffin. Once the interment was complete everyone returned to the house. Jean sat in a corner of the sitting room and wept. "Where do you think Madame Monet is now?' Suzanne asked, breaking the silence, her question directed to no one in particular. "She is in heaven," Germaine assured her older sister with a steady nod. "She's waking up from sleeping and she's talking to Jesus."

Claude went to his room and remained there until nightfall. When he emerged, his eyes were rimmed bright red. Everyone in the house went to bed early. The next morning, Alice discussed financial matters with Ernest, felt they were agreeably settled, and watched him leave. She then dutifully set about re-arranging Camille and Claude's bedroom. She sent Camille's few clothes to the church and with the help of Gabrielle and Lisette dusted, washed, and polished every surface in the room until it shone. Her efforts to maintain household order were not entirely in vain, but within the next weeks the Vetheuil housing arrangements changed. The weather pleasantly warm, plans were made for a move to a larger house which had become available not far away on the Mantes Road. When Alice wrote to Ernest to inform him of the move, he was infuriated by the fact that he had neither been consulted nor considered in the decision. Of course he would still be expected to pay part of the rent and share in expenses, he was told, but clearly, awkward personal arrangements were being made. Claude and his two children would leave his house, Alice and her six children would leave theirs, and all would now share the same dwelling.

"You cannot do this!" Ernest immediately wrote back to Alice. "I won't have it! I will come to Vetheuil and bring the children back to Paris to live with me before I allow this embarrassing arrangement!"

"What you are planning is scandalous!" he shouted upon arriving at Vetheuil. "Alice you are setting the worst possible example for your own children. Don't you see what you are doing? I will take legal action if necessary. My children will not remain here in the middle of this unspeakable situation! Alice, pull yourself together! I insist that you come back to Paris with me. You've been under a great strain here what with Camille's illness and death. You need rest and you need to be away from all this chaos. We can all stay with my mother until I make permanent arrangements."

"Alice laughed. Stay with your mother? Ernest, how can you suggest such a thing? The woman hates me. No, I will not be coming back to Paris to live with you or your mother and Ernest, don't threaten me. You will not be taking my children anywhere! I would remind you that a central condition of the fifty-thousand-franc fine my Uncle Julian paid in order to keep you out of debtors' prison clearly states that for ten years and under penalty of immediate arrest you are not to engage in legal actions or legal entanglements of any kind."

The new house was rented from a Madame Elliot and her sister. Although an improvement in every respect over both the former Monet and Hoschede Vetheuil residences, some things hadn't changed. Further debt was accumulating. The green grocer was demanding payment, as were the butcher, the laundress, and the cook. Her patience worn thin, her purse empty, Lisette returned to Paris a week before the move and saintly Gabrielle was threatening to do the same. She had not been paid in months.

From his modest rooms in Paris, Ernest seethed. Deeply humiliated by the implications of current housing arrangements at Vetheuil, he outwardly conveyed no particular dismay but under the veil of optimism he presented to the outside world he carried the great burden of defeat. His only hope for the future remained stubbornly tied to the belief that something marvelous would come along for him and soon. Tomorrow or next week or next month something would surely present itself; an opportunity, an introduction, a fortuitous encounter that would set things right. In the meantime there was additional income from his columns which were now expanded to include society news, this responsibility requiring exactly the sort of elbow rubbing, café frequenting, and boulevard strolling for which Ernest possessed a genuine talent. His mother continued to indulge her son's constant requests for extra money and he was managing to pay rent and buy adequate food, but in a vengeful strike he wrote to Alice and demanded Claude give him paintings in exchange for at least part of the monthly funds he was contributing to the combined Vetheuil households. Neither Alice nor Claude could agree to such a demand, citing the fact that there were six Hoschede children and only two of Claude's, but through the efforts of Jean DeLille who never admitted to buying them, several of Claude's paintings did make their way into Ernest's hands. He promptly sold them for whatever prices he could get, quick to report back to Alice that from what he could see, Claude should not expect prices for his work to rise beyond a hundred francs per painting any time soon. The market for his work had dried up, he wrote after selling a Vetheuil subject to the writer, Theodore Duret, for just over one hundred francs.

November came, and with it during Ernest's unannounced visit to the new house another shouting match. "Have you no pride; no sense of propriety at all? How can you destroy my family this way?" Ernest roared to Claude. "I trusted you to be my friend! I let you into my life, allowed you to befriend my wife and children and now you insist on embarrassing all of us and most of all, yourself! I demand that you immediately end this intolerable situation and move yourself and your sons to another house in another fabled village!"

"How dare you accuse me of destroying anything!" Claude shouted back. "It is you who are the destructive one! You do not support your own children and you do not communicate with them. You are in no position to make demands! Go back to the city, back to your little magazine and your little life! Leave us alone!"

By December, gossip was circulating in Paris. In the cafes where the chatty artists, journalists, and their patrons spent long afternoons, embarrassing questions were being asked about the Hoschede-Monet living arrangements at Vetheuil. Have you heard the news? Monet's wife has died. What need is there for Madame Hoschede to remain at Vetheuil with Claude Monet and his children now? How far does friendship go? "When is Alice coming back to the city?" Ernest was repeatedly asked in the marble floored Riche. "You must miss her."

Late in October, Claude had traveled to Paris with paintings he was determined to sell. Ernest had not been meeting so much as a fraction of his financial responsibilities and something had to be done. Generous advances from Caillebotte had continued and he had also purchased paintings, but the sums

Caillebotte presented, however generous, did not begin to cover the needs of the large family housed at Vetheuil. Contrary to Ernest's earlier warning, while in Paris Claude did sell several paintings for more than one hundred francs each, but only because he took matters into his own hands. A tenuous situation had arisen, one affecting a long, successful relationship.

Durand-Ruel was experiencing serious financial difficulties and although he continued to accept paintings, his sales were poor and he could barely maintain his lease and keep his doors open. As a result he was no longer in a position to advance funds to individual artists. Sympathetic to his dealer's circumstances, reluctant to seek other solutions but desperate, Claude met with Georges Petit, a gallery owner as well as a publisher of prints and artistic periodicals who conducted a brisk business at Number Eight Rue de Seze, an address behind the Church of La Madeleine.

Petit was known for self-aggrandizement and a love of ostentatious luxury, a personal indulgence he displayed in his sumptuous gallery which created an opulent setting for the pieces he sold with enviable success. He had had served as Expert-Valuer at the Hoschede bankruptcy auction and had sold the Monet pictures in it, including *Impression Sunrise*. Claude knew that Petit had not begun purchasing Impressionist paintings until 1878 and that he was not a supporter in the generous Durand-Ruel mold, so he could barely hide his surprise when Petit immediately purchased *Winter Effects* and promised his support. While in Paris, Claude also met with Georges de Bellio, the homeopathic physician who had purchased *Impression Sunrise*. De Bellio was a Romanian aristocrat and avid art lover. He had lived in Paris for many years, practiced at the Hahnemann Hospital, and was a member of the Societe Medicale Homeopathique de France. He owned paintings by Franz Hals and Jean Honore Fragonard and had begun buying Impressionist paintings. When not seeing his many homeopathic patients at the Hahnemann, Dr. de Bellio could be found seated at the table under the chandelier at the Café Riche and it was there that Claude found him, promptly selling him five paintings for which de Bellio immediately advanced him a thousand francs. Like Georges Petit, Georges de Bellio also promised continuing support. Unlike the dealer Petit, however, de Bellio could, at almost any time, be relied upon for an extra hundred francs or two in quick exchange for a Pissarro or Renoir painting he had barely looked at. Greatly encouraged by his transactions with Petit and de Bellio, Claude proceeded to explore additional opportunities for independent sales. He did well. For one hundred francs he convinced the opera singer Jean-Camille Faure, Edouard Manet's most loyal patron and Ernest Hoschede's nemesis, to buy one of his Lavacourt paintings. Back on Rue Laffitte and for three hundred francs he sold another Lavacourt canvas to Alphonse Legrand. Legrand was Durand-Ruel's former assistant. On a rainy day five years earlier he had helped to prepare *Impression Sunrise* for delivery to Ernest Hoschede and a short time later had opened a Street of Pictures gallery of his own at 22A, his one and only investor the ever generous Gustave Caillebotte. Reassured by his independent sales and with money in his pocket, back at Vetheuil the Eliot sisters were paid rent that was overdue, the grocers and butchers were paid, the cook was also paid and reluctantly stayed on, but the laundress said she was overworked. She insisted upon an increase in wages. Alice immediately dismissed her and taking matters into her own hands made the decision to take the family laundry to the washhouse at nearby Follainville. With Jacques and Marthe assisting in the loading and unloading to and from the pony cart she borrowed from a neighbor, Alice herself took the laundry to the washhouse on Mondays, paid for the services of a young laundress to do the scrubbing, and every Wednesday retrieved every sheet, shirt, and pair of trousers returned wet and in need of either being hung outdoors to dry or, in bad weather, strung out on two lines of rope Marthe quite capably stretched between two walls in the family sitting room. As winter set in, Alice was chopping firewood, tending to a constant round of children with sore throats and colds, comforting two babies who were teething, and along with Marthe and Blanche, assisting the cook in the preparation of two meals each day.

In December a freeze set in and the Seine began to rise. From the kitchen windows Alice could see a coating of ice covering the banks of the river. On the tenth of the month, Ernest braved the bitter cold and journeyed to Vetheuil with every intention of reconciling with Alice and returning his family to Paris. It was his Christmas visit and he was bringing them the gift of wonderful news. The opportunity he had been waiting for had presented itself. He was euphoric. A group of Paris investors had proposed he manage the new restaurant they were planning. They had encouraged his many ideas for a good location and an elegant setting where patrons could enjoy fine food and wine and staged cabaret entertainment. They had applauded Ernest's reputed gift for understanding public taste. They had also advanced him funds adequate enough to cover costs of equipment and furnishings with just enough left for settling his family into a modest Paris apartment. At last, life would return to normal, just as he had planned. Alice would be thrilled.

Arriving at Mantes in the wake of a particularly severe snowstorm, he was told the carriage ride to Vetheuil could take three or four hours. Much too exuberant to care about personal inconvenience he paid no attention to the discouraging driver, enthusiastically offering him twice his normal payment. As predicted, the snow drifts were immense, the roadway barely passable. The carriage was stuck over and over again. By the time the church at Vetheuil came into view the horses were exhausted, the driver was demanding not twice but three times the agreed payment, and Ernest shook with cold in the white winter sun. The strenuous journey was in vain. Although pleased by the prospect of her husband's new venture and what it could mean to the support of his family, Ernest's repeated pleas for reconciliation and a return to Paris fell on deaf ears. Alice flatly refused to return to Paris with him. To add to the adversity, Marthe and Blanche now understood the extent of difficulties existing between their parents and the reasons for them. They took their father's side.

"Mama, please let us go back to Paris with Papa!" the two begged. "We hate it here and soon we will hate you for forcing us to stay. Papa has a new career. He is looking for an apartment for us and he wants Blanche and me to live there with him. Mama, please!" Marthe pleaded. "We can go to school in the city and see our friends. The little ones can stay here with you. Please!"

Alice was adamant. She refused to separate her children from one another. They belonged together and in their mother's care they would stay together, she insisted. She was, however, wisely open to compromise. "Once the weather warms, perhaps in April, we will begin to visit Paris together for short periods of time," she announced to them before Ernest left for Paris. "We'll stay with Aunt Beatrice for one or two weeks at a time. She has written to invite us. Marthe and Blanche can visit with their city friends and all of you can plan on outings with Papa, but make no mistake. When our city visits are over we will return to Vetheuil together, all of us. This is our home now. I want you to understand that."

Plans for occasional visits to Paris were met with great enthusiasm and for a brief time, Marthe and Blanche seemed satisfied, but shortly before the Christmas holidays were ushered in, all Alice's children were made aware of the truth behind the circumstances now affecting their lives and the truth was not what they wanted to hear. Dreading what she knew she must do, Alice asked for Claude's help.

"I want to help, my dearest," he assured her, "but we both know it is you whose lips must form the words. Those dear young people you love may be unhappy for a while when they hear what you have to tell them about our relationship, but they adore you and they must be told the truth. I will do all I can to make the next days and weeks go smoothly because I love them too, but in the end I am very much afraid they may hate me. I do hope, though, they can understand that I have no intention of taking their father's place. Their relationship with him must always remain strong. You must be sure to tell them I said that."

Shortly before Christmas Day, Alice gathered her children in the sitting room and closed the door. She sat in a chair by the fireside, prepared to deliver the words she had rehearsed over and over again. She forgot every word. "Life is difficult for us right now," she began hesitantly, her heart racing as she gazed into first one set of anxious eyes, then another, "and I know some of you are not happy here at Vetheuil. All of you have been waiting for the day when we return to Paris to take up the same life our family had there. I hope what I will be telling you now will help you to understand why that will not be. As I told you earlier, from now on we will visit Paris together when we can and we will enjoy being in the city, but your father and I will not be living together, not ever again. This means that we will not be with Papa as a family the way we were, not in an apartment in the city and not in a country house such as the Chateau Rottembourg. All that is of the past and we must forget it. From now on, Papa will have his own home and his own life and all of you will live with me and Monsieur Monet and his children."

Suzanne began to cry. Jacques leaped to his feet and ran to the door. Germaine jumped into Alice's lap, tears streaming down her cheeks. Marthe and Blanche froze in place and stared straight ahead. "Why don't you like Papa anymore?" Jacques shouted out, his back against the door. "Why are you letting Monsieur Monet take his place? He is nothing to us! I hate him!"

"He is not our Papa!" Suzanne sobbed. "I want us to go home. Please, Mama!"

"You are at home," Alice said quietly. "We are together and this is our home."

"Will you and Papa be divorced?" Marthe asked. "Are you going to marry Monsieur Monet?"

"No," Alice answered. "I promise all of you that I will never divorce your father. He and I will lead separate lives, but I will keep the promise I am making to you today. There will be no divorce and your relationship with your father must continue always. You must love him and pray for him as you always have."

Alice had suspected that the question of divorce would eventually arise but she also knew she would never go against teachings so inextricably ingrained in her. She loved Claude and she wanted to spend the rest of her life with him, but as committed to him as she was, she would never be able to confront a breach with her Church and her God, excommunicated and denied the sacraments. Awash in rivers of guilt and confusion and holding Germaine close to her heart, Alice buried her head in her youngest daughter's arms and sobbed.

It was a pitiless winter at Vethueuil, the significance of its human trials borne by Alice with a heavy heart. As Christmas of 1879 neared, one monstrous storm after another paralyzed Vetheuil, piling fresh snow over old. In some places drifts reached rooftops. Temperatures dipped and hovered well below zero for days. The level of the Seine rose along with the prices of food which, due to the difficulty of transport, was difficult to obtain. The sellers of root vegetables, fresh meat, and fish had to shovel their way through deep snowdrifts along the central road to the Vetheuil church where they were met by anxious shoppers shocked by the high prices being demanded for their strenuous efforts. Unsuspecting travelers died from exposure in the Siberian temperatures, a few hardy village residents made a sporting contest of racing across the frozen river from one bank to the other, and every day without fail Claude braved the frigid temperatures to paint the winter Vetheuil landscape. Wearing his fingerless gloves, he stood for hours in the middle of the frozen Seine to paint *View of Vetheuil in Winter* as nearby, Alice and the children played and skated on the ice, trying to restore the spirit of old country games and ignore the fact that all the children were quickly outgrowing their clothes, the once plentiful supply of well-worn hand-downs severely depleted.

By the time Germaine had grown into her older sisters' dresses, colors were faded from frequent washings, collars were frayed, and buttons were missing. Jacques suffered most. There was nothing for him to grow into. He refused to attend Mass on Sundays because he had nothing suitable to wear. Neither did Jean Monet. The two babies, Jean-Pierre and Michel, fared best. In the luggage she had brought from the Chateau Rotttembourg, Alice had packed a plentiful supply of her children's outgrown infant wear and it continued to serve the two babies in her charge very well, both of whom were now walking. Much to Alice's surprise, a package from Ernest's mother arrived on the twentieth of December. In it were two sets of new clothes for each of her grandchildren. Once again, Ernest did not travel to Vetheuil to observe the holiday with his family but he sent another box of tea to Alice and books for each of the children.

On Christmas Day of 1879 there were no presents, but in the morning after Mass, all the children, including a noticeably happier Jean, created paper stars and cut-out dolls which they exchanged with one another. The afternoon was spent singing French carols and playing cards. Claude joined in the singing, delighting the entire household with the sound of his hearty baritone voice in solo renditions of Bel Astre que j'adore and Dans le silence de la nuit. Having never before heard him sing, the children clamored around him and applauded, laughing happily when he took his dramatic theatrical bows. From the piano, Alice watched her children closely. They were being deprived of so much and they were not unified in their attitudes toward the life their mother was choosing for them, but they were celebrating Christmas together with smiles and surprising joy. Overall, as the year of 1879 came to a close, conditions in the Monet-Hoschede household were imperfect but tolerable. Marthe and Blanche prayed for an early spring and the promised visits to Paris. Pretty Suzanne was struggling to adapt to reduced circumstances, and precocious Germaine was being herself; inquisitive, observant, and the darling of the family. Intrigued by Claude's painting and inspired by his encouragement, Blanche was becoming ever more interested in drawing and painting with water colors, but at the age of sixteen, Marthe, although continuing to supervise her siblings' at-home schooling with loving good humor, was frequently at odds with her mother. For the most part, Jacques was sullen and Jean, although more involved with the family still mourned his mother's death and was retreating into himself too often, but Claude was right. Alice's children loved their mother. She knew it. She felt it. It was enough.

On the last day of December, there was a rise in the temperature and rain pelted the windows. A thaw was setting in. The entire village breathed a sigh of relief, but their complacency was ill-advised. In the early hours of New Year's Day 1880, loud, explosive sounds rocked the village. At first they were difficult to identify but it was soon evident that the raging, dangerous breakup of the frozen Seine had begun. In the dark of night, huge blocks of river ice cracked and snapped and thundered down from the hills of Garenne in a fierce, loudly rolling tide. Crashing against one another, they surged over the riverbanks at Lavacourt and sped directly toward Vetheuil. Garden walls were smashed to bits in the process. Old trees lining the riverbanks were sliced in two as the Seine heaved and belched and fought to rid itself of winter's grip. At daybreak Alice was met by a dismal gray dawn and what she would later realize was a sweeping barrage of jagged ice stretching from the Ile Namur all the way down the river to the port at Saint-Getoise. The little snow-blanketed islands so recently picturesque and memorable had completely disappeared, their legendary inlet lines of ancient poplars destroyed in one blunt winter stroke.

Far from discouraged by the Seine's temperament and immensely grateful for the drama, the breakup of winter ice at Vetheuil led a delighted Claude to paint some of his most important works: *Sunset on the Seine, Breakup of Ice, Floating Ice*, and *Winter Effects* among them.

Although unrecognized as such at the time, this was a momentous period for Claude and for the evolution of his body of work. In future years he and Alice would look back and clearly see the winter of 1880 at Vetheuil as the first truly high mark in Claude's successful progress as a working artist. They would also realize that nature in all its guises, the nature Claude loved and revered, adamant and unyielding, was the great catalyst for the successful work of that impetuous winter of 1880.

A few days into January the flood plains were no longer underwater, but gray pack-ice littered the fields. Claude studied their leaden pallor and painted scene after scene of dull deterioration as once again temperatures dipped below zero. The dirty, rain-drenched snow turned rock hard and unchallenged by bursts of occasional, warming sunshine, the river continued to flow with ice blocks until late February. The garden walls of the house were destroyed, the snow-packed roadway at the front door was strewn with tree limbs, the roof leaked, and the basement was flooded. Miraculously, Claude's studio boat was only slightly damaged. The Eliot sisters promised to have the roof repaired as soon as the weather broke. They also agreed to repair the garden walls and white-wash the badly water-stained basement.

Her life in an elevated state of confusion, news from Paris struck Alice like a lightning bolt. At the end of January, Le Gaulois, a widely read Paris journal, published an article on the life of the Impressionist painter, Claude Monet at Vetheuil ……"where he lives with his unusual…….and large family," the anonymous writer suggesting the presence of a so-called indulgent mother to Claude's two sons and describing in some detail the unconventional, combined family arrangements at Vetheuil, naming Ernest Hoschede as a close friend and devoted patron of Claude Monet, and a man "ruined by buying Impressionist paintings at very high prices, and an individual who today has become a mere admirer."

Le Gaulois failed to print Claude's immediate letter of objection. Angered and dismayed, he wrote to Ernest, demanding he use his influence to print a defending letter in Voltaire. The letter never appeared, due, Ernest maintained, to the co-incidental serialization of Emile Zola's latest book, *Nana*, and its city-wide popularity. As a result the matter of Ernest and Claude's relationship to one another and to Alice was never publicly resolved. In fact, L'Artiste went so far as to reprint the Le Gaulois article unchanged.

Alice was devastated. The gossip and chatter reached Beatrice and Julian Raingo. It also reached members of the Raingo family as well as Ernest's mortified mother, Armel DuCasse, Jean DeLille, Paul Durand-Ruel, and all the Impressionists. It even reached the ears of Mother Catherine at the Abbey of Notre Dame at Yerres.

As far as his closest Impressionist colleagues were concerned, Claude's personal affairs were his business and his business alone. Not one of them pronounced judgment or even cared about the whole business. They said as much to him during meetings at the Nouvelle Athenes and the Café Riche. Claude, however, felt that the gossip could negatively affect the group's already tenuous reputation and the progress of its path to success. In early March of 1880, he defected and although his defection was not entirely due to personal circumstances, his attachment to Alice was affecting his most important decisions. At her repeated urging he decided to take a deep breath, follow Renoir's lead, and submit to The Salon.

"You must try," Alice said to him in quiet moments when of an evening they sat alone in the sitting room, Claude smoking, Alice mending holes in children's undershirts and socks. "What is there to lose except a small piece of ego if you're rejected? But you won't be refused. I feel it. Please Claude, it could open the door to the acceptance you have yearned for. It could also make our situation more tolerable."

In preparation for meeting the March 20th jury deadline, he worked furiously on completing several large paintings. Two Vetheuil winter scenes were submitted: *Lavacourt* and *Floating Ice*. Caillebotte was aghast when he heard the news. Degas fumed. Pissarro ignored the whole issue and continued to work in preparation for a Fifth Impressionist Exhibition, but Sisley, Morisot, Cezanne, and Renoir had already defected from the group, and now there went Monet. The rebel band was truly fractured. At odds with his colleagues but undaunted, Caillebotte once again decided to stir the ashes of revolution and as self-appointed architect of the Fifth Impressionist Exhibition was faced with a complicated challenge. Without a majority of its core group painters, namely Monet, Sisley, Morisot, Renoir, and Cezanne, the game had changed. As yet unnoticed by idealistic, untroubled, and wealthy Caillebotte, its lesser players were also changing. Like Claude, they too were looking toward independence, not only as a group but as individual painters responsible to no one but themselves. Could it be that the democratization of the Paris art world was underway?

Easter arrived. The wait for word from the Salon Jury seemed interminable. Claude fretted and smoked incessantly. Alice busied herself with unnecessary tasks. Ernest did not visit during the long, traditional holiday week. The children were disappointed and Alice wrote him to say that she would never again encourage them to expect his arrival for special occasions. As arranged, she was coming to Paris with the children at the end of the month, she added, and if he cared to see them, he could call at Beatrice's home.

The Fifth Impressionist exhibition opened on April first, 1880. Seen by critics as diluted in talent and short on substance, the Fifth reflected increasing disparity and overall was deemed inconspicuous. Claude's absence from its roster and his submission to The Salon was noted by several prominent critics.

"...and here we have Monet, one of the most authoritative leaders of the movement divorcing himself from the little phalanx of Independents for reasons that are also unpardonable," wrote Gustave Goetschy, a journalist colleague of Ernest's in Le Voltaire.

"With the exception of work by Degas and the newcomer, Raffaelli," highly influential Albert Wolff wrote, "the exhibition is not worth taking the trouble to see and even less worthy of discussion. These men never change," he published in Le Figaro. "They cannot forget anything because they never knew anything. Why does a man like Degas dally with this pack of incompetents?"

Based on such disappointing results it was generally believed that Impressionism had finally taken its last breath and died a horrible death. Rather appropriately, though, in the days following Easter, Claude's reputation and Impressionism's stature were resurrected. The Salon Jury notified him that *Floating Ice* "had not found favor." *Lavacourt*, however, had! Alice was ecstatic. Claude was speechless. Each of the two paintings had been officially valued at 1,500 francs.

The Salon preview was held on April 30th and the next day the doors of the Palais d'Industrie were opened to the public. *Lavacourt* was hung in Room 15. It occupied a place too close to the floor but even this disadvantage could not dim its color and delicacy. In La Gazette, the former director of the Ecole des Beaux-Arts, the Marquis de Chennevieres, reported that the Monet painting made all the landscapes surrounding it seem dark. Emile Zola, a new supporter, himself criticized the placement of *Lavacourt*. Writing for Voltaire in mid-June, he went so far as to name Claude as an incomparable landscape artist, suggesting that Monet should now devote himself to finished, important work and what he called "major" pictures without dealing with the haste and pressure of exhibition. Later in the same month, Zola further predicted that "Monet's great and beautiful art" would one day be highly regarded and sold for very high prices.

"I knew it would happen! Acceptance at last! I knew it would come!" a delighted Alice remarked repeatedly, tears glistening in her eyes. "My prayers have been answered, my darling. Emile Zola himself is praising you! And the Marquis de Chennevieres! The Marquis!"

Satisfaction brought a new level of contentment into her life, but Alice's joy exceeded all expectation when Claude was invited by Georges Charpentier to present a one-man-show at his magazine, La Vie Moderne's, premises. Now that Claude was officially seen as worthy of the revered Salon, Charpentier was receptive to furthering his career by offering him use of his gallery space at Number 7 Boulevard des Italiens. The journey to greatness was underway. Alice was sure of it.

Georges Charpentier was attracted to Impressionist paintings and their struggling painters, particularly to Renoir, but he did not bother with struggling or first-time writers for his magazine. For La Vie Moderne he had only the famous Paris notables: Gustave Flaubert, Emile Zola, and the Goncourt brothers. His interest in the Impressionists had been piqued during the First Exhibition of 1874 when he had become a friend and patron of Renoir. Several years later it was the large Salon-accepted painting of Charpentier's wife and children commissioned from Renoir for 1,500 francs that had firmly secured his loyalty. Now though, apart from her delight in Claude's Salon acceptance and George Charpentier's consequential invitation to exhibit, Alice was confronted with another concern.

The April visit to Paris she had promised the children did not materialize. In March, Beatrice wrote to say that her husband Marc was opposed to having Alice as a guest in his home. Beatrice did all she could to soften the blow but it was abundantly clear that establishment-minded, devoutly Catholic Marc Pirole had heard the gossip and decided he could not be seen as supportive of Alice's illicit Vetheuil lifestyle with Claude Monet. "Alice Hoschede is living in sin!" he emphatically declared to Beatrice. "She is a shameless, adulterous woman! I cannot allow her to be in my house! Do not dare to invite her or her children here ever again!"

Beatrice and Marc attended the Salon exhibition as they did every year, and in spite of her husband's attitude toward Alice and her lifestyle, Beatrice felt great pride in finding Claude's painting in the company of works by the Paris notables Marc admired most. "His work is nothing, nothing at all," Pirole commented, walking past Claude's painting of *Lavacourt*. It doesn't belong here. Tomorrow that disaster should be cut into pieces and put in the trash bin along with the mistress its painter has taken up with."

So hurt was Alice by Beatrice's letter that she tore it to bits and burned it. Returning from the barn, Claude found her at the sitting room fireplace, lighting a match to the elegant sheet of ivory velum. "I won't be going to Paris with the children this month," Alice said to him, tears filling her eyes. Marc Pirole no longer approves of me. Beatrice says he will not have me in his house."

"Then we will go to Paris all together," Claude responded, taking a distraught Alice into his arms. "I'll ask Gustave Caillebotte to find a flat for us, something we can take for a week or two, something big enough for the children. I know he would be happy to find something."

"No, Claude, I don't think so," Alice whispered. "Where could we go together in Paris and not be ridiculed? No, it's best I stay here. Perhaps I will be forced to allow Marthe and Blanche to go back to Paris to live with their father after all. Yes, perhaps next time Ernest comes, I'll tell him. The girls and Jacques miss the city so much. The little ones don't know it the same way they do, so at least I can keep them here with me."

"Marry me," Claude answered with a smile. "Yes, divorce Ernest and marry me and together we will stroll the Bois du Boulogne, the Boulevard des Italiens, and the Luxembourg Gardens. We'll greet everyone we can, especially perfect strangers, and you will wave your left hand in the air and show off your gold wedding ring."

"Oh, Claude, if only that could be, but divorce is unthinkable. I can't do it. You know all the reasons. Please don't ask me to. Aren't we happy with things as they are?"

"Yes, my darling, of course we're happy, but you cannot remain imprisoned and forever afraid of what people will say about us. Someday we will have to go out into the sunshine together and face the inevitable."

The serious implications of her lifestyle and society's prevailing attitudes concerning adultery and co-habitation were eating away at Alice. Beatrice's letter had not only wounded her deeply, it had laid out the cold harsh truth of what she was facing. Her impeccable reputation was a thing of the past. She was not only unwanted by the people who had once loved her, she was likely to be scorned for the rest of her life by people who barely knew her name. The hideous shame, the whispers and smirks would always follow her. Members of her own family would shun her. In better days she had heard the cruel things the Raingo women said when they decided to harp on "certain ladies" caught up in situations such as hers. Over sips of tea and nibbles of warm macaroons they could be cutting and cold, and they enjoyed their cruelty. They laughed their vitriolic laughs and raised their penciled eyebrows and made their vicious remarks. Alice's personal life was no one's business but her own, she repeatedly reasoned, and yet the outside world would always be there, ready to pounce, its moral compass at the ready. Ernest wanted her back; wanted his children back. He wanted everything to be as it once was and in light of her present situation it sounded appealing, but it was too late. She couldn't go back. There was nothing to go back to, yet the pain and loss of the past remained vivid. It lay there, tucked somewhere in a bruised corner of her heart where with very little encouragement it could invade nightly dreams and taunt fondest memories of a life that had faded into lost shadows and aching emptiness.

Into the early summer of 1880, Alice was once again haunted by self-loathing. It was a condition she had endured at the start of her affair with Claude. Now the self-loathing had returned and this time although it was a condition she struggled to ignore, it was one she helplessly nourished daily. Her outward demeanor gave off no hint of her depression, but in the next months she would have reason to further estimate the high cost of her role as the mistress of a determined, yet constantly struggling artist.

La Vie Moderne's exhibition of eighteen of Claude's paintings opened on June 21st. Lacking the courage to be seen at his side, Alice stayed behind at Vetheuil, but she was well-aware that an event under the auspices of Georges Charpentier was all about quality and inclusion of only the best people. For Claude's show, a print copy of Edouard Manet's portrait of Claude accompanied the introduction written by DeLille's friend, Theodore Duret. Charpentier had enthusiastically promoted the event with articles published in his magazine and in a move that was the first of its kind for Claude, Charpentier wanted to send one of La Vie Moderne's regular contributors, Emile Taboureaux, to conduct a personal interview at Vetheuil.

IMPRESSION SUNRISE — 539

The request caused great consternation at Vetheuil. Of course the interview had to be granted, but in advance of Taboureaux' arrival, Claude and Alice worried and fretted, taking great pains to consider at length exactly to what extent their personal lives could be exposed in print. Aware of her compromised position, Alice was very nervous about the possible exposure of embarrassing details. Claude must discuss only his work and his interest in Vetheuil painting subjects, they agreed. No questions on family life would be answered and no names of family members would be mentioned for any reason. Claude must divert conversation back to his work and irregardless of his triumphant Salon acceptance, to his abiding loyalty to Impressionism and its practitioners. There was plenty to talk about there, he assured Alice.

On the surface, the decision seemed simple enough, but it was this first agreement between Alice and Claude that would form the lasting basis for all future interviews Claude granted. From this time forward his caution when it came to protecting Alice, their children, and the life they shared from close public scrutiny and gossip would remain at the heart of his unusual but natural skill in public relations. For the rest of his life these parameters would guide his every discussion with representatives of the curious outside world.

"I'll take the children with me to Garenne for the day," Alice said. "They like the market there and we shouldn't be here with you when Taboureaux arrives. "Make sure he leaves by four o'clock. We'll be on our way back by then." This casually announced arrangement for a family absence lasting several hours and during an interview would form an additional protocol for the future.

On arrival, Taboureax was shown into the sitting room which he described in his column as "covered with pictures." When he asked to meet the family he was told they were away with relatives for a brief holiday, which was not entirely a lie. When he asked to see Claude's bedroom he was told it was a private place he showed to no one outside the family, which was also not a lie. When he asked to see where Claude worked he was shown outside and led away from the house to the rickety, yet to be repaired ice-damaged dock where the studio boat was moored. "But where is your studio, Monsieur Monet?" Taboureaux asked. "Monsieur Charpentier asked specifically that I see your studio. He said our readers will want me to describe it in some detail. Surely there is a building or room in the house where you paint."

"This is my studio," Claude answered with a sweeping gesture to the river and the inlets and hillsides. "This is where I work."

"How did it go?" Alice anxiously asked, coming through the door with the children shortly after four o'clock. "Oh, it went very well," Claude replied, calmly lighting a cigarette. "Monsieur Taboureaux was charming and says he has everything he needs. We talked in the sitting room for a little while but we spent most of our time on the studio boat. It was such a beautiful spring day. I took him on a tour of the river. He seemed to enjoy it. Before leaving he thanked me and said it was one of the most pleasant afternoons he had ever spent. He is staying overnight at Madame Voulliard's boarding house and leaving for Paris first thing in the morning."

The Vie Moderne exhibition was well attended. *Floating Ice*, the Vetheuil painting refused by The Salon, was listed as Number 1 in the catalogue and was promptly purchased for 1,500 francs by Madame Charpentier as a birthday present for her husband. Spring of 1880 progressed and Claude painted the La Roche-Guyon Road from a variety of vantage points. It was this road that led from Vetheuil to Chantemesle and Haute-Isle. A number of glens and hollows along the way attracted his attention. Although Alice appeared in several of these 1880 spring paintings, it was difficult to accurately identify her since her facial features were painted in blurs, the figures she represented in the landscapes too small and vague to be identified with any certainty. This was not an accident. Claude had previously painted and would continue to paint Alice and her children, posing them in countless landscapes and scenes, their features, except for Suzanne's, always vague and blurred, their identities absolutely clear only to the family and to Paul Durand-Ruel who, unlike many outsiders, understood and respected the loving but unconventional relationship between Claude and Alice. Exceptions in style had applied to earlier portraits of Germaine, Jean Monet, and the two babies, Jean-Pierre Hoschede and Michel Monet where, in order to savor the delight and charm of the beautiful young children in the family, Claude had implemented a traditional approach to his talent for portraiture, but from 1880 forward, as with interviews and all future matters related to public scrutiny, protective habits were being cleverly established in order to shield all members of the unconventional Monet-Hoschede household from an increasingly inquisitive world. In the process, Claude's painting was, along with his personal life, evolving constantly. Struggling at Vetheuil with continually nagging issues; with a constant shortage of money, the daily needs of a large family, Alice's emotional dilemma, and a growing list of impatient creditors to whom Ernest Hoschede remained oblivious, he was at the same time living every day within a relentless but blissful cycle of observation; with distracting study and contemplation and with the driving application of a vast, uncommon vision through which he sought to capture one elusive thing: perfection.

 He walked every day. He watched and studied the daily workings of nature, which in all types of weather and all seasons of the year remained a great, endless marvel to him. Like a delighted, inquisitive child and as if he had never seen such things before, he stopped to examine trees and the light and shadows flickering across their leaves, a smile often crossing his face in the process. He studied the river for hours and he smoked almost constantly, the strong smell of his pungent Caporal Rose cigarettes and its pale blue smoke as much a calling card as his palette and easel. He had gained weight since Alice's arrival at Vetheuil. The delicious rich sauces to which she had been accustomed in the past accompanied the most stringent cuts of meat and fish, the precious ingredients of butter, fresh thick cream, and beef and chicken stocks carefully measured out in the process of preparation the necessities upon which, regardless of the cost, she insisted always be available in the kitchen. Alice, by contrast, had lost weight. The strain under which she lived had taken its toll. There were deep hollows in her cheeks but her lovely eyes were clear and bright and on those days when small, tired lines did not surround them, she was a woman in full. Her complexion, though often pale, remained flawless and as had been the case at the Chateau Rottembourg, Vetheuil's fresh country air agreed with her. Her figure now slimmer but shapelier, had grown more attractive than ever. Watching her move smoothly and effortlessly through her many tasks whenever he visited, Ernest was acutely aware that his wife was taking on a handsome aura of mature reserve. He came to visit during the July 14 Bastille Day festivities. Like Paris, the village of Vetheuil was decorated with a profusion of flags and bunting appropriate to the celebratory mood and once again he brought news. It was not good. The restaurant-cabaret project so enthusiastically anticipated had failed to materialize. At the last minute, its investors had decided against embarking on the overly ambitious plan Ernest had proposed. In typical fashion, he had overreached, taking a viable project well poised to meet clear budget parameters to a level beyond which, in light of the high costs of the many additional enhancements he proposed, his investors felt no profit could possibly be made. Not to worry. Now, he was proud to announce to Alice and the children that he had been appointed manager of L'Art de la Mode, a smart, new monthly magazine promoting and reporting on the most elegant lifestyles in Paris. Not only was the position perfect for him, he told them, but the long list of distinguished contributors he intended to publish in la Mode's pages would ultimately rival and eventually surpass any called upon by Georges Charpentier. The first issue was to appear in August.

In view of ongoing hostilities, Claude thought it best to be away from Vetheuil and in Paris during Ernest's stay. It was a timely decision and once again set a pattern for the future. Knowing Ernest's visit was planned to last for two weeks, after spending a short time in Paris, Claude also decided he would travel north to the familiar environs of Le Havre and the Normandy Coast. He felt the need for a visit with family members. Once there, he enjoyed time with many of his Monet relatives, but his interest in them quickly waned as once again he sought inspiration for painting along the Normandy Coast. At Rouen he visited with his brother Leon, a successful chemist and art lover who took him to Petites-Dalles, a small resort in the Pays de Caux known for is high cliffs rising dramatically above the churning sea. Claude created several studies here and it was this experience at Petites-Dalles with Leon Monet which turned his attention to seascapes and which resulted in a series of painting expeditions to the Normandy Coast over the course of the next years.

Returning to Vetheuil with noticeably heightened affection for his extended family, he painted additional portraits of his two sons and as summer of 1880 came to a close he had moved on to a series of flowers and fruit. In November, Ernest again came to visit Alice and the children with yet another announcement and repeated pleas for a permanent reconciliation, requests which, not too surprisingly, went ignored. He had been replaced as manager of the L'Art de la Mode, but there was no need for concern he was quick to add. His talents had been "underutilized" in management and he had been promoted to editor-in-chief. His title elevated, his income for the year had remained negligible, but in December an unexpected, albeit sad event, provided a fresh influx of funds. His mother died early in the month and Ernest was left a bequest adequate enough to cover his basic living expenses for an extended period. Undeterred as 1880 drew to a close, single-minded Ernest continued in his determination to reconcile with Alice and restore his family life. At the same time, Claude had restored his relationship with the supporter most equal to his own developing strategy.

Paul Durand-Ruel had recovered his financial position and was now able to access a fresh line of credit with Jules Feder, Director of the Union Generale Bank. Conveying no sign of displeasure in light of Claude's success with his rival Georges Petit and pleased to restore their relationship, in October, Durand-Ruel bought two of Claude's Vetheuil paintings for 250 francs each, and in February of 1881, visibly stunned by the high quality of the paintings Claude was bringing in to him, within a month he bought 15 additional canvases for a total for 4,500 francs which was immediately paid. These paintings included *The Chateau at Roche-Guyon*, a picture so recent that although paid for, was only finished and delivered to Durand-Ruel two months later. So firmly re-established was the restored Monet-Durand Ruel association that an eminently confident Claude made a firm decision never again to submit to The Salon. Nor would he exhibit in the Sixth Impressionist Exhibition being discussed.

Alice voiced great concern, not so much over Claude's decision to absent himself from a Sixth Impressionist Exhibition, but over his firm determination never again to deal with The Salon. "You cannot do this, Claude, not when you're well on your way! The Salon is the where you belong. It's what every artist wants. Can't you see that? People respect your Salon acceptance. It has changed everything for you! The director of Ecole des Beaux Arts himself compliments your work. You should enter again and again. Edouard Manet does. You could be making a good living on your art with the Salon solidly behind you. Why are you turning away from such an opportunity? It lies in the palm of your hand! Acceptance! Recognition! The respect of the establishment! It's what you said you wanted more than anything in the world. Don't you remember?"

"Alice, my dearest, I know how you feel, and yes, I remember very well, but please understand. I want to proceed on my own now. With the sale of so many of my Vetheuil paintings and Durand-Ruel's encouragement behind me, I feel I can manage myself independently, free of Salon burdens. Perhaps in submitting to The Salon this time I had something to prove to myself and, perhaps most of all I had something to prove to you, but I will not do it again, not ever, and we will not discuss it ever again."

Alice was furious. She did not speak to Claude for days. Their polar opposite worlds were colliding. Common ground was nowhere in sight and they both recognized the dangers, but Claude felt more confident than ever. This newfound confidence however, and an accompanying yearning for fresh subject matter in new, distant locations would require long absences he told Alice. He had tired of the local color, he said, and with Durand-Ruel's encouragement and hearty approval, he had decided this was the way forward.

If, as the new decade flared out before them, any serious difficulty would stand between them and reveal the slightest hint of tension or discontent, it was the knowledge that separation and loneliness would remain a fact of life brought about by the requirements of Claude's approach to his work. Although he and Alice were at the threshold of a new phase in their lives, one promising the recognition he craved, Claude was becoming more intense than ever before in his search for the elusive dot on the horizon. Sensitive to his self-demanding nature, Alice was convinced he would not hesitate for a moment to leave her totally alone to deal with the issues of their large combined family and the mountain of debt that never seemed to diminish. Claude's cavalier attitude was of great concern to her and for the first time she began to wonder if she would ever be able to come to terms with his frequent desertions. Now, as never before, she sympathized with Camille and understood the emotional challenges of her all too brief life. Simultaneously and of little solace, Ernest's attitudes toward involvement in his family's life were also changing. He was rather enjoying a return to his bon-vivant Paris lifestyle. With proceeds from his mother's will he was dining out with friends more often and dressing with much of his former attention to detail. He was also seeing more than a few women, but his relationships with a number of attractive Paris females, although sincere at the start and fondly pursued, never lasted. Under the bravado and complaisance, in his heart Ernest remained completely devoted to Alice who, he confided to Jean DeLille, was and always would be the love of his life.

At Durand-Ruel's urging and inspired by the great enthusiasm he had shown for the results of his earlier Normandy Coast experience, Claude completely disregarded Alice's wishes that he not abandon her for a long painting expedition and against her repeated wishes he returned to the Normandy Coast at winter's end. Leaving her alone to bear the household burdens at Vetheuil, it was to the great fishing port of Fecamp he now turned. He arrived in early March and took lodging on the Grand Quai. He had planned on spending three weeks, but working furiously he stayed until April, painting the Fecamp cliffs. To Durand-Ruel he wrote, "I came here for a brief spell by the sea and am in such good form that I am very keen to stay for a little while longer. I have worked hard but I am somewhat short of money, particularly since I have a lot to pay out before the end of the month. I am thus writing you to ask whether you could kindly make a note for 600 or 700 francs available to me."

Attracted by Fecamps' foaming sea spray and dramatic rock formations, he set up his easel at the dangerous sheared edge of jagged high cliffs, his view not at all to the far horizon but directly into the deep ocean itself. The work was challenging and tiring, but when he was not painting, fatigue was overlooked and the adventurer in him took hold. He walked long distances along the rugged coast, exploring and watching, judging his perspective and assessing his intention. Deeply moved by the area's raw beauty, he returned from these forays to paint the rough Fecamp seas with renewed interest and yet greater vigor. On the 10th of April he left Fecamp to celebrate Marthe's seventeenth birthday with the family at Vetheuil, an event at which Ernest did not make an appearance.

Marthe, oldest of the children and more devoted to her father than her younger siblings who now frequently called Claude, Papa Monet, was bitterly disappointed by her father's absence on her birthday and withdrew into a disillusioned shell out of which Alice could not shake her. But for spontaneous and only occasional bursts of gaiety, Marthe appeared resigned and never again regained the carefree, joyous personality of the vivacious, city-loving young girl whose adolescent development had been cruelly interrupted by the loss of all she cared about most. Alice's many concerns, including her sensitivity to Marthe's worrisome detachment were set aside at least for a time when the success of Claude's Fecamp painting expedition was made abundantly clear

Durand-Ruel had visited Claude's Rue de Vintimille studio, so impressed by the quality of what he saw that he bought 22 of Claude's paintings for 300 francs each. They were everything he had hoped for. He praised the 18 scenes of Fecamp and those of the idyllic seaside town of Petites-Dalles where Claude had visited with his brother, Leon, the Street of Pictures dealer's degree of satisfaction such that he strongly suggested Claude take on similar painting expeditions in the near future.

His Normandy Coast expedition successful, his dealer solidly behind him, for the first time in his life Claude found himself satisfied but thoroughly exhausted by weeks of non-stop work. He left his easel and rested. He and Alice set schedules and worries aside and in a one-horse carriage borrowed from a neighbor they enjoyed leisurely excursions into the nearby countryside. They visited the small island paradise of Chantemesle. They browsed the market there and bought the first of the springtime peas at Saint-Martin-la-Garenne. At home they read, slept, and made love. His energies restored, Alice happy to have him all to herself, Claude returned to his work and painted closer to home, enamored not only by Alice's attention, but also by Chantemesle where he returned to create *The Rocks of Chantemesle*.

By early summer he was painting the Lavacourt plain and scenes of the nearby island of Saint-Martin-la-Garenne. He was feeling like a true working artist, at least moderately successful and confident as never before. Having exhausted Vetheuil's surrounding themes and at Alice's frequent urging, he remained close to home, painting many views of the garden leading from the roadway to the river. So satisfied did he seem with his work that it was difficult to say exactly when the boredom set in.

Alice noticed the first signs of change when he began to focus totally on domestic themes. She knew that at Argenteuil, when he had lost interest in its increasingly industrialized environs, he had withdrawn from the outside world to paint domestic scenes: Camille in the garden, Jean on the steps of the house, the blue and white porcelain planters, the pots of flowers by the door and now, like a return to a mirrored past, he painted Alice seated in summer shade, a glimpse of the fruit orchard behind her. Jean and Michel stood on the stone steps, the house on the Mantes Road where they lived behind them revealed on canvas for the first and only time. In all its comparative elements, the Vetheuil summer of 1881 was for Alice, much the same as it had been at Argenteuil three years earlier for Camille, and in July along with a dip in artistic inspiration, an old tune was replayed.

The rent had not been paid since January and the Elliot sisters were demanding their money. More then 900 francs was due within twenty-four hours. The three-year lease was to expire on the first of October and the Elliots, like Madame Aubrey-Vitet at Argenteuil, were in no mood to discuss further extensions, nor were they agreeable to accepting Claude's paintings in exchange for overdue rent. Once again Claude was called upon to abandon expectations and search out a new beginning.

During a Caillebotte-hosted luncheon at the Café Riche a few months before, Emile Zola had told him about a village not far from his own home at Medan. It was Poissy. On the left bank of the Seine, Zola had said it was closer to Paris and much more conveniently located than Vetheuil. Always in search of subject matter, Claude had occasionally passed through Poissy on the twelve-kilometer journey from Mantes to Vethueil. He remembered its location at the bend of the river and without much encouragement from or conversation with Alice, he proceeded to rent the Villa Saint-Louis at Poissy, promptly announcing to her one morning that he wished to close the Vetheuil chapter of his life. "We will be happy at Poissy. I promise you we will," he said, "and I will not be away from home so much."

Caught off-guard, Alice was at a complete loss. In two houses she had endured a period of intense struggle and dramatic change both in her marriage to Ernest and in her relationship with Claude and so much had happened. A young wife had died. Alice's husband and Claude's most devoted patron had turned against him. Innocent children had been forced to adjust to the most unconventional domestic arrangements imaginable. In the process, debt had continued to mount and too many personal issues went unresolved, but it became abundantly clear to Alice that completely disregarding these details Claude now looked forward to happier days at Poissy, encouraged by its fresh prospects and the recent turn in his artistic fortunes. Privately uncertain of what the future might hold in yet another village where she and her children would be strangers once again, at first Alice failed to join in the enthusiasm, but she had promised to participate in the battle no matter what, she reminded herself. The uphill climb to the top of the mountain was turning out to be far more difficult than she had anticipated and the rules had changed, but for now the encouraging plateau was offering Claude a fine view. She loved Claude and she courageously decided she would make the best of it.

For Ernest, the prospect of a move from Vetheuil to Poissy held potential of another sort and an encouraging one at that. Claude's relentless search for fresh inspiration was presenting exactly the opportunity he had hoped for. His patience was about to be rewarded. He was sure of it. Alice would never agree to another move. Claude was asking too much. For two years and at some distance from Paris, Vetheuil's thinly veiled façade of two separate families temporarily sharing household costs had offered at least a modicum of face-saving protection from the curious and intrusive, but now with Claude selfishly determined to be off to Poissy, if Alice decided to join him, the gossip and public humiliation would not only begin anew. It would do further damage to her reputation and bring an intolerable level of embarrassment to her children. Alice really would have no choice but to return to Paris and her waiting husband. Where else would she go? Claude may have been asking too much this time, but the egotistical artist's growing self-centeredness was providing the perfect solution. Alice would clearly see what was happening to Claude and she would find his selfish mindset intolerable. His spirits higher than they had been ever since the terrible day when he had found Alice with Claude in the Rue de Vintimille studio, Ernest promptly set about preparing for his family's return. They would need a suitable place to live, but money was short. Excited by future prospects, he swallowed his pride and went to Julian Raingo, requesting his assistance in leasing a spacious apartment he had found available on the Rue de Rome, not far from Beatrice and Marc Pirole's address.

It was the first time since the 1878 bankruptcy and auction of the Chateau Rottembourg that Ernest and Julian Raingo had seen each other and it had taken a good deal of courage for Ernest to appear at the elder Raingo's door. He was indebted to the elder Raingo for keeping him out of prison and he knew how the Raingo family patriarch felt about him but he was spirited on by the conviction that Alice and the children were finally coming back to him. That was all that mattered. The downward spiral had run its course. He was on the way up again. He could feel it. With his family restored to him and the Monet episode over, there was nothing he could not do. Within the next year he would perform miracles. He was sure of it.

"Ernest, you are the last person I would have expected to come to me with such a request," the persistently direct Raingo said slowly and deliberately to Ernest from his chair by the fireside in his eternally beautiful drawing room. "And, no, I will not lease a luxurious Rue de Rome apartment for you and your estranged family, not unless I talk to Alice first and hear for myself that she intends to return to you," he continued. "Ernest, I must say in all honesty that I do hope Alice returns to Paris. I miss her very much. I miss our luncheons and outings, and especially our long talks. I hope she is still reading a lot. I really do wish she would come back, but frankly Ernest, it is my belief that she should have divorced you a long time ago. You know how I feel about all that bankruptcy business of yours and the loss of the Chateau Rottembourg and my family's clocks. It is one of my greatest disappointments. I had such faith in you. If Alice had divorced you when I wanted her too, life would have come with its difficulties what with the Church and all that religion she cares about, but this gossip about her living in sin with Claude Monet would have died down. It would mean nothing by now. They could have married and with my help Alice and her artist could have continued to live in the city or anywhere else with some semblance of respectability. It wouldn't have taken long for her to regain her ground. I would have helped her. She's very resilient. So am I, but I will say this: if Alice comes to me and I hear for myself that she truly wants to return to you, I will allow the two of you and the children to live in one of the Raingo apartments on Rue du Temple. For a few years my nephew, James, has lived in one of them. It overlooks lovely gardens but now that he is finally married and his wife is expecting a baby he says he needs a proper home. He moved close to the Parc Monceau just last month. Ernest, the apartment on Rue du Temple will not come free of charge. There will be a minimum rent due each month. I'll decide what it will be and I will make it commensurate with whatever your income can withstand but I will expect it to be paid in full and on time, or mark my words, I will put all of you out on the street. I do hope you are making some semblance of a decent living these days."

"Thank you, Uncle Julian," Ernest said quietly. "I'm managing right now and in a short time I fully expect to see my finances improving further. The apartment on Rue du Temple sounds perfect for us. The Marais and its Place de Vosges are areas Alice and I have always liked. I'll tell Alice you want to see her. She will be happy to hear that. I'm leaving for Vetheuil next week. Once I tell her about the apartment I know she will be as excited as I am. Now I'm absolutely sure I can convince her to come back to Paris with me."

The silver-haired Raingo family patriarch returned to his chair and back to his book, exactly as he had in years past. This process had always signaled the end of a visit and apparently it still did. "Oh, and Ernest!" he called out as Ernest turned to leave, "I was out at Montgeron a few weeks ago. I called at the Chateau Rottembourg. The new people there are very happy with the place. They have children and dogs." He paused and looked up. "I hope you know you broke Alice's heart. And mine."

Julian Raingo had no intention of waiting for Ernest to talk to Alice about a visit and a discussion concerning the prospects of a fine apartment in the Marais. He immediately sat at his desk to write her a letter. In it he urged her to come to Paris for a few days. She could stay in the pretty yellow bedroom she had loved as a child. "Please do come, my dearest Alice," he wrote. "I long to see that lovely face and hear the voice I have missed very much. We'll talk about books and go to the theater."

Vetheuil was at its best that summer. But for the occasional afternoon shower, the weather was warm and sunny and in spite of complaints from the entire household about its necessary maintenance, by August the small garden at the back of the house was putting on a great show. The asters and dahlias Alice and Suzanne had planted in the spring were blooming profusely against the fence and the two rows of beans, onions, and carrots Germaine had learned to protect from ravaging rabbits with chicken wire and cloches were providing the house with fresh ingredients that every day the faithful family cook, Marie, was adding to dishes she prepared in a variety of delicious ways. After a long period of uncertainty, a daily rhythm had fallen over the household. There was the regularity of children's activities and the ritual of meals over which conversation and laughter came more and more easily. All the children had something to contribute, Alice noticed. They had grown so much. Jean-Pierre had celebrated his third birthday on the twenty-second of August, and in March, Michel would also turn three. Although the older children no longer seemed resigned to periods of sulking and sharp bursts of anger, the prospect of a move to Poissy was clearly upsetting the entire household she had worked so hard to hold together and yet again she had reason to agonize. Like Ernest, she knew what a move to Poissy with Claude would mean. There would be no turning back. There would be no further hiding behind convenient facades and vague exaggerations, not from her children, not from her Raingo family, not from anyone. What little was left of her reputation would be completely destroyed and there would be no excuses left to make. Her children would suffer countless encounters with retribution. How would they grow into the secure, accomplished adults she wanted them to be?

She read and re-read her Uncle Julian's letter and when Ernest arrived to share the news regarding the available apartment on Rue du Temple, his enthusiastic plans for a new life in Paris came as no surprise. "Yes," she said to him, "I will travel back to Paris with you to visit with my Uncle Julian, but only because I have a great wish to see him. We'll discuss Rue du Temple later."

She hadn't said no. She hadn't argued and insisted and sent him on his way. She was open to discussing matters. It was more than he could have hoped for. "It will all work out, my darling Alice," he assured her on the train to Paris. "I promise you it will. We will all be together again and our lives will go on just as they should. We'll put all this behind us and never talk or think about it again."

The plan was for Alice to be in Paris for a week. Claude had urged her to go. "This issues regarding our lives together at Poissy must be resolved, difficult as they are," he had said to her as she prepared to leave. "It tortures me to see you suffering month after month with indecision but the doubt must end. I love you so much, but the move to Poissy must feel absolutely right to you, my darling. There can be no doubts, no indecision, no looking back. You know how I feel and how much I love and need you, but Ernest will want you to go back to him. He has wanted that all along. Why wouldn't he? Were I walking in his shoes, I would want that too. He sees Poissy as his opportunity. I understand that, but I want you with me. That will never change, but we have lived suspended between two worlds for too long. A visit to Paris with your uncle may be all you need to see things clearly. I hope it is, even though in many ways I dread what it could mean."

Insisting that Ernest leave her at her uncle's Rue de Miromesnil door and go on alone, Alice found herself warmly received. "How I've missed you, my dearest Alice! I'm so happy you've come," Julian Raingo said, greeting his niece with a warm embrace. "Here, let me take your things."

"I've missed you too, my dear Uncle Julian, so much," Alice responded with tears in her eyes, handing him her cape and gloves. "I've thought about you so often. I would have written but I didn't think you would understand my position and I wasn't sure I could explain it well enough. I know how you are about propriety and such, but thank you for inviting me."

"Let me have a good look at you!" the Raingo family patriarch gushed with a broad smile. "Oh, my goodness! Even prettier than before! How have you managed that? It must be the country air. The yellow room is all ready for you. Go on upstairs and settle yourself. I'll have your bags taken up. I'll be waiting for you in the drawing room and we can have a long talk, but nothing too serious for now. We'll just talk about the books we've been reading and I'll tell you all about the plays I've seen. Before Beatrice was married she was a reliable companion for these things. Marc Pirole is too much of a bore to enjoy anything with, so now except for a few of the professional people I deal with here in the city, I have no one whose company I really enjoy. I do hope you haven't read du Maupassant's La Maison Tellier. I put a copy in your room. We can talk about it while you're here. And perhaps out there in Vetheuil you haven't yet heard that Sardou is working on something new for next year. It's expected to be his best. He says he's calling it *Fedora*. Sarah Bernhardt will be the star. Oh, it's so good to have you back!"

The yellow room was just as she remembered it; cheerful, quiet, and facing the garden, the soft yellow toile on the walls, the pale yellow silk bed hangings and the curtains at the two mullioned windows trimmed in bands of creamy white. She had almost forgotten what such a luxurious room looked like or felt like and for the first time in weeks she allowed herself to think back to rooms like this that she had lived in and loved for so much of her life. She sat at the edge of the bed and let the tears roll down her cheeks as she remembered luxurious canopied beds and long endless hallways filled with the precious voices of a family secure and happy in its lovely surroundings. The remainder of the afternoon was another fond reminder of times past, Julian Raingo typically ebullient and throughout their dinner alone together that evening endlessly engaging, no talk whatsoever of future plans, only wanting news of the children, their activities and developing interests.

"You probably don't want to hear much about Claude," right now, Alice found an opportunity to say at the dining room table, "but, uncle, you must know that at Vetheuil he is at the center of my life."

"Alice, I want to hear all about your life at Vetheuil and of course I want to hear about Claude. I was at Durand-Ruel's last week. I saw some of the Vetheuil and Fecamp paintings. They aren't to my taste, as you must know, but Durand-Ruel was quite enthusiastic about them. I respect his opinion and he told me about the La Vie Moderne exhibit. I didn't attend, but Beatrice did. She said it was wonderful. She liked Claude's paintings very much. I tried to make her understand it wasn't that she liked them but that she was getting used to the look of them. I don't think she believed me. I did see Claude's painting at The Salon, though. Again, not to my taste, but Zola liked it, didn't he? What was it called? *Lavacourt?*"

"Uncle Julian, Claude is doing well," Alice was quick to inform her uncle. "His Vetheuil and Fecamp paintings are selling, not in the quantity or at the prices we would like, but Monsieur Durand-Ruel is very encouraging and Claude is more motivated than I've seen him in quite some time. With Ernest out of the collector world, little by little, others are coming along to take his place. As I keep reminding Claude, we must be patient."

Alice said good-night directly after dinner and went to bed. Settling against the fine linen sheets and under the cloud-soft quilt she immediately fell into an exhausted sleep. Downstairs, Julian Raingo poured a glass of brandy and sipped at it from the comfort of his favorite chair. It bothered him that Alice had said Claude's paintings were selling, but not in the quantity or at the price "we" would like. She had used the word "we" as if to imply that her affiliation with the painter from Le Havre had taken on a serious, almost permanent note. She talked about him affectionately and with openness and ease, the way a woman talks about the man she cares about most in the world, the man who is her lover and confidant, but that was all right for now. Tomorrow the campaign to bring her to her senses would begin. To start with, Julian Raingo would see to it that Alice began to enjoy the Paris she had known all her life. Ernest Hoschede didn't understand. He was going about things in his typically selfish way. The man had to be blind. Alice felt something more than mere affection for this Claude Monet person. And there was something else. Alice was facing great difficulties in her life and she was handling them well. That was a very new Alice. Where had the woman who all her life had chosen to sweep unpleasantness under the rug disappeared to?

In the next days and nights Alice was caught up in a whirlwind of Paris activity. She lunched with Julian Raingo at Polidor, dined with him at Laperouse, and at Worth was, at his insistence, fitted for three new dresses suitable for the Paris scene. They saw Sarah Bernhardt in *Lady of the Camillias* and in elegant evening finery they arrived at the Opera and enjoyed a performance of Camille Saint-Saens' *Samson and Delilah*. Alice had been nervous about being seen in Paris, especially at the Opera, but no one snubbed her or looked away when they saw her on the arm of Julian Raingo. Everywhere they went friends greeted them with regard and respect. There were polite remarks, smiles, and hand kisses all around. It was as if she had never left.

The moment of truth was not long in coming. Alice had been expecting it, but she had waited for her uncle's cue. What the wise, elegant senior Raingo could not know as he launched into his discussion regarding her future and a permanent return to Paris was that his beloved niece's time in Paris with him, however pleasant and gratifying, had not resulted in a change of heart at all. In the city she loved and in a room she had known since childhood, all doubt and indecision had vanished. Somehow, in the heady swirl of Paris restaurants and theaters and wrapped in the security of her uncle's affection, every worrisome thing had melted away and she was able to clearly see that throughout a long, tedious set of years, one day had disappeared into the next and thrust into an alien world, she had survived. She had lost her beloved Chateau Rottembourg and for a time she had lost herself, but hour by hour and day by day she had found strength and love and she had managed to remain standing. Her energies had been depleted and she had doubted herself and everyone around her, but her heart was still beating, her blood still flowed, and she could think clearly. Most gratifying of all, she had her children. In spite of emotional ups and downs, they were healthy and yes, very nearly thriving. Yes, hour by hour and day by day she had moved forward with Claude and the children had moved forward with them. She had managed it all: the loss, the doubt, the reversal, and in the comfort of a beautiful yellow room on elegant Rue de Miromesnil Alice arrived at that all too rare moment in human life when she was able to define the boundaries of her happiness.

The expected conversation with Uncle Julian began on a highly optimistic note. "I hate to think about your leaving in just a few days," he said from the drawing room's long damask settee. "I'm enjoying the visits to our old haunts, and wasn't Madame Bernhardt marvelous? No wonder she's called divine. That tour in America was a huge success I hear. I hope we don't lose her entirely to the American audiences. If you could stay in Paris we could see her in *Art of the Drama*. It opens in September."

Alice came to sit beside him. "I love being here with you, Uncle Julian, and Paris is, well, it's Paris. There is nothing in the world like it." She laughed. "I live so differently. There are no Polidors or Sarah Bernhardts in Vetheuil, no filets of sole gently sautéed by a maitre at my tableside, no massive silver gueridon keeping my boeuf-en-croute warm, but there are other things; very good things. There is watching my children making necessary sacrifices and laughing and sharing and baking their own bread and exchanging hand-made paper ornaments at Christmas and working hard to grow a garden and failing, and trying and failing and trying again. Most of all, dear uncle, at Vetheuil, there is life; a good life, a life filled every day with a river and clouds and color and hope. Uncle Julian, it's a wonderful thing to live with hope when that's all you have. When it all comes easily and anything you want is handed to you just because you've asked, hope is just a word. It's something other people need, never you. But hope is a wonderful thing, I've found. It makes every day important. You're never bored, and no matter what happened yesterday or the day before, you look ahead. Why? Because the tomorrows are always coming. Next month, next year, they lie there stretched out before you. They're yours for the taking. And it will be better, always better. It may be snowing in the morning and the frozen river could flood overnight, but the next hour could bring something wonderful; an idea, a dream, a promise, a pledge."

Julian Raingo sat back and looked into Alice's eyes. There was no need to pursue plans for her return to Paris. It was too late. Ernest Hoschede had lost her. Somewhere in the country, with an impoverished painter as her guide, she had found her center and she had fallen in love, really in love. In the process, she had discovered herself and along the way she had triumphed over the constraints of her own privileged background. "I am very proud of you, my dearest," Julian Raingo said in a hoarse whisper, tears glistening in his faded blue eyes. "You have become even more than the woman I expected when you were a bright little, curly-haired girl at my side and we were reading storybooks together and meeting here for lunch every Thursday. You won't be coming back to live in Paris. I understand that now. Ernest will take it very badly. He has all those grandiose plans in his head. I feel very sorry for him."

"He's coming tonight," Alice said. "I'll talk to him. It will be fine."

It was a brief visit and it wasn't fine. Ernest was stunned and hurt and he hated showing that he was. "Alice, this must end!" he raged. "You simply cannot do this! You cannot possibly move to Poissy with Claude and you cannot take my children with you! I won't allow it! I never expected such a thing. We have a chance for a new life here in Paris! You don't know what you're doing! Alice, you're not thinking clearly. Surely you must know I cannot allow my wife and children to continue to live openly with Claude Monet. This is madness. Have you thought of the gossip? The scandal? The effect on the children? Get hold of yourself, Alice!"

"I have a hold on myself, Ernest," came Alice's steady response, "and I intend to move myself and the children to Poissy with Claude Monet."

"I'll take legal action!" Ernest raged. "You cannot do this to me, to us!"

Alice took a deep breath. "Ernest, yes, I can do this and I will do this and no, you will not take legal action against me. Let me remind you once again that during the bankruptcy proceedings you were kept out of prison as a result of my Uncle Julian's generous intervention and that a primary condition of the bankruptcy order's dismissal clearly prevents you from being involved in any legal action whatsoever for the next ten years."

"Only in France!" Ernest shot back. "I can leave France for a while and take up a case with Belgian or Italian authorities."

"But you won't. You can't afford it! You'd be required to take up residence there. Don't be ridiculous! It is you who is not thinking clearly. Ernest, I am a French citizen and your children are French citizens. I was born in France and so were they. No French court would hear the rantings of a man taking up temporary residence in another country only to launch a case against his own wife and the mother of his children, regardless of the circumstances. And what would you be demanding? Full custody of the children? Protection for them from their terrible mother? Ernest, how would you explain to a French judge your plans to support six children on your modest and erratic journalist's income? Where would they live? Would you be doing the cooking for them? Hiring a cook? Paying a governess? Buying their clothes? Sending them to expensive schools? Ernest, it is I who should be bringing a case against a French father who is delinquent in the support of his children and whose wife, as a result, has no choice but to enlist the help of friends be they in Vetheuil or Poissy or anywhere. I'm sure there is a legal term for it but right now I'm thinking of abandonment. I will allow one thing, however. I'll continue to bring the children to Paris to visit with you on a regular basis. You are and always will be their father, but you in turn are not to come to Poissy for any reason. Is that clear? Say you agree. Say it, Ernest!"

"All right! All right! I agree! You leave me no choice!" Ernest shouted.

It was too much. He had been listening to a strange, demanding woman he didn't know at all. From the outside she looked like the woman he had married and still loved, but under her familiar face was a remote, cold figure from a vague, only dimly remembered past. She was an unfaithful wife, a woman who had lost herself, and without so much as the barest expression of regret she was proceeding with plans to openly cohabitate with her lover. Worst yet, she was about to take his children further and more irretrievably into her confusing world of altered values and makeshift morality. All of it was more than he could handle or retaliate against and all of it, he told himself, was his fault. He, and he alone, was responsible for this predicament and he, and he alone, was paying the ultimate price.

Alice left the city on the Fourteenth of September. "Thank you, dear Uncle Julian," she said in parting. "Thank you for understanding. You have helped me more than you know. And don't worry. I'll be coming to Paris more often now. Ernest has agreed its best to have the children visit with him here. There's more for them to do together in the city. Before this visit, though, I was afraid to come, afraid of what people would say and think of me, but I really don't care about that anymore. I may not be ready to be seen here in public with Claude just yet but you've led me over a very rough patch and I love you for it."

"Bring the children when you come to see me next time," Julian Raingo was quick to suggest. "There's plenty of room for everybody and I'm going to talk to that pompous ass, Marc Pirole. Beatrice misses you, the children too, even the dog. You should be visiting her at her home whenever you wish. Pirole thinks I don't know about his Madame Fontaine and their Thursday afternoons!"

It was near one o'clock, when she settled into her seat on the northbound train. Claude and the children would be at lunch, she told herself. They would be talking about Mama in Paris. They would be speculating about who she had seen and where she had gone with Uncle Julian. Marthe would have set the table with the yellow tablecloth and the white plates. Marie would have one of her hot soups waiting. After lunch, the little ones would nap, Jacques and Jean would run out to the riverbank, Blanche would be drawing, Germaine would be playing with her dolls, and Claude would be waiting for her return. He might walk along the riverbank, watch the river activity with the boys for a while and then return to the house to read. Every few minutes he would look up to the clock on the wall to check on the time to be sure he wasn't late meeting the land coach arriving from Mantes. Alice looked up to the luggage rack. Beside her brown leather suitcase was the box of chestnuts she was bringing to him. Next to it was a blue box from the Dore. It was filled with peach croustades and two dozen madeleines.

At about that same hour, Ernest lunched with Jean DeLille at the Café Riche. "It's all come apart, DeLille," he announced. "Alice is moving to Poissy with Claude Monet. She has no fear, no doubt. It's over between us. There won't be a divorce. I really don't want one and Alice is too Catholic to consider such a thing. She tells me she promised the children she would never divorce their father. She'll bring them to Paris now and then to see me. Needless to say, Poissy is the last place I ever want to visit."

"I'm so sorry, Ernest," DeLille responded. "I know how much you wanted to put things back together, but maybe someday you and Alice can set aside the past and at least be friends. You should both try."

"Yes, that's good, DeLille, very good," Ernest responded from across the table in his throaty voice. "Yes, maybe we can be friends now, Alice and I. We'd be good at that. And perhaps we can write little letters to each other and inform one another about friendly things such as the gossip in Paris concerning Claude Monet and a particular married lady he's living with, or the status perhaps, of a poor former art collector who didn't pay quite enough attention to a particularly friendly summer visitor."

The clocktower at Sainte-Chapelle was chiming two in the morning when Ernest pulled the covers up over his shoulders and gathered Alice's green shawl close to him as he had every night for years now. He had found it lying in a heap on the bedroom floor at Rottembourg during the final hours he had spent in those beloved rooms and that last night, when everything was gone and there was no longer a real home to go to, Alice's shawl had provided him the only comfort he could find. It still did.

CHAPTER 25

Poissy
1881–1883

In the sweeping beauty of the French countryside, from the regions of northwestern Brittany and neighboring Normandy to the Loire Valley and as far south as Provence, people were living out their lives much as their ancestors had lived them for generations. Rich or poor, their loyalty to the past was tied to country tradition and family heritage. Their devotion to the land was legendary. Most lived and died in the same sturdy houses built on the same solid ground where their fathers, grandfathers, and great-grandfathers had lived and died. They ate the same types of food, drank the same types of wine and baked the same types of bread the family had known from one set years into the next. Secure in their habits, they lived peacefully in their houses and walked safely along village paths, their lives untouched by startling innovation or the intrusion of change. Poissy, a delight to the eye and rich in natural beauty was the embodiment of just such a village.

Securely tucked into a cleft of densely wooded Central France and cleverly designed by some thoughtful hand for head-clearing walks in springtime rain and idle star-gazing on warm summer nights, Poissy's massive old trees sprawled over its gently winding lanes and paths. Long, overarching branches of oaks and elms framed gated entrances to handsome gable-roofed houses peering out from their evocative settings on the banks of the bend in the River Seine. The people who lived out their days under these enviable circumstances were solid and stable and protective of their bit of heaven on earth. These were the agreeable conditions of life in the Poissy of 1882 as on a cold March afternoon, in one of the gable-roofed houses set along the bend in the river, the older children at school and young Jean-Pierre and Michel taking naps, Alice sat at her desk writing a letter. His work finished for the day, Claude was reading in a chair nearby. Alice had convinced him to start Emile Zola's latest novel, Pot-Bouille, a copy of which her Uncle Julian had sent, its title (Pot-Luck) a metaphor for the moral corruption of the bourgeois, the story revolving around the complicated lives of an apartment house landlord, his children and tenants, all residents of the same building.

"I thought of you immediately when I saw this at the Laurent Bookstore," Julian Raingo had written in his accompanying note. We've both been such fans of Zola and I know he is a supporter of Claude's. It's just out, and although I know you have your hands full with the many adjustments necessary to moving, I thought it might serve as a pleasant diversion perhaps in the evening when the house is quiet."

Zola's novel had indeed provided Alice with a pleasant diversion late in the evening when the children were asleep and she and Claude could sit quietly by themselves, Claude reading through the letters he was receiving from his Impressionist colleagues, Alice happily exploring the escapades of the largely dysfunctional family Zola brought to life with his typical ease and satirical indictments. Julian Raingo would have been pleased to see his niece at ease against her new background; comfortable, happy, and at peace, the many adjustments to which he had referred in his note having been made with no difficulty at all. From their very first day at Villa Saint-Louis in December the extended Monet-Hoschede family had found a level of profound happiness, their satisfaction largely due to the villa's beautiful setting.

Almost entirely surrounded by water, the attractive three-story house was in every respect a welcome departure from the houses Alice and Claude and their children had occupied at Vetheuil. Spacious and strategically situated, from all the front rooms there was a fine view across the river to the old village bridge and the stretch of picturesque residences lining the Boulevard de Seine. Even in the austerity of late winter the children had adapted quickly, the older ones largely because they were immediately enrolled in schools, delighted to find themselves busy with new schedules and new friends. At home there were larger rooms, a larger garden, and like Montgeron, Poissy was a convenient twenty-kilometer train ride from Paris. Alice envisioned a time when the older girls would be allowed to take the train into Paris alone to visit with their father. Pleased with her new home and it range of possibilities, the agreement she had secured with Ernest allowing her a welcome level of peace and Claude well satisfied with Poissy's potential for his painting, Alice had no regrets concerning her decision to come to live at Poissy with Claude. Three months had passed since their arrival at the pleasant house situated along the east side of the riverbank. Now, on a cold March day, the older children at school, young Jean-Pierre and Michel taking naps and with a few precious hours to herself, she was writing to her uncle, Julian Raingo. Her view was to the stately row of houses lining the opposite bank of the half-frozen river.

Snow had fallen the night before, cloaking chimneys and rooftops in iridescent shrouds and etching the ice-rimmed shoreline in a magnificent ribbon of white. She tried not to be distracted from her writing. There was so much to tell Uncle Julian, but every now and then she looked out to admire winter's talent for commanding the landscape and holding it majestically still. Nothing moved. No bare tree branch swayed in a gust of curious wind. No lost bird flew across the winter sky seeking refuge in a convenient knoll. All was so still and quiet that the loud knock at the door startled her. "I'll go," Claude said, placing his book on the table beside his chair.

"It's probably another neighbor bringing us a cake," Alice remarked. "Everybody's trying to be welcoming, but at this point we have enough cake and bread to last for quite a while. Of course, the children love it."

Claude laughed, but Alice was right. Since their arrival at Poissy everyone in the houses bordering the river had been trying to appear welcoming. They came to the door full of pleasantries. They brought cakes and loaves of bread and the occasional bottle of wine, but under the flood of pleasantries and abundance of comestibles, Alice and Claude knew exactly what they were doing. They also knew why they were doing it. They wanted to know about the large family who had recently moved into the Villa Saint-Louis. Rumor had it that the man and woman living together there were not married and that there were eight young children. Of course it was not a rumor. Expecting either a friendly but inquisitive neighbor or another hand-delivered notice of debt, Claude answered a second heavy rapping at the door, shocked when he opened the door to see not another neighbor or debt collector at all, but Ernest Hoschede.

"I've come to assure myself of my family's well-being," he said, stepping across the threshold without waiting to be invited in. Claude stood speechless as Alice came into the hall, curious to see who or what had arrived with the unusually loud knocking she had heard from her desk.

"My goodness, Ernest, what are you doing here? I wouldn't have expected you to come to Poissy!" she said, a look of total astonishment clearly etched across her face. "I thought we had an understanding and that you were not to come to Poissy at any time, for any reason! In Paris at my Uncle Julian's, we agreed that once I was here in Poissy I would be bringing the children into Paris to see you there. I thought it was all settled. What happened? Is someone ill in Paris? Beatrice or my Uncle Julian?"

"No Alice, everyone is fine but I've had a chance to think about things," Ernest said, standing just inside the open door, his remarks directed at Alice, "and I decided they weren't settled to my liking. I further decided I wanted to see where my wife and children were living."

"I don't like all this cold air coming into my house," Claude said, reluctantly gesturing the unexpected visitor inside and firmly closing the door behind him. Ignoring Claude and stepping further into the hall, Ernest delivered a stern reprimand, one which left both Claude and Alice furious.

"Alice, I am still your husband and the father of our children!" he said, his voice strident and shrill and not at all the throaty well-modulated voice of the old Ernest. "Nothing about our family relationship has changed simply because you have chosen to live outside the respected boundaries of marriage and motherhood so I've decided I'll be coming to Poissy whenever I please and I expect to see you and my children whenever I do so!"

"Such words are uncalled for!" Claude interrupted. "There is no need for attacks and rude demands here in this house! As Alice has said, I too believed the arrangements were such that from now on the only visits with your children would take place in Paris."

"Well, Claude, is it that you feel uncomfortable with the thought of my turning up here in Poissy at an inconvenient moment? Too bad! And don't you dare to call me rude! No one has been ruder than you!"

Claude was incensed. "If this is what you plan to do, then I expect you to carry the financial responsibilities that must come with your free access to my home and its occupants!" he thundered out. "And by that I mean sending proper amounts of money to your family on a regular basis and not only when the thought occurs to you after a little rendezvous at the Riche!"

Claude's face was aflame. His nostrils flared. Finally, he exploded. "You are a disgrace as a father!" he shouted. "Your children go to school without proper clothes and shoes while you are flitting about Paris like the wastrel everyone knows you to be! Do you think people don't know that you loll about at the Riche every night and that you sleep until noon every day?"

"Wastrel? How dare you!" Ernest shot back. "You didn't think I was much of a wastrel when I was buying your paintings by the dozen and passing you an extra hundred francs or two whenever you presented your pitiful self at the Guerbois hat in hand!"

"You never paid me for the panels at Montgeron! You still owe me on those! It's been four years now!"

"Consider the debt settled! You have my wife as full payment!"

Claude stepped close to Ernest, his fists clenched at his sides. "No!" Alice shouted. "Stop this! Stop!" Claude turned to look into Alice's eyes. "This cannot continue," he said to her, his gaze unblinking, his voice oddly strained. "It must be resolved and Alice, it is you who must do the resolving. I cannot stand all this uncertainty and confusion. None of us can."

Claude left Alice with Ernest and stormed outside. Close to the kitchen door, he fumed and paced and lighting a cigarette outside the house in which he had fully expected to make a new beginning with the woman he loved, he felt he had no choice but to escape into the only refuge that ever made sense to him. He returned inside, gathered his painting supplies, packed some clothes, and in barely half an hour announced to both Alice and Ernest that he was leaving for the Normandy Coast and a return to Fecamp. There was no warm farewell embrace for Alice and she said nothing to stop him. Instead, she dropped wearily into a chair, tears glistening in her eyes.

"I hope you're satisfied, Ernest," she said. "You have a great talent for upsetting me. You should have had this out truthfully with me in Paris. I gave you every opportunity. Why were you so stoic then, so tolerant and resigned when we talked at my Uncle Julian's?"

"Because I love you and I was worn out by your hard game of resistance, that's why!" Ernest shouted. "I foolishly thought I loved you enough to give you up and allow you to go off with another man and take my children with you, but I suppose I really am the selfish, arrogant bastard you make me out to be! And I couldn't care less who can hear me or how upset anyone in this house is when I come here. Know this my pretty one, and be sure to tell Claude that if I have to fight for you I'm ready. No matter how long it takes or how difficult it becomes, I'll keep on fighting until I win! And I will win! Alice, I know you. You will never divorce me. You love the Church too much. You're too afraid of the consequences that will be visited on you by priests swinging their incense and nuns twirling their rosary beads. And your children will never let you forget that I am their father. They're my greatest allies! You will never be rid of me!"

"Ernest, please," Alice said. "Please give us a chance here."

"A chance? A chance at what? At embarrassment? At setting the wrong example for your daughters? At carrying on with a man you will never marry? Is that the chance you want? Alice you are living here with Claude Monet poor and disrespected. You can be poor with me! At least some respect can be salvaged for both of us in that arrangement! You have my name, my love. We can manage it. Alice, if you can manage here, you can manage in Paris with me! Just say you will and all this madness will be over."

Alice swallowed back tears and rose from her chair. "Ernest you are making this too difficult," she said, her voice and her hands trembling. "I know what you want, but can't you see there is nothing left between us? There is nothing for us to take to Paris and manage there or in any other place. Please, let me go. If you love me as much as you say you do, you must see that things between us will never be the way they were, not ever again. Ernest, in a corner of my heart I will always love you, and whenever you need me, really need me, I'll come, but please end this terrible confusion once and for all. Ernest, you must forgive yourself for the past. More than that, you must forgive me. Please, please go on with your life and let me go on with mine."

Suddenly Ernest reached out and pulled Alice into his arms. She was sobbing and he held her very close. She let him. She let him bury his face in her hair and she let him kiss her. "I can't forgive myself for what happened," he whispered against her cheek. "I never will." Alice looked up into her husband's eyes, brushed away his tears, and smiled. "Yes you can," she whispered, "and you will. And no matter what happens, you will always be my Ernest, my handsome, charming Ernest. That will never change. Never."

He returned to Paris on the late afternoon train. From his seat by the window he watched the countryside rushing by, prevailing in its cloudy winter ritual as every year it could be relied upon to do. Once again and all too soon, tree limbs had been bared of their leaves under cold, graying skies. Time was passing too fast and like winter itself, life was feeling cold. He was in Paris by seven. He headed for the Café Riche. It was always high summer at the Riche.

Claude took a room at the Hotel du Nord on the Quai Henry IV at Fecamp. The view of the seashore met with his expectations as well as his mood. It was rugged and raw, its cliffs stark and jagged. In the next days he searched for his dot and the resolve that always came with it. He walked for miles in freezing cold winds. He scanned the horizon. Nothing leaped out at him, nothing appeared, but the adversity and bad weather did not disagree with him altogether. It urged him on to Dieppe. The all too sudden parting from Alice and Poissy nagged at him, adding remorse to his anger and speed to his step, but the cold rain and thick morning fog became his enemies. The muscles in his legs ached as his search along the coastline became less of an adventure and more of a campaign. Finally, he found only moderately satisfactory subjects in the houses along the quay and Dieppe's Church of Saint-Jacques. Alone in the freezing coastal air the situation at home worried him constantly. He had left too abruptly, he told himself. He was miserable and his misery overwhelmed the normal strength and strategy of his decisions. He wrote letters to Alice expressing his deep love for her and his hope that matters could be settled soon. "If only you knew how much it pains me to see you suffer like this," Alice read and re-read from the fireside at Poissy.

Every day he walked farther and farther, but away from Poissy there was no escape from all he now knew mattered most in all the world to him. He missed Alice terribly and in a way that surprised him he also missed the children. He thought of Marthe and her struggle to accept him. He would never take the place of her father but he would do better at befriending her, he vowed. Blanche showed a great talent for painting. He would encourage her efforts more enthusiastically in the future. Suzanne was growing more beautiful every day. Her mere presence in life was enough. Jacques and Germaine were often at odds but they enjoyed their sparring and lately they seemed a bit more tolerant of one another. Germaine was strong, like her mother. She brought light into a room and laughter into every corner. Jean worried him most of all. The boy's health was delicate. He was first to catch a cold and last to have it cured. The small ones, Jean-Pierre and Michel, were happy and robustly healthy, all thanks to Alice and Marthe who fussed over them constantly. They thrived on the attention and had no memory of a life without Alice as their mother or the man called they called Papa Claude.

Every night, discouraged and disheartened by a fruitless search, he returned to his hotel exhausted and worried. What would he do if Alice decided to return to Ernest Hoschede? She and six children he loved would leave him. The house would fall quiet. He and his two sons would be alone. The thought tortured him. He couldn't concentrate. His work suffered. He had to go home. He settled his hotel account and with every intention of giving up on Dieppe and leaving the Normandy Coast, determined to maintain life with Alice under any and all circumstances, during a last introspective walk, six kilometers from Dieppe he found Pourville, a small fishing village tucked between Varengeville and Offranville. He had never heard of it; had never dreamed of so enchanting a spot for painting, but at Pourville, lonely and deserted for the winter, he found his dot. The cliffs were beautiful, the small beachfront casino situated so that ocean waves broke dramatically at its foundation stones. He moved into a room at the casino's hotel, welcomed by the restaurant's chef, Paul Graf, and his engaging wife, Eugenie, who were delighted by the rare winter visitor whose profession they found intriguing.

Paul Graf himself was an artist, but of another sort. He was a talented chef whose abilities quite fully met the requirements of Claude's sophisticated Paris tastes, Graf's abilities considerably enhanced by the presence of his wife, the warm and engaging Eugenie Graf and her dear little dog, Follette. Comfortably settled and warmly welcomed, Claude began studies immediately, including one of Follette, the friendly little Brussels Griffon who was most curious about the gentleman who stared at him constantly and held a strange stick in his hand. During a spell of bad weather forcing him to remain indoors, Claude painted a portrait of Paul Graf in his white chef's hat as well as a portrait of Eugenie, the pleasant woman everyone called Mere Graf, wearing her bonnet and holding her beloved Follette. During his stay with the Grafs at Pourville the winter weather was dramatically unpredictable. In one moment the sun shone, in the next a cold rain or snow storm blew, reminding Claude, who stood out in the open ocean air sketching and painting for hours, that there were no convenient cliff caves in which to retreat during stormy weather as there had been at Fecamp. Planning his return to Poissy, his energies restored, his spirit greatly comforted by Alice's loving letters assuring him that the relationship with Ernest had been satisfactorily resolved, he arrived home at Poissy in a changing world racing headlong into the final years of a tumultuous century.

The decade of the 1880's was one of new ideas in France. Rapidly expanding industrialization, particularly in manufacturing and in the expansion of the railway system had resulted in a financial recovery and by 1880 prosperity had returned. Political stability had come with it. Comte de Chambord, the last male Bourbon heir had died and French law was amended to forever exclude members of former royal dynasties from its presidencies. In 1879, Jules Grevy had been elected President of France. Regarded as the first true President of the country, The Third Republic of France would remain unchanged for the next sixty years.

From the Villa Saint-Louis in northern Poissy it was a simple matter to ignore the world's accelerating pace. Newspapers were usually delivered more than a week after publication and the untimely collapse of the distinguished merchant bank, Union Generale, went completely unnoticed until the long trail of debt following

Claude from Vetheuil to Poissy propelled him once again to Number 16 Rue Laffitte, only to find Durand-Ruel in a state.

Jules Feder the Generale's chief executive had been arrested and as yet unknown to Claude the Generale's bankruptcy had been officially declared on the Second of February. Feder had made a number of substantial loans to Durand-Ruel and now he was being required to pay them back. The Street of Pictures dealer found himself short of ready cash and unable to offer advances to his artists, but being the astute businessman he was, he realized he must now find an efficient way to raise some much needed capital, and quickly. He decided to do what he did best. He would organize an exhibition. Once Claude arrived to see him, anticipating a generous advance, Durand-Ruel informed him of his financial dilemma and his plan to schedule a Seventh Impressionist Exhibition which would include work of the core group of Impressionists as well as that of a few newer artists. He expected Claude's participation. Having made his decision to leave the Impressionist group once and for all, Claude did not know how to respond. "When I approached Renoir he said he would think about it," Durand-Ruel said to him. "That surprised me, and now Degas tells me he refuses to take part unless his protégé, Jean Francoise Raffaelli, is included, a suggestion I am seriously considering."

Renoir's ambivalence was understandable. He had not forgiven Degas for his open disdain when his painting of Madame Charpentier and her children had been accepted for Salon exhibition and he wasn't at all sure he wanted to participate with him or the group ever again. Claude found Renoir's hesitancy to participate disappointing, but even more appalling was the news that among the unknowns and at Pissarro's urging, Durand-Ruel was planning to include Camille Pissarro's protégé, Paul Gaugin.

"Newcomers such as untried Gaugin and other mere protégés edging into the group will create a very different climate for an exhibition of Impressionists," Claude insisted, "and without Degas who has developed a loyal critical following, I will agree to exhibit only if Renoir exhibits." To Durand-Ruel this was an intolerable remark and in a stern departure from his natural graciousness, he did not mince words.

"Claude, I must remind you that it is due to the monthly support I have been providing not only to you but also to Renoir, Pissarro, and Sisley that you have been living with regular income for some time. Of course, with the collapse of the

Union Generale, the monthly arrangements will be coming to an immediate halt, but I must also remind you in particular that it is as a result of this reliable income that you have been able to lease your villa at Poissy and live reasonably well."

Claude was beside himself. It was true that Alice was managing to run her Poissy household with some degree of stability all thanks to Durand-Ruel. His generous monthly support uppermost in her mind, Alice had intelligently determined that Claude's output of paintings could be staggering and that now he was more prolific than ever. Past debts aside, she had pointed out to him that if he could turn out just four paintings each month and be paid two hundred francs per canvas, she could realistically hold things together. This in mind, eight hundred francs each month from Durand-Ruel was exactly the business agreement Claude had struck with his dealer, an arrangement that, ironically, had made Claude's steady monthly income considerably more than any amount Ernest Hoschede earned as an art critic and commentator on the Paris world.

Durand-Ruel's agreement had been brilliantly conceived. In 1881, he had begun acquiring not only Claude's paintings in volume, but those of Pissarro, Renoir, and Sisley, and occasionally Degas when Degas was in the mood to sell, which was not very often. In exchange for this exclusive agreement and instead of purchasing paintings outright, Durand-Ruel offered monthly payments tailored to a painter's basic needs. With a rise in economic fortunes and prior to Jules Feder's demise, sales had picked up. Monthly payments set as commensurate with individual needs, the security of regular income allowed a painter to take care of his family and work without worrying about keeping a roof over his head or where his next meal was coming from. In turn, Durand-Ruel received his artists' entire output, the growing dissention within the core group of Impressionists by February of 1882 and just as his fortunes fell, a matter he handled with the foresight and skill of an international diplomat.

A Sixth Exhibition of Impressionists or Independents, as the exhibiting group had wished to be officially known for purposes of their 1881 show the year before, had been hastily organized, spurred on by Edgar Degas. Durand-Ruel had watched its progress with his usual grace and good manners, not at all surprised to observe the childish behavior of those concerned. Held from April second through May without Claude or Renoir but with Morisot, Pissarro, and the American, Mary Cassatt, it was held at exactly the same 35 Boulevard Capucine address as the First Exhibition, the event ignored by Caillebotte who refused to exhibit, citing his great disappointment in the destruction of community among the "real" Impressionists.

Appearing to have been taken over by Degas, The Sixth was felt by many observers to be an attempt at moving forward with new blood. It was also seen as a spiteful and deliberate public slight to what Degas called "the turncoats" Renoir and Monet, as well as to Sisley and Cezanne who had also submitted to The Salon. As far as Degas was concerned, these traitors had surrendered hands up to the enemy. As if all this were not enough for the art-loving café crowd to digest over multiple glasses of wine, a dramatic turn of municipal events in this year of 1881 provided a shocking finale. The State had abandoned its supervision of the official Salon Exhibition. News that an Association of Artists had been formed and assigned the responsibility of organizing the annual Salon event spread through Paris like a firestorm. Now, remarkably, any artist whose work had been accepted on at least one occasion was allowed to participate in the selection of the jury! At first, the concept was loudly applauded and nominations for jury membership were promptly presented in a huge stream of names known and unknown, but before long the Association of Artists initially based upon democratic principles would be found to be as autocratic as the original Salon itself. In consideration of the disparity existent in the original renegade band of Impressionists and now with the formation of an even more imperious Salon system let loose on itself and provided generous opportunity for favoritism, Claude made it known that he would never again submit to The Salon, neither would he ever again participate in future Impressionist exhibitions. He would for all time become and remain an Independent.

Durand-Ruel's proposal for a Seventh Exhibition in March of 1882 and Claude's expected participation in it had come at a bad time. It placed Claude in an awkward position. He would be seen as nothing more than a painter who every day put his finger in the air to see which way the most favorable wind was blowing. But how could he say no to the man who had done so much for him? Unwilling to injure his relationship with his dealer and against his better judgment he agreed to exhibit in the Seventh Exhibition of Impressionists, but this was "absolutely the last time," he made clear to Durand-Ruel.

Critics were, as a whole, conservative in their praise of what they saw exhibited at 251 Rue Saint-Honore, but their recognition of a distinctive Monet style and a heretofore unharnessed grace did not go unnoticed. Several published reviews fell handily into what a future generation of critics would call "raves."

"To my mind, Monet is not only the most exquisite of the Impressionists, he is also one of the true contemporary poets of the things of nature," wrote Armand Silvestre in Charpentier's La Vie Moderne. "He does not merely paint it, he sings it. A lyre seems hidden in his palette."

Claude had decided to show *The Ice Floes* which, refused by the Salon and in the catalogue titled *Les Glacons*, had been loaned by its owner, La Vie Moderne's editor, Georges Charpentier. "It is with pleasure that I see once more Claude Monet's *Glacons* shown two years ago at the Vie Moderne," wrote Georges Riviere in Le Chat Noir.

In a room designed by Charles Garnier of Paris Opera fame and rented by Paul Durand-Ruel on Rue Saint-Honore, after eight troubled, often confusing years, the Seventh Exhibition not only succeeded in establishing a high point for Claude, but in Durand-Ruel's hands the sum of its parts presented a solid definition of Impressionist Art at last. The small regiment of combatants had heard General Paul Durand-Ruel's bugle call and falling at first into sorry ranks, had, at the end, responded with exceptional precision. The general public witnessed the subtle victory and were joined by members of Paris high society making its elegant appearance at the trooping of the colors, alighting from gleaming carriages lined up on opening day along the entire length of Rue Saint-Honore to view the most and best-publicized art-moderne event of the year.

Notably absent from the roll call were Paul Cezanne and Edgar Degas, but added to the Durand-Ruel-led-ranks was the newcomer, Paul Gaugin, his inclusion met by the original group with resistance but stubbornly supported by Durand-Ruel. On opening day and throughout the month of March, Claude's thirty paintings joined by a stunning array of "real" Impressionist work stood as a sterling example of Durand-Ruel's skill and expertise in the art of exhibition. Much to the delight of its participants, paintings were well hung and arranged in understandable sequence. With assurances of continued support and the suggestion of a series of one-man shows in the new gallery space he was considering on Boulevard de la Madeleine once his cash flow improved, Paul Durand-Ruel had convinced the disgruntled band of picky, bickering artists to put aside their differences and use the opportunity of a Seventh Exhibition to show off and enjoy themselves. To Alfred Sisley who was uncomfortable with the prima-donna behavior of his colleagues and quite uncertain of his ability to prepare enough work in time, Durand-Ruel recalled a personal experience from a rehearsal of Richard Wagner's Die Meistersinger he had attended at the Paris Opera to which the rehearsal conductor, Monsieur Balfe, an art lover and client, had invited him. Hans von Bulow himself was due to conduct the performance and Balfe, known to be extremely demanding of his singers, was not pleased with the rehearsal progress of the tenor. "You are exquisitely prepared, Monsieur Rothier!" Durand-Ruel mimicked. "Your voice is beautiful! Magnificent! Your phrasing is impeccable! Each and every note is a joy! Now, please, please, please! Just sing!"

And sing the Impressionists did, their harmonics and brilliant high C's testament to Durand-Ruel's own virtuosity. Adding to Monet's thirty-five paintings, Pissarro showed twenty-five, Renoir twenty-five, Sisley twenty-seven, Berthe Morisot nine, Gaugin thirteen, and Caillebotte seventeen. Although invited, Degas maintained his stubborn distance and did not show at all. Following her mentor's example, neither did Mary Cassatt.

Critics' reviews were mixed. Not all had heard the music. "When Caillebotte is not demented, he has as much talent as anyone," wrote Albert Wolff in the popular Le Figaro. "If he had learned to draw, Renoir would have a very pretty picture," Wolff further commented on *Dinner at Bougival*.

"We are a little embarrassed to mention Gaugin. He is the Independent who has the most to do to earn the name! His exhibition is the least consequential as well as the least interesting," said Sallanches in Le Journal des Arts.

"Well it is not Gaugin who will give us the note that sings!" wrote Louis Leroy in Le Charivari.

His own reviews pleasantly digested, his spirits high, as the summer of 1882 approached, Claude thought back to Pourville. Through the winter he had spoken repeatedly to Alice and the children about the seaside casino on the Pourville beach, describing to them the hotel, the charm of Paul and Eugenie Graf and delightful little Follette. So infectious was his enthusiasm and his desire to paint at Pourville once again that when the fine summer weather arrived in June, the full Monet-Hoschede household found itself off to Pourville, soon comfortably installed in the rented Villa Juliette, a charming, airy house secured for Claude through the efforts of the Grafs. At the seaside Claude was on a painting holiday with his family, thoroughly delighted to have everyone with him. Here, for the first time, Alice saw him on location.

He enjoyed pointing out to her the views that had formed the subjects of his earlier Pourville canvases, pleased by her comments and praise, most of all pleased by her agreement with and understanding of his choice of subjects not only at Pourville, but at nearby Varengeville as well. Her interest in his work was growing more concentrated, her attention to his use of color, her understanding of his grasp of movement across water, of light over hills and abandoned fields more focused, more intuitive and more admiring.

"You have a very great talent, Claude Monet," she said to him in a moment of deep introspection when he pointed out the small fisherman's house at Varengeville which he said would be one of his summer subjects. "It has taken a long time for me to understand why you choose to paint the subjects you do, but it really is all about what you feel isn't it? All along I've thought it was in your eye, in that wonderful piercing gaze you use so well, even on me, but it really isn't what you see at all that matters most. Unless your heart and your eye feel connected to a river, a sky, a shore, a field of flowers, a stand of trees, a house, you look away; you walk away. That's it, isn't it? You wait for a connection. That's what you intend when you search a horizon for your dot is, isn't it? The dot is the whole of Claude Monet, isn't it?"

He smiled. "My darling, don't analyze me too much. I don't want you to be disappointed, but yes, I need to feel something."

At Pourville, eighteen-year-old Blanche often painted at his side. She was watching him more and more closely and learning to choose color, see light, and execute views of the shoreline and the forever intriguing boats that passed in the distance, their unpredictable movements in the constant motion of water never ceasing to fascinate Papa Claude. Through these summer months Claude was feeling both happy and adventurous. While Alice and the children enjoyed the beach and the summer sunshine, he painted from the precarious top of the Falaise d'Amont. He explored the cote path and at Varengeville he painted the rustic fisherman's house as well as the village church. At the Ailly Gorge, he painted the custom officer's cottage from several angles. He also painted the trees on the nearby high ground by the seaside. He favored the view from the foot of the cliff which he could easily reach from the Pourville beach and it was there that he set up his easel to paint views of fishermen's nets spread out to dry and repair along the beach. The tradition of net-spreading on the sandy shore fascinated the younger children, but another heightened view soon captured Claude's greater interest. Atop the high cliff, quite close to its precipice and in full length, he painted Alice and Suzanne watching the boats, Alice carrying a pink parasol, Suzanne at her side, wearing a flower-trimmed hat. Again, facial features were obscure, the identity of the two female figures in the painting undecipherable to the casual observer.

In July, en route to his summer holiday at Dieppe, Durand-Ruel stopped to visit, observing at first hand the Pourville landscape to which Claude was magnetically drawn. He was introduced to the Grafs and Follette and along with Claude, Alice, and the children enjoyed warm hospitality as well as Paul Graf's culinary talents, in particular his galettes, the fruit-filled, light-as-air puff pastries for which Graf had become justly famous at the Pourville restaurant appropriately named, a la Renommee des Galettes. To meet and see for himself the Grafs, their enchanting little dog, and Paul Graf's galettes, all affable subjects of several of Claude's most intimate Pourville studies and paintings, provided Durand-Ruel with a fresh perception of the painter's eye and indomitable will. At Pourville, Durand-Ruel saw a transformed Claude Monet, a man who had at last found joy in life, a genuinely happy man at the head of the large family for which he had assumed full responsibility. He heard his easy laughter, saw the spontaneous delight he took in the simplest moments of family life, and he watched Claude's eyes light up when the lovely woman at his side made no secret of the fact that her faith in him was as indomitable as his will. Durand-Ruel left Claude at Pourville with sincere words of encouragement and the assurance of a set of good years ahead. He also offered him a commission for still-life panels to decorate the drawing room doors of his Rue de Rome apartment. Not only had Paul Durand-Ruel seen Claude's Pourville, he had felt the artist's relationship to it. In natural settings and from eye to canvas he had seen for himself the translations in Claude's unique visual language and through the prism of his own deep sensitivities he had observed the eye of a master, the irrepressible style of a renegade, and the colors chosen by a happy, gifted painter in complete control of his medium. Claude Monet was a man who had come into his season, Durand-Ruel decided at Pourville. He was born to shine and soon he would.

Alice rested at Pourville. It was her first real holiday in years and it came at a good time. She was making her peace with the past. When disappointment and loss had left her paralyzed and afraid, somewhere deep inside she had found that hidden place the heart reserves for storing wounds that never heal and dreams that crack and die. It was a place through which she still traveled and one she had never quite succeeded in ignoring, but before leaving Pourville, Alice had discovered she no longer feared its grip on her. The pain of the past had not gone away. It never would entirely, but now it was just there; suspended, harmless, and for the first time, completely devoid of anger. Her greater focus was on Claude who suddenly was not at all pleased with the results of the summer's work.

Alice could not understand his disappointment. To her, the Pourville work was his best to date. Attempting to boost his spirits as at summer's end the family prepared to return home to Poissy, she turned his attention to a review of the summer's more positive achievements. The family was unified and happy, she pointed out. The long summer outing had benefited the entire group of eight plus the ever-loyal Gabrielle and dear Marie, who, under Paul Graf's supervision, had often cooked meals over beachfront campfires, triumphing one day with a mountain of oysters and mussels, their shells charred to perfection. Claude admitted to having enjoyed the family as never before, and yes, he had taken great pleasure in the satisfaction of warm, sunny days when everyone had laughed over sunburned noses and delighted in rainy nights when sausages were blistered and blackened in the fireplace. They had read books and played card games late into the night. Schedules and bedtimes had been tossed out of the windows, and in October when they left the Grafs and Follette, Claude said good-bye to Pourville with a new, deep commitment to the large family he now felt was truly his. Returning to the demands of life at Poissy however, by November as the first hoar frost coated the landscape, he once again found himself at odds with the slow progress of his career even though new collectors were appearing and sales of his paintings were improving. To further stimulate sales, in late autumn he approached Durand-Ruel with an idea for smaller exhibits of his colleagues' work, perhaps just two or three painters, perhaps an exhibition for the following spring. No Eighth Impressionist Exhibition was being planned for 1883 and considering the rivalry and pettiness now overwhelming the original group, leadership of which it appeared Degas was taking over, it was concluded that the movement had run its course and was at an end.

His mood following a happy summer generally defensive and difficult for Alice to deal with, Claude was now also finding himself completely disinterested in Poissy and its environs. None of its subjects pleased him; not the river, not the inlets, nothing. Again at Durand-Ruel's suggestion, in January of the New Year of 1883, he decided to return to the Normandy Coast to paint, and once again Alice was furious. After the great pleasure of a family summer spent at Pourville, her own dissatisfaction with life at Poissy, like Claude's, illuminated a need for change.

Unnoticed in the course of a few contented months spent at the seaside, life had taken on important new dimensions. Returned to Poissy and its demands, both Claude and Alice felt it; the well-being, the sense of belonging, the ease of life lived happily in the company of a loving partner. Now, into the New Year of 1883 there was no question of their commitment to one another. Nor was there the slightest doubt regarding the permanent nature of that commitment. There would never be a return to unresolved relationships suspended in cloaks of secrecy and there would never again be a return to vague levels of satisfaction in a succession of unsuitable environments. They had been together for five years and it was clear that they were inextricably bound to one another for all the years ahead. Moreover, they now knew they needed a large family home where they could settle comfortably with their eight children. Where the money for this accommodating family home would come from was unknown, but it would come. They were both certain of it, and very much in keeping with this trail of loving optimism there arose a most encouraging development.

Before leaving for the Normandy Coast, Claude had completed the Pourville studies and in October of 1882 had delivered a series of thirteen finished paintings to a thoroughly delighted Durand-Ruel. Two weeks later, thirteen additional canvases followed, all but one, of Pourville. In two separate transactions 11,100 francs were paid to Claude before he left Poissy for Normandy and the dramatic rocky shoreline of Etretat which was his destination. The regular monthly income from Durand-Ruel had come to a sudden halt, but left with more financial security than they had known in recent years and left as well with far more than the 800 francs to which they were accustomed each month, now there was a substantial 11,100 francs which could last through a comfortable year or longer. Alice was thrilled with this good fortune. She would still manage the household with great care, she expressed to Claude, but now she felt she was a serious partner in a seriously developing career. Claude's absence would be difficult to bear, but she would do her best to deal with its demands.

At Etretat's Hotel Blanquet he took a room with a magnificent view of the sea. It was perfect: cliffs, boats, a raging sea, a beachfront deserted by tourists in January, a room from which he could paint in bad weather. He could not have asked for more, especially since now there was a new project for which to prepare. In the course of their last meeting, Durand-Ruel had suggested not a two-man or three-man show as Claude had proposed, but better yet, a one-man show for which he suggested Claude actively prepare. Captivated by the prospect of a solo exhibition at Durand-Ruel's new Rue de la Madeleine gallery, he immediately planned for two large Etretat-themed paintings. Studies were promptly begun with the thought that the paintings would be completed at home in Poissy where he had carved out studio space again, as at Vetheuil, in the barn. Arriving at Etretat on a Sunday, he wasted no time in exploring the possibilities open to him. He was out examining the wild wind-whipped Etretat shoreline as dawn broke on Monday.

The cleft in the rugged Jambourg of Etretat ran down dramatically from the top of the Falaise d'Aval and offered a spectacular view of the landmark formation called Needle Rock. The cleft would serve as his vantage point, he decided. By Tuesday morning all the pieces were fitting into place, but on Wednesday and before he had even completed his basic exploration and planned his subjects, Durand-Ruel's letter informing him that he had been able to secure the date of March first for the opening of his one-man show arrived. The news made him nervous. March was just two months away. He wrote to Alice. "It isn't enough time," he complained. He loved her very much he also wrote. He hated being away, but for now it was the only way. He ended his letters with kisses and caresses and love to the children. He didn't mention that he was indecisive or that his plans for the large paintings had changed or that the weather had turned stormy and the magnificent view from the comfort of his room was blurred by torrential rain and gusting winds. Then there was the matter of the fishing boats which although of great interest, had been moved to safe ground. Discouraged and once again disheartened, the Etretat studies remained just that, studies; beautiful, expansive Monet studies of a rockbound shoreline magical in its dramatic winter formation and dimension. The paintings were finished at Poissy and were not to be included in his one-man show.

At this same time, Ernest also wrote to Alice. He had heard about Claude's upcoming one-man show and he immediately fired off a letter to Poissy. "I insist you not accompany Claude Monet to Paris to attend his one-man exhibition at Durand-Ruel's," he dashed off, "and I further insist that you not accompany him to the preview or attend on any days whatsoever of the show following the preview. His exhibition is not at all the same as the show of '77 where I was the biggest lender and figured prominently with you proudly at my side, nor, as you are well aware, is your relationship to Claude at all the same as it was to me at that time. I will not be embarrassed and have my name and my children's names dragged through the mud simply to satisfy Claude Monet's ego. Alice, you must give the details of your role in Claude's life and developing career a good deal of thought. I have and will continue to do so. I cannot turn back the clock, but you have not heard the last of me."

Claude left Poissy for Paris a week before the opening date of March First and took rooms at the Hotel Masse. Alice did not accompany him. Ernest's letter had upset her, but his insistence was not the only reason for her decision to remain waiting at home. She had wanted very much to attend the exhibition, but even before receiving Ernest's letter she had feared that her presence with Claude at such a significant event could easily provoke a scene capable of distracting public and more importantly, critical opinion, thus overshadowing and possibly destroying the very purpose and importance of Claude's moment in the sun. It was a delicate time. Potential buyers might be influenced. There could be published articles filled with embarrassing innuendos. Impressionism itself was controversial enough without adding more spice to the boiling pot, she pointed out. Much to his regret, Claude left Poissy without her. Unwilling to be influenced by Ernest's letter or Alice's own reluctance, until the last minute he had urged her to come to Paris with him. He didn't care about gossip and stares, he insisted. It was an important time for him. He wanted her there, at his side, but in the last moments he had understood the significance of her decision. Their life was shadowed by infidelity and the implications of moral impropriety and perhaps those implications could affect the success both he and Alice felt really was within reach. For now their love required shielding and protection, but how would they hide from the world forever?

The private view was held on February 28th at Durand-Ruel's new gallery, Number 9 Rue de la Madeleine. The catalogue listed fifty-six paintings, most bought and owned by Durand-Ruel, others loaned by their owners, among them Georges de Bellio, Theodore Duret, Georges Charpentier, and Paul Graf who loaned the portrait of himself in his chef's hat which Claude had completed and given to him at Pourville. Included also were the paintings of Follette and the painting of Graf's puff pastry specialty which until the last minute Alice had felt was too trivial to be included. The Varengeville and Pourville paintings were the most numerous in the show and as the first of the Impressionists to exhibit singly, Claude was extremely nervous.

Invitations had been sent out well in advance but attendance was poor, public interest even poorer, critical comment completely absent from newspapers and magazines. Days passed and not a single word about the event appeared in Paris print. Claude was devastated. He returned home to Poissy humiliated and angry, his solo debut on the Paris stage deemed a failure.

"I am being sacrificed so that my so-called colleagues can all follow in my footsteps and profit from my mistakes!" he ranted to Alice. "Durand-Ruel did me no favor! He insists I need the publicity that comes with singular exposure no matter what the critical outcome in the first trial. He tells me it is a process. Process indeed! He should have prepared his process more carefully! He should have done more to alert favorable press to his process. But what good would it have done? All journalists are stupid!"

Claude's ire was short lived. After sending off a furious tirade of accusatory letters to Durand-Ruel and in keeping with the tradition of delays in the delivery of mail, it was not until late March that press cuttings from Courrier de l'Art, Le Gaulois, and Le Journal des Artistes sent by Durand-Ruel began reaching Claude at quiet, unremarkable Poissy. They were few, but highly favorable. Phillippe Burty wrote a long complimentary article for La Republique Francaise and Emile Bergerat's glowing assessment appeared on the front page of Le Voltaire. Claude's one-man show had been a victory after all. Attendance had been minimal and critical praise had not come soon enough to suit, but Durand-Ruel's intention to show his work before an ambivalent press and public had endured its first trial after all. Claude's one-man show had not caused a sensation but it was a very good beginning. There would be no looking back now and there would be no further fury vented, especially once the words of Alfred de Lostalot appeared in the April issue of none other than the widely read La Gazette des Beaux-Arts.

"Monsieur Monet ……sees things differently from most of humankind, and as he is sincere, he makes an effort to reproduce what he sees," Alice delightedly read aloud to Claude and all the children. "………The poetic quality of his work is very striking; I admire the audacity and sobriety of his treatment……To perceive M. Monet's paintings correctly and appreciate their exceptional qualities, one has to go beyond the first impressions; soon the eye grows accustomed and the intellect is awakened; the magic does its work……….he knows his trade and he goes about it in no uncertain way. This is, I believe, a description matching the concept formerly entertained of the true artist."

More than any work of Claude's the children had seen in progress at home, and more than any moments of the diligent work of painting they had closely or routinely observed indoors or out, this critical accolade published in the Beaux-Arts

Gazette affected them in such a way as to imbue the man who functioned as the head of their household with a clear identity. To all but Marthe, he was no longer "our friend" and he was no longer "our Mamma's friend." He was Papa Claude. Marthe, although respectful and outwardly agreeable to an ongoing situation over which she exerted no influence, remained intensely loyal to Ernest as the only man she would ever call, father. The Beaux-Arts Gazette article acknowledged with respect, she continued to call Claude, "Monsieur."

His vision for the future focused on a career that in his mind was now solidly defined, it was time to find the permanent home he and Alice had discussed; a place far enough away from Paris to inspire the natural landscapes he was now convinced were where his best talents lay, and most importantly, a place where he and Alice would be happy together always, even once the children were grown and living in homes of their own.

"I have been wandering about the countryside of Normandy, looking for a new home," he wrote to Durand-Ruel in early April. "At Gisors and Vernon I am walking for miles every day, searching out a suitable property."

"I have seen a number of houses at Vernon," he wrote to Caillebotte just a few days before the lease ran out on the Poissy house in mid-April. "Vernon is lovely and the landscape there appeals to me, but yesterday, as I traveled west on the Le Havre train and along the line between Pacy-sur-Eure and Gisors I happened on a small village situated along the River Epte. There is a nice house for rent there which is entirely enclosed by walls. There is a big garden and in addition to the house, which is blessed by a studio-appropriate barn, there are outbuildings which include a woodshed and a cottage with its own stable and cellar. I am quite thoroughly enchanted by the place. It is called Le Pressoir. I took Alice to see it and she has fallen quite in love with it. That alone makes me happier than I can say."

CHAPTER 26

Giverny
1883 – 1884 - 1885

Ernest flew into a rage when Alice wrote to inform him of the decision to move again, his mood clearly conveyed by the boldly scrawled handwriting in his responding letter. "What? Moving? Again? Aren't things difficult enough? You are ruining my children's lives with this nomadic existence! You assured me they were happy at Poissy and I expect they still are, or doesn't their stability matter to you at all? Is it that whenever temperamental Claude becomes bored with the scenery around him that all heaven and earth must immediately be moved to suit him and no one else? The situation is intolerable!"

He arrived at the Villa Saint-Louis door well before his letter reached the hands of the time-tolerant train station master who, in the prevailing tradition of country life held mail for the residents of Poissy until such time as they came to claim it, whenever that might be. Confronting Alice in the midst of packing and preparations for the move to the sleepy village Claude had discovered on the right bank of the Seine in the Epte Valley of Normandy, his letter unread, Ernest found her reaction to another of his unexpected visits one she met with admirable calm.

"And where is to be this time?" he blared at her angrily in the sitting room littered with boxes and bundles of clothing tied up in quilts. "Varengeville? Pourville? Dieppe? An unknown planet perhaps?"

"We've been fortunate enough to find a wonderful rental property at Giverny," Alice replied ignoring Ernest's annoyance. "It's a very small village between Vernon and Gisors," she added quietly as she led a visibly annoyed Ernest to the two chairs facing each other at the table by the window the children had been using as a desk. "Claude took me to see it and I was more than pleased," she continued in a steady tone. "It's a roomy, two story house with an attic and gardens and a few outbuildings, about eighty kilometers from Paris. For many years it was a thriving cider farm. Beautiful old apple trees still stand at the front of the house. They were fully budded and ready to bloom when Claude took me to see the house for the first time. I hadn't realized that in that part of the country apples of every conceivable variety are still grown, plums too. The property hasn't been lived in for a while, so it needs attention, but there's a quality about it, Ernest, a welcoming feeling in its rooms I thought I would never experience again in any house of mine. Ernest, it's a safe place, a good place for the children and for Claude and me."

What Alice failed to tell Ernest was that the house she had seen at Giverny restored happy memories of the Chateau Rottembourg. Its scale and grounds were not the same at all, but it had not gone unnoticed that a center pediment focused its architecture in much the same way Rottembourg's center pediment had focused its view to the grassy park where Claude had painted *Turkeys at a Chateau*.

"Alice, another move seems excessively trying," Ernest said, attempting a parallel show of patience. "Can't you see that? It isn't good for children to be displaced again and again this way," he insisted, oblivious to Alice's calm assessment of a rural property at obscure Giverny. "They need permanence, a place to call home no matter what happens. You are asking them to live like wandering gypsies. It's a good thing they have each other. They certainly can't be forming lifelong friendships at their schools, but I suppose this move is to be merely another step in Claude's quest for greatness; another rung on his ladder of pitiful little triumphs that lead nowhere. Alice, you know better than to sacrifice yourself and our children to one more place he will soon tire of and abandon. He keeps on asking too much of all of us. Alice, you've known the meaning of a secure life.

You've lived with substantial people and had the finest of everything. How can you settle for so little now?"

"I'm happy, Ernest. I know that must sound too simple, but it's the truth. We are happy, Claude and I and the children, his and mine, and now we can look forward to living in a very nice house, better than Vetheuil and much nicer than even this house with its delightful views. Ernest, the house at Giverny is a lovely place. It's a rambling Normandy farmhouse with low ceilings and lots of light. It isn't a fancy Paris apartment with artfully carved marble mantels and cornices atop the windows, and it isn't the Chateau Rottembourg, but Ernest, there's something wonderful about the place. It has nothing of the elegance I loved in the past, but turning away from the road and opening the latch on the gate, I felt the same warmth and simple grace I always felt when I arrived at Rottembourg's gates. Ernest, the children can be happy there. There's plenty of room inside and out. The house sits on two full acres of ground and there's lots of privacy. Neighbors are few and far between and there are lots of trees, spruce and pine along the path leading to the house. Over time we can plant and work on the gardens and live a good life there. Please be happy for us."

"Happy? I will never be happy for you and Claude. You should know that by now."

"Then at least accept things as they are!" Alice snapped back. "Ernest, please! Once again I thought we had come to terms with a situation that won't change. I also thought that once again we had come to a sensible understanding about the children's visits, you and I, and just as I promised I have kept my end of the bargain by bringing them to see you in Paris as often as I can. I encourage those visits in spite of the fact that I feel forced into them. If moving the children to Giverny is all that is upsetting you now, please put your concerns aside. It will be much easier to travel to Paris. Giverny is farther away from the city but there are direct trains from Vernon. The children can come to see you more often, but Ernest, they really are looking forward to living in a big house with big rooms and grounds to explore and feel part of, perhaps for a long time to come. You should hear them talking about it. They love the idea of living at an old cider farm. Ernest, there are schools, good schools, at nearby Vernon. I'd like to board the older children at one of them next year. It means another expense and I'll need your help, but they need to apply themselves to their educations. Don't you want that for them too?"

Alice stood and faced Ernest squarely, her hopeful eyes intent on his reaction, her hands in the pockets of the flowered cotton apron she wore. Meeting her gaze, Ernest explored the face he had never stopped loving. For the first time he noticed the few strands of silver in his wife's dark lustrous hair. He saw the few small lines that had settled into the corners of her eyes. He wanted to reach out and touch them. He wanted to take her into his arms and beg her to grow old with him; to weather the storms and trials of the years ahead and turn white-haired and wizened beside him. And, as always when he saw Alice and looked into her dark, quiescent eyes, he wanted the past swept away, all its disappointment and pain forgotten as if they had never been. But it was too late. It was always too late. It had been too late for too long. He turned away and stared out of the window. What Ernest wanted most in the world, more than any house or any painting or any possession continued to elude him. It always would, he told himself, focusing on the row of picturesque houses across the river. He would not grow old with Alice, he also told himself, looking back to her and into her questioning eyes. He would not triumph in some new gloriously successful venture for which she would praise and admire him. He would not die in her arms. His children would never live under his roof. He would, from now on, be resigned to watching the wife and the children he loved from a distance, like the accommodating, understanding friend Alice was asking him to be.

"Write to me and let me know the address at Giverny," he said stiffly, tugging nervously at his sleeves as he stood and turned to the door. "I'd like to come out for a visit with the children once you are settled. And Alice, regardless of what you may think of me, I do want you to be happy. I've always wanted that."

"Yes, come to Giverny. I'd like you to see the house at least once. You'll have no trouble finding us," Alice graciously replied with a grateful smile as she walked toward the door beside him. "There are only two roads," she was quick to add, her manner pleasant, her smile warm and kind, the way he remembered it whenever he thought of her. "We'll be between the Rue de l'Amiscourt and the Chemin du Roy at the House of the Cider Press. There's a slate roof on the house and grayish shutters on the windows. Through the apple trees in front you'll be able to see the house from the road. It's pink."

"Oh Alice! Pink?"

They moved into the House of Cider Press in April, just as spring was turning the Seine Valley into a hundred hues of green and the hillsides of it sandstone quarries came alive in bursts of color. The age-old apple trees in the orchard at the front of the house were in full bloom, the cultivation of apples as important to the farmlands of old Normandy as the production of wheat was to the Brie Valley Alice had known so well, their varieties and color shadings as numerous as the Montgeron roses she had loved and nurtured at Rottembourg.

It didn't take long to fall in love with the house. The rectangular, north-south design of the long, rambling stucco structure provided splendid northerly views of the spring landscape from the glass paneled doors of all four first floor rooms. At the south, through the roadside gate and at the end of the tree-lined walkway, the front door opened onto an entrance hall where a modest staircase ascended to the second floor. On the first floor, the dining room and kitchen were to the right of the entrance hall, the drawing room, a second hall and staircase, and an adjoining room to the left. On the second floor there were four additional rooms. Two at each corner of the house enjoyed views both north and south, and in the third floor attic, several more rooms completed the generous plan.

Alice was more than accurate in revealing to Ernest that the House of the Cider Press was not the Chateau Rottembourg. Although the largest house in the village of Giverny, it was no formal estate. It was a simple Normandy farmhouse set into a simple valley nurtured by farmers, market gardeners, and keepers of cows and sheep. Its inhabitants were people of the land who had lived in the same small, tile-roofed houses for generations. They farmed and kept company with whims of nature and they had never been to Paris. From the beginning, Alice understood them. She understood their lives, their beliefs, and she appreciated their hard work. At Montgeron she had known people exactly like these; fine, hard-working citizens of the Brie who planted and ploughed and harvested and celebrated their achievements all their lives and every year in the annual French country tradition of seasonal abundance and cyclical change, and although at first she and Claude were seen as suspicious city oddities in Giverny's small, close-knit agrarian community of less than three-hundred souls, Alice's consistent attendance at Mass every Sunday morning with eight children in tow slowly but surely broke the ice. Her first caller, however, was not her nearest, most curious neighbor, but Father Toussaint, the village priest, a young cleric devoted to his small flock and Alice's new confessor at Giverny's Romanesque Church of Sainte Radegonde.

Two weeks after the move from Poissy, he came unexpectedly to the House of the Cider Press expecting a cool reception, largely because outsiders never came to live in Giverny and also because he had heard that the "new people" were city folk and not at all like any of the Givernese. Alice's warm welcome disarmed him completely, her cordial ease with conversation pertaining to country life, to the geography of the Plain of Ajoux, to matters of loyal church attendance in Paris, at Montgeron, Vetheuil, and Poissy, and her great affection for the Abbess, Mother Catherine at Yerres and the Sisters of Notre Dame, providing more than an hour of spirited exchange.

"A relative of mine was among the first colony of Sisters of Notre Dame to go to America," a soon relaxed and engaged, black-cassocked Father Toussaint related to an attentive Alice over cups of tea and slices of lemon cake served in the drawing room where Alice had arranged the sitting room furniture from Poissy.

"My mother has the letters she sent from California more than fifty years ago," he continued, dabbing at the corners of his mouth with one of Alice's finest white linen napkins. "The pages are yellowed with age, but when I visit her at Rouen we sometimes take them out very carefully and re-read them." They reveal that American California was hardly a welcoming place for a small group of French nuns forty years ago. They spoke no English at all but in this case were fortunate enough to encounter a local resident, a landowner, who spoke fluent French as well as English and translated for them. I often think of their courage and determination to serve the Church under such adverse circumstances, but these are the ways of spiritual life."

He sat at the edge of his chair, his manner gentle but attentive and poised, his subjects of conversation sensitive and thoughtful. Alice could not help but notice how young he was, and how very handsome. Brown-haired and of slim build, Giverny's village priest was slight, almost frail in appearance. He was also pale, his eyes a watery blue, but his was the face of a kind, benevolent cleric and Alice felt completely at ease in his company.

"Father Toussiant, in so small village as Giverny you must surely know every family and every member of it by name," she said to him, taking advantage of his prominent role in the rural community that was now her home. "We are newcomers, my family and I, but we hope to live here in Giverny on cordial terms with its residents. For many summers I lived a country life in the Brie Valley. I know the habits of people who love the land and devote themselves to its cultivation from one generation to the next. I also understand the suspicions they can have about newcomers and strangers. With this in mind, I would deeply appreciate any kind word you could advance about me and my family."

"I hardly think you, Madame, will be in need of my intervention," Father Toussiant replied. "You obviously understand the reluctance of the residents of our rural community of Giverny to befriend strangers, but I have a feeling you, Madame, will succeed very quickly in gaining their trust and respect."

"Then I shall continue living as I always have," Alice said. "I am devoted to the Church and its teachings and I will trust that my loyalty will serve me well both here in my house and in the Church of Sainte Radegonde."

"The ways of spiritual life become welcome rituals to all those committed to Christ," the priest responded before asking the burning question that had preyed on his mind.

"Madame Hoschede, since you seem eager to settle into a cordial life here at Giverny I know you will tell me how it is that you and your husband bear different names. "Monet is the name of the family I received from the prelate at Poissy with his letter informing me of your expected arrival in Giverny, but I notice that you and six children bear the name of Hoschede while only two are named Monet."

"Father Toussaint, my life is not without its complications. We are two families combining our energies and financial resources as best we can in difficult times. You are my confessor now, and there are things I must eventually tell you. For now, though, please let us be on friendly terms and discuss other matters. As you may know, Monsieur Monet, the father of the two Monet children you mention and the head of this household, is an artist, a painter. Come, let me show you some of his work. And I believe I see Jean and Michel out there in the garden. They are Monsieur Monet's two boys and they come to Mass with me every Sunday. I'm sure you've seen them."

Of course it would never be known what, if anything, Alice confessed to Father Toussiant. It was apparent, however, that shortly after his initial visit with her, a wave of the hand or a friendly smile came from a few of her new neighbors as she and the children passed along the dusty King's Road to Sunday Mass, and although most of Giverny's close-knit families remained suspicious of the seldom seen artist, the church-going woman, and the many children living at the House of the Cider Press, Alice anticipated at least a satisfactory relationship between them and her large family in the community that was her new home.

Matters of spiritual life comfortably settled, life in a new setting at Giverny began to take on increasingly satisfactory dimensions. As Alice had described to Ernest, the House of the Cider Press, situated on a gentle slope facing the Epte and the Valley of the Seine to the south, quickly succeeded in stirring her affections. More spacious and because of its privacy more inviting than the Vetheuil and Poissy homes she had lived in with Claude, from the very first day she spent in its light-filled rooms she knew this was a house she could nurture and love. The children called it 'Le Pressoir' (The Press)," an affectionate label immediately adopted by the entire household.

A rambling old house with the lingering fragrance of aged apple wood and sweet moss-covered rootstock locked into its low-ceilinged rooms, The Press offered Alice's older children a level of grace long absent from their lives and they, along with Jean, Michel, and Jean-Pierre, who had heard stories about the elegant Chateau Rottembourg all their young lives but had never been there, soon adapted with ease to its accommodating spaces both inside and out.

For Alice, The Press filled, to a great degree, the emotional void left by the loss of Rottembourg. Most of all, it succeeded in healing many of the wounds she had carried under her heart, and in the way that weathered old country houses with character and talents for mixing doses of rusticity with surprising touches of stylish urbanity can reach the sensitive and troubled, The Press soon diverted her attention away from the old doubt and regrets she had carried within her for more than five difficult years. Adding to this new lease on life and in spite of continuing financial challenges, she and Claude immediately embarked on establishing a stylish country life centered on a family, its gardens and activities, and the career of the head of its household. So enamored of the house and the potential of its two acres of ground were they, that merely leasing it for a year or two was soon thought not to be enough. A short time after settling in, they decided they wanted to buy The Press one day, to own it outright and live in it for the rest of their lives. In turn, this energizing dream of truly owning The Press deeply affected Claude's motivation and he immediately embarked on plans for turning the first floor's extra room into a studio where he could work uninterrupted. Within mere days of organizing his materials and settling into it, on April 30, he received word of Edouard Manet's death, an event which was to make a lasting impact not only on Claude personally, but on all artistic circles in Paris.

Manet had been gravely ill for some time. Suffering through the final ravages of venereal disease, he had painted almost nothing in the previous year. The past summer of 1882 had been spent with his wife, Suzanne, and his mother at Rueil, near to his brother Eugene and sister-in-law, Berthe Morisot who had taken a house at Bougival. In the following winter months he had failed rapidly and before the Paris lime trees he loved lining the walkways of the Coeur d'Honneur had budded in the warmth of spring sunshine, he had died a painful, Berthe Morisot said, agonizing death. His last work was a small painting of roses and lilacs arranged in a Japanese vase.

Edouard Manet's passing affected the Impressionists more deeply than had any other recent event. Firmly tied to the traditions of the Salon system, Manet had nonetheless and with unfailing approval, encouraged their efforts to reach the public and he had generously advanced funds whenever asked. In many ways he represented the transition from past to present and Claude, who had become a particularly close friend and passionate admirer of his work, saw his role as critical to the very tenets of Impressionist painting. He took the loss as a great personal blow. He was asked to attend the funeral and serve as a bearer along with Fantin-Latour, Antonin Proust, Emile Zola, Theodore Duret, Alfred Stevens, and Philippe Burty. Without a proper black suit to wear, once again Paul Durand-Ruel came to the rescue, this time with francs adequate enough to purchase appropriate attire for Claude's participation in the sad, but well-attended occasion. On May third, Manet was interred at Passy, in a cemetery plot purchased by his brother Eugene, his legacy and the power of his prolific body of work now merged with the futures of all those painters he had supported and loved.

Manet had never seen The House of the Cider Press at Giverny, but in the way that friends who stand on common ground understand, Claude knew his former advocate would have heartily approved of its setting along the peaceful, willow-banked waters where the Epte meets the Seine, its quiet marshlands alive with fern and wild iris by June, its vast, nearby poppy fields a vibrant mass of red by mid-summer, Louis-Joseph Singeot, who owned The Press, entirely agreeable to having the gardens at The Press cared for in any way the new occupants would choose.

"But do not cut down the trees," Monsieur Singeot cautioned. "They are to be left as they are, trimmed perhaps, but please understand that most of them have been undisturbed for many years and in this part of the Seine Valley we respect all talents for survival."

It was a good summer, a very good summer; good in the sense that at The Press a genuine family structure fell into place; good in the sense that once again and at last, Alice had a house to love, and good because the family could fully embrace the novelty of taking up life in spacious surroundings. Before moving in and arm in arm, Alice and Claude walked through the rooms of The Press; planning, deciding, and even arguing over which of the chairs or which of the tables would look best here, which there, and which of the second floor rooms should be assigned to the children. They went so far as to discuss which pieces of furniture should be considered for purchase when the budget allowed. Happy and content once they had moved in, they also walked the grounds every day, discussing how the garden could develop and thrive over time and what would do best planted here and what would look best growing there.

It was a summer for caring and dreaming and looking fearlessly into a future that had begun to shine with a faint glimmer of promise. Finances continued to worry them both, but now so accustomed were they to living under tightly restricted circumstances, that the question of money no longer loomed quite as invasively as it had, and in the stable comfort of The Press they changed. Faith came to them in that first summer at Giverny, the kind of faith that brings purpose to life. In the full blush of its promise, their long, passionate romance blossomed into a mature closeness and trusted friendship they respected but could never fully explain either privately to themselves or to each other. Soon, peace also came to them at The Press, for together there Alice and Claude found what all devoted lovers of old houses find: that a special house of a certain age and seasoned merit can cast a magic, contented spell over its yearning inhabitants; that it can touch and move the hearts and minds of those people who effortlessly find love and joy within its walls, and that because of them it can make its greatest imprint on life within that span of years randomly chosen for its prospering. Such was to be the legacy of The House of the Cider Press.

In late May they began work on the vegetable garden which, due to the distinctly agricultural nature of the Giverny community, had been cultivated directly at the roadside front of the house and not at the back, or in a less prominent location, as Alice would have preferred. Putting her natural wish for elevated exclusivity aside, Alice conformed to village precedent and pressed all the children into service. They attacked weeds left thriving on neglect for years. With spades and hoes they turned over rock-hard soil that had gone untouched for decades. Once the tough, overgrown copeswood, spathe, leafstock, and caulicle were pulled and cleared and the soil was smoothed and prepared, Marthe, Suzanne, and Blanche were assigned to organize the seeds the family had received as a welcoming gift from their nearest neighbor. Alice, Germaine, Jean-Pierre, and Claude planted, while Jacques, Jean, and Michel fetched pails of water. They put in beans, onions, lettuce and cabbage. Flowers were added: asters and dahlias. It was hard, dirty work and it took ten, intensely motivated days, but in the process of clearing the frontage land and planting their garden in neat rows they laughed and joked together. Now and then tempers flared and arguments erupted over how deeply seeds were to be planted or how much water was required each day, but disagreements were eventually followed by apologies, compliments accompanied words of polite appreciation, and in the course of that first summer at Giverny, the full, loving, maddening, frustrating range of a large family's interaction with one another in their first real home was explored in ways that would remain dear to Alice and remembered all their lives by the eight children she loved.

Claude soon turned from planting and took up his painting of the new landscape. By late August he was creating scenes of the church at Vernon and the hill at Notre-Dame-de-la-mer and before year's end he sent a packing case of seven canvases to Durand-Ruel. In December he left Giverny for a brief period to paint along the Italian Riviera with Renoir. As 1883 came to a close and the early winter of 1884 set in, he worked indoors on the floral-themed wall panels Durand-

Ruel had commissioned for his Paris apartment on Rue du Rome, more grateful than ever to the man the Impressionists now affectionately called Monsieur Durand and with good reason, for exceeding all normal boundaries of client-dealer relationships and with no guarantee of sales, Monsieur Durand was readily advancing funds for paintings that had not yet been finished or were virtually forgotten and casually left in studios. He was also generously settling accounts with schoolmasters, tailors, art materials suppliers, and framers in exchange for paintings by his young lions, thus acquiring hundreds of Impressionist pictures which, for the most part, went unsold.

"I know our life here can be wonderful," Claude had expressed to Alice, several weeks prior to his departure for the painting expedition with Renoir, "but I must work harder now. I must find a way to truly succeed, and it must happen soon if we are to live here at Giverny as we have envisioned. Monsieur Durand suggests I continue to expand my outlook and perhaps spend some time in Italy. He mentioned Bordighera. The climate is tropical and the natural growth is unlike any I have attempted in France. I am anxious to see it but it would mean a separation of a few weeks."

When Claude left to join Renoir at Bougival before traveling on to the Italian Riviera in mid-December, Alice was sad to see him leave, but this time his absence was not quite as deeply felt as it had been in the past at Vetheuil and Poissy. Conditions had changed. He would be away for a very good reason and in his absence she would be living in a house she cared about. Her precious children would be there with her and as she waved good-bye from the gate, her thoughts turned happily to plans for the family's first Christmas at The Press.

Claude met up with Renoir at Port-Villez and the two left France to set up easels at Genoa and Bordhigera. Pleasant as it was to absorb fresh perspectives in the friendly ease of Renoir's good-humored company, it was soon apparent to Claude that something had changed. His fondness for Renoir had not waned in the least but he was not enjoying the dual painting expedition as he had in the past. Nothing was fitting. He was not painting well, he told Renoir. He could not seem to grasp the quality of the environment. It was a magnificent locale, rich in color, but something was wrong. Renoir felt it too. Palettes and easels were soon packed away and the trip was cut short, but not before the two visited with Cezanne at L'Estaque and shared with him their mutual disappointment in failing to grasp on canvas the natural essence of the glorious Italian Riviera.

"It is the speeding light on the thick, lush plantings," Claude moaned. "It is the impossibly rapid variation of shadows, the fronds of palm trees that won't stay still and insist on waving and turning and driving me crazy even in the gentlest sea breeze."

"Yes it is all that," Cezanne agreed, "but it is the colors along that part of the Italian coastline most of all; the impossibly hot, dense colors of exotic plants that nature wants to lock up for herself and watch us fight for."

Renoir returned to paint at La Roche-Guyon and Claude returned to The Press in time to enjoy a Christmas filled with Alice's special touches: doorways decorated with the traditional paper cut-outs, pine branches and ribbons, the stuffed goose and chestnut pudding waiting at home after Midnight Mass, and the traditional Christmas Eve "pain calendeau," a part of which, Alice reminded Claude and the children, "is by tradition to be shared with a poor person."

The appearance of the pain calendeau at lunch on the day before Christmas was met with no little humor, Claude quick to point out that there was no need whatsoever to seek out a poor person with whom to share the special "calendeau" since, as a collective whole, they were the poorest people he knew. His humor aside, income for 1883 had not been poor at all. In addition to frequent advances from Durand-Ruel, he had been productive enough to sell close to 30,000 francs worth of paintings. Durand-Ruel had not been sitting on his hands either, but once again the wolf was at the door.

His finances shaky, resources shrinking, the rent on his Rue Madeleine space increased, Durand-Ruel saw the need to expand his horizons beyond French borders. In mid-winter he mounted an exhibition of Impressionist paintings in London and a short time later sponsored a similar show in Berlin. Sales were weak, but attendance was good and once again people were talking. Mary Cassatt, the American painter who had exhibited both at the Paris Salon and with the Impressionists, had seen the London exhibit and suggested Durand-Ruel plan a similar show in America. A close friend and admirer of Edgar Degas, Cassatt was from a well-to-do Pennsylvania family and had connections to the newly wealthy New York crowd. She spoke of a Mister James Robertson, an American gentleman connected in some way to the Art Students League in New York. She suggested Durand-Ruel contact him. Durand-Ruel said he would think it over.

In mid-January of the New Year of 1884, Claude kissed Alice good-bye and was once again off to Bordighera, this time alone, newly curious, and determined to find his dot on Italy's horizon, hopefully one resulting in a series of canvases linked both by location and theme.

Ten miles from the French border and dominated by the Maritime Alps, Bordighera lay on the western Riviera, superbly poised on an indented fringe of sea in the province of Imperia at Liguria, between Vintimiglia and San Remo. The spectacular tropical landscape and warm temperatures were those for which the winter resorts of Bordighera and neighboring Nice, Cannes, Saint-Jean-Cap Ferrat, Beaulieu-sur-Mer, and Monte Carlo had become justly famous. A number of Paris celebrities lived there, among them Charles Garnier, the Paris Opera's designer. Claude took lodging not far away from Garnier's address, at the Pension Anglaise in the "Citta Alta," Bordighera's old town. Durand-Ruel had told him that before deciding on subject matter he must see the Moreno garden just to the west of the Citta Alta. Letters of recommendation were required before the discriminating, French-speaking Monsieur Moreno admitted visitors to his garden, but bearing Monsieur Paul Durand-Ruel's praiseworthy document in hand and impressed by the artist who spoke such beautiful French, Claude gained admittance to a lush, private Riviera world resplendent in its proliferation of flowers, palm trees, olive trees, orange and lemon trees, and views to the bluest of blue Mediterranean seas. He began studies immediately, experimenting with the hot, intense, elusive colors of Paul Cezanne's world, but exactly as before he had no control over the vagaries of light on restless palms and the forever unpredictable state of the sea, his initial attempts disappointing him and leading him to distracting excursions into the nearby towns of Sasso and Vallebona.

"I must believe that progress comes with increasing familiarity," he wrote to Alice. "I am working on as many as six canvases at a time."

By February there was a series of fourteen.

"I dare to put in all the shades of pink and blue I can. It is enchanting and I hope you will like it," he wrote to Renoir. At home, Alice waited, occupying herself with looking after the three youngest children, Jean-Pierre, Michel, and Germaine, who attended the public school. She wrote to the older ones at their Vernon boarding school where they once again made new friends and progressed in the basics of their educations. On the Nineteenth of February Ernest appeared at the front door. It was Alice's fortieth birthday. On the same day, Claude began work in Monsieur Moreno's Bordighera garden, by now so well thought of by the distinguished Italian gentleman that he was entrusted with a key to the garden doors which allowed him to come and go at will.

At first he painted the olive trees, but the work was labored and uncertain. Nothing came together on the first try. Colors were all wrong and the incessant warm breeze kept every branch and leaf in a state of perpetual motion. Brushes were cleaned and put down. In his room he worked on studies for Durand-Ruel's drawing room doors. Bad weather set in, an event which annoyed Claude as little else could, except, of course, for the news from Alice that Ernest Hoschede had come to Giverny, his clear intention, Alice confessed, to reconcile with his wife and put an end to their six-year separation. Again, brushes were cleaned and put down, the situation at home taking center stage in his mind, his confidence in Alice's love for him remaining strong enough in spite of moments fraught with frequent doubt to allow events to play out and take their course as he felt they must.

He decided not to return home immediately, but to stay on in Italy as planned and wait. Seeking diversions, he spent three days in Monte Carlo with a group of Italian friends introduced to him by Madame Moreno. When he returned to Bordighera the weather had cleared and with no word from Alice he set out on an excursion to charming Dolceacqua where with renewed but forced energy, he painted not the flora and fauna, but the Doria Castle and the Chapel of San Filippo Nero. Constantly haunted by thoughts of Alice and Ernest alone together at Giverny, his concentration lagged and his work suffered. None of his pictures pleased him. How long would Hoschede be staying, he wondered? What were he and Alice saying to each other? The heat bothered him but not more than his frame of mind and despite the warm temperatures, he took on a nasty cold and went to bed for three days. In the next week, his health stabilized and he returned to work in his room, facing twenty canvases in progress. He fretted and fumed. It wasn't good. Again, nothing was fitting together. He took a larger room where he could work on his studies with improved perspective. Dissatisfaction prevailed. He was very tired, his eyes were swollen and irritated, his clothes were in unwashed tatters, and Monsieur Moreno's kind offer of an excursion to another of his properties several hours away in Andora did little to improve matters. He had been away from home for a month. His attitude at an intensely negative pitch, he anticipated staying away from Giverny even longer, perhaps for as much as two more months if he was to produce the results he wanted.

In the next days he painted ceaselessly, morning to night, struggling with color and theme. Late at night he wrote long, loving letters to Alice, eagerly anticipating her encouraging responses but increasingly convinced that Hoschede would somehow manage to steal her away and that once he returned to Giverny there would be no one there to return to. Under the Italian Riviera's demanding sunlight he continued to work displeased and discouraged, worried and anxious, but he was turning out a remarkable volume of work. Alice's reassuring letters had begun to reach him with encouraging regularity, but still, he was not at all sure exactly what awaited him at The Press. Word of an excursion Alice had taken to Paris was particularly bothersome.

In mid-February, she had written from Paris to say that Ernest had arrived unannounced at Giverny and had managed to talk Michel and Jean-Pierre into convincing her to spend a few wintry days enjoying a beautiful fresh snowfall in the city. After much cajoling and for the sake of the boys she had finally agreed. She and the boys were staying with Beatrice Pirole, but only for a few days, Alice had assured him.

The thought of such a visit to Paris had worried him constantly. Beatrice Pirole's affection for Ernest Hoschede was hardly a well-kept secret and Alice had not gone into enough detail to satisfy him. The circumstances surrounding the Paris visit were impossible to unravel completely and he imagined all sorts of scenarios. He could think of little else. He continued to fret and worry, so much so, that unlike Ernest, he completely forgot Alice's fortieth birthday.

"Why do you insist on doing this to me?" Alice had asked Ernest when he arrived at Giverny, Claude would later learn. "Just when the pieces of life are fitting together for me, you appear," Alice had shouted out. "Why, in the names of all the saints, can we not come to terms with your visits? I need to be notified of your plans. You come at me out of nowhere."

"Alice, I seem to recall that you invited me out to Giverny. When I saw you at Poissy you were packing up and quite magnanimous in suggesting I come to see the place where you were taking our children. "Look for the farmhouse between Rue l'Amiscourt and the Chemin du Roi. Its pink!" you said to me. "Well, here I am at the pink house and I admit that I'm happy to see I've once again disturbed the balance."

"Ernest, the most basic civil behavior calls for a brief note or letter telling me of your plans," Alice interrupted. "We've not heard from you in months."

"Of course. Forgive me. What could I have been thinking to be so unforgivably rude? It must be that rudeness is at the center of my life. My wife and children have been stolen from me. They live under another man's roof and I must ask permission to gain access to their home. How very rude of me to expect a warm welcome!"

"Ernest, please. It you've come here to taunt me again, I must ask you to leave."

"No, Alice, I've come here because it's your fortieth birthday and I knew Claude was away. Durand-Ruel mentioned some sort of long painting expedition to Italy which gave me the perfect opportunity to come out here to see you without that self-indulgent snake around, but enough about Claude. I have a birthday present for you."

"Oh Ernest, you needn't have done that. Please don't."

"Alice, I have always remembered your birthday," Ernest insisted. "In the past few years I've been unable to bring you a gift but I want you to know that I've thought of you every year on the 19th day of February, just as I did when we were together. Of course I think of you every day of my life, but this year I set aside a little birthday fund in your honor and here is the result."

Ernest proceeded to open the briefcase he always carried and from it he removed a small, beautifully wrapped package. "Let's sit down on the sofa there while you open this," he suggested.

It was with great reluctance that Alice began to unwrap Ernest's gift. She glanced at him repeatedly, unsure of what to do. But for his occasional bank drafts which never adequately covered his share of monthly expenses as was the original plan, it felt wrong to accept a gift from him. She knew he could barely afford to pay his own rent. Nonetheless, in no mood to spar with him, she went ahead with typical grace, taking great care with the thick white wrapping paper, commenting on its fine satin finish. Ernest watched as she folded the paper neatly and set it aside the way people do when they have learned to save every small scrap of life's niceties. For a moment she held the black velvet box the white paper had covered in her hand and despite her reluctance, she smiled.

"Go ahead. Open it!" Ernest said with a broad smile. "I can't stand the suspense!"

Alice laughed and opened the black velvet box. In it she found a gold cross on a thin gold chain.

"Oh Ernest, its lovely!" she said, tears filling her eyes, "but you can't afford something like this. I want you to return it and get your money back."

"Don't be ridiculous, Alice. I want you to have this. Now, let me put this little token of my love around that beautiful neck of yours."

There he was again, the familiar old Ernest, the perennially optimistic, once very rich Ernest Hoschede who now struggled every day to create opportunities for himself and restore the privileged life he and his family had been forced to sacrifice. "Do you remember when the necklaces I gave you were covered in rubies and diamonds?" he whispered, placing his gift around his wife's neck and fastening the clasp. "This will do for now my dearest and at least its gold, but before long you'll be wearing rubies and diamonds again. I promise."

"Thank you, Ernest, but I don't need rubies and diamonds," Alice said standing and turning to face her husband, her voice tinged with weary impatience. "Other things are more important to me now. I thought you understood that. You said you did. Thank you, though. It's a beautiful necklace and it means a great deal to me to know that in spite of everything you wanted me to have it. Now, tell me, how are things in Paris?" she asked, once again changing the subject as well as the mood. Have you seen your cousin Beatrice or my Uncle Julian?"

Beatrice and Marc invited me to dinner last week," Ernest replied with the wry smile that always crossed his face whenever he talked about his eccentric cousin and her mercifully tolerant husband. "Beatrice has done the dining room over," he went on, leaning back against the blue sofa cushion. "Wait till you see it! As might be expected it's really dreadful. The lovely wall panels we both liked so much are gone and this time big purple flowers are painted on bright lime green walls. It's horrible! I could hardly eat my dinner. Beatrice told me she had commissioned Jacques Limone to do the painting and that it cost Marc a fortune. I told her I thought Limone should be arrested for robbery and sent off to prison. She thought I was joking and laughed herself silly. Of course she asked about you and the children. She misses all of you and she admonished me for not coming to see you at Christmas. I told her I wasn't ready just then to see you and the children there at Poissy with Claude. Your Uncle Julian was there at dinner, silver-haired and as elegant as ever, and of course as wary of me as ever. He has never had to tell me he didn't like me, which as you know he has, and on more than one occasion. Now though, with all that has happened, the disapproval is plainly engraved on his face. It sounds as if he and Beatrice are seeing quite a lot of each other; luncheons, dinners, that sort of thing. Marc doesn't seem to mind...........Oh well. He's such a bore......"

The idle conversation focused on a dinner with his cousin Beatrice and two men he cared nothing at all about was not what Ernest wanted to talk about in those moments alone with Alice. He had come to Giverny for one last attempt at reconciliation. It wasn't too late at all he had repeatedly told himself in the weeks since he had visited at Poissy and saw Alice there, excitedly preparing for the move to Giverny. Seeing her calm and happy, he had assumed that friendship was all he could expect from her and that all he could look forward to was a sad, lonely future without the woman he loved, but there was still time and he intended to make the most of it.

He missed Alice terribly. He missed the contentment of days and nights they had shared through the years of a marriage he had always thought of as ideal. He missed their passionate lovemaking, their shared confidences, their reliance on one another. He knew he would never stop loving Alice, and despite the circumstances that had torn them apart he was convinced she would never stop loving him. They had done so much and they had cared so much, but time was quickly passing and although his optimism in the future was unfailing, sitting inches away from the woman he loved on her birthday Ernest was not at all oblivious to the new confidence and sense of satisfaction he saw in her. Clearly, here at Giverny her priorities had changed.

He took notice of the unflattering gray wool dress she wore. Its white lace collar, although perfectly acceptable, was too common for her and failed to reflect what he knew of her elegant past taste. It was limp and small and did nothing to draw attention to her regal neck and flawless complexion. Not so long ago she had place great emphasis on such things. Of course in the country at Rottembourg daytime life was informal and Alice had worn simple dresses, that is until evening and the formal dinner hour when the beautiful gray tulle gowns she was known for came out, but regardless of the day or hour and when she wasn't in the garden at play with the children, Alice had always paid careful attention to what she was wearing and how her hair looked, even when she was spending the morning or evening at home alone in one of her comfortable but beautiful satin robes. Now none of that seemed to matter to her, but gracefully launched into her forties Ernest saw his wife as more beautiful than ever. Time was being kind to her he acknowledged, but she was no longer the privileged heiress, chatelaine of the historic Chateau Rottembourg and keeper of its famous Raingo clocks. Somehow, in the span of a few years she had evolved into a confident woman content with much less than the abundance and access she had known all her life and now, in a rambling farmhouse at Giverny, Ernest was becoming all too aware of other changes in her. They were apparent in her measured tone, her deliberate manner and gestures, even in her well-modulated voice, but on her birthday in the drawing room of a house she shared with another man, all that mattered to him as he watched his wife unwrapping the present he had brought to her was her nearness and the unwavering conviction that soon she would return to him and that once with her life would fill with the soaring happiness he craved.

Unaware of the assessments Ernest was making, uncomfortable with his presence at her Giverny home and with Claude away, Alice approached her own line of conversation, eager to establish some semblance of neutral ground.

"Tell me Ernest, how are you managing these days?" she asked, well aware that he had sent nothing to help support the children in months.

"Oh, as best I can," came the honest answer. "I'm sorry I haven't been able to send you anything for a while, but making ends meet is a challenge for me these days. My mother's bequest, saw me through the difficult months after she died. Now, I get by on my writing. Le Monde and La Vie d'Art keep me in francs adequate enough to pay the landlord and keep my account open at the Café Riche.

It's a good thing one can sit in Paris cafes for hours on end without ordering more than a coffee."

Alice laughed. "Well, maybe I can offer you more than a cup of coffee today, perhaps some hot chocolate, but since you're here, first let me show you through the house. It's really a wonderful home, Ernest. You'll like the children's rooms. The boys have taken over the third floor. The little ones, Michel and Jean-Pierre are with Gabrielle right now, but soon she will be bringing them home from one of their music lessons. The nice widowed daughter of one of our neighbors here has this set of what she calls rhythm instruments, and as she plays the piano and sets the beat, they bang at a drum, click a pair of little sticks together, or shake a bell, keeping up with the beat of the music as they go. It's really wonderful for them. They've even started singing little songs together as they bang and click and shake. I think it's good for them to start enjoying music this way, don't you?"

"Of course I do," Ernest replied, "and I imagine Jacques loves the drum and Jean-Pierre loves the singing."

"You're absolutely right!" laughed Alice, "but now they want to make their own little instruments. I'm being asked to save the boxes of macaroons I buy at the Vernon market on Saturdays when the budget allows. They put a little dried rice or a crisp crust of bread inside, shake it up, and voila! An instrument! Ernest, they'll be happy to see you. Jean-Pierre has grown so much. He's a lovely, inquisitive boy. Michel is his best friend."

They walked together through the rooms of The Press, their thoughts not at all too away far from days very much like this when together they had strolled the halls and chambers of the past, talking about the children and taking great delight in the beauty and harmony they had effortlessly harnessed around them.

"I can see why you like it here," Ernest commented peering into the bedroom that was Alice's. "The house is very pleasant, and somehow it feels right for you. I'm glad, Alice, really I am."

Alice's room in one of the corner rooms on the second floor overlooked the rear garden. Next to Claude's bedroom and dressing room, of all the bedrooms it was the brightest and most pleasantly located. "Is that where you write your letters?" Ernest asked, gazing toward the small desk at the window with its view across the garden and toward the Epte.

"Yes," Alice answered. "It's especially lovely to look out there when the mist covers the valley in the early morning," she commented, moving ahead more quickly, eager to return downstairs when she heard the Gabrielle and the boys coming through the hall.

As predicted, Michel and Jean-Pierre were surprised but happy to see Ernest. He hugged each of them, commenting on how much they had grown since his last visit.

"Is it a cold winter in Paris? Has it snowed?" Jean-Pierre asked between bites of the small cakes Alice always had ready for them in the afternoon and sips of the hot chocolate she had prepared. "We have had three bad snowstorms in Giverny so far this winter and Madame Choubier, our music teacher, told us today that one February when she was a small girl, it snowed every day for two weeks and school was closed during all that time."

Ernest laughed. "You must promise me you will not start praying for two weeks of snow this year. You must keep up with your studies. When you grow up to be rich lawyers or bankers you will be glad you did."

"Is Paris beautiful in the snow?" Michel asked. "Mama has told me it is. She says that the church spires and steeples look like white ghosts in the sky and that the parks look exactly like Papa Claude's snow pictures. Do they?"

"Why don't we arrange for you to see the steeples and parks in Paris for yourself?" Ernest suggested with one of the broad smiles that brought out the crinkled lines at the corners of his eyes. "Every time you boys have come to Paris with the family, it's been spring or autumn. You must see Paris in the winter, in the snow. I highly recommend it. As a matter of fact, snow was falling when I left the city this morning. I expect the avenues and boulevards are covered in a blanket of white by now. Why don't we go to see! Now! Right now, today! Yes, let's go to Vernon and leave for Paris on the next train! The driver and for-hire carriage I engaged when I arrived at Vernon are waiting outside to take me back to the train station. You probably saw them when you came up to the house. Why don't we go to Vernon together, then on to Paris to see the snow? "

"Oh, Mama, please let's go!" Jean-Pierre pleaded. "The snow must be so beautiful in the city. I'd love to see it! Please, just for a little while! Michel and I can get ready very quickly. We have warm clothes and everything we need."

"It's a wonderful, but ridiculous idea!" Alice quickly announced, staring at Ernest with utter contempt, her eyebrows arched high up into her forehead with the "how dare you" expression that spoke volumes and was among the tender myriad of Alice's more memorable habits Ernest very much missed.

"Cousin Beatrice loves having you visit," Ernest went on with great emphasis. "She told me so just a few days ago when I was with her in that great big house of hers with no children in it. How lonely the poor woman must be, and how very quiet it must be for her on snowy winter afternoons. She must sit by the window and watch the falling snow all by herself with no small children to talk to about the wind and the flurries that must be falling across the long garden stairway at the Palace of Saint-Cloud and the beautiful white drifts and curls of ice that coat the windows of the Palais Royale and the walkways of the Louvre opposite the court."

"Oh, Mama, please, let's go to visit Aunt Beatrice! We love her and she loves us," Jean-Pierre called out," and she is lonely in the snow!"

"There is no time to write Aunt Beatrice about a visit and it is rude to arrive at someone's home without prior warning," Alice said sternly, her knife-like pronouncement aimed directly at Ernest.

"Nonsense!" Ernest said with an agreeable chuckle. "Beatrice is ready at a moment's notice for any visit from you and the children, Alice. She has made that perfectly clear on a number of occasions. We talked about that very thing just the other day. I think we should all go to Paris right now. What is there to worry about? The older children are boarding at school and for just a few days Gabrielle will look after things here. By the way, I've wanted to tell you how happy I am to know that my little Germaine has been enrolled with Jacques and her sisters this year. She's been ready for school since she was three."

"Well, I do have a few matters to take up with Uncle Julian," Alice confessed, "and it would be lovely to have Beatrice's company for a while, especially with Claude away."

Snow had indeed fallen on Paris and its suburbs that February day. The train from Vernon had been delayed by rapid accumulations across the tracks but the traveling party of two adults and two five-year-old boys had miraculously arrived at the Gare de Saint-Lazare only an hour later than scheduled.

Ernest's intention in skillfully elaborating on young Michel's question regarding the beauty of Paris in the snow had not escaped Alice's attention, but somehow his spontaneous enthusiasm for the whole ridiculous idea had struck a memorable chord in her and not just one small surge of affection. She marveled at the fact that his sparkling bright light of schoolboy playfulness had not dimmed at all. Perhaps she really was being too hard on him. When all was said and done there was no need to fight him quite so fiercely, was there? He was, after all, still her husband and he had every right to see the children. He loved them and they loved him. One outing to Paris in the middle of winter with two five-year-olds wouldn't hurt anything.

"Something told me you'd be coming," Beatrice called out happily as she welcomed her unexpected houseguests with predictably open arms. "I just had a feeling. Ernest, be a darling and bring the suitcases upstairs, will you?"

"Forgive me for not taking the time to write you about a visit," Alice said, holding Michel's hand in hers while Jean-Pierre raced up the stairs ahead of Ernest, "but this was all Ernest's idea. I hope you don't mind. He wanted the boys to see Paris in the snow and decided at the spur of the moment that we should come. Michel has never met you or come to this beautiful house. I do hope it's all right. We can leave in the morning if it is inconvenient."

"It's more than alright, Alice, my dear, and Michel, I'm so glad to meet you. You're a fine looking young man. Oh, this is marvelous! I've needed someone lively around, and if it's a snowy Paris the boys want, they've come at the right time. From the looks of things we could be snowed in by tomorrow morning! Listen to that wind whipping up!"

Ernest talked non-stop to Alice and Beatrice long after the boys had gone to bed. "Why don't you stay the night, Ernest," Beatrice offered as the clock on the mantel struck eleven. "It may be difficult to find a cab and driver in weather like this. You may have to walk all the way home, but it's very cold."

"Oh, Ernest is a very hardy soul!" Alice chimed in quickly. "He loves cold, snowy weather, the colder and snowier the better. Isn't that right, Ernest? And

Rue Lisbonne is not so far. I'm sure it is absolutely beautiful there in the snow."

There were those eyebrows again, Ernest noticed with a small smile, and that withering glance. "Yes, I adore cold, snowy weather, especially when I know the people I love are safe and warm," he replied, standing to leave, his eyes looking directly into Alice's. "I'll come by tomorrow about noon and take the boys on the Paris snow tour. Why don't you come too, Alice?"

"Oh, no, I don't think so," Beatrice quickly interrupted. "It's best you have time alone with the boys, Ernest," she insisted. "And besides, Alice is too delicate to be walking around in cold, icy weather," she added dismissively. "She's been living in the country and sitting by those big roaring fireplaces with her knitting every afternoon for a long time. She isn't used to getting around on her own in slippery city winters anymore. We'll bundle up the boys in their warm mufflers and caps and you can enjoy showing them the sights. Do remember to wear a scarf yourself and do drop into a café now and then for hot chocolate. It will be wonderful day for the boys," Beatrice concluded, "and for you, Ernest."

"Yes, it will be wonderful," she repeated slowly, her intention in encouraging Alice's absence from the proposed snow tour meant to do all she could to affect in some decisive way the reconciliation she knew Ernest wanted so desperately, the reconciliation Beatrice herself felt Alice must surely want as well. How could she not want to return to a man who loved her so much? She was all he talked about. Alice was always on his mind, in his conversations, in his dreams and memories. He had never stopped loving her. She had abandoned him for a penniless artist and yet he spoke of her only in the most glowing terms, recalling her kindness, her intelligence, her devotion to her children, and her ability to handle the challenges she had faced with strength and dignity. Tears had often filled his eyes, Beatrice remembered, when he told her about his many attempts at finding a substitute for Alice; a lover, a companion, a woman to share his life and force him to forget. At first he had thought it would be so easy. He was good-looking, charming and clever. Someone would surely come along: a beautiful temptress, a wealthy but needy heiress, a lonely young widow, an only slightly impoverished but titled countess.

The widows and impoverished countesses had come and gone, the needy wealthy heiresses were few and far between, the temptresses although satisfying for the moment were selfish and demanding, and eventually the knowledge that no woman would ever replace Alice in his life became all too apparent. He loved her. She was the only woman he wanted, and seeing Ernest out into a snowy Paris night, Beatrice decided that within the next day or two she would do all she could to help him win her back.

"I have come to Paris for a few days, and am visiting with Beatrice," Claude had read and re-read in Alice's letter. "Ernest wanted Jean-Pierre and Michel to see the city in the snow. They begged to come and of course I could not allow them to travel to the city without me. I am sure you agree that was the right decision. The boys are enjoying every minute here. You will be pleased to know that Michel drew a picture of a snow-capped window at the Palais Royale and that little Jean-Pierre has described the Parc Monceau's statues draped in white better than you or I ever could."

His work came to a halt. His confidence wavered and he gave serious thought to returning to Paris on the very next train to have it out with Hoschede. If only Alice would forget her piety and agree to a divorce they could be married and none of this would matter. Yet again, Hoschede was placing Alice in a compromising position, testing her, tempting her while he was miles away, but he had to trust in their love. Alice would not fail him, he told himself. He had to have complete faith in her ability to decide what was best for their future together and as a family, but at the same time he was uncertain and indecisive. Perhaps it was best to get back to Paris and have it out with Hoschede after all. At least he would know what was going on. But no. He had to trust in Alice. Unfortunately, once again she was being required to make the decision she alone must make and it was critical that she come to a firm and final agreement with Hoschede. In Paris, however, at the same time and with Ernest's full cooperation, Beatrice was doing all in her power to fulfill Claude's worst fears and affect a permanent reconciliation between two people she loved very much.

"It's so good to see you in Paris," Beatrice said to Alice pouring hot coffee at luncheon the next day after they had seen Ernest and the children off. "You've probably missed the city very much. You were so involved with your wonderful life here. I myself have missed you more than anyone, anyone that is except Ernest, of course. He talks about you constantly, about the life you two shared for so many wonderful years. Do you ever think about those times, Alice? Do have one of these warm rolls."

"Of course I think of those times," Alice replied, placing the suggested roll on her plate, the faraway look in her eyes taking her back to the difficult adjustments she had been forced to make, "and you must know that at the beginning, when I moved to Vetheuil I dwelt on them all the time. It was hard not too. Every day, while I scrubbed and worried about how to pay for food and clothes for growing children I thought about the thousands of costly luxuries I had left behind me and taken for granted both at Rottembourg and in the city: clothes, beautifully appointed rooms, an army of servants, manicured gardens, lavish picnics, delicious meals prepared by invisible hands and beautifully served to me and my family each and every day by people in my employ. Yes Beatrice, I thought about the leisurely, gay life we had all shared without a single solitary thought toward the impossible difficulties the unknown future might hold. At Vethueil I was thrust into a world I felt didn't belong in. It was quite a comeuppance and I wasn't always happy, but I had Claude to help me through and I had my children to think about, so I decided to swallow my pride and do all I could to survive. There was always so much to do. I was constantly busy, but I lived one hour, one day, one week at a time and I waited to see what would happen next. It wasn't easy and I don't quite know what I expected, perhaps that Ernest really would magically restore the past to all it had been and that somehow we would regain the trust between us that we had built up over time with so much love and so much devotion. As you well know Beatrice, none of that happened and I suppose I knew early on at Vetheuil that I would be forced to kiss the past good-by and teach myself to forget. That part was the most difficult of all and I admit that over the next months I was torn, really sick inside much of the time. Had I done the right thing for myself and my children? Had I reacted too quickly? Was I expecting too much from Claude? Had I been fair to Ernest? Was I so deeply hurt that I did not seen things clearly? Was I being selfish and spoiled? It was endless, but once we were settled at Vetheuil, Ernest began spending less and less time with us. He was more and more distant, sent fewer and fewer francs to support us, and in the meantime one day dissolved into another and the happiness and new life I was finding with Claude came to conquer any thoughts I might have had about returning to the past. Besides that, I was busy from morning to night doing things I would never have dreamed I'd be doing. Beatrice, you should have seen me. In some of my best clothes I was cutting wood, feathering chickens, washing bed linen, and in the process the past became the past. Eventually there was nothing left of it, nothing to return to. It all began to fade away, not completely, but enough so I could look ahead and see some fresh light. Through those times Claude grew to be much more than a caring lover. He became a strong guiding force for me. He was a father to my children, a reliable companion with whom I was immensely happy, and a man to whom I committed myself without reservation. Best of all Beatrice, Claude returned me to myself, to the pieces of myself I'd lost. It's taken me these past seven years to see that every day, slowly and bit by bit, he gave me back my bearings, those fragile but necessary foundations we all rely on every day of our lives and don't take time to notice until they're knocked out from under us and we're left floundering in mid-air, not knowing how to stand or where to go."

"But Alice," Beatrice said, reaching for her second serving of warm rolls, shirred eggs and Parma ham, "you can't be truly happy living with a selfish artist who leaves you alone with all those children for weeks to paint somewhere. Ernest is not that inconsiderate type of man at all, not when it comes to his family," she continued, dabbing at the corners of her mouth with her napkin. "He would never leave you or the children for such a selfish motive. Alice, sooner or later you must realize that you have been sacrificing yourself to the wrong man. I don't want to confuse you, my dearest one, and your estimation of Claude Monet is commendable, but someone has to point out the truth and it might as well be me. Ernest has never stopped loving you," she said, putting down her fork and staring directly into Alice's eyes, "and even in light of his compromised financial state, I think you are a foolish woman to cast love like that aside. Together you could start over again and build something wonderful. It's not too late. You both have it in you to start again. Surely you feel that."

Alice breathed a deep, uncomfortable sigh, Beatrice's intention now very clear.

"Beatrice, I never cast Ernest's love aside. He did that. My dear, dear Beatrice, I know what you are trying to do here, but please understand. There are many different facets to love I'm finding, and each of us responds differently to the light and shade of it." Alice took a deep breath. "I have a special place in my heart for Ernest and I always will, but he hurt me and he hurt the children. He destroyed everything I believed we had built up between us, and I don't mean our lovely houses and the things we had in them. He destroyed the trust, the respect, the peace of mind, those safe, solid bearings that hold couples together, and in the process I found he didn't give a single thought to my feelings or my willingness to share the burden and help when things turned against us. He wouldn't let me in, wouldn't include me in decisions. His ego got in the way. It always does. He was handling everything he told me, but he wasn't handling anything at all. He kept secrets, he lied, he deceived me into thinking he was stronger, more capable of righting things than he really was. When we were first married I allowed myself to function as his anchor and do all I could to help him prosper. I trusted him to do all the right things. I tried to talk to him about everything I thought he cared about. I made myself available for business dinners and parties and visits to his suppliers and purveyors, but he failed me and he lied about failing me, and what did I get in return for my trust? A childish, immature man incapable of explaining to me or to himself the reasons for his obsessive overspending. Beatrice, in his inimitable way Ernest made a terribly serious situation seem idiotically simple and simply solved. You know how that turned out. Beatrice, I love you for what you are trying to do, but please stop. I am not returning to Ernest, not now, not ever. Our life together is over."

"But at least hear him out, Alice! You owe him that much."

"Hear him out? Owe him? Beatrice, I have heard him out more times than I care to remember: over and over again at Vetheuil, at Poissy, here in this house, at my Uncle Julian's and just yesterday at Giverny, and it is always the same. Beatrice, I don't owe Ernest a thing. He does all he can to intimidate me, make me feel guilty, and make it seem as if I alone hold the key to recovering his old success; as if I alone can guide his ability to deal with whatever it is he feels he must deal with to succeed and get back on his feet. He expects to restore our past with a touch of the old charm and a hopeful gamble. It simply will not happen. His childish ways, his childish vision, his constant need for approval, all of it is flawed. It goes nowhere. Don't you see? With the negative experiences of the recent past I expected Ernest to change, to grow and mature because of them. Instead I'm the one who has changed and grown and matured. Simply put, I cannot live my life with a child as my husband. I have found a better way, with a stronger, more responsible man. My life with Claude Monet is far from conventional and may never be exactly what it should be. Don't you think I know there's gossip all over Paris? I don't care, not anymore. Beatrice, please be happy for me. I have triumphed in all this. It has been very difficult, and it continues to be, but I have done it and I will continue to do it."

"You should divorce Ernest," Beatrice said flatly. "Yes, your Uncle Julian is right. If you feel that strongly about Claude, you should forget the Church and excommunication and everything connected to it. Marry him and then your old life with Ernest will truly be over. That's what you want, isn't it?"

"I will never divorce Ernest," Alice said. "Of course I am committed to my faith but I promised the children long ago that I would never divorce their father and I intend to keep my word."

"Then one of you will just have to die!" Beatrice said, laughing in the way people do when words pop out of their mouths without a thought to their impact. Alice could not suppress a laugh herself. "Yes, one of you will have to leave this life and allow the other to live," Beatrice went on. "I can't imagine I have said that, but it is what I am thinking. God forgive me!"

"Darling Beatrice, I love you for taking it upon yourself to find a solution that makes everyone happy, but please stop. Let's continue to be the close friends we are and enjoy the time we spend together without any of the old debris. You must come out to Giverny. Our house there is very special, at least I think it is. I'd like you to see it. It's a big old cider farm. The house itself is rustic and worn out in many places. The garden needs work and the neighbors aren't very friendly, but I have this wonderful feeling of belonging there. I belonged at the Chateau Rottembourg. I felt it every day I spent there, but after losing it I lost my sense of belonging anywhere at all. That's all changed. Now I belong at Giverny. We're leasing the house for now, but we want to buy the property one day. I hope you understand all this. Beatrice, it's what I want. I'm sure of it."

Alice talked privately with Ernest that evening. He was in a buoyant, carefree mood, immensely pleased to tell her all about the boys' responses to snow-covered Paris.

"I wish you could have seen their faces in the wonderland that was the Parc Monceau. Jean-Pierre was absolutely intrigued by the puffs of white perched exactly like pointed hats on the heads of the statues," Ernest gushed on. "He and Michel laughed themselves silly and plunked themselves right down on one of the iron benches that stood almost invisible under a huge sidelong drift. A brave vendor came along out of nowhere and provided us with warm beignets and chocolate sticks and then it was off to walk some more. What fun it was to point out the snow shapes created over the windows, doors, and cupolas. What a beautiful city our Paris is. I never tire of it. It lives so well with its character and the pace of its seasons. Too bad the sun was so warm today, though. The snow is melting away. Tomorrow most of it may be gone, but today was a truly wonderful day."

"You should be very pleased with yourself, Ernest. I can see that the charm of Paris in the snow has worked its miracle," Alice said in Beatrice's drawing room where they sat in the two chairs facing the fireplace. "The boys have had a grand time with you. They told me all about the Parc Monceau draped in white. Thank you for spending time with them and caring about them."

"Alice, I could care about the children and you forever if you'd let me. There could be days like this every winter. Alice, can't you see how happy we all could be here in Paris? There is so much for us here, especially for you. The theater, the music, the people you love. Tell me you'll think about it. At this point I could be happy with only that."

"No, Ernest, you couldn't be happy with only that at all," Alice answered, her voice touched with a tenderness he hadn't heard in years. "You will only be happy to have me tell you that I want to return to life with you here in Paris under any circumstances, and I never will. Ernest, we've been through this again and again. Please give it up. Give me up and look ahead. Please, find someone else to love. I want you to. Find a lover, a companion, a woman who can give you what I no longer can. Please, Ernest."

"We'll discuss this further at another time," Ernest declared emphatically, his tone suddenly cold. "I once said you would never be rid of me, and I stand by that. Go ahead Alice, go on with your long romantic fling with a poor painter who will never amount to anything and never put you first. For all your loyalty and all your sacrifice, you'll never compete with his canvases and color. Those are his real lovers. Those are his real mistresses and he will leave you for them at a moment's notice and for whatever time it takes to engage with them and trifle with them and complete his so-called work on them. On one of those misty Giverny mornings you described to me so well, when you're sitting at your lovely little desk by the window in your room, you'll have grown tired of him and his endless selfishness, and when you do I'll be waiting. In the meantime, for the sake of keeping peace between us, I'll strike a compromise with you. I promise to notify you well in advance of my visits to Giverny if you promise to bring my children to Paris more regularly than you have. If you find you are too busy with Claude and your new house, the older girls are perfectly capable of chaperoning the younger ones on the Vernon train now, and one more thing, Alice: when they do come, you can keep Jean and Michel Monet at home with you."

Alice was shocked. "Jean and Michel? Ernest, where does this cruelty come from?" she asked, her face shadowed with disappointment. "Claude's children are like my own and your own children love them," she blurted out. "Oh, I see. You were kind to Michel and Jean-Pierre today, but it was all a big show to get me here, wasn't it, the birthday present, the chocolates, Paris in the snow? Of course! But, it's fine. I'll agree to keeping Claude's boys with me at Giverny while our children are with you if you promise never again to have a discussion with me concerning a reconciliation. Our marriage is over and done with, but as usual you have tried to manipulate me and force conditions that suit you and not me. I can assure you that you will not be doing that in the future."

Alice was infuriated by Ernest's stubborn persistence and more by his negative reference to Claude's sons. His terms and refusal to free her from the grip of the past fueling her determination, she decided to set boundaries as never before.

"Ernest, there can be no divorce as you well know, but there can also be no door left open in our lives, not any longer. You leave me no choice. If you do not halt this ongoing harassment, and that is exactly what it is, I will be forced to take legal action to restrain you. I may live in the country, with simple country people who keep cows and sheep and have never been to Paris, but I still have influential friends in the city who take a dim view of fathers who do not support their children. Ernest, as I told you before we moved to Poissy, you are in no position to be named in legal actions and due to your bankruptcy you won't be for some years to come, but now you force me into doing what I must. Ernest, as far as the law is concerned you are still a debtor and that status still keeps you only one small step away from prison. Short of divorce, I will do whatever I must to bring our relationship to an end. Do you understand me?"

Again, a visit begun under favorable circumstances and initially conducted with good intentions was ending in anger and resentment. The abyss between Alice and Ernest, once only narrow and easily bridged, had been further widened and further deepened by threats. Ernest was clearly bitter.

"I could say a number of things to you right now, Alice," he snapped, "but I won't. I'm sure you know, though, what some of them are. Scandal, adultery, and co-habitation come to mind. But I do have some honor left in me, and alright! Agreed! I shall abide by your rules and cease the so-called harassment of my own wife."

"I have one last demand," Alice added, confronting a final concern, "and that is that you behave impeccably with Claude when and if you ever do come out to Giverny for the children's birthdays or on any other occasion. That means polite, civil behavior, and it means cordial exchanges and gentlemanly conversation or I shall take the necessary legal steps to keep you away permanently. I've heard it said that practiced behavior once applied with regularity and at least some degree of sincerity can result in surprisingly positive results. You must try it, Ernest. I have."

"Your request may be difficult to fulfill, but Alice, I can assure you I won't be staying long when I come to Giverny to see my children, and if I come at all I certainly won't be coming to see Claude with the intention of exchanging pleasantries or applauding his feeble efforts, but it's not Claude I care about. It's you and what I know about you that tells me that wherever you are I will always be there. I will live in your dreams, in your prayers, and in that corner of your heart that can't forget me. I may be less than I should be. I may even be less than Claude, but we will always be homeward bound together, you and I. Always."

Three days later, Alice thanked Beatrice and took Michel and Jean-Pierre into a waiting carriage. They arrived at the Vernon station well before dark and in the unpredictable way that anxieties and worries can be swept away, nothing Alice could have said to Claude about arriving home at The Press after the confrontation with Ernest could have proven more reassuring or meaningful to her than the quick phrase Jean-Pierre shouted out as he anxiously ran along King's Road and toward the gate of The Press.

"Home!" he said. "Home! We're here! It's the best place!"

That night she wrote to Claude, taking great delight in expressing her happiness in having returned to The Press after a visit to Paris and a meeting that had left her confident of having reached a clear and final understanding with Ernest. Now, she emphasized, she would look forward to Claude's return with a clear conscience. She prayed his work was going well and that he was taking care of himself. In the meantime she would wait for his letters and continue to enjoy just being at home. Gustave Caillebotte had sent one of the newly published seed catalogues from the gardens at Tours, she added. "I will study it she wrote, "and circle the flower seeds we might order for planting in the spring." If Claude found cuttings of plants at Bordighera that he felt would do well in Giverny's climate, she suggested he bring them home.

Her letter was received at Bordighera with immense relief. Claude responded immediately, his sentences filled with repeated references to their love and the unencumbered future they would share. Secure in the knowledge that Alice loved him and in her inimitable way had settled things with Hoschede, he took up palette and color and returned to work, writing again the very next day asking Alice to join him at Bordighera. She made preparations immediately, but within less than a week before she was due to depart for Menton where it was arranged Claude would meet her, she wrote him to say that Michel had come down with a cold. It had quickly settled into his chest and his cough was such that Alice decided she could not leave him. It was just as well. In a short time, Jean-Pierre caught a similar cold and developed a similar cough, his fever, which was worst than Michel's, a great worry to Alice, who nursed both boys through the next two demanding weeks. Dr. Aubert was summoned from Vernon twice. Once the fevers broke, at Alice's insistence he came regularly to look in on the boys well into March, reassuring Alice that her excellent care and insistence on good nourishment was successfully seeing them through the sort of serious bronchial difficulties many of the local children did not survive.

Losing sleep, worried about sick children, Claude away since January, Alice felt very lonely at times and through the month of March she had frequent occasion to recall Ernest's observation that she would never come first with Claude. He was right, and she must face it. Claude loved her and needed her, but at a moment's notice he responded to the beck and call of the true mistress in his life and it was impossible to compete with her allure. She was the provocative, invisible rival, the faceless, nameless muse who sang her sultry songs and reached him like the siren voices reached Ulysses, his war-worn body lashed to the mast of his aimless ship no match for the power of her seductive melodies.

True to form and in extraordinary volume the work continued at Bordighera: in Monsieur Moreno's Garden, at the Valley of Sasso, at Dolceaqua, the Via Romana, and la Citta Alta. At the end of the Bordighera expedition he had forty paintings to show for his efforts, scenes of la Citta Alta, the Via Romana, the Sasso Valley, the Nervia Valley, the Bay of Vintimiglia, the palm trees, the lemon and lime trees, the olives of the Moreno garden, and the beautiful village town of Dolceacqua and its bridge over the River Nervia. Every canvas represented his determination to persevere, move forward, and produce under what remained highly unsettled emotional circumstances. In April, packing cases filled with paintings shipped, the three-month Bordighera expedition completed, Claude was aboard the express train leaving Menton for Marseilles, and although comforted by Alice's reassuring letters, he was still not sure what might be awaiting him at The Press. He had, however, found a plant in Italy of which he had become very fond and he was bringing clusters of starter roots home. In 1884, along the sun washed coast of the Mediterranean, Claude had discovered Italian parsley.

He needn't have worried about his homecoming. It was much warmer than expected. Alice flew into his arms. "You are doing something very different here," she said to him when she saw examples of the Bordighera work. "You have dwelt on one motif at a time. In that single slim display of nature you seem at one and completely at ease with the environment in these canvases. The warm Italian climate and its natural beauty has agreed with you, my dearest. Your colors are extraordinary."

Durand-Ruel did not see the Bordighera canvases of 1884 for weeks after Claude's return to Giverny, the need to apply final studio touches to his work a habit that would now be carried into the coming decades. In May he was at last preparing to pack and send what he called "polished" Bordighera canvases to Durand-Ruel when he received a letter from Renoir, one of the only friends to whom he had written while on the Italian Riviera, eager to describe to him many details of his progress and schedule.

"As you have been away for some time and immersed in your work, you may not have heard that Monsieur Durand is suffering financial trouble once again," Renoir wrote. "The flat art market is affecting him badly and as if that were not reason enough to complain, once again he faces the demands of creditors who were part of the Union Generale debacle. "Pissarro has told him to sell his paintings for whatever he can get for them. I am telling him the same thing. You may wish to consider something similar."

In mid-May, thirteen Bordighera paintings arrived at Durand-Ruel's Street of Pictures door. Later in June, there would be nine more. The average price placed on each canvas was 800 francs, but for the time being Durand-Ruel could advance only a fraction of the entire sum of the 10,400 francs Claude had expected. Upset and of two minds, Claude chastised himself for requesting advances from Durand-Ruel at a time when the stalwart man could ill-afford to comply with pressing needs as he had in the past. At the same time, he needed to sell work. He reluctantly considered the likelihood of becoming his own agent, forced, out of necessity and under the circumstances of Durand-Ruel's financial trouble, to make contact with another circle of dealers and patrons who might be favorably inclined to buy or sell his work. At first, he made every attempt to sell paintings directly to a few patrons of the past. He quickly succeeded. Dr. Georges de Bellio made purchases, and in a surprising turn of events, so did a newly enthusiastic supporter of his work.

Claude had found favor with Ernest Hoschede's first serious collecting competitor, the opera singer, Jean-Baptiste Faure, by now the Paris Opera's leading baritone and an acclaimed art patron who had abandoned his interest in the work of Impressionists of the previous decade in favor of Edouard Manet, but who now had renewed his interest in the Impressionist group, particularly focused on Claude Monet whose increasingly favorable reviews were enough to prompt his purchase of several Monet paintings, an activity which continued late into 1884 when Claude met with Georges Petit, the dealer who had come to his rescue in the past and the competing dealer to whom a number of Durand-Ruel's painters were now turning.

"Claude, your work is becoming well-known," Petit said in the luxuriously gilded world that was his gallery. "You are being absorbed into the Paris art world's fickle vernacular. That's very good, and I congratulate you, but don't make a bad mistake now. I'd be very foolish indeed not to take anything you bring to me, even in this deflated market, but you mustn't lose sight of the fact that Durand-Ruel has watched over you and your career from the start. What is it? Ten years? More? You have a moral obligation to him and absolutely none to me. All that being out and cleared up between us however, I will tell you that I would like very much to include your work in the International Exhibition I am holding next May. Something has to be done to generate sales in this terrible art market, but it may be short notice for you. Do you have enough work to show? Can you in conscience leave Paul Durand-Ruel?"

"Rest," Alice advised to a conflicted Claude as 1884 drew to a close. "Don't decide anything now. Work in the studio, then look through those seed catalogues Gustave Caillebotte has sent. Think about those young plants we'll put in. The answers will come. They always do. Why don't you spend a little time with Gustave? He is wise beyond his years and will understand your dilemma. You always come away from a visit with him feeling better about everything."

"There is no time to dally with visits," my dear one, Claude was quick to reply. "Monsieur Petit wants my decision now. My brain tells me to go ahead with him, but my heart tells me such a move could jeopardize my relationship with Monsieur Durand and perhaps damage it forever. On the other hand, Petit is becoming very active in the Paris art market and with Monsieur Durand's current money problems which could last for a long time, Petit could take on new prominence with painters and buyers. Oh, it is confusing, to say the least."

Desperate to promote his sales and in need of income adequate enough to support life at The Press, deeply concerned at the same time about the future of his heretofore untarnished relationship with Monsieur Durand, Claude agreed to exhibit ten paintings at Georges Petit's 1885 International Exhibition. The event was to be but one in an ongoing annual series of lavish shows at which in the past the flamboyant Petit had promoted artists such as James McNeil Whistler and the young American painter, John Singer Sargent.

Everything about a Petit exhibition was elegant and grand. The Petit catalogue itself was a work of art. Seemingly unaffected by financial concerns, the Rue Seze dealer's recent sales were consistently surpassing those of any art dealer in Paris and he had expanded his imposing art gallery interests to include printing and monochrome, a move that along with his high-pressure, grand social occasion approach to public exhibitions, had led to a highly successful, money-making venture in the reproduction of good quality paintings by in-demand contemporary artists such as Braquemond, Desboutins, and Bonvin.

As was the case with Durand-Ruel, Georges Petit had inherited his art gallery business from his father. Unlike Durand-Ruel, however, Petit had become interested in the Impressionists at an early age. Twenty-five years younger than Durand-Ruel and determined to make a big name for himself in the international art world, he had been happy to take almost any of the Impressionist work Durand-Ruel rejected and was known to buy outright from painters who came through his doors with work he liked. Also, and as was the case with Durand-Ruel, Petit was a certified auctioneer, his commanding auctioneer talents shown off for one of the first times and at the tender age of 22 when he had held the hammer at Ernest Hoschede's auction of 1878.

 Claude took the invitation to show at Petit's 1885 International Exhibition as no small compliment. Like Georges Charpentier, who depended on an accomplished group of literary talents for the success of his magazine, Petit accepted nothing for his exhibitions that he felt he couldn't sell. His reputation was growing rapidly and with the assistance of a long list of wealthy American collectors who were coming to Paris in droves, wary of its depressed art market but once meeting the imposing Georges Petit and understanding the attractive monetary exchange, discovering they could acquire contemporary French paintings for comparatively few American dollars. Preparing for his exhibition, Petit carefully assessed Claude's ten paintings and in the spirit of dealer cooperation also remained open to exhibiting whichever of Claude's current paintings Durand-Ruel was finding difficult to sell and might wish to loan him. Savvy, equal-to-the-Petit-challenge, Street of Pictures-wise Durand-Ruel loaned Claude's *Strada Romana*, his Bordighera painting of the roadway linking the new and old Italian cities. It reigned as the star in Petit's international exhibition. Buyers came forward, but desirable *Strada Romana* was not for sale. Durand-Ruel owned it and he intended to hold on to it. A painting shown, well-received, and not for sale? Unheard of, but it was a masterful move. Durand-Ruel was a seasoned survivor and he knew how to hold on in choppy waters, especially when confronted by sudden squalls. Petit's exhibition was a critical success, but sales were soft. Claude was disappointed. Once again and as in the past, he had been required by personal circumstances to accept the invitation presented by an attractive open door. He had walked through with his eyes wide open, but once again his only reward lay in the fact that his work had been seen by a fickle public and was now talked about by critics more for having been shown at Georges Petit's elegant, upper-crust gallery than for its quality. He was devastated, and all the more so since at the same time Georges Petit was being seen and talked about more than ever. He, Petit, was being seen as the new promoter of Impressionist painting and as a result he was also becoming Paul Durand-Ruel's nemesis.

In July, relations between Durand-Ruel and Claude continuing frosty, Claude finally followed Alice's advice and together he and Gustave Caillebotte sailed the Seine on The Condor, one of Caillebotte's own boats. "Berthe Morisot has written to me," Claude told him, his bearded profile etched against the soft summer sky, the blue cotton jacket he wore over dark trousers tucked into his boots a perfect foil for the tonality of the cloudless azure haze. "She is offering a commission for a large wall panel. I've accepted. Seems I am destined to paint such pieces. I'll be doing a view of the Strada Romana at Bordighera with Garnier's villa in the foreground. Well, at least Madame Morisot has the means to pay me."

"It will be good for you," Caillebotte added looking up to the masthead of his favorite boat. "If I weren't painting panels for myself, I would commission you to do some for me this summer! As to how you should think about proceeding with sales and the rift you say you have with Monsieur Durand-Ruel, all I can suggest is that you do what must be done in order to survive until the art market rallies," he replied when Claude raised the question of Petit's ongoing support and his interest in becoming Claude's exclusive dealer. You may not think so right now, but I believe Monsieur Durand will understand. He has been your greatest ally, but he is also a fine human being and an unusual man who understands the plight of painters. Claude, although the air may seem tense between you, Monsieur Durand cannot possibly be suffering any affront whatsoever with you right now. Talk to him. Make the first move. He knows your circumstances and your needs, but enough about problems and concerns for today. Tell me, what have you been doing to enjoy yourself?"

"What a question!" Claude responded quickly. "I have been painting. I have been fretting about unfinished work and storms and bad weather and worrying about money and my relationship with my dealer. That is my life and it is all I do. Gustave, sometimes I think I am a complete failure. Nothing is working. Nothing is happening for me and I certainly am not enjoying myself much."

"Claude, you need a hobby, like sailing," Gustave declared to the battle-weary, exacting friend he admired, a man he knew was driven every day of his life to triumph over the challenges of living, hovering all the while like a tortured genius at the fragile edge of greatness.

"What do you love best to do in all the world when you are not painting and arguing with Mother Nature?" Gustave asked with a chuckle. "We must find a suitable diversion for you, something irresistible and ongoing."

"Gustave, the sort of diversion you suggest cannot exist for me, even if I were so inclined. I am not wealthy enough to indulge in boats and regattas, nor am I inclined to the idle pursuits of thoughtless dilettantes. Not that I am suggesting you are one. Far from it, but I don't ride and I don't hunt, as I once pointed out to Monsieur Hoschede at Montgeron who, by the way, I recall appeared quite shocked by my admission. No, the spirit of my insane world is too restless, too guarded for the discipline and demands of strict rules and proper forms and all those prescribed directions so easily followed by others in their pastimes. I read and I think and I must be a sorry companion most of the time. I have very little of interest to talk about but my work, the books I am reading, or the activities of Alice and the family. My home is important to me and Alice sees to it that I have peace and pleasure in it. I don't know how she does it really, but the Giverny house is providing a good deal of pleasure for her. The garden requires a great deal of attention and our landlord allows us to proceed with it as we wish. Alice enjoys planning for the flowers and trees we'd like to plant when we can afford to, and she loves the freedom of more outdoor space than she has had since leaving the Chateau Rottembourg. It pleases me so much to watch her reach for the yellow straw hat she keeps on the rack in the hall and set out from the house to walk the grounds. She never did anything like that at Vetheuil or Poissy. A short way down the path, she glances over her shoulder to wave and smile at me or one of the children. It is only two acres of land, but Alice takes pleasure in every inch, unkempt and overgrown as most of those inches are. We talk about the possibility of buying the property some day and perfecting the garden. I hope I can find a way to make that happen. It would make up for so much of the past."

"That's it then!" Gustave smiled to his good friend, his own white sailing shirt and jacket in sharp, crisp contrast to the opalescent river and brilliant blue sky overhead. "You are in touch with nature every day of your life and now you and Alice have found a wonderful place in which to enjoy it on your own terms. Claude, when you aren't painting and worrying about the weather, why not apply your creative energies to making a garden you can enjoy fussing over and filling with the color and shade you understand better than anyone else I know? You admired the gardens at Rottembourg. You studied and painted the pond, the bowers of specimen roses, the dahlias, the trees at the edge of the Senart, even the crazy wild white turkeys. You visited my father's gardens at La Casin and marveled at their beauty, and on many occasions you have complimented my own small efforts at Petites Genevilliers. It sounds to me as if at Giverny you could develop at least a small garden of your own to fit your vision of nature, which apart from the satisfaction developing a landscape would bring you, would give us more to talk about. We could write to each other about our great cultivated successes and our embarrassing, disastrous failures with plants instead of paint. It would be good for both of us."

In August, the family left Giverny for a summer holiday on the Normandy coast. Jean-Baptiste Faure had invited Claude and the entire family to stay at his villa at Etretat where he housed a large part of his Impressionist painting collection. Again, for Claude it was a painting holiday with his family, this time infinitely more luxurious than the summer holiday at Pourville. Most mornings and with Blanche carrying canvases, he set out to paint the Etretat cliffs which Faure himself had painted. Claude also painted at Petites-Dalles while Alice and the children enjoyed the spacious Faure house, its array of Impressionist paintings, and the fine coastal weather as once again by the summer sea, schedules were thrown out of the window.

The children swam and splashed in the crystal-clear water between the dramatic cliffs, delightedly shrieking when Papa Claude returned, rolled up his trousers and waded in to join them. Sitting on the rocks with him, they studied the tides and watched the gulls. They wondered where birds go to die and if the very same seawater that broke onto the Etretat shoreline traveled long distances to other, faraway shores, perhaps to exotic Morocco or ancient Alexandria. In the evening they played card games by candle light. They cooked meals over campfires, fished in small inlets, and at the end of the day watched the blazing sun set from their perches on beach cliffs where in rising tides the waves pounded and crashed and the sky above filled with millions of stars.

The unceasing struggle for perfection. The unending battle for technical mastery. A family doing its best to make sense of itself. A marriage dissolved but for legalities and against all odds a pair of polar opposites finding deep, lasting love. Time racing by, speeding ahead, the unknown future a frame surrounding an incomplete canvas, the keen eyes ever watchful, ever vigilant, never satisfied, and under it all, a rift between a dealer and an artist gnawing away, reminding all concerned that unhappiness took on many disguises.

"Monsieur Durand has been there for you all along," Alice reminded him that summer when he became pensive and buried himself in a book to fool her into believing he was truly reading and not thinking about his friend and mentor. "Talk to him, my darling. Don't let too much time pass. Friendships are like plants. Marriages too. Without proper attention they wither and die."

"What can I possibly say to the man? He knows I need to sell my paintings in order to live and if he can't sell them, then I have every right to engage with a dealer who can, Georges Petit or anyone else. Furthermore, I think Monsieur Durand should return some of my unsold pictures so that I can sell them myself. He is holding on to everything Renoir, Pissarro, Sisley and I bring to him. I'm not Manet or Caillebotte, born to those high ceilings you, yourself, know so well. "

"No, Claude, you are not anyone but yourself, and because you are the strong, driven individual you are, you must be the one to take the first step. Go to Paris as Gustave suggested and see Monsieur Durand. Do it soon. You must mend your relationship with him. Come to an understanding with him. It wouldn't surprise me to know he's waiting for you to walk through the door there on Rue de la Madeleine right now."

Waiting? Yes. Alice was right. Durand-Ruel was waiting, but he was also thinking as he waited. The dealer of thoughtful decision and wise counsel was not unnerved by Claude's defection to his rival, Georges Petit, not at all. It would be temporary. Big talent had its big egos and in Claude Monet's case, big ambition came with every canvas, but what should be done? Another Impressionist Exhibition in Paris? Another stab at seducing the French public away from its comfort zone? No. It was no longer enough. There had to be another way, another avenue, a newer and better road to genuine success and the money that was needed at the end of it.

Through summer and into the late months of 1885, Durand-Ruel worked diligently at developing his ideas for a new strategy and a new approach to exhibiting the work of the Impressionists. In the past he had made attempts at stirring the interests of a broader European audience with exhibitions in London, Berlin, Rotterdam, and two years before, in 1883, he had gone so far as to test American waters by crossing the Atlantic and exhibiting a number of Impressionist paintings in Boston, Massachusetts at the International Exhibition of Art and Industry at

Mechanics Hall. The exposure at all locations had resulted in only minimal interest and equally minimal sales, but through the early autumn of 1885, barely able to pay the rent and keep his doors open, Durand-Ruel was encouraged by a number of New York and Boston collectors visiting his Paris gallery filled, as it was, with Impressionist paintings. A number of these American collectors and art group representatives offered opportunities for Impressionist exhibitions in the United States. Durand-Ruel sent letters and print material to groups and individuals recommended to him in New York and Boston, including copies of critical reviews and biographical sketches on those artists who formed the Impressionist core. As late as mid-summer summer of 1885, he had heard nothing back from contacts in America, but in July, Claude came to see him in Paris, renewing not only his relationship with his supportive and understanding dealer, but at the same time forming a valuable new friendship with a highly influential Paris man of letters.

Octave Mirbeau was the art correspondent for La France, and although still in the early stages of his career, he was a widely read journalist and pamphleteer. Considered a highly authoritative Paris art world source, he was interviewing artists for a series of articles he was writing and one afternoon he had come to Durand-Ruel seeking introductions to one or more of the Impressionists. Claude's presence at Durand-Ruel's gallery that same afternoon could not have proven more fortuitous, for it was there that Mirabeau conducted an interview immediately. Shown a number of Monet paintings which Claude proceeded to discuss in detail, Mirbeau's resulting article appeared in the haut bourgeois La France brimming over with admiration and praise for the landscape artist "so complete, so vibrant, that every play of shadow, every magic of the moon is a masterpiece of precision, perspective and tone."

Writing in the decorous style for which he would soon become famous and thorough to a fault in reviewing Claude's themes and subjects, Mirbeau's interpretation of the several Monet landscapes he had been shown at Durand-Ruel's went so far as to compare Claude to the revered Courbet, a highly favorable comparison La France's conservative, Salon-oriented readership could readily understand, accept, and most important of all, remember and hopefully discuss. By clearly expressing, in his adjective driven, romantic style what Claude was then and what he was to become, Mirbeau, in one authoritative and successful attempt, made himself the official Monet interpreter, becoming at the same time

Claude's lifelong friend. In appreciation for his enormously helpful promotional effort at a crucial time, Claude presented him with The Customs House, the Pourville painting of the customs officer's house and the cliff between Pourville and Dieppe.

CHAPTER 27

State of the Art
1885 – 1886 - 1887

At Giverny, Claude was slow to apply himself to local subjects, his work at Bordighera and Etretat far more compelling. Into the early winter of 1885, however, he began a series of paintings of the village, the Seine and its banks, and the outer fringes of Giverny. Only one diversion could distract his single-minded focus on his work. On cold winter nights or when he wasn't creating studies or painting, he and Alice sat by the fireside and took great pleasure in perusing the seed catalogues Gustave Caillebotte had been sending on to them regularly. They began ordering, only a small representation of flower seeds at first, mostly perennials and no vegetables. From the beginning, the location of the vegetable garden at the front of the house had not pleased Alice, the unwieldy, random heights of its tight rows of produce by mid-summer at the roadway entrance a visual disappointment, but in her inimitable way, Alice found a solution. During the previous spring, Father Toussaint had helped her to secure a small plot for growing vegetables at the nearby farm everyone in the village called "the blue house," a project supervised and cared for by the farm's accommodating owner who happily responded to his new neighbor's clear understanding of farm life, applying enough of his experience and expertise to produce a thriving collection of beans, onions, peppers, and potatoes for the large family living at the house of the old cider press. Its flourishing productivity put an end to the growing of vegetables in the front garden of Le Pressoir and new plans for it were discussed.

By late summer of 1885, in the studio created in the room to the immediate left of the drawing room, Claude was working on Durand-Ruel's wall panels once again, complaining to Alice that the work was too demanding and too time consuming. He was also complaining that he missed his friends. He had continued to see Renoir and Caillebotte on a fairly regular basis, but since moving to Giverny he had been out of touch with the others and he confessed to longing for their news.

"Invite them here to Giverny and we'll have a luncheon," Alice suggested. "Marie and I cook for ten every day. A few visitors shouldn't disturb us too much. We can keep everything very simple, but very delicious."

"No, Giverny may be too far to come for most of them, but my dear Alice, you have given me an idea. "Perhaps our old group could meet in Paris again, the way we used to, not at the Guerbois or the Athenee, but perhaps for dinner at a restaurant."

Claude began to write to his Impressionist friends. All wrote back, responding enthusiastically to meeting for dinner. Renoir suggested they meet at the Café Riche.

Claude was not alone in missing faces of the past. Members of the old group had been feeling the same way and welcomed the idea of a reunion. Dinners at the popular Café Riche, a prominent Paris establishment well above the status of the Café Guerbois of earlier days, quickly became a tradition, given over to the first Thursday of every month, the members of the now vastly scattered group immensely pleased to reassemble, restore old friendships and sentimental ties, but in the interim of passing months, life had changed. No longer lost to the vagaries of café sawdust, fierce shouts, and clicking billiard balls, much to their surprise, the reunited band of rebels was now being heralded in a number of Paris sectors as heroic. They were veterans of a long and gallant mission. Many patrons of the Riche now knew their work. They recognized the faces gathered at the long table along one of the mirrored walls, defining by their mere presence and together, the meaning of tenacity. People watched to see what they ate and what they drank. They noticed how they dressed. There were whispers and nods of recognition. Café Riche patrons stopped to exchange greetings as they passed the table where Pissarro, Degas, Sisley, Renoir, Caillebotte, Cezanne and Monet sat assembled for the first time in many months, their animated dinner conversation driven, as in the past, not so much by their work or its progress, but by the personal events affecting those same individual lives with whom they had become closely allied more than ten years before. One particular onlooker observed much more than friendship and survival at the Riche. On a Thursday evening he sat with a female companion in a quiet shadowed corner. He saw no gathering of social friends, but a small army of gallant warriors he knew well and by name. He was Ernest Hoschede, and watching the proceedings at the long table under the mirrored wall, he found himself not at all disturbed by the view.

He had known them from their earliest beginnings. For a time, he had supported their every effort and objective and he had been their loyal friend, but he hadn't seen them together this way in years. Watching them come through the door and waiting until they were all assembled, he left his companion and in a few confident strides, reached their table with a broad smile and the self-assured posture of a man who had made peace with the past. At first, an awkward silent hush fell over the group. The discomfort was palpable, but the Ernest Hoschede of old seemed to have recovered his charm and incomparable gift for engagement.

"Wonderful to see you together!" he exclaimed, his smile and demeanor as he greeted each man by name entirely disarming to Claude who sat back in his chair amazed by Hoschede's friendly approach. Where was the anger of old? Where the resentment and graceless behavior of the past few years? Could this be the same man who Claude thought would forever hate him, hate his every action, his every word and deed? This strange man was behaving exactly as he had in the Guerbois years ago when all the world was at his fingertips and few things other than Alice and his children were more important to him than his Impressionist friends and their paintings. So disarming was the new Hoschede, that for a brief moment it seemed entirely appropriate to forget insulting affronts and invite him to join the table as he had in the past. Ernest's display of good manners, however, made it clear that he had no desire to intrude on what had apparently been planned as a rare reunion.

"I'm sorry to see that Madame Morisot has not joined you this evening," he said, his eyes sweeping over each figure at the table, "but of course, she would never be seen here at the Riche by herself."

"Monsieur, I doubt the day will ever dawn when Madame Morisot will join us at evening dinners, or any public meetings whatsoever," Renoir moaned, shaking his head, his momentary discomfort vanished as he addressed his good friend, Claude's, romantic rival. "And what a shame!" he added. "She is one of us, and a refined lady of great talent, but women of her class play only certain roles in Paris today and unfortunately those roles do not include dining alone with a group of male contemporaries in a public restaurant, no matter how talented. Tragique!"

"Tragique indeed!" Ernest replied, "but you may be interested to know that I am including a life profile of Madame Morisot in a series of articles I am writing for my column in Le Monde. Don't be too surprised if I publish something on the present status of your group, which I believe has established a rather strong foothold in the city's life. Don't think I haven't been watching your progress. In spite of those early exhibitions we saw as complete failures, the exposure meant something, just as Monsieur Durand-Ruel said it did, and today people aren't finding your work too shocking at all. Well, I must get back to my guest. Enjoy the evening and I'll be listening for your toast, "A la belle France!"

Change. Elements of forgiveness and a truce of sorts. Time flying past on the wings of dimming pain. Wounds mending. Healing. Memory fading. A la belle France!

By year's end of 1884, Ernest had settled into an acceptable way of life, his monthly income enough to sustain him in the simple manner to which, try as he might, he had never become accustomed. Making every attempt to restore his optimism and feel at least minimally productive, he wrote for several arts and Paris lifestyle publications and appeared once again to be the Ernest of the previous decade: a man in love with life, cheerful and well-met, but seasoned and finally at peace with conditions over which he no longer had power to influence or change. The only person to understand the truth of his great difficulty in having arrived at this delicate point was his long-time friend, Jean DeLille, whose loyalty had withstood long bouts of anger, depression, drunkenness, and years of overwhelming periods of self-loathing and regret. The only other person to know the truth behind Ernest's recovery from the painful past was Valentina Perrett, his frequent companion at the Café Riche and a woman who in the past year had fallen deeply in love with a man she had never known as anything but bereft.

Valentina Perrett bore no pedigree and no connections to a life of prosperity. She had invented her name and her only known human condition was loneliness, a quality with which Ernest immediately identified. Orphaned at the age of six, she had run away from the Sisters of Mercy at the age of ten. By the time she was twelve she was begging on Paris streets during the day and sleeping under bridges, in darkened doorways, and occasionally with a friendly gentleman at night. One day, hungry and attracted by the baskets of coins a group of street musicians collected from passers-by, she joined a similar troupe of itinerant, corner-based musicians, her audition conducted by the mandolin player who had handed her a tambourine and taught her a few dance steps which over time were expanded into ambitious routines capable of drawing a large, coin-tossing crowd and which, in a few years, had led to Valentina's gainful employment as a leading dancer at the Folies Bergere. It was there, in the company of fun-loving Jean DeLille, that Ernest had noticed the raven-haired young beauty on the stage, attracted as much by her impressive Venus Dance as by her dazzling smile.

In The Folies' elaborately staged scene based on the ancient Greek beauty contest, the Homeric Age's Trojan Prince Paris is asked to judge the merits of three Greek goddesses, Venus, Minerva, and Juno and to choose the most beautiful of the three. The three appear for his close scrutiny and after careful deliberation he chooses Venus, presenting her with the prize of a large golden apple, the triumphant Venus then proceeding to dance a celebratory dance with the large golden apple as her partner amid thunderous rounds of applause. Very much taken with Valentina's beauty and elegant depiction of Venus, Ernest had sent a note, inviting her to join him for supper at the Riche, a café Valentina had only heard about from girlfriends who eagerly befriended the sorts of sophisticated gentlemen who frequented such distinguished Paris addresses.

Unlike many of her Folies friends, Valentina did not take to airs or affectations, and although at first she was drawn to Monsieur Ernest Hoschede's fine manners and elegant tastes, Ernest soon discovered she was not at all impressed by luxury and its trappings, and that in fact, she was uncomfortable in the presence of wealth. Although proud of her affiliation and current starring role with the Folies Bergere, Valentina was basically a strong, street-wise individual far more content to live with simplicity and independent honesty than with wealth. From the start, she had expected nothing from Ernest and since there was little to give, their relationship had developed from common ground. After her Folies performances and over a few weeks of intimate suppers at the Riche and long conversations, Ernest had gradually revealed to her the details of his life and past; his children, his marriage to Alice, her affair with Claude Monet, and the fairy tale quality of life once lived at a place called the Chateau Rottembourg. Providing the undivided attention and compassion he had craved for so long and with her lighthearted approach to life, Valentina was teaching him to forget. She was fun for him to be with and she was earning her own way in life. In a short time she became his lover, his friend, and by the start of the New Year of 1886, as an event being planned some distance away from Paris began to take shape for Alice and Claude, Valentina alone held the key to Ernest's happiness.

In January of 1886, news of an opportunity for the further expansion of Claude's career was received. He and Pierre Renoir were invited to participate in the Belgian exhibition of a group of artists known as The Brussels Twenty. Alice was more impressed than Claude, her undiminished affection for all things Belgian from chocolates and tea to lace tablecloths and fine linen a constant source of amusement to the family, especially when she spoke excitedly and very rapidly when any bit of news of Belgium reached her.

"Oh, this is the most prestigious invitation, Claude!" she announced all aflutter. "You must exhibit!" she insisted, her vocal speed accelerating with every syllable. "This is the last year the "Twenty" will be holding their great event at the Palais des Beaux-Arts. In his last letter, Uncle Julian said that next year the event will move to the Brussels Museum of Modern Art. He doesn't like the change, but of course, that's to be expected. Anything called "modern" annoys him."

Les XX was a group of twenty Belgian painters, designers, and sculptors formed in Brussels in 1883 as a reaction to the conservative policies of L'Essor, the official Belgian academic Salon equivalent to the Paris Salon. "The Twenty," as they called themselves, held an annual exhibition of their work and each year invited twenty additional international artists to participate, including poets, playwrights, dramatists, and composers.

"One of the aspects of the Belgian event is the added feature of lectures and performances of new music," Alice noted, reading through the pamphlet which had accompanied Claude's invitation. "This year, Caesar Franck is debuting a violin sonata and Verlaine and Mallarme are discussing their work. Oh, Claude, I would love to go. And it's Belgium. I haven't been there in years. I suppose, though, I wouldn't know anyone there anymore. Claude, do you think my being at this event with you would distract from things, I mean cause gossip?"

"Of course it wouldn't. And I would love having you there," Claude responded immediately. "Alice, at some point you must stop this worry over what the public may or may not think about us. It doesn't matter."

"Oh, but it does," Alice responded quickly. "It does matter. We can never allow anything about our personal lives to affect or interfere with your progress as a painter, not ever. It would kill me to know that my place in your life had anything at all to do with a critic's negative review or the failure of a sale. People can be very judgmental and cruel. They draw conclusions and make decisions based on what they've heard, even if they're lies. You know that, and the nastier they can be the better they seem to like it. Claude, we can't escape the fact that I live with you and am still married to Ernest Hoschede. It's a condition not everyone ignores or accepts as we do."

It was still there in Alice; the self-reproach she couldn't shake off, the fear that an illicit relationship could at any time affect not so much her own reputation but Claude's, and always deep within the inbred fear of offending the Paris establishment remained. None of her concerns escaped Claude's notice. He appreciated her consideration and loved her watchfulness over his career, but he did all he could to encourage her escape from her relentless battle with culpability.

"We are going to Brussels together," he declared in no uncertain terms. "Begin to prepare for the trip and take out a few of those wonderful hats you've put away. Apart from our summer holidays, the trip to Brussels will be our first public outing of consequence and I intend it to go not well, but perfectly."

Renoir arrived in Brussels with Odilon Redon, one of the founding members of "The Twenty." Claude showed ten paintings, among them *Le pont d'Argenteuil* and *La Mannes-port d'Etretat*. It was decided in advance that he, Alice, and Renoir would attend the formal opening together. Upon arrival they were impressed by the attendance. Well before the opening bell, hundreds of people had gathered at the entrance to the Palais.

"Somehow, our work always looks better away from home," Renoir shared with

Alice as the three reviewed the many paintings and pieces of sculpture exhibited, pleased with the hanging and display arrangements of their work. "Why do you think that is, Madame?"

"Because at home you pay too much attention," Alice replied with a laugh, thrilled to see Claude's work and that of his colleague so prominently shown. "I'm sure you fuss and fret the same way Claude does. At home, in familiar surroundings, the intensity is always there, the feeling that it isn't quite right or quite ready and may never be, but once the work leaves home, it flies off alone, like a brave young bird, prepared to face the world and deal with whatever consequences come with the wind. It is a great risk you take each time you exhibit and I think what you and Claude do is very, very brave."

She was so pretty in the flattering light, her dress so old, but still so beautiful, so elegantly finished, so appropriate. It was the blue wool dress and matching jacket she had worn the day she and Ernest had lunched at Laperouse and she had told him a new baby was coming. Much to her delight and although she was a bit slimmer, the ensemble still fit and flattered her figure, a pleasant surprise which very much contributed to her confidence. That morning in Brussels, as she had dressed for the exhibition opening, the nine-year-old memory of a luncheon with Ernest at Laperouse did not escape her, but there in the hotel and in the excitement of being in Brussels, her Raingo family's Belgian roots very much on her mind, she somehow overcame its old impact and wearing the blue wool now along with a wide-brimmed darker blue hat, she was enjoying every minute she spent at Claude's side.

Together, they attended the Caesar Frank violin sonata debut and while Claude met and socialized with fellow artists, Alice attended the literary discussions led by the Symbolist, Paul Verlaine, forbear of the Symbolist movement and later the poet and critic, Stephane Mallarme, author of the famous poem, *Prelude to the Afternoon of a Faun* which was soon to be set to music by Claude Debussy.

They were invited to luncheons and dinners and returned to Giverny reassured and at peace with the overall success of their venture together into the public arena. They had interacted with like-minded people. They had dined with authors and musicians and they had succeeded in simply being together and being themselves. More important to Alice were the international reviews which were highly favorable to both Claude and Renoir, the accepted avant-garde nature of

"The Brussels Twenty" allowing for few, if any, traces of friction in terms of public opinion. Pleased with his participation in the Brussels event, Claude's greater satisfaction as he returned home to The Press came with the knowledge that confident at his side, Alice had not endured a single moment of distress.

In years to come Pissarro, Caillebotte, Sisley, Cezanne, and Gaugin would show with the illustrious "Twenty." Georges Seurat would exhibit his *Sunday Afternoon on the Island of la Grande Jatte* in 1887 to great acclaim while Paul Gaugin's *Vision After the Sermon* would meet with a less than lukewarm reception in 1889.

Encouraged by the success of the Brussels trip and Alice's increasing confidence in their way of life, Claude suggested she plan a luncheon, perhaps one inviting Paul Durand-Ruel to Giverny.

"Yes, of course, but it will have to wait until you return from Etretat" she responded. "Monsieur Durand-Ruel will be a wonderful guest. I'll plan everything while you're away."

Alice was encouraging of the proposed Etretat expedition, exactly as she knew she should be, but there it was again, the seductive call of the irresistible mistress, her demand this time in the month of February, her directive to a striking, mid-winter clad Etretat. "I'll write every day," Claude promised. "It will be as if you are there with me."

"And while you're away don't forget to answer Gustave's letters and those of the young man who has been writing to you with questions about Giverny," Alice reminded him; that American, Monsieur Sargent."

Correspondence was piling up. Letters were coming in every day. Fellow artists, critics, and now a crop of young American painters including Carolus Duran's protégé, John Singer Sargent, were contacting Claude, eager to hear directly from the Impressionist painter known to be living in a rural country village where he worked quietly and simultaneously on as many as four or five canvases of the same outdoor subject at various times of day. At the same time the issue of Durand-Ruel's role in Claude's life remained both central and vexing. Georges Petit's encouraging correspondence and repeated requests for an exclusive artist-dealer association did little to help. Claude had placed himself in a complicated corner, one dealer offering the glitter of showy public exhibition and the secure promise of sales, the other his old friend and mentor selling his paintings at a disappointing loss while enduring his own financial difficulties and at the same time the man to whom he bore deep feelings of loyalty and respect. Alice shared his concerns. She was well aware that Claude's reputation was developing solidly now. His star was rising, that much was clear, but solid reputations and rising stars did not generate the income they needed. He had to sell his paintings. As tempting as the formal affiliation and attractive promise of sales Monsieur Petit was envisioning might seem, Monsieur Durand-Ruel could not simply be cast aside, Alice advised strongly, not now, not after his long history of support and generosity and especially not now when he himself struggled to remain afloat in the murky sea of only mildly interested patrons and mounting debt. The painting expedition to Etretat could very well provide the diversion Claude's state of confusion required, Alice reasoned. She encouraged him to go with time to think things out.

He arrived at the Hotel Blanquet in late February and immediately set to work on studies of the Manneporte, the magnificent huge vaulted cliff over the sea so large that a ship could pass through it.

In the dead of winter, he positioned himself at the foot of the ocean shoreline's closest cliff, his concentration one morning so intense that he failed to notice the changing tide and mounting waves quickly rising and lapping at his knees. Suddenly knocked into the icy water by an immense crashing wave, his easel was splintered, his canvas and materials dashed against the jagged rocks.

"I do not know how I found my way out of that deep mass of frigid water," he wrote to Alice that same afternoon. "I tried to rescue my things, especially the canvas I was working on, but I was so wet and cold and the waves became so wild that I just left everything and returned to my room. I have no idea where it has all gone, but don't worry, my dearest. I am fine."

He wasn't fine. A lingering fright had come over him as a result of the Manneporte experience, one which affected him far more seriously than he had confided to Alice. In his letter to her he had failed to mention that the water had been so deep and had knocked him so far out to sea that he thought surely he would drown. He had also failed to mention that he feared he would have damaged his hands if he had tried to rescue his materials from the raging waves at the jagged Manneporte. Hand injuries were the secret dread of every painter he knew. He couldn't remember how he had found his footing or the safety of the shore, but in the days that followed, uncertainty and nervousness were his constant companions as he made every effort to calm himself and return to work, rubbing his hands together every now and then, grateful they had survived undamaged, but once again nothing was fitting. Nothing was right. It was the old story. The sky was too gray. The sea was too rough. He was too wary. He had too few supplies left to continue. He was cold. He was lonely. It was time to leave for home.

The trip to Etretat a failure, his mood as cold and gray as the winter itself, he returned to Giverny to find the household in utter turmoil. Marthe, Blanche, and Suzanne were in tears. Jacques and Germaine were home from school and sulking. Only the behavior of the youngest children, Michel and Jean-Pierre seemed normal. It took hours, but Claude was finally told that during his absence, Alice had endured long, raging tirades from Marthe, Blanche, and Suzanne.

They were now of an age to understand exactly what was going on between Claude Monet and their mother and had made it very clear that they had abhorred their mother's behavior over a long period of time with a man to whom she was not married and who was not their father. They demanded she break all ties with him. No longer were they adamant about a return to their father's household, but they demanded their mother leave Claude and begin to live a life of respect, especially as now they were of marriageable age and felt entitled to husbands of means and at least some position. Suzanne was 18, Blanche 20, and Marthe 21. All three girls were slim and attractive and had inherited much of their father's natural charm.

"Who will want to marry us?" Marthe had shouted to her mother. "Who will have us? The poor, old widowed farmers of Giverny? The miller's son? The fishmonger's ugly offspring? You are a disgrace to your own daughters!"

"You are a selfish, unfeeling woman!" Suzanne had added to the lethal mix. "We should all be in Paris where we belong. We are ashamed of you; ashamed of the way you have made us live! Our Papa has wanted us back all along. He has wanted to restore his family's standing and respect. He has begged and begged you to return to him, over and over again. We've heard it all, the pleadings at Vetheuil, at Poissy, and at Aunt Beatrice's house in Paris, but no, our dear Mama has turned away from all his pleadings and has preferred to have us live in sin with her and Claude Monet!"

"It's too late now anyway!" Blanche had also cried out, tears streaming down her cheeks. "Papa has a woman now. Yes, Mama, a woman!" she screeched.

"Her name is Valentina and she dances at the Folies Bergere! She's beautiful, yes beautiful, and she's fun for Papa to be with. They have suppers at the cafes he once took you to. They laugh and joke and they sleep together in his bed. Yes, Mama, in his bed! It's too late now for you to end your adultery! Even Papa doesn't want you anymore!"

Alice had heard the relentless ugly rage in voices she loved and barely recognized. She had looked at this trio of daughters ranting and thundering against her, but hearing their scorching words and feeling their anguish she hadn't seen a beautiful eighteen-year-old, a tearful twenty-year-old and a bitter twenty-one-year-old. Standing defenseless against an endless deluge of painful tirades she didn't see The House of the Cider Press. She didn't see Ernest storming through the door as he had at Poissy, and she didn't see Camille dead and veiled in white at Vetheuil. All she saw were three little girls playing at statues in the bright summer sunshine of vanished hours, their carpet an emerald green lawn, their walls the safe, protective trees of an August lost to memory and regret. She heard their happy, childish voices ringing out in clean, undamaged country air. She saw herself with them, stroking their cheeks, hugging their precious small bodies close to her heart, their young lives vibrant and whole in their chateau world of tall chimneys and wide hallways and an abundance of roses and gates open to the bluest sky and the kindest voices, and in the half-heard music of an afternoon Alice understood the great magnitude and price of her transgression. She had climbed the stairs to her room and barricaded herself within its walls. It was there that returning from Etretat, Claude found her in bed, hollowed out and broken.

"Oh, my dearest, what has happened?"

"Please, Claude, just leave me here," she begged, all color drained from her face. "Let me stay here alone for a while. I need to be here by myself. Please."

He brought trays of food. She wouldn't eat. For four days following his return from Etretat Alice languished in her room, speaking to no one, seeing no one, caring for no one.

"I hope you are happy," Claude said to the girls when from Marthe he learned the details of the attack against their mother. "You have succeeded very well in hurting your mother very badly. She may very well become ill as a result of your behavior. I want you to know, though, that I understand all too well what lies beneath all this and I know I bear most of the blame, but you have forgotten one very important thing. Your mother loves you, all of you, more than anything else in the world, even me. She would give her life for any one of you and as things stand now she may indeed be doing that, but remember this: If one of you were ever in a situation like hers or in any sort of difficulty at all do you believe for a moment that she would call you names and rage at you and forget what you mean to her? Never! She would always be there, kind and understanding and helpful. You are all eager to face your futures and live your lives on your own terms. I understand that. But for my interference you might be looking forward to privileged lives in Paris. You might marry rich men and live in beautiful houses. Right now, at your ages you must find Giverny boring and offering none of the glamour you feel you were born to. Understanding and patience may not be settled in you yet. Your lives are stretched out before you and as you look ahead you feel you are at a disadvantage. Well, you are not. You have strength of character and good, useful minds. Your mother saw to it. I think you're just afraid of life right now."

Alice did not die. She did not retaliate against her children or show the slightest sign of disappointment in their behavior. There was enough disappointment and self-loathing in her own bruised heart to last a lifetime and, as in the past when facing difficulty, she maintained her stoicism and displayed the loving attitude toward her children that no cruel outburst of any dimension would ever diminish.

"I thought it would be so different," she confided to Claude as days passed and she slowly rallied. "I thought my children would grow up and be happy because I was. When you came to Rottembourg you watched them and called them my five young fireflies. You said their gossamer wings fluttered around me constantly. They wanted to touch me, be near me. I thought the power of my love for them was all they needed. How wrong I was. I hadn't counted on having them grow up to question their identities or their places in the world. I never looked that far ahead. How stupid I was."

"My darling, you brought them through a very difficult time. Life presented you with challenges no mother could have anticipated or prepared for, but you have given them good, secure lives in spite of shortages of everything but love. Together you and I have done what we could and I believe that under all their resistance they know that."

"I don't worry so much about the younger ones," Alice said to him. "They love you. Our being together is all they've ever known. Oh, Jacques is sometimes torn and sides with the older girls who have always wanted me to return to Ernest and live with him as before. I've tried to explain how the tricks life plays can change everything we thought we'd believed in; people, feelings, memories. I've told all of them that in the space of a few years their father changed. I changed. I found you, but I see now that they have never understood all that. They've been too busy growing up and without knowing it I've placed barriers in their paths."

"They will understand one day, and perhaps sooner than you think," Claude assured her, relieved week by week to watch his beloved Alice gradually recovering her strength and high spirits, admiring as he admired few things in life, her ability to deal with her children as if absolutely nothing had happened to alter the chemistry in the household. More than that, he remained in awe of her loving devotion to him and the unwavering confidence she continued to place in his talent and his ability to eventually succeed beyond his wildest dreams.

In the next weeks, although Alice's mood improved, Jacques grew more sullen. Jean was more distant than ever, never having quite adjusted, Alice knew, to the massive Hoschede invasion into the quiet, only-child life he had lived with a fragile mother he adored and a father whose love he had never expected to share. At the same time, Marthe, Blanche, and Suzanne were withdrawn and uncharacteristically quiet, but out of habit they remained attentive to their mother's every word. They helped to prepare and serve meals and they were quick to clear the table and assist Marie with the dishwashing and drying. Ten people, eight of them children varying in age and attitude, sat at the dining room table twice each day and Alice worked very hard to see those ten people re-engaged on better terms. She encouraged conversation and humor and she insisted on discussions concerning whatever books were being read. Her efforts, noble and effective as they may have been, were currently being overwhelmed, however, by the chorus of highly favorable comments on the quality of food now being served at The Press.

It did not go unnoticed that meals were of increasingly better size and quality than in the past. Generous cuts of tender beef were finding their way to the ten places at the dining room table, as were a wide variety of tasty cheeses and an abundance of delicious dessert puffs of delicate flakey pastry filled with cream and baked slices of one of the many varieties of apples stored in the cellar. Claude's income had improved sufficiently to provide for the large family living at The Press for which he now felt solely responsible.

By September, his income for the year had reached more than fifteen thousand francs. Some paintings were being sold for as much as one thousand francs each. It was a substantial improvement over sales of the past, but now he had made the decision over which he had agonized. He decided to break his exclusive arrangement with Paul Durand-Ruel and wanted to sell with Georges Petit in an unusual combined arrangement he hoped to strike with the two competing dealers.

When approached, Petit was immediately agreeable. Inviting Durand-Ruel to the luncheon at The Press that Alice had planned the month before, Claude met with his dealer at Giverny on familiar ground, taking far more time than he had with Petit in explaining his position fully and honestly, pointing out as a means to soften the rough edges, that competitive dealers selling Monets would only add to their value and prices. He hoped Monsieur Durand would understand and remain his supportive friend and ally. His thoughtful efforts rewarded somewhere between the soup and the apple tart, fences were indeed mended and affections quickly restored.

Paul Durand-Ruel rose to the occasion brilliantly and with an idea of his own that would benefit both parties. His finances satisfactorily recovered, his account books on remarkably even footing, he agreed to continue representing Claude in spite of the artist's wish to also engage with Petit. At the same time, he called on Claude to supply a dozen pictures of Giverny and Etretat subjects in return for funds adequate enough to enlarge the existing studio at The Press, a space which the dealer saw as ideal for Claude. The offer was irresistible. Claude and Alice had talked about an extension to the studio to include large windows, a fireplace, and a slate floor. On the last day of December 1885 and following still another lengthy expedition to Etretat, Claude delivered said paintings to Durand-Ruel for a total of more than ten thousand francs and the additional advances that would make improvements to the Giverny studio possible. The year was ending on a highly positive note. The largest of the Etretat paintings found pride of place in the resourceful dealer's gallery and most canvases were priced at slightly more than one thousand francs each, but the astute and tireless Monsieur Durand-Ruel had yet one more tantalizing prospect to present before immodest Georges Petit and the New Year entered in. He had heard from one of his American contacts. Late in the year, a Mister James F. Sutton representing the American Art Association in New York had come to Paris and had visited him, inviting him to bring a large collection of French Impressionist paintings to an exhibition to be organized at the Art Association's premises in America.

James Fountain Sutton collected Oriental Art and was one of the first Americans to visit China and bring Chinese porcelains into the United States. Inspired by his visits to Paris and aware of Durand-Ruel's close affiliation with the Impressionists, along with his American Art Association colleagues, R. Austin Robertson and Thomas E. Kirby, James Sutton, the son-in-law of R. H. Macy, proprietor of the dry good establishment on 14th Street in New York City, was prepared to host and support an exhibition of French Impressionist paintings under the auspices of the American Art Association in close cooperation with the Durand-Ruel Galleries of Paris. In behalf of the Association, Mr. Sutton had suggested April dates.

"America? Why should I show my work in America?" Claude responded, the shock in his voice ringing out along the carmine red walls of Durand-Ruel's gallery. "There is no audience for me or my colleagues there! Monsieur Durand, you cannot be thinking clearly at all. The tasteless Yankees are satisfied with copies of paintings and a few meaningless amateur canvases influenced by the British. Of course this is because they have none of the great museums of Europe. Unless they come to Europe, they don't see high quality art, and my God, they can't have any developed taste at all for modern art. No, I do not believe this is a good idea. Besides, I understand the Americans are very busy with big new industries and fancy inventions."

"Exactly," Durand-Ruel agreed, nodding his head, his blue eyes twinkling, his thumb flicking at his gold watch chain. "Claude, there is money being made in America, very big money. The wealth is there, especially in the city of New York, and contrary to what you may think, so is the taste. I've already spoken to Pissarro and Degas. They are agreeable to having their paintings cross the Atlantic for a big exhibition. I'd go so far as to say they are enthusiastic. I may already have a buyer for several of Renoir's paintings and Degas was born in America, so he will want to show his best and he could sell very well."

A business in existence for a number of years, The American Art Association was re-organized in 1883 by Sutton, Robertson, and Kirby. Becoming known as both an art gallery and a New York auction house located at 6 East 23rd Street,

Thomas Kirby was its popular auctioneer. Before affiliating with Sutton and Robertson, he had independently conducted sales in works of fine and decorative art throughout the United States and had developed a good reputation. In future years and through a succession of owners, The American Art Association would move to several New York locations and on the occasion of Kirby's retirement in 1923, would be sold to a new owner who contracted with Hiram Parke and Otto Bernet to manage the auction house. Fifteen years later, in 1938, the firm would be taken over by Parke and Bernet and re-named The Parke-Bernet Galleries, Inc.

Through the course of its long history and many incarnations, The American Art Association, better known by the mid-twentieth century as Parke-Bernet and later as Sotheby, Parke, Bernet, would find itself at the center of the burgeoning American art market as an interested, ever-widening circle of wealthy, well-traveled American collectors formed great art collections and built and donated to a number of American museums. In 1886, however, the Association under the direction of Sutton, Robertson, and Kirby, was barely three years old. The first step toward its remarkably rapid maturation would be directly related to the arrival of three hundred French Impressionist paintings at its lavish galleries in Madison Square and would mark the beginning of historic events for which Paul Durand-Ruel would singularly and forever be credited in the pages of Impressionist History.

Business in Paris weak, competition more heated by the day, Durand-Ruel wisely recognized the need for a more aggressive marketing strategy, but before the invitation to America was accepted and dates for a New York exhibition were decided, he wisely traveled to New York to examine the Art Association's gallery rooms and attend to final details. Encouraged by this advance trip, on his return to Paris he immediately embarked on plans for a three pronged attack which he hoped would alter the fortunes and reputations of all concerned.

If the American exhibition of Impressionists was met with the level of success James Sutton was advising him to expect, Durand-Ruel would present similar exhibitions in rapid succession in both London and Berlin. Although sales had been flat, three years before he had shown more than sixty Impressionist works at Dowdeswell Galleries on New Bond Street to an influential, interested audience. His return to London and the Dowdeswell would be seen as no great surprise and after an American debut, the public would likely be more receptive with news of increasing international success. Two competing events in the hectic year of

1886, unrelated to but involving Durand-Ruel would, however, complicate but not destroy his vision.

Georges Petit's Annual International Exhibition was scheduled for May and much to the surprise of many Paris dealers and artists alike, an Eighth Impressionist Exhibition extending from May 15th to June 10th was also being planned. Degas and Pissarro were its organizers. Their combined efforts and intention to show once again resulted in the cooperation of only one additional member of the original core group: Berthe Morisot. Degas and Pissarro intended the Eighth to emphasize a group of independent artists formed this time not only as a continuing show of resistance to the Salon, but as an emphatic act demonstrating a new independence from the domination of dealers and their individually emerging markets. Singling out Paul Durand-Ruel, in their discussions they went so far as to point out to their colleagues that in order to be avoid being seen as living under Durand-Ruel's continuing patronage, and "in light of his frequent financial distress" they should make every effort to distance themselves from identifying too closely with his role in their artistic lives.

"Why are they doing this?" the furious, always well-informed Ernest Hoschede wrote in Magazine Francais Illlustre where he was enjoying a renaissance of sorts as its remarkably well-paid art editor. "Monsieur Durand-Ruel has established the market for Impressionism and as a result of the upcoming American Exhibition of French Impressionism in New York, could likely become the most important commercial advocate of modern French painting in the world."

With interest in the Impressionists accelerating, by the mid-decade Ernest was finding himself possessed of a gravitas he had never before possessed. Of course, he liked the feeling. He didn't understand it altogether, but he was very much enjoying what re-established self-esteem could bring to life. The old swagger was back. It wasn't the affected Street of Pictures strut and bluster of the gilded past, but Ernest now bore an air of self-assured reality about him; a sincerity of spirit which he carried elegantly and with the background of one who has come to terms with painful loss.

His history as the earliest, most avid patron of Impressionism was well known in art-loving Paris. The large number of Impressionist paintings he had once owned, *Impression Sunrise* in particular, as well as his intimate knowledge of the earliest beginnings of the core Impressionists themselves were also becoming well-known facts. As for years he had struggled with fear and doubt and Alice's affair with Claude Monet, the rich facts of his own life had been forming an expanding tale capable of piquing not only gossip and rumor, but serious public interest, a condition which was successfully restoring Ernest's self-confidence and never quite diminished love of the limelight. His position with Francaise Illustre was not what he had wanted following the destructive events of 1878, but now he was using his sharp eye and discriminating taste to great advantage in his writing and he enjoyed the hard work of gallery browsing, café hopping, and exhibition attendance. His long-standing anger had subsided, he was happier than he had been in years, and he had Valentina. His wife's long affair with Claude Monet now relegated to a page of ancient history by many and no longer newsworthy, Ernest was by now also well aware that its existence, however interpreted, was only adding color to the living chemistry of the heady mix he now represented. He hadn't forgotten Alice and he still loved her, but he had found a satisfactory hiding place for his memories of her and their life together.

"Too much undergrowth this time!" wrote Lucien Masseret in La Vie of the Eighth.

"Such weedy pettiness has no place in the art world, but alas, it exists."

Pissarro was eager to include emerging younger artists in the Eighth Exhibition. He continued to mentor Paul Gaugin and introduced him to Durand Ruel who refused to represent Gaugin, citing his Synthetist style and stock-broker-turned-artist reputation.

Held in the old Impressionist Rue Laffitte neighborhood, above the Restaurant Dore at the angled intersection with Boulevard des Italiens, The Eighth Exhibition of 1886, twelve years after the First, formally introduced work of young Georges Seurat and Paul Signac. It also included paintings of Odilon Redon and the never-say-die Bracquemond, Forain, Zandomeneghi, and Guillaumin. Berthe Morisot's good friend, Henri Rouart showed, as did Degas' devoted American friend, Mary Cassatt. She showed seven paintings, Degas fifteen, Morisot fourteen, and

Pissarro twenty. Advocating further his interest in promoting the work of young painters, Pissarro's son Lucien also showed for the first time, demonstrating in eleven entries his talent not only for painting, but for printmaking and wood engraving. In what some saw, Ernest Hoschede most vocal among them, as an organizational move intended to soften the obvious affront to Durand-Ruel, two stipulations were placed on participants of the Eighth Exhibition. In order to be admitted, no entrant would participate in another group show (such as Petit's) that year, nor would an entrant submit work to the Salon Jury, but in his own stubbornly vindictive way Degas insisted that dates for the Eighth coincide with those of the annual Salon.

"But we will be seen as being rejected!" Guillaumin argued, "and forced into mounting our own show because we are second-rate!"

"It is what we must do and will do!" Degas insisted. "And we are not second-rate! Do not ever say that again! In handling ourselves this way we are standing our ground and chipping away yet one more time at the old ways! Our small stabs will eventually take down the big old tree!"

Degas had his way and until the last minute attempts were made to tempt the four remaining members of the core group to join their independent colleagues but Monet, Renoir, Sisley, and Caillebotte had had enough. They felt the original focus and enthusiasm had been lost and but for Sisley who would struggle all his life, and Caillebotte who was wealthy enough to paint for the sake of painting, they were finding independent commercial and exhibition success satisfactory enough to financially encourage their individual efforts, but the Eighth was the last of the courageous Impressionist Exhibitions.

Moving forward and into the future, each of Durand-Ruel's original young lions would now work on his own and show on his own. Some would personally handle sales, others would entrust their work to a variety of dealers. Some would submit to the Salon Jury and find acceptance. Some would receive national honors and enjoy the patronage of respected European collectors, but an expanding global art market was hovering overhead and its complexities would require much more than the temperamental voices of a few old lions. The tightly bound group born in the studio of Gleyre in 1868, set free in French forests, and nurtured on the sawdust of the Café Guerbois had grown up and run its rebellious course, but now its members were veterans cut loose. The cooperative of the past was over, but all was not lost. An old enemy had been wounded. Unbelievable as it was, the reputation of the Salon was dimming. Attendance at the annual exhibitions of the past two years had fallen off dramatically. There was competition, serious, deliberate, well-planned competition. The continuing stubborn reluctance of the French Academy and the Salon Juries to accept the work of artists classified as Avant-Garde or Impressionists, had led to the formation of other breakaway groups who also held public exhibitions. The Salon du Champ de Mars, or Nationale, as it became known, was formed by Rodin, Puvis de Chavannes, and Meissonier. By 1881 the Ecole des Beaux-Arts had given up control of the Salon to the Society of French Artists and in a few years the list of influential societies and numbers of annual exhibitions held by them would grow and multiply, weakening the influence of an institution that had been in existence since 1740.

The artistic Paris air of 1886 rife with elements of dissatisfaction and defection, the three hundred Impressionist paintings to be exhibited in America packed and shipped, the painters themselves at bitter odds with the project and one another, in March, Paul Durand-Ruel left his son Charles in charge of his Paris gallery and set off for America and a New York exhibition which in an exciting flurry of new people, new enthusiasm, and welcome acceptance, would leave the frequently beleaguered dealer's deepest concerns well behind.

Met at Pier Four by Monsieurs Robertson and Sutton, the New York weather was balmy and like America itself, tailor-made for brave new ventures, but it was not the first time Paul Durand-Ruel had been to America he recalled, stepping off the gangway and onto American soil. The "Foreign Exhibition" had been held in Boston in 1883, but examples of French modern painting had also been provided through Paul Durand-Ruel and included in the Statue of Liberty Pedestal Exhibition at New York's Academy of Design.

The Pedestal Exhibition was a public exhibition held to raise funds for the building of the base for Bartholdi's Statue of Liberty. Among the five thousand works in the exhibition which included old medals, stained glass, suits of armor, and musical instruments, were three paintings on loan from an American collector. They were Edouard Manet's *Boy with a Sword*, his *Woman with a Parrot*, and Edgar Degas' *Dancer*, all three purchased by Edwin Davis and all three purchased from Durand-Ruel in Paris in 1883 by J. Alden Weir, an American artist, a member of the Pedestal Exhibition Committee, and a man commissioned months before by

Davis to travel to Europe on an art buying trip. More than equal to the irresistible task and setting his earlier disdain for the Impressionist style aside, it was during this time that Weir purchased the Degas and two Manets for Davis. It had not gone unnoticed by Durand-Ruel as he had prepared *Woman with a Parrot* for shipment to Davis in America, that Ernest Hoschede had been Woman with a Parrot's first owner, or that for a time she had hung at the Chateau Rottembourg, or that she had fallen sad victim, along with four additional Manets, to Hoschede's 1878 bankruptcy auction. In New York, shown at the Pedestal Exhibition, the *Woman with a Parrot* suffered travail yet again, this time under the pen of a New York critic.

"Degas' ugly little ballet girls in pink occupied a place of honor in the large south room facing Edouard Manet's *Boy with a Sword* and a very homely young person holding up her petticoat……the title of which I do not remember," wrote the editor of The Art Amateur of Manet's *Woman with a Parrot*, a painting destined to find its way into the collections of Boston's Museum of Fine Arts, gift of Edwin Davis.

America. 1886. A new class of wealthy Americans in love with all things European. An elegant French art dealer in their midst. He is well-met, well-spoken, in command of just enough deliciously accented English to charm, and above all he is imminently gracious. His appearance, his stylish dress, and his refined continental manner are completely at home in the Art Association's luxurious and newly renovated galleries in Madison Square which in 1886 is at the center of New York City.

A business arrangement Durand-Ruel could never have afforded without Sutton and the Association make it possible to have all his exhibition costs covered, including shipping, insurance, publicity, and catalogue printing. It was heaven. Better yet, the Art Association, classified as a quasi-institutional organization, customs officials allowed duty-free and as temporary imports the forty-three cases of paintings sent from Paris, the normal thirty percent tariff on imported foreign art which American collectors found a great hindrance, magically waived.

Valued at just over eighty thousand American dollars, the precious cargo contained twenty-three paintings by Degas, seventeen by Manet, forty-eight by Monet, forty-two by Pissarro, thirty-eight by Renoir, fifteen by Sisley, three by Seurat, also paintings by Caillebotte, Boudin, Guillaumin, Morisot, and finally paintings by Mary Cassatt, the American whose affiliation with the Impressionists and with Durand-Ruel had proven fortuitous in establishing Durand-Ruel's earliest contact with James Sutton and the Art Association. Mary Cassatt went further yet in paving Durand-Ruel's American way by introducing him to her brother Alexander, an avid art collector, and to her closest friend, Louisine Havemeyer, also an American art collector and a wealthy woman, who, on several occasions Cassatt had brought to Durand-Ruel's gallery during visits to Paris.

Paul Durand-Ruel arrived in New York City at a brilliant moment in American life and like a gift shipped directly from the world center of culture, taste, and refinement, he did not disappoint. Quickly catching on to the fact that Americans liked first and foremost to know the person who was running things, he capitalized on his expertise in organizing and running exhibitions and did so in the direct, decisive manner which he was also quick to understand was critical to the success of things in America.

Robertson, Sutton, and Kirby liked him from the start, as did the admiring staff at the Association. In preparing the exhibition, they all watched him more carefully than he knew, observing that in every decision affecting the display of the work of his lions and those of their French contemporaries which he wisely included, he insisted on perfection, a word which they learned in Durand-Ruel's terms was defined by sequence, scale, visual rhythm, and a public presentation that of itself elevated the common act of hanging pictures to an art form. Eventually, everyone connected to the organization of the exhibition wanted to watch him.

"It must tell a story," he declared emphatically to the gloved, attentive installation staff, flicking with his thumb at his gold watch chain from the center of the room, the tables around him covered with the pictures designated to its walls.

And tell a story it did. Under Durand-Ruel's watchful eye, The New York exhibition told the story of modern late Nineteenth-Century French art at its best, and although it included a wide variety of paintings from what future afficionados would call "lesser known moderns," the Impressionist story of new color, new light and life, new subjects and themes, new angles, new viewpoints and fresh new energy took center stage in the city coincidentally also called New.

It was an entirely novel view of the world applied to canvas and it was exactly the correct view for an America alive with new ideas, new viewpoints, new angles, and new energies of its own. It was a view, however, that alarmed more than a few jealous New York art dealers who found the lenient tax arrangement outrageous and unfair since they enjoyed no such exemptions.

"The Art Association is not a quasi-institutional or educational institution at all," they complained to New York officials. "It is a business and a profit center!" was the loud cry, "and since all the artwork these French invaders plan to show is for sale they should be required to pay the same tax any American dealer must pay on imported artworks!"

Quickly grasping the positive impact the large exhibition of French art would be making on the public and art critics alike and highly sensitive to envious New York dealer claims that a fancy European dealer appeared to be receiving preferential treatment, James Sutton promptly arranged to move Durand-Ruel and his three-hundred paintings to the accommodating walls of the National Academy of Design, an institution completely devoted to educational principles and entirely within its right to sponsor and hold exhibitions for the educational benefit of the public. The exhibition re-opened on May 25th, with twenty-five additional Impressionist paintings on loan from American collectors including Edwin Davis, Mary Cassatt's brother, Alexander Cassatt, and H.O. Havemeyer, the latter loan having come about as a direct result of the developing interest of H.O. Havemeyer's wife, Louisine in Impressionist paintings. By closing day of the exhibition, so interested was Mrs. Havemeyer in the scope of Durand-Ruel's expertise and the quality of the Impressionist work she had seen, that at the dinner she hosted the evening before he left New York for a return to Paris, she suggested he consider opening a gallery in New York. She would discuss the matter with her husband and find something suitable she assured him.

The move to the Academy of Design was well publicized and attendance was good. Onlookers were more prominent than buyers, but Durand-Ruel managed to sell approximately twenty-thousand dollars worth of paintings. One glaring technicality did arise to dull the overall success of the New York show. Durand-

Ruel found that a work of art imported to America lost its tax-exempt status when it was sold. He was required to pay the thirty percent duty. Although infuriated at first by this unforeseen development, Durand-Ruel once again looked to positive considerations. His artists had done well, Claude Monet, in particular. His paintings were the biggest sellers. Once Durand-Ruel sailed for home, at least seventeen Monet canvases remained in America and along with respectable sales of Pissarros, Degas, Morisots, and very good results from pictures by Edouard Manet, whom Durand-Ruel now classified as an Impressionist, there was a good deal to be happy about. Critical success had not been as enthusiastic as he would have liked, but it had certainly been an improvement over the blistering waves of negative comments to which he had become accustomed in Paris.

During the seven-day sea voyage returning him to Paris, Durand-Ruel took advantage of the opportunity to review the American debut of Impressionism from an objective point of view. Standing at the ship's rail, his eyes scanning the white-capped gray North Atlantic, he determined that the American public's overall reaction had been dramatically different from that of Europeans. It was more positive in every way, but there was something else. Though sales had not met with Mr. Sutton's expectations, the Americans had reacted the way they lived: in clear-cut, no-nonsense terms that left no doubt that either like or dislike was immediately in play. By contrast, the French needed to take time for long nicety games before coming to the point. Durand-Ruel laughed aloud just thinking about the contrasts.

"How is your lovely mother?" one was likely to ask in Paris before coming to the real point of a meeting or rendezvous, or "Is your son still interested in sailing?" a question that could lead to a half-hour of meandering until the true objective of the conversation was finally addressed, its significance often lost, more often forgotten altogether as the merits of sailing, the incomparable quality of silk sails, and the direction of the wind at last Saturday's regatta were explored in the Athene or the Café Riche over glasses of wine or several delicious, worthy-of-lengthy-comment cups of café noir served at exactly the right temperature.

When it had come to the paintings Paul Durand-Ruel had chosen to bring to America and the trail of interest left by the exhibition he had supervised with unparalleled skill, like had prevailed handily over dislike in a fiercely driven America the insightful dealer now felt was ready to buy paintings in quantity and as was more increasingly the case in Paris, strangely reluctant to invest in the work of its own native painters, looking instead to the approval of distant shores. Perhaps the idea of a New York City gallery was a good one after all.

In truth, a far bigger story than was yet understood by Durand-Ruel had begun to unravel in those moments during which he had been met by James Sutton at New York's Pier Four, for in memorable words and music the Impressionist song was played and heard loud and clear in New York City during the spring months of 1886. Not only did its bold staccato reach the minds and hearts of a sharp-witted population ready and eager to experience a breathtaking new pulse of color, light, and life, its haunting lyric had lingered and touched the lives of a small circle of immensely wealthy, well-traveled Americans who admired and respected all things European, from the pages of its history to the architecture and decoration of its houses and the cut and color of its clothes. An American art collection of serious content, focused on European painting, spoke to rarified cultured interests and a sophisticated view of life in a manner nothing else could and few Europeans arriving in New York in 1886 for the first-class ocean-crossing cost of five-hundred francs or one-hundred American dollars could have set a better standard for those views or ideals more fully than the well-met Paul Durand-Ruel, his embodiment of the modern European art world a breath of welcome air circulating in a city ready to define its own set of cultural standards.

Elegantly poised, the Paris dealer bore no trace of pretension. New Yorkers had seen a man who walked and wore his well-cut clothes with the ease and authoritative air not of a haut Parisian, but of a refined citizen of the world; a confident, clear-minded individual on good terms with the inner workings of a well-lived, well-connected life, his wardrobe most certainly left in the classic hands of the very best old-world tailors, his human grace tangibly exemplified by the creative touch of a fine, handmade, red silk cravat by day, or in the evening at receptions and dinners by the textured layering of a black brocaded vest under a dark gray frock coat. Able to change the dynamic of a room of art lovers by his mere presence and the reliably well-noted charm of his thumb flicking at his gold watch chain as he spoke, he smiled and turned his head slowly from person to person when involved in the group conversations on which he thrived and which at times required assistance in translation.

It was at these times of pause that Paul Durand-Ruel's natural poise appealed most to the Americans with whom he engaged, especially as his English rapidly improved, the practice of which he had begun during his earliest visits to London years before. His knowledge of art history, his father's and his own long dealer experience with the Barbizons together with his strong support of the intriguing Impressionists were endlessly alluring topics to the Americans he met, and as spring descended on an energetic American city ready to embrace its own potential for greatness in tangible ways, that small circle of admiring wealthy Americans eager to build monuments and create legends, fell head over heels in love with his every convincing word.

Having made a number of friends while in America, few of Durand-Ruel's New York relationships were more personally pleasant or more meaningful to him than his association with Mrs. Louisine Havemeyer, the good friend and confidant of Mary Cassatt. Mrs. Havemeyer and her husband were avid collectors of Barbizon and Old Master paintings, favoring works of Corot, Courbet, Rembrandt, the Flemish School, and an occasional Delacroix. The Havemeyers were not only wealthy New Yorkers, they were also civic-minded. Just that month they had given the Metropolitan Museum of Art a Gilbert Stuart portrait of George Washington. Appreciative of their taste as qualified, experienced collectors, Durand-Ruel soon found that unlike her husband, Mrs. Havemeyer was strongly influenced by Mary Cassatt and with her guidance had grown quite interested in Impressionist artists and their subjects. Durand-Ruel appreciated Mrs. Havemeyer's thoughtful, insightful approach to collecting and found her developing passion for the Impressionists reminiscent of similar qualities he had known some years ago in a young Paris collector named Ernest Hoschede. He recognized traces of that same elan, that same talkative enthusiasm for collecting. Hoschede had displayed that same unabated interest, that same inquisitiveness, that same infectious delight.

Continuing to fume over the shipment of so many of his paintings to America, as Durand-Ruel made his way back to Marseilles, Claude worked at Giverny with renewed vigor as well as a growing resentment toward his dealer for having taken so much of his work across the wide Atlantic to a tasteless, unimaginative country.

"I will do all I can to prevent this from happening again!" he stormed to Alice. "I want my work to remain in France, or at least in Europe where it belongs! I must have this out with Durand-Ruel. He has told me I have yet to learn that success on distant shores can bring with it twice the value and three times the money. Well, who does he think he is to tell me such a thing? I haven't been struggling for all these years to calmly accept American support for the sake of Yankee popularity or to watch my work disappear into unknown Yankee hands at rock bottom prices. Where is the success in that? Let someone else provide that new world with its bargains and a new view of art!"

Alice voiced her sympathy for Claude's feelings, but once again she feared that another breach would surely destroy an old, important relationship.

"But, it could be Monsieur Durand is right," she ventured, Claude's vehemence striking the reliable chord of broad-mindedness in her that could quiet his raging heart. At times such as these hers was the only note of reason to which he listened. "Name-value in other countries can mean so much," she added. "Claude, look at the success you enjoyed in Belgium, which is just next door, and London too. I know America is something else, but at least try to see beyond our national boundaries. You could like the idea."

"No, I cannot. My dear, I appreciate your attempts at placating me, but I have heard that now in America, our Monsieur Durand is lumping Manet in with us and calling him an Impressionist. I can't say I object. Edouard Manet was a great artist and my good friend, but you know as well as I do that he was an Impressionist only in his heart! "

Claude's concerns for exports of French art to America, Edouard Manet's Impressionist classification in America, and the temperament of the fiercely territorial French citizen Alice loved were overwhelmed only by the increasingly complicated state of family life. Still at odds with the unorthodox situation in the Hoschede-Monet household, Marthe had expressed her wishes to spend an extended period of time in Paris with her father. Knowing that Ernest had absolutely no room for her, Alice had written to Beatrice asking if Marthe could stay with her on Rue Rome. As expected, Beatrice agreed, arrangements were promptly made, and by early May twenty-two-year-old Marthe left Giverny for Paris, intent on living the sophisticated life to which she felt entitled. Much to Alice's dismay, Suzanne also wanted to go to Paris. Her enthusiasm for living in the city and away from home not quite as high as Marthe's, at the last minute Suzanne found she was not as willing as her sister to leave her mother and the family members to whom she remained deeply attached. A week before the scheduled departure she had tearfully changed her mind and much to Alice's relief, had decided to stay with the family at The Press. By the following summer of 1887, Suzanne would have good reason to appreciate her decision to stay. Claude, however, would find himself wishing she had gone to Paris. The New York exhibition of Impressionist paintings to which the entire family had paid almost no attention, was about to bear unexpected fruit. Giverny was about to be discovered by a few American painters who had been inspired by the Impressionist work they had seen in New York, in particular the landscapes of the movement's acknowledged leader, Claude Monet and specifically his painting titled, *Meadow with Haystacks in Giverny* which was said to have defined the New York Impressionist Exhibition, its theme preceding the Monet *Grain Series* soon to follow.

Although they would deny it in years to come and insist they had found Giverny by chance and perhaps at the suggestion of Willard Metcalf, suddenly American painters were coming to Giverny to work and hopefully learn at the knee of the master. Some were more talented than others, but most were young and handsome and all knew rudimentary French. They were appreciative of attractive female company and not all were painters. The musician, Edward Breck, accompanied by his mother and his artist brother John Leslie Breck were among the first Americans to arrive at Giverny in the summer of 1887 along with several companions. Preceded in their interest by the picturesque inspiration of Giverny and the surroundings with which they had been told Claude Monet lived by John Singer Sargent, Willard Metcalf, Theodore Robinson, and Theodore Wendel, the Brecks were among the very first Americans to assemble a small American artist colony in a small Giverny house, and much to Claude's dismay, Mrs. Breck was soon inviting the Hoschede girls, "Claude Monet's wards," as Suzanne and Blanche were becoming known, to their frequent luncheons and picnics.

Not too surprisingly, Claude took an extremely dim view of these social occasions with the Americans and hotly discouraged them, but as a result of Alice's intervention he did not insist on putting a complete stop to Suzanne and Blanche's participation, choosing instead to assert his paternal position by questioning Alice and the girls at great length not only about the motives of their hosts, but also by questioning the exact locations of such ridiculous interaction with the tasteless Yankees. Adding fuel to his fire, Claude was not at all pleased to further learn that at the recommendation of the local café proprietor, Lucien Baudy, the Americans were taking lodging in the village at the small, rustic Ferme de la Cote, which was owned by members of the local Baudy family, a situation that would soon lead to the necessary and profitable addition of several guest rooms at the back of Baudy's café, yet another condition which Claude would find increasingly disturbing, his disdain for the growing American invasion and his refusal to allow any of its warriors into his world or anywhere near his knee only adding to the power of his growing legend.

His attitude was only mildly affected by Durand-Ruel's draft for more than sixteen-thousand francs on the sale of seventeen Monet pictures in America, the biggest overall sale Claude had ever made. Another New York Exhibition was scheduled for October and adamant in his objection to the whole idea as well as unmoved by Durand-Ruel's enthusiasm for it, his output continued more remarkable than ever. At the end of 1885 Claude had completed more than forty Giverny paintings, another forty from Etretat. By the end of the following year, he would complete twenty five paintings of Giverny subjects and thirty nine of Belle-Ile.

As a continuing thorn in the Impressionist side, in the Paris Salon Exhibition of 1885, among the best received paintings by prominent artists were *The Queen of Sheba* by a Swedish professor named Kronburg; *The Death of Bianca Capello* by M.H.F. Schram, and *Bal des Ardents* by the realist, M. Rochegrosse. Edgar Degas was beside himself and for several days he stormed along Boulevard des Capucines, dragging his cane along the sidewalk muttering obscenities.

Durand-Ruel's two oldest sons, Charles and Joseph, were sent ahead to New York to receive the paintings planned for the October showing, but now there was even greater opposition from agitated New York dealers who, reacting against the great competitive buzz created by the French Impressionists, were now closely allied in their protest against the exhibition of imported French art in any venue whatsoever without payment of customs duty, their legally filed complaint maintaining that under the protective banner of the American Art

Association, James Sutton was not an educator running a tax-exempt educational institution at all, but a businessman running a profit center regardless of where in New York or indeed all America he decided to hold his exhibitions of imported art. A further stipulation in the official complaint made it necessary for a buyer to have his purchases sent back to Paris and re-shipped to New York where the import tax would then be appropriately levied. After long deliberations and much to the dismay of allied New York dealers who had expected the strength of their combined actions to put an end to the French invasion, Paul Durand-Ruel and James Sutton calmly agreed to comply.

The paintings sent from Paris remained in bond for more than six months. Their fate hanging in the balance, it was not until May 25, 1887 that once again the National Academy of Design opened its doors for the Second Exhibition of French paintings shown in America through the auspices of the American Art Association in cooperation with the Durand-Ruel Galleries, Paris.

Understandably, Sutton and Durand-Ruel enjoyed the moral victory, but Durand-Ruel was not at all pleased with the tax demands placed upon him. In control however, of his unfailing ability to find personally acceptable conditions in times of sharpest controversy, he saw that the very public six-month dispute had elevated his exhibition's importance to a level of interest neither he nor disgruntled New York dealers had anticipated at all, the event, quite contrary to all competitor expectations, extremely well received by a highly supportive public who voiced great admiration for an art event they now took very seriously, the tenacity of its organizing figures admired and seen as altogether in keeping with the spirit and ideals of a proud, fiercely independent nation undaunted by the threat of international competition and its requirements.

Appealing to a variety of tastes and appreciative of his position in affecting the opinions of his American audience, Durand-Ruel wisely exhibited the work of his Impressionist lions expertly and to great advantage, but once again he also showed paintings by the better established, more experienced artists of whom many American had heard both in Paris and New York such as Daubigny, Rousseau, Courbet, Delacroix, Dupre, Pauvis de Chavannes, and Jean-Jacques Henner, the painter of several Raingo family portraits which had hung at the Chateau Rottembourg.

At the close of the American exhibition, sold or not, all the paintings were returned to Paris and as in the past Durand-Ruel rose to address an untenable situation brilliantly. There was now no doubt in his mind that an audience in the land of independent spirit existed for French painting. Sales in New York had been far better than expected, those of the modern Impressionists and Claude Monet in particular, but the complex import tax situation had discouraged many potential buyers. Quickly moving forward with his convictions and exploring what he felt could be a viable solution to the customs problem, he visited with Mrs. Louisine Havemeyer and with her blessing and assistance promptly leased premises at 297 Fifth Avenue, establishing there the Durand-Ruel Galleries of New York City, soon turning over operations to a third generation of Durand-Ruel art dealers, his three sons, Joseph, Charles, and George who professionally paid U.S. customs charges at point of entry and set gallery prices to absorb their costs with no significant consequences to their rush of American clients.

CHAPTER 28

A Gifted Man
1886 - 1891

The next five years raced past in a haze of relentless activity, its frenzy of events so significant and complex that one day, one month, one year melted into the next not in an orderly succession of calendar days but as if at the whim of an invisible hand. Prophecy and promise no longer lived as bitter rivals and although personal challenges having to do with the unconventional nature of their lifestyle persisted, Alice and Claude had come to accept the passage of time and its impact on their relationship with the knowledge that they could not change the hard, cold metal of the past, not the pain or loss, not the gossip or rumors, not even the opinions of their children who, by 1888, ranged in age from ten to twenty-four.

They did not discuss certain topics anymore. So many had been worn thin by years of repetition and the uneasy companionship of anxiety, but difficult decisions had been made and old ties severed. There were still moments of an evening, though, when Claude searched Alice's eyes for the concern that from time to time he found there, but assured more and more now by the brightness in her voice and the security of their relationship that all was well, he would kiss her cheek, find his favorite chair, and settle into its comfort to light a cigarette, puffing at it three or four times in rapid succession. The curling smoke would fill the air and he would lean back slowly watching it, satisfied to have seen for himself that yet another day had passed happily for the woman he cared about more than anything in life but his work.

Patience and contentment had once loomed as elusively as the isolated cloister of success, but at the pink stucco farmhouse in Giverny, as the decade of the 1880's drew to a close, habit had begun to form tradition. The dull, gray shutters Claude had spotted through budded apple trees during a springtime walk in 1883 had been painted in the bright shade of green that would remain a hallmark of the Giverny house for years to come.Soft, welcoming fragrance too had become infused into the distinctive personality of The Press. Hickory logs burned in the fireplaces every day in autumn, hot chocolate wafted through the scented air on cold winter afternoons, and in every season of the year a large family pursued daily life on its own set of complex terms as more and more their Giverny home provided a comfortable setting in which to live and work.

Marthe, so anxious to live in Paris, close to her father and in the city they both loved, had returned to the family life she had missed much more than she had expected. Her return to Giverny was heralded with no particular ceremony by anyone but Alice, and soon her presence was absorbed into the routine of The Press as if she had never been away at all. The painting Edouard Manet had created of her seated with her father in the pavilion at the Chateau Rottembourg and one of the only artworks Armel Ducasse had allowed Ernest to keep due to its family subjects, hung over the fireplace in Ernest's small Paris sitting room. It had served, Marthe had noticed during her extended stay with Beatrice Pirole and her almost daily visits with her father, as a powerfully symbolic reminder of the distant past, a past which on her return to Giverny, Marthe found had been softened and mellowed by memories that no longer hurt or haunted her and by the love of a family who had found strength not in old dark shadows but in the promise of a shared, bright future.

Ernest did not visit at Giverny. The older children traveled to the city on their own to see him and Alice occasionally took the younger ones there herself. The estranged couple still married and named Hoschede but living very separate lives had, at last, come to terms with broken dreams and empty promises and in the process had become friends. Alice no longer resentful and defensive, Ernest no longer demanding and arrogant, their meetings now were brief but cordial, at times surprisingly warm, and always their conversations in a Paris café or restaurant centered on the lives and activities of their children as at each meeting there was more and more family news to share.

Alice experienced more personally satisfying times in Paris when she and Claude attended the theater together, especially the opening nights of a man who by now had become a close friend and admirer, Octave Mirbeau. They took great pleasure in serious drama, but they also enjoyed irony and satire. One of their favorite plays was the Moliere social-climbing satire, Le Bougeois Gentilhomme, and once they befriended the actor, Lucien Guitry, they became great fans of his stage work and especially enjoyed him in Chantecler and Pailleron's L'Age ingrate. At their invitation, Guitry and his wife, Marie, began visiting The Press regularly.

At the age of twenty, Jacques Hoschede often left rural Giverny to explore the faster-paced urban attractions of Rouen and Paris. Marthe told Alice that he had one girlfriend in Rouen and another in Paris. Informed of this development, Ernest chuckled and said he heartily approved. Jean Monet, also twenty, had joined the military and was away for months at a time, taking well to the discipline and structure of military life. Blanche, at twenty-three, was Claude's assistant. She carried canvases and supplies and stood at his elbow while he painted scenes of Giverny and its environs, Claude finding now that in the constantly changing light of any given day, two canvases for the same subject, one for sunshine and one for graying skies, no longer sufficed. He was becoming obsessed not by the minute or the hour but by the instant and by the immediacy of air and space in that instant.

More patient and home loving than her sisters, Blanche willingly helped her mother to look after The Press, her great fondness for the house in evidence every day as she dutifully applied herself to the tasks of dusting, shaking out rugs, replacing towels at washbasins, and in spring and summer placing fresh flowers in every room, but Blanche was a talented painter herself and in 1889 had courageously submitted to the Salon, a move which had disturbed Claude greatly, until one day she received word of her acceptance.

Suzanne, beautiful and playful, was Claude's favorite model, but she was enjoying the influx of handsome young American men into Giverny a bit too much he complained to Alice, yet one more consequence of the American invasion to distress him.

Germaine remained the darling of the family, as inquisitive, talkative, and bright at fifteen as she had been at five, well-adjusted and at one with her environment and its conditions, her company as delightful to Claude now as it had been on an August morning long ago when Rottembourg's white turkeys had been the object of their mutual concern.

Michel and Jean Pierre were ten. Energetic, often mischievous boys, they loved the outdoors. In every season of the year they freely roamed the grounds, the gardens, and surrounding countryside, but lately they were being told they must avoid running and playing in those garden areas which had been planted for each of the past years with an ever increasing variety and volume of thriving, but delicate flowers.

Ernest followed the Impressionists more closely, not with the collector's passion of the past or with resentment for the personal debacle to which their leader had contributed, but with a journalist's interest and a natural talent for detailed observation. He attended their individual exhibitions and wrote critical essays on their work and as the unique group he knew them to be. Alice read his published critiques and appreciated his encouragement, far more poignantly aware than anyone of his long attachment and devotion to the Impressionist language. She had little time, however, to dwell on the progress of Ernest's new career. Guests were coming to Giverny more often now, Lucien Guitry one day, Octave Mirabeau another. Luncheons had to be planned and prepared. Guests were invited only for luncheon, seldom for dinner. Eager to get started with his painting every day, Claude rose much too early in the morning to linger at long, late evening dinner parties. Caillebotte, Renoir, Degas, and Cezanne were frequent attendees at the luncheons Alice planned with her typical care and close attention to detail. Soon Auguste Rodin came too, a lovely, interesting woman always on his arm. Michel and Jean-Pierre, young as they were, stood enchanted by the stage actress, Isadora Duncan and the beautiful, famously buxom blonde pianist, Monique Leroy of whom they spoke for hours after she had left.

Belle-Ile in 1886. A Brittany never painted before. Seaside paths and little inns. A wonderful swarthy man named Poly met along the way; part volunteer manservant, part guide, mostly cheerful companion. Painting campaigns conducted away from Giverny in weeks of rain and cold and against dangerous rages of the angry sea he loved. Overcast skies, fatigue, wonder, devoted Poly, and always thoughts of Alice and Giverny. What was she doing this very moment? What were she and the children having for luncheon? What new books were they reading?

1887 and the Belle-Ile paintings exhibited at Petit's in May. Glimmers of recognition, a little more money, a little more security, and always work. The handsome essayist, Gustave Geffroy, is full of admiration for the painter he met at Belle-Ile and called the "Prince of Impressionism" in La Justice. All this, but by February of 1888 the solid forester still lives in tangled webs of doubt and dissatisfaction, enduring long periods of nothing fitting, time wasted, not enough speed, too little accomplished. Off to Antibes.

A falling out with Petit. Heated negotiations, prices too low, more anger, more disagreement, suspicion that he is not receiving the money due him. Fresh conversations with Durand-Ruel, and now with his son, Charles Durand-Ruel. Time racing away, children growing too fast, finding the world, leaving home, searching, running exactly as he had. At the same time, hesitation, alienation, regrets, and bouts of worry.

"There is a promising new young face in the Paris art world," Ernest writes in La vie moderne. Theo van Gogh, the new young face and Vincent's brother, is visiting Giverny regularly.

"A ripe new art market is emerging," the pleasant, shy young Theo tells Giverny's master. He fails to mention heated competition, but soon there a rise in prices paid for Monet paintings. Theo van Gogh, rising star in the Paris art world, latest talk of the town, his small gallery on the Boulevard Montmartre and a branch of the popular dealers Broussod et Valdon, quickly sells six of Claude's paintings for four thousand francs. Sale, re-sale, profit. Accolades. Dazzle. Take that, Georges Petit!

Money was coming in. Genius, he was called. Monet! Monet! Soon some paintings were selling for as much as two thousand francs. And still, mixed critical reviews, but the irascible Albert Wolff had capitulated and purchased a Pourville painting. "Small victories and excessive bravura," the critics insist, Monet's work consistently "unrefined, unfinished." they also continue to insist. Emile Zola and Stephane Mallarme, most famous of the Paris writers and supporters of the late Edouard Manet whose popularity had only increased after death, are showing interest, mentioning his name, writing about his work more and more often. Monet! Monet!

Enter Broussod and Valdon, art dealers extraordinaire, strong-armed angels on horseback, Paul Durand-Ruel suddenly required to negotiate with their representative, Theo van Gogh, for special arrangements related to the handling, exhibition, and sale of Claude Monet's paintings. Outrage. Insult! Rudeness. Bitter arguments. Ingratitude. Amnesia. Theo van Gogh visiting The Press more and more often, taken on walks through the summer gardens in June, met in the city at the mirrored Café Riche on cold winter days when skies threatened snow. He organizes a one-man Monet exhibition of ten Antibes landscapes.

Luncheons, family dinners, more accolades, more guests to plan for. No outsiders at The Press, only creative minds: fellow-artists, stage personalities, and a few trusted writers, Alice still the only family member allowed to visit the studio. Seed catalogues arriving, an increasingly ambitious garden being planted each spring. Plans. Strategy. Love.

In 1889, three paintings are shown at The Exhibition Universelle in Paris as a stream of internationals crowd into the polished city by the Seine. Paris sees a sudden influx of Russian grandeur, Italian grace, Spanish allure, British elegance, and American energy. Here are the Swiss, the Danes, the Austrians, the Americans. Accents, money, waxed mustaches, rouged lips, pomaded hair. Handsome men, beautiful slim, satin-clad women, long gold cigarette holders twirling everywhere, the onset of the glorious Belle Epoque setting yet another new glossy stage for life lived night and day in Paris through the bejeweled lens of the Nineteenth Century's fast approaching last decade at its most lavish, most excessive best, its American counterpart a pageant of wealth and glamour called the Gilded Age.

Oblivious to all the glitz and glory, at Giverny he walks a country lane. That winter, much against Alice's wishes, he is painting on the frozen Seine and then comes the first of the *Grainstack*, pictures, or "*Meules.*"

Stacks of hay sheltering sheaves of wheat until threshing time. Layers of corn, stubble, piles of rye straw, shaped round in Normandy. Motif. Series paintings? The grainstacks dotting the Clos Morin seen just west of The Press? Perhaps those.

Late February. Hello again, Georges Petit! Where have you been? Plans for a Monet-Rodin Exhibition at Petit's during the Paris World's Fair in June. Yes, brilliant timing, an important event, millions of people coming into Paris, and in June the retrospective of not just a few but one hundred twenty-five of his paintings publicly exhibited for many of those millions to see along with Rodin's deeply pocked, controversial figure sculptures. Well-publicized, well-attended, rave reviews from the important critics, international interest from the gold cigarette holder crowd now also waving their oversized, superbly printed, gold-tasseled souvenir Petit Catalogues along avenues and boulevards, the name "Monet" emblazoned on thick white Petit parchment covers set down on gleaming marble topped tables at the Polidor, the Lerois, Laurent's, and always the crowded Café Riche and La Nouvelles Athenes.

Inland now, to paint at Fresselines in March. Extremes in climate along the Creuse in central France. Cold, rain, then a burst of sunny warmth. Plants thriving one day, dead the next. The outdoorsman in his element. He is tireless. Observant. More than twenty paintings by the end of the month. Goupil Exhibitions in Paris and London and again, Theo van Gogh, now Goupil's representative, the Goupil firm famous for handling more Salon painters than any dealer in Paris. Established names in the Goupil mix include those of old masters and academic painters. More than ninety Monet paintings shown at Goupil, London.

And all the while, Claude's long absences. The mistress calling, seducing, demanding his color and canvas. Come to me, bend to me, kiss me good day. Opening of the spectacular new Palais des Beaux Arts. Alice far from the excitement of openings and new monuments to art. Waiting, waiting, always waiting. Tending, watching, and writing letters. To Claude. To Jean. To Beatrice. To Claude. To Uncle Julian. To Claude, always to Claude.

A world away, in America, the fresh market place of new ideas, the great financial trusts are being organized. The Rockefellers had formed the first with Standard Oil in 1870 and in 1887 another prosperous New Yorker named Harry Havemeyer is busy pioneering the second, his Sugar Trust. Mr. Rockefeller understood the myriad uses of the commodity of oil in a country aimed full speed ahead toward fueling industrial development and Mr. Havemeyer now sweetened the journey with his sugar refining business and its voluminous production from the largest sugar refineries in the world. In the first years he had earned profits in excess of twenty-five million dollars annually. Those numbers quickly multiplied and more remarkable profits swiftly followed. In a short time, and with the encouragement of his art-loving wife, Louisine, art collecting became a serious pastime Harry Havemeyer could well afford, as were plans for the large new Havemeyer house to be built on East 66th Street, its interiors designed by Louis Comfort Tiffany, its architecture by Samuel Coleman, its paneled walls shouting out for decoration.

The American Sugar Refining Company grew and prospered, the Sugar Trust securing its monopoly to the degree that it crushed competitors and dictated tax schedules, leading to an annual profit of more than $55,000,000, well before the Sherman Anti-Trust laws of 1890 ignored during the assassinated President McKinley's administration were very much noticed by ever-ready Theodore Roosevelt.

In June of 1889, the Havemeyers left New York for Paris, the World's Fair, and its two million visitors. Mr. Havemeyer was particularly interested to see the Eiffel Tower, construction of which he heard had led to the prevailing opinion that the massive iron maze was nothing short of a disgrace to the city of Paris and must be taken down and done away with at the close of the Exposition. Mrs. Havemeyer, no stranger to Paris and looking forward to a visit with her good friend, the American artist, Mary Cassatt, who now made her home in the city she had adopted as her own, was anxious to experience the effect of the new electric lights she had read would be illuminating all the wide Paris avenues and boulevards by night. These attractions, grand and jaw-dropping as they were, could not for a moment compete, however, with the impact made on Louisine Havemeyer by the hundreds of paintings she saw at the Beaux-Arts Exhibition held in the palace of the Champ de Mars, the international, sensation-causing attraction the brainchild of Antonin Proust, the French Minister of Fine Arts, its magnificent catalogue printed in both French and English, a nod to the growing presence in Paris of British and American audiences.

Representing the Impressionists and not at all understood in America as being an Impressionist in name only, Edouard Manet's astonishing *Olympia* stood with Monet's *The Tuileries*, Pissarro's *The Road*, and the Barbizon School's Gustave

Courbet's *Stone Breakers*. In time, Mrs. Havemeyer would own several of the paintings exhibited in the Proust exhibition of that year, but in the Paris summer of 1889, Harry Havemeyer had a few ideas of his own and they did not include modern pictures. He was far more interested in the upcoming auction of the art collection of a Monsieur Secretan, a European copper magnate who was finding himself in severe financial distress.

Secretan's "vente judicaire" or court-ordered sale which was to begin on July First and continue on for several days, would dispose not only of his widely acclaimed collection of Nineteenth-Century French paintings, it would also strip him of a vast collection of works by Harry's favorite Dutch and Flemish masters. Anticipation for the elite event had stirred great interest among American and European millionaires alike, many of whom had come to crowded Paris specifically intent on purchasing a few of disgraced Monsieur Secretan's treasures at bargain prices, but as the sale progressed and the high quality of offerings became apparent, they saw that final knock down bids were higher than any they had seen at recent, similarly anticipated European or American auctions.

Bidding was especially spirited for Jean-Francois Millet's *l'Angelus* and included the efforts of James Sutton's agent as well as those of a representative of the Corcoran Gallery in Washington, D.C. Mr. Havemeyer watched the French Ministry of Fine Art prevail with the shockingly high bid of $111,000 made in the Ministry's behalf by Antonin Proust himself. He also saw James Sutton extremely disappointed to have failed with *l'Angelus*, immediately offering to donate more than $10,000 to the poor of Paris if the Ministry would sell *l'Angelus* to him. Sutton's offer was promptly rejected, Harry Havemeyer related to Louisine, but in an ironic turn of events Harry and Louisine and all New York would later read in The New York Times that Sutton had indeed become owner of the coveted Millet picture when the French Government failed to appropriate adequate funds for its purchase, their attempts through Proust to keep *l'Angelus* in France unsuccessful. "The Angelus Surely Coming!" read the New York Times headline on July 27, 1889, shortly before James Sutton returned to New York, his wife Florence, and his Westchester County home aboard The Lahn. Customs issues and a duty of $16,500 imposed on the painting would keep *l'Angelus* and Mr. Sutton in the news for some months to come, but the Angelus issue was exemplary of the serious interest Americans were taking in European art.

Through Mary Cassatt and at the urging of Louisine, Paul Durand-Ruel was engaged as Mr. Havemeyer's agent and succeeded in obtaining a Delacroix and a Millet pastel for him at the first Secretan auction session. At the second, he went considerably further in delighting Harry by securing a few of the old masters he had seen at the pre-sale exhibition and wanted very much to own. De Hooch's *The Visit* was ensnared for $55,000 and two Hals panels were readied for shipment to the Havemeyer's New York address for $9,000 each. Courbet's *Landscape with Deer*, a painting that Louisiene admired very much and one on which she had repeatedly urged her husband to bid, went to the Louvre for the highest bid of $15,000, a situation which caused Harry pangs of great regret but one which at the same time elevated his opinion of his wife's good taste and astute eye for Louvre-worthy paintings.

The warm friendship between Mary Cassatt and Louisine was renewed during the Paris Exposition. In 1887, Cassatt and her family had taken an apartment just off the Champs Elysees and it was there that the Havemeyers visited with the artist during her convalescence from a fall and the broken leg she suffered when it was said her horse had reared on the rain-drenched pavement of the Champs Elysees, an event which later collectors would note had fortunately come at the close of the most productive decade of her life. Delighted with news of their success at the Exposition and equally delighted to know that Paul Durand-Ruel was now actively involved in their art collecting life, Cassatt now urged the Havemeyers to see the Monet-Rodin Exhibition at the Georges Petit Galleries, her great enthusiasm for Monet's 145 paintings and Rodin's 36 pieces of sculpture in bronze and marble not quite in keeping with the more structured tastes of Harry Havemeyer who did not share his wife's appreciation for Claude Monet and seemed unwilling to be introduced to a Durand-Ruel competitor such as Petit so early in the satisfactory client-dealer relationship he was enjoying with Durand-Ruel. The international impact of the well attended Monet-Rodin exhibit during the Paris World's Fair lost, at least for the time being on Durand-Ruel-loyal Mr. Havemeyer, its most lasting effect had been superbly achieved, for the name Monet had crept into the conversations of influential internationals from every corner of Europe and America. Petit may have been at odds with Claude from time to time, but by closing day of the Monet-Rodin show the name Monet was officially synonymous with Impressionism and French Impressionist painting. The two went hand in hand and no longer would there be a crisis of identity.

"The genie has sprung out of his bottle!" Lenoir wrote in l'Art de Jour in May of 1889. "He has glimpsed the world and there will be no catching him now!"

More than two million people had come to the Paris World's Fair and at one time or another an influential representation of that two million had found its way to Georges Petit's Galleries. They had seen the Monet signature on paintings that were changing the way the world looked at its pictures and when it came time to pack away the satin gowns, top hats and diamond-studded gold cigarette holders, they carried the message home.

Havemeyers. Durand-Ruel. A warm, trusted personal and professional relationship established. An American interest in Impressionism expanding to the degree that in no time at all Paul Durand-Ruel and his sons were purchasing back from European collectors many of the Impressionist works previously sold to them, but together and as a couple, Harry and Louisine Havemeyer remained of separate minds when it came to paintings by the Impressionists.

Louisine was highly receptive to the work of Monet and Degas, but it would be three years after Impressionism's arrival in New York City before Harry could admit to perhaps liking "just a little bit" a few works by Monet, Degas, and Mary Cassatt, his privately tolerated acquiescence the result of his dear Louisine's relentless enthusiasm for the French moderns. As for himself, Harry soon depended exclusively on the Durand-Ruels to advise him of the availability of the Rembrandts, El Grecos, Goyas and the Delacroix and Barbizons he admired. The Durand-Ruel New York and Paris Galleries complied magnificently while at the same time in Paris, Claude was involved in an ambitious project of his own.

In early June it was rumored that an American collector had voiced interest in buying a controversial painting he had seen at the Proust-organized World's Fair art exhibition. It was Edouard Manet's 1865 Salon exhibited *Olympia*. Manet's impoverished widow, Suzanne was said to be willing to sell. Visiting with Suzanne to verify the news and much to Claude's dismay, the rumor was verified as true. Unable to tolerate the idea of his friend's twenty-four-year-old masterpiece in the hands of foreigners, Claude wanted to buy *Olympia* from Suzanne Manet himself and donate it to the Louvre, thus establishing his friend's lasting legacy and aiding his widow. Hardly in a position to pay the twenty thousand francs required for Olympia's purchase, he quickly organized a subscription drive and wrote to a long list of potential supporters, friends, and patrons of the late artist requesting their donations. Early returns in amounts of one and two thousand francs soon arrived, but a scathing commentary by Emile Zola made it clear that although he had been Manet's good friend and regarded the artist as a master, he would not contribute a single franc to such a trite and shallow benefit drive which by its cheap nature besmirched the reputation of a great artist who would eventually find his way into the Louvre on his own merits. Further criticism followed.

"*Olympia* is simply not appropriate for display in the Louvre," some said. "A naked woman reclining on her chaise lounge? Never! Don't waste your money!"

"Official acceptance of *Olympia* will never occur! How could it?" Mary Cassatt and Faure agreed, declining Monet's request for a donation.

Most surprising was crusty Degas' generous contribution, influenced, Claude presumed, by the generous donations of Degas' long-time friend Madame Berthe Morisot, Manet's sister-in-law. Contributions came in as well from Renoir, Pissarro, Caillebotte, and Durand-Ruel and four months after the subscription drive's start, 15,000 francs had been donated. By November, donations totaled 18,000 francs, but as Claude was often reminded, in spite of this success, there was no guarantee that the State would accept Manet's *Olympia*.

Dissent among the old guard. Too modern a painting for our Louvre! Too risqué, too revealing, frankly pornographic! I'm shocked! Poor impoverished Madame Monet. Too bad, but alas, *Olympia* will likely go to America after all. They have a high tolerance for such things.

"Why are you involved in this?" Alice asked repeatedly as across the drawing room at his desk Claude labored over the names of subscribers on his list, many of whom he was finding had distanced themselves and were writing to ask for return of their donations when they learned that the State was "deeply committed" to maintaining its standards for admittance to the Louvre and highly unlikely to accept *Olympia*.

A myriad of French officialdom became involved. Soon everyone who mattered had an opinion. The Director of l'Ecole des Beaux-Arts, Gustave Larroumet, had his say, as did Armand Fallieres, Minister of Education and Fine Arts. The Louvre, the newspapers, the journals, and most significantly, Antonin Proust, a childhood friend of Manet's and the State's representative at the Exposition Universelle, stirred an exceedingly hot, confusing brew which when served up to the public through weeks of lengthy dissertation, debate, and argument, succeeded in emitting an exceedingly weak "maybe" from Minister Fallieres.

"It is insane!" Alice remarked to Claude over and over again at The Press. "No one is fonder of Suzanne Manet than I, but even she must see that you have stirred up a completely unnecessary muddle with all this. You have better things to do and if you ever so much as suggest something similar in the future I shall confiscate all your paperwork and burn it!"

Only after Proust's intervention in arranging an audience for Claude with influential Armand Fallieres, not only Minister of Fine Arts but future President of the Republic, was the matter only partially settled. Since it had been determined that no artist's work could enter the Louvre until ten years after death, Claude suggested the Musee du Luxembourg hold *Olympia* until the required ten years had passed. Impressed by the subscriber list and the several courageous officials in favor of "consideration," Fallieres proceeded to instruct the Consultive Committee of Museums to "examine the nature of the donation in keeping with all regulations." This was no guarantee of acceptance, but in their final conclusion regarding the complex matter, the Consultive Committee acted with its own degree of negative complexity, determining that *Olympia* was not acceptable to the Louve at this time, nor was the painting to be held by the Musee du Luxembourg with a definitive commitment for acceptance at the close of the required ten-year waiting period. All that remained, Monsieur Proust assured Claude, was the simple question of settling whether or not *Olympia* should be admitted to the Musee du Luxembourg with no commitment at all as to the determination of its final resting place.

It was this undetermined determination which at last settled the matter for French officialdom, but not for Claude.

"Is the painting then owned by the subscribers if you decide against these terms and simply buy *Olympia* from Madame Manet?" he was being asked by subscribers who had followed the confusing developments and the fate of their donations closely. "And in that case exactly where will it be held? In someone's home? Yours? At Durand-Ruel's or Georges Petit's galleries?"

The fate of Edouard Manet's Olympia and his own reputation in the balance, Claude decided that the offer for admission to the Musee du Luxembourg with no future commitment should stand accepted but, he insisted in a letter to the Committee, there must be an assurance that the painting remain in Paris, on public view, and with no exclusion of eventual consideration for admission to the Louvre. This Monet requirement set the Consultive Committee as well as the

Ministry of Fine Arts and its Director into yet another tailspin of undetermined determination.

"I thought it was all settled!" a clearly frustrated Alice declared to Claude. "What else could possibly go wrong?"

Enter the elegant new Minister of Education and Fine Arts appointed in March, Monsieur Leon Bourgeois, whose first task was to immediately study the interpretation of the Consultive Committee's indecisive decision on *Olympia*. In accordance with the dignity of his office, Monsieur Bourgeois deliberated, interpreted, and decided in favor of his own singular approval, the promise set that *Olympia* would indeed remain in Paris and on public view at the Musee de Luxembourg, the question of the painting's ultimate placement in the Louvre, however, a decision remaining open to the future. Claude conceded. Bought from Suzanne Manet for 20,000 francs in March of 1890, *Olympia* entered the Musee du Luxembourg as officially designated. It remained in Paris, was placed on public exhibition, and by order of Prime Minister Georges Clemenceau was at last admitted to the Louvre seventeen years later, in 1907.

The Olympia Matter concluded, contributors hotly divided on the Ministry decision, his own role in its very public fate substantially elevating his reputation and lasting significance of his link to Edouard Manet, his heir, some said, Claude now returned to painting. For too long the demanding Olympia affair had distracted him and now he felt compelled to move forward at full speed. His effusive output by summer's end of 1890 included the *Isles at Port-Villez*, scenes of Giverny's fields, the famous Normandy poppies in *Poppy Fields*, and *Oats and Poppy Fields*. All were quickly sold to Boussod et Valadon.

Living now in a borderless world and in a period of financial comfort, the novelty of accessible luxury made its presence known. Claude was nearing fifty. Alice was forty-six. They had been together for more than twelve years and the struggle they had shared was behind them. Secure and comfortably settled into a home they loved, they were able to hire two kitchen maids to assist the cook, Marie, and three gardeners to tend the property daily. At Alice's suggestion, Claude began to order English tweeds, lace-cuffed shirts, and fine leather boots from London. In Paris, he frequented the Irish tailors, Auld and Reekie, from whom he bought the cheviot wool jackets he paired with his wide pants and laced ankle boots. His wide-ribbed sweaters and the oilskins he reached for in wet weather came from Petit Matelot. Always a stylish man, he wore custom-made berets and brimmed felt hats when painting. Alice, herself, patronized the best Paris dressmakers, milliners, and custom furriers of which there were many more than had been the case when she had dealt exclusively with Worth and could count on the high quality merchandise at Hoschede's to supply her with hats, gloves, and handbags. The children too acquired clothes for every occasion. Through the autumn and early winter Marthe, Suzanne, Blanche, and Jacques traveled into Paris to see their father as often as they wished. They stayed with their Aunt Beatrice or Uncle Julian and in their company often attended plays and concerts, always appropriately dressed.

Demands for the best quality in food and wine were gradually becoming lifestyle hallmarks of The Press, Alice now planning meals a day or two in advance so that the kitchen could obtain ingredients from the expanded local market gardens, fishmongers, and poultry farmers in time for preparation as required. With visitors coming and going, it was often difficult to accurately determine how many people to plan for, but venturing out to nearby produce vendors and poultry farmers herself from time to time, she purchased more than adequate supplies of fruits and vegetables, still hoping as she engaged the local farmers, to befriend her neighbors. In a way she would never fully understand, as the years had passed, except for short, polite exchanges at the roadside, the local residents Alice called "the Givernois" had never taken to the people at The Press, continuing content to assign to the strange Monet-Hoschede household the label of "odd."

Odd or not, entertaining was becoming a pleasant tradition at Giverny, Alice in her element and more than capable in planning and presenting the luncheons and special family occasions for which her talents had never waned. Claude would watch her closely as guests complimented the decoration of the house, the flowers on the table and in the garden, the food preparation and choices of wine, his thoughts at such times never too far from recollections of the lifestyle Alice had known at the Chateau Rottembourg, his pleasure in having grown able to provide her a satisfactory substitute an accomplishment he held quietly but very close to his heart.

Berthe and Eugene Manet came to visit during that summer of 1890, Stephane Mallarme with them. Claude felt indebted to Mallarme for having failed to comply with his request for an interview during the Olympia affair. As an apology he offered him the choice of several recent Giverny area paintings. Mallarme chose *The Train at Jeufosse*. The Morisots and Mallarme stayed a week and took lodging at the Café Baudy, its proprietor, Lucien Baudy's timely addition of guest rooms to the premises of his café found quite satisfactory in a village where hotels were unheard of.

Theo van Gogh had also planned to visit that summer, but in a stunning blow his brother Vincent died that same month, leaving the grieving young man so distraught that by autumn he was seriously ill. Although still months away, in January of the New Year, 1891, Theo too would die at the age of forty-four in the Netherlands at Utrecht, Claude very much aware by then of the fact that of the six dozen paintings Theo had purchased from him, almost a full five dozen had been sold before spring of 1891 had arrived. Arrogantly assured of Claude's continuing relationship with Boussod et Valadon after van Gogh's death, Valadon was boasting to Paris dealers of an agreement with the artist to take his entire production, but as the months dissolved one into the other, it would become clear that there was little if any substance to the claim, especially in view of the fact that Paul Durand-Ruel had returned to his prominent position in Claude's life.

Lacking confidence in Boussod et Valadon and at Alice's repeated urging, Claude renewed his relationship with Durand-Ruel who was encouraging the series paintings of haystacks they had discussed months before, the relationship between the two re-established so well that Durand-Ruel advanced Claude funds adequate enough to change the equation with Boussod et Valadon. Painting of a haystacks series and dealings with the offended Valadon were temporarily set aside, however, in favor of a more distracting matter, this time a situation having to do with far more personal endeavors than those for which Claude and Alice had planned. Their landlord, Monsieur Louis-Joseph Singeot, came to see them in August bearing unexpected news.

"I wish to retire to my native islands in the Caribbean and have come to let you know I must sell this house and its land," he announced in the blue drawing room. "I am offering it to you first. You have done so much to beautify the property and your family has seemed happy here. I do hope we can come to terms, especially now, since it seems Monsieur Monet's paintings and this village have become rather intertwined."

Intertwined indeed. Giverny and the standard bearer of Impressionism were no longer strangers, not to Paris, London, or Berlin, or to the numbers of American painters finding their way to Giverny every year. The ever-growing numbers of Americans said they had come to paint the local scenery, but their protests were weak. Clearly, they sought introduction to the famed Claude Monet who was living and working in the bucolic village that had inspired paintings they were seeing in Boston, New York, Philadelphia, and Baltimore, hoping to emulate their themes and style in their own work.

In November of 1890, Claude became owner of the Giverny property where he and Alice and their children had lived since 1883. The price was just over 22,000 francs, a sum payable, according to the agreement with Singeot, in four annual installments beginning due not until the first of November, 1891.

They were homeowners. And unabashedly ecstatic. The Press and its two and one-half acres of ground officially belonged to Claude, but its ownership and the journey to that ownership was, in many ways as meaningful and heartfelt to Alice as the Chateau Rottembourg had once been. She cried tears of joy from the town hall at Vernon all the way to the gate of the house on Chemin de Roi.

"Champagne!" Claude called out to Marie when they arrived home with the happy official news. "And then more champagne!" he added, eager to sit down and examine his deed of ownership carefully.

A house in the country. A man's property, his statement of personal success, his haven, his freedom to escape the interference of the world, his family and the woman he loved rooted at last. Yet once more Durand-Ruel had come to the aid of the party, advancing Claude the funds necessary to complete his purchase of The Press. The proposed Grainstack Series of paintings previously discussed and strongly urged by Durand-Ruel formed the basis of that advance, the variations on the theme of local haystacks a project Claude now assumed with vigor and great purpose. With loyal Blanche often standing at his side, handing fresh canvases to him as from hour to hour the daylight and its color changed, he was hard at work throughout autumn. Winter came early, with a light frost in late October, but it was a winter somewhat warmer than in the past, until December, when temperatures plunged and the Seine froze over, much to Claude's delight and Alice's chagrin. Out came the fingerless gloves, the heavy woolen socks and fur-lined caps, the rugged, now fifty-year-old painter of nature in all her moods oblivious to the cold, delighted to be in her grip for hours, alert only to the chiseled prisms of Mother Nature caught in the act of being her gleaming self as one after another came *Grainstacks in White Frost, Grainstacks in Morning, Grainstacks* in overcast weather, in thaw, in snow, at sunset. And then in May of 1890, a Salon-competing exhibition opened its doors at the Champs de Mars, among the paintings exhibited, a black crayon portrait of Ernest Hoschede by Louis Picard.

Life altering events and brushes with fame had not remained exclusive Monet domains. Ernest Hoschede had not been sleeping as fortunes were reversing themselves. Claude Monet's name may have become widely known in Paris, but by 1890 Ernest Hoschede was among the most popular of the Paris art critics. He was far from wealthy and his future was insecure, but unlike Claude who was enjoying his hard-won success, even in the face of local fame and in the company of respected fellow journalists and the creative, forward-thinking minds with whom he had always preferred to engage, Ernest was dissatisfied with life. He thought often of Alice and Claude and against all odds the remarkable great triumph of their loyalty to one another. It was difficult to bear. On the surface he remained jovial and glib and seemed possessed of the natural roguish charm that all his life had served to define him, but more and more frequently he was dwelling on the past and re-living long-lost moments at the Chateau Rottembourg. As if the passing years had gone untainted and unchanged, he could see himself watching for small wild game at the shaded edge of the Senart Forest. He could feel the warm sun on his back. He was sure he heard the treeswifts chirping overheard, and in one of the rotunda's brightly flowered chairs he was absolutely convinced he heard himself laughing and joking with his amiable country neighbor, Jean DeLille.

In his own disappointed world he saw paintings against walls of the past. He heard the summer rain pounding on a country roof. He heard barking dogs as black iron gates were opened at the top of a drive. He saw a pair of urns to each side of the entrance gate overflowing with red blossoms, he watched children playing in December snow, the sounds of their happy laughter music to his ears, and always, in the fragile moments he had locked into the hallowed portals of memory, Ernest took Alice into his arms and in the soft bed at the end of the hall he made passionate love to her. She was warm, receptive, ardent. Her skin was made of satin, her hair smelled of tuberose and lilies, and under the handsome persuasiveness he presented to the outside world, Ernest remained a deeply troubled soul, his heart and mind never far from Alice and his haunting memories of their vanished past.

Christmas, 1890. At Giverny the family gathered to celebrate, love and laughter in abundance, enough money now for presents and festive food, time for singing around the piano in a house alive with peace and plenty, but on December 28th, came news of Marc Pirole's sudden death in Paris.

"It was a stroke," Beatrice wrote in a hand-delivered message sent from Paris by special courier. "Alice, please come. I need you."

Marc's funeral at La Madeleine was well-attended by his friends and relatives as well as a number of prestigious members of Paris' financial world. In Julian Raingo's company, Alice attended along with the four oldest children. Claude did not attend but Ernest did, visiting briefly following the funeral with the family at Beatrice's home. Alice and the children stayed on with Beatrice and looked after her for the next two weeks.

Beatrice took Marc's passing very badly. She cried constantly after Alice and the children had returned to Giverny, but Julian Raingo soon became a daily visitor, his affection for Beatrice, his kindness and talent for looking ahead allowing for the healing that eventually came. By late summer Beatrice had sold the house on Rue de Rome and had taken up residence with him, she and her devoted silver-haired lover resuming the ardor of their own personal past at Julian Raingo's Rue Miromesnil address and together facing whatever remained of life content, and not unlike Alice and Claude, unmarried and unapologetic.

CHAPTER 29

The Rule of Three
January 1891

Doors and shutters painted green. Floors in blocks of black and white, a long sofa against the wall, books everywhere, plants in baskets, and come the first warm day of spring, a yellow straw hat waiting on the rack in the hall.

"I suppose that's they way it will be for them there now, a happy home for happy people, " Ernest said to Valentina looking up from the latest issue of Le Galois where, in the sitting room of his small apartment, they sat on the sofa by the fire on a chilly January afternoon. He had just finished reading Tremaine's lengthy and highly complimentary article on the leader of Impressionism.

"I expected it to come to me one day; the success, the name recognition, the money," he stated, gazing into the fire. "All along I had intended to buy Rottembourg back and put life together the way it was, but now it's Claude who's doing well enough to buy a nice house in the country. Ironic, isn't it? Claude Monet has actually succeeded where I failed. It is he who has the nourishment of satisfying work and the gift of time. He must feel like a very rich man."

At fifty-three, Ernest was still impressively handsome, his distinguished profile still enviable, his beard trimmed close to his chin just as he had always kept it. The one obvious sign of age other than the deep lines at the corners of his eyes when he smiled was to be found in his hair which with the years had not thinned at all, but had now turned almost snow white, remaining thick enough to brush attractively against his perennially starched white collar exactly as it had in former days.

"Ernest, please," Valentina said to him, leaning forward to kiss his cheek, her hand brushing his shoulder as he abruptly left her side and walked to the window with the limp he had taken on in recent months.

"You mustn't do this to yourself," she said watching him, concerned as she always was that he could not let go of old hurts. "Lately, you've been so good about putting all this hostility behind you. Please, Ernest, don't stir it up again. It leads nowhere but to pain for both of us, and do you think I like being reminded of your sublimely happy past with Alice?"

The afternoon had turned gray, the darkening skies threatening snow. The gloom suited his mood, the room's dull light a mirror of his heart's freshly open wounds.

"I'm sorry to burden you with my eternal pessimism," he said without turning to Valentina, his gaze to the north view of Rue Baudin, the street where he had lived for several years. "It's just difficult for me when I read about them and how wonderful life is for them, and you, Valentina my dear, are more patient with me than I deserve, but I will always wish you had known me before all the trouble began, before I changed into this sour, unpleasant me," he went on. "I wish you could have known all that sharp, new thinking, all that promise, all that heart I had in me not only with Alice and our children, but with that motley group of Impressionists. It was a wonderful time in my life. And think of it, I was the first owner of the painting that named them and gave them their label. I chose that painting. I'm proud of having done that."

His mind and spirit at one of the lowest ebbs Valentina could remember, Ernest's reflective mood was nothing new. He often looked back to that spring day in 1874 when swept up by his love of all that was newest and best and most cutting-edge he had purchased *Impression Sunrise*. So clear was his memory of the experience that now, sixteen years later, his world turned upside down and never set to right, he could remember every detail. He could describe the exact hue of brownish-red color on the walls of Durand-Ruel's gallery and precisely the way the lengthening shadows of a fine spring afternoon had fallen soft as velvet against the painting called *Impression Sunrise*. Neither selfish wishing nor humbling fear amassed at memory's door had ever changed his view of that one fleeting hour as more and more often now he had cause to wonder what would have happened if he had never purchased Claude Monet's *Impression Sunrise*, never wanted it so desperately, never cared about it so much, never felt the power of its ownership.

"Come, sit down Ernest," Valentina insisted, patting the sofa cushion next to hers. "I know that look. You're getting overtired, my darling. You've been standing by that window for too long and instead of thinking needless, unhappy thoughts you should be thinking about what Doctor Gachet has told you to do. Sit with your leg elevated as much as possible, he said. Rest, he also said, and the pain won't be so difficult to bear."

"I'm beginning to think Doctor Gachet offers the same advice to all his patients, even to expectant mothers," Ernest responded with a chuckle. "Sit with your leg elevated. Rest, and the pain won't be so bad," he mimicked.

He laughed his infectious throaty laugh, but following Valentina's advice, he limped back to the sofa and dropped down beside her. "And there I go again. What's the matter with me, Valentina? I can't find pleasure in anything or anybody but you these days. I must be getting older and sourer than I thought. Look at my hair! It's the color of old, used-up iron. I'm probably turning the same color inside!" He laughed again, but it was a brittle, empty laugh, the expression in his eyes as he faced the woman who now shared his life still revealing the great measures of distress she had found in them when they had first met and which, in spite of the closeness and love they had shared for several years, had never quite vanished. Only now that he wasn't feeling at all well was she beginning to understand the true toll that his distress had taken.

In recent months it had become clear that her companionship, good humor, and the passionate nights spent in her arms had done little to halt the personal battle Ernest waged with himself every day of his life. He constantly fought to find himself and make sense of all that had happened to him, but most distressing of all was the fact that he had never stopped struggling to achieve and triumph, and always in endeavors too ambitious, too out of reach. It had taken immense patience and a level of devotion Valentina had not known she possessed to convince him that he tried too hard, expected too much, and that he envisioned a world that wasn't there and never would be.

She stroked his cheek and smiled, leaning back on one of the sofa pillows. She hadn't convinced him of those things at all, she now told herself. Ernest loved her. She had no doubt of that, but for all the intimate, happy hours they spent together, it was an incomplete love. Ernest was caught in the web of his own past and he had no real desire to escape it. The world of past glories he envisioned was the only world he really loved. It was a world Valentina knew no woman other than Alice could ever truly understand or be a part of, but it was a world she would continue to tolerate with all the love of which she was capable.

"If I really am the only person you can stand to be with, then I shall continue to love you and look after you as best I can," she said to him, her voice bright and cheerful, "but, really, my dear one, you must follow the doctor's advice. Please try harder. Promise me."

Over-indulgence in rich food and an abundance of alcohol had soothed Ernest's bitter heartbreak for years. Now, gout had come to settle in and penalize him further. The pain in his right leg and knee was unbearable at times.

"Follow the doctor's advice?" he joked. "My dear, did Henry the Eighth follow the royal physician's advice when he developed gout?" I have never heard that he did any such thing. He just got fatter and meaner and died anyway."

Gout was incurable, doctors had told him, but with proper nutrition and rest the condition could be managed and lived with.

"I am producing too much acid," Doctor Gachet tells me," he continued, elevating his foot with difficulty onto the stool Valentina brought to him. "My kidneys and liver may not be functioning at their best, he says. Imagine that! I am in possession of a sluggish and likely faulty set of organs!"

The attacks had been mild at first, a cramping, arthritic-like pain in his foot in the middle of the night, but lately excruciating pain and swelling had centered on his knee and a bluish-green skin discoloration was running all the way down to his foot which was chronically painful. It was impossible to walk during an attack which could last for as long as two interminable days.

"No meat, no alcohol, no rich sauces whatsoever!" Doctor Gachet had advised with his first diagnosis, "and be sure to eat plenty of fruit, especially cherries, and drink several glasses of water every day. Your kidneys need to be flushed out. You might also try Vin Mariani. Take a full wine glass with or directly after your meals. It helps with the pain. My patients have done well with it. Interestingly enough, Pope Leo himself endorses Vin Mariani!"

But for the suggested Vin Mariani which he consumed punctually at every meal and with frequent toasts to Pope Leo, the recommended diet plan was ignored, the ridiculous suggestion of adding plain water to his daily intake of alcohol far too insulting to Ernest's preferred tastes, the influx of recommended cherries into his system substantially and healthfully increased he insisted, by way of the flaky pastries layered with cherries and the thick cream he loved and consumed religiously every day. Valentina had done her best to coax him into following the prescribed regimen, but old habits were hard to break. Ernest was addicted to the flavors and textures of foods and beverages he had found could provide him the satisfaction nothing else could, not even beautiful Valentina's love and undivided attention.

Despite his predilection to rich desserts and sauce-laden foods and because throughout his life he had walked so much, hunting in the country and exploring the Paris he loved with a curiosity that never waned, until gout had set in to restrict his activity, Ernest had not gained excessive weight. Now, though, he was noticeably thick around the middle, but so were most men in Paris who had reached the age of fifty, he assured himself when he caught a glimpse of his expanding waistline in the washstand mirror.

The first two months of the year had passed in reasonable comfort, his attacks manageable and of short duration. In early March, however, he suffered an attack so severe and debilitating that he could no longer manage the short walk from his apartment to his office at La Vie Moderne just three doors away. He tried a cane, but hated the compromised image it conveyed. Confined to the apartment, often to his bed, he grew worse daily as Valentina fretted over him and did all she could think of to make him comfortable.

"Gout can be an insidious disease," Doctor Gachet informed her during one of several visits, "and in Monsieur Hoschedé's case, as I have told him, I believe his kidneys have been badly damaged by an excessive accumulation of acid. Right now he is at a dangerous stage. I can give him something for pain and more of the laudanum which I know he has been taking, but this episode could continue on for some time and may not improve at all. I'm so sorry."

Doctor Gachet left Valentina with Ernest at the Rue Baudin apartment on March first. On March second Valentina wrote to Alice.

"Please come, Madame. Monsieur Hoschede is very ill. The gout with which you know he has suffered for some time is very bad right now. I am doing all I can, but I know he would like to see you. I would not write to you if I felt he was recovering well."

Alice wrote back immediately, assuring Veronique that she would come. She left Giverny on the tenth of March and alone on the train from Vernon to Paris, thoughts of Ernest being as desperately ill as Valentina had led her to believe in her letter were difficult to comprehend. Ernest was too energetic, too involved in life. He liked his work and was managing well. The woman had undoubtedly exaggerated and was probably the type to jump to conclusions.

Alice arrived at Rue Baudin on the afternoon of the tenth. She was greeted at the door by the woman in Ernest's life whom she had never met and about whom she had only heard, finding that she was as beautiful and as pleasant as the children had said she was and that contrary to expectations, she was not distraught at all.

"Thank you for coming," Valentina said in a kind, reserved manner as she took Alice's small brown leather suitcase. "I received your letter yesterday. I won't be staying," she quickly added, handing Alice a small sheet of paper, "but you can reach me at this address whenever you wish. Ernest will be happy to see you. It's that door there by the blue chair. A woman named Cece comes every day to help with the cooking and straightening up. She will stay overnight if you wish. I have sent her for more laudanum but she should be returning with it soon. You will find Cece very pleasant and very helpful. You may send her to my address for any reason."

Valentina was gone in seconds. The apartment was quiet and still. Alice placed her gray cloak on the blue chair and without so much as familiarizing herself with the apartment Ernest called his home and which she had never seen, she walked directly into the bedroom where he lay. His eyes were closed, his hands stretched down by his sides over the neatly arranged bedclothes.

She made no sound but immediately settled herself into the chair close to his bedside. She looked closely at Ernest's face as he slept, pleased, in spite of the circumstances existing between them, to see him. They hadn't talked or written in months. She leaned forward to stroke his forehead. It was hot and feverish under her hand. Her fingers stroked his cheek and when she adjusted the bedclothes around him she heard him calling out her name.

"I'm here," she answered, "right here beside you, my dearest."

"I could tell it was you, even with my eyes closed. I know your touch. Alice, how good of you to come."

He struggled to sit up. "No, no, you must lie back and rest," she insisted, adjusting the pillows and managing a broad smile as their eyes met.

"I couldn't believe that you were ill at all," she said. "I had to come and see what you've done to yourself. Tell me all about it."

Ernest fell back against the pillows and ran his hand through his thick, rumpled hair.

"I must be a sorry sight," he said. "This has been going on for a few months. Until now I've been able to manage it and continue with the daily routine, but this time has been the worst. How did you know?"

"Valentina wrote to me. She asked me to come and check up on you. She met me at the door just now, but said she had to leave for a while. She'll be back soon."

Ernest began to breathe hard. He suddenly lurched forward and called out in pain.

"It's all right. It's all right, dear one," Alice said, trying to remain calm as he lurched forward again and again. "Hold on to me. Here, hold onto my arm. Hold tight, tight as you can. I'm here."

The episode lasted for what seemed an eternity, the hard grimace on Ernest's face difficult to watch. Alice breathed deep breaths and remained locked in his grasp until she could feel no sensation in her arm. The woman Alice assumed to be Cece came into the room as the episode at last subsided and Ernest fell back onto his pillow, exhausted, and pointing with relief to the laudanum Cece had brought.

"You must be Madame Hoschede," she said. "Valentina told me you were coming. I am Cece and I will help in any way you want me to. Here is the laudanum. Doctor Gachet said only three times each day, no more. Monsieur has already had one dose today. I'll fetch some fresh water."

"He has fever," Alice said. "It's too high. He is burning up. Can you go for Doctor Gachet? He must come. Do you know where he lives? It's late now. He must be at home."

"Yes, I know where the doctor lives. I've gone for him before. It's not far. I'll go right now if you think I should."

"It is more than gout at this point, Madame Hoschede," Doctor Gachet told Alice. "I'm afraid the symptoms we might have controlled early on, have only worsened. The kidneys are very badly infected. I'm sorry to say that Monsieur Hoschede is not a good patient. He is unaccustomed to illness and no one has to tell me he has ignored all my advice. I can see that for myself. Cool compresses will help with the fever which may last for another day. It will break, though, and the pain will lessen, but only for a while. After that we will wait. I wish I had better news for you, Madame Hoschede. I'll come again tomorrow if you wish."

"Are you saying what I think you are saying, Doctor?" Alice hesitantly asked at the door, her heart racing. "You make it sound as if my husband is desperately ill and may die. He can't. He's much too young and active. He has children. Surely there is something more to be done to heal him."

"Madame, there is no cure for gout. As I have told Monsieur Hoschede many times over, the disease can be controlled with proper nutrition and rest, neither of which he subscribes to. He has led a very full, very rich life, but I'm afraid too much good living can come with consequences."

"But he is in so much pain," Alice insisted. "The laudanum isn't strong enough."

"Three times each day is what I recommend, but at this point you may add another dose if you find it necessary. He's a big man. He will tolerate it."

She returned to Ernest's side, but not before asking Cece to move the blue chair into the room for her.

"I've made up the bed in the spare room," Cece said. "If you want to go to sleep there for a few hours, I'll sit and watch Monsieur Hoschede. I'll stay as long as you need me. I told Valentina I would."

"Cece, I'll be fine here, at least for tonight. And thank you for staying."

Tonight. Tomorrow night. How long would it be? She hadn't been able to ask Doctor Gachet the question that burned at her. How long could Ernest tolerate this? How long could she?

She wrote a brief letter to Claude and the children, careful not to alarm them unnecessarily. She also wrote to Beatrice. Ernest was ill with complications related to gout, she informed them, an ailment with which they all knew he had suffered for several months, but Doctor Gachet was attending to him. She would be staying on to look after things for several days. She would notify them of any change.

The nights were the worst. She barely slept. The lightest touch to his knee, the barest brush with bed linen could generate anguishing pain. She arranged the bedclothes to expose his leg and make him as comfortable as possible. She applied compresses to his hot forehead and did her best to make conversation and maintain a level of steady optimism. In two days the fever passed and the pain subsided, just as Doctor Gachet had predicted. Ernest was able to sit up, enjoy a meal, and attend to physical functions without help. Alice was exhausted but encouraged.

On March seventeenth, everything changed. The pain returned, the fever too, and now Ernest's swollen leg and foot were turning deep purple. Alice administered the laudanum as directed and for periods of time Ernest fell back into an exhausted sleep, his pain relieved, the anguish gone from his face for a precious hour or two, his eyes closed, his body limp with fatigue. On the morning of the eighteenth, he rallied. The pain was much less, he told her. Yes, he felt much better.

"You're working wonders on me," he announced as she spoon-fed him the chicken broth Cece had made and then forced him to drink a glass of water and eat the slices of apples and pears she had sent Cece to purchase from the produce vendor stationed each morning at the corner of Rue Baudin.

"Alice, I've been thinking about something," Ernest announced with unexpected spirit and the broad, boyish smile that even with advancing years and illness had not faded. "When all this is over and I'm back to normal, let's you and I take a ride together on the train. Just the two of us on the private train out of the Gare de Lyon the way we used to. Just one more time on the train. Say we can do it, Alice. Say it."

Alice laughed. "What goes on in that head of yours?" she asked. "I will never understand it. And stop smiling that way! A train ride? To where?"

"Alice, I'm serious. Fever has not affected my capacity to think, and a ride on our train just once more is not so far-fetched. It's just sitting there you know, waiting for us in the station. Think of it, we could ride right out of Paris in that dark blue beauty and into the station at Montgeron without a worry in the world. We could bring a box of pastries from the Dore to Madame DeLage and then go right up to Rottembourg in the carriage; yes, the open gray landau you like so much. It will be wonderful, Alice. At the top of the Raingo Road we'll turn in at our gates and everyone will be waiting for us at the house. They are waiting, you know. Promise me we'll go. Promise."

"I promise," Alice whispered, tears filling her eyes. "Now let's finish these apples and settle you down for a nap."

She had never worked so hard at maintaining her composure and swallowing back tears. Ernest was hallucinating, drifting between past and present, living in that portal between what was and what he wished for. He was returning to Montgeron and the Chateau Rottembourg with no memory at all of loss. It was where he had wanted to be all along. He remembered the pretty little gray landau and amusing Madame DeLage eating pastries behind her jail-like bars at the rose-covered station. "Everyone will be waiting for us at the house," he had said, convinced it was so. Alice kissed his cheek, took his tray, brought it to Cece in the kitchen, and went to her room where she fell into bed and sobbed.

By nightfall, Ernest was quiet, his eyes open, his head resting comfortably against the white linen pillow cover. Alice lit the candles and sat in the blue chair at his bedside, making idle conversation, talking about the children, laughing as she told him about the antics of the pair of recently acquired spaniel puppies that were terrorizing the household.

"I don't know how those little monsters got hold of the new hat I bought for attending church, but they almost destroyed it," she related. "Suzanne rescued it just in time. I really couldn't be too angry at them, though, they're too adorable. They'll grow out of this stage, just as all our dogs have. Ernest, do you remember Igor? Wasn't he just the most loyal little companion? Germaine still talks about him. I don't think any dog we've had since has quite lived up to him, at least not in her eyes."

Ernest managed a smile and a nod and near ten o'clock he fell asleep. Alice prayed and lit fresh candles.

"Promise me," he called out weakly near midnight, his voice a grating rasp, his face ashen. "Promise me we'll go on the train once more, to the country, just you and I, Alice. They're waiting for us at the house. You know they are."

She arranged herself beside him on the bed. Careful not to brush against his foot or leg, she put her arms around him, kissed his cheek, and gently laid her head on his chest. She could hear his heart beating. It was steady and strong. She smiled, closed her eyes, and felt his warm arm coming around her shoulder as she fell into a drowsy half-sleep against him. In seconds she awakened, startled. There was no sound. She listened at his chest. There was no beating heart. There was nothing. She looked up to Ernest's face. His arm fell away from her shoulder. His eyes were closed. He was pale, his expression serene and calm.

In the not quite darkened shadows that welcome midnight, when one day ends and a new one is born out of the soul of eternity, Alice had held Ernest in her arms as he died, his life ended only when he had felt her near to him, safely clasped close to his heart where he had always wanted her to be. She stayed there, lying quietly next to him on the bed, holding his cooling hand, stroking his forehead, thinking and remembering, alone with him in the small, quiet room. There was no need to rush away now. There was no urgency to say good-bye, not to Ernest, and not to a past that had once meant so much to both of them.

Alice would never be able to remember exactly how long she stayed at Ernest's side that night, reliving images of faces in the spacious rooms of a country house, the flicker of candlelight in its long wide halls and arms full of roses coming in from the garden, but she would always recall that it was only when Cece came through the doorway that she dissolved into a disabling sea of sobs and hot tears.

"Cece, go to Valentina and tell her what has happened. Tell her to come at once," she instructed, trying between gasps to regain some small measure of composure. "And then go to Doctor Gachet and tell him too. I know it's the middle of the night, but he must come."

Waiting in Ernest's room and continuing to watch over him from the blue chair, a swirling rush of disconnected images went speeding through her mind. She closed her eyes. Heavy blue damask curtains were drawn closed on a hot summer day. Perfume bottles sparked color on a sunny windowsill. A piano was covered with tassels and fringes. Hoar frost covered a meadow. Pyramids of oranges and lemons were piled high on a table. She heard music. She smelled jasmine and tuberose. She saw polished floors and shadows falling soft as velvet against an orange-hued painting. A large, handsome man was seated in a wicker garden chair under a stand of old copper beech trees. He smiled to her in autumn sunshine. He had brought her branches of the berried orange bittersweet she loved. He threw back his head and laughed in high summer's warm glow. He had brought her baskets of beautiful things. They littered the grass: white rosebuds for her hair, lantana for the window boxes, white marguerite, primroses, bunches of jonquils on the first day of spring, and for her birthday a small cross on a golden chain.

"Valentina is not coming," Cece announced quietly from the doorway. "I told her what has happened. She wants me to tell you that she will not be coming here anymore. She says she does not belong here and that it is you, Madame Hoschede, who belong here now, at Monsieur Hoschede's side."

In the morning, arrangements were made. Doctor Gachet had come in the middle of the night to examine Ernest and sign the certificates of death which would be taken to the Registrar of the Municipality. Alice then sent Cece to the priests at the nearby Church of Sainte Marguerite to arrange for delivery of the coffin and placement of the body by the Brothers of Carmona. She and Cece bathed Ernest and dressed him in his best clothes. Alice kissed him and stroked his cheek one last time before the dignified Brothers of Carmona, wearing long, black cloaks embroidered at their sleeves with white garlands of marguerite daisies gently placed Ernest in a simple pine coffin, closed its lid, and carried him to Sainte Marguerite's where no Mass was held, but where that same evening his coffin covered with a blanket of white lilies lay before the altar as vespers were sung by the choir in a beautiful blaze of candlelight and Alice and a small group of mourners prayed. Beatrice and Julian Raingo attended as did Cece, Jean DeLille, an assortment of Ernest's fellow journalists and the many art critics DeLille had notified, as well as a procession of nuns from the convent next door to the church. Unseen by the mourners but also wearing a black veil, Valentina slipped into the back of the church and was gone before vespers were concluded.

The next morning Alice met the funeral carriage she had engaged to take Ernest to the train station. She watched him placed aboard a private train car for which, with Julian Raingo's assistance, she had also arranged, and pulling away from the Gare de Lyon in the puffs of steam and whistles he had loved, she took Ernest home; not home to a house at the end of a gated drive at Montgeron and a beloved past that was no more, but to Giverny; to the waiting tears of his grieving children, the prayers of Father Toussaint, and to Saint Radegonde's churchyard cemetery where on a cold March day Ernest was laid to rest in a plot of simple country earth purchased by Claude.

"Jean Louis Ernest Hoschede, aged 53 years, Man of Letters, died shortly after midnight," the announcement read in Le Figaro on March eighteenth. Except for naming his surviving children and his deceased parents, few details followed.

There was no mention of Alice or Claude or Impressionism or Impressionists.

Seated at his gallery desk scanning the pages of Le Figaro as he did on Thursday mornings, Paul Durand-Ruel was stunned to read the read the announcement of his former client's untimely death. He sat back in his chair unable to fully comprehend the printed words before him and all they conveyed. He hadn't seen much of Hoschede in recent years. The paths of their lives had changed, but the passage of time and its wide range of triumphs and trials had never altered his high regard for the young collector he remembered with great fondness and occasionally saw at gallery openings and in the cafes along Boulevard des Italiens where his throaty laughter rang through the air like a familiar musical strain.

The now famous dealer's clear recollection of Ernest Hoschede's passion for pictures and the transaction that had made him the first owner of *Impression Sunrise* had never dimmed, nor had his view of the overwhelming heartbreak and struggle that he knew had followed in its relentless wake. And even when the gossip and finger-pointing had begun and the devil nibbled at every corner, he had preferred always to think back to that incomparable day, wishing he could recapture the rare poignancy of its innocence, the triumphant, confident smile on Hoschede's face in the old Street of Pictures gallery, his unfailing charm, and his delight in having concluded the transaction that had made him the first owner of a painting now so significant that surely one day it would be housed in the Louvre.

As sensitive and patient a visionary as Durand-Ruel may have been through the difficult days, it was only now, with news of Ernest's death and after legends had been crafted and battles won, that he came to terms with the dramatic role the young, enthusiastic Ernest Hoschede had played in setting the remarkable course of Impressionism. Later that morning, Jean DeLille came through his gallery doors, bearing the news of which the dealer was already keenly aware.

"What did he die of, Jean? Such a young man. Fifty-three. Was it his heart? A fever?" Durand-Ruel asked of the grief-stricken portrait painter Ernest had befriended long ago and who now sat across from him at the same desk where once the young enthusiastic collector had come to sit, eager to engage in long, spirited talks concerning a rebellious new group of young painters who were thumbing their noses at tradition and calling themselves Impressionists.

"No, Monsieur Durand-Ruel," came the slow, sad reply from DeLille. "It was no heart attack, no fever. Our Hoschede died of Impressionism."

The End

AFTERWORD

Eight weeks after Ernest Hoschede's death, Paul Durand-Ruel exhibited fifteen of Claude Monet's twenty-five haystack paintings, the legendary series of agrarian pictures whose humble concepts and ranges of rural color defined him and solidified for all time the success of Impressionism, lending credence to Victor Hugo's belief that nothing is more powerful than an idea whose time has come, the Haystack Series establishing so significant a Monet identity that from this time forward the name Monet was enough to ensure interest in a painting, regardless of its title or date.

Alice and Claude married at Giverny a year after Ernest Hoschede's death and for the remainder of their years together they conducted a very private life at The House of the Cider Press. Much to the delight of the many American painters who found their way to Giverny, on an occasional Saturday they lunched at the nearby Cafe Baudy, Claude consistently annoyed by the stares and whispers which invariably accompanied his presence. At home, Alice and Claude entertained only family, close friends, and those creative colleagues whose interests were related to Claude's career. Together and over time they expanded their garden, its thriving development and eventual great beauty intended not for public view at all, but for their own personal introspection and pleasure and for the cultivation of those natural subjects to which Claude was drawn in his painting. The passage of time and events of the Twentieth Century would elevate their beloved home and gardens in the quiet village of Giverny to a legendary international prominence neither of them could have imagined. By contrast, the dimensions of their personal relationship as the auspicious years of success evolved remained theirs alone, their long premarital relationship and the nature of its many consequences generally overlooked, unspoken, or unknown to all but their family and closest associates. To this day, the name of Claude Monet in all its throbbing singularity echoes through rooms and gardens of the green-shuttered farmhouse which was most definitely shared by Alice and eight active children, but which in fact and in the universal mindset is a house of rooms exclusively assigned to Claude Monet. And this is the way Alice and Claude wanted it, the protective system meticulously ensuring their personal privacy, in particular Alice's intimate role in Claude's life having been effectively put into place in 1878 at Vetheuil when Claude's gave his first significant interview to a journalist from La Moderne prior to which and after much worrisome deliberation it was decided that Alice and the children would visit a distant village market for the day, leaving Claude quite capably alone to handle and enjoy his earliest climb to the top of the rocky Impressionist mountain with no need to explain the details and complex nature of his personal living arrangements with a house full of children and a woman who, until 1892, remained married to another man. This plan as successfully implemented in 1878 was a brilliant exercise in the arena of public relations and served as a protective buffer against the threat of scandal which Alice always feared could affect Claude's career in a negative way.

Into the Twentieth Century, white hair and the habits and experiences of lives bridging two remarkable centuries settled in and the constancy of devotion between Claude and Alice remained unassailable until the time for parting inevitably came. Alice died of leukemia at The House of the Cider Press in 1911. She was 67. Following a long period of mourning, Claude continued to live and paint at Giverny, completing a monumental body of work crowned by the Water Lily Paintings and the Eight Water Lily Panels installed at the Musee de l'Orangerie in Paris according to plan in 1927 just a few months after his death in December of 1926 at the age of 86. Both Alice and Claude are buried in the Giverny cemetery plot where Ernest Hoschede has been at rest since 1891.

About the Children

The first of the family weddings was Suzanne's. In 1892 she married Theodore Butler, a young American painter from Columbus, Ohio who had trained with Carolus-Duran in Paris and was one of the many aspiring American painters drawn to the inspiration of Giverny and its famous resident. In 1893 Suzanne gave birth to a daughter, Lili, and in 1894 to a son, James. Tragically, in 1899 and following a lengthy illness, Suzanne died at Giverny at the age of 31, the first of Ernest Hoschede's children to be laid to rest beside him. It was said that Alice never recovered from this loss and that her beautiful dark hair turned snow-white almost overnight. In 1900, Theodore Butler married Marthe Hoschede who became step-mother to her sister's children. For the rest of their lives the Butlers lived in a house very near The House of the Cider Press. Marthe died there in 1925, Theodore Butler in 1936. Suzanne and Theodore Butler's son and Ernest and Alice's grandson James, grew up to become a botanist. Through the early decade of the 1970's as the House of the Cider Press and its gardens were being restored and until his death in 1976, James Butler led the important botanical restorations at his grandparents' home, researching and listing the many plants known to have surrounded the House of the Cider Press season by season and as he remembered them. Lili, Suzanne and Theodore Butler's daughter and Alice and Ernest Hoschede's granddaughter, grew up to be a fashion designer and married Roger Toulgouat, a designer of children's furniture. Their son, the French painter, Jean-Marie Toulgouat, born in 1927, grew up in the Butler house at Giverny, was taught painting by Blanche, achieved notable success as an artist, but left a uniquely personal legacy to the art world in having served as French Consultant to the restoration of his great-grandparents' Giverny home during the 1970's where his childhood memories of life at The House of the Cider Press following his great-grandfather's death and in the company of his many aunts and uncles proved invaluable to restoring the property's authenticity. Jean-Marie married Claire Joyes, author of *The Taste of Giverny* and *Monet's Table*, and lived all his life in the Giverny house left to him by his grandfather, Theodore Butler. He died in 2006.

Romantically linked for a time to John Leslie Breck, also one of the young American painters attracted to Giverny, in 1897 Blanche Hoschede married Claude's oldest son, Jean. They lived first in Rouen where Jean pursued a career as a chemist and later at Beaumonte-le-Roger, the picturesque Normandy village in the valley of the Risle. In ill health through much of his life, Jean died in 1914 at the age of 47. There were no children. After Jean's death Blanche returned to live at The House of the Cider Press where she devotedly assumed domestic responsibility for the household and served as Claude's trusted aide and painting assistant until his death in December of 1926. A gifted Impressionist painter in her own right, one-woman exhibitions of her work were held at the Bernheim-Jeune Galleries, Paris in 1927 and 1931; also at Gallery Daber, Paris in 1942, and at Gallerie d'Art Drouot Provence, Paris in 1947. One of Blanche's haystack paintings hangs at The Press and a Giverny street bears her name. During World War II, following the Landing at Normandy and as the Allies pushed eastward and skirmishes broke out, Blanche painted a sign for the front door at the Press. It read: Please, This was Monet's House. Faithful to the end, Blanche Hoschede Monet died at Giverny in 1947 at the age of 82.

Jacques Hoschede, born at the Chateau du Rottembourg, married Inga Jorgensoen and established his household in Norway. Alice and Claude visited them almost every year, Claude very much taken with the wintry Norwegian landscape and the collection of warm fur vests and caps he brought back to Giverny to wear during his winter painting expeditions. Jacques and Inga had no children. Jacques died in 1941.

Born at the Chateau du Rottembourg in 1873, in 1902 Germaine Hoschede married Albert Salerou, a Rouen lawyer. The Salerous lived in Rouen and kept a second home at Giverny not far from The Press. They became the parents of two daughters, one of whom, Simone, married Robert Piguet in 1928. Simone and Robert had 12 children. Germaine died in 1968, at the age of 95.

Jean-Pierre Hoschede, born at Biarritz in 1877, married Genevieve Costadue and was the author of several well-received books and articles on Claude Monet who is rumored to be his father, an attribute which during his lifetime Jean-Pierre was privately known to accept with no small degree of pride. A lifelong resident of Giverny, for a time after Blanche's death he assisted Michel Monet in caring for The Press. Jean-Pierre died in 1961. He and Genevieve left no children.

Michel Monet, born in 1878 was his father's heir. Claude Monet left no will and as a result everything was left in Michel's hands. Michel entrusted to Blanche the maintenance of The Press as well as the preservation and periodic sale of the many paintings Claude left there upon his death including a little known personal collection of paintings he kept in his bedroom. A lover of African Safaris and fast automobiles, in 1931 Michel married a beautiful fashion model, Gabrielle Bonaventure. Known for his stylish wardrobe and love of elegant living, Michel was killed in an automobile accident at Vernon in 1966 at the age of 88 while returning home from Giverny to the house he and Gabrielle had built at Sorel-Moussel, the Loire Valley village located between Fermaincourt and Oulins. He and Gabrielle left no children.

The House of the Cider Press, its gardens and water lily pond were bequeathed by Michel Monet to the French Academy of Fine Arts. Without adequate funds to maintain the property as it had been in Alice and Claude's lifetimes, after Blanche's death in 1947 a long period of harsh neglect ensued and it was not until 1980, following a long decade of devoted work, that the extensively restored property was open to the public. Following his father's death, Michel stored many of his father's paintings at Sorel-Moussel and on his own death he bequeathed many of them to the Marmottan Museum where *Impression Sunrise*, gift of the family of its second owner, Georges de Bellio, who purchased it at Ernest Hoschede's Auction of 1878, is exhibited today in an octagonal room. To add further to its significance, *Impression Sunrise* was stolen from The Musee Marmottan in 1985 but recovered in 1990.

The Monetary Exchange of the Period

As pertains to U.S. Dollar and French Franc values in the late Nineteenth-Century: I have implemented the generally accepted Five French Francs to One U.S. Dollar exchange of the period. A number of art historians dealing with Nineteenth-Century exchanges of Francs and Dollars translate French Francs into today's U.S. Dollars. I have preferred to use the Five French Francs to One U.S. Dollar average ratio of the Impressionist period and not a present day conversion. As for example, *Impression Sunrise* for which Ernest Hoschede paid 800 francs in 1874, would have cost an American in the Paris of 1874 with U.S Dollars, $160.

About the Four Panels Painted by Claude Monet Commissioned by Ernest Hoschede for the Chateau Rottembourg, 1876

Panel 1: *Les Dindons, (The Turkeys) Musee D'Orsay, Paris; (Wildenstein Number 416)* in which we see the façade of the Chateau du Rottembourg as it appeared during Claude Monet's visit in 1876, was purchased unfinished from Monet by Ernest Hoschede in 1876. *Les Dindons* shows the north side of the Chateau du

Rottembourg and the estate's pond and grotto concealed amid the foliage to the left. In 1877, when Ernest Hoschede was the Third Impressionist Exhibition's biggest lender, *Les Dindons* was Number 101 in the Exhibition Catalogue. Labeled "decoration non terminee" (unfinished decoration) it was listed as loaned by M.H. (Monsieur Hoschede). Sold either during or soon after the Hoschede bankruptcy auction of 1878 to Giuseppe De Nittis, (1846-1884) the most influential of the young Italian painters in late Nineteenth-Century Paris, this painting has been in the hands of a number of distinguished owners including those of the collector and art critic, Theodore Duret, Comte de Brie (1837-1927), the Hoschedes' Brie Valley neighbor who acquired it after De Nittis' untimely death in 1884. Ultimately finished by Monet in 1899 yet still dated 1877, *Les Dindons* was sold to the Paris art dealer, Georges Petit, in 1894. Acquired thereafter by Francois Depeaux of Rouen in 1903, Depeaux sold it back to back to Petit in May of 1906 and a month later, in June of 1906, it was sold to Princesse Edmond de Polignac in whose hands it enjoyed a long and particularly distinguished stay.

The Princesse de Polignac was Winaretta Singer, an American born in Yonkers, New York in 1865. Twentieth of the twenty-four children of Singer Sewing Machine founder, Isaac Merritt Singer and brother of Paris Singer, one of the architects and financiers of the resort of Palm Beach, Florida, in 1893 Winnaretta Singer married Prince Edmond de Polignac, soon establishing a lively Paris salon in the music room of their mansion on Avenue Henri-Martin, today the Avenue Georges-Mandel. The Polignac salon quickly became a haven for avant-garde music. First performances of Chabrier, d'Indy, Debussy, Faure, and Ravel took place there. The young Maurice Ravel dedicated his famous "Pavane pour une infante defunte" (Pavanne for a Sleeping Princess) to the "Princess Winnie," as Winnaretta was affectionately known within her intimate circle. After her husband's death, Princesse Winnie used her great fortune to benefit the arts, letters, and sciences. She commissioned Igor Stravinsky's *Renard*, Erik Satie's *Socrate*, Darius Milhaud's *Les Malheurs d'Orphee*, Francis Poulenc's *Two Piano and Organ Concertos*, Kurt Weill's *Second Symphony*, and Manuel de Falla's *El retablo de Maese Pedro*, the harpsichord part premiered by Wanda Landowska. Princesse de Polignac was a patron of Arthur Rubenstein and Vladimir Horowitz and a close friend and patron of Nadia Boulanger (1887-1979, the highly regarded female composer, conductor and most significantly the teacher of a long international list of composers and conductors including Aaron Copland, Phillip Glass, Virgil Thompson, Walter Piston, and Quincy Jones. Princesse Winnie's foundation, created in 1928 and under Nadia Boulanger's direction, continued to present concerts and recitals in the Polignac mansion's music room long after Princesse Winnie's death in 1943.

In her possession for thirty-seven years, *Les Dindons* was bequeathed to The Louvre. It was exhibited in the Galerie du Jeu de Paume until 1986 when it was transferred to the Musee d'Orsay where it is exhibited today. This author likes to imagine Claude Monet's painting of the Chateau du Rottembourg's white turkeys enjoying pride of place during Princess Winnie's lifetime on an accommodating Avenue Henri-Martin wall, silent witness for many years to a range of artistic efforts equal to those of its creator.

Panel 2: *Coin de Jardin a Montgeron*, (*Corner of the Garden at Montgeron*), Wildenstein Number 418: According to M. Rostand who is quoted by Daniel Wildenstein, Ernest Hoschede was unable to pay for this panel and never took possession of it. All that remains known is that sometime in 1899 it was sold to the Paris opera singer, Jean-Baptiste Faure, likely through Paul Durand-Ruel. This painting was exhibited at the Third Impressionist Exhibition of 1877, Catalogue Number 112, titled *Un Jardin*, listed as loaned by M.H. (Monsieur Hoschede). By 1907 it was in Paul Durand-Ruel's hands and that same year it went to the Second Museum of Modern Western Painting, Moscow. It is currently at The Hermitage, St. Petersburg.

The Study for Panel 2 is titled *Les Rosiers dans Le Jardin de Montgeron*, or *The Rose Bushes in the Garden at Montgeron*; Wildenstein, Number 417. This study shows the park at the Chateau Rottembourg and although according to Wildenstein it was purchased from Monet by Ernest Hoschede in December of 1976 and is listed in the catalogue of the Third Exhibition, Number 93, this painting is not noted as loaned by M.H. (Monsieur Hoschede), yet it was sold for 130 francs to Jean Baptiste-Faure at Hoschede's June 1878 Hotel Drouot bankruptcy auction, Catalogue Number 58. This study was in Buenos Aires private collections from 1930 until 1970 and as of this writing is in a private American collection.

Panel 3: *The Pond at Montgeron;* Wildenstein, Number 420. It has been impossible to accurately document the provenance of this painting and it is unknown whether or not Ernest Hoschede ever took possession of it. What is known is that the woman barely visible to the right is Alice Hoschede and according to Wildenstein, that the painting went from the Paris dealer, Vollard, to a private collector in Moscow in 1907. By 1918 it was in The Second Museum of Modern Western Painting in Moscow and in 1931 was transferred to The Hermitage Museum where it remains today.

Study: *Coin d'etang a Montgeron, (The Pond at Montgeron)*; Wildenstein, Number 419). This Study for Panel 3 was purchased from Claude Monet by Ernest Hoschede in December of 1876 and was exhibited at the Third Impressionist Exhibition of 1877, Catalogue Number 91. This painting was in the United States by 1891, sold by Parke-Bernet in 1945, sold once again in 1957 to a private American collector.

Panel 4: *La Chasse, 1876* (*Hunting*); Wildenstein, Number 433. Delivered to Ernest Hoschede by Claude Monet in December, 1876, *La Chasse* shows Ernest Hoschede in his hunting clothes on a forest path of the Senart Forest which bordered the Chateau Rottembourg estate. Theodore Duret, who for a time owned *Les Dindons* (*The Turkeys*), acquired *La Chasse* some time during or soon after the Hoschede Hotel Drouot bankruptcy auction of June 1878. By 1894 it was in the hands of the dealer, Georges Petit. A short time later, Paul Durand-Ruel sold it to the Comtesse de Brecy. It is widely believed that *La Chasse*, depicting Ernest Hoschede and his companions enjoying his favorite country pastime at the Chateau Rottembourg, hung for a brief time at Brecy, the Comtesse's Seventeenth-Century Francois Mansart designed chateau ruined during World War II and lovingly restored by the Mid-Twentieth-Century French writer, Jacques de Lacretell, member of the Academie Francaise, who has been at rest in the chapel at Brecy since 1986. By the early Twentieth Century *La Chasse* had returned to Paul Durand-Ruel where it remained in the highly distinguished Durand-Ruel Collection of Impressionist paintings until it was deposited into the collection of the Musee de la Chasse et de la Nature, Hotel Guenagaud, Paris.

Additional Monet Paintings Created at Montgeron

Portrait de Germaine Hoschede Avec Sa Poupee, (*Portrait of Germaine Hoschede With Her Doll,* 1877); Wildenstein, Number 434. Exhibited at the 1877 Third Impressionist Exhibition held at 6 Rue le Peletier, Paris, Catalogue Number 99, this charming portrait of Germaine with her doll was loaned by her father, Ernest Hoschede. Likely a gift to Alice in 1877 and later gifted to the subject of the painting, today it remains in a private collection.

Sous Bois, Automne, (The Wood Lane, Autumn); Wildenstein, Number 432 was purchased by Ernest Hoschede in December of 1876. It sold for 95 francs to Victor Chocquet at the June 1878 Hoschede Auction, Catalogue # 57. In 1899 it was sold at the Chocquet sale, thereafter to Georges Petit, and subsequently to Paul Durand-Ruel. This large painting along with another large canvas also titled *Sous Bois* (Wildenstein, Number 433) shows the same forest path we see in *La Chasse* where Ernest Hoschede is seen hunting in the forest adjacent to the Chateau Rottembourg.

L'arrive a Montgeron, (Arrival at Montgeron); Wildenstein, 421 shows the train from Paris which sped through the French countryside and ran along the Chateau Rottembourg's lower boundary, its smoke and whistles announcing its pending arrival at the Montgeron village station. Purchased from Monet by Ernest Hoschede in March of 1877, *Arrival at Montgeron* was later in the hands of the dealer Georges Petit, then at the galleries of Boussod, Valadon, et Cie. Obviously of great sentimental value, in 1892 Monet bought the painting back and gave to Alice. Today it is in a private American collection. In a remarkable turn of events, when Monet bought *Arrival at Montgeron* for Alice, he discovered another of his paintings nailed to the same stretcher. It was *La Maison d'Yerres;* Wildenstein, Number 422. Attached to a new stretcher, *La Maison d'Yerres* was later and after his father's death, in the hands of Michel Monet. Exhibited in the Third Impressionist Exhibition of 1877, the painting had been loaned by Ernest Hoschede and titled *Le Chalet*, Catalogue Number 109. This painting remained in several German and Swiss collections until it reached an American collector in 1972. The house depicted stands today at Number 37 Avenue de l'Abbaye in the village of Yerres and looks much as Monet painted it. As of this writing, *La Maison d'Yerres or Le Chalet*, as Ernest knew it when he loaned it to the Third Exhibition, is in a private collection in Argentina.

While at Montgeron and specifically at La Lethumiere, Monet painted four views: *Yerres River Near Montgeron, View of the River Yerres, Willow Grove at the Water's Edge, and Willows on the Banks of the Yerres*, these scenes likely those he viewed every day from the charming riverbank lodge he occupied while artist in residence at the Chateau Rottembourg.

The Biographical/Historical Novel

The form of the Biographical/Historical Novel has allowed me the creative freedom to apply the color of imaginative circumstances, dialogue, and events to the factual details of well-researched, accurately depicted historic material, thus creating a relatable story capable of breathing life into accomplished, definitive people who would otherwise and forever remain silent and immutable at the fringes of history.

- *N. Joaquim*

In *Impression Sunrise*, Alice and Ernest Hoschede, their parents, their children, the French Impressionist Painters and their dealers are themselves in historically documented settings. The major events in their lives: Ernest Hoschede's interest in and collection of Impressionist paintings, his bankruptcy, the loss of the Chateau Rottembourg as well as the Boulevard Haussmann apartment, and the Eight Impressionist Exhibitions are factually recounted, related conversations and emotional conditions although for the most part logical, obviously created. Claude and Camille Monet and their sons Jean and Michel are themselves in historic settings, their domestic life, their conversations, their financial challenges, their personal observations and Camille's death based on both anecdotal, documented, and historic research.

I have advanced Germaine's age by three years, but since she lived to be ninety-five I don't believe she would mind. Julian Raingo, Beatrice and Marc Pirole, Armel Ducasse, Jean DeLille, the DeLages, Valentina, and members of the Hoschede household and estate staff, although very real to me now, are characters of my creation. Based on real people, their conversations and activities mirror traditions and events of the times.

Among publications verifying Alice Hoschede's relationship to the distinguished Raingo family of French-Belgian clockmakers and Paris purveyors of fine art bronzes is that of Claire Joyes Toulgouat, wife of Theodore and Suzanne

Butler's grandson, the late artist, Jean Toulgouat. Madame Toulgouat is a resident of Giverny, noted Monet historian, and as previously noted, author of *Monet's Table, The Cooking Journals of Claude Monet*; Simon and Schuster, New York 1989, originally published in French by Societe Nouvelle des Editions du Chene, Paris, 1989 and titled *Les Carnets de Cuisine de Monet*.

Exhibited at the Paris Universelle Exhibitions of 1867 and 1878 and winner of the coveted Gold Medal in 1889, Raingo clocks are world famous, well-chronicled and featured in prominent volumes of horological history as well as a vast array of resource catalogues focused on important clocks and their makers. In 1824, George IV purchased an Orrery Clock containing a music box directly from Raingo of Paris. Prized for their beauty and fine workmanship, Raingo Orrery Clocks are in the Royal Collection at Windsor Castle, other outstanding Raingo examples in collections of The Soames Museum, London; Scotland's Glasgow Art Gallery; the Conservatoire des Arts et Metiers, Paris; the Musee de l'Horlogeries, Besancon; the Palais de Cinquentenaire, Brussels; the Royal Collection in Madrid, and in private collections in Paris, Madrid, Brussels, and the United States, including that of this American author.

I have advanced by one year (to 1876) the date of Renoir's famous *Woman With Her Cat*. Officially dated as painted in 1875, it is today one of Impressionism's most recognizable works. It was sold at the Hoschede auction of 1878 where it fell under the hammer at 84 Francs, or in the currency exchange of the times, just over $16 U.S. Today, Renoir's *Woman With Her Cat* is in the distinguished Impressionist Collection of the National Gallery of Art, Washington, D.C.

Although the love affair of Alice Hoschede and Claude Monet coincided with Ernest Hoschede's financial ruin and frequent absences from home, at the same time it is also true that the Paris Recession of 1872–1879 was largely responsible for fueling not only Ernest's decline, but with cash reserves dwindling throughout France, the widespread economic downturn can also be seen as responsible for negatively affecting sales of and interest in early Impressionist paintings, coming as it did, directly in the middle of the New Group's first fledgling efforts to reach the public.

Jean DeLille's painting of Ernest Hoschede's portrait and their resulting friendship is based upon Paul Jacques Baudry's 1876 portrait of Ernest. Known to paint portraits of illustrious men of his day, Baudry also painted decorations for the foyer of the Paris Opera House as well as a portrait of its designer and his friend, Charles Garnier. The location of Ernest Hoschede's 36 X 48 inch portrait by Baudry is unknown.

A Crayon Noir of Ernest Hoschede was created by Louis Picard in 1890. This artwork can be seen by appointment in The Louvre's Print and Drawings Study Room.

Circumstances regarding Gustave Caillebotte's pivotal dinner in anticipation of the Third Impressionist Exhibition is based upon material from The New Painting, Impressionism 1874-1886 (see Acknowledgements).

Ernest Hoschede's Impressionist Paintings

On the whole, accurate information regarding original prices is sparse and prices are usually confined to averages and handwritten notes kept by art critics, journalists, dealers, and patrons of the period, most of which, this author has found, are often at odds when compared to one another. One of the few transactions for which there is accurate record is that of Ernest Hoschede's purchase from the dealer, Paul Durand-Ruel, of Monet's *Impression Sunrise* in May of 1874 for 800 francs and its subsequent sale to Georges de Bellio in June of 1878 for 210 francs.

The original "procese verbaux" (sales records) of the Hoschede auctions of 1874 and 1878 as well as catalogues of the Eight Impressionist Exhibitions (1874-1886) have served as important source materials, in particular the Hoschede Auction Catalogues of the two-day June 1878 Hotel Drouot public sales at which forty-eight Impressionist Paintings out of a grand total of 138 paintings, (that number including paintings by other artists of the time such as Diaz, Rousseau, Jundt, and Leclair) were sold at embarrassingly low prices, as for example, Monet's La Liseuse, (*The Reader*); (Walters Art Gallery, Baltimore, Maryland). This painting, also known as *Springtime* (at the Walters Gallery) and *Jeune Femme Assise dans un Parc*, (in the *Hoschede 1878 Auction Catalogue*), which according to its provenance was painted at Ville d'Avay, was purchased from Paul Durand-Ruel by Ernest Hoschede on April 28th of 1873. It was sold at the Hoschede Hotel Drouot Sale in June of 1878, Catalogue Number 54, for 160 Francs according to the handwritten catalogue sale price noted beside it which is believed to be in the hand of Alfred Sisley.

Along with Monet's *Impression Sunrise* at 210 francs, or $42 U.S., Ernest Hoschede's five, now priceless, Edouard Manet paintings are exhibited in several of the world's most prestigious museums including The Metropolitan Museum of Art, New York; The Museum of Fine Arts, Boston, and The Norton Simon Museum, Pasadena. At the Hotel Drouot in 1878, all five brought a total of less than 3,000 Francs, or approximately $600 U.S. The Library l'Ecole des Beaux-Arts in Paris holds the original procese verbaux of both the 1874 and 1878 Hoschede sales, as well as the catalogues of the Impressionists' own 1875 sale.

Of all the valuable sources available to me in researching and preparing the manuscript of *Impression Sunrise*, the 1878 Hoschede Auction Catalogue proved extremely valuable in providing an assessment of and guide to Ernest Hoschede's remarkable taste in paintings. Although far from being a complete inventory and true measure of his extensive art collection, its spectacular list of contents, the twelve Monets and *Impression Sunrise* and *La Liseuse* in particular, inspired and motivated much of my work on this book. It was not at all difficult to imagine what living with these treasures on the walls of the Chateau Rottembourg or the Boulevard Haussmann apartment must have been like or what would have happened had Ernest not been forced to sell a single one. Had the conditions of his life remained unchanged or had he, by some miracle, found a way to bring the auction proceedings at the Hotel Drouot to a halt during those two agonizing days in June of 1878, the course of art history as we know it today might exist dramatically altered, for held together in its entirety with the cooperation of his children, in just one additional generation and given the meteoric rise and corresponding values of French Impressionist works in America and around the world, the entire Hoschede Collection of Monets, Renoirs, Sisleys, Pissarros, and Morisots (Degas, Cezanne, and Caillebotte only minimally represented) would have become priceless and superbly important for their range of content and scope of market value.

Starting out as a novice collector in 1873 with his purchase of Corot's *Dance of the Nymphs* (Musee D'Orsay, Paris) at the Laurent-Richard Sale and continuing on to the acquisition of modern pictures to which through Paul Durand-Ruel he was attracted long before Impressionism gained its earliest foothold, Ernest's heirs, in two generations, would have found themselves the proud and fortunate beneficiaries of his courageous and generous support of the universally beloved phenomenon known as Impressionism.

La Lethumiere

La Lethumiere is, by long tradition, known as the riverbank cottage Claude Monet occupied while painting studies and wall panels for the Chateau Rottembourg in late summer and autumn of 1876. Municipal records show that for a time this property belonged to J.P. Jazet, father-in-law of one of the Raingo brothers and an engraver of note. Officials of the Montgeron Historical Society reveal that during his stay at Montgeron, Monet may also have painted in the estate's orangerie as well as in a pavilion Ernest Hoschede had built which was one of the estate alterations and additions made by the architect, Paul Sedille following damages resulting from the Franco-Prussian War.

The Chateau Rottembourg

The Chateau Rottembourg was and is today a real place. Built in the early Nineteenth-Century by Baron Henri du Rottembourg, one of Louis XVI's youngest military officers and later one of Napoleon's most decorated generals, his name inscribed on the Eleventh Column of the Arc de Triomphe, Alice Hoschede's father, Denis Raingo, purchased the property in about 1860 and on his death in 1870 left it to Alice. Denis Raingo left a legacy of 2.5 million gold Francs and at the time of the 1878 auction, the Chateau Rottembourg was valued at 175,000 Francs.

Much has changed in that part of France in the more than one-hundred-forty years since Ernest and Alice left the quiet village of Montgeron. Made famous as the first stage of the Tour de France in 1903, Montgeron has been called "the Capital of the Tour de France." An impressive municipal sculpture marks the 1903 starting point of those first cyclists. Home to approximately 1,000 residents when Claude Monet stepped off the train from Paris at the village station in 1876, today Montgeron numbers more than 24,000 residents. There are hotels, gas stations, shops, restaurants, movie theaters, schools, newspapers, and on the village outskirts, a shopping mall.

My husband and I have visited the Chateau Rottembourg at Montgeron, privileged to be taken through its estate gates and allowed into its rooms and hallways. Many renovations have taken place over the 200-plus years of Rottembourg's existence, but the quiet beauty and solidity of the estate remain unchanged. The grounds and gardens are not as lavishly planted as they were in Alice and Ernest's time, but from the lovely old terraces the Concy Hills can still be seen in the distance, the train arriving from Paris can still be heard from the house and the meadow, and although Rottembourg's once rose-colored façade as shown in Claude Monet's famous painting of Rottembourg's white turkeys is now stony white, during our visit the two tall pine trees seen just over the rim of the meadow in the Monet painting still stood prominent and proud in their grassy park. The convenience of automobiles, good roads, and the onset of suburban sprawl in once bucolic Montgeron have resulted in housing developments encroaching onto the chateau's original boundaries and well into the Senart Forest where Ernest Hoschede loved to hunt. It is true that the Chateau Rottembourg's gardens were beautiful in their day, its hosts legendary in their time, their children delightfully at home in the privileged Nineteenth-Century chateau environment few people enjoy today. It is also true that the most famous of the Impressionist Painters and their families visited Rottembourg during the brief but memorable Hoschede years none, of course, more famous or more impactive on its history than Claude Monet.

- N. Joaquim

BIBLIOGRAPHY

The National Gallery Company Limited, London; Published to Accompany the Exhibition: **Inventing Impressionism and the Modern Art Market**; **Paul Durand Ruel and the Modern Art Market**; The National Gallery, London, March-May 2015. Edited by Sylvie Patry.

Pierre Assouline: **Discovering Impressionism, The Life of Paul Durand-Ruel;** The Vendome Press, New York, 2004; Distributed in North American by Harry N. Abrams, Inc., New York.

MFA Publications; **Monet Paintings at the Museum of Fine Arts, Boston**; Published to Accompany **Monet and Boston; Lasting Impression**, Exhibition 2020.

Daniel Wildenstein: **Monet or The Triumph of Impressionism;** Taschen Books, Wildenstein Institute 2003.

John Rewald and Frances Weitzenhoffer: **Aspects of Monet, a Symposium on the Artist's Life and Times**; Harry N. Abrams, Inc., New York 1984.

Wildenstein & Company, New York; **Claude Monet, A Tribute to Daniel Wildenstein and Katia Granoff**; Published to Accompany the Exhibition, April-June 2007

Bernard Denvir, Editor: **The Impressionists at First Hand**; Thames on Hudson, Ltd., London 1989.

Sylvie Patin: **MONET, The Ultimate Impressionist**; Discoveries, Harry Abrams, Inc. Publishers, New York, 1993.

Richard Kendall, Editor: **MONET by himself**; A Bullfinch Press Book; Little, Brown, and Company; Boston, Toronto, London; First U.S. Edition 1990.

Anne Distel; **Impressionism: The First Collectors**; Harry N. Abrams, Inc. New York, 1990; Translated from the French by Barbara Perroud-Benson.

Museum of Fine Arts, Boston: **Renoir**; Exhibition by the Arts Council of Great Britain in Collaboration with the Museum of Fine Arts, Boston, October 1985-January 1986.

Pierre Willlmer: **Caillebotte and His Garden at Yerres**; with excerpts from *Treatise on the Design and Decoration of Gardens* by Louis Eustache Audot, Paris; 1859. Harry N. Abrams, Inc. Publishers, New York 1991.

Theresa Ann Gronberg: **Manet, A Retrospective**; Random House Value Publishers, New York 1990.

T.J. Clark, **The Painting of Modern Life**; Princeton University Press, Princeton, N.J.1984.

Anne Willan: **Chateau Cuisine**; In Association with Friends of Vieilles Maisons Francaises; Photography by Christopher Baker; Conran Octopus Limited, London 1992.

Francesca Crespi: **A Walk in Monet's Garden**; Frances Lincoln Ltd.; Bullfinch Press; Little, Brown, and Company, Boston. 1995.

Caroline Mathieu, Curator: **Guide to the Musee d'Orsay, Paris**; Translated into English by Anthony Roberts; Editions de la Reunion des Musees Nationaux, Paris 1987.

Editions Francois Bibal: **Chantilly, Domaine Princier**, 1989

Sotheby's Monaco: **Tableaux, Mobilier et Livres Appartenant a Mgr le Comte de Paris et Madame la Comtesse de Paris**, provenant de la Quinta do Anjinho, 14 et 15 Decembre 1996.

Academie des Beaux-Arts, Paris: **The Guide, Selections from the Collection, Musee Marmottan Monet.**

Claire Joyes: **The Taste of Giverny, At Home with Monet and the American Impressionists;** English Language Edition: Flammarion Inc, Paris, France, 2000.

Milton Keynes UK
Ingram Content Group UK Ltd.
UKHW050919261024
450169UK00013B/123/J